Sex in the
Hood Saga

Sex in the Hood Saga

White Chocolate

URBAN Renaissance

www.urbanbooks.net

Urban Books, LLC
97 N18th Street
Wyandanch, NY 11798

ISBN 13: 978-1-62286-972-5
ISBN 10: 1-62286-972-9

First Trade Paperback Printing May 2016
Printed in the United States of America

10 9 8 7 6 5 4 3 2 1

Distributed by Kensington Publishing Corp.
Submit Orders to:
Customer Service
400 Hahn Road
Westminster, MD 21157-4627
Phone: 1-800-733-3000
Fax: 1-800-659-2436

OCT - - 2016

Chapter 1

Duke Johnson towered over a fucking, sucking tangle of bodies at his feet. The wall-to-wall carpet of black, brown and beige asses, titties, legs, arms and dicks extended up the huge staircase and under tall archways on each side. To the left and to the right were huge rooms where hundreds of people were bouncing and banging and blowing to a deafening bass beat and nasty rap lyrics.

Straight ahead, double glass doors reflected Duke's six feet six inches of smooth, dark muscle draped in white linen pants and matching shirt. The dim light cast a crown-like glow around his bald head and made his diamond ring sparkle as he surveyed his enterprise, including the dozens of Barriors, black warriors who flexed like the ninja motherfuckers they were supposed to be if some fool went crazy in the middle of all this pussy. Wearing black from head to toe, the Barriors were double-strapped at the hips, watching to make sure everybody followed the rules in the hot, intoxicating fumes of booty, booze, and blunts.

Yeah, it looked and felt like the kind of pussy party that made Babylon the baddest in the business, but something didn't smell right. So, The Duke was about to collect the bank his damn self and remind everybody who was the boss. Not Izz, the host of this Sunday afternoon fuck fest. Not any of these warriors who worked for him and were conspiring with Izz to steal his cash. And not Knight, who was reputedly trying to call the shots from behind bars.

Hell naw. The only one in charge of Babylon and beyond was The Duke—and only The Duke, now and forever. Especially after today, when he would meet the goddess who was going to help him take Babylon coast to coast.

"We gon' be in an' out in a Motor City minute," Duke told his boy, Beamer, who stood beside him. "I ain't gon' let Izz's bullshit make me late to get my Duchess."

"You trippin'," Beamer said. "You crazy if you think that half-white rich bitch from TV is gon' come down to D-town worse hood an' get wit' yo' gangsta ass."

"Watch me," Duke said, staring each Barrior in the eye. He had no time for anybody's scheme right now, since Knight would be out in two weeks. Duke had to make everything perfect, to show he was handling business himself and building Babylon even bigger and better than what his older brothers started.

The four Barriors at the front door approached, handing Duke a miniature gold treasure chest full of cash.

"Babylon!" They shouted the way Marines would say "Attention!" with the loudest emphasis on the last part of the word. As they bowed to Duke, the tall, muscular men each pounded their right fists over their hearts and said in unison, "Massa Duke rule Babylon!"

"Wha'z up." Duke's nod let them know they could march back to the door.

"A lotta dicks is what's up," Beamer said, taking the heavy money chest and sliding it into his sleek black shoulder bag.

Beamer was usually obedient and reliable, but right now Duke wanted to slap the silly out of his boy's big Bambi eyes. A goofy glow always seemed to jump off Beamer's face, from the cinnamon-hued freckles on his plump, peanut butter brown cheeks to his thin brown lips. His wide, flat nose was pointed down at the tip. His hair, dark brown with a slight red cast, snaked back in cornrows that gathered in a ponytail down his neck as he watched a girl's titties flap while she fucked.

"Stop gawkin' like this the first time you seen pussy," Duke said, biting down to make his jaw muscles flex.

"Yes, Massa Duke." Beamer wrapped his chubby fingers around the BMW medallion hanging over his red, white, and blue Detroit Pistons jersey. His fast-talk was even more jovial than usual as he said, "This ain't nothin' compared to what your birthday party gon' be Friday. Check out homegirl. She earnin' her keep today."

At the foot of the stairs, a Slut was working two guys. They were laying on their backs, their heads pointing in opposite directions. She was squatting down, fucking one guy with her ass pointed toward his face, while she bent over to suck the other guy's dick. Both of them wore condoms to protect her mouth and her pussy, according to Babylon rules. She was like a pump; her ass went up when her head went down, and vice versa.

The dude under her pussy was squeezing her ass, with one black hand on each of her big, brown booty bubble cheeks. The guy under her mouth had his redbone fingers all up in her black braids. They were flying all over his belly and hips as she worked it to the rhythm of some rapper chick squealing lyrics about how she loved to "bounce that ass, make it fas', make it last, bounce that ass." That's what hundreds of people were doing on each side of this foyer, where big archways opened onto huge rooms full of sex.

"Damn," Beamer said, scanning the scene that was littered with rubbers and wrappers. "They 'bout to play musical pussies."

Duke looked to the right, where about fifty Sluts stood facing the four walls, pressing their hands to the red paint, bending over, and sticking out every size and shape of booty. Some orange Victorian-style lamps, the kind with the fabric shades and hanging beads, cast an orange light on the chicks' asses, which were every color from almost white to blue-black.

In the middle of the room, a Barrior stood with a whistle, surrounded by fifty nude dudes with condom-covered cocks ready to rock. The whistle blew, and every guy found a pussy to drill. Thirty seconds into the act, the whistle blew again, and all the dicks had to swing to the next pussy on the right. All kinds of dicks—from that huge-ass licorice stick covered in cream to that brown pencil prick in the corner to that fat, brown sausage to the left—they all came out, shining like a mug with sex juice, then disappearing under some of the prettiest asses in Motown. They did this over and over, until each guy made his way around the room, sticking his dick into all fifty of those hot, wet holes. They were healthy holes, as the Sluts were checked by the doctor every week back at Babylon

HQ, and the mandatory jimmy rule made sure all that pussy meat stayed clean.

Duke watched this symphony of sex being played by every kind of human instrument: titties that were pointed, flat, swole, bite-size, natural, silicone, suntanned and freckled, with nipples that looked like pepperonis, pink frosting, licorice discs, copper pennies, or bronze slots at the casinos, all with a little point or a big udder tip on the end.

He watched asses of every shape and size: huge, ripply ones that looked like if somebody put his hand on it, the booty would ripple like a rock in a pond, and tiny butts that were so skinny the whole asshole was exposed when they weren't even bent over. But mostly, perfect booties filled the room—big and round, firm and smooth, muscular, and athletic—as if the bitch could buck and ride for hours and never get tired.

There was pussy hair that sprayed out like afros or was shaved into shapes like hearts, stars, and lips. Others had just a little strip of hair at the top—a Brazilian wax like Duke's first baby momma, Milan, had—so everything else, including the pussy lips, was bald. Some of the chicks were shaved completely hairless. Other girls had pussy hair that was so nappy it looked like little black ants crawling around the tops of their thighs. Others had silky black fur that made a nigga just want to pet it like a cat while he was lapping up the milk in her steamy bowl.

The Sluts wore the hair on their heads in every imaginable style, all of it bouncing and flying around as they fucked like rabbits without getting tired. Lee Lee worked them in the gym as tough as she conditioned Babylon's Secret Service because this was their job, and they had to be in shape . . . and healthy. But if Milan kept acting crazy, Duke was going to have to replace her scheming ass with somebody who could concentrate on keeping the Sex Squad schedules, doctor's appointments, and income on time and accounted for. All of it.

Sudden vibration on his waistband made Duke pull the cell phone from his belt. MILAN flashed across the blue screen for the fourth time in an hour. He pressed his thumb to the little silver button to put that wanna-be-who-ain't-gonna-be into voice mail. He'd heard enough of her bitching and whining for today, because this was a day for the history books of Babylon as ruled by The Duke. This was the day the black god that he was would meet the ultimate female partner—in business and in bed—and give her the power and glory that every bitch in the hood would kill to have as The Duchess.

"She trippin'," Beamer said, holding up his red-flashing phone which read: MILAN. Duke shook his head. Beamer reattached the phone to the pocket of his saggy jeans. "Dog, I got a bad feelin'. Just like that night Prince got shot."

"Shut the fuck up," Duke said. "Don't jinx my shit, ma'fucka. Don't never say that to me again. Jus' let me work. An' tell me if Pound call. We gotta be on the spot right when Duchess come."

"Yes, Massa Duke."

"We rollin' strong," Duke said, referring to the back-up he had outside the kitchen windows and door, just in case. "But if you act like a bitch, I'll treat you like one."

A girl to the right screamed. "Fuck ma pussy, punk! Not ma assho'!"

In a flash, the nearest Barrior was on him, saying, "You out."

"Aw, man, I won't do it again." The rule-breaker had a punk look on his face.

The Barrior's big hand on homeboy's shoulder made him sober up. "I said you out," the Barrior repeated, pushing the punk toward the door. "Go to the Black Room. Ain't no rules in there."

The booty-poker stroked his cock as he left. He walked across the foyer to the room that was pitch black except for a few purple lightbulbs, which cast a lavender glow over the twist of shiny bodies. They were grinding and banging and shaking in every inch of the room.

"Look like a bowl of purple chitlins," Beamer said with a laugh. "And if somebody get they period, it's gon' look like they poured hot sauce on the chitlins."

"You a nasty ma'fucka," Duke said, turning back to the musical fucking, where another dude took the booty-poker's place.

"Shit!" another Slut shouted. "My pussy ain't the Windsor Tunnel, an' I ain't lettin' yo' eighteen-wheeler bust through!"

"Ooh," another girl purred. "Send 'im to me."

The Barriors rearranged the guys, blew the whistle, and let the fucking begin again.

Duke loved to look at all this sex. No matter how many times he had seen this, his dick would get cocked as hell. But right now, Timbo wasn't swole for any of these bitches. Timbo was as big and hard as a tree trunk with only one pussy in mind. Her ridiculously fine face on TV this morning was stuck in his head like a hologram, touching every thought, shooting a laser beam down to his dick. Even his fingertips were tingling with the need to give that virgin pussy the Mandingo dick-down of the millennium, which The Duke would do before the night was over.

Even though he'd never met the girl, he just knew he had to have her the first time he saw her beautiful face and heard her brilliant, sultry voice on the news a few weeks ago. "And so it is written," he had said, quoting the Ancient Egyptian pharoah Ramses from *The Ten Commandments*. "And so it is done."

And it would be done in a couple of hours. But for now, Timbo was hard as hell for another reason. Every one of those pussies and every one of those dicks represented big dollar signs in Duke's mind. Big, big dollar signs. Money he learned how to make from Prince. Money he earned by building the Sex Squad to three times what Prince had started. Money he planned to make even more of once he got Duchess in on negotiating and strategizing to make every part of Babylon bigger, better, badder.

With a brilliant business mind, a pretty, light-bright face and the Queen's English, that chick was about to become the money-making face and voice of Babylon. And if he had any concern about how her lily white suburban-raised ass would react to this, he knew she would get over it in a Motor City minute. The sex power in her eyes was so strong he had felt a chill when she looked into the TV camera and out the screen, right into his soul.

She'll be all into this. Might like it too much. But I'll be bangin' her fine ass so tough, I'll give her some Timbo ten times a day if she want it. An' she will.

Gold-tipped titties came bouncin' his way. Long fingernails tickled his cheek. Like a brown Barbie with straight black bangs, a bob-style haircut that swayed just below her ears, and thick fake eyelashes, Chanel's face came at him.

"What'cha need, Massa Duke?" she whispered, her sparkly gold pasty crushing into his arm along with her big, ripe, caramel brown titties. She smelled like expensive perfume as she did a pole dance on him. Standing on one gold six-inch stiletto boot that came up over her knee, she rubbed the side of his thigh with the gold lame crotch of her thong. It was held up by three gold chains that draped over her hips and came down to the crack of her ass, where they disappeared. Her other leg was up in front of him, in the gold boot, and her knee was stroking Timbo.

"I need somethin' ta suck," she whispered through big, swollen lips shining with coral-colored gloss.

"Chanel, baby girl, you fine as hell," Duke said, loving that intoxicated-by-lust look in her big, dark eyes. It was a look that he would soon put into Duchess' eyes and keep there. Forever.

He reached down, squeezed her soft ass and said, "I got bidness ta han'le. Hook up ma boy, Beamer. He hurtin'."

Chanel puckered and squinted those false eyelashes together. She mouthed "I miss you," then she slid to her knees, kicked her spike heels up to her pretty ass, and worked Beamer's jeans with those long, gold fingernails. His big, peanut butter brown dick came flying out like an arrow, making a bulls-eye into Chanel's shiny mouth. Didn't take but a minute to blow his nut. Chanel knew right when to stand up, turn around and bend over, letting Beamer jack his hose as he sprayed a white fountain all over the caramel curves of her ass. His cum dripped down her round, mouth-watering booty like sugar glaze on a golden brown donut.

"Hell yeah," Duke groaned. For a second he was tempted to pull them gold chains to the side of her booty crack and drill himself some relief in a pussy that had never disappointed

Timbo. But he had work to do, and he didn't need the mellowing powers of pussy to dull his mind when he was talking with bad-ass niggas about his bank.

Sex transmutation. That was the term in one of Duke's favorite self-help audiotapes based on the book, *Think and Grow Rich* by Napoleon Hill. It said most men didn't earn their fame and fortune until after they turned forty because they were so distracted by chasing pussy. In the hood, forty was the equivalent of ninety in the white world. Duke was damn lucky he was about to celebrate twenty-one, let alone fucking forty. So, on the hood accelerated life plan, he was right on target. And he was going to stay that way, with Duchess' help.

Once in chemistry class in seventh grade, the teacher talked about "shelf life," how a chemical lost its full potential because it would start decomposing or getting weaker after a few days, months or years. All of Duke's friends started talking about "hood life," how they only had a few years to do what they were going to do before they got shot, went to prison or got killed. And it was true. Most of his boys were either dead, locked up, fucked up on drugs or bums with babies they weren't taking care of. No plan, no goal, no vision. Just living down to the sorry-ass expectations the white world had laid out for them since the first slave ship left Africa four hundred and some years ago.

So, when Duke listened to that book hoping that someday he could actually read it, he decided he needed to focus his sex energy into his work and find just one woman to take care of it for life. That way he wouldn't be squandering his sex power on every ho in D-town. He'd be building his business every time he was fucking his sexy-ass partner in business and in life. His wife. Duchess. Even though all this pussy was his for the taking any time, any way, any day, he knew no pussy could compare to the one he wanted. Now, rather than snack on some always available chicken wings, he would wait for the rare cut of premium filet mignon.

First he had to make dog meat of Izz and any one of these Barrier motherfuckers who were giving each other looks that let Duke know something was up. And wrong.

"Let's roll," Duke said to Beamer, who had zipped up his pants and was on the phone with Pound, checking to see if Duchess had arrived in the hood yet. Beamer tapped his phone to his heart, his signal that everything was cool for now.

Duke stepped toward the hallway leading under the staircase to the back of the house.

Where Izz might be stealin' from me right now.

He walked fast, with purpose, into the kitchen. Izz was at the table counting bricks of Benjamins. Two handguns sat like black eggs in a nest of cash. One of Izz's titty bitches was standing behind him, braiding his hair, and shaking her butt-naked ass to the beat of the music. Some orange platform shoes were sticking out from under the table where another of Izz's own hoes must have been sucking his dick.

Dumb-ass ma'fucka can't concentrate on cash and cummin' at the same time.

His boy, Rake, who was supposed to have Izz's back, was standing at the counter, scarfing down a deep dish pizza. And catching bricks. First Rake would take a bite of pizza then look over at Izz, who would toss a brick. Rake would catch it and toss it into a brown leather backpack next to the pizza box on the counter. They did it again, and Rake didn't even look up. He just held out his hand and caught the cash.

My cash. These ridiculous ma'fuckas makin' a game outta tryin' ta get ova on The Duke.

Duke hit that switch in his head marked BAD-ASS NIGGA-TURBO-DRIVE. He moved so fast, he was like a cat pouncing a mouse.

Before Izz could blink, Duke was on him, with the silver tip of a gun on each of Izz's ashy ears. Duke's voice was deep and hard. "Ma'fucka, fin' the rest o' ma bank you an' Rake stashed, an' you can keep havin' yo' dick sucked."

Izz froze. Beamer was in front of the table, double-aiming at Rake.

Izz groaned. "I ain't—"

Duke pressed the cold metal into his ears harder, to help him think more clearly.

Izz grunted. "Yo, man. Rake." The brown leather bag came flying. It landed on the table, making money flutter up.

"Put it all in the bag." Duke pressed the barrel tips harder into this empty-skulled motherfucker. "An' listen close, bof y'all. One mo' whispa that y'all even *thinkin' 'bout* takin' wha's mine—" Duke loved the power of his deep voice that put the whole room on freeze-frame. "An' you bof gon' get a up close an' personal introduction to ma favorite brotha, Prince."

Chapter 2

Babylon Street was jumping as Duke screeched his ivory convertible Porsche between TV trucks, Escalades and hoopties. Folks packed the porches in every direction, dancing, barbecuing, and talking about this mixed rich bitch from TV who was moving into their hood. Whether they loved her or hated her, they couldn't touch her. Duke had big, bad Barriors standing guard on every corner, just like they did for school kids and grandmothers and anybody else who hired Babylon's protection services.

Now, all eyes were on Miss Green's crumbling little wood-sided house with faded, peeling blue paint, a sagging porch, and dirt for a front yard. A media mob was already camped out on the cracked front sidewalk. A strip of dirt stretched between them and the curb, where Pound Dog sat inside a black Hummer. TV trucks were parked in front and in back of the big vehicle that was holding the hottest spot in the hood right now.

"It's on," Beamer said into his cell phone.

In a flash, the Hummer pulled out and Duke pulled in, just in time to watch his Duchess get dropped by fate right into his lap.

"Tell me I ain't the baddest ma'fucka in the galaxy," Duke said, loving how his voice was vibrating as deep as the funky electric beat of his Bang Squad CD. "Ain't no otha ma'fucka got his own theme song to rock wit'. Jamal finally finish cuttin' Duchess' jus' in time." Duke's diamond "D" ring sparkled as his enormous left hand fell from the polished teakwood steering wheel to the tentpole in his white linen pants. "Damn, Timbo ain't neva been this cocked. An' I ain't even seen her in person yet. This bitch gon' rule."

"No joke, Massa Duke," Beamer said, pulling a thin gold box from the dash. "If I didn't know you better, I'd ask what you been smokin'."

"B, why you think TV here?" Duke nodded toward reporters and cameramen who were running around like ants, jockeying for a spot on the three-foot swath of dirt between his gold rims and the sidewalk. "'Cause e'rybody wanna see the mos' wild, whack give-you-a-heart-attack love story ev'a!"

"She gon' look at you an' run!" Beamer laughed then shouted to the media mob. "Yo! We security. Y'all can't block us."

A white female reporter cut her eyes at him and shook her head, but she got out of the way anyway. So did the big black dude with the camera on his shoulder, and some other reporters with notebooks and tape recorders.

"You definitely on pussy patrol now," Beamer said, nodding across the street where Sha'ante and her hoochie crew were blasting "Move Bitch Get Out Da Way" from the porch of their second story flat. They were also smirking down at the news trucks raising their poles to broadcast live from this urban warzone where the *rat-tat-tat* of gunfire was as common as sirens and screaming.

"Media on one side," Beamer said, "and them blown-out hoes across the street at Sha'ante house, plottin' a bitch hunt."

"Hell no." Duke stiffened with the overwhelming need to protect his Duchess. Sweat prickled down his solid muscles that he had pumped tougher in the gym with the Barriors this morning. He glanced up at those jealous, hard-ass hoes then he looked down at the silver metal nestled between his leather bucket seat and the center console. "Let a bitch try."

Above, the rhythmic beat of helicopter blades stirred up frenzied noise and movement amongst the kids on bikes by the weed-clogged lot next door, the dark faces crammimg every inch of porches on crumbling Cape Cod-style cribs, and the brothas and bitches parked in cars up and down the street sparkling with broken glass. Duke cranked the Bang Squad on the stereo and nodded with Beamer to the deep, steady drumbeat, like marching soldiers, and a chorus of Barriors chanting "Babylon!" Their voices vibrated through Duke with the powerful force of the black warrior motherfuckers he created.

Jus' like they boss. Me. Duke flipped down the mirror. His black wrap-around sunglasses were cool as hell against the angular planes of his dark-dark brown, clean-shaven face and his bald head. The shades rested on an exact replica of King Tut's nose as it appeared on the gold masks Duke had at Babylon HQ. His heart was hammering so tough, he could see it pumping through those thick veins on each side of his wide neck, all the way from the white linen collar of his shirt to the little silver hoop earrings in each ear. They flashed in the late afternoon sun as Duke nodded harder and pointed to the stereo.

"Here go Jamal." The background chant continued as Jamal preached. It was like the ghetto gospel according to rap.

"Babylon rule, wit' D-town cool, urban jewel, win any duel, jack a fool, sexy seductive, serve an' protect, in Babylon, Duke an' Duchess get respect."

The male chorus got louder then faded as the girls rapped over a belly dancer beat. "Babylon men, I'll take ten, rock this ass, oh, so fast, they last an' last, like a rocket blast. The Duke, he rule, wit' D-town cool."

"Watch," Duke said. "She got a light-bright face, white voice, white brain—wit' black balls big as mine."

A week's worth of TV reports flashed in his mind about the girl who would soon be formerly known as Victoria Winston. She had worked for her millionaire daddy in his business. Got straight A's at private school and was scheduled to start classes this week at the University of Michigan in nearby Ann Arbor. She was star of the debate club and school play.

"B, read 'bout how her daddy let her do deals."

Beamer snatched the newspaper from the back seat and read aloud. "Victoria Winston was apparently so wise and mature beyond her years that her father who was known for his distrust of others, entrusted her to secure six-figure negotiations."

"Tha's what I call good home trainin'," Duke said. "She perfect for helpin' me manifest my urban destiny, 'specially when we meet wit' the Moreno Triplets and Mr. and Mrs.

Marx out west. They an' the rest o' the world betta sit down an' shut up. 'Cause Duke Johnson and his Duchess takin' ova, side by side."

"Who you kiddin'?" Beamer said, laughing. "You know damn well that bigger, badder Knight gon' come back an' snatch Babylon back from baby br'a."

"Hell naw." Duke bit down, making his jaw muscles ripple so they'd stop trembling like the rest of him. "Knight know I be runnin' it as good as him an' Prince was."

Even though I shoulda had all this shit from when Knight firs' got locked up. But it took me this long to figure out what the fuck I was doin', all by my damn self. Now I know, an' I'm gon' make Knight finally give me my props.

"Yeah," Duke said. "Me an' Knight gon' be equals, like him an' Prince was."

"Then why you look scared jus' thinkin' about it?" Beamer asked. "Can't nothin' or nobody else scare The Duke."

Duke cranked the music louder.

"Except Knight," Beamer said. "An' you should be scared o' your girl, Milan. She gon' go off! If you make some new, light-skinded, long-haired, blue-eyed *bitch* yo' Duchess, it's gon' be baby momma mutiny."

"Milan ain't it." Duke ignored the vibration of his phone flashing her number. "Blowin' up my phone. She all external. Got too damn skinny, tryin' to be like a model, obsessed wit' looks an' clothes. Greedy, powa-hungry bitch who'd stab my back if I didn't have her watched. Talkin' white, perpetratin' like she so smart."

"She ain't stupid." Beamer put the newspaper on the floor.

"Yeah, she stupid, thinkin' she can get over on me. I hate how she be perpetratin' like she so bougie. The spa. Her aromatherapy. Tellin' me spaghetti ain't spaghetti, it's vermicelli. Michelle ain't Michelle, she fake-ass Milan."

"No joke, Massa Duke, I'd take Milan in a Motor City minute if you 'bout to put 'er out wit' the trash."

"What bank you think you got to get that gold-diggin' diva?"

Scheme flashed in Beamer's goofy-ass eyes as he slid his Glock between the ivory leather seat and the console. He ran his hand over that gold box on his lap, pulled off the lid and stared at a dozen chocolate truffles.

He inhaled loudly, then said, "I'ma get my treasure. But while we on it, how you think yo' num' a one boy feel gettin' trumped by some snowflake you fell in love wit' through a TV screen?" Beamer popped a chocolate ball into his mouth. "Damn, these good when they half-melted in the sun."

Duke shook his head. "Listen to you, ridiculous ma'fucka. Lookin' at chocolate like it's some good pussy. An' you want The Duke to take you serious about havin' juice at Babylon."

"Why you lookin' at me like I ain't shit?" Beamer turned pale.

"'Cause you lack vision, ma'fucka."

"I got vision, man." Beamer nodded at a dark blue Caddie turning into Miss Green's driveway. "Here come Lily White."

"The gods 'bout to deliver my Duchess. Delivered into some Timbo temptation she can't neva resist."

"Mo' like Miss Lily White 'bout to get delivered into Terror Nation," Beamer snickered. "She probably the mos' scary, prissy-ass brat who gon' get here, say 'hell naw,' then do jus' like her daddy and take the quickest exit off Planet Black!" Beamer pointed his Glock at the sky and imitated that nursery rhyme, "Pop Goes the Weasel."

"Pop go the white girl!"

"I'ma pop yo' ridiculous P.O.W. ass like I thought about when I captured you," Duke said. "You ain't said it yet today."

Beamer looked down and bowed his head, just like he did two years ago when Duke decided to let him live. "You gave me life, Massa Duke. You give me life every day, so I serve The Duke in every way."

"Don't forget it, neither." Duke cut his glare away from Beamer and focused on his goddess inside that Caddie about fifteen feet away. All he could see was the back of a white man's head in the driver's seat. The sun glare on the window was blocking her.

His heart hammered so loud, it made static in his ears.

The car door opened. Her long, black hair appeared like a silky, swaying cape as she stood up. "Hell yeah!" Duke groaned with his hand on his dick. Timbo was damn near doing flips. She slammed the door like she was mad at the world. She should be, the way the media was blackwashing her Daddy's scandal all day and night. It was a good thing, too, otherwise Duke never would have seen her on TV, thanks to Henry "Pound Dog" Green, who had pointed to the screen and said that was his cousin who was coming to live on Babylon Street.

Welcome to my urban empire. Duke was like King Tut and Ramses and Caesar and Alexander the Great, all rolled into one. She would become his Cleopatra, conquering new territories, plundering the treasures and the pleasures of their kingdom together.

All in time for Knight to come home an' see I ain't a stupid, scared ma'fucka. I'm gon' be rulin' coas' ta coas' . . . an' he gon' be proud to join back wit' me. Talk to him e'ryday about e'nythang . . . me an' big br'a, tight as ev'a.

And fate was helping them out right now, delivering the face, the mouth, the brain, and body they needed to represent Babylon.

It wasn't a coincidence that Victoria Winston just happened to come on the news while Pound Dog was up in Duke's office at Babylon. Her cousin was a soldier who understood there was no such thing as coincidence when a great leader was manifesting the destiny of Babylon. When shit was divine, all the loyal folk a man needed to make it happen just came, like magic. Like the universe just called them up and said, "Yo, go see The Duke. He got a job fo' ya."

And now his top diva was appearing before his eyes. Cameras were snapping. Reporters and their video crews were running all up on her. She walked tall, proud, and regally down the driveway. Her pink sweater hugged round, ripe titties. Her tight-ass jeans squeezed almost-thick thighs. Her legs were as long and graceful as a giraffe. That hair swinging down to her ass was like a shiny black cape that had to be sexy as hell over them creamy shoulders when she was naked. On red sandals that matched her purse, she stopped at the popped-open trunk, bent over and—

"Ka-pow!" Duke said, his mouth watering at the two ripe cantaloupes pointing his way. "I'ma slurp all ova that juicyli-cious booty."

"Dang, Duke." Beamer laughed. "Close your mouth, dog. Wit' all the bitches you got, why you—"

"Look at them big chocolate kisses on that ass!" Duke groaned. His dick was marble.

She yanked out a suitcase like it didn't weigh anything, then she turned around.

"Check out my Duchess, man. Got a poker face like a mug. Can't never tell her daddy blew his brains out last week. Now e'rybody know she black, broke and comin' to live in the hood wit' her grammomma."

Sha'ante and her crew were blasting their music so loud, it was rattling the windows. They sneered down at Duchess and shouted, "Move, bitch! Get out da way!"

"If she scared," Duke said, "she ain't showin' it. Like a true Amazon. Look at that sexy-ass mouth, like that ma'fuckin' pucker-fish I seen at the zoo wit' my kids." Duke's mouth watered. Her lips were plump and puckered, and red. Extra red against a face that looked like it came straight out of one of Duke's books on Ancient Egypt.

"Damn, this some scary shit, like this chick just popped straight outta one of my dreams." Duke could not believe how her face looked so much like the golden Cleopatra masks they had back at Babylon. Her skin was golden-bronze, her cheeks were pink, and her nose was just like a Barbie doll. Her big, metallic-blue eyes had to be the answer to Duke's silver-dollar wishes shining back from the Zeus fountain in Vegas.

For New Year's Eve, he had taken his crew to Caesar's Palace. In the Forum Shops, after the fiery, thunderous display of the Greek Gods show, he had stepped to the fountain, tossed a handful of coins, closed his eyes and wished for his Duchess to walk into his life like Momma said she would someday. And he'd just know it was her.

Now I know. Fo' sho'.

His dick was throbbing so hard it hurt. Bangin' it up into that virgin pussy couldn't come soon enough if it had happened yesterday.

"Timbo hard as hell. 'Cause she gon' take one look at this six-foot-six Mandingo warrior ma'fucka, an' she ain't neva gon' think about anotha dick. In life."

"We need to work on yo' self esteem, br'a," Beamer said playfully. "No joke. Maybe crank up the confidence a rung or two."

The reporters clustered around her like a swarm of bees. They had already stung her dead daddy and her momma. Now they wanted to suck the honey out of her. Like a reflex, Duke grabbed the side of the door, raised his knees to leap out and shield her from those vultures.

"Massa Duke!" Beamer grabbed his arm. "The las' thing you need is yo' face on TV! You can't be brawlin' wit' the media 'less you want 'em jamin' they cameras down the street at Babylon."

Duke froze. *Prince. He would pimp-slap my ass right now, 'cause I know betta.*

This was just like the day, three years ago, when the mayor walked through the hood with a national TV crew talking to folks about urban renewal. Duke wanted to give them and the world a peek at Babylon HQ from the outside only, to show how he and his brothers had transformed the 100-year-old warehouse into apartments and offices. He wanted them to see how the Barriors were patrolling the streets to keep everybody safe. But as soon as Duke had said it, Prince smacked his bald head and shouted, "Li'l Tut! You wanna audition for a future episode of *America's Most Wanted?* 'Cause I guarantee one ma'fucka watchin' the news gon' say 'Look at that proud nigga. Can't be doin' nothin' legal to pay fo' dat, so let's bring 'im down.' Then they'll write a script for the perfect crime, frame it wit' yo' face, an' put it all ova TV 'til yo' mortals call in to bus' on they enemy."

Prince's eyes always had that wiser-than-you look, just like Knight's did. His big brothers had the same face as Duke, except Prince was a little lighter, and Knight was a little darker. But both brothers were always looking at Duke and talking to him like he was a knucklehead.

Even as Duke held Prince in his lap as he died, his eyes still looked up like *I'll always be smarter'n you, ma'fucka.* Prince looked at him that way even as his last breath bubbled through his lips with a gush of blood and the worst gurgle sound Duke ever heard. It was a sound Duke didn't ever want to hear pass through his own mouth. The sound of death.

Duke slid down in his seat, hoping no cameras had already caught him in pictures or on video. Damn, Knight would probably kick his ass for this too. That was why he hadn't told his brother about The Duchess yet. Duke needed to transform her into a hood goddess before she could come close to passing Knight's ridiculous standards of excellence.

He gon' love her an' think I'm a genius.

So, for right now, Duke could break the rules for a minute because he was here to collect the female treasure being dropped from the sky.

"You are all wicked!" Her strong but satin-smooth voice, deep and sexy, came at him as she faced the TV cameras and reporters. "Everything you printed and broadcast about my dad and my mom was malicious and racist and wrong. Wrong!"

She stomped through the swarm, tossing her head with a slight jerk to her neck, making all that hair fly up, like at the end of a movie when the screen faded to black. It was like she was dismissing all the Motown media with a toss of her pretty head.

"Tol' you baby girl got balls big as mine," Duke said, the corners of his mouth curling up as he watched her strong, elegant stride on the sidewalk.

"Bof y'all crazy," Beamer said, smacking on his chocolate.

"Naw, just watch her," Duke said. The way she carried herself so tall and proud reminded him of his mother—regal, no matter how hard life was. Now, Duke took care of Momma the way she deserved to live, like the Queen that Big Ma named her.

But how would Momma react if Duke brought something that bright home to dinner? When Momma had seen her on the news the other night, she said, "Po' chil'. Don't nobody deserve that. I'd give'er a hug if I could."

His mother sure couldn't stand to see the dollar signs flashing in Milan's eyes, or the bossy, fake proper way she started talking since she went to that white prep school and renamed herself after the fashion capital of Italy. But something about this chick Victoria Winston, she looked and sounded one hundred percent real.

She was all natural, without a lick of makeup. Perfect black eyebrows arched over lashes so long and thick they looked like awnings over windows with her long, black hair falling straight around her face and an Indian-style necklace on, she looked like a Native American princess, walking toward the chief.

She was about three feet away on the sidewalk when she turned to him. Locked those silver-dollar eyes right on him. Her face wore no expression, but the sex power in her stare hit him like two blue-flamed blow torches. Sucked the air out of him. His mouth, nose, and throat burned dry as the desert. It felt like a firestorm inside him.

His heart beat fast and hot, blowing blood up to his brain like a hot air balloon. His head felt light and swirly, like steam was shooting out of his every pore, from his bald head to his toes in his brown leather loafers. His eyes bugged as big as doorknobs behind the sunglasses that steamed up and blurred his focus as she checked him out.

And Timbo, he was flipping around like a giant, caught fish just laid out on the dock under the burning sun, trying to dive back into familiar waters. But it bit that juicy bait worm, so now he was caught. Used to being king of the sea, it was now about to be served up as a feast for a creature who was bigger, better, smarter.

Ma'fuck me! What the fuck kinda crazy feelin's am I settin' off? This bitch gon' kill me wit' one glance!

"Duke?" Beamer knit his thick eyebrows, leaning close. "Look like you havin' a heart attack. What the fuck?"

It was as if Duke's eyes were a magnet and she was a rod of gold. He couldn't separate the two. He was paralyzed on it.

"Dang, she got The Duke kronk'd wit' a right look," Beamer exclaimed. "He out cold!"

The hot spotlight of her stare turned cool as she looked to her left, toward Miss Green's house. Duke sucked in air. She turned her back, walked up the front walk toward the porch. Her ass was bouncing, *Bam! Shazam!* with every step.

His every muscle was trembling, like when he didn't eat for three days after Prince died. His stomach was jumping, and his whole body felt like he was cumming, wracked with delicious spasms. That light-headed feeling was rolling down his whole body, like he was about to float away.

His soul had just found its mate. In fact, it was the same soul, born in two different bodies, in two different worlds. Now it just wanted to run over, dance around with its other half inside her, and come right back here inside Duke.

"Duke, you look possessed. I'm 'bout to call a priest, sprinkle some holy water over yo' exorcist ass."

"Ridiculous ma'fucka," Duke said coolly despite his jittery insides. "That Mexican food we had fo' lunch crampin' my gut. Stole my breath for a minute."

Duke watched her walk up the steps into the house.

"You the ridiculous one, Duke," Beamer said. "Sayin' 'my' about some chick who might be crazy as hell after what she went through. Black momma got fucked to death. Daddy blew his brains out. Now she gotta move outta a big-ass palace an' move into that ghetto shack." Beamer nodded toward her as she ascended the stairs.

"It ain't a question," Duke said, watching her ass cheeks pop as she stepped up. "She gon' move into Babylon tonight." Duke deepened his voice to imitate bad-ass Yul Brenner playing Ramses in *The Ten Commandments*. "And so it is written, and so it is done."

Chapter 3

I am Alice in Ghettoland.

Victoria Winston wished she could pop a pill to escape back to her white wonderland. Then she could get away from the wicked media, the big black guys in that Porsche and the hostile girls across the street. But right now, she had only one magic trick—rubbing her fingertips over her throbbing clit and cumming so hard that her mind, body, and spirit would be transported to another dimension where she felt nothing but raw pleasure.

I'm gonna faint if I don't make myself cum. Now.

Every time her knee rose to step up the stairs, the hard crotch of her jeans rubbed against her hot, wet pussy. Her extreme craving to cum made her sleep-deprived body feel wobbly and off-balance. She concentrated on putting one red leather sandal after the other up the five porch steps. Lumpy shreds of brown indoor-outdoor carpet were a trip-and-fall waiting to happen.

I want two fingers in the pussy and that special flicker-stroke on the clit. Non-stop. That was Celeste, her sex power voice, dictating exactly how to deal with this nightmare. Celeste was Victoria's best friend and worst enemy, because even though Celeste screamed for attention twenty-four/seven, she always responded with intoxicating sensations that defied words. Celeste didn't just make Victoria cum; she gave her power to make dreams and visions come true, especially when Dildo Dick joined the party.

Now, Victoria's sweaty palm gripped the handle of her suitcase, where Dick was nestled between the few jeans, sweaters, and shirts she had salvaged as the feds seized Winston Hill this morning. If her pussy weren't making such a hot, creamy mess of her panties, Victoria would feel a horrible ache and emptiness. For a hug. For assurance that everything would be okay. For the kind of loving gaze her parents used to give her and each other.

Now I have nothing and no one except Celeste as my constant companion. Without that luscious relief, Victoria would have lost her mind the minute she walked into Daddy's blood-and-brains splattered office.

No, she could not let those horrible memories replay in her head. She had to get inside this house and soothe herself the only way she knew how.

I need you to slide your fingers outta your pussy . . . rub your wet fingertips over your hard nipples . . . then cum like your life depends on it.

It did, because orgasms were the ultimate brainstorms for Victoria Winston. In the middle of shivering and gasping, the best ideas always popped into her head. Or, if she already had a goal or a dream, thinking about it while she came would always give it the power to make it come true. Now her goal was getting the hell out of this ghetto, finding some money and starting college forty-five minutes away in Ann Arbor.

After she satisfied herself, she could finally, after half a week with no sleep, slip into a peaceful slumber for a day or two. Now, though, the less she slept, the more irritable and panicky she felt. That made her crave her pussy power all the more. It was her pacifier, her valium, and the closest thing Victoria had to the little pills that Alice popped to grow, shrink or escape from one terrifying experience to the next.

"White bitch!" those girls screamed from across the street. "We gon' stomp yo' ass!"

Would those ogling thugs in the black Porsche parked at the curb—whose stares were burning her backside—stop those chicks from hurting her? What about all the muscular guys and girls in black who were standing on the corners and mid-block like undercover cops? Were they gun-toting drug dealers? Pimps? Friends of her cousin Henry?

A sinister bass beat vibrated from the Porsche, from those girls' upstairs porch, from every car that rattled past, and from inside Gramma Green's house that was smaller than the garage at Winston Hill.

"There is absolutely no money," John Stanley, Daddy's top lawyer, had said when he dropped her off. "Even the insurance policy was seized to pay your dad's debts. Including your college fund. I'm sorry, Victoria. If anything changes, I'll contact you here." And with the slam of a car door, life had booted her into the gutter.

Now, tears blurred the banged-up, dirty aluminum door, its blackened screen ripped and ragged. She coughed on the odor of bacon, dogs, and cigarette smoke. If it was this choking on the porch, she would suffocate inside.

I have to escape, but I have nowhere to go. No credit cards to check into a hotel, no car, no cell phone, no friends.

The sadness felt like her insides were melting. The worse she felt, the more ferociously Celeste throbbed for attention. *God, get me to the bathroom!* She'd been indulging this secret pacifier for as long as she could remember, with the orgasms starting around age eleven. Stroking Celeste was just like when her former best friend Tiffany would ease nervousness by smoking cigarettes, or like her sister Melanie, who calmed stress with chocolate chip cookies and milk. Her brother Nicholas was a neat freak, always washing his hands. And her boyfriend, no, ex-boyfriend Brian, did tequila shots to mellow out. But Victoria's tried and true stressbuster was to dance her fingertips over her always hot, quivering clit then shiver away anxiety and angst. Worked every time. The ultimate opium. All-natural. Free. Safe.

She'd even written a poem about it in her journal, which was crammed in a box along with dozens of others. Years' worth of her most private thoughts were left in her closet at the house she was evicted from today. Victoria tried to remember what she'd written.

I touch Celeste when I'm stressed the best, whether rubbed or pressed . . . like a button, all of a sudden I'm electric, ooh eclectic, feel eclectic . . . in my nerves as my hips swerve to get what I deserve, my fingers serve me so well . . . this hot swell, never tell or go to hell, can't let anyone under my spell . . . or I will kill with my skill, my sex power thrill . . . so good that it could make history repeat, like Mom and Dad, so sad to defeat the men that I meet who want to eat my meat, so erotic and exotic but toxic . . . so I gotta keep it virgin, even though it's surgin' with hot cream, lusty steam, and it seems to possess me, ooh caress me, I'm feelin' so sexy . . .

Victoria almost smiled. She'd performed poems in the spoken word style at the cool coffee house where she used to hang out with Brian and Tiffany, but never that poem, of course. They were more innocent ones, about life and love and whatever came to mind at the moment. Brian never believed her when she said she'd made it up as she went along, but she did. And she could remember them, too. Only problem was that the one she just recited in her mind was making her pussy *burn*. And making her feel a million miles away from the hip coffee house in the rich suburb with her fancy friends. They were fake friends who loved her "exotic" Native American look, until they found out her creamed coffee complexion had some real black coffee in the mix. It was as if she turned to chum before their eyes, because once they sniffed black blood, they bit like sharks and left her with a bleeding heart.

Right now, she was going to counter every bit of sadness and rage with an equally powerful orgasm.

I'm gonna have hot pussy meltdown if I don't get inside and find the bathroom.

The screen door creaked as Victoria pulled it open. A hot gust of thick air that reeked ten times worse than on the porch, assaulted her nose and mouth.

How in the world am I gonna breathe in here? Much less breathe hard as I cum.

"Com'ere, sweet chil'," Gramma Green wheezed from the plastic-covered yellow couch facing the door. An oxygen tube extended from her nose to a dark green tank beside the couch. Her swollen legs protruded from a quilt over her lap, and a crusty black sore dotted her heel. "Thought you was neva gon' get here."

If Victoria hadn't seen her grandmother at her Daddy's funeral the day before, she wouldn't even recognize her. When Mommy died, Gramma Green had a full, nutmeg-brown face with beautiful, flowing black "Indian" hair. But the past ten years had etched a dark, raccoon-like streak around her watery eyes, and an ashen gray pallor accentuated her sunken cheeks. Who knew what was under that ratty auburn wig?

Victoria froze. Dogs were barking in the room at the end of the little hallway that led back from the front door.

"Lawd, if Henry 'nem don't get them animals out ma house—" Gramma Green doubled over, hacking. Her movement exposed the framed pictures on the table next to the couch. Among them was Victoria's first grade school picture, when she was six, the last time she came to visit here with her mother. After Mommy died, Daddy said it wasn't safe or wise for Victoria to come here and be influenced by her cousins.

Gramma Green sat up, blocking the picture. She spit a wad of slime into a tissue then looked back up at Victoria.

How is this sick old woman gonna take care of me? And how did Mommy grow up in this place? She escaped, scooped up by her white knight, who made her princess of his castle. But now some wicked spell was reversing the good fortune.

"Grrrrr!" Victoria glanced to the right, down a dim hallway. A white pit bull with red-rimmed eyes was charging at her. She screamed, dropped her suitcase and raised her arms over her head. Her mind flashed with news reports she had heard about those vicious attack dogs clamping their teeth onto a person's neck, shaking violently, and killing men, women and children.

The dog's sharp white teeth flashed. It leaped up at her.

It's over. Three minutes in the ghetto and I'm killed by a pit bull. Yet another tragic tidbit for the media to sensationalize Daddy's scandal. Maybe the TV stations would even show her chewed-up, bloody body being dragged out of this little hut while all those people on the street cheered, "Whitey's dead!"

And I didn't even get to make myself cum one last time. Male laughter shot into the room along with a high-pitched dog whimper and a rattling chain. Victoria peeked between the pink sleeves of her shirt. The dog was flinging backward on a leash held by a young black guy who was cracking up.

"Henry!" Victoria shouted. She hit him on the arm playfully, like when they were kids in the backyard or at the family's annual picnic at Belle Isle Park. "Don't you remember I'm scared of dogs?"

"Welcome to da hood, baby!" Finally, a familiar, vibrant face. Henry's big, dark eyes sparkled from his oatmeal-colored face. He had a cool goatee and mustache that was so finely groomed it looked painted on. His oversized, super-white teeth flashed as he grinned then leaned down to tighten the dog's leash. His black hair was carved with block letters that spelled POUND across the back of his thick head. The same word scrolled across the wide back of his red football jersey, which hung long over his baggy jeans. He dropped the leash and kept the dog in one spot by pressing a red leather gym shoe onto the chain.

"Henry, you scared me!" Victoria pressed her right hand just below the C-cup curve filling out her soft pink sweater. If only she could caress her nipples and take care of Celeste right now! The terror of that moment intensified her self-sex craving so strong, Victoria was dizzy.

"Girl, you ain't gotta worry 'bout nothin'," Henry said as the dog growled. "You my favorite cousin. An' I got' cha back!"

"Then can you take me to the bathroom."

"Grandbaby, this Joe," Gramma Green said over a soap opera blasting from the giant-screen TV. It was next to the window facing the street, but the heavy drapes were closed. Bluish light from the screen illuminated a corner where a white-haired man with dark skin sat in work pants, a white wife beater and suspenders. He nodded.

Gramma Green held out her arms. "Give me some suga, girl."

Victoria felt Joe's eyes on her body as she bent to kiss Gramma's clammy forehead. She wanted to say, *Thanks for taking me in when everybody turned their back,* but putting it into words would somehow make this feel real, and right now it still felt like a bad dream.

As she inhaled Gramma's perfumed medicine scent, Victoria's mind flashed with the images of Daddy's waxy white face, the eery stillness of his elegant hands crossed over his chest, all those folds of beige satin, and the casket closing on her life, too. None of his family had come to the funeral. In their eyes, Daddy had died when he said "I do" to life with the woman he loved. Those nameless, faceless relatives had never met Mommy, never seen Victoria or her siblings. And they certainly hadn't come forward to take any of them in.

"You gon' stay in Kay-Kay room," Gramma said, pointing with chipped fingernails splotched with the remains of red polish. "Slow that fas' chil' down. But first, Henry, take her to eat in the kitchen. I know you hungry."

"I'm starving," Victoria said. She was starving for satisfaction from food, and her fingers. A heaping plate of chicken, rice, and salad would be perfect. "But I need the bathroom!"

Henry led her into that dark hallway ringing with foul language carried on by deep male voices, along with the sound of growling dogs and loud, chewing-smacking sounds. He stopped at a door, turned the knob, and pushed it open.

"Eh!" a man yelled.

"Yo, ma bad," Henry answered. "Sorry, Vic, the throne room occupied. C'mon."

Victoria followed him into the kitchen. To her left, on the stove, pots and pans held pork chops in gravy, cornbread, green beans overcooked with chunks of bacon, and super-fattening macaroni and cheese. Yuck. She never ate artery-clogging crap that would make her butt as wide as that old refrigerator.

Oh my God.

"Day-um!" exclaimed one of four guys kneeling around four pit bulls that were ripping raw steaks to shreds in the middle of the floor. In the corner, a dog was running on a miniature treadmill.

"This *can't* be little Victoria," said another guy who was Henry's younger brother, Hank. "Ain't nobody that fine in this family."

"Her momma was," Henry said. "Our momma was, 'til she hit that pipe." Henry glanced back at a table in a sunlit alcove. Beyond three black handguns and a box of bullets, Aunt Harriett sat dazed, her skinny, scarred legs crossed. Bony brown shoulders protruded with grotesque skinniness from a halter top as she smoked a cigarette.

Victoria's stomach burned with disgust. How could *that* be Mommy's sister? Something about the shape of Harriett's dark brown eyes resembled Mommy's so much. A sour heave bubbled up in Victoria's throat.

"Git!" Henry shouted at his dog. It scampered to the others to slurp that meaty mess on the floor.

The guys circled Victoria, steamrolling her body with four pairs of eyes. She wished she hadn't worn the pink sweater that always made Brian so hot and bothered, the way it pushed up her C-cups and exposed just a slice of stomach above those black jeans that were too snug for this ghetto family reunion.

Brian. *That bastard said he loved me.* He said they'd be together forever . . . graduate together from The Academy, attend business school at the University of Michigan, then open their own company.

"Pretend we never met," Brian said just days ago, his blue eyes turning to ice as she sobbed her fate. She begged him and his parents to let her live in one of the wings of their mansion across the lake from Winston Hill.

His dad looked up from the Sunday newspaper with Daddy's picture on page one along with a story that revealed Mommy was black. "You deceived us, Victoria," Mr. Martin said. "We knew about your Indian grandmother, not your black mother." Mrs. Martin flinched as her husband continued. "Had you been open and honest with us, perhaps we could be more obliging to your tragic plight right now, but I'm afraid we could never trust you."

Then, after Brian ripped out her heart, he smashed it to bits by reading—with an executioner's accusatory tone—the newspaper's sidebar article about Mommy's mysterious death. "An unnamed source tells *The News* that thirty-two-year-old Lynnette Winston's dark beauty— with her caramel brown skin and black satin mane—was so bewitching and seductive, she literally aroused her husband to make love to her with such frequency and force that it killed her."

Brian looked up from the paper. His sandy hair clumped on his sweaty forehead, his angular cheeks reddened, his blue eyes glowed with disgust as he growled, "Your mom was a little freak and you won't even fuck me!" Then he read more. "'Mrs. Winston's death certificate read: cardiac arrest from an undiagnosed congenital heart defect.' Shoulda said sexual overdose! You little freaky bitch! It's a good thing you're finding this out now, before you let me or anybody else fuck you to death too!" He snatched her arm, yanking her into a little room where his parents would never hear him act on the rape roiling in his eyes.

She kicked him in the dick she had sucked so many times. And she ran, crying, trembling, and hating the world. She ran a whole mile to Tiffany's house, where her parents were also reading the Sunday paper.

"Earth to Victoria!" Henry shouted, laughing. "Girl, you trippin' up in the Twilight Zone! You in'a hood now. Betta pay attention, front, back, and sideways."

"You gon' live *here?*" asked a guy with cornows and denim overalls. "Yo, Pound, dis dat chick you was shown' us on da news? Da one who daddy suck down some lead?"

"Shut the fuck up," Henry shouted at him. "Dog, you sho' she black?" another guy asked. "Booty don't lie," Henry said, his eyes scanning her jeans.

"Girl, I got your back around these fools, too. Kay-Kay, though, she crazy. Keep your legs crossed when you sleep, else she'll try to lick your pussy all night long."

Victoria kept her face a stiff mask, just like Daddy taught her.

"Her girl stay here half the time, so she straight," the guy in overalls said. "I mean she gay, but she straight when her girl—" The other guys cracked up.

"Let me get you away from these clowns," Henry said, putting his arm around Victoria. "'For they scare you half to death."

As he led her down the hallway, Victoria remembered how Henry taunted her in the church dinner hall after Mommy's funeral. "Yo' momma got fucked to death. Yo' daddy loved black pussy so much he banged it up, dead."

Victoria, who was six, had no idea what Henry was talking about. All she knew was that whatever Mommy did to die that way, Victoria was never gonna do when she grew up.

Ever.

Chapter 4

Milan Henderson's insides were a pent-up coil about to spring loose if Dr. Reynolds didn't hurry up. It had been three hours, and ten more Studs and Sluts were still lounging around the plush red couches up here in Sex Squad HQ. Above them, in the tall paned windows set in exposed brick, the late afternoon sun cast an orange haze as they watched TV, flipped through magazines and missed five o'clock sexercise.

"Madame Milan, you fine as hell in them pants," said Johnny "Flame" Watts, flashing those famous smoky gray bedroom eyes. His black-as-leather linebacker body stretched on the couch, facing the TV, barely covered in white cotton bike shorts and a tank top. The shining black head of his legendary dick stuck out of the waistband, resting on his flat abdomen. Against the white fabric of his cotton tank top, it was so swollen that it looked like the mangle-shaped head of a big snake, lying in wait for a treat. He was one of the most requested Studs, who could slither like no other.

"Yo' ass look like two tiny apples," he said. "Madame Milan, if you was my woman—"

"Yo, G, she ain't," Dante Williams snickered. "So, 'less you wanna get Duked, put cha eyes back in ya head and zip them pretty-ass lips. Let a brotha watch the news in silence."

Sharon "Lollipop" Barnes sucked her teeth. "Niggas."

The way she was sitting, she looked like an indigo wishbone. Her black sundress was raised around her waist, and each long, elegant leg was hoisted over the arms of the chair. She was holding a hand mirror and examining her pussy.

"Madame Milan, that new chick down in the salon jacked my cunt up wit' her no-bikini-wax-havin' self. Shit! When you gon' get Freida back? That girl can work wit' some pussy hair."

"I need some ointment for the same thing," Dante said, running a hand over his pecks that were bulging through a muscle T-shirt. "Call herself waxin' my chest. Sheee-it! Coulda done a better job wit' a lawnmower. What's takin' Doc so damn long?" Milan crossed her thin arms, closing her eyes, trying to block out Dante's prattle. "Ma clients ain't tryin' ta lay up agains' no nasty-ass rash."

Milan ground her teeth to make the sudden wave of nausea stop. Why did they call it morning sickness when it lasted all day? And what was the name for the extreme horniness she always felt when another baby was growing up in there?

I have to talk to Duke. Now.

It was time for him to make good on his childhood promise to marry her and call her Duchess. No more of this grunt work, overseeing the Sex Squad, their checkups and all their drama. It had been two years since she graduated, thanks to a scholarship at the exclusive prep school. She had come to work for Duke instead of going to college. Now it was time for her ultimate promotion to Duchess, wife, and mother of two, soon-to-be-three, of his babies.

Her breasts felt swollen, extra sensitive and too tight inside her lace bra. She had a serious Dolly Parton look in her green silk blouse. She reached under, to the green alligator belt around her slim waist, where she unclipped the cell phone. The metallic jade rectangle flashed 5:03 p.m. on the display.

That bastard hasn't called me back all afternoon. Beamer either. He'd better not be out fuckin'.

Her muscles tensed, as if that coil inside her was tightening even more. Sobbing echoed from the exam room. Milan's green gator pumps tapped the polished hardwood floor as she made a beeline to the orange door marked EXAM ROOM. When the next Squad member came out, Milan was going to talk some sense into that dingy broad, Dr. Reynolds. Was she fucking one of the Studs? Eating some Slut pussy?

"I will fire her rule-breakin' ass if she even thinks about it," Milan mumbled under her breath as her knuckles rapped on the door. "And sic Uncle Sam on her house out in West Bloomfield. Let him ask her how she can live so large with her little clinic in the hood."

"A few more minutes," Dr. Reynolds called. Somebody was crying. A woman.

"I don't have time for this drama," Milan said, opening the door. Duke needed to understand that her brainpower, her class and sophistication needed to be put to more challenging and important work, like negotiations with the Moreno Triplets and strategizing the future of Babylon. Not what she was doing now, opening the exam room door to see Janelle Rhodes, a.k.a. Hot Box, slumped like a big heap of butt-naked brown sugar on the table. Janelle's platinum blond braids were all over the place like Medusa's snakes, all the way down to the red heart tattoo over her plump ass.

Milan's nipples hardened. She remembered the feel of Janelle's smooth ass and the taste of her pussy at one of the Duke Joint parties. That was well before Janelle started to look so used up and through.

"You look like hell," Milan said, closing the door and crossing her arms. "You must have this medical exam room confused with a psychologist's couch. And *greet* me when I enter the room!"

Janelle stared through bloodshot brown eyes ringed by plum arcs of fatigue from fucking for a living. No words passed over her chapped, quivering lips.

"I said greet me," Milan ordered. Her every muscle was tensing so hard it hurt. "I don't care how bad you look or feel, Slut. Show your respect."

"I ain't callin' you Madame Milan no mo'. Fake bitch, stuck-up snob. Walkin' 'round like you da queen when all you really is is a prissy-ass p-i-m-p!"

Milan ground her teeth. *I will not waste my energy going off on this worn-out wretch.*

"Janelle, you've obviously been smoking something or taking a hallucinogen, both of which are grounds for termination from the Squad. Not to mention your appearance has been going from bad to worse by the week."

"Excuse me, Madame Milan," Dr. Reynolds said. "It's time for Janelle to retire."

"What did you catch, Slut?" Milan noticed purple bruises dotting her thigh and upper arms." And who beat you?"

"My client," she sobbed. "He seen somethin' on my pussy after we fucked."

"I just tested Janelle. She's got genital warts. And HIV."

Milan stared hard into Dr. Reynolds' almond-shaped eyes behind those big, purple glasses. "Why the fuck didn't you see this at her exam last week? Thank goodness I didn't send you to the party on Chicago this afternoon. Stupid bitch."

Dr. Reynolds said, "As you know, HIV can take three months to register on a test. And Janelle's vagina was so swollen and red from a yeast infection last week that the warts were not visible."

"Janelle, did you use condoms like you're supposed to with clients?" Milan asked.

Janelle sobbed into the crinkly paper on the exam bed.

"Stupid bitch," Milan said. Her neck muscles were so tense she was sure that coil was going to spring and she'd just go off. "I recommend that you leave town for a while. Visit your family in Texas," Dr. Reynolds said.

"Just go," Milan said. "Get dressed. Go to your room. Pack your things. Leave out by six o'clock. You know the drill. If we catch you tryin' to do business on Babylon turf—"

"I ain't got no death wish, bitch," Janelle shrieked. "You always walkin' 'round here like you a drill sergeant. Maybe if you act like a woman, the man you think yo' man would give you the time o'day!"

Nausea made Milan want to grip the edge of the exam table, but she stopped. She didn't want to touch Janelle's nasty-ass germs.

"I know Babylon gon' pay for my HIV drugs," Janelle snapped.

"Out," Milan ordered.

Janelle darted from the room.

"It'll be a few minutes, everybody," Milan told the Squad members in the lounge. All of them were staring up at the TV. "That is Duke," Flame said. "Him an' Beamer."

"That's the mixed chick who been on the news all week," Dante exclaimed, sitting up straight.

Milan glared up at the TV. If Duke thought he was gonna jump on that half-white bitch right under her nose . . .

"Hey," Flame said, shooting up like a rocket over to the window. His hard, round ass looked better than any male underwear commercial as he looked through the horizontal blinds, down and to the right. "That's all down at Pound Dog house."

Milan sprang to the window. There was Duke in his Porsche. There was the bitch on the porch, cameras, eyes and probably a few guns all aimed at her fat ass. A hot, burning sensation shot up Milan's throat. She ran to the bathroom, a door beside the exam room. She barely made it to the toilet before she vomited. That coil of tension inside her was sprung, and it was bringing up the seafood salad she ate for lunch, along with all the toxic thoughts and feelings.

Her mind tripped forward over so many scenarios. She could go down there right now, tell Duke off to his face and put him and that bitch on notice that Milan Henderson was Duke Johnson's first and last, his one and only. She could call him real sweet, plan a candlelight dinner, and convince him how much he loved her and only her. Or she could bitch-slap him into submission by treating him the way he needed to be treated until he acted right.

She splashed water on her face, brushed her teeth, gargled then stared at her diamond-shaped face. Her usual complexion was more gray-green. But one good thing about morning sickness, all this vomiting was making her cheeks look chiseled like those fashion models she saw on the runway during Fashion Week last fall in New York. Duke was so sweet, sending her there to enjoy the glitterati and stay in one of Bang Squad's penthouses. Since then, she had starved her five foot three inch hourglass from a size eight to a size four. Now, her little triangle of a nose looked more pointed than ever. Her eyes, the same rich light brown color as maple syrup, appeared bigger, more intense. Her relaxed, straight, brown hair was thick and shiny, parted at the side and pulled back to show off the raisin-sized rocks in her ears. The earrings were gifts from Duke, of course, on the day one year old Hercules was born. The diamond studs were double the size of the ones he gave her in the hospital when their first baby, two year old Zeus came into the world.

She fingered the necklace at the base of her much skinnier neck, displayed so richly between the still collar of her green silk blouse. *Milan,* it said, scrolled in diamonds. She remembered the love in Duke's eyes five years ago when he gave her that and said, "You in ma blood, baby girl. E'rytime ma blood pump through ma heart, you there."

And I will not let him get a white blood transfusion to flush me out or deprive me of the best dick in Detroit. Duke is mine.

Horny as she was, carrying their child, Duke *was* going to take care of her pussy, her life, their family. The right way. With a ring. A wedding. A proper household. Not that either of them had ever had that, but Milan wanted it, and she always got what she wanted, even if she had to take it.

"And no suburban cream puff is going to steal my spot at Babylon," she whispered. "Never."

Milan walked calmly back into the lounge just as Flame was coming out of the exam room. She took his hand, led him into her office and closed the door. Then she stepped to the window, rested her elbows on the ledge, and stared down at Duke in his Porsche with one hand holding his phone to his ear, the other hand on Timbo, eyes on Miss Thing's ass.

"You like my pants," Milan said lustfully back at Flame. "Pull 'em down and fuck me."

As his huge hands unbuckled her belt and pulled her pants down over her pooted-out ass, her phone fell to the floor and began to ring. DUKE flashed on the screen. She was watching him call her back finally, but she let it ring. She was busy moaning, grinding her back on the baseball bat and big balls connected to this Stud. No, she couldn't hear Duke ringing her phone now. Not when she cried out as Flame slammed her hot, wet pussy into the outfield.

Chapter 5

"Henry, it's beyond urgent!" Victoria exclaimed outside the bathroom door. She crossed her legs and squatted a little, as if she were holding in pee. She was actually rubbing her clit against her jeans and squeezing the muscles between her legs. The massage sensation teased like a crumb when she was craving the whole cookie.

Henry banged his knuckles on the door. An angry male grunted back. "Yo, let a nigga take a shit."

"Ugh," Victoria groaned, standing up. "If I don't get in there, I'm gonna faint. Seriously."

"Seein' Kay-Kay gon' make you faint," Henry said, leading her to another door. He grabbed her suitcase from the living room and said, "Anyway, let them fumes air out befo' you come back. Lonnie stink bombs notorious!" Henry opened the bedroom door. Sweet-scented smoke stole Victoria's breath.

"Girls only!" Kay-Kay shouted from somewhere beyond the cloud.

"Iss ma fav'rite cousin!" Kay-Kay emerged from the smoke. Her skinny brown arms were extended, her raisin-colored nipples were hard, pointing forward, and a silver ring formed an "O" at the center of what looked like a black olive in a dark nest.

Victoria gasped. Kay-Kay's marijuana breath was so strong, Victoria could taste it. She stared hard at Kay-Kay's face. "What happe—"

Her resemblance to herself and Mommy was eery and freakish. They had the same big, round eyes with long, thick lashes, same Indian priestess cheekbones, pillowy, puckered lips, and luxurious hair. A center part divided two thick black plaits extending down her bony shoulders. But her skin was horrible, splotchy, with scaly patches. A dark scar streaked across her stomach and upper thigh like a tire track.

"Girl," another female voice cried out from the smoke. "Why you ain't tell me she *that* fine?" She leaped out of the smoke and put her arm around Kay-Kay. She was a little plumper, with skin the color of corn chips, and nipples that looked like the tips of those snack sausages on the counter in party stores. The girl extended a joint pinched between long, blue fingernails with sparkles and stripes. "New girl, I'm LaKwonda."

Victoria held her breath. Her eyes burned. They were wide open, staring. As the smoke thinned, bunkbeds came into focus behind the girls. Threadbare, dirty yellow comforters hung over their edges. Nearby, studded jeans and T-shirts covered a wooden chair. Clothes covered the chipped, faux-wood desk, the dusty green tile floor, and hooks on the closet door.

"Dorothy straight outta Kansas." LaKwonda giggled, sucking on the joint, which glowed red. "Girl," she squinted, "you in the hood now. Look, she even got red shoes."

"I have to open the window," Victoria gasped. To her right, late afternoon sunshine sliced through a rip in the yellowed window blind and dust particles danced in the smoke. No way was she going to jeopardize her health, or the track scholarship she now needed to attend college, by breathing their toxic air.

College, right. She was supposed to be at the University of Michigan *right now*. But the money was gone. So now, as soon as she got settled in this rathole, she would figure out how to apply for a track scholarship and get to the Ann Arbor campus right away. There was no other option; not a community college, or worse, missing out on higher education altogether. No, she had to get up and out. Now. Without breathing all these toxic fumes.

"I can't deal with smoke," Victoria said, squeezing her pussy muscles to calm her nerves.

"Pull that stick out yo' ass, girl." Kay-Kay laughed. "Ain't nobody tryin' to be prissy down here. Show some love fo' yo' kin now that you comin' back to yo' black roots."

Victoria stared. Looking at Kay-Kay was like looking in a carnival mirror that distorted color rather than size. Her face was the darker, drugged-out, unhealthy, and a haunting version of her own. And her mother's.

This is the freakish and deviant extreme of unleashing our mix-race woman power.

Kay-Kay had it, too, from her mother Harriette, the crackhead in the kitchen, who got pregnant by a Mexican migrant worker a year after Victoria was born.

All this was silencing Celeste. Numb.

Victoria hated that she could see her mother so strongly in Kay-Kay's face. It was taking her back . . . ten, eleven years, to their big, pretty house, when Mommy took her on her lap on the frilly vanity chair, pointing at the ornate mirror where, in the soft perfumed air of her bedroom, mother and daughter reflected back the identical face—one girl-sized vanilla, the other full-grown caramel brown. Both were framed by flowing ebony hair that shone in the soft light. Both had big, sparkling aquamarine eyes fringed with thick black lashes, natural ruby lips parting over perfect white teeth, and smiles beaming with mother-daughter love.

"Victoria," Mommy would say, pressing her soft, Indian priestess cheek to the girl's plump one. "You inherited a special power, a force. I call her Celeste. She will always be within you. And when you're older, I'll teach you how to use her to get any and everything you want and need in life."

"Where does it come from?" Victoria asked.

Her mother tapped an elegant fingertip to Victoria's forehead. "She's in here. My grandmother, she was Blackfoot Indian, she taught me that mix-breed women like us possess the power of many races. African plus European plus Native American, all contained in a beautiful female form, is the most potent power in the universe."

Her mother smiled. "Our female essence activates that power, and it makes us magic. And there are ways you can draw in even more power. Back when I had nothing, Celeste made your daddy fall in love with me and bring me here to live like a princess."

But Mommy died before she could teach Victoria how to summon and use Celeste. That was okay. Little Victoria figured out that any power so strong it made daddy fall in love with mommy and ultimately kill her, was too strong of a power and Victoria didn't want anything to do with it—neither the race mix that brought it on, nor the sex that brought it out.

So, Victoria vowed to stay a virgin forever. Despite overwhelming adolescent hormones and a pleading boyfriend, Victoria made a deal with herself. As long as she controlled her body and never shared Celeste's power, she would never risk killing herself, or someone else. And she learned to channel this magic power. While masturbating, she would envision a goal: winning the 100-yard dash at the school track meet, getting an A on her chemistry final exam or being a perfect, charming lady in formal gowns at all those black tie events Brian's parents hosted in their ballroom. As she orgasmed, she would hold that image in her mind in perfect detail.

Life imitated eroticism every time. She never failed to win track medals, straight A's, and praise from Brian's parents. Victoria never outright made a mental call to Celeste in the way her mother had described, like an angel or a fairy godmother.

"Vic, what you been smokin'? I don't want nothin' that make me that spaced out." Kay-Kay and LaKwonda giggled then dove onto the bottom bunk.

The stillness and silence snapped Victoria out of her flashback. The girls came into focus. Their limbs were tangled together and they were French kissing.

Victoria dashed from the room. A swath of light shined from the bathroom. She ran in, closed the door. Whether it reeked or not, she'd never know. She pulled the top of her sweater up over her nose and inhaled the soft floral scent of the perfume she abandoned at her house. The doorknob jiggled when she turned the lock from horizontal to vertical.

"Oh my God, finally." She unzipped her jeans, pulled them and her pink satin panties off, and hung them on a hook on the back of the door. The filth of the bathroom barely registered as the cool air hit the steaming hot gush between her legs. With her sandals on, Victoria raised her right foot onto the chipped blue tile of the sinktop vanity. She balanced on her left foot, spread-eagled with her right leg bent at the knee to expose her red-hot, throbbing pussy. She washed her hands. There was no soap, but she scrubbed them together hard under hot water. She balanced her right fingertips over her swollen clit.

Why was that music so loud? And those guys's laughter.

One of them was saying, "Whoo-wee!" She scanned the wall. *Oh my God!* Hank's dark eyes flashed in a hole in the wall between the toilet and the mirror. About the size of a man's fist, chipped plaster ringed a circular peephole into the kitchen.

"Excuse me!" Victoria exclaimed as she bent at the waist to cover herself. If questioned, she would say she was about to insert a tampon. "Never complain, never explain," Daddy used to always say. So no, she wouldn't say anything. Instead, she stepped to the wall, pressed her back against the hole and raised her foot onto the lid of the toilet.

"Yes," she whispered.

Touching her clit was like pressing a button that released tiny purple lightning bolts from a super-charged warehouse between her legs. Each bolt shot with tingling intensity, zigzagging up to every inch of her skin, making it tickle. And as her fingers made little circles round and round the swollen ball, the lightening bolts danced behind her closed eyelids in streaks of orange, red, yellow. Her pussy was pulsating so hard it was like her heart, pumping, pounding, beating the life through her. And that sweet, salty smell was so intoxicating, she pulled her shirt off her face so she could inhale loudly.

She would use this energy, the most powerful energy available to humans, to conceive an idea, a plan, and a vision for how she could escape this inner city nightmare immediately. Without violating her vow of celibacy for Celeste. For a second, she remembered Dildo Dick in Kay-Kay's lesbian lair. He would make this all the more awesome, but no way was she about to go back into that room. She'd have to make do on her own.

Victoria shoved her left middle finger into the hot, tight hole while her right fingers rubbed away angst and anxiety. With all the questions quiet, her brain was a silent workshop where innovative ideas could stand up and shout.

Celeste, Victoria thought as wonderful shivers rippled through her flesh. *I am calling on you right now to give me the power to leave here and live like I'm used to.*

"Your mix-race woman powers," a voice answered. Victoria's fingers stopped midstroke, even though she was about to cum.

A voice answered! She moved her finger in and out of her slick hole, rubbed her clit with perfect precision, so that her body was trembling.

"Mix-race woman powers," the voice said, "will get you up and out. But you—"

Victoria's every cell exploded in orgasm. Her arms and legs convulsed. Her nipples poked through her pink sweater. The sensuous intoxication was so strong, such a relief from the horrors of the day, her face twisted into a sob.

The voice screamed in her mind, "But you have to share your sex."

"No!" Victoria cried. Alice found the little pill to pop and escape from Ghettoland, but the bottle was marked with a skull and crossbones! "No!" Victoria was gasping and sobbing and saying with a tone that was erotic and anguished all at once. "No! No! No!"

The bathroom door burst open. Henry's eyes bugged. A silver gun flashed at his side. "What the fuck, Vee! Sound like somebody hurtin' you, but you in here havin' a freak party all by ya damn self! Shit!"

Victoria glared at him through tears. Her lips trembled as she shouted, "Get me out of here!"

Chapter 6

As Duke wove the Porsche through the clog of trucks and cars on the Lodge Freeway, Beamer sat in the passenger's seat, popping another Godiva chocolate truffle into his mouth. It was like lobbing a Cocoa grenade into his gut to blow up and sugarcoat the fucked up feelings he had right now about Duke and that almost-white chick.

But he had to speak. Couldn't hold it in no longer, even though there was no tellin' how Duke would react. "Yo, dude, that's some whack shit about makin' Snow White your partner," Beamer said. "I been yo' devoted servant two years now. Time to make me Lieutenant o' Babylon."

Duke tossed back his head, opened his mouth wide to the sky. A deep laugh busted out. Beamer's heart rattled. Duke's laughter was like poison fangs stabbing every inch of his skin. Rage seeped into his blood. He was dizzy.

"You workin' on a routine for open mic night down at the comedy club?" Duke laughed.

Beamer hated that emotion was making his voice sound shaky. "I'm serious as a heart attack, dude."

As he laughed, Duke's big, white teeth flashed along with his diamond "D" ring on the hand holding his stomach.

Beamer had to state his case. "I know how e'rythang at Babylon work. Top to bottom. The B'Amazons, the Barriors, the Secret Service, the Sex Squad. Now, I'm puttin' you on notice. Beamer up for promotion in the biggest way."

Duke's big hand gripped the steering wheel. Other than that and his foot moving on the gas pedal, he was still as a statue, even when he sped up to squeeze through what looked like the eye of a needle between two cars to get into the fast lane. The speedometer moved from ninety-five to ninety-seven to ninety- nine. Beamer put on his seatbelt. "Yo, dog," Duke said with that smooth, deep voice that always made everybody in the room shut up. Now he mimicked a game show host. "Mr. Beamer, you're the lucky winner of two choices."

Beamer laughed and popped another chocolate into his mouth.

"Choice number one," Duke said, "you can keep kidding yourself through the helluva magnifying glass you got between yourself and reality. Or you can focus in on the twenty/twenty now, before the hindsight at your last breath makes you see you were fucking up in grand style."

Beamer sucked the chocolate, laughing loudly, but he spoke in all seriousness. "Ain't squat distorted. I'm speakin' for Milan too."

"Now you really in the comedy zone. Milan look at the world through eyes so greedy and jealous, half the time she don't know a dolla from a dick."

"Dude," Beamer said, "she know Babylon even more 'n me. She—"

"She a professional ho. Two kids and knowin' her my whole life, b'lieve me, Milan ain't nobody friend. She out fo' num'a one. And damn the foo' who think she ain't gon' back, front, and side—stab 'im to get her way."

"So, you diss yo' girl but think Miss White Thang gon' want some thug love? Milan'll kill bof y'all." Beamer popped another chocolate into his mouth.

"All that chocolate mus' be helpin' you grow some balls," Duke said. "That's good, but dig this: You ain't my partner. You my assistant. Helper. Servant. You owe me your life. You oughta wake up every morning and kiss my feet before you take your first breath."

Beamer froze. The chocolate melted on his tongue.

"I am God, ma'fucka. I gave you life. I give you life e'ry day. I'm the king. You're the servant. When I get my pretty-ass, half-white Duchess, who prob'ly got more brains and balls than ten o' you put together, you gon' serve her too. So, get that scheme outta your eye."

Duke stared hard, right into Beamer's eyes. "To put it on repeat fo' ya. You my servant, not my partner. I'm the king. I need a queen, and she it. And so it is written, and so it is done."

Beamer was already spinning back, remembering vividly the carnage that Duke spared him from, working as second in command for Duke's archrival, whom he dominated and defeated. But when it happened, Beamer had vowed to someday reign over Duke.

"Know why it was so easy for me to bring Pinks down? 'Cause you was holdin' him up. Some people was born to lead, some to follow, some to serve. You serve me. Now, what was the exact words?"

Beamer said, "I promise to protect and serve you with my life forever."

"And what is the punishment for breakin' that promise?"

"Finish what you was about to start."

"Cool. Now that we got that refreshed, shut the fuck up. Speak to me when spoken to, ma'fucka. Speak about me, schemin', we gon' hopscotch back to square one wit' my gat up yo' ass."

What the fuck am I thinkin'? I would be one dead son of a bitch if it wa'n't fo' Duke. Damn sho' wouldn't be sittin' in no Porsche eatin' gourmet chocolate, wit' my own laid apartment back at Babylon.

He glanced at his savior. "Duke, man, lemme call an' set up yo' manicure and pedicure," Beamer said. "Hit you wit' a facial too?"

"Yeah, gotta be soft as black satin when the Duchess rub her face all up in mine," he said raspily, turning onto Babylon Street. "Now, do it quick. We almost there."

Chapter 7

Victoria perched on a ratty lawn chair on the porch, wishing Henry would wait until she was gone before he played biscuit toss with those three pit bulls. He was sitting right beside her, refusing to say who was coming to get her.

"Those are the scariest dogs," Victoria sneered, hating their smell and their chewing and chomping noises. She curled her feet under the chair so that the growling animals couldn't trample her red-painted toenails. "Hardly anybody's best friend."

"Naw, but they tight wit' Benjamin," Henry said playfully. "An' Benjamin keep me rollin' in style." He nodded toward the black Hummer parked at the curb where those thugs had ogled her from that pearlescent Porsche. Thank goodness they and all those reporters were gone. Didn't they have anything better to do than hound an eighteen-year-old girl as she descended into hell? Sitting here, literally, with the hounds.

"Are you a breeder? Is that why they call you Pound?"

"Som'm like that," Henry said, grasping the brown dog's ear to examine a huge, oozing sore. "Damn," he groaned. "Yeah, I'm in the dog business."

"You're almost as vague about what you do as you are about who's coming to pick me up. And why are those girls across the street still staring at me? If looks could kill."

"Vee, you in the best hands," Henry said. "If it's anybody 'round here you can trust, it's me and the boss man."

"Oh, great," she said sarcastically, wrapping her arms around herself to rub away a shiver in spite of the warm weather. Even her still-throbbing sex couldn't stop the terrifying barrage of questions assaulting her brain. "I'm in the middle of Detroit and now the boss man is coming to get me. Sounds like a really bad scene from an even worse superhero comic book."

Henry laughed. "Yeah, he definitely got supa' powas!"

"Who?" Victoria snapped. "When we were little, Henry, you used to say stuff like, in code. Now I still have no idea what you're talking about. One day I'm gonna beat you at your own game, so tell me or don't laugh."

"I got orders," Henry said, dumping the box of biscuits in front of the dogs. Their claws screeched as they lapped up the crumbs.

"Well, I got needs," she said seriously. "I have to get a job and my own place, somehow. I am not going back into Kay-Kay's lecherous lair."

Henry let out a deep laugh. The dogs growled. "Girl, you be sayin' some words! Now I see why he want you."

Victoria stared hard at her cousin. "Who wants me?"

"You ain't heard it from me," Henry said, "but you gon' get offered e'rything you need and much, much more, so chill."

"If it's anybody around here," she said, glancing toward the street where a souped-up Monte Carlo with window-rattling rap music and three barely visible black heads was rolling past, "then the offer probably has far more strings attached than I want to pull."

"You a trip wit' yo' words."

She tapped his shoulder and said, "I need a job, I'm a snob, no urban mob to rob, make someone sob."

Henry grinned. "Yo, lay some beats an' we got Eminem half-black sistah in'a house!"

She smiled, rhyming to her own beat. "I need cash in a flash to live away from Kay-Kay and lay in peace. Eat, sleep, and breathe, free to be me."

A white blur made her turn toward the street.

"Do *not* tell me *they're* here for me," Victoria said. Her heart was pounding as two big black guys, the same ones who'd been here before, got out of their Porsche. "They were front row spectators earlier."

Henry leaned close. "Listen, cuz. I know you ain't used ta seein' six-foot-six brothas unless you in yo' daddy suite at the Palace watchin' the Pistons." Henry's voice deepened. "But you in anotha world now. You asked me to help you, so I went straight to the top o' hood hierarchy." He smiled. "That sound like one o' yo' words, don't it?"

As the guys walked toward the porch, the tall, bald one moved so gracefully and powerfully, he reminded her of an animated superhero. Wow, Henry wasn't joking. That guy's expensive-looking leather sandals seemed to barely touch the ground as he approached with a step as soft as a cat's, like a giant black panther—powerful, stealthy, quick, dangerous, and elegant.

"Always follow your instincts and make decisions quickly," Daddy would say. She glanced back at the house. Inside, she could suffer with roaches, hunger, smoke, and Kay-Kay's debauchery. If she got past those wicked little dogs. Or outside, she could step into the urban version of a fairytale. He was probably the neighborhood drug lord. Probably didn't even finish high school. Probably had a gun, or three on him. And a criminal record. A whole bunch of out-of-wedlock babies by different teen mothers who were probably part of a whole bus load of those flashy, sexy girls who shook their butts in rap videos. Besides, who knew what STDs were dripping into this petridish of a neighborhood under the lowest rung of the socio-economic ladder? It seemed like a news report about HIV and gonorrhea was always coming out to say Detroit was one of the most infected cities in the country. Yuck.

These were two more reasons Victoria wanted to stay a virgin—to stay healthy and not get pregnant. No, the longer she looked at this guy, the more she thought about all the statistics he could help her become, and none of them were good.

But the same media that had filled her mind with so many stereotypes about young black men had also made her father sound like a psychotic criminal for the past week. And today that same media was after her.

Daddy's deep, comforting voice echoed in her head. "Never prejudge," her father used to say. "Remember, the black farmer in overalls and a straw hat may be holding a sack full of hard earned cash to buy a new pick-up truck, while the white man in the Brooks Brothers suit driving the Cadillac may be on his way to federal prison for bribery and murder."

Victoria's head ached from hunger. Her stomach cramped. Her pussy was finally quiet and calm.

"Vee," Henry whispered. "Tha's the only cat you got *to* know 'round here. Let me at least introduce you. Then decide if you wanna go wit' him."

Victoria nodded, taking Henry's hand as he led her down the steps. They stopped on the sidewalk where a golden beam of sunlight was slicing through the trees. The guy in the Pistons jersey was looking around, casting a mean look at those girls on the porch across the street, his hand on the right front pocket of his baggy, saggy jeans.

She would talk with the bald guy first and figure out if he felt safe. Even though his whole image, when viewed through her lens of aristocratic suburbia, was screaming "Drug dealer!" he actually looked just like that new NBA star, Tyrell Jackson. Victoria knew, because her brother was a basketball fanatic. He was always talking about games and players and statistics.

I have no way to reach my own brother. Don't even know where he is . . . Or my sister. Melanie is probably going straight to the convent. I'm all alone.

Her jittery insides were making her pussy ache for attention. This fear, on top of the grief of losing her father and her whole life, made her throat burn with dryness. Maybe it was because all the moisture in her body was getting sucked between her legs. She was so hungry and horny and sleepy, she could pass out right now and sleep for three days.

She shivered because this guy was hot, so physically gorgeous that he didn't look real. His vibe was so cool, so sexy, so powerful that it stunned her. All she could do was stare.

He was so tall, her eyes were level with his solar plexis, the center of the chest that Da Vinci was always diagramming as the central point on human beings. His open-necked shirt made a little frame around that swath of hairless skin. It contrasted with the white linen so vividly, it mesmerized her. She couldn't help imagining what it would look like if their bodies were tangled together—her buttermilk legs, arms and ass wrapped all around his dark chocolate muscles.

"Vee, this The Duke. Duke Johnson," Henry said. "Duke, Victoria Winston."

Victoria looked up into his eyes.

Oh. My. God. Her pussy creamed. She felt dizzy because his eyes were like giant onyx jewels, just like the ones in her necklace. The way he was looking at her, his eyes were sparkling down with equal intrigue.

His face was as masculine and sculpted as Michelangelo's David. His skin was taut and flawlessly stretched over a broad jaw, angular cheekbones, a wide forehead, and a thick neck so dark in the creases that it shimmered with iridescence.

His arms, from where his shirt ended just above his elbows, all the way down to his enormous and elegant hands, were just as beautiful. The distance between the base of his thumb and the tip of his index finger, which all the girls at school swore equaled the length of a guy's dick, seemed to stretch from here to eternity.

Victoria's body ached for the comfort of cuddling up and curling up in his length and his strength. What she was feeling was far more than physical. Just standing there, gawking at this god-like statue, she felt like his spirit was wrapping around her like the sheared mink coat she abandoned at her house. Right now it felt like she was connecting with this complete stranger on another level. A soul deep dimension where she'd known him forever.

Her pussy throbbed. Celeste was going wild with the idea of hopping up on this guy and solving the mystery of what fucking was all about. At the same time, she had the urge to run. Fast and far. But that hot, gushing sensation surged up to her brain, which flashed an image. *She leaps up to embrace him . . . he's holding her up around his waist by cupping her butt with those giant hands . . . and she's kissing him as if the very touch of her lips to his keeps her heart beating . . . and if she pulls away even to breathe, the spark of electricity that makes blood pump through the body would fizzle out and she would dry up and blow away, leaving him with two hand-fuls of white confetti . . . but she doesn't have to pull away to breathe because his expelled air, the oxygen molecules dancing around his windpipe with carbon dioxide and heat and moisture, that's all she needs to sustain her own life . . . just him, inside her, his big dick inside her hot, hungry pussy.*

A boiling sensation sizzled across every inch of her skin. Her cheeks were burning. Lips were scorched. And Celeste was bubbling, as if that geyser inside her turned upside down and was blowing steam and frothy splashes onto the pink velvet shores of her pussy.

She had to run, get away from this overwhelming feeling. No way could she maintain her vow of celibacy if she were around someone who, in a split-second, aroused more potent sensations than she'd ever felt. And even though Celeste told her, during that awesome orgasm inside the house, that she had to share her mix-race woman powers in order to set off their true, phenomenal potential, she didn't believe it. Her physical and emotional state of mind today was so crazy, Celeste was liable to say anything in the heat of the moment.

Your sweet little cherry is about to get plucked, sucked and fucked by this black superhero, Celeste said through the inner voice in Victoria's head. Victoria's mouth watered with a hunger for—

Oh my God, this guy could turn me into a certified nymphomaniac serial killer.

She turned around and ran toward the house. "Vee!" Henry called.

She stomped up the first two steps.

The pit bulls growled. They got into attack stance. The brown one glared with red-rimmed eyes and leaped at her.

A blur of white teeth . . . brown fur . . . claws dog-paddling midair. Pow!

A red splotch exploded on the side of the dog's round belly.

Chapter 8

Duke couldn't stand the sight of fear in her huge eyes. They were like blue-tinted mirrors, flashing code that only he knew. Good thing he was seeing this message here right now, because he was going to make it his life mission to erase it and never let it flash on her fine-ass face again. Ever.

And so it is written, and so it is done. Like right now, Duke just knew this chick was going to be putting herself out of her virgin misery in a Motor City minute. Tonight. On his dick. If she thought she was in shock now, she couldn't even imagine the raw dog dick-down that was about to rock her world like a meteor. And make her fly . . . tonight.

She gon' be so ridiculously horny she gon' be throwin' that sweet pussy at me befo' midnight tonight in my penthouse.

Timbo was burning and tingling just as tough as Duke's right hand from the kick-back. He balled it up, along with his left fist, to stop himself from rushing up on her and sweeping her into his arms. She'd probably pee on herself if he did that. If she hadn't already. She was a suburban, half-white princess one day, and standing in the hood with dog blood on her pretty toes the next. A dead pit bull was staring right up at her. Now she knew never to run from The Duke, but she also knew if she were in trouble, she would be safe.

Damn, fate was a motherfucker, the way stuff was happening at the right time to help The Duke manifest his destiny with The Duchess.

"Oh my God!" she shrieked, spinning around. Her big eyes were trying to figure out who shot the dog, but she'd never know. Henry was walking as cool as he could up to the porch to take the other dogs inside and grab the hose to rinse off her feet.

Beamer was strolling back to the car with the smoking dog defense.

And I'm standin' here cool as Luke. The fastest, slickest ma'fucka on the planet. He wanted to say this to Beamer and Pound, *That quick draw was some wild, wild, west shit!* But Duke had to play it cool, standing there waiting for her introduction as if he hadn't just popped his top fight dog. The way she was looking at him before the bullet, Duke knew there was no question. She was already struck. On Duke.

Ain't gon' take but a minute to crown her queen o' Babylon. And queen of my bed.

"You coulda shot me!" she screamed. Her right foot stomped the patchy grass. All that long, black hair swayed like a cape from around her back, tickling her ass and swooshing around her right hip. "Who did that?"

"Divine intervention, baby girl," Duke said. "Immaculate ammunition. Don't matta the who, jus' the what. That we gon' protec' you."

"Who's gonna protect me from *you?*" she snapped back. Just as quickly, she stared down at her bloody foot.

"Yo, Vee," Henry said, splashing her feet with water from a green hose. "It's cold but clean."

She kicked off her shoes. Henry handed her a small orange towel to dry her feet as he washed her sandals.

"Now," Henry said, kneeling to slip her feet into the clean shoes. "I know you starvin'. Duke takin' you out to eat." Henry put his hand softly on her back and guided her toward Duke.

"From the frying pan into the fire," she said, striding so elegantly, even though she was mad, on those long giraffe legs.

Damn, Duke, be cool, man.

She stopped so close that he could have rea

ched out and squeezed her big, juicy titties, pointing at him in that innocent pink sweater. She was close enough for him to smell that hot, virgin pussy, sweet, salty, and served up fresh, just for him. It was probably as wet as his watering tongue right now. She was ripe, ready to get plucked like a big, juicy grape bursting under his tongue, squirting sugar every which way.

Timbo was throbbing like a mug, aching to poke into that tight jar of jelly and stir it, spread it, whip it, dip it, flip it, and sip it dry. But if the look in her eye was any indication, this chick was the type who would stay wet because she liked it so much. Duke just knew. He had pussy radar like that. Some bitches had a dry look in their eye. They'd fuck you, but they weren't in it for the pleasure. They were in it for the treasure. This chick, she was hungry as hell for something she hadn't tasted yet. She was scared to take the first sample because she knew she would be addicted. Fiending.

"As we were saying, I'm Victoria Winston." She held out her hand in a business-like way. Her exotic eyes were hard but sexy and soft, too, fringed by thick black lashes. She was the perfect chameleon to snow plow the Moreno Triplets. She looked white enough to make them lose their minds, but once he brought out the sista in her, she would be fatal.

And Duke would reign.

Duke's mind was a filmstrip of Duchess going into meetings, representing him, putting folks at ease with that creamy skin and drop-dead beauty, using her King's English and brilliant business mind to manifest the Babylon that was his birthright.

The touch of her fingers snapped him out of his visions. She was taking his hand, the one that was still burning from the gun, and shaking it. Her baby-soft fingers disappeared in the hot wrap of his huge hand. She felt so hot, he imagined steam shooting out of his palm like Iron Man. Sweat prickled up through his skin, from his head to his toes. And Timbo . . . good thing his shirt was long and swaying, or else she'd see the tree trunk with her name written all over it.

I ain't neva felt like this . . . like I'm 'bout to bust. "I'm Duke. Duke Johnson."

It felt like time stopped when he stared into her eyes. Every time he looked at her, those creamy cheeks turned pinker and those lips became redder. Her chest rose and fell as he took hard breaths. He almost couldn't stop himself from bending down to taste that smooth, pretty skin on her chest where her sweater made a U-shaped scoop on top of her pretty titties.

"I'm hungry as ten men," Victoria said. Her voice was deep and smooth, like warm honey in his ears. "Let's go." Still holding his hand, she pulled him toward his own car.

"I'll have you at any restaurant you want in a Motor City minute," Duke said. He nodded toward the car. "That mean zero to sixty in five seconds."

"Thanks, but I don't need a translation. I'm pretty quick. So, let's rock."

Duke's feet would not move. It felt like he was wearing cement boots and his whole body was numb. Except for his pounding heart. His pulse was so strong and loud, it sounded like a hammer inside his ears. *Damn, Duke. Be cool, man. Ain't no woman ev'a sucked yo' powa. She s'pose ta make you stronger.*

She turned back. "What are you waiting—"

Duke made his right foot take a step, then his left. He remembered Momma telling him, Knight and Prince at the dinner table, "Be careful what you ask for, 'cause if you get it, you bett' be ready. I loved y'all daddy mo' than life itself. Finally got him, blessed me wit' three babies, but stole my heart, my soul, an' my settlement check. I jus' wasn't ready to take on somebody so slick." Then Momma would always get that sad look in her brown eyes. Duke never knew if it was for losing his daddy or for the baby that died, or both. Her lawsuit against the hospital won her $200K, but gave the man she loved enough loot to book while she raised three babies in the ghetto. Now, Duchess' sad expression made him realize they had both lost their fathers.

"Where is there to eat around here?" Duchess asked, sliding into his passenger's seat. Henry closed the door, leaning over it.

"Vee ain't hip to Grammomma Green ghetto-style cuisine," Henry said with a laugh.

"I'd be as wide as this car if I ate things that are fried and smothered beyond recognition," she said as Duke slid into the driver's seat. "No wonder there's epidemic obesity and diabetes in the black community."

"Baby girl got the socio-economic analysis of our inner city plight down like a mug," Duke said, speaking in exaggerated proper English. He had learned it by studying the newscasters on TV.

Shocked amusement flashed in her eyes.

"Perhaps, Miss Winston," he added, "we can discuss some statistics to illustrate your point over our evening meal. I want you to dine like a queen."

Henry laughed. "Quit, dog. Soundin' like a white boy." Her eyes blazed, making him feel like he was about to burst into flames.

"Anywhere you wanna go, baby girl. D-town your oyster tonight."

An' I'm yo' dessert.

Chapter 9

Now that Duke was with Lily White, Beamer had the freedom to meet Milan at a hotel room. As he walked down the hallway, he thought about how to focus on his coup. And what better partner in crime than Milan, who wanted exactly what he wanted: money, power, and Babylon. Being a 'round the way girl at heart, Milan was smart and sexy enough to pull it off right under Duke's nose. Plus, he was so caught up with that suburban creampuff who would no doubt crumble after a day in the hood, Duke wasn't good for anything right now. This hostile takeover was going to be a done deal before it even started.

Check it out, world. We the new Duke an' Duchess.

"Damn, you gotta be the finest female in D-town," Beamer said as she opened the door of the Presidential Suite.

"You're early."

"Naw, you said six." He flipped up his watch. Six on the nose. "The Swiss Army don't lie."

The disapproval in her light brown eyes made his blood bang through his veins like rattling pipes. Maybe she was mad because she was standing there in a dark green silk robe. She must have been butt-naked underneath because her titties looked like two of those little dum-dum lollipops poking at him, tempting him to take a lick. How could a bitch so small have such big nipples? And damn, her toenails looked like more candy, all shiny pink and curled into the plush white carpet. "Why Duke ain't on you twenty-fo'/ seven, I jus' don' know."

"You would know better than anyone," she said with those intelligent, analytical eyes. They looked like they were moving back and forth with little quick movements from one of Beamer's eyes to the other. Like she was looking in each eye, real close, to see what he was thinking.

No chance. I got this.

See, Milan was slick, having them meet at this fancy hotel in the suburbs, far away from all those nosy-ass, jealous niggas in the hood who would love to see them both shot for doing what would look like a triple taboo booty call. But it was all about business right now for the future bosses of Babylon.

Future boss, really. Milan thought it would be a partnership, but Beamer was going to be the new sheriff in D-town. She would take her proper place for a female, at his side, doing what he told her to do. Nothing like what Duke was talking about with Victoria Winston, wanting to share the power with the woman he hoped would someday be his baby momma.

"What's the password?" Milan said, crinkling her little nose that was more pointed than Lily White's. Her big, light brown eyes looked devious and delicious. Her straight, dark hair was bouncing off her shoulders as her bitch-stare dissolved into a smile. "Say it or you can't come in and play."

"Damn, you look sexy," Beamer said playfully, stopping in the threshold. His dick was so hard, it felt like it was going to rocket-launch straight at her, even though Chanel had just given him the supreme dick-suck over at the party on Chicago Boulevard.

"Wrong answer." Milan screwed up her face like he was stupid.

"Bonnie an' Clyde," he said with a more serious tone.

She closed the door. A lock clicked, a bolt slid. "Milan, if you gon' change it, let me know first." Silence.

He knocked. "Milan?"

An old white man in a hotel uniform walked past. Then he turned around, came back and asked, "May I help you, sir?"

"No," Beamer said, his heart beating faster. If he were to get kicked out of the hotel, he would not be able to talk with Milan about their plan. And it wasn't like he had a lot of time, either, because if Lily White were telling Duke to kiss his black ass right now, the first thing he would do would be to call Beamer to handle the business that Duke had put on hold to chase some almost-white pussy.

"My fiancée mus' be 'sleep," Beamer told the hotel man. "I'll call her cell phone."

Beamer turned so the man could see the cell phone clipped to his jeans pocket. Otherwise, the man might think he was pulling a gun, then he would call the cops, and the next thing he knew, Duke would be riding up to ask why Beamer was at a hotel with his female. With sweaty palms, Beamer flipped open his red, white, and blue Pistons phone. He scrolled down his missed calls— the whole screen said MILAN from top to bottom. Six times. Every time she called him that day, Beamer followed Duke's orders to let it ring. Otherwise, she would just be asking too many questions about who they were with and where they were. But now *she* was playing let-it-ring.

The white man stepped close, stared down hard, and asked with a snooty tone, "Do you have a room key, sir?" Adding the "sir" on to a sentence that was spit out with so much disrespect was like adding insult to injury because it was so false.

"She'll answer," Beamer said calmly, but his insides were spinning. She did not answer.

The hotel man knocked on the door. "Madame, are you there?"

Dang, why Milan playin' me? Beamer knew better than anybody what kind of tricks Milan had played on Duke. It was crazy shit that nobody but a devious bitch could come up with, like crashing her brand new Benz into a pole, with the kids in the back seat, just so Duke would come home early from the trip to the Superbowl in Jacksonville. If she were that mad thinking he was fucking around with a couple chicks, Milan would lose her mind if she knew the truth. Duke had been down there fucking a whole team of cheerleaders by the hotel pool.

"Let me try one more time." Beamer dialed again. "She must be 'sleep." The man's hostile stare—which Beamer did not look up into—felt like fire on his cheeks. The man had his arms all crossed, breathing in hard, acting like he was going to let his stress make like an army and attack his damn heart, all over a nigga in the hallway who was trying to get with his girl.

"Sir, I'm going to have to escort you to the lobby."

"A'ight."

A few minutes later, the man was on the phone behind the polished wood reception desk. "Ms. Henderson, a young man claiming to be your fiance is trying to reach you."

A lady next to him, who wished she were still as fine as she might have been twenty years ago, turned her skinny ass that looked like a board under her St. John skirt. She pulled her Prada purse up against her half-starved-looking body and looked at Beamer like he was crud in an old, dirty shower. The bad way she was looking at Beamer only made the already angry hotel dude cut his eyes harder.

"Darling," the bitch said to her husband, "aren't there hotels down in Detroit for people like him?"

The hotel guy cleared his throat. Then he coughed, as if he were going to keel over if Milan said no and he had to sweep Beamer's ghetto ass out of this snobby lobby.

"Darling!" the wife-bitch said in a way like she was used to being ignored.

Her husband, a clean-cut white man with brown hair and a dark blue suit, looked up from handing over his credit card to the receptionist who was checking them in. The man turned red. His eyes got big as golf balls. In fact, his eyes were now as big as his own balls, which Beamer had seen slapping against three Sluts' asses Friday night at a Babylon freak party. That one was three times bigger than the one they had attended today on Chicago Boulevard. It was all white men, all in from out of town, trying to get their freak on in the Motor City during some kind of automotive executives' convention.

This guy here, with his snooty-ass wife, was the host. He had requested three flavors of ass: licorice black, chocolate brown, and coffee with cream Beamer smiled. He couldn't help it, because the image in his head of this dude's wife walking in on her husband with his head bobbing between two blue-black thighs would have given her cardiac arrest her damn self.

Ain't this some shit! That dude was the one who had given Beamer the bulging bag of Benjamins when he and Duke stopped by as planned. That scene was some crazy-ass shit, filling up the whole penthouse of one of D-town's most exclusive apartment towers. All white men. All black Sluts.

Barriors doing protection, with all the right people on notice so no shit could go down to jack up the operation.

Beamer would bet that freaky automotive man's wife was *not* getting her freak on. That bitch looked like she hadn't had any dick since Kennedy was president.

Sandpaper pussy bitch. Damn, I wonder if Duke hittin' it wit' Lily White. Wonder if she as juicy as she look . . . an' if she gon' stick wit' Duke like he want. Not after me an' Milan get through . . . an' take ova Babylon.

"Yes, Ms. Henderson," the hotel dude looked relieved. "He's—"

"Barb," the woman's freaky-ass automotive executive husband said, trying to nod real cool at Beamer. It wasn't necessary, since the husband already knew Babylon's strict code of confidentiality, which Duke had gone over with him at their first meeting. Normally, Duke did not handle the details like that. Milan did all of that, but with monster deals, Duke had his hands all over them, just to make sure all the dollars got delivered to the right place.

Right now, the man was talking to his wife like she was a child. "Barb, you really should keep up on the kids' music. That young man is one of the most famous R&B artists in America."

"Wha'z up!" Beamer pointed real quick. The hotel dude smiled.

"In fact," the freaky husband said, "we used his latest hit in our ad for the Sports Coupe ZX. It's been airing around the globe for three weeks now."

The woman turned as pink as her lipstick. She pivoted toward the receptionist, talking about the spa. At the same time, her husband nodded, flashing a look that said, "Can't wait to see ya at the next pussy party." Then he looked at the hotel dude and said, "Your hotel should feel honored to have a man of this stature patronizing your establishment. I feel privileged just to shake your hand. Your talent is phenomenal." His eyes flashed something real sneaky, like he wanted to ask, "Where da party at?" As if he were going to put his wife to bed and come creeping up to a suite full of black pussy.

Beamer cracked up. He patted the auto-freak on the back. "Thanks, man. I 'preciate yo' props."

The hotel dude was all flustered, hurrying around the corner of the counter so fast, he bumped himself in the hip. He took Beamer's arm, leading him to the elevator. "I'm so sorry about the inconvenience, sir. We get all kinds of riff-raff here and make sometimes aggressive efforts to filter out those who don't belong. We have a very particular clientele."

"It's a'ight."

"May I offer you and Ms. Henderson a bottle of champagne to make up for the misunderstanding?" The elevator stopped and the doors opened.

"We already got the Cristal on ice," Beamer said, knocking on Milan's door. She opened it instantly, flashing a smile and holding out her arms.

"Oh, baby, I'm sorry. I was in the shower," she said all sweet, pressing her hard nipples into Beamer's chest.

"If there's anything you need," the hotel dude said as he walked away, "please don't hesitate to ring me."

Milan pulled him inside, closed, and locked the door. The high-ceiling suite was all white, from the leather couch and matching chairs to the marble fireplace, the chaise facing it and the TV in a glass-and-silver cabinet holding plants and books.

"Oooh, Peanut, you look delicious tonight," Milan said, posing on the chaise. Beamer was sure that if she took that robe off, she'd look just like a centerfold, no joke. Her sexy playmate attitude rattled Beamer inside. It felt like steam was shooting out of his ears.

"I know I'm delicious," Beamer said playfully, "but no joke, Bonnie an' Clyde don't need no romantic distractions."

"Bonnie and Clyde," she said in her white girl way of talking. "Damn, why you gotta say e'ry letter?"

"I know it's a crime to sound intelligent where you come from—"

"We grew up around the block from each other, Michelle Henderson." He sucked his teeth, wishing her big brown eyes and her still-hard nipples were not so distracting. He wanted to talk about their coup, but his dick was trying to talk louder. He needed to tone down her attitude before they got down to business.

"You could blow them airs up e'rybody else ass, but wit' me, you gotta keep it real. Michelle Henderson always gon' be a hood rat. I don't care if you havin' tea wit' the queen o' England. You from the hood in D-town, so keep it real wit' yo' boy."

She stood, stepping toward him with that fake-sophisticated walk that she'd been perpetrating ever since she went to the fashion shows in New York. Every time she took a step, she would put one foot directly in front of the other, to make her hips sway, sashay, or straight-up switch. It made her look sexy as hell with those titties bouncing, the satin flowing around her, and her lips opening as she came at him.

"I learned to keep it real at my prestigious prep school," she said, poking his chest with a fingernail. "Private school taught me that in the *real world,* you have to know how to—" Her lips got real tight and her hard nipples looked like they were going to cut holes in that robe as she said, "Speak like a white person."

"You trippin', Michelle."

"My name is Milan. Obviously you need training before you're ready to embark on our plan."

"I don't need shit but some cooperation from yo' ass. You might be in charge o' the Squad by day, but when you an' me is workin' this deal, you gon' call me Boss."

She threw her head back, laughing. "As if I would bow down to your dim-witted mumblings."

Damn, how could somebody look so sexy while they were being so mean? Beamer's whole body was shaking as he thought about pulling open that robe, laying her on that lounge chair and fucking her until she started talking like she used to. Something about her made him feel weak as hell, like a nigga could think tough all he wanted, and say it, but when he looked in those eyes, he turned to grits inside.

She clawed her fingernails over his cheek, stopping to tickle his lip. "If you think it's cool to dumb yourself down to the lowest common denominator of every hoodlum you know, then I'm going to smarten you up until you're intelligent enough to partner with me on our Duke Deal of the day."

All of a sudden, something in her eyes made Beamer remember when they were eight, she sweet-talked him into going to the corner store and stealing some Blow Pops for her. "I'll kiss you if you get me three green apple ones," she said. But when he came out and delivered the goods, she was sitting on the porch with Duke, so Beamer gave each of them a sucker and kept one for himself. Never did get his kiss.

Right now, the way she was cracking up just looking at him—and he hadn't said squat—it was making him feel retarded. It made hot energy, like steam, blow through him, making him want to punch something.

"You know, Peanut, there are two kinds of people in the world: leaders who make decisions, and imbeciles who wouldn't know how or what to think if it weren't for the leaders thinking for them. Duke and I, we're the leaders. And you, sorry little punk, happen to fall in the second category. Now, here's my plan that you're going to help me execute."

"Aw, hell no!" Beamer shouted, balling his fists. "You nothin' but a trick! Fulla tricks!"

She looked at him with excited eyes. Her lips poked out the way models always look in pictures like they were about to kiss their own picture.

"What the fuck you doin'?" he asked, sounding much more angry than he had intended. "I coulda got arrested up in this snobby-ass joint. The suburbs ain't no place to play."

"You didn't get the password right, Peanut. And if you're going to do business with me, I need you to pay attention to the details. Now, what is the password?"

"Don't fuck wit' me."

She tossed back her head, making that straight hair bounce all over the place. She leaned on one hip, spreading her fingers out on her thighs to press the fabric down. The robe fell open wider on her chest.

Damn, if I could fuck her jus' once . . .

Beamer's dick was ramming up against his jeans. Benzo wasn't even this hard when Chanel was sucking it this afternoon. Something about Milan's bitchy drill sergeant way of talking made Benzo iron hard.

If he closed his eyes, she would sound white, but looking at the way she jerked her neck when she talked, there was no question she was a sista when she said, "I'll fuck with you every second of every day, you stupid motherfucker, until you can concentrate on business."

He stomped closer. Their bodies were almost touching. "Don't call me a stupid motherfucker, you bougie wannabe, two-timin' bitch."

She craned her neck forward. Her eyes grew bigger as she said, "You don't have the balls to make this happen with me."

Beamer stared hard into her eyes. His right hand yanked open the top button on his jeans, which he pulled hard enough to unzip. He whipped out his big dick in his right hand and cradled his balls in his left hand.

"These some big muthafuckin' balls," he said angrily, "an' a big black dick ta go wit' 'em. So don't tell me—"

"Maybe you have the equipment, but you're scared to use it." Milan shook her head. "Put that little mess away. I been dealin' in dicks way bigger than that all day long."

Beamer could feel something inside snapping, like his rattling veins had just blown a pipe and steam was blowing every which way but out. He was like a pressure cooker, and Milan's haughty expression, her words, her sexiness, were making his gauge tick even more violently.

"I said put the dick away before I jump up on it."

Benzo throbbed harder, like that pressure cooker was about to blow right through the head of his dick. All that steam would shoot straight back into Milan, where it came from. And either pair of her lips would do.

"Peanut, if you think I want that little earthworm of a click—"

I got this. No joke.

Beamer lunged. He wrapped his arms around her waist, lifted her up and let that robe fall open. He slammed her down on his dick like she was a bubble and he was sticking out a pin to pop it.

"Peanut, stop!" She clawed the collar of his Pistons jersey. Was she trying to hold on or get a grip so she could fuck him back? She didn't exactly wrap her legs around him, but she didn't push off either. Her pussy was hot, wet, and gripping him like she'd been wanting it all along.

"Damn, yo' pussy wet." She was so small, all he had to do was hold her in place, lift and lower her real quick, and bang up. He inhaled the smell of her designer perfume and salty pussy. That put Benzo on swole even more.

This some good pussy. No wonder Duke—

Beamer's whole body went cold.

I am one dead mothafucka. No joke.

He looked up into Milan's eyes. She was loving this dick. She was evil, just like Duke said. She'd sell her own momma to get her way, to get paid, to get some dick, just to be a bitch.

Then how could her pussy feel so good?

"You started now, Peanut. Don't you dare get guilty an' pull some *coitus interruptus* unless you're lusting for rigor mortis in return. 'Cause the number one way to royally piss off Milan Henderson is to get stingy with the dick."

I'm double-crossin' Duke, now she's gonna double-cross me. Threaten me, too! An' I'm too stupid to have known better. Talk about stuck between a cock and a hard place. Beamer would laugh if he were thinking about some other dumb-ass fool. Duke was right. The reason it was so easy for him to knock down Pinks was because Beamer had been holding him up.

Then why does Duke rely on me so much?

"Fuck me!" Milan ordered. She tossed off the robe, letting it fall to the floor. Her fingernails clawed under the collar of his jersey, scraping over his shoulders. Stripes of pain burned his skin. Her hair was bouncing all over. She pulled the holder off his braids, letting them fly wild.

She was making her ass bounce like she was riding a horse. The sharp little heels of her slippers were stabbing his thighs, and he was galloping right underneath her. Yeah, galloping toward the barrel of a gun if Duke were to find out.

They fucked until they were both dripping, then they each blew a nut so hard, they collapsed on that couch and guzzled champagne straight from the bottle. After she put on her robe, Milan picked up the remote, pointed it at the TV and clicked.

"Where is it?" she asked, pushing buttons.

The screen flashed with images of green fabric sliding to the floor . . . brown hair bouncing . . . redbone braids flying . . . and Duke Johnson's number one baby momma getting fucked by his number one boy. His servant. His back-stabbing right hand with a death wish the size of Michigan.

Beamer's whole body shook so violently, he was afraid he was having a convulsion. He half wanted to tell Michelle to call 911. "Why the fuck—"

She raised her eyebrows, crossed her arms and looked at him like he was stupid.

"Give me the tape," Beamer said with a dead-serious tone. "Thought you'd like a copy," she said, pushing a button and ejecting a tape.

Beamer threw it on the floor. His gym shoe slammed down on the tape, making the plastic crackle.

"Why you laughin', bitch?"

"My new camera is so handy," she said, aiming the remote at the TV. There they were, still fucking on the screen.

"Erase that shit. Now!" Damn, Beamer's voice sounded just as deep and powerful as Duke's usually did. "'Fore I tear up this room to find yo' hidden camera."

"Cameras," she said, pushing buttons. "See, I have multiple angles. Do you know anything about digital film? It's wonderful. You'll never guess where it's hidden. I can download the images, print them out, copy them to tape, e-mail them around the world if I want to. And the way you came at me—"

Beamer shot up to his feet.

I'm gon' fin' e'ry last one o' them cameras an' break 'em. No joke.

"Of course, if you act up, Peanut, I can ring our friend down at the front desk, who'd be happy to call the police about the unruly nigga up in the Presidential Suite. Then you'd have to call Duke to bail you out of jail. After he and I enjoy our home movies."

Beamer stomped back to the couch. He stood over Milan and glared down. "What the fuck you want from me?"

"I want you to make sure that Duke Johnson does not do whatever he's planning to do with that white bitch." Her lips got real tight against her teeth and the words came out like a growl, like she was biting down hard. "Whether he plans to fuck her, hire her, pimp her, I don't know. I don't care. Just make sure she doesn't step one foot into Babylon."

Milan opened her robe again, lay back on the couch, and spread her legs wide open. Her body looked like an evil face: nipples for eyes, an "outie" belly button for a nose, and that gapped-open brown-and-pink pussy was the mouth trying to suck him into hell.

"You're going to do all of that, of course," Milan said with that playmate/drill sergeant voice, "after you eat my pussy."

Beamer's mouth watered because her pussy was beautiful. It was still tight, even after two babies, and it was still good, real good. But that bitch who was attached to it made everything sweet about her body go sour.

"Don't make me have to cum by myself." She pressed her long, gold fingernail onto her inch-long clit, rubbing it in circles. Her nipples pointed at him like poison darts.

Damn, that pussy look good. But she makin' a triple-dead sucka mothafucka outta me.

"Eat my pussy. Now!"

If I'm gon' die, I might as well get as much good pussy as I can first. He pressed his face into his own sticky nut all over her pussy. He rubbed his face around. He wasn't just going to drink the poison; he was going to savor every sip.

"Ooooh, shit. Think about how you ain't gon' let Duke fuck that white bitch. Think about how if he try, you gon' tell me so I can get a fresh manicure before I kill the bitch with my own pretty little hands."

Chapter 10

Even though she was dizzy from hunger, the first thing Victoria did when they arrived at the upscale restaurant on the river was go to the bathroom and make herself cum. The whole drive there, she had squirmed in her seat, making a soaking wet mess of her panties. Panic was gripping her throat, anxiety about her life turning her insides into a nest of wasps stinging her from the inside out. Something about that guy—that enormous, dark chocolate god who twenty-four hours ago she never would have even considered talking with much less going to dinner—was turning her into a boiling vat of cum cream. And that rap music, the kind Brian was always playing, was arousing something rebellious and wild within her. She'd almost made herself cum in the car by squeezing her pussy muscles in rhythm to that music that Duke said was Bang Squad.

I can't believe how hard I just came, in the bathroom, thinking about his lips.

Making herself cum mellowed her mind. It cured the sting. Especially when she thought about his dick and how he would feel. Fucking was a totally abstract idea because she had no real life reference point. All she knew was what her friends told her, and they'd all complained that losing their virginity was painful and disappointing. Even Tiffany complained, though she was like a little rabbit with Jake because, she said, "Once you pop it, you just can't stop it. You crave it constantly."

If that were true with nerdy-looking Jake, then what would happen with sexy, studly Duke? Whatever it was, Victoria wanted it. But she would never, ever get it.

This is so dangerous. I'm already a nympho by myself, but if I let Celeste loose on him, I might never get out of bed! My deathbed. Or his.

So, walking back through the restaurant to Duke Johnson, sitting so cool at a table framed by the bright blue Detroit River and the downtown skyline, Victoria focused on her goal tonight. She had to strategize how he could help her find a better place to live. If this guy had so much pull, maybe he could help her get an emergency loan.

Henry said he wants to help me, so—

As she sat down, a gray-haired white man in a business suit glared at her from a nearby table. He said something to his frothy-haired wife, who shook her head with disgust. Had they seen her on TV? Had they known Daddy? "Why is everyone staring at us?" Victoria asked. "The whole drive here, people in other cars were looking at me like I'm some kinda freak."

The corners of Duke's mouth raised up slightly. His eyes sparkled. "They tryin' to fig'a out what NBA ma'fucka wit' a vanilla shorty."

"Oh, I love those," Victoria said, remembering her favorite coffee drink at the Java Joint, which just days ago was her favorite hangout with Brian and Tiffany.

"With cinnamon and whipped cream on top."

"They're just some jealous ma'fuckas," Duke said playfully. "Hatin' on a brotha for ridin' with the finest shorty in D-town."

"I'm not short. I'm five-eight." Victoria pointed to her red leather mules. "Make it five-eleven in these heels."

"You short next to six feet six inches o' this Mandingo warrior ma'fucka," Duke said coolly, his eyes roving down the exposed "V" of her cleavage to the round curves of her breasts. His stare made her nipples pop so hard against the pink satin of her bra, they made two points on her sweater. Then he said, with the sexiest deep voice she'd ever heard, "See, you hearin' me loud an' clear."

She squirmed. His bad boy command of cuss words made Celeste throb even hotter and wetter. The simple act of looking into his eyes made her feel out of control. She had the same feeling as when she was dieting with perfect discipline until she walked into Mrs. Fields Cookies. All her discipline melted under the warmth of that fresh-baked goodie in her hand. The sweet chocolate scent literally turned off the part of her brain that said "no" to all other fattening treats.

But if Victoria succumbed to the temptation of this male god sitting in front of her, how could she make up for that? What if she got pregnant? What if she caught something? What if she loved it so much she lost her mind and become a slave to her sex?

"Wherever your mind takin' you right now," Duke said, "let me go too. 'Cause the look on your face be sneaky as hell. Sexy as hell, too."

She glared at him.

"One look in your eyes," Duke said, "and I got a fuckin' all-access pass into your horny-ass mind."

"Don't talk to me like that," she snapped.

"Oh, sorry, Miss Daisy," Duke said. "You ain't used to hearin' words like that."

"My dad had a potty mouth too. I hated it."

"Then I'll speak," he said with that playful proper white cadence, "like a perfect gentleman."

Victoria smiled. *But I don't know if I can keep being a lady with you.*

"My pops booked. Never met him. You lucky you had one."

"I can't talk about my dad right now." Victoria squeezed back tears, closed her eyes, and inhaled the delicious cologne scent that was wafting from Duke. She kept squeezing her pussy muscles to soothe away the stares, the worries, and the sheer terror that was gripping her soul.

The scent of salmon made her open her eyes.

"I ordered fo' ya," Duke said with an adorable smile. It was like his eyes sparkled and tenderness washed over his face, which was all the more dramatic because he was so enormous and tough-looking at first glance.

"Mmmmm, exactly what I had in mind," she said, ogling the big slab of grilled salmon over mixed greens with gorgonzola cheese, walnuts, and dried cherries. "Duke, I can't remember the last time I ate. Or slept. It's been, like, half a week. I don't know how I'm staying awake."

"You gon' sleep good tonight," Duke said with a warmth in his eyes that made her shiver. It wasn't just in his eyes; it was radiating from his entire being. Just like it did from Daddy and Mommy. The energy registered in her mind like *I'll take* care of you no matter what. Duke flashed those big, beautiful white teeth and said, "I tol' you I got cha back, baby girl."

"I'm not sleeping a wink at that hellish house of dogs," Victoria said as the waiter placed a bread basket overflowing with hot whole wheat rolls. "Paradise." She smiled as the waiter set a plate of steak and lobster before him. A platter of giant crab cakes descended between them. "No, I'm in paradise right now, and if this is my last meal in life, I'm gonna savor every bite."

Duke let out a quick, deep laugh. "Oh, baby girl, it ain't the las'. It's jus' a little taste o' what gon' be yo' life e'ry day."

She stared hard into his eyes, looking for answers, but radiating back was pure male domination that told her without words, *Your wish is my command as long as it fits into my mysterious master plan.*

"The house specialty," the waiter said, putting on the table an elaborate arrangement of fresh pineapple, strawberries, and blueberries with a dish of fresh whipped cream. "Indulge."

"Thank you," Victoria said between bites that transformed the acid burn of hunger in her gut into a warm, mellow fullness. "Damn, baby girl," Duke said playfully, his dark eyes sparkling.

"You eat like a man."

"Thank you! This is so good!" she said, savoring every flavor. She speared a big piece of pineapple, dipped it in cream, stuck out her tongue, and chomped in an exaggerated way. "All my friends were always starving themselves. They were so scared to eat in front of guys. Stupid."

"I love a girl wit' a big appetite," Duke said with a mischievous smile. "Can't stand them salad-eatin' chicks. Always mad 'cause they so hungry."

Victoria laughed. His eyes were mesmerizing. She could not look away from the rich, black depths of his pupils and irises, the super whiteness of his eyes, the beautiful radiance of his flawless, coffee bean brown skin. She had never really looked this hard into a black face. Gramma Green and other relatives, of course, but somehow a man, a young handsome man, was different. Way more intense. And scary.

He represented everything opposite her, and her body was electrified. If she were to put her fingertip to the bottom of a lightbulb right now, it would no doubt glow brightly. She never felt this electric, even after hours of heavy petting with Brian. But now, all of a sudden, she was analyzing the whole race-sex vow that she had made to herself. She ached to talk to Mommy, to hear the adult version of what she had told her in the vanity mirror.

What if the power that Mommy described only worked on white men? What if an inner city tough guy like this was so used to sex power that he was immune, so nobody would get hurt? If so, then Victoria could satisfy the incredibly distracting craving to indulge her virginal body in sex—especially a hot mouth on her pussy. Celeste would go wild. Oooh, what would it be like for Duke to wrap those full, chocolate brown lips around her clit? And his dick was probably huge. Would it hurt? Or would she love it so much that her pussy sucked him inside her forever?

"You a'ight, boo?"

"Why do you keep calling me that?"

"What?"

"Boo. Like you think I'm scared or something."

"We alike like that," Duke said. "You got a poker face like a mug."

"A what? I've never had a mug shot. Don't plan to."

Duke laughed. "Girl, I gotta school you on the language of the street if you gon' make it."

"That's not a question," she said. "I'm gonna find a job and move out as soon as I can."

"I know," Duke said.

"How do you know?"

"I see it in your eyes. You and me, we just alike. You'll see. We got the same soul, but it was split apart and born in different worlds. But now—"

"I'm trapped since the lawyers took away my car," Victoria said. "What can you recommend that's close to my grandmother's house, where I can work?"

"Work for me."

"Doing what?"

"Represent me. At meetings. Help me run my business. The way you talk and carry yourself, that'll give me a lot more credibility."

"With who?"

"Various business partners."

"Duke, I'm eighteen."

"I'm twenty, and I'm runnin' the shit. I learned it from my brothers startin' when I was twelve. I took ova wit' Knight when Prince—" Duke looked down. "Jus' say we on the fas' track business plan here in'a hood. Life short, so you gotta shoot to the top quick or—"

Victoria's stomach cramped. "Where's your brother?"

"The same place a whole lotta niggas go befo' they see twenty-one. Elmwood Cemetery."

"Was he a drug dealer? I'm not doing anything illegal."

"Hear me now," Duke said, taking her hand. "You help me out, I will make sure your fine ass never takes a fall. I'll confess it right now, you are my new reason for living."

Victoria stood up. "I'm sorry, but you know nothing about me. I'm going to college to start my own business someday, and I don't want anything to do with whatever business you're in."

"Think about it," he said. "Workin' at McDonald's by yo' Grammomma house or workin' for me with your own apartment, a car, and protection."

Tears stung Victoria's eyes.

"Now come on," he said. "I'm takin' you grocery shopping so you can get some white girl food for your gramma house. Anything you want."

His eyes scanned her body. "And you can come to my crib for a shower if you still want."

Celeste throbbed, but Victoria shook her head and looked at him like he was crazy. "Your crib?"

He laughed. "That's ghetto for home."

"I feel like I need a Berlitz book when you talk," she said playfully, ticking down a grocery list in her head: green apples, yogurt, tuna, baked chicken, peanut butter.

"A what book?" he asked.

"It's a travel guidebook, for when you visit a foreign country. It has a bilingual dictionary of common words and phrases. You say something, I look it up, and get a translation."

"Yeah, write that book," Duke said. "Whitey's Guide to the Hood."

She stopped, turned, glared at him. "I don't like racial jokes."

"Nobody ever called you a nigga bitch, have they?"

"You just did." She stared back without flinching.

"Nice," he said, those piercing eyes glowing with approval as they walked past tables toward the exit, that white man and his wife who stared at her earlier stood up.

"Victoria Marie Winston," the man said. Her heart pounded. Not that she was scared, just that after being all over the media for a week, she was expecting lunatics, perverts, and racists to come crawling out of their gutters to say or do vile things.

Duke wedged himself between her and the man. He was so tall and wide, he entirely hid her like a big, black wall. "Can I help you?"

"No," the man said, stepping around Duke.

"Victoria, I worked with your dad."

"She don't want to talk right now," Duke said.

"Wait," Victoria said, allowing the man to approach.

Maybe he was looking angry because he was grieving. "The apple doesn't fall far from the tree," the man said with furious eyes. A bit of spit landed on his lip.

Duke blocked her as gracefully as a giant cat. "Yo, step back."

The man did, but he shouted, "Your dad was a despicable, nigger-loving bandit!"

"A criminal!" the woman shrieked. She shook her over-powdered cheeks, which were dusted with giant ovals of rouge. "You're obviously following in his footsteps!"

Duke swept Victoria away from them so quickly, it felt like she was floating. His big, strong arms curved around the back of her waist so quickly and powerfully that he lifted her up and out, away from those freaks.

Her brain was like an out-of-control radio, spinning past dozens of ear-splitting stations. *People hate Daddy. Now they hate me. Can't go anywhere public with Duke. Arouses racist hatred in strangers. Makes people think I'm bad. But I like him. He protects me. And I've never felt so comfortable with a guy . . . like when I move he moves . . . when I think he feels . . . when he breathes I melt. We're connected on another level.*

And the way he was looking down at her right now as they walked past the scowling maitre d', Victoria shivered with a sense of *us against the world.*

And she loved it.

Chapter 11

"There they are!" that crazy-ass white lady from inside the restaurant screamed as Duke and Duchess stepped to the valet stand facing the water.

Hell no. We out two hours an' 5-0 on us like a mug.

That old geezer and his cow were leading the cops straight their way. Duke kept his usual stance, cool as a cat.

"Are you all right, ma'am?" the young black cop asked Duchess.

"We were both fine," Duke said with his TV voice, "until this gentleman confused us with somebody else."

"This is Tyrell Jackson," Duchess said with a strong business voice. She looked up at Duke. "Don't you recognize him from all the media coverage? He's like the talk of the NBA right now. The hottest draft pick since Shaq."

Duke raised his chin a little as four pairs of eyes rolled up and down him, along with a dozen others waiting for their cars at the valet. All of their eyes were going from glaring to staring, from mad to glad, in a Motor City minute as Duchess worked the magic Duke knew she had in her.

The white cop shook his head, smiling as he said, "Jump shot Jackson! From the University of Texas. Forward."

The other cop, who had a smile as goofy as Beamer's, added, "Congratulations on your contract that could run a small country!"

"Thank you. Give me your info an' I'll get you into the suite for the celebrity charity game tomorrow," Duke said. "We got everybody from the mayor to Motown stars comin' out to support a good cause."

"It's gonna be hot," Duchess said, smiling. "I work for my school newspaper, and I was interviewing Mr. Jackson over dinner, about the game. It's raising money for kids with cancer because Mr. Jackson's nephew—"

"We've already got tickets!" the angry white man, who was happy now, interrupted. "Our grandson has the same lymphoma. Bless you, sir." The man shook Duke's hand.

The old white witch put her hand on Duchess' shoulder. "I'm sorry, dear. I apologize for both of us. You're the spitting image of a young lady we knew in a very bad situation. We thought—"

"That's okay," Duchess said with a big smile. "It happens all the time. I just have one of those faces." Duke knew the sound of his car coming without turning around.

"Becky," Duke said, as he opened her door. "We still gotta run out to the Palace for the pictures."

"Oh, your car," she said with that happy white girl cadence. She waved as she stretched her long giraffe legs onto the seat. "Nice meeting all of you."

"We'll be lookin' for those passes," the white officer said, handing over their business cards.

"I'll hook you up tonight," Duke said as he got in the car.

"Keep up the good work," the angry white man said as Duke drove away to the blasting beat of the Bang Squad.

"Oh my God," Duchess said, laying her head back and looking up at the lights on the Ambassador Bridge. It looked like a sparkling necklace draping over the river between Detroit and Canada. "That was hilarious and horrible all at once."

"You talkin' about life," Duke replied.

"Whoah," Duchess said, leaning toward him over the center console. The heat of her body made the hairs on his arm raise up. "That feeling of being wrongly accused," Duchess said in a way like she was about to cry. It made Duke hurt inside. "Is that how my dad felt?" she asked. "Like no matter what you say to explain the truth, it's pointless because your accusers are already so convinced that you're bad."

"Soun' like you describin' a whole lotta brothas I know in the joint right now. But baby girl, you get a Oscar fo' that performance. They ate it up!"

"What a relief," Duchess said as he blew back past the restaurant with the deep blue river flowing to their right. "Love how you just played along. I didn't even have to tell you."

She got quiet, like she was realizing what she was about to say.

We so natural, no words required.

She answered with a fresh windful of pussy perfume. The smell of her sex was so strong, it was like a sweet cloud, like when Gramma in Alabama used to crack the oven door open to check on her famous sweet potato pies. Everybody in the room would be sniffing and smiling because they knew if it smelled that good cooking, it was going to taste like a big, juicy slice of heaven.

Duchess was quiet as they passed all the abandoned warehouses on the left, the huge silos at a cement company where a tanker docked on the water, and Chene Park, the outdoor theater on the river with pretty grass, a pond, and a curvy white tent for a roof. She lay back, closed her eyes, and didn't open them until he pulled up to Astoria Bakery in Greektown, a crowded, block-long strip of bustling restaurants, bakeries, and a casino.

"There's too many people," she said, glaring at the packed sidewalk where street artists were sketching pictures and people were standing around eating ice cream. "I'm not getting out. I don't want anyone to recognize me or bother us like at the restaurant."

"Come wit' me. I know you like ice cream," he said, opening her door and guiding her past a sidewalk musician who was blowing a saxophone. They entered through the glass-and-wood door, past the mouthwatering display of chocolate-covered strawberries, the Greek honey-nut baklava pastry, and ridiculously gooey cookies.

"Oh my God, it smells so good in here," Duchess said, inhaling the heavy-sweet scent of waffle cones cooking.

Duke's fingertips brushed the small of her back. She responded with a fresh breeze of pussy perfume rising up to his nose. Damn, her cunt smelled ten times sweeter than any waffle cone.

He was sure that nobody around them could smell her. No, their senses weren't tuned to pussy scents or sense. They probably just picked up on that lemony-flowery white girl scent coming from her hair—hair that he couldn't wait to twist up in his fingers while fucking her doggie style. It *would* happen. Soon. First he had to strip away the stiff white layers and unleash the wild black beauty within. She was horny as hell, and her animal instincts were trying to claw out anyway.

An' I'm gon' let 'em run free. He felt like God, taking white clay and molding it into the perfect black Eve. He inhaled. Her heavy-sweet sex smell made Timbo surge with red-hot blood.

"Every flavor looks good, but I already know what I want," Duke said as they stood in front of the ice cream counter. She was beside him, ogling the pink Michigan cherry, brown Mackinac Island fudge and his favorite, the blue-yellow-pink swirl of Superman. Duke opened his mouth to ask her what she wanted, but no words came out.

Damn. What's her name? In his mind he'd been thinking of her as Duchess so much, he couldn't remember the name her parents gave her.

"Baby girl, tell me yo' flava," he said, licking her up with his eyes. He could feel the girl behind the counter pitching hardball attitude at them with her eyes, her snarled-up lips and her head cocked to one side.

"I don't usually eat ice cream," Duchess said. "I'm like a chocolate addict. One bite and I totally lose control."

Miss Attitude cut her off. "Den you ain't gotta be havin' no chocolate." The girl cut her eyes at Duke then slammed her scooper in the vanilla. "Yeah, honey, you betta leave da chocolate fo' dose o' us who can han'le it." She raked her eyes all up and down Duke.

He stared back hard and said, "My baby girl want a double scoop o' that Godiva dark chocolate fudge decadence." Duke pointed to the label in front of a tub of the flavor that Beamer ate almost every damn day. "Make it extra big. Mandingo size."

The attendant sucked her teeth and mumbled to herself as she dragged the scoop through the glistening dark chocolate ice cream. She filled a waffle cone then handed it to Duchess.

"Now fo' me, a triple scoop o' Superman." Duke didn't look at the chick behind the counter. He locked his gaze on Duchess' tongue, which was coming out slowly, wrapping around that huge tower of black. Her candy-pink tongue licked up the side of the dark chocolate. She closed her eyes like it was the best thing she had ever tasted. So far. She'd have the same look when she slurped up on his dick for the first time, and an even more lustful look after he fucked her good and she truly knew the powers of Timbo.

Duke smiled, imagining how someday he would lay her on the kitchen counter at his crib, fill up her pussy with ice cream then hold his mouth open at her pussy lips and let it melt out.

Duke took his cone, tossed a ten at Miss Attitude and led Duchess back to the car. They sat in the convertible, in a no parking zone, watching the crowded sidewalks and flow of cars on Monroe Street. Greek music played from overhead speakers, mixing with rap from niggas on cruise with their females, and white folks walking up and down the street, their bellies full of lamb and that *opal* cheese they set on fire and let sizzle before they sloshed it up on some bread.

Duke tucked a napkin into his collar so no pink, blue or yellow Superman ice cream could drip and stain his white linen.

Damn, Duchess looked gorgeous, sitting right next to him where she was destined to stay. His pulse was pounding.

"Baby girl, why you look so scared?"

"I think I have a chocolate addiction. It makes me feel totally out of control. I mean the first drop on my tongue, it sets off this crazy, runaway train of thoughts, like I wish I could eat chocolate constantly. I wish I could taste this—" She took a lick, closed her eyes and said, "Mmmm . . . every second of every day."

"My boy Beamer always eatin' chocolate."

"It shows."

Duke laughed. "See, you ain't scared. Half my crew be scared to say a damn thing 'bout Beamer 'cause he my boy."

"He's fat. That shows no control. Disregard for the consequences of your actions. Just like teen pregnancy. Emphysema in smokers. Wrinkles in girls who lay in the sun, like my friend Tiffany. She's only eighteen, but years of frying herself, sunbathing—"

"Don't wanna be black, but tryin' ta look as black as they can," Duke said.

"I tan easy and I get dark in a heartbeat. It looks beautiful, but I usually only do it on our boat in the summer." She moaned. "Used to."

"Baby girl, I got a yacht that'll make you feel right at home," he said, licking his Superman scoops like they were the little man in her boat getting swept over by a giant tongue wave.

She stared blankly at the street with a look in her eyes like her mind was far, far away.

"Seriously, baby girl, you got all the right instincts. You know its death to show fear, 'cause now you know you gon' get eaten alive in'a hood an' in'a fancy white world you used to. You need protection. From me."

"No, I don't." Her neck jerked ever so slightly in a way she wasn't even aware of. Her silver-blue eyes flashed with defiance.

He smiled. *I seee sista-girl inside tryin'a break outta white girl bondage already.*

"You do need protection. Already proved it tonight, twice. Pit bulls, ghetto hoes, the media, the cops, and angry white men. An' the brothas. Walk down Babylon Street an' e'ry thug gon' try an' stick you on they dick an' roas' you like a marshmallow."

"Do you have to say it like that?"

"By the look in yo' eye, you hear ma point loud an' clear." His motor hummed loudly. "Ma brotha Knight always say, 'Show, don't tell.' Now I showed you what I do. Serve an' protect."

She licked fiercely, looking down on the ice cream. The way her thick black eyelashes constrasted against her milky skin looked sexy as hell. She shifted her feet and something made a crinkle noise. It was the four-day-old newspaper Beamer had been reading earlier. About her. She snatched it up.

"Are you like, a stalker? You planned to meet me!" she accused. "I mean, why would Henry call you when I—" She turned as gray as the newspaper.

"Listen, baby girl, you got balls. Wit' five-oh no less! Balls as big and black as mine."

"You are so crass." She crossed one arm over her ripe titties. "Can you say, 'Victoria, you speak with such confidence and courage. I'm impressed with how you think on your feet to resolve problems with finesse.'"

"Naw, I can say, 'We the D-town new dream team,'" Duke said. "The Duke an' Duchess dream team."

"I was thinking I'm actually in a nightmare. But if this is a dream team, then what, exactly, is our game?" She took a big lick, like it would sweeten her situation.

"Manifest Destiny fo' my company, Babylon. All my turf in Detroit, we call it Babylon, named after the street we on an' the ancient Arabian city known for the wildest shit in history. Crazy gold, the sexiest goddesses . . ." He let his eyes lick all over this chick who had to be finer than any bitch in the real Babylonia. "An' straight-up ridiculous wild abandon."

"And wickedness and sexual obsessiveness," Duchess added in a way that was sassy but innocent. "So, what do you sell at Babylon?"

Duke tossed his head back and let a deep laugh boom up and out. "We sell what e'ry body want, any kinda way. Its always a fresh supply, e'ry flava, e'ry style, for e'ry taste. Ain't nothin' like Babylon anywhere, an' you gon' love it."

"What do you sell?"

"Pleasure and protection," he said. "We mostly do parties and patrols. Now, we rollin' west an' east. An' Knight, he got two mo' weeks."

"Of what? Two more weeks of school?"

"He in the pen, framed for somethin' he didn't do. He finally comin' home, so we got a tight deadline. I gotta make a whole lotta shit happen, 'cause by time you meet Knight, you an' me gon' be flexin' from Cali to da Bronx. An' we gon' have my boys wit' da Bang Squad at his comin' home party."

"Why do you sound excited about your brother but—" She looked hard into his eyes. "You have a weird look in your eyes. Like he intimidates you."

Duke bit down hard. Her comment started that game of hot potato in his head. Instead of hands holding a potato, it was his emotions pitching his brother back and forth, shouting "Love!" and "Hate!" so no area of his body or brain would get burned. Sometimes "Love!" won, other times "Hate!" got the last word. Right now, they were both screaming at equal volume.

"I learned e'ry thang I know from Knight an' Prince. So naw, I love 'em to death. They blood. We got a vision."

Victoria's face scrunched with confusion. Her eyebrows drew together, the corners of her mouth drew back, her eyes got big, as if all that would help her figure out what he was saying.

"How do you expect me to help you with your 'vision' to sell protection and pleasure? What in the world! That could mean anything from a condom company to porno flicks. And having a brother in prison, that's serious. Did you guys get audited like my dad?"

Duke imitated her white girl way of talking. "Did you guys get audited like my dad?"

She snarled, "Don't mimic me!"

"You so sexy when you mad. Make me wanna instigate somethin' jus' to see how them pretty lips curl up an' yo' eyes flash like lightnin'."

She bit the waffle cone, crunching as if it would shut him up. "It's a'ight, 'cause you gon' be bilingual in a minute."

"*Je parle franais*. So, what's the third language? Espanol?"

"Naw, Black. Ghetto. Street. Ebonics. You gon' converse like Becky when we be steamin' the Moreno Triplets, but you gon' be rappin' like a hardcore bitch when we deal wit' Izz an' any otha sorry-ass ma'fucka."

"Duke, translate. What the hell does 'we be steamin'' mean?"

He licked his cone. "Cool it, baby girl. This meeting, it's about turf. About me holdin' the Moreno Triplets to their promise. Just before Prince got shot, he made a pact that Babylon would take ova they turf, from Jersey down to the Keys."

"Sounds like mega-bucks. As in, help me pay my college tuition if I agree."

"Millions, baby. It's a win-win situation for everyone."

"Then why do you need me?"

"To soften them. Yo' exotic face—when I get through makin' you ova to fit my vision—gon' distract 'em."

"So it's like *My Fair Lady* in reverse. He took a street urchin and made her into a proper English lady. Now I'm the next contestant on *Extreme Ghetto Makeover*."

Duke laughed. "You sexy as hell, naturally. How you think Cleopatra made Caesar an' Mark Anthony do whateva the fuck she wanted? The power o' pretty pussy, an' knowin' how to use it to whip any ma'fucka into submission."

Her whole face blossomed into the biggest, most blinding-bright smile she had flashed all day.

"See, baby girl, you gon' be dangerous wit' a Big D!" Laughing, he admired his diamond "D" ring. He felt like a snake charmer—he had to bring it out of her without getting stung himself. "So when these dudes see yo' light-bright face, you gon' come off like beige Barbie wit' a business degree from Harvard."

"Then you'll help me to go to college."

Yeah, Inner City College, where you gon' major in Streetology, get a masters in Babylonology, an' a PhD in Sexology.

"Anything you need, baby girl."

"Then what's the catch? Daddy always said if something sounds too good to be true, then it probably is."

Duke shook his head. "It's a straight-up equal exchange on the table. I help you, an' you help me make sure they can't get over on a nigga."

"Get over. Get over what?"

"Take advantage 'cause we from the hood and they from a big white dynasty on a hill. They still gangsta as they wanna be."

"I hope I've never seen them before," Victoria said. "I mean my ex-boyfriend's parents are the richest, but they had some mafia-type friends. This one guy, with slicked-back hair and the most gorgeous Asian girlfriend—"

Duke glanced at traffic on the busy street. Five-oh in an undercover squad car crept past, nodding.

"Keep your voice down low, on the cool gears," Duke said to Miss Daisy, who was eating that ice cream like she was going to cum. "Don't let it ride up. Slow, steady, cool at all times."

"Duke, I haven't agreed to do anything for you."

"Protection, baby. Just like I protected you twice tonight. From that dog—"

"So it was you! How did you draw so fast?"

"Practice," Duke said. "Wit' warrior protection. We guard the hood-old ladies to the bus stop, kids walkin' to school. Twennie-fo' se'en."

"That doesn't make money." Her words shot back like a question mark.

"We got legit contracts for sports events an' political rallies at all the stadiums an' convention centers in Metro Detroit."

"Oh, then that would earn a lot of money," Duchess said, "and you get minority business status. That's why my dad put my name on the company." A glazed look spread on her face as if her brain had just pushed the in-case-of-emergency TOO MUCH INFORMATION button. She licked her ice cream, staring up at the colorful signs outside the row of restaurants and shops.

"What in the world could I possibly do for you, Duke?"

"You work at HQ. My building is that warehouse down from your grammomma house. It's laid like you gotta see to believe—hundreds of employees, 'bout to be thousands—an' it's all legit. You handle my books, keep things runnin' smooth, and work with my clients to arrange what they need. Travel to the wes' coas' an' eas' coas', help me expand."

"What's in it for me?"

"I set you up to live like you wanna live. You'll have time to go to college and study too. Just think on it tonight, especially when Kay-Kay creep into your sheets, smackin' her lips."

Her eyes widened. "Can we stop for a newspaper, please? I need to look at the Want Ads for a job. And an apartment."

"Who gon' hire the crook on the news who, if you listen to Mr. and Mrs. Mad back at the restaurant, people be thinkin' you jus' like yo' daddy?"

"I can't work for you. I have to get my old life back."

"Look like the media blackwashed that all away," Duke said, peeling away from the curb between two sweet-ass red motorcycles and a black Escalade with silver spoke rims. "Your secret out, shorty. You black and everybody know it now. And once you go black, you can't go back. ''Specially when I can see it bubblin' out your blood."

"What?"

"You ain't wearin' no makeup," Duke said, but ev'a since I saw you, your lips been gettin' redder and redder. I see it. A strong, sexy diva bitch that's beatin' you up inside to escape the stiff- ass way you talk and carry yourself."

"Don't talk to me like that. You don't know my life. Just take me home."

Duke let out a sinister chuckle. "Home, right. Miss Daisy gon' wilt up in that mug. And that other bitch inside you gon' come out, come to me, neva look back. You'll see, 'cause I see it. I'm a visionary, and you the vision."

Chapter 12

The only vision Victoria had right now was her naked body next to his. As he drove with his left fingers draped so cool over the bottom of the steering wheel, she imagined hers clasped with his, like the posters for that Spike Lee movie, *Jungle Fever*—a black and a white hand, fingers intertwined. She'd never seen a black dick, just Brian's, which was like beige and dark pink when it got hard.

"What? What is that enormous black fist in the middle of the street?" she exclaimed. He stopped at a red light on downtown's huge, car-clogged Jefferson Avenue. "Is it supposed to be there?"

Duke's deep laughter boomed through the car and up into the early evening air. "Damn, you ain't neva even been downtown Detroit?"

"I saw *The Nutcracker* ballet at the Fox Theatre on Christmas. Daddy took me to the opening of the Hard Rock Cafe and the Auto Show at Cobo. But I've never . . ." She was mesmerized by the black iron fist and forearm that were parallel with the ground. It was suspended by wires hanging from the center of a long, pyramid-shaped frame of posts or pipes.

"Coleman Young, when he was the mayor, he put it up to remember Joe Louis. You know, the boxer."

"Right, I read about it in history class. The Black Power fist."

Duke imitated her. "The Black Pow-werrrr fist."

As he drove, blasting rap music, she closed her eyes, squeezing her pussy muscles. She stuck her butt deeper into the clean, butter-soft leather bucket seat. It embraced her ass, and her full stomach pressed into her waistband.

Now with her stomach satisfied, an overwhelming hunger for Duke Johnson made her want to yank down her jeans, sit on the steering wheel, and spread herself wide open in his face. Her pussy was as pink and creamy as that vat of ice cream inside the bakery.

How's this for a Michigan cherry? she could tease while popping her pussy-fruit into his mouth.

Her crotch felt like a wild animal screaming and squirming and starving to spread open its lips and suck down that big, juicy sausage bulging in his pants. Yeah, his dick would get squeezed, chewed and slurped up and down by Celeste. Then they *could* sit quietly for a little while, satisfied and full, until the raging and insatiable hunger made them devour each other all over again.

If Duke felt half as good as Dildo Dick . . . Victoria smiled. Maybe the fact that she'd been using her dildo would make it easier to take all of Duke. Did that mean she was still a virgin? Would she still feel like a virgin? Would he be able to tell?

Victoria couldn't stop thinking about how it would feel to straddle his lap, kiss him like there was no tomorrow, and slide down on his dick while his giant hands cupped her butt cheeks. He would be like the Greek god Atlas with her whole world in his fingertips. He was so big and strong, he could lift her up and down. She saw that once, in one of the porno movies she found in Daddy's bedroom while he was out of town.

"Duchess." That deep, delicious voice rumbled through her chest, snapping her out of her thoughts. "You thinkin' 'bout my proposal?"

"Kinda," she said as she came back to reality. *I can't work for this guy, no matter what definition of legitimate he's working with. I'm stuck in hell.* Her eyes stung with tears. She kept them closed.

She thought of the works by Faust she'd just read in Honors English. *Do I have to make a deal with the devil just to survive? Could I ever escape? And if I deal with him, will I break my race-sex vow to myself, about Celeste? Then where does that leave me the rest of my life?*

Chapter 13

Duke turned off Jefferson onto Iroquois, where giant oak trees shaded huge, fancy houses built by auto barons like the Dodge family. This would make Duchess feel more relaxed, like he wasn't as much of a hood rat as she thought. For now.

"I've been here," Duchess said softly. "Indian Village. My dad's ex-partner lived right"—she pointed—"there. You should see how they restored it to its tum-of-the-century grandeur. It was even in *Architectural Digest.*"

Duke pulled up to a brick colonial with white shutters and pink flowers blooming from window boxes and along the brick walk leading to the white wood double doors.

"Pretty," Duchess said.

Duke got out, grabbed a brown leather backpack from the trunk, and opened her door. "C'mon."

"Who lives here?"

"The real boss," he joked.

"Henry said you're the boss. Is this like, an investor in your company or something?" The curious flash of her silver-blue eyes made his heart pound. His dick swelled harder.

His every cell was on fire, but he had to stay cool. He couldn't confess yet that with one look, he'd lost his mind through those windows to her soul. No, Duke would never just blurt out some corny sounding Casanova bullshit lines like that.

In fact, this was the first time they had ever formed in his head. Milan, she was his childhood girlfriend, but fine as she was, he hadn't felt anything this deep about her. Maybe it was because she could be so evil when she didn't get her way. Maybe it was because she could be so sexy when she wanted something, but as soon as she used sex to get it, she would go right back to being evil.

Duchess, on the other hand, who should have been a raving crazy bitch after what she had gone through, was as cool and as calm as he had been when Prince got killed, when Knight went to prison, and when Pinks staged that hostile takeover of Babylon.

Stupid dead ma'fucka.

"This way," Duke said, keys jingling in his hand as he led her up the sidewalk. He walked behind her, resting his fingertips on her back, so he could watch her ass cheeks pop as she took long strides on her giraffe legs. At the same time, he inhaled her wind trail of pussy and lemon-flower shampoo. He almost moaned, sniffing like a dopefiend.

He put in a key, turned, then pushed open the door.

"Do you live here?" Duchess asked with wide eyes. It smelled like furniture polish and hazelnut gourmet coffee. At the center of the foyer, pink tulips sat in a vase on a table. Above it, the crystal chandelier sparkled with sunlight beaming in through little square windows around the door. Duke watched Duchess check it all out, from the white marble floor to the white-carpeted staircase and the polished banister that led upstairs.

"This is beautiful," Duchess said, turning around and looking up. "Where are we?"

"You'll see in a minute. Hold up." Duke walked down the side hallway to the garage door. He opened it, but inside all he saw were a lawn mower and extra patio furniture.

"This way, baby girl," he said, leading her into the kitchen. "There's a guest bedroom wit' a full bath." He pointed down the tiled hallway. "I know you wanted ta take a shower."

"If you think I'm gonna get naked in a big house alone with you—"

I do, but not right now. Duke kept his face serious, but he wanted to laugh because she was fooling her damn self. *She wish I would just take the pussy and put 'er outta her horny-ass misery right now.*

"Lock the bathroom door." He handed her a phone. "An' dial nine-one-one if you hear me breakin' it down." Duke smiled. "It should be some stuff yo' size on'a vanity table. 'Cause I put it there, knowin' you'd wanna freshen up when you stepped down into the hood."

Duchess stared up at him like she was trying to figure out what was really going on. She crossed her arms. "I'm *not* putting on your wife or girlfriend's clothes."

"The tags still on e'ry thang. Don't belong to nobody but you. Anything else you need, we can go shoppin'."

She glanced down the hall, which looked like an enchanted garden with all the pink pots of English ivy vines hanging over the high white window sills and walls. She looked at the phone in her palm then glanced back up at Duke.

Damn, she beautiful. That little nose, he just wanted to bite it off. And that skin, he wanted to slurp every inch, suck the pretty out of it. But this definitely was neither the time nor the place. Duke's heart was pounding already about how folks would respond to this visit once they got home.

Duchess sharpened her eyes on him and said, "My dad always advised me to listen to that little voice in my head. The instinct in your gut. Mine is always right. And right now it says this is safe."

"You ain't gotta convince me," Duke said with a laugh.

She spun toward the hall, all that hair slapping him in the chest. If he hated her, or if any other bitch flipped her long-ass hair on him like that, he'd hate her even more. But something about this chick was so humble, so unaware of just how fine she was, it would be impossible to hate her. It was like she was so busy thinking from the inside out, she forgot how she looked from the outside in. Most chicks, especially Milan, were always thinking from the outside in, like, "I'm so fine an' sexy, he betta buy me a Prada outfit an' take me to dinner at the Ritz."

That was the opposite of what Momma had taught him, Prince, and Knight "Judge men and women by how they is on the inside. Close yo' eyes an' feel 'em. The looks department be the devil's workshop. He know how to paint a pretty picture over the wors' nightmare, just ta fool you an' get you into the wors' trouble. An' you can't escape the nightmare once you done paid big bucks for the artwork."

Duchess' silky-sweet voice snapped him out of the memory.

"Duke," Duchess called, standing in the arched white doorway to the bedroom. "Thank you." She flashed the biggest, brightest smile then closed the door.

Click. It sounded like she put a chair up to it too. Duke's heart pounded as she laughed a little. She was trying to protect herself from her own pussy.

He smiled as he walked into the kitchen, but returning Milan's call and hearing her bitchy attitude made him stiffen and scowl.

"What took you so fucking long to call me back, Duke?" Her voice shot through the phone like every word was a nail. He held the phone away from his ear, hating how she was always trying to sound so white and proper.

He stepped to the white-tiled kitchen island, where the brown backpack sat next to a cake plate full of fresh-baked oatmeal raisin cookies. Duke raised the clear glass lid and sniffed his favorite home baked treat. He took one, bit down, and savored its thick, chewy sweetness.

I bet Duchess' pussy jus' like this, washed down wit' a steady stream of her own warm milk.

"Duke!" He went to the refrigerator and grabbed the milk, concentrating on the delicious cookie to block out Milan's voice. "What evil, stiff-ass bitch," he said, "took ova the sweet, natural Michelle I use ta love?" He remembered riding his bike with her to their secret spot in the tall grass. In the empty lot beside her mamma's house on Babylon. They were only six years old, kissing as the wind blew the grass all around them, promising each other that one day they'd get married, have some kids, and be happy.

Right now, if she knew he was fantasizing about loving and fucking Miss Daisy, Milan would straight up try to bite his dick off, chew it up, and spit it up his ass. But the thought of touching the bag of bones around her evil spirit made him shiver as if he were watching a scary movie. Even the oatmeal cookie suddenly tasted bad as he thought about sex with Milan.

"I saw you on TV, Duke. I don't know what you have in mind, but you need to delete any vision you might think you might be having about our new neighbor."

"You one crazy bitch." Duke stuffed the cookie into his mouth as if it were medicine to sweeten her bitterness, just like when Momma would give him honey to soothe a bad cough.

"No," Milan said, "I'm afraid you haven't seen crazy. If you even think about giving that girl my position at Babylon, the position I earned by building everything with you, Knight and Prince—"

"Oh, hell naw." Duke swallowed the cookie. "Listen up. Firs', you been so mad since Mahogani an' the baby moved into Babylon, you been miscountin' money an' makin' mistakes wit' the Squad schedules. Yo' evil ass say you lost the appointment book for the Sluts and the Studs."

Right now, Duke couldn't even picture Milan's face that he'd been kissing more than half his life. His brain drew a blank when he tried to remember what he thought was the finest face in the hood, and the world, for a while. Now, all he felt was evil, like the taste of cold, hard metal, making him remember the time Knight shoved a gun in his mouth to scare him. His big brother was trying to toughen him up, saying something about what that philosopher, Nietzche, said, "If something didn't kill you, it would make you stronger."

Knight loved that quote so much, he had it tattooed over his left bicep. And it proved true for Duke, because the next week, he got jumped by some thugs from a hood across town. They pulled a gun, but Duke was one fearless ma'fucka. Now he couldn't say "Boo!" to those same punks without them shitting on themselves.

But fearlessness in Milan's case was what made her so dangerous.

"You was mad about e'rything under the sun," Duke said, "but soon as I show you some love, you had a coincidence an' *found* the book and my twennie-five K you had los' wit' it. So play e'rybody else, Milan, but you don't play The Duke, 'less you wanna lose in the wors' way." Duke glanced down the hallway. The shower was still running behind the closed door.

"You don't scare me, Duke. But if you even think about getting with some dejected suburban slut who's whiter than me, I will show you crazy."

Duke scarfed down another cookie and guzzled milk. "I don' know nobody like that. You an' me ain't married, an' you ain't got no claim on who I talk to or work wit'."

"You belong with me, Duke, the lightest, prettiest girl on the block who gave you two babies and believed your promises that we would get married and rule Babylon."

The hiss of the shower stopped. Duchess would be walking in soon, and she never needed to even hear the name Milan, much less meet the bitch.

"Milan, you need to look in the mirror and see how small a speck you is in Duke's big picture. We grew up together, fucked around, had some kids. Now you work for me. Don't act right, and you know I will pull the plug on your glamorous life."

"I'll get immunity and you'll get life," Milan said.

"Now you really crazy," Duke said. It was time to take care of her for good. "Maybe you forgot what happened to Sunnie."

"I want to know what happened to us," Milan said. "You don't even call me to check on business." She sounded white as snow until she said "business." It came out "bee-yass-niss," like a certified sista.

"Duke, how do you know I haven't been dealing with a crisis here with the Sex Squad?"

"You woulda tol' Beamer when I was in my meetin'."

"I need to tell you something very important, Duke."

"Tell me."

"In person."

"Milan, if you tryin' ta script anotha soap opera scene, I ain't comin' to the set. So jus' say it."

"I'm not going to play by your bad rules right now. I'll brief you on everything, including the baby, if you can schedule me into your rotation." Click. Baby? The baby she wished she could have.

Ain't no way her skinny ass could get pregnant again. The way her hip bones were sticking out lately, that womb was nothing but a hostile environment for his sperm. And as little as they been fucking—he was just turned off by how she was wasting away, a sack of bones with no ass to hold on to—no way she could be knocked up.

This jus' anotha o' Milan tricks. Work wit' tricks all day, schemin' wit' her own the rest o' the time. I ain't got time fo' no drama.

Footsteps in the hallway made his heart hammer, and his skin prickled with sweaty excitement to see Duchess. They'd been apart fifteen minutes and it felt like forever.

She walked toward him wearing the baby blue velour warm-up suit with matching satin gym shoes and a white tank top that held her titties up just right. She was drying her hair with a big, pink towel. Her face was clean and shiny. Her cheeks and lips were naturally red.

"A shower never felt so good," she said. "I was so dirty."

"Come in here," he said, guiding her to the family room off the kitchen, where he sat on a plush, pale green couch.

"Duke, who lives here?" she asked, lowering her ass to the cushion beside him. "Would they mind if I spend the night in that guest bedroom? I mean, just one night. Then tomorrow I'll figure out where I'm going."

"We'll see how it go when you meet the owner," he said, keeping his voice low and steady to mask his excitement. "You handle ya bidness just like me. The mo' shit come at cha, the cooler you get. E'rybody know, when Duke calm and quiet like a lion, I'm thinkin' about how I'ma pounce somebody or something. An' I get my way e'rytime."

"I noticed that," Victoria said, sitting Indian style on the couch cushion, facing him so that her knee was touching the side of his thigh.

Timbo was pounding, but this was the last place he needed to get busted trying to mix ebony and ivory. Yet.

"During dinner," she said, "when you were watching me eat and walk and talk, you get so still you're like a mannequin. I wanted to reach over and take your pulse."

Duke let out a low, sexy laugh. "Oh, my pulse 'bout as strong as it's gon' get." He raised his hips slightly, shifting to let huge, hard Timbo roll to a looser spot under his white cotton briefs. "My pulse poundin'."

Her big blue eyes cut at him in a way that only a sista could do. She just didn't know it yet. "Please," she said with her white girl business tone, "whatever private detail you were about to share, keep it to yourself."

Damn, her sexy-ass voice, especially with that prim and proper in-the-boardroom talk, put his dick on swole. Her voice was deep, kind of raspy, not slow but not fast, just right, and every word came out like she was in complete control of how she pronounced each letter. If she could suck his dick into her mouth as elegantly as she blew out words and sentences, Duke was in for one helluva treat. One helluva life.

"You walk like a panther, too," Victoria said. "Like every step has this feline grace, like your joints are liquid and you're just flowing along silently. Like the most powerful, most treacherous king of the jungle."

"Make a nigga scared, too." He laughed, remembering how he pounced on Izz this afternoon. It was exactly how she described it, and she didn't even see it. "Callin' me a treacherous panther. Miss Animal Planet. Baby girl, I could listen to you talk all day long." The lust in his voice hung in the warm air. A fresh waft of hot, clean pussy made him dizzy.

Damn, that girl horny as hell. Prob'ly made herself cum in the shower and she still hot an' bothered.

"You a virgin?" he asked.

She got perfectly still. Her thick black eyelashes lowered then that giraffe neck turned with a slight jerk. She pulled all that black hair to the opposite shoulder and fixed her gaze on him.

He stared back. Her unblinking eyes were like blue ice, cold, hard as picks. That would come in handy when she was negotiating for him. Otherwise, all he would have to do was blow on her horny ass and she'd melt in a creamy puddle all over his face. Yeah, someday very soon she was going to squat on his face, take some tongue up that virgin pussy, and blow her nut all over his nose, cheeks, mouth, and eyes.

"Baby girl, if you think you can beat the Duke in a staredown . . ."

"You have panther eyes," she said in a way that made her lips look extra sexy. They stuck out, pouting, and shining like she had just licked them.

"I won!" she laughed. "You looked at my lips!"

His body and eyes were still, facing her as she tossed her head back, laughing.

"Tough guy." She giggled. "But seriously—"

"Seriously my ass." His hard voice cut her off. "Don't trick me."

"Don't lose your own challenge," she said with a slight neck jerk. "See, look at your eyes right now. They shimmer like a panther's eyes. Like, they're so rich in color and texture. During our stare-down, they were tough and like, aroused. Now they're analyzing the situation."

Timbo was jumping with every word.

Someday I'm gon' fuck her while she talkin' just like that. "Damn," he exclaimed. If she kept it up, he was going to have to taste that intelligent language. Kiss her. Suck that skill right out of her mouth and try to pull it into himself. That was why she was going to work for him, so she could literally be his mouthpiece; an extension of his brain.

"My dad was like that," Victoria said slowly. "After my mom died, he would just sit and stare at people. Like he was figuring out who was on his side, and studying people. Then, boom. He put everything he'd learned to work and built his business bigger and better."

"That's my plan for Babylon," he said, his lust now turbo charged by exciting visions of her at his side, building their kingdom bigger and better than any inner city thug could ever imagine.

"What's that?"

"My company. You'll see, tomorrow, when you agree to work for me."

"I can't work for you," she said, crossing her arms. "Don't say that again."

His heart skipped a beat then pounded harder than ever. The hot surge of blood went straight to his dick. It made Timbo hurt.

A nigga could get some lead pointed toward his head, just to scare him, for talking to Duke Johnson like that. Cussed out, beat down, showed out. But this white bitch was talking to him like she was the boss, and that hard glint in her eyes, sharp as a knife blade, as she sliced a look his way.

"Damn, baby girl, you like that movie, *Clueless,* about them valley girl chicks in California. Ain't got no clue. You got balls as big as mine, and ain't scared to swing 'em right in Duke Johnson face!" His voice rose on his last name in a mock shocked tone.

Her cheeks turned almost as red as her lips. She crossed her legs, squirmed her ass deeper into the seat. The idea of that hot pussy cradled inside the baby blue velour, shooting flames against the couch, made Duke want to lift her up and pull her down on the telephone pole that was jolting so hard it felt like it could split his pants.

But footsteps in the hallway made his dick deflate. Instantly.

Chapter 14

Victoria felt more hope than she had in a week when an older woman's cheerful voice echoed into the family room. Maybe it was Duke's mom or his aunt, and she would let Victoria stay there until she figured out where in the world she was going to live. Anywhere but that horrible house of hell on Babylon Street.

"My baby boy," the woman called.

His expression was still cool and calm, but his eyes flashed something different than she'd seen all afternoon and evening: nervousness. He stood, smiling like a kid who wanted his mom to tell him he'd been a good boy.

"Lawd ha'mercy," the woman called. "Ma baby boy come see his momma."

Victoria smiled, letting all the love in the room give her the hug she'd been aching for all week. Not that she expected a hug from Duke's mom, but she was giving off such strong mother love, it was enough for Victoria too.

The woman, who was a good foot shorter than her son, whisked toward them, raising her hands to grasp Duke's cheeks. She was wearing a pink straw hat with big flowers on top and a delicate net covering her full, bronze face. Her pretty pink dress was belted against her trim hourglass. Its chiffon skirt floated behind her as she approached on white pumps and stockings that matched the satin gloves dangling from the pink straw purse over her shoulder. Her face glowed as her dark brown eyes focused only on Duke, as if Victoria were invisible.

"My baby, Knight! You come home early!" The woman's sing-song voice echoed with gratitude so strong it gave Victoria goosebumps.

"Naw, Momma, it's me, Duke," he said as her hands cupped his cheeks and he wrapped his arms around her back for a hug.

"Lawd ha'mercy. I miss that boy so much I be 'lucinatin' my baby boy done turnt into my biggest boy," she exclaimed, stroking the back of his bald head. "Call me bad as e'rybody else, mixin' the two o' you up like you one an' the same."

Duke's jaw muscle flexed and something bad flashed in his eyes. Did he resent that he looked like his older brother?

"That's okay, Momma. Two more weeks you'll have him back." He glanced at that brown leather backpack on the coffee table. "I brought—"

"You brought Ellie Mae wit' a suntan up in ma home, boy." She kept hugging Duke, but her voice turned from sweet and soft to razor-sharp. "You tryin' to follow in yo' big brotha footsteps? How you 'spect me to love somebody who look like the reason Knight in jail? Ain't no half-white girl welcome in ma house."

"Momma, she black."

Victoria's brows drew together. *I am?* If that was what it would take to sweeten this lady's voice, then—

"Can't nobody who grew up that white be black in they heart," she said. "She might could be mulatta, but hist'ry show you can't neva trus' somebody wit' that much enemy flowin' through they blood. Knight the locked-up proof o' that."

"Momma!"

"You wanna see twenty-one next week, don't let Knight hear 'bout ya new little friend. An' don't ev'a let 'im see you makin' a mockery o' his sit'ation."

Duke's tall, broad shoulders appeared shorter and narrower as she spoke, as if his mother's words were hammering him down.

"Momma, she different," he said softly. "This the girl we seen on the news when I brought you Chinese food Tuesday night. You said—"

"Boy, don' tell me what I saw or said. That was in general, not a invitation to come up in here wit' her an' you lookin' all love-struck. Now y'all go 'head."

Victoria's heart was pounding. She was almost as scared as when that pit bull came at her, when the police approached outside the restaurant. What in the world happened between Knight and a white girl that got him sent to prison? And how could this lady in pink who looked at Duke with so much love possibly transfer her hate for Knight's white female friend onto Victoria?

She doesn't even know me. She's letting the bad feelings she has about the whole White race taint her view of me. Just like Brian's parents and Tiffany's parents. They did know me, like a daughter, yet their negative attitudes about the Black race made them hate me too. And all of them, just like Duke's mother, said they couldn't trust me.

The white people who used to love her hated her blackness. Now this black lady wouldn't love her either, because she hated white. And all of them were hating her based on their malice toward the whole race, not her personally. She hadn't done anything but show and crave love.

This is so unfair. It had nothing to do with what a sweet, intelligent, polite girl she was. And judging how big, bold Duke had that wimpy expression and even wimpier posture under his mom's disapproving glare, Victoria was going to keep her lips zipped.

Chapter 15

Duke could not believe he exposed himself like that. He never let anybody see the power his mother had over him. Nobody. And the only person who had even more juice over him than Momma? Knight. Momma was wrong comparing Duchess to that bitch whose family went crazy when they found out she was trying to kick it with Knight.

Duchess one o' us. Momma gon' see. Soon.

As for now, the sooner he and Duchess drove away, the better. Maybe when Momma opened the backpack and saw the cash, she would feel better.

It was just a matter of Duke bringing out the black in this beauty, and Momma would warm up in a Motor City minute.

Something pink flashed to his right. Duke turned. Momma was in the front doorway, throwing Duchess' sweater, jeans, pink panties and bra and red sandals out on the front walk.

"Oh my God," Duchess gasped with huge eyes. Momma slammed the door.

Duke walked up to collect her clothes. He folded them and put them in the trunk.

"I'm sorry she actin' like that," Duke said softly as he drove away from the curb. "In time she'll see."

"I guess I should get used to arousing hatred in complete strangers," Duchess said in a way that made his heart hurt. "Now what? I am not going back to that filthy house with dogs, smoke, and roaches."

"I know a spot where we can talk and relax for a minute." Duke turned onto five-laned Jefferson Avenue, driving past apartment buildings on the river to the Belle Isle Bridge. He loved how the bridge's white arcs extended across the deep blue Detroit River to the lush green island park. It was city folks' only place to play on a hot September night like this.

"Did you say relax?" She turned to him, glaring as if he were crazy. "Take me to my grandmother's. They find bodies on Belle Isle. People get shot there!" Her head snapped and a sista-rhythm rang in her words. "And if black people hate my appearance so much, I am not tryin' to be somebody's target practice."

A laugh from deep in his gut made Duke toss his head back. He cracked up at the deep blue sky.

"This gon' be quick," he said.

"What! Turn around!"

"It's your transition, baby girl. Your fade ta black. Know this at all times: Anyplace you go wit' The Duke, anytime, you safe. I rule D-town. Don't nobody mess wit' The Duke."

He pulled into the first parking lot near the river's edge. The setting sun was a huge orange fireball casting a wide red stripe over the rippling river. The mirrored round towers of the General Motors world headquarters in the Renaissance Center looked like five gold fingers stretching into the pink sky.

"What if people decide to mess with you if they think you're havin' jungle fever?" Victoria glanced around at black folks barbecuing at picnic tables, fishing, and rolling past in SUVs with the jams blasting. "If you expect me to sit here chit-chatting—"

"Ghetto survival lesson numba one: Be fearless. If you scary, e'rybody smell it. If you act like you the boss, like can't nobody touch you, then people respect that."

"My dad told me that too."

"Then do it."

"He meant in business."

"If you ain't scared here, then you won't be scary in a board room facin' some pit bull ma'fucka who wanna rip yo' throat out if he don't get his way." Moreno's sneaky eyes—all three of those dudes were just as sneaky as the next—flashed in Duke's mind. Victoria Winston would disarm those sleazy bastards so tough, none of them would even know their own name.

"Duke, when you say I'm scary, that means I scare you."

You do, but I ain't neva gon' confess it. He stared back, silent and still.

"If you say 'I'm scared,' that means 'I feel afraid.' The words 'scary' and 'scared' are not interchangeable."

"Let me go get an apple for the teacher. Ain't that what white kids do? At my school, kids gave teachers a knock upside the head."

She leaned close. His lips parted. Was she doing a 180, about to kiss him?

"See, your eyes." She stared the same way that doctor did in the emergency room when Duke cut his eye as he was trying to save Prince. "Panther eyes."

"So, doc, you ain't scared. I'm 'bout to pounce your fine ass?"

"You want something from me. You wanna butter me up."

"Ain't like you got no chips."

"I am my own trump card." She raised her chin, poking her chest out. "And only I choose how and when to play it."

"Damn, girl. Soundin' just like me."

"See," she said, her hot breath tickling his cheek as she stared into his right eye. "When you get excited, your eyes sparkle, like onyxes, these beautiful black jewels. My mom had an onyx choker and earrings, but they didn't sparkle as much as her eyes."

The sadness in her eyes made his heart hurt.

"But what am I thinkin'?" When she looked into his eyes, could she see the fantasy film strip playing his mind, of them fucking on the hood of this car in the orange haze of sunset, right here on Belle Isle? Could she see how he wanted to bend over that round ass and bury Timbo deep up in that virgin timberland, make her cum so hard she wouldn't be staring hard at anything but him when she begged to get fucked senseless all over again?

"Well," she sounded real scientific. "Since thoughts are electricity popping between the neurons, I mean the cells in our brains—"

This chick was seriously concentrating on his eyeball. Her face was close enough to kiss. If she didn't move back and stop pushing her left titty up against his arm, making her soft, sweet sex smell make him want to pounce like that panther she was describing.

Duke shivered, not just with lust but with fear, because when he kissed her and she agreed to work for him, when she became his Duchess ruling over Babylon with him, could he handle that? Just like Momma always said, "Be careful what you ask for."

The only successful relationship partnerships Duke had seen between a man and a woman in love, were on TV. He'd never met his own daddy. Never knew any kids whose daddies were around for a long time, living like the ridiculous Huxtables. What made him think he could succeed at it himself?

Because I'm The Duke, and when I want somethin', I make it happen. According to my vision. Just like Ramses. And so it is written, and so it is done.

"We literally think at the speed of light," Duchess said.

"I'm gon' kiss you at the speedo' light if you don't stop teasin'me."

"Your eyes captivated me," she said with that scientific stare into his eyeball, "when we met at Gramma Green's. The way your irises shift, it's so cool, like I see these fascinating sparkles of bronze and copper and onyx all set in dark brown velvet."

The way her lips were wrapping around all those big words and blowing them out, right in his face, it was just too much. If there were a big CONTROL switch in Duke's brain and he had been holding the lever back as tightly as he could, then something just sucked away all his strength and he let go. Let that ma'fucka slam into the red, alarm-ringin' OUTTA CONTROL zone. It could have been worse, in the black, LOBOTOMIZED BY DUCHESS. Pussy zone. Naw, right now the red zone just meant he had to kiss her.

Duke pressed his mouth to hers. Her words jammed into his lips. She tried to close her mouth, to pull away, to push his chest with her long, elegant fingers, but the scent of her sex coming up like a cloud from her pussy let him know that her mind over matter didn't mean a thing when he took control of her body. She got still. Her lips were open, letting him nibble them like the juiciest barbecued ribs in sweet-spicy sauce that been smoking all day, the smell making his mouth water for hours. Now he was going to slowly savor every bit, knowing he could feast on this for a lifetime.

Chapter 16

Victoria felt dizzy. She hated that Duke's hot mouth on hers was erasing every bit of stress, sadness, anxiety, and fear. She loved the physical sensations of his lips, his delicious, expensive cologne mixed with his macho-as-hell guy smell, the huge bulk of his body, his exotic dark skin, and the tenderness in his eyes.

His affection feels so good to my love-starved body, mind, and soul.

This was the first time she had been touched since all those hugs at the funeral, and her whole body was aching for a warm touch, for assurance that she could somehow get her normal life back, her safe, pampered, privileged life back. She could go to sleep right there because when she closed her burning eyes, the physical sensations of his kiss sucked her mind and body into a luscious lullaby where she was sure he would hold her in his arms and rock her all night long.

"Mmmm." Her heart pumped boiling blood with such ferocity that her ears were ringing. It was threatening to drown out her resolve to keep her mix-race sex power in check. Duke didn't know it and wouldn't believe it, but by kissing her, he was literally flirting with suicide. He would laugh if she tried to tell him, but every second longer that he electrified her soul like this, he was unleashing her danger within. Danger that would be unstoppable if they went to second, third, and fourth base.

No way. But never had she been kissed like this. Duke's lips were so soft and full and gentle. His breath was clean and slightly spicy. His nose against hers was more warm satin against her face. He nibbled slowly, and she responded the same way. It was the total opposite of Brian's frenzied oral assault with pursed, hard lips.

I could do this 'til I die.

Just this afternoon, at first glance, Duke Johnson looked like the worst stereotype of an inner-city, drug dealing gang member thug. But now she was kissing him and loving it. Was this what he meant by her transformation, her fade to black?

One of Duke's giant hands raised up. He ran his fingertips down her hot cheek, as if touching to prove she was real.

She sucked his bottom lip into her mouth, wishing he would do the same to her clit right now, because Celeste was writhing like a wild pink animal trying to claw her way out of these comfy velour pants. Even the blue panties fit perfectly, but now they were so wet, Victoria was sure she'd look like she peed on herself if she stood up. Tonight, she would stroke her pussy again.

I have no idea where I'm going to sleep tonight. I am not going back to Gramma Green's house.

Right now, she would be happy to spend the night right here, kissing him, not thinking about tomorrow or school or her life or her dead parents or her femme fatale mixed race sex power. Nope, if she could stay in this safe, innocent bubble, kissing this gorgeous knight in a shining Porsche at sunset after he rescued Alice from Ghettoland. . . .

Can't stand the hand that fate just slammed and rammed me, damned me. Don't understand this man who planned to demand that I hand him my soul that he stole with one look, all it took, and I'm hooked on this god. Yes, this god whose eyes can't disguise love 'til he dies. No lies, just whys. Why is it me that he sees on his dream team? Yes, dream team. I will scream if he touches the seam between my legs. Make me beg. No, I will never beg.

She begged Brian so many times to kiss her pussy after she'd given him enough oral sex to make his eyes pop. But all he could do was talk about "secretions" and "period blood" and "yeast infections," which she'd never even had. "It's disgusting," he'd say. When he begged her to finally go all the way, she demanded to know why he wanted to stick his penis without a condom, into a place he'd called disgusting.

Thank God l never had intercourse with that jerk!

A soft moan from Duke, a deep, wonderful sound that vibrated through her chest, drew her from her thoughts. Would Duke kiss her there? Would she have to ask? Would his giant dick feel as good as movie stars made it look on the silver screen?

Suddenly, her lips felt cool. Exposed. His mouth was like a thousand feathers dancing over her cheek; soft, slow, air-brush kisses that made Victoria's head swirl. Over her nose, across her forehead, down her eyebrows and onto her eyelids. He was kissing her eyelids with such exquisite softness, she gasped. Moaned. Her eyes burned with tears.

Love. That was love, kissing someone's eyelids like that. For a moment, she had no mental picture of him, couldn't remember what he looked like. She couldn't even think of his name. She had never felt this in her brain, her body or her spiritual being. The feeling was similar to the rock solid sense of comfort and security she had felt with her parents, but this was more delicious. Intoxicating. Exhilirating. And terrifying.

Oh my God. He sucked both her lips between his then ran his tongue between them. Victoria moaned. She grasped his jaw, her fingertips on his hot, thick, baby-soft neck. She had to suck on it, taste it, smell it. Her lips trailed down his jaw.

The rosy haze of sunset was casting a surreal glow, as if this were a scene in a movie she was watching and it wasn't really happening to her, even though her chest was rising and falling violently. For the first time ever, she was panting with need. Sure, she had breathed heavy with Brian, but he never made her feel dizzy. Never made her tingle down to her fingertips with the desire to do that mysterious act that men and women were supposed to love so much.

That was so good it killed Mommy.

Silvery explosions of fear and panic and resolve snapped her brain to attention for a second, but they were splashed down, melted, drowned by the gush of molten lava that was her body's blood boiling away her brain's ability to reason and control her lips, her limbs, and her pussy.

Her tongue trailing down Duke's neck inspired him to tip his chin up, offering a wide plane of delicious, dark chocolate skin. Victoria inhaled it loudly.

"Oh my God, you smell so good," she whispered. Her mind was spinning. "And you're so soft." Her wide-open mouth took in his flesh, sucking, tickling the sensitive nerves underneath.

"Oh, baby girl," he groaned. "Feels like fireworks in my neck."

She squirmed in the seat, rubbing her clit against the crotch of her pants, squeezing her pussy muscles. She could cum just like this.

No! I can't. This is beyond wrong. I have to stop.

But as she nuzzled his neck and ran her hands over his rock hard pecks, wishing she had the nerve to touch the huge bulge in his pants, he was as irresistible as Mrs. Fields brownies. His lips and his skin were as moist and sweet and rich tasting as her favorite confection, but if she could exercise and bum off the extra calories from a brownie, how could she make amends with herself for this? For shimmying from the white elite at the top of the socio-economic ladder, all the way down into the black pit of inner city blight. How could she ever climb back up and out? If she got involved with this guy even for a minute, if he were a true thug, then he would never let her leave. Or maybe she'd get tangled up in his illegal enterprises and get in trouble with the law. Maybe she'd get pregnant. She stiffened. Pulled away. Leaned her head back on the seat. Languid, she kept her eyes closed, slowly wiped her mouth with the back of her hand.

"Please take me away."

Chapter 17

Duke tapped the stereo to turn on his favorite R. Kelly CD as they crossed back over the Belle Isle Bridge. Beamer better have his ass back at Babylon with a good explanation about why he hadn't answered his phone when Duke called from the restaurant. Twice. It wasn't like Beamer's goofy ass could forget what happened the last time he didn't pick up the fucking phone when Duke called.

As he drove, glancing at the dark blue river under the shadows of sunset, he flexed his jaw muscle to bite down the anger he felt toward Beamer and mixed-up-in-the-head Duchess. They needed to straighten out a few things before they got back to Babylon Street, which was just a few minutes away on the East Side.

"Yo, Miss Daisy." She was still lying back with her eyes closed. "If you tryin' to snooze so you can wake up from this black dream, I got some news you can use as a reality check."

Her nipples poked through her shirt.

Timbo was an iron rod. Damn, he couldn't stay mad at her because she was so damn sexy. But that was what got him in trouble with Milan, being blinded by her sex and not seeing the evil scheming in them eyes.

Naw, Duchess was different. The complete opposite, as a matter of fact, however he was feeling right now, it was all right. It was all going to work out perfectly, according to his vision.

Part of him wanted to wait until Duchess was ready, which wouldn't be long. If he changed his mind, he had plenty of pussies back at Babylon to take care of it in the meantime. Chanel, yeah, she was looking so fucking sexy at the party today. She'd be the one he'd call. But she was all sex.

I want more. A chick who excite my body an' my brain. Any other bitch who teased him like Duchess just did would never get away with it. He'd have something loud to say. Not that he'd do anything. Duke never took pussy that wasn't offered. Shit, this afternoon he didn't even take the pussy that was offered. But if a chick were a tease, he'd tell her something about herself. But Miss Daisy, being in such a clueless state of mind, was so horny she didn't know up from down. No surprise then, that one taste of Duke and she was hooked. She would be back for more, especially after that nasty-ass cousin of hers tried to do a dyke dive on her tonight. If losing her daddy was making her feel anything like Duke had felt when Prince got killed, her mind was as mushy as a bowl of grits right now. He was surprised she hadn't straight up lost it, at least for a minute.

"I believe I can fly," he sang softly as they wove through traffic. "I believe I can touch the sky."

She slapped the stereo, but rather than turn it off, she switched it to the radio. A male newscaster was saying, "New developments in the suicide scandal of millionaire business-man Dan Winston. The IRS is now producing documents that prove the suburban family man was laundering money for a powerful crime cartel that is expected to be named in an indictment."

Victoria sat up, eyes wide open, reaching to poke the dial into silence, but her fingers stopped midair.

"Authorities are also re-opening the investigation into the mysterious death of Winston's young black wife, and are now trying to locate the couple's three biracial children for questioning."

"Oh my God," she whispered, turning as white as her teeth. "One daughter in particular, Victoria, worked in Winston's offices and may have crucial information about his suspicious business dealings."

Duke focused hard on the metallic green Crossfire sport coupe ahead of them. His left hand kept a cool grip on the bottom of the black leather steering wheel, but inside, he was grinning like a mug.

I got her now. She gotta hide.

She would hide in style, though, at Babylon, doing things that would flip a big ass middle finger at those fed ma'fuckas who killed her daddy and now wanted to rape her fine ass with their wicked ways of the white world.

And what better way to hide than to turn black?

Chapter 18

Victoria slapped the stereo button.

"Oh . . . my . . . God. They say it like I'm some armed and dangerous mafia princess. I'm eighteen!"

She crossed her arms hard. Her bottom lip poked out and trembled. That news report set off a sob that was slicing through her gut, squeezing her chest, threatening to burst out of her sleep- deprived body.

No, I will not have a breakdown in front of Duke. Never let 'em see you sweat. She maintained her hard, serious tone. "I'm never gonna talk to those wicked pricks again. After Daddy died, they questioned me with this accusatory tone, as if I'd shredded all the documents then pulled the trigger myself!"

Actually, she had fed box after box of files into the shredder, all late on a Wednesday night while Daddy rummaged through boxes of papers he'd pulled out of the storeroom. Was he trying to hide something wrong that he'd done? Or had he been wrongly accused and wanted to make sure nothing in the office could be used against him?

That sob zigzagged up her neck, making her throat swell into a hot, aching lump. Her head was light, spinning like a tornado inside. Fatigue fogged her mind.

If she had helped Daddy destroy evidence of wrong-doing, did that make Victoria guilty of a crime? If the feds caught her, could they prosecute her and send her to jail?

"Miss Winston," Duke spoke with a cool, flat tone. "They got you on a BWB."

"No, I am totally innocent." The corners of her mouth curled down. That sob was surging up, ricocheting around her mouth with her words. "I'm the victim! I have no parents, no nothing, now I'm thrown into the ghetto with a perfect stranger driving around aimlessly with no place to sleep tonight."

Duke swerved to the right. He screeched to a stop in front of a tall apartment building.

"Now I really can't go back to Gramma Green's. The FBI is after me! Right?"

The sob shot out. It was a gut churning groan that filled her burning eyes with tears. Hot droplets spilled down her cheeks. Her shoulders shook. She gulped air, exhaled hard. She couldn't let Duke see her like this. He might think she was weak. Her open palms met her face as she bent toward her lap. There, in the darkness of her hands, with stinging eyes closed, she sobbed into the baby blue velour of her long legs.

A huge, hot hand stroked circles on her back. It was as if he were smoothing over her jagged emotions. His hand on her back, rubbing in slow, gentle circles, reminded her of the way her mom used to tuck her in bed and tell stories while she rubbed her back. "Let it out, baby girl." Duke's deep voice was like a cozy blanket over her senses. "I got cha back. I always got cha back, baby girl."

Victoria's every cell trembled as she expelled a week's worth of anger, anguish, and anxiety. She was breathing violently, loudly sucking down lungfuls of air then heaving forward as her lungs flung it out just as quickly. Was she hyperventilating?

I gotta get a grip on myself before Duke drops me off at the mental ward at Detroit Receiving Hospital. Wouldn't that make a hot news story! Never! I will make it. And I'll be bigger and better than anyone ever imagined. So much so, they won't even know it's me.

How? She was as clueless about the world as Duke said she was. Green. Naïve. Totally unprepared to make her way in what looked like a wicked world. But she knew, deep down, she could do it. Duke would help her. She would figure out a way to make it happen so that she would be untouchable if things came crashing down like they did for Daddy. Whether he was right or wrong.

"Duke," Victoria whispered, rising. Her face felt hot, wet and swollen, just like her pussy. "I have to tell you something."

His eyes glowed with tenderness as he said, "My station is tuned to all Duchess, all the time. Ev'a since I firs' seen you on the news last week."

"Well I got a news flash, and I can already hear you saying 'ridiculous.'"

He smiled.

"I have like, a sex curse. It could hurt you."

"A curse," he said playfully. "You mean like a witch? You already put me under a spell."

"Stop laughing!" she shouted to stop another sob from exploding up, out, at him. "You and the whole world think I'm a stupid little girl who—"

He grabbed her wrist. His touch made her gasp. If only she could press up to his chest, let him wrap his arms around her trembling body, and just sleep in the soft, sleek protection of this sexy panther named Duke Johnson.

"Ooooh, them eyes stormin', like lightnin' shootin' at me."

And they'll strike you down if I'm not careful.

A fresh, hard sob made Victoria burst into tears. Her whole body was shaking, hurting with sadness, fear, extreme sleepiness. She was crying like a baby. She couldn't stop. Didn't want to stop. Didn't care what he thought. She bent at the waist, cupping her face in her hands as her knuckles pressed into the soft velour covering her knees.

What if she just gave up? What if she just gave in? She could let her sex-crazed body take over her mind, let her circumstances take over her life, let her curiosity run free into the darker side of her heritage. Her first grade school picture in Gramma Green's living room flashed in her thoughts.

My roots really are here, on the black side. The white side doesn't want me, never has. I could see Daddy's relatives in the next car and wouldn't know they were my own blood.

But the delicious smelling man leaning over to stroke the back of her head, with the soft, soothing lullaby voice and the warmth she felt without opening her eyes, was all she had right now. It felt like more than she'd ever had outside of her mother's lap and Daddy's hugs and guidance to groom her into an intelligent person in business and in life.

But how can that be? Duke and I are opposites. Or are we?

Sobs made her whole body tremble under his gentle stroke on her back. The overwhelming grief and anger and unknowing of the moment swirled in her head.

"It's a'ight, baby girl," Duke whispered into her hair. I'd be scared, too, if I was fallin' in love with some big black dude from the hood. An' come to find out the feds was after me too? Shoot, you deserve to go off. In full effect."

"If you knew the truth, you wouldn't touch me." She sobbed, feeling light-headed. "My curse could hurt both of us. Plus if I work for you, those blood-thirsty investigators—"

"Would never find you."

She raised up, staring at him through tear-blurred eyes. "This is so bizarre I feel dizzy. The job you have in mind would only get me in more trouble, whatever you do at your so-called company. Whoever you are!"

"Yo' stomach full?" he asked softly.

"I could've found something to eat—"

The tenderness in his eyes hardened. He had a scolding tone when he said, "An' I coulda lef' yo' white ass in yo' Grammomma house wit' roaches, pit bulls an' yo' dyke-ass cousin. I coulda let that dog attack yo' pretty face. I coulda let you go hungry. So, go back tonight and think about exactly who I am. Duke Johnson the hand that feed you. So don't bite."

"I already did," she said with a sassy tone. She sat up straight, staring hard-as-nails right back into his beautiful onyx eyes. "I bit you on your neck. And you loved it. Now, what crime did you say they got me on?"

Disbelief flashed in Duke's gaze. Then he said, "A BWB."

"What in the world is that?"

"Breathing While Black."

"I'm not—"

"Ain't no gray area in them white ma'fuckas' eyes. One drop of nigga blood, you black. So now, to them cock-suckin', sell-they-own-momma-up-the-river FBI cats, you black. And they wanna get cha, 'cause they couldn't get cha daddy. He gone. Stay wit' me, baby girl, an' they'll neva fin' Victoria Winston. She jus' changed her name to The Duchess."

Duke screeched into traffic. She laid her head back, staring up at the darkening sky. Suddenly, a rhyme spun in her mind. She recited it with spoken word rhythm. "I'm so confused, bein' used as a news scandal muse."

Duke turned. His eyes sparkled with intrigue.

"Don't know where to go, feelin' so sad, so mad, so bad, 'cause the life I had," she looked closer into his eyes, "went up in gun smoke. A cruel joke, like a yoke around my neck. What the heck am I doin', thrown into the hood? Am I no good? Misunderstood?"

"Yeah, baby. Rap that." Duke smiled, touching the stereo. A deep bass beat by Bang Squad played under her poem.

"Now I'm black, catchin' flack, with a lack of money. It's not funny. My life was honey, now it's—" She hit the radio. "That music is distracting."

"You rappin'. Tha's all rap is, rhymes wit' music."

"I suppose you want me to put pasties on my boobs and say vulgar things about sex. I'm a poet, not a rapper chick."

"A flower by another title still a flower," Duke said, trying to remember what he learned in eighth grade English.

"Ugh, get it right or don't say it.' A rose by any other name would smell as sweet.'"

"You a'ight, baby girl," Duke said with a laugh.

She laid her head back, yawning like she could sleep for three days, but soon as he turned onto Babylon, she turned white as a ghost. Her pretty hands gripped the sides of her seat. She shook her head, fear flashing in her eyes. Her chest was rising up and down quickly like niggas had a tendency to do when Duke pulled them aside and evaluated their performance at Babylon.

Duke ached at the sight of Duchess looking so scared.

Ain't no way I'm gon' let her back up in Miss Green house. She mine now.

Chapter 19

Beamer's whole body shook as he sped down the Lodge Freeway after leaving Milan's hotel room. He had to get back to Babylon with a good excuse for why he didn't answer his phone when Duke called twice. Doing that once was enough to get jacked. But twice?

'Cause I was fuckin' his girl?

If Milan still was Duke's girl. She wasn't officially, because Duke was probably on Lily White right now, getting her hooked on his power and his dick. But with Duke being so super-mack, the unstated rule was "once his lady, always his lady." This made her off limits for anybody else to take a taste. Or a fuck. Or scheme an overthrow.

"What I'ma do?" Beamer cried into the loud beat of Tupac inside the black Hummer. It was Babylon's Hummer, of course. Beamer wouldn't have shit if Duke hadn't given him life two years ago.

Fo' real.

"I mus' have a death wish. Nineteen years old, plottin' my own murder."

By bein' stupid. Clownin' wit' my job, my life.

He'd been writing out the instructions with his own nut. Why hadn't he known Milan couldn't be trusted, that trying to work with her was like trusting Judas? Impossible. He was thinking with his dick that was why. What could he do now? He could tell Milan that he wanted out, but she would bust on him, no joke. If he tried to tell Duke it was a set-up, boss man would ask why he was in a hotel room with her in the first place. He could confess to Duke what happened. Beamer let that conversation play out in his head, but he felt like he had an audience: all the ghosts of too many other dead motherfuckers who also jacked up their own lives and got themselves killed. They were proof that nobody could fuck around on Duke and get away with it.

Hell naw, I ain't goin' out like that. Especially over some ma'fuckin pussy. Beamer slammed his foot down on the accelerator. He had to get back to Babylon and fast.

Chapter 20

No, I can't faint. Victoria focused hard on the garbage heaps, rusting cars, and abandoned houses on Babylon Street. The surrealness of it, like the set of one of those futuristic movies about a city destroyed by war, made it harder to hold onto her consciousness.

I'm okay. I'm okay. I'm awake . . .

She felt like she was about to faint, like that time last year when Brian told her she had a fat ass and she didn't eat for nearly a week. Right now, she felt the same as she did back then, when an ear-ringing blackness rumbled into her brain. She closed her eyes and slept until her sister Melanie shook her awake, forced her to drink orange juice and eat a good meal.

"Duke," she said. Her voice sounded like it was at the end of a tunnel, echoing back at her.

Celeste, help me. Give me some strength.

"Baby girl, you white as snow right now. I'ma take you in, let you sleep."

She shook her head. Panic was transforming her insides into a live electrical wire, buzzing and sparking and jolting her senses. "Check this out," he said, pulling up to a ten-story warehouse building with big wooden double doors, sandblasted brick and new paned windows. The sidewalk was clear of the broken glass that glittered everywhere else.

"When I was growin' up right there"—Duke pointed to a neat Cape Cod-style house next door—"this buildin' was abandoned. All the windows was broken out." He was talking fast. Somehow Victoria knew he was trying to keep her conscious.

"Crackheads used to smoke up in here, an' a girl got raped while she was walkin' to school. Man, I was 'bout to kill a nigga when that shit happened."

Victoria strained to hear him over the constant scream of sirens, the bass beat of rap music, loud voices, and old cars rumbling past. The noise, at least, was helping to push back that dark cloud in her head that was trying to knock her out.

Duke turned toward the building on their right. "So I built my own Trump Tower. Me, Prince, an' Knight was visitin' some associates on the East Coast. Soon as we seen that shit on Fifth Ave, took my vision to another level."

The empty lot next door and the boarded up, graffitti covered house beside that made Victoria want to ask why he'd build a palace in the ghetto. But she didn't have the energy.

"This home base, baby. I'm a leader. E'rybody 'round here look up to Duke and the Johnson brothers. Right now, though, I'm solo, rulin' like a king."

The deep drone of a military style chant made Victoria glance to the right. Her mouth dropped open.

Jogging toward the car, up the almost dark street, was a column of shirtless men in black-white-gray camouflage pants and black combat boots. Their skin glistened with sweat over muscles rippling in a mosaic of colors: jet black, cinnamon, nutmeg, oatmeal, redwood, Cocoa, and cream as white as hers. Some were bald, some had huge, wild afros, others had tiny braids, loose and bouncing or curving against their heads.

There were dozens. Yeah, four columns of twelve. As they jogged past the car, each man let out a deep call to Duke that vibrated through Victoria's chest.

"Babylon!"

They accented the last syllable, *"Babylon!"* with a sort of upward swing on the end, like a call out with the greatest pride. The word was also tattooed in small scroll across each of their right pecks.

Victoria stared with wide eyes. If she had stepped out of her former life and into this spot without the past week's events, she would faint from fear. She still felt like she could. This was just part of her wild-and-getting-wilder Alice in Ghettoland experience.

Maybe if I live through this I can write a book and use it to pay for college.

It looked like an NFL team was coming at her, and it was making Celeste absolutely roar.

Oh my God. Those guys are like letting off a cloud of sex power. If I go anywhere near that—

At the academy, there were two black guys on the football team, and Victoria's pussy would cream as she watched them run in those little tights. That's why she loved watching Lions games at Ford Field from the private suite Daddy's business paid for. All the clients and friends thought it was cute that Dan's daughter had such passion for the game of football. Little did they know that all her staring through the binoculars let her ogle those athletic asses, their curving hamstrings, and their super-strong quads as they ran and tackled.

Now, Victoria crossed her arms to hide the fact that she was panting so hard. Her chest was rising and falling as hard as it had when she kissed Duke.

"Baby girl, you safe. Chill. This my army. My Black Warriors. The women, they B'Amazons." Duke was beaming as the men thundered past. As he nodded proudly, his diamond ring sparkled when his hand fell to his lap.

The cloud of testosterone exploding from Duke and all those men made Victoria melt into the bucket seat. All she could think about was sex, but not in a way that she'd ever experienced. The only frame of reference for sex she had were memories of Brian's erections. Movies with love scenes. Suddenly Victoria was overwhelmed with curiosity at what it would be like to do it with Duke, and all these men.

"Huu-uuut!" A deep female voice called.

Victoria turned around. More soldiers were coming.

Women! They were wearing fatigues, boots, and tank tops. Their heads were adorned with braids, ponytails, bald heads, and afros. Their skin represented every hue from pinky white to black satin, and it glistened with a super sexy sheen of sweat.

Their faces were so beautiful. One reminded Victoria of the black Barbie dolls her mother bought when she was five. Daddy had taken them away after Mommy died, just like he stopped bringing her to Gramma Green's house for visits with the black side of her family. Not because they were black, he said, but because this part of town was "treacherous and crime-infested" and "a bad influence."

Now Victoria felt a burning pang of resentment that she'd been shielded from this part of her roots. Who, in her past privileged life, would believe this sight? It was surreal even as she stared through her own fatigued eyes.

She felt a jolt of sex energy as the women jogged past. It was impossible not to feel a prickle on her skin or a hardening sensation in her tingling nipples or a hot gush in her pussy, because those women were like Amazon goddesses. They radiated nothing but power, strength, confidence, and sex.

As the women, they ranged in age from about thirteen up to a woman with silver hair-jogged past, they charged the air with sex. They looked so powerful, confident, and strong. She watched the way their nipples were poking through tight tank tops. Each had BABYLON tattooed on chiseled biceps, triceps, and deltoids.

They followed the men through the field, around the back of Duke's building. He drove the other way, down an alley. A huge door opened. A futuristic, neon blue light glowed from the opening as Duke wheeled inside.

The enormous garage could hold a football field. The three-story-high ceiling was a silver network of exposed pipes and whirring fans. Brick walls displayed airbrushed murals of ghetto fabulous city scenes in vivid cobalt blue, magenta, and bright yellow. A giant sign, made from neon blue block letters, said **BABYLON** across the left wall.

It shined on the silver floor, which was made of metal tire tread. It seemed to stretch forever as Duke drove past rows and rows of black Navigators, Hummers, and Escalades. A yellow H2, a cobalt blue Corvette and a baby blue Bentley were also on display. To the right was a set-up worthy of an authentic rock or rap concert hall: a grand, black stage with enormous speakers. The far corner looked like a nightclub with a long bar and sleek silver stools. Behind that, a mirrored wall held endless glass shelves of liquors.

Victoria looked up and back as the garage door closed. Near it, a spiral staircase, also made of that silver tire-tread metal, led up to a balcony furnished with cobalt blue plush couches and silver tables. A glass elevator connected the garage floor to the balcony and upper floors.

All those male and female soldiers were inside now, their chants echoing through the cavernous garage. They were filing up an industrial-looking staircase that led somewhere beyond the elevator. Motors revved, drowning out their chants. Lights glowed on four Navigators. The vehicles filed out.

Victoria felt dizzy. Awed. What the hell kind of operation was this? Was this legal? What were all these people doing here? And what in the world did Duke want *her* to do here?

"Duke," she said, turning to him. "What—"

A blue light flashed through his white linen shirt. Duke stopped the car in the center of the garage. He raised the bottom of his shirt, reaching for one of two phones clipped to his waistband.

Oh my God.

His stomach was exposed for a second—a flat, hairless expanse of skin as smooth, beautiful and soft looking as his bald head and gorgeous face. His belly button was perfectly round and taut. Without thinking about it, she licked her lips as if she were tracing his "innie" with her tongue.

Victoria shifted, making the fabric of her baby blue velour pants rub her pussy. Celeste and her hungry imagination had already made a puddle in these fresh panties.

"Mass' Duke," a male voice echoed through the garage.

Did he say Master Duke? Victoria squinted, as if that would help her hear better.

It was that guy in the Pistons jersey, the chubby one with the little braids and the BMW necklace. The guy who'd been with Duke when she arrived at Gramma Green's, and when he picked her up, the one who helped kill the dog.

The guy's pudgy fingers wrapped about the edge of Duke's door, but he did not look up from his phones. Instead, Duke pressed a button on the center console. The window raised.

Beamer moved his hands.

"Yo," Duke said deeply into the tiny silver square. "It's three-six-one down."

He squinted toward the speedometer. She heard a male voice so deep it reminded her of that rapper Tone Loc, one of Brian's favorites. His voice was so bass it felt like it could rumble through her body and alter her heartbeat. It was the same feeling as when she would stand too close to a giant speaker during a concert. The vibration upset the body's rhythm. Now that voice on the phone was so deep, Victoria could not decipher any words.

"Ain't it." Duke flexed his jaw. Over the past few hours, she had noticed that when he seemed irritated or lost in his thoughts, the little muscles under the smooth skin on his jaw rippled, as if he were grinding his teeth. But something was different. Duke's super-cool expression had suddenly transformed into that same look he'd had at his mother's house.

Fear. Subservience. Nervousness.

Who in the world was on the phone? It was a man, for sure. Was Duke in danger? Was it the person or the subject matter of the conversation that was making Duke like that? Or was he just annoyed that Beamer was standing on the other side of the car window, looking even more scared?

"Yeah," Duke groaned. "Straight up." He tossed his head back and let out a hearty laugh that echoed through the garage, and returned Duke's usual machismo to his face and eyes.

"Like beamin' up some shit!" Duke said the last word with a high pitch so playful it made Victoria smile, even though she had no clue what he was saying.

Duke hung up, clipped the phone to his waist, and kept his shirt pulled up longer this time. Victoria's mouth watered. She could not look away from that incredible skin on Duke's bare stomach. If she could just plant her lips there for a few seconds and taste . . . suck . . . lick . . . She leaned forward. Her mind felt foggy with fatigue, curiosity about this place, and raw lust. She imagined her body twisted up with his, their skin hot, their sweat gluing them together, their complexions contrasting in a way that would be breathtakingly sexy and dangerous in ways Victoria didn't even know. Her pussy was gushing. She kept bending forward, and re-tied her shoes.

"Baby girl," Duke said, "you remember Beamer from earlier."

"B, this Victoria Winston."

"Hi," Victoria said. "Are you named after a car?"

"Naw, I'm jus' goofy," he said. Why was his voice higher than earlier? Why was he so nervous? The way he kept looking back and forth between her and Duke, it was like he was waiting for someone to scold him and tell him he'd been a bad boy. But he kept talking as if everything were fine.

"As a kid I was always clownin', crackin' jokes an' carryin' on. My auntie said I beam like the sun, so she nickname me that. "Beamer, no joke. Then cats got hype to the luxury ride." He tapped the BMW medallion that dangled at the point where his belly bulged outward. "It's natural, you know?"

"You a crazy ma'fucka," Duke said playfully, but in a split second his tone got deeper and threatening.

"Why the fuck ain't you called me all night?" Duke glared up at Beamer, who quaked so hard his braids shifted on his thick shoulders.

"Dude, I got sick. All that chocolate I ate—"

"I don't care if you laid up in the ma'fuckin' morgue. You betta write a note on yo' toe tag, tellin' somebody to call The Duke an' tell 'im where Beamer at."

The hair on the back of Victoria's neck stood up and her nipples got rock-hard. The toughness, the machismo in Duke's voice made Celeste squirm so wildly, Victoria squeezed her pussy muscles to make her favorite milking motion, like the whole length of her vagina squeezed from top to bottom, making the milky cream squirt down onto the swollen, slippery lips as they massaged her clit.

Duke's deep voice vibrated through her. She wasn't even hearing his words as he scolded Beamer; it was just the macho power potency shooting out of his voice box that was making her dizzy.

Right now, her pussy reminded her of the pretty little purse she took to the prom. It was velvet, with a satin drawstring, holding her lipstick and cellphone within its folds. Now her pussy felt the same way, holding her nerve endings that were sparkling like diamonds and jewels. It was a wet, sunken treasure waiting for a pirate to dive down and crack open the chest.

Victoria poked her butt deeper into the seat.

Oh my God, I could cum right now.

Except Beamer looked like he was about to pee on himself.

Why aren't I scared? I'm in a garage in the middle of a Detroit ghetto with a big black guy who's talkin' about a toe tag . . . and I'm horny as ever. What is wrong with this picture? Everything. Because Alice is starting to like Ghettoland.

Victoria felt dizzy. This whole scene was so unreal, it couldn't possibly be happening. She was going to simply wake up from a bad dream, look around her pretty aqua blue bedroom overlooking the Winston family's private lake, get dressed in her giant walk-in closet, then go to the University of Michigan to start college. Nightmare over.

The machismo radiating from Duke on her left made her want to climb out of the bucket seat, straddle him and suck on his lips for three days. She wanted to rub her pussy all over his bald head and spear herself on that log he couldn't possibly think he was hiding in those loose linen pants. How could she be in such mental turmoil, and still her body was more on fire than it had ever been?

It spelled only one thing: D-a-n-g-e-r, for herself and everyone around her. She remembered what Daddy used to say, quoting Eleanor Roosevelt, "Anger is only one letter away from danger." Daddy would add, "Never let anyone see your anger."

The danger of this new world felt deliciously rebellious against a world that had suddenly scandalized her. The media, the FBI, the white family whom she'd never met, her boyfriend, and her best friend, all turned against her when she needed help the most. Yeah, hanging with Duke and immersing into this urban black world felt seductively lawless, as if she were screaming, "Fuck you!" to all the people who let her down.

But it was terrifying too. How could Duke's business possibly be legitimate? Even if he did supply bodyguards for sports events, how could that finance this operation? It didn't feel one hundred percent legitimate. Not that army. Not this garage. Not Duke's mysterious phone call, or his domination over Beamer. No, this whole scene, especially this garage inside this nondescript building, was like something straight out of one of those *New Jack City* type movies Brian was obsessed with watching.

If I stay too long, the only way I'll ever get out of here is in a police car or an ambulance. I'll stay just long enough to get what I need and get out.

"I'm sorry, Massa Duke." Beamer dropped to his knees, lacing his hands as if he were praying. "Please forgive me."

All that for not calling? It was just a few hours ago they were together at Henry's. Beamer laid his elbows and forearms on the car, bowed his head and sobbed like a baby. It reminded her of Roots when a slave would beg not to get whipped.

"Sorry ain't gon' erase my worries 'bout jumpin' back on yo' ass. You know what happen to e'rybody who ev'a thought about schemin' on me."

Beamer shook his head. "I serve you, Massa Duke."

Duke reached out with his left hand, grabbed Beamer's jersey and twisted it under his chin. Beamer's eyes bugged as the fabric cut into his neck.

"Act like a punk, you get treated like you one," Duke said. "Now, go take yo' pussy-stank ass an' think about how you s'pose to act an' what gon' happen if you fuck up again." Duke's voice was ice, completely void of sympathy.

"Now, me and the lady got some serious bidness to han'le."

Duke glanced at Victoria with the same tender gaze he'd had all evening, but he glared back at Beamer. "Y'all two get used to each other. Vee 'bout to plug her white business mind into the engine that drive Babylon. Fo' real."

Victoria let his words vibrate through her head. *Drive, hmmm.* She might drive this car. She might climb on top of

Duke and drive his dick-stick at every gear. But drive this mysterious, inner city empire?

"Duke," she said with a sultry-serious tone. "We still need to talk. I haven't agreed to anything, so until you give me a tour and tell me exactly what you do here, I am not a Babylon employee. And you are not my boss."

Beamer's mouth dropped open. He stared at her with envy glowing in his eyes.

Duke tossed his head back, flashed those beautiful white teeth, and let his deep, sexy laughter echo through the garage.

Chapter 21

Milan threw the binoculars so hard against the exposed brick wall of her apartment, the glass and plastic shattered all over the hardwood floor. She stood by the window, where she had just seen Duke drive up with that white bitch in his Porsche.

"I told Beamer not to let her onto this property!" She trembled, seething inside, hating him. She'd done everything to please him; got the best education, took care of herself so that she was still the finest of the fine, worked her ass off for his empire.

"And he is not going to just toss me aside like a used piece of trash. Especially for that white bitch."

Milan crossed her arms. Nausea washed through her. She hated this goddamn morning sickness that lasted all fucking day and night! Milan's mind spun. She had to figure out how to take over.

Beamer was too much of an idiot to execute a plan. Who else could she recruit to her side? Knight. He was coming home soon, and nobody scared Duke more than Knight or their momma.

Duke was always so worried about Knight coming back and trying to regain the power he and Prince had back in the day, before Prince died and Knight was wrongly convicted.

Yes, Knight was definitely the way to bring Duke down. It would probably happen anyway, but if Milan played her cards right, she could do better than Duchess all together. She could be Knight's queen. Now all she had to do was figure out how to get in touch with Knight and seduce him into seeing things her way. Then putting Duke in his place would be easy.

"We can take control of Babylon together," Milan said out loud. "Easy." No matter how tough Duke thought he was, he quaked in his damn boots when Knight just looked at him. Knight didn't even have to speak. He was even worse than his mother.

"Punk!" Milan screamed.

"Madame Milan." Renee came running from the boys' room. "Sound like you kickin' somebody ass out here."

"Are the babies okay?"

"Sleepin' like little angels," Renee said, her thin lips breaking into a grin. "You shoulda seen how little Zeus was teachin' Hercules how to count on that computer game Duke got 'em for Christmas."

Milan hugged herself, hoping these awful waves of nausea would stop.

"Madame Milan, I tried calling you earlier, but—"

"But what?" Milan snapped. "I told you don't bug me while I'm working unless it's an emergency."

"Well, it wasn't an emergency, but—"

Milan sucked her teeth, rolled her eyes, and wished this nausea would stop getting even worse.

"That rash Zeus has on his leg," Renee said. "Seem like the ointment ain't workin'."

"Isn't working. Can you say 'isn't working'? 'Ain't is not a word you will ever speak around my children. And we put a 'G' at the end of i-n-g words. Say it!"

Renee's eyes grew huge. "Isn't working," she said, bowing her head.

"Unless you want to go back to working in that disgusting nursing home up the street, you'd better take your work as my nanny more seriously. In fact, I'm going to get you a tutor so you can speak properly around my children."

"Yes, ma'am."

"Call the pediatrician about the ointment."

"Do you want to see it?" Renee said every letter clearly and deliberately like she should. "I can show you while Zeus sleeps."

Milan grasped her stomach. If she took one step, she'd throw up. And looking at a nasty rash certainly wouldn't make her feel better, nor would looking at two little faces that were mirror images of Duke Johnson.

"I trust that you'll take care of it."

"Yes, ma'am." The nanny returned to the nursery.

Milan talked herself out of heaving up the crackers she tried to eat in the car while driving home from the meeting with that imbecile named Beamer, who didn't know his dick from a donut.

The thought of fucking Peanut and his silly ass made an acid burn surge up her throat. "Ugh."

I will not throw up in an apartment that I shouldn't even have because me and our babies should be living up on the tenth floor in Duke's penthouse. Our penthouse. As a family.

She should not have been down here with the other baby mommas in their apartments. Those stupid, gold digging hoes!

Those two bitches were so far beneath Milan Henderson. She was educated, knew etiquette, had a strong business mind. She had vision, like Duke.

"I'm the whole package. Brains, beauty, and companionship," she said out loud. They were just a piece of ass for Duke, like so many he'd had, all under Milan's nose, since they grew up together.

Of course he'd been with countless girls. After all, he was a gorgeous twenty-year-old black Adonis whose business was the hottest sex in Detroit.

We deal in sex. And I've sampled more than a few Studs myself, but Duke is my number one. Always has been, always will be. I will be moving myself and our two little baby boys up to our rightful home, with him or Knight when he gets back and helps me take over.

Milan needed to talk to Knight, now, to set this in motion. She needed to tell him something that would make him all the more eager to wrench power back from his baby brother.

What about the upcoming meeting with Moreno? What if Milan called Knight, let him know that Duke was mishandling Knight's vision to partner with Moreno to expand the Sex Squad into five major cities across America? That upcoming meeting, if it went right would be worth a fortune, but only if it were done with the kind of finesse and sophistication Milan could bring to the table. Yet despite her insistence, for months, Duke had ignored her pleas to let her represent Babylon at the meeting. After all, who knew the Sex Squad army of Babylon's affairs better than the brilliant business mind who ran it every day?

That would be me. Madame Milan.

Now she just had to enlighten Knight on these points. He'd be so grateful she gave him the heads-up on baby brother's incompetence, Knight would only be too happy to hand over control of all five cities and the millions they'd make, to Milan. Then she'd be in charge of Sex Squads in six cities.

And I'll be tellin' Duke what to do.

To make up for all the humiliation that would create in him, maybe Milan would be kind enough to let Duke keep his little cream puff. No, no, definitely not. Duke deserved nothing but misery. The same misery he'd inflicted on Milan all these years, ignoring her, fucking her so she'd keep sharing her brilliant business mind with Babylon to run the Sex Squad as efficiently and profitably as possible.

Maybe Milan could kidnap the white bitch Duke just brought into Babylon. Maybe she could open up her own business and sell expensive white pussy all day long until Duke's cream puff was blown out as a five-dollar trick in the Cass Corridor.

That could work.

But first she had to see for herself what Duke was doing with that Victoria Winston who was all over the newspapers, the TV, and the radio. She had to see if Duke really had the idiotic idea that it would be all right to bring that suburban rich bitch up in here.

Milan's heels pounded the hardwood floor as she headed to the door of her apartment. She'd start down in the garage. If they weren't there, she'd go up to the penthouse.

She swung open the door. Two Barriors stood in the hallway, facing her door, arms crossed. She'd seen them around, but didn't know their names.

With so many new recruits lately, 250 to be exact, on top of the 500 who lived in the area and 500 others on reserve, it was impossible to know all their names.

Besides, Milan's department was the Sex Squad, and Studs and Barriors were two different things. Studs fucked for a living. Barriors did bodyguard work, and if they fucked in the line of duty, that wasn't on Milan's watch.

Her heart pounded. Her gut cramped with nausea. No Duke wouldn't have her on lock-down in her apartment! That would mean either he knew she was scheming as he always accused, or he wanted her kept far away from whatever he was doing.

Milan wanted to scream, but she bit it down, along with the vomit burning her throat. "Excuse me," she said, stepping into the hallway, turning to dash to the elevators.

"Go back inside," the taller Barrior said. And he was tall, like as tall as Duke. Six-six, with huge muscles. Like the Hulk. He looked like he was going to pop right out of his black T-shirt and sweatpants.

Milan said, "I need to go downstairs to my office to do some work."

The other Barrior nodded, making his Afro sway as he said, "You want somebody to pick it up? We can do dat."

The Hulk grunted. "But you gotta stay here, Madame Milan."

She flitted past them. A huge arm came down like gates at train tracks. His forearm pressed into her chest.

"Don't touch me!" she shouted. Hot, sour vomit burned up her throat. "I'm going downstairs!"

"No, you not," Hulk said. "Go back inside befo' we follow orders to carry yo' skinny ass back into yo' crib."

"Don't talk to me like that, you overgrown barbarian."

They came at her. She spewed stomach acid and chewed-up crackers all over their big, bulging chests.

Chapter 22

Duke watched his Duchess' juicy ass pop as she walked in her baby blue velour pants toward the glass elevators. Those two fat, round bubbles of undeniably black booty were the perfect size to squeeze like ripe melons then bounce, bite and bury his face in.

Her ass had personality. The way it rose up with every step on her long giraffe legs then lowered down when she stepped with the other leg, it was like two giant pens handwriting a secret love note that said, "Come get this good pussy, but only if yo' name is Duke."

Timbo felt like a big, heavy log. One look at Duchess' booty, it was instantly rock-hard, because she had just as much attitude in her ass as she had on her face.

This chick crazy.

She still didn't have a clue who she was talking to, or what she was dealing with. Or what kind of bank just dropped into her sexy-ass lap. But she would in a minute.

Wit'in twennie-fo' hours, max, she gon' be signing her life away to me. Not wit' ink, not wit' blood, but wit' cum. Hers mixed wit' mine.

It would be the ultimate power potion that would rule, coast to coast. And so it was written, and so it was done.

"Massa Duke," Beamer whispered, "I cain't b'lieve how you lettin' her disrespec' you."

She turned around, looking straight in Beamer's eyes.

"I hate girls who are scared to speak up," Duchess said. "Meek, mild, letting others make decisions for them. My parents taught me to be a very take-charge person." She started to turn around, but looked back at Beamer. "And what do you know about self-respect when you call another person Master? Emancipation Proclamation of 1864. You should look it up."

Beamer's goofy eyes looked like hardboiled eggs, they were so big right now. He looked at Duke, but Duke was staring at Duchess. He was smiling down into her big, silver-blue eyes. He loved how she handled herself.

"I still have my integrity," she said.

"An' you got The Duke, yo' black knight in shinin' armor," Duke said.

Beamer stared at her like he was so shocked he couldn't see straight, and he said, "You so pretty you hard to look at. Like how a man s'pose to look in them eyes an' think wit' his head?"

Duke smiled. "Maybe you can't, ma'fucka, but The Duke ain't got a problem."

Duke laughed, leading Duchess into the glass elevator near the staircase. He and Beamer dropped some names of musicians, comedians, and athletes that Warrior Protection provided security for, including a highly promoted concert that night.

"If I work for you," Victoria said as the elevator rose, "I want you to agree to pay my college tuition. I'm supposed to be at U of M right now. That's my number one priority. The lawyers said my college fund is gone, so I need to find another source."

Duke stared down with amused eyes. She wouldn't need college after she got her undergrad degree in Dukeology, her masters in Streetology and her PhD in Babylonology.

"And one more thing." She looked up in Duke's eyes with a serious expression. "My dad always stressed, the first thing you do when you enter a deal is establish the out clause."

"The out clause." Duke echoed flatly.

Timbo went soft. He couldn't believe this bitch who had nothing but the brains and beauty he needed, who was on a private tour of Babylon that nobody ever got, who was up for a job that a whole lot of niggas would kill for, was talking about an out clause.

"You bold as hell an' don't even know it," Duke said, staring down at her hard. Her big, silver-blue eyes flashed with defiance but not fear. "A nigga could get jacked for talkin' shit like that to me."

She blinked. "Shit like what?"

Duke bit down, making his jaw muscles flex. He glared hard at her; she stared back without flinching. Beamer was just as still and silent as he was supposed to be. Part of Duke was amused by her innocence and impressed that she wasn't scared to speak her mind to get the business done. Even with him.

"Damn." He shivered with self-satisfaction. Timbo surged again. Even his nipples were hard against his shirt. He could take her right now, let all this ridiculous energy he hadn't ever felt before just go wild on her pretty ass. And she'd love it. She would love it. It wasn't a question. Tonight.

"Miss Winston," he said with a playful business tone. "You know how many ma'fuckas cringe when I look at 'em like that? And you just sittin' there, starin' back? You a triple threat: brains, beauty, and balls as big as mine. You gon' be bad—"

She drew her brows together. "No, I don't want to be bad. At all."

He smiled. "Bad. That's black for 'good.'" He laughed long and hard. "You and me gon' be so good together, I'll let you do whateva you want. Go to college, start yo' own bidness—"

"Let?"

Duke nodded slowly. "However you want to do this, it's done. On one condition."

"What?"

"Yo' name Duchess."

"My parents named me Victoria Marie Winston."

"Ain't that the chick the feds is lookin' fo' right about now? The chick who was on the news tonight, bein' left at her Grammomma house? The firs' place they gon' look."

"Well, obviously," she said with a slight neck jerk and very attitudinal tone, "I'm not there. I'm here with you in this urban underworld called Babylon."

The elevator stopped on the second floor, where the doors opened onto the gym. The three of them stepped into the huge expanse of mirrored walls, red mats on the floor, silver-and-black weight machines and rows of cardio equipment. If kissing him at sunset didn't get her ready for the dick-down of the millennium, then this would.

Duchess' eyes were all over the Barriors and B'Amazons, who were pumping iron, jumping rope, doing push-ups and sweating on Stairmasters. Her eyeballs rolled up and down their fine-ass bodies on display in snug shorts and sports bras.

"I love this gym!" Duchess said, swaying to the relentless bass beat booming from the top of the line sound system. "It's huge, and the equipment, it's better than my fitness club. And that was state of the art."

"You ain't seen nothin' yet," Duke said as Lee Lee stepped to the front, by the mirrors, and blew her whistle.

All seventy-two of them one of four Squads, filed onto the big open space on the red mats. Standing in three rows of twelve, they peeled off their clothes. Noah and his assistants walked between them with baskets. Everybody tossed their clothing, including shoes, into the basket. Then they walked by with a basket of condoms; all the men took one.

Miss Daisy stared like a mug. She didn't know what the fuck was about to happen. When the first dick, then another, then another came swinging out of so many pairs of shorts, her eyes popped.

Duke bit his lip to stop from laughing. He wanted to tell her to close her mouth, but the way she was looking at all those titties flying loose and all the pretty asses, Duke wished he had a video camera.

Milan. Stupid scheming bitch. Did she really think she could take Duke's video camera and get away with trying to blackmail Duke's boy in her plot to do whatever she thought she was going to do? She had never been more ridiculous than today, fucking Beamer's pudgy ass on camera.

Didn't she know Duke knew everything? The Duke had godlike powers. God was in charge, no doubt. But certain men, like Caesar and Alexander the Great and the Egyptian pharoahs and Moses and Ghandi and Martin Luther King, Jr., they had superhuman powers to help them do what they did. Make change. Rule. Improve people's lives.

That's me. I give folk jobs. I provide needed services, whether protection or pleasure. I take care of Momma in grand style. Got her Livin' like she ain't neva imagined she would. I'm a role model to the kids in the ghetto who see a young, black man can become somethin' great. A leader. A visionary.

So, if gold digging Milan Henderson thought she was going to bring him down by tossing some of that skinny ass at his boy who never turned down pussy, and she was going to use some kinda whack videotape scheme to do it, she was beyond crazy.

That was why she was on lock-down right now, the first step toward booting her out of Babylon. It was going to happen while Miss Daisy was getting schooled on the ways of the world here at this "urban underworld," as she called it. Duke was sure she had never dreamed she'd be in what she called a "fitness club," where seventy-two motherfuckers were banging booty like the turbocharged, robo-dicked warriors that The Duke had made their asses into.

The sight of all of them made Duchess gawk. She was creaming those pants like nobody's business. Her pussy was blowing gusts of pheromones, the natural scent that people and animals gave off when in heat.

He inhaled, loving how the hot, sweet fumes of her pussy rose up and tickled his nose. Timbo was rock hard and ready, just like she would be in a minute.

Chapter 23

The prison guard who was passing Knight Johnson's cell was the meanest one in the joint. When that hillbilly bastard's face appeared between the bars, Knight focused harder on his book, *As a Man Thinketh* by James Allen. He was on the top bunk, lying on his stomach in the arc of soft light glowing from the mini reading lamp Momma had sent him. The small, yellow book was open to pages sixty and sixty-one, propped up on a fold in the dark blue wool blanket on his bed.

Bang! The guard's baton hit the bars. The guard passed to the next cell and hit their bars.

Knight read his favorite sentence in the book, which he had highlighted in orange, "He who cherishes a beautiful vision, a lofty ideal in his heart, will one day realize it." It was only being in prison though Knight Johnson was wrongly accused and wrongly convicted, that had prepared Knight's mind to believe and appreciate that incarceration had been a blessing in disguise.

Here at Monroe Prison, in its library, through books, audiotapes, and volunteer tutors, Knight had learned to read, write, and speak the King's English.

An' I can still rap as raw as any otha ma'fucka.

Now he had the ability to speak the white man's language. Moreno's language. Wall Street bankers' language. Business moguls's language. He would be able to communicate with them on an intellectual ground. Actually, he would be on superior intellectual ground, but they didn't need to know that.

In his peripheral view, the guard was standing there, still and silent, just staring into the cell, radiating evil energy as usual.

Knight put up his Teflon mental deflectors to stop and push back the literal gusts of hatred that were hurling into the cell, at him and his cellmate, from the guard.

In the lower bunk, Knight's cellmate, Lonnie, rattled the newspaper he was reading. He spoke in a tone just loud enough for Knight to hear. "Look like somebody wanna play gladiator."

Knight focused harder on the page, refusing to poison his thoughts with stories about that secret sport when guards bet money on which inmate could beat the shit out of another. Gladiator was just like the dog fights back home, but here in lockup, they used niggas, rednecks, spicks, even a couple Indian brothas.

The guards never dared mess with Knight, although lately this guard, who either was not aware of Knight's status or didn't care, had been mumbling about "bringin' a proud nigger down a peg or two."

Knight barely let that man's presence register in his mind. Instead, he was envisioning every detail of himself walking out of this place, into the wildest welcome home party Babylon could pull off, and taking his proper place at the helm of an empire begun by Prince, rest his soul. First on his list: giving Moreno an offer he couldn't refuse to surrender—not share or partner as Duke was planning, but straight-up hand over territories a.k.a. Erotic Zones throughout the Midwest, East Coast, and the South that Moreno had promised Prince.

Two more weeks and I'm free to cash in on a broken promise.

It was a promise buried with one brother and banished by another brother's fear. Not so with Knight. He was ready to go after what was rightfully his, the property, and domain of Babylon.

The West Coast operation was basically a done deal, since Priscilla and Larry Marx were leaving the business to start Question Marx, a multimedia company. Just the other day, Knight had read an article in *The Wall Street Journal* about how the couple planned to produce Hollywood movies, documentaries about the sex industry, entertainment Web sites and a glitzy, mainstream magazine for couples who, they told The Journal, ". . . want to keep their love life sizzlin'."

Knight had met the couple years ago, when they were in Detroit and contacted Babylon to arrange a party on a yacht. That was Knight's first deal. Sure, Prince was watching over his shoulder, checking every detail to make sure it was perfect. And it was.

Mr. and Mrs. Marx were phenomenally impressed with the Sex Squad, from the flawless transactions to the extreme discretion to the documented health status of all fifty Studs and Sluts. The Marxes were most pleased with the quality and performance of the fifty Sluts and Studs who fit the exact profiles that were desired, requested and enjoyed by the Marxes and the twenty-four couples who were their guests on the luxury yacht that summer night on the black waters of Lake St. Clair and the Detroit River.

"If you ever want to follow the American tradition of Manifest Destiny," Mrs. Marx told Knight.

"That means moving west and taking what you want," her husband said, handing Knight a champagne flute in their plush master suite on the yacht. "Like when the white man snatched everything west of the Mississippi from the Natives."

"Call us first," Mrs. Marx said. "We've got a vision, a plan for a whole new game in a couple years. Right now we're just recruiting folks who we think are worthy when we pass our golden baton."

With that, Mrs. Marx's left hand, the one with her grape sized diamond wedding ring, wrapped around the hard-as-lead pipe in Knight's slacks. In a flash, she was on her knees, sucking it all as her husband jacked the biggest dick Knight had ever seen on a white man. She bent over, legs apart, hands grasping her ankles, husband standing in front of her, steadying her suntanned skinny ass. Knight instinctively knew to lay pipe in the foundation of what would become the Taj Mahal of business relationships.

Now, after frequent communications from the pen, Knight was going to luxuriate in their generous accommodations, in a business sense. That pipe was hot, about to burst right now.

Two weeks can't pass fast enough before I'm free.

Every time Knight talked with Duke, his little brother sounded recklessly power hungry. It made Knight realize that Duke's ambition was about to inspire premature moves and fatal growing pains, like taking over more turf than he could manage, expanding the ranks of the Squad to such huge numbers that quality control would be impossible, or promising protection for notorious celebrities whose parties and concerts were always known to have a gunbattle sideshow.

Bang! That guard slammed his baton on the bars then walked past, doing the same at the next cell.

Knight gripped his book, staring at the pages, feeling so confident in its message that it was only a matter of time until his own dream became reality. He knew it would happen even if his dream clashed with Duke's dream when big brother got free.

Li'l Tut was twenty, going on twenty-one. That wasn't nearly as wise or as capable as twenty-five, like Knight. And in inner city black man years, a quarter-century was ancient, venerable, and respectable. Sage. And highly qualified to take charge of Detroit's most unique underground entrepreneurial venture ever. As the boss.

Knight's eyes focused back on his book, to a yellow highlighted spot on the next page. "Ask and receive." Below that, he read, "Dream lofty dreams, and as you dream, so shall you become. Your vision is the promise of what you shall one day be; your ideal is the prophecy of what you shall at last unveil."

For Knight, that dream, that vision, that ideal was multi-faceted: Freedom. Power. Happiness with one woman who loved Knight for Knight, who believed in strong family values, who shared his vision, his passion, his purpose. And my voracious libido. It had been self contained and self satisfied for two years and six months. Nobody had even thought about trying to do unnatural acts with Knight's muscle-pumped six-foot-seven inches of brawn. Even if he were a pee-wee runt, his special status as top Babylon Barrior would be all the protective shield he needed.

Now I need a wife, one woman who'll cherish and celebrate me. I don't want to swing Shane left, right, at every pussy in sight. That reputation is what got me locked up. Now I only want a single female for life who's a spellblinding beauty on the inside, first and foremost. Being beautiful in appearance is appreciated but not mandatory. And if she wants some sexual adventure, she and I can certainly indulge together by bringing extra playmates to our party.

Knight's dream for his life and for Babylon required security for himself, for Momma, his family. And he wanted fulfillment, by spending money on his community to improve it and make it safer. On that last one, during his two years and six months here, Knight had decided to start a foundation for people in his hood. Feeding hungry children, providing prenatal care to mothers to remedy the high infant mortality rates in the inner-city, and building safe playgrounds and community centers; that was what he planned to do with the millions he'd make after Moreno agreed to submit to Babylon in five cities. That would make Knight Johnson's business the biggest of its kind, anywhere. Duke, of course, would help as second in command.

Bang! Bang!

"Mister Knight Johnson," the guard called.

Knight looked up, facing the man without letting his eyes focus on the windows of that evil soul. His mind felt so pure and inspired and focused on his vision of freedom and fulfillment out in the world, there was no point letting anything leap out of the guard's miserable mind and try to ride his evil stare into Knight's brain.

The guard laughed as he unlocked the bars. "Yo' momma named you right, Mister Knight Johnson, 'cause you sure as hell is black as night." He slid the bars back. "Come with me, sir. Some folks up in the office picked yer name outta somebody's lucky hat. They wanna tell ya the prize."

Knight sharpened his eyes on the guard's face. Was this just a ploy to take him off to the gladiator pit?

Chapter 24

Victoria wanted to scream. No way could she stay here and not become a sex addict or a nymphomaniac rabbit, as Tiffany and her friends back at school liked to call themselves.

If I unleash my wild, pussy power in this place, whatever it is, it will kill me or Duke or some of these other people.

"Is this like a sex army?" she asked Duke, who was standing close, to her right. His body heat, his delicious scent, his overall sexiness made her head swirl. Looking at all those naked bodies—beautiful, toned men and women of every hue, their bodies already glistening with sweat from their workout—this was an impossible situation. Even a nun would get horny up in here.

Nobody back home would believe her if she told them she'd been in a gym watching three rows of twelve men, all gorgeous, laying on the floor as thirty-six women fucked them. And it wasn't anything close to normal, missionary-style sex.

The women were squatting over them, their butts pointing to the men's faces. Just like Victoria learned at the fitness club to do squats, either on the barbell machine or free standing with weights in her hands, the women were doing squats down onto big, swollen, shiny penises!

The girls' knees were all pointing out, and their hands were on their knees. It was as synchronized and graceful as a ballet.

Knowing how painful squats were to the quads, Victoria was doubly amazed that they were so in shape they could go and go.

All those dicks were enormous. The music was too loud to hear if they were moaning, but the mellow expressions on their faces left no doubt they were lovin' it.

"Oh my God," she whispered, her cheeks on fire as Duke glanced down and over at her. He smiled.

Was this a normal, everyday activity in the hood? What in the world were they training for? Was this some kind of porno video shoot? Even the movies Brian watched never had anything like this. They always had orgy scenes in someone's living room, but never this many people in a gym!

"Faster!" shouted the woman with the whistle. She looked like a model—tall, thin but muscular, in skin—tight black leggings and a ballerina tank top. Her skin was deep tan, and the slight slant of her eyes reminded Victoria of a girl in her school whose father was black and whose mother was Vietnamese. The sexercise coach had a wild mane of curly, jet-black hair with maroon streaks framing her dark eyes, button nose and full cheeks. She was very hip, with a sort of Bride of Frankenstein look.

"Okay, girls. Slow down," she shouted. Her voice was raspy and commanding. "Faster . . . faster . . ."

The girls were literally slamming their butts down on the guys's six-pack abs. One guy in particular looked like Duke. He was tall, muscular, and dark chocolate, and he had gray eyes. The woman fucking him was even darker, like blue-black, and she looked like that popular New York runway model from Africa who was showcased in all the fashion magazines—super tall, thin, with strong facial features, and short hair.

Every time she rose up, Victoria stared at the guy's giant dick, which was pointing straight up, covered in a glistening red condom. A few veins zig-zagged on the side.

Did Duke's dick look like that? Was it that big? Bigger? How could all that go inside that girl? It looked like she was sitting on a telephone pole!

The scent of sex made her dizzy. It was salty, sweet, intoxicating.

This is sheer torture.

Her hands were trembling with lust, with fear, with excitement. There was no way she could stay here and remain true to her vow to stay a virgin. No way.

But what about her mix-race sex power? Did it only have lethal effects on white men? Did everything that Mommy said apply if she were with a black man? Or woman? These women looked just as delicious as the men. And what if she made love with Duke and wanted more men? Could she control the power?

Her mother said she could use it to get whatever she needed or wanted. But how? She had died before she could explain any of that.

Victoria squeezed her pussy. It was so wet that if she stuck her fingers in it, she could pull them out, make a scissor motion with her fingers and form a web of clear pussy juice. One touch to her clit right now and she'd cum.

"I have to leave!" She stood on her tiptoes to shout into Duke's ear over the loud music. Celeste throbbed in the heat of his body, his scent, that mesmerizing onyx sparkle in his eyes that were devouring her like candy. "Duke—"

"Ain't no way in hell I'm gon' let you leave right now," he said with a hard tone. Every word sent a wave of goosebumps over her hot skin. Inside, she felt numb. An icy fist of fear squeezed her breath.

"What, are you gonna kidnap me?"

"Betta me than the FBI. B'sides," he shrugged, "who would know?"

"My grandmother." She crossed her arms.

"What she gon' do? Duke Johnson the police around here. That sick old woman can't do a damn thing."

"Henry."

"Pound Dog work for me. He ain't gon' bite the hand that feed him. He put you in my hands. Remember, Miss Daisy?"

"Don't call me that. The lawyers would find me."

"Lawyers want one thing—money. And your daddy money gone, so now that massa dead and they shipped yo' pretty black ass off to the ghettolands, they work done. 'Less they gon' take you in themselves, which they ain't. They don't give a damn about a little spoiled half-black bitch wit' no dough."

Victoria glared at him. She did not blink as her brain focused on her mother, her power, Celeste. She had to use that power to escape this situation. Now. She had to use the female wiles Mommy told her about—the mix-breed woman power of many races packed into her brain, body and spirit—to get her way. She had to gain control over her life by figuring out how to tap into that power.

It was the power Duke thought he was exerting over her right now. In a Motor City minute, though, she was about to harness it, hone it, and hurl it right back at him. She would do it so fast and sweet that he wouldn't know what hit him. He didn't even realize the monster that he wanted to create would someday dominate him with the same sex that caught his attention.

And so it was done in Victoria's mind.

She wouldn't fight it, for now. She would stay. She would work for him. She would learn any and everything. She would go inside Duke Johnson's mind, sit down, takes notes, and train herself to be the female version of him. The Duchess.

Then, forever holding onto this feeling of frustration, fear, and unfairness at life, she would lash it all back on him, crush him under her submission. And rule over the Duke and his Babylon. Finally, she'd break away, go to college, live her original dream of opening a business, and climb the traditional ladder of success with the stealth and street smarts she was about to learn from Duke.

I'll be his Duchess all right. I'll learn his game and beat him at it in grand style. Celeste style.

"Checkmate," she said flatly, staring into his eyes, unflinching. Not sweating. Not breathing hard anymore. Motherfucker. Let's do this.

"Checkmate what?" he asked.

"I'll work for you. Teach me everything I need to know. Now."

Duke's onyx eyes sparkled down on her. They were smiling, probing, questioning.

"Bet," he said, offering a hand. "Let's shake on it."

Victoria shook, squeezing his hand hard so he wouldn't feel that every muscle in her body was trembling. She was lying to herself when she vowed to maintain her virginity and only work for Duke for as long as it would take to move away for college. But for now, she had to go along to get along as Duke put her on a crash course to learning street life, his vision for Babylon, and the rules of the game.

She would start her education with this bizarre gym class orgy where, for the moment, all her fear and frustration was exploding in the hot throb between her legs. Her palms were so hot, she could hold a piece of bread between them and make toast. She squeezed her pussy lips to get a grip on her lust so it wouldn't take over her mind, but they were so slippery and swollen, it made her shiver.

She leaned closer to Duke. Her right nipple rubbed against his arm. A moan escaped her lips. "Duke, what is this?" she asked.

He turned slightly, staring down at her with those big, gorgeous dark eyes with the bejeweled irises. His face was as luscious as his bald head, with all that coffee bean brown skin she wanted to slurp, suck, lick, and bite.

"Duke, I feel dizzy," she whispered.

"You should," he said playfully. "Anybody would lose they mind, seein' all this pussy an' ass."

"No—"

"Yes," Duke said. "You probably so on fire right now you can't think straight." He put his arm around her back, resting a hand on her shoulder. She shivered. The hot scent of his cologne, the heat of his body, the hardness and height of him next to her was so intense, her chest was literally rising and falling as if she'd just sprinted at a track meet.

If he touches my bare skin, I'll faint. She couldn't believe how electrified she felt with his hand on the velour fabric of her zip-up jacket. She looked into his eyes; the deep, penetrating tenderness of his voice made her cheeks burn.

"Baby girl, you look like you need some love so bad."

He pulled her closer. Her lips felt hot and swollen with lust. She wrapped her arms around his waist.

Oh my God, he is so warm and strong.

Victoria's lips pressed directly into the center of his chest.

His hot skin under her mouth was soft and sweet. She inhaled his scent of designer cologne, spicy male musk, and sex.

The rise of his pecks touched the sides of her mouth, her cheeks. This was her spot. She rubbed her face in small circles there, not caring that all these people were around them or that Beamer was watching. The men and women who were fucking on the floor were so into their groove they probably couldn't care less.

A whistle blew and a deep male voice boomed through the gym. "Ladies, on your knees!"

Victoria turned to see a man, he was small, with dark, wavy hair and a white warm-up suit, taking over from the Asian looking chick.

Duke grasped Victoria's shoulders and spun her so that the back of her body pressed into his chest, stomach, thighs. A huge, hard, hot rod pressed into her butt. She arched her back slightly, but stopped herself.

What the hell am I doing? This is a set-up. Henry probably told Duke what he saw me doing in the bathroom at Gramma Green's house. So, Duke would know I'm easy prey. I am.

She imagined Henry saying something like, "Dude, she want it. That horny bitch need some dick bad." So, now Duke felt it was his duty and part of his premeditated plan to basically abduct her to take care of her hormonal crisis, which was bad enough for any eighteen-year-old girl.

But I'm different. Celeste has dangerous powers.

"Check this out." Duke's deep voice vibrated through her more potently than ever, since their bodies were touching.

She leaned her head back into his chest. His chin rested on top of her head. He planted a kiss in her hair. Victoria closed her eyes. The warmth of his body, the comfort of it, made her want to stand there forever. It felt so good, nothing mattered at the moment. Not the wild, crazy fuck fest in front of them. Not the fact that she was an orphan in the ghetto with nowhere to go. Not the fact that she wanted to indulge the very urge that terrified her with the threat of deadly consequences. All that mattered right now was the affection and protective embrace of the urban god behind her.

Oh my God, I'm finally getting some love. A hug. A kiss.

Hot tears stung her eyes, blurring the sextravaganza before them. She blinked hard, letting the tears fall down her burning cheeks. With her eyes cleared, her body calm, she watched the action.

In one graceful motion, all the women rose up out of the squat position, aimed their open palms at the red floor mats, and dove forward with the liquid motion of acrobats. They fell to their knees, straddling the men's legs at their shins.

The men didn't just fuck them doggie style, they alternated and balanced on each leg as they pounded away.

"Harder!" the man commanded. "Pump it!"

The men fucked furiously. A few women cried out. Their boobs were bouncing, hard nipples pointing down at the floor.

They looked like Victoria did in the mirror when she made herself cum. She was sure the giant dick rubbing into her ass right now could only make that sensation a million times more amazing.

"Now, slow and controlled," the man commanded.

The men slowed down, still moving in unison as gracefully as a dance troupe.

A guy who was grimacing cried out, "It fuckin' hurts!"

The commander's legs sliced like white scissors as he strode toward the whiner. "Look like you love this shit or you'll get twenty minutes straight!"

The sternness on the commander's face and in his voice made Victoria sober up for a second. This wasn't for fun. This was serious training for something. If Babylon did executive protection, what did fucking have to do with being a bodyguard?

Unless these men and women provided a different kind of secret service . . . Prostitution.

So, right now they were working out to be strong and lean, but also to fuck with Olympic strength and endurance.

Sexercise. Daddy used to always tell her the key to success in business was to do what nobody else thought of, then market, market, market!

The whistle blew. "Switch!" the commander shouted.

What in the world kind of place was she in?

Her skin was soaked, sweaty, and prickly from how horny she felt. Her mind was like melted butter, dripping through the rest of her, making a puddle in her panties. She was trembling. Her mind was spinning. She wanted to run far away from this temptation, but at the same time she wanted Duke to ram his dick deep inside her hot, slippery pussy. What would it be like if she were naked, grinding on Duke's dick right now?

"I can't," she whispered. "I can't."

No, she didn't want to end up like her mother, killing someone, or herself with her mix-breed woman power that came out in sex.

No! She wanted to scream.

"Don't ever let them see you sweat," she remembered hearing Daddy say so many times about the backstabbing cheerleaders who teased her when she had trouble doing a double flip; about the chemistry teacher who told her girls never got A's in his class (she did anyway); and about the blood-thirsty reporters who hounded her and her siblings at their school during the scandal just before he killed himself.

Now, Victoria wanted to cry, run, scream, and fuck all at once.

I won't. If I have to make myself cum every ten minutes, I will.

She couldn't let Duke win. He planned this whole situation, to get her in here, horny out of her mind, so he could talk her into working for him. For now, since she had nowhere else to go, she would let Duke think he was winning. But she would always be beating him at his own game.

"Market this." She turned, looked up at him and whispered with a cool expression, as if she were seeing this every day. "Call it Sexercise, and you'll be an instant millionaire. All you need is a video camera and a Web site."

Duke stared down hard at her. "We don't give away our secrets. Not for any price."

The power of his eyes pulled those satin strings on the velvet drawstring purse between her legs. His scent made her dizzy. She turned to face him all the way. His beautiful face made her want to never look away.

That huge rod poking into her stomach made her pussy convulse. She squeezed her pelvic muscles as he pulled her close.

Her nipples pressed into him. His lips brushed against her trembling mouth and Victoria shivered.

Oh my God, I'm cumming from just a kiss.

Chapter 25

Duke knew she was ready to let him pop that juicy cherry.

I can't wait no longer or Timbo gon' explode. An' she gon' faint from needin' some dick so bad.

He picked her up like he did his kids when they would fall asleep in the car and he had to carry them up to their mothers' apartments here at Babylon. With Duchess, he was so smooth, he picked her up without unlocking their lips.

Damn, ain't no kiss neva felt like this. Even the air around them was on fire, just like his skin, his dick, his heart, his head. He had his right arm under her knees, his left arm under her back, and she was kissing him while he walked past the sexercise to the elevator.

Ain't no secret. She gon' be e'rybody Duchess in a minute. They gon' bow to her jus' like they bow to The Duke, so might as well come out wit' it now. An' fuck Milan if she get a attitude. Ain't nothin' she can do about it from her apartrnent.

Duke pulled Beamer a few feet back, so nobody would hear him say, "Yo, B, I ain't available fo' nobody. Anything happen, han'le it."

"I'm on it, Massa Duke."

"I know 'bout e'rythang you be on." Duke stared down hard into Beamer's big eyes, which popped like Buckwheat on them old-fashioned black and white re-runs of *The Little Rascals* he loved watching.

"But I ain't mad," Duke said. "Can't no normal man keep his dick to hisself when Milan lay on her evil ways. 'Specially yo' stupid ass. An' I don' give a fuck who she screwin', long as they ain't 'round my babies."

Beamer quaked.

"So, B."

"Yes, Massa Duke." His voice was all wavery and high pitched like a girl. "You still ma boy."

Beamer nodded.

"If you wonderin' why I ain't gon' jus' pop yo' dumb ass, let me explain. It's Dominology 101. You gon' kiss ma ass even mo' fierce now, 'cause you know, one wrong move an' you"—Duke raised the last word to a higher octave—"th'ough." He tossed his head back, laughing, stepping toward Duchess.

In the elevator, she sucked on his neck again, like she did in the car. No girl had ever kissed him like that, making the little muscles under his skin ripple and send sex shocks through his body. Whatever nonsense she was mumbling about in the car, about a sex curse, that was the craziest shit he had ever heard. The only curse she was going to have was liking it so much she would want it twenty-four/seven. She would be tempted not to get anything done because she would always want to be fucking.

He still had to keep an eye on her, though. Yeah, she agreed to work for him, to stay here, but she didn't have a choice. Those pretty eyes were glowing with scheme, but whatever kind of break-out plan she was thinking, it wouldn't work. Couldn't trick The Duke. Beamer, Milan, and his other baby mommas had already tried, along with half the niggas trying to make something happen in Detroit and beyond. So, this white bitch here, his Duchess, the girl he would cherish and protect forever, wouldn't succeed at whatever she tried.

The elevator rose to the tenth floor, opening onto the sharp-ass black marble hallway of his penthouse. It was all black marble, top, sides, and bottom, with custom lights that glowed cobalt blue from behind silver BABYLON sconces, three on each side, leading toward the all-cream living room.

Duke carried Duchess through the foyer, past the couches, fireplace, and floor-to-ceiling sliding glass doors that opened onto his terrace overlooking the city's skyline and river. Walking with her in his arms was easy. She felt light, like part of his own body.

He heard something that made him freeze. It was their song, "Duchess' Theme Song," which the Bang Squad had written, composed and produced for this night right here.

Now it was pumping through his top of the line stereo system that played in every room of the penthouse.

"Listen, baby girl." Damn, looking down in those eyes made his heart stop a minute. She glanced up as if it helped her hear better. The tune was as soft as she was, with piano and a soft rumble of drums, just enough bass to make it sound masculine.

Jamal was crooning like Marvin Gaye.

"Duchess, be my girl. Help me rule the world. Duchess, be my wife. Share this dream of life." Duke sang along, looking so deep into her teary eyes that he felt like he could dive in and swim around.

"Duchess, be my girl," Duke sang. "Help me rule the world. Duchess, be my wife. Share this dream of life."

She nodded slightly, never looking away from his eyes. He stepped into the bedroom, decorated like an Egyptian pharoah's palace. Custom lights were set behind tall columns along the walls, inlaid with colorful tiles in Egyptian patterns and hieroglyphics. They were already adjusted to cast a sexy peach haze through the huge room, especially on the two eight-foot-tall mummy cases on each side of the black lacquered dresser.

The face paint of the cases always gave Duke this look like they were adding their power to his purpose. He loved the black eyeliner around the round, direct eyes, the richness of the gold covered faces, the sharp contrast of the black stripes on their headdresses. The cases were arranged so they were facing the bed, focusing their power on Duke for when he finally made love with Duchess.

He stepped to the dresser, where he unclipped his phones from his belt, turned them off and set them down. They sat next to candles that were already burning, making the room smell like butterscotch. The burning logs crackled inside the white marble fireplace.

He had his Duchess in his arms, ripe and ready. She was kissing him like she wouldn't be able to breathe if she unlatched her lips.

"Baby girl," he whispered, carrying her toward the bed. She put her hand behind his head and pulled his mouth back to hers.

He stepped up the four white marble steps to the king-sized mahogany playpen surrounded by a canopy of sheer gold panels of shimmery silk. He angled Duchess' head so she parted the curtains. He laid her on the gold silk bedspread. Her black hair fanned out around her head.

"You look like a angel," he whispered.

Her blue flame blowtorch eyes incinerated him. Timbo flipped harder than ever. Duke was actually trembling from head to toe. He was a little scared because he didn't want to hurt her. The way he felt, it was so overwhelming, he knew he would lose his mind up in that pretty pussy. And he hadn't even seen it.

"Take your shirt off," she whispered, lips and cheeks red as ever.

He unbuttoned his shirt, tossing it to a nearby chair. Her eyes trailed all over his chest, over his shoulders, down his arms and back again. It seemed like forever before she whispered, "Undress me."

He pulled off her gym shoes and her socks. He knelt down, sucked her pretty toes, sliding his tongue between each one. Duke ran a hand between her legs, fingers outstretched to tickle the insides of her thighs. Then with his middle finger only, he ran it straight up the stretched-tight fabric over her pussy. It was hot, wet, and meaty, like a meat flower all bunched up in there that would open up and suck him in like a big-ass stinger on a bee, dripping honey all over the place.

Duchess cried out. It was like agony and ecstasy all rolled into one sound. She was so horny it was hurting her, and it was his duty to relieve her of this suffering. She was his, and he needed to brand her with his tongue, his juice, his love. To burn their souls together into one, forever.

He put his fingertips on each side of the waistband on the pants he bought her. Touching the baby-soft skin of her hips, he pulled slowly. His fingertips, which caught her panties too, trailed down the outsides of her hips, her thighs, her knees, her calves, and her ankles. Then he just stood there, staring at her long-ass legs smooth, creamy, and toned. She had skin the color of the inside of an almond, white with a little bit of yellow-tan, on the prettiest legs he had ever seen. She raised her knees and just stared up at him from between the valley of her legs like they were framing her face from where he was standing.

Her jacket still covered the tops of her thighs. He unzipped it, peeled it off her shoulders. He lifted each hand, kissed every finger, then pulled the wristband over her hand and laid her arm gently back on the bed.

She shivered when his hands passed over her nipples through the white T-shirt. She let out a little moan. She could start a fire the way she was looking at him.

Duke peeled off her T-shirt and unhooked her bra, letting loose the most beautiful nipples and titties he'd ever seen. Full, round, plump, with cinnamon-color circles that came to a point. And they tasted as sweet and soft as they looked. Duke sucked like a baby, twirling his tongue around that nipple that he would never let go of.

Her back arched; her hands grasped the sides of his head. She pushed him up. "Look at me," she whispered. "All of me."

First he stared into her eyes, which made his skin feel like flames were dancing up and down him from head to toe. Her face was too pretty to believe. His eyes traveled down that elegant, swan like neck. Some of her straight black hair covered her creamy shoulder and made a fan against the gold silk under her. Her titties pointed straight at him. Her stomach was so pretty it was a sin, the way her waist curved in below her ribs. Her belly button was like a little eye, winking at him as her stomach rose and fell because she was breathing so hard already. He wanted to take a fork and eat all that smooth, creamy skin over her hips, down to the black hair at the "V" of her pussy.

"Oh . . . hell . . . yeah," he groaned.

Her clit was big, red, and so wet it was shiny. It looked like a red rose pinned to a black mink coat. He wanted to stare at this forever, but he didn't want her to clamp up and push him away. He had to get it while it was hot, before her mind took back over her body.

"Baby girl, you got the prettiest pussy on the planet."

"Her name is Celeste," she said matter-of-factly, staring up at him. "And she's been wanting you to kiss her since we first saw you this afternoon."

Day-um! Baby girl had a name for the pussy, talking about "we." All of a sudden he heard Momma's voice saying, "Be careful what you wish for, 'cause if you get it, you betta be ready." Duke knelt on the bed. He bent down, wanting to kiss her pretty thighs and that stomach . . . and that pussy!

The sweet scent made Timbo so hard it hurt. He looked straight into her eyes. She was on her elbows, watching him over the smoothness of her stomach. He almost didn't know where to start. But the tip of his tongue couldn't resist the tip of her clit. The way she was looking at him, her eyes were fiending for him to slurp on it all night.

"Baby girl, you ain't neva had nobody eat yo' pussy?"

"No," she groaned as if the thought hurt.

"I'm the first and the last," Duke whispered into the salty sweet cloud of pussy vapors making his face feel hot. He had to go there first. It was so soft, so sweet, so clean. He stuck out his tongue as far it would go.

"Oh my God," she cried out. "Oh . . . my . . . God."

Then he wrapped his lips in an "O" shape all the way around that big, red clit. He sucked it into his mouth.

Her whole body heaved. "Duuuuuke!" she moaned.

It sounded so sexy. If he never heard another word, the way she said his name was the most beautiful sound ever to pass into his ears. And he knew she was through. His mouth on her pussy was his magic pass to getting any and everything he ever wanted from her. Didn't need to string her out on drugs like some thugs did to keep their bitches under control. All he had to do was turn her pussy into his own all-you-can-eat buffet, and she'd serve him every day, every way, forever.

The way she was arching her back, sticking the pussy up into his face harder, grinding her hips up into his mouth, she must have wanted this for a long time. Even if some suburban punk had tried it on her, there was no way he could have done it like The Duke.

"Oh my God," she gasped.

He went back down, sucking on each lip, slurping up that sweet cream. It was so sweet it was like the lemon cake batter he used to lick off of Grammomma's bowl when he was little.

This chick pussy tasted like lemon cake batter!

That made Timbo throb even harder with the idea of sliding up into that never-been-entered pussy. He stuck his tongue in, wrapped his lips around her clit, just to suck it in for a minute, like a scoop of strawberry ice cream melting under his kiss. Now it was time for his sure fire trick to make her cum hard, so he could make her his forever.

Chapter 26

Tiny dots of light danced behind her eyelids as Duke ate her pussy. So many times she had practically begged Brian to perform oral sex on her, after she'd given him countless blow jobs. Brian always said it was disgusting to put his mouth there, especially when he thought about how period blood and pee came out of the same spot. *That punk motherfucker.* But right now, she knew the disrespect she got from Brian in so many ways was preparing her to take this incredible love from Duke. Nothing that felt this good, from just looking into Duke's eyes to listening to his voice to feeling him touch her this way nothing could possibly be wrong.

There has to be a purpose, a reason that I am in this place called Babylon. Feeling like I never knew a person could feel. Because Daddy said everything, even the bad stuff, happens for a good reason.

"Duke," she whispered. "Yeah, Duke, do that to me."

His forearms were under her hips, and his giant hands gripped the insides of her thighs. He squeezed her soft flesh then rose up, looking into her eyes.

"Baby girl, you got me. Fo' ev'a. Fo' ev'a." His head descended back down.

"Love what you do," Victoria moaned. "My pussy, Celeste, loves what you do."

The way his tongue was moving, it was beyond words. The rhythm reminded her of a windshield wiper. The tip of his tongue was like the end of the blade; the thicker part of his tongue was the length of it. He sloshed it back and forth over her clit, first soft, then harder, then soft again, increasing the pressure with every stroke. It went back and forth, back and forth, in a half-circle motion, applying more pressure with every wipe.

That was what it felt like on the outside of her clit. The inside of her clit felt like a starburst, a ball of fire between her legs. Every time Duke licked her, the fireball got hotter, sending out sparks farther and farther through her body. Pretty soon she knew it was going to explode, making her whole body shimmer with heat and light. But right now, she was loving the psychedelic sensations making her mind, body and spirit look and feel like a Fourth of July fireworks display.

This is unbelievable.

She gripped her fingertips into the soft skin of his head, holding him there as she moaned softly, never wanting this moment to end, except for when he took her all the way to relieve this horrible curiosity and ache. After so long without a hug or any love, after the trauma of losing life as she knew it, she finally felt safe. Loved. Happy.

She felt this, even though she was going against her lifelong vow to never, ever unleash the femme fatale between her legs. *If this is the way I'm gonna die, then so be it, because this is heaven on Earth.*

"Duke, you are a god," she whispered. "You are a gohhh-hhhd." She thrust her hips up higher, spread her legs wider. Never had she even imagined anything so incredible.

Celeste was in seventh heaven. She never would have believed it felt this good. Tiffany had oral sex and said it was great, but she said the prick who did it to her was sloppy and impatient, then ran to the bathroom to gargle for a full five minutes afterward. And she hadn't even cum.

Not Duke. He acted like he wanted to stay down there all day and would drink a glass of her pussy juice if she gave him a straw.

"Duke," she cried, "what are you doing?"

A finger slid into her pussy. In and out, in and out, all while he did the windshield wiper tongue motion on her clit.

"Aaahhhh," she moaned, her whole body trembling.

The starburst was getting bigger, hotter, radiating through her every cell as if the sun were rising between her legs, as if the black dome of Duke's bald head between her white thighs was the cataclysmic fusing of two worlds. Lightning, meteor showers, tidal waves, volcanic eruptions would surely follow.

She was breathing so hard, her ears were ringing.

And now another finger pressed up into her pussy.

Brian was always begging her to go all the way, pressuring her by saying if she didn't fuck him, they'd have to break up so he could find someone who would fuck. He would threaten this, even though he was constantly refusing to do exactly what Duke was doing right now.

I'm glad Duke is the first because this has got to be the best, anywhere, ever.

That starburst was sparking, flaming. It was spraying red hot sparks up her abdomen, through her chest, making the points of her nipples tingle and burn. Her fingertips were tingling. Her toes were twitching. The muscles in her legs were trembling. Her pussy was quivering around his fingers and under his tongue.

Duke let out a deep moan like this was the most delicious thing he had ever tasted. Like it was his oxygen.

"Oh my God," she whispered. "Oh my God."

The fireball was roaring, rumbling . . . exploding.

Great flames of red, orange, and yellow licked out through her limbs, flashed behind her closed eyelids, made her heart glow white-hot.

"Oh, hell yeah," Duke groaned as her pussy pulsated around his finger. Another white-hot flash of fire shot down her legs, up her belly, over her nipples, down her fingertips, into her head, which glimmered in a psychedelic swirl of color and light.

"Yeah, baby girl," he whispered. "You ready for me now."

He kissed her mouth. She licked and sucked off every drop of her own sweet juice. It felt so nasty, so liberating. And she felt drunk on champagne.

Finally, her pussy powers filled her head with the idea that from now on, she would never go without a man who could make her cum like that. She would settle for nothing less.

Duke ran his hand over her still-throbbing clit, down into the juices, to the satin soft, soaked skin where Celeste was about to suck him in whole. With his face so close to hers that their noses touched, he stared into her eyes and whispered, "Let Duke make love to his Duchess. I'm gon' anoint you. Make you mine."

Victoria thrust upward, impatient, wanting to shove that big, beautiful dick inside her like the world was going to end tomorrow and they had to fuck right up until they died. She wanted to take every inch of this black god, this Mandingo warrior, this knight in a shining Porsche who rescued her in the middle of Ghettoland. This man she was studying, learning from, so that one day this very act that made him feel like he was dominating her, helpless, homeless, with nowhere to go, would enable her to whip him into submission. So she could dominate.

"Now," she whispered. "Fuck me now, Duke."

Chapter 27

Duke stood at the side of the bed, staring down into two silver-blue moons begging him to make love like he had never done before. Her lips were redder than ever. Her perfect little nipples were pointing at him, calling him. Her pussy hair was a soft black bush at the "V" of her juicy thighs.

Thinking about being with Duchess for the dick-down of the millennium didn't even come close to what it would be like in a minute. If she could cum that hard with his mouth, then she would no doubt damn near kill him when Timbo slid up in the prettiest pussy God ever made.

Duke had seen thousands of pussies, but he had never seen a pussy like that in a titty bar, even in Vegas, or in a magazine. And the way she looked right now, laying there waiting on the big dick, this was some shit right out of the movies. The movie of my life, The Duke, starring Duke Johnson as himself, and introducing The Duchess.

"We 'bout to make magic," he said deeply as he unbuttoned his white linen pants. Timbo bulged and never throbbed like this. He had never wanted a woman so bad, not even the first time. He pulled down his pants and his white cotton briefs at the same time.

Her blue moon eyes grew huge. Her lips opened. She rose up, crawled over, put her hands up like she was praying, one hand on each side of Timbo, with her fingertips touching. And she stared into his black eye.

Chapter 28

Victoria couldn't believe her eyes. She knew it would be huge, but it was breathtakingly beautiful. A giant, shiny head the way the edge of the head curved around reminded her of Darth Vader's helmet in Star Wars. She could almost hear his deep voice saying, "Welcome to the dark side."

I'm already here.

She just wanted to stare at it, let her gaze trace that long vein that ran from the head back to the silky nest of hair. She ran her fingertips along the length of it. The skin was soft as satin and smooth as glass. She glanced up at Duke, letting her eyes study the perfection of his body, from his slim hips to his tapered waist, his muscular chest, his beautiful delicious neck to his strong-jawed face with those spectacular, sexy eyes and sensuous mouth.

His palms gently stroked the hair on top of her head.

"Duchess," he said softly.

"Yes." She stared into his eyes.

"I want you an' Celeste to meet somebody. Timbo."

She looked at the hole at the end of his penis. The bulging ball of black flesh all around it, the gorgeous head of his dick, almost did look like a face, with the hole as the mouth.

Victoria puckered. She placed the softest kiss over Timbo's mouth.

"Enchantee." She whispered the French word for "enchanted," which people say when they first meet.

She wanted to suck him down whole, but first Victoria leaned close to the soft nest of hair and inhaled deeply. "Ooooh," she moaned. "I loooove that smell."

"Damn," Duke whispered.

She leaned down a little, cupped his big, hot balls in the palm of her hand, raised them toward her nose. "Oh my God," she groaned. "Get me a bottle of this so I can smell it all day. Call it Essence of—"

"Essence of Bo-Bos," Duke said, laughing. "Can't b'lieve you like smellin' ma balls."

"It's delicious. Sweet and musky. I knew I'd wanna stick my face right here and stay for a long time."

"Day-um," Duke moaned, gently gripping the top of her head with one hand.

She stuck out her tongue, ran the tip of it against the mauve black skin of his balls.

He sucked in loudly. "Yeah, do that, baby girl."

Just like she'd done his neck earlier, she sucked in a mouthful of the skin and gently sucked, tickling the flesh beneath.

"Ma'fuck me!" he groaned.

Victoria gave his balls a tongue bath, slurping up, down, all around. Then, cupping his damp balls in her hand, she took his huge dick into her mouth. She slid her wet lips down the length, sucking at the same time, until Timbo hit the back of her throat.

"Yeah, swallow that cock," he groaned.

She sucked for a while longer, never gagging, just savoring the sensation of him inside her as she inhaled his intoxicating male pheromones. Slurping up and down, over and over, with a very wet mouth and slightly open lips, she made super-sexy nasty, wet-sucking noises that made Duke moan. The slippery hotness of her lips against his iron-hard dick, and the feeling of taking him whole into her hot mouth made her pussy drip.

The sex smell, all those sweet-musky male scents set off something inside her that made her want to fuck until she couldn't see straight. Victoria pulled back, looked up at him.

"I love the way your dick feels in my mouth," she said as she slid her tongue up and down his shaft.

"Hell yeah," Duke groaned. "You do that so good, baby girl."

As she slurped up and down his dick, suddenly a rhyme came to mind. *This is bizarre . . . Won't I scar this chocolate bar? I'm 'bout to cum as I suck. What luck, I'm so struck to let him pluck my cherry, my virgin berry.*

"Oooh, baby girl, com'ere."

She stood on the bed in front of him. He kissed her stomach then with his hands on her hips, turned her.

"Prettiest ass I ev'a seen in my life!" he exclaimed.

His lips tickled soft kisses all over the round mounds of her butt. His hands traced the curves of her hips, her butt cheeks, her thighs. Then he rubbed his face all over her ass, squeezing it, moaning, raising it up, sticking his tongue down in it, licking it.

"This beautiful ass all for me," he groaned, sucking the curve of her cheek. "Juicylicious. Like a big white chocolate kiss meltin' in my mouth."

Victoria smiled, loving every second of his praise. His appreciation for her size and shape thrilled her after all those cold comments from Brian about how she had a fat butt and needed to lose weight, how she needed to make it flat like all the other x-ray thin girls at school.

That punk. If I ever see him again, I'm gonna kick his ass like I shoulda done a long time ago, especially when he tried to rape me when he found out I'm black.

"Baby girl, let me lay you down."

Chapter 29

Duke wanted to stop because he was about to lose his mind in his own bed. He couldn't build up Babylon and impress Knight when he got out in two weeks if he were stone cold crazy from some pussy. Even if it was sweet, virgin pussy that was spread out on gold silk waiting for him to just take! What made it even more hype was that this was happening on the same day he met this goddess whom he had just picked right out of the headlines.

I got what I wished fo'. Now I ain't ready.

Maybe Momma was right, talking about white chicks like she did. They definitely were the reason Knight was in jail, after those hill billy motherfuckers got mad that their slutty little sister was sniffing around a big black dude who didn't even want her stank ass.

Now maybe Duke needed somebody who wasn't everything all wrapped into one perfect package. Shit, the way Duchess was talking to him earlier tonight, with balls as big as his . . . maybe he didn't need an equal. Maybe he needed somebody less than him, somebody he could control.

"What are you thinking?" she asked, looking up with the kind of eyes that love songs were written about.

"You too much, baby girl. You too much."

An' I'm fuckin' ridiculous, standin' here wit' the biggest, hardest dick of the century, wit' the finest chick on the planet who waitin' to fuck me, an' I'm hesitatin'.

Earlier tonight, when they had pulled into the garage and Knight called, his big brother had said, "Hesitation will get you killed. But a premature move will get you jacked too."

And that was what this was. Now that he was taking a closer look, this chick was too damn pretty. Too bold. Too sexy. She sucked dick too good. She took a tongue job too good. Her body was too bangin', she was too smart, and could talk like a queen.

What if she turned around and tried to beat The Duke at his own game? No, not try, just straight up demolish his ass with all the tricks he was about to teach her. No doubt, he had seen some scheme in her big, pretty eyes all night long. He saw it even though he was playing her, especially in the gym, when he knew she'd get so damn horny she wouldn't care about nothing but sliding down on this tree trunk and trying to break it off for a few days straight.

"Duke, if you're just gonna stand there contemplating life and love, I'm gonna take a nap." She pulled one of the half-dozen gold silk pillows from the head of the bed and rested her cheek on it. "I don't remember the last time I got some sleep."

He stared at the way she turned her body. She was lying on her side and her hip was pointing up, with those long legs across his bed and her candy toes touching his thighs.

I ain't neva had a mo' ridiculous chain o' thoughts than what jus' went through my head. Standin' here wit' Timbo swole, a goddess in my bed, an' I'm playin' fuckin' philospher.

Even his favorite self-help book, *Think and Grow Rich,* said successful men made decisions quickly and changed them very slowly. *Meaning, go wit' yo' firs' gut' reaction an' stick wit' it.* And that was what Duke was doing with his Duchess.

'Cause The Duke don't choke.

He smiled, then said deep and raspy, "Naw, baby girl, you so beautiful, I was jus' paralyzed for a minute. Like when I firs' saw you, I couldn't breathe."

A seductive smile beamed up at him. She said with a business-like tone, "Duke, I want you to wear a condom."

"I'm clean, baby girl."

"So am I."

"We both clean, we don't need—"

"I'm not doin' it without one," Duchess said with a shrug.

He stared into her blue-gray eyes. What if she wasn't a virgin? Her pussy smelled clean, looked clean. No way did she have anything. And if she got pregnant, then good. They'd have the prettiest baby in Babylon and beyond. Plus, that would definitely make her stay forever.

"Baby girl, I get tested all the time."

She pulled her knees to her chest and wrapped her arms around her legs.

"I want you to feel all of me," he whispered. A condom gon' block the—"

"Exactly," she said. "Pregnancy is not on my agenda right now. And I don't want to have to worry about STDs. Nothing personal. It's just a fact, whether I'm with some rich white guy from the academy or with you. HIV doesn't discriminate."

"You right," Duke said. "I can't argue when you tryin' to be safe." He went to the nightstand, opened the top drawer and pulled out a condom then rolled it down on Timbo. "There. But after this, you an' me gon' go get tested together an' neva have to worry about it again."

Timbo looked like a black rocketship shooting toward her as he knelt on the bed, crawled over to her, and sucked her pretty mouth between his lips.

Chapter 30

Victoria loved the way Timbo was sliding between her legs. Not penetrating, just sliding down over the wet slick that couldn't wait to suck in that big, black dick.

"I don't want to hurt you," Duke whispered. His hot, damp cheek pressed against hers. The huge head of his cock pressed into the wet lips. He had put a towel under her, in case she bled when he popped her cherry. Tiffany said she made a huge mess when her boyfriend fucked her the first time. It was like her period all over her thighs and the bed.

Ugh, I hope that doesn't happen with me. Seems like Dildo Dick would've already softened the ground.

"I want you to look into my eyes while you come inside me," she whispered. Her legs were spread wide. That totally exposed feeling made her pussy dance with anticipation. She studied the sparkles in his eyes in the dim light. He reminded her of a genie . . . his bald head, his bright eyes, and the way his black eyebrows were so perfectly arched, as if they were painted on. It made him look happy, sexy, picture perfect.

She grabbed the round curves of his butt, one cheek in each palm. His glutes were rock-hard. Solid muscle, no fat. The skin was soft, smooth, hairless. Victoria pulled his butt toward her. The flesh of her pussy felt so swollen and hot, she imagined his dick slicing into it like a hot knife in already half-melted butter. Easy. Smooth. Painless.

"You sure you ready, baby girl?" he whispered.

She thrust her hips up. He slid deeper. Sharp pain. The voice of her pussy, Celeste, screamed in her mind. *What the fuck are you doin' to me? This torture can't be what I've been craving for so long!*

He shoved his dick even deeper.

Victoria cried out.

He froze. "My baby okay?"

"It feels like a knife."

"Wanna stop?"

"No. Will it get better?"

"Yeah," he whispered. "If I do if soft and slow."

"Okay." In just a few strokes, it felt like Tinkerbell was waving her magic wand over them and tiny gold stars were lighting up every inch of her body.

Her pussy throbbed, loving the iron-hard rod pounding in and out. The more he pumped, the more her whole body shivered. Her cheeks felt like fire. Her mouth sucked on the beautiful black skin of his shoulder, right where the deltoid muscle formed that little groove that rippled when he moved.

The fucking made tingly waves wash through her, from head to toe, and the more he pounded her pussy, the more intense it got. The waves-big ones, little ones, giant ones-they were hot, rippling through her in a way that made her skin tingle, her nipples harden, her lips quiver, and her insides sizzle.

"Oh, baby girl," he groaned. "I ain't never had no pussy this good in my whole life, baby girl. Fo' real."

The sex on his voice, the passion, the adoration, and the intoxication made Victoria feel drunk. She reached between her legs, pressing her fingertips onto her clit, rubbing, rubbing.

"Oh my God!" she screamed. Her mind splashed with stars. Her skin, her muscles, her bones, her soul felt as if stars were exploding inside her. Hot, potent, beautiful. She convulsed with orgasm as Duke continued to ram Timbo into her hot, hungry hole.

Her pussy pulsated as she came, squeezing around him, welcoming him into her soul.

This is the power, a sultry voice whispered inside her head. *This is the essence of the power*. It was Celeste.

And then her mother's voice, *Use it here, everywhere, to get what you want.*

"Duke," Victoria moaned. "Duke, I'm yours. All yours."

Chapter 31

Duke savored every stroke. He never wanted to touch or kiss another woman in his life. This queen would be his wife.

Ain't no way I'll ev'a let go of this. Let another nigga even think about tryin' to get some o' this sweet stuff. He'll have a sure-fire ticket to join Prince over at Elmwood Cemetery. Nobody. 'Cause this is heaven, and I'm stayin'. Forever.

The way Duchess was responding, even though this was her first time, she would never let go either.

"Duchess, you like my love?"

"No," she moaned. "I looooooove it. Love it."

Duke hoped their heat would melt the condom away, shred it, rip it, so she'd get pregnant right now. Seeing that pretty stomach bulge with his flesh and blood growing up inside this goddess, that would make him Triple Massa Duke. No better present God or the Universe could give him for turning twenty-one on Friday. When he presented his official Duchess to everybody at the party, the shit would be on.

"Oh, baby girl, you just don't know."

"Now I do."

"I been tellin' yo' sex all day. 'Bout ta drive me crazy. I ain't neva met a girl horny as you. Damn, I could make love to you for a week straight."

"I'm game." She giggled. "Wear me out."

Duke groaned out a little laugh as he fucked her harder.

"Soundin' like a sista already."

Chapter 32

Victoria loved every second of his pumping and pounding.

All I gotta do is lay here and get fucked.

She gripped the round curves of his beautiful shoulders, his deltoids, which were as toned and lean as all those men down in the gym. She pressed her open lips to the soft skin of his shoulder, sucking, kissing, and licking. Did Duke work out like that, to that sexercise routine?

I want to. With him as my partner.

Someday she would squat on him like the women in the gym. But right now, she just wanted him to keep on banging relentlessly, with that wild look in his eyes.

A rhyme came to mind. But this time, she spoke it out loud to Duke.

"Oooh, jackhammer," she moaned, gasping for breath. "I stammer, wild pussy rammer . . . Wham! Bam! Slammer!" She glanced up at the beautiful sheer gold fabric around the bed.

"Love this glamour. Anybody jealous? Damn her."

"Rap that shit," he groaned, fucking her ferociously.

She rhymed, "Love that sound when you pound the round mound of my ass." She giggled. "Dick me, stick me, lick me, pick me"—she gasped—"with Timbo, I'm in limbo. Ain't no bimbo."

Duke tossed his head back, laughing, flashing those beautiful, big white teeth. "Girl, you rappin' like nobody business."

"I ain't rappin' while you slappin' an' you tappin'." She drew her eyebrows together. "Wait, Duke, isn't that an expression, 'tappin' that ass'? Did I say it right?"

Duke bust out laughing. "Don't make me laugh, baby girl, else I can't fuck you senseless like you need. Matt'a fac', I'ma fuck you 'til you can't rhyme to save yo' life."

"Oooohh," Victoria gushed. "Bring it on, bring it out, make me shout, leave no doubt."

Duke wrapped his giant hands around her legs, just above her knees, then pressed her legs forward. That opened her pussy wider so he could really bang it.

"Fuck me fast, squeeze my ass, make me gasp." The jack-hammer action made her voice waver like she was sitting on a washing machine and the load was off balance, making it shake violently.

She loved the union of their bodies. His dark hips over her milky ones. The base of Timbo looking like a log disappearing into a cave covered with black vines. Her thighs raised in a "V" shape as if her body were making the peace sign that hippies made with their index and middle fingers.

"Don't stop," she moaned. He pressed her knees into her boobs then banged harder. "Make my eyes pop out . . . shout . . . your cock . . . knocks me out." She sucked in air. He rammed and rammed and rammed.

"You're bionic . . . supersonic . . ." Orgasmic waves made Victoria go limp. Her arms and hands fell to the bed. Her head turned to one side. Her legs flapped in his grip. "Kronked," she whispered, "out cold."

Yeah, he was bionic. Felt like they'd been fucking forever and a day. Like he could fuck her for eternity and then some.

And I love it. The slap of skin on skin, their bodies gliding on a soft sheen of sweat, the fiery heat between them, their panting. . . . Victoria was just lost in erotic euphoria. No more sadness, no more worry, no more fear. Just pure pleasure, because this was the most mind-numbing indulgence, more than wine, more than eating a brownie, more than watching a good movie.

Sex was pure opium. The perfect escape from all her worries.

It was something she would take every day, her magic remedy for stress, anxiety. Yeah, Duke could sex her up every day as therapy to the mind, body and soul. She'd never worry again.

"Oh my God, what are you doing?"

His hands were reaching behind her, beneath her, taking her ass in his palms, squeezing his fingers gently into her flesh, tilting her hips up even higher, stimulating her even more. He pounded with more ferocity than ever, like he was going to split her in half, pummel her pussy into a banana split full of marmalade.

"Oh, baby girl, we just gettin' started. Before this life is through, I'm gonna flip you every which way you never imagined. Make you cum so tough you won't know which way is up or down. The only word you'll be able to say is 'Duke.'"

She exploded in laughter because that was exactly her plan for him.

"Go for it," she whispered, thrusting her hips up.

Duke wrapped his hands around her ankles, raised them into the air, and thrust from his knees. He pounded and pumped, making her shiver and scream.

"I'm 'bout to cum," he groaned, laying down on her, kissing her forehead, her eyes, her cheeks.

"Cum for Duchess," she whispered. "Cum for me, Duke."

"Oh, baby girl. Baby girl."

He thrust with so much force, her whole body shivered. It was like a heat blast that was mashing their bodies into one delicious mix. Duke and Duchess, cream and coffee, blending into one exotic-erotic fusion of flesh, passion and purpose, power and potency.

"Yeah, baby girl. Oooh yeah." He shuddered, pressed his hot cheek to hers, sucked her lips into his mouth.

She wrapped her arms around his smooth, broad back, tickling the baby-soft mounds and valleys of damp skin, pulling him deeper.

"Oh, baby girl!" he shouted. "Duchess, baby!"

He pulled Timbo out, yanked off the condom, and jacked his dick over her. A fountain of white cream sprayed over her bare, quivering stomach. His face twisted, but he focused hard on her.

"You mine now," he groaned then lay next to her, kissing her face. "I'm yours, Duchess baby. All yours."

Victoria couldn't get close enough to him. She wanted to press her body right through him so their souls could touch.

She had no words for this feeling. She couldn't describe the magic he just worked on her body or explain the whole race-sex phenomenon she thought about constantly.

Mommy spoke to me! She said this is the way to get what I want. Now I know . . .

She suddenly felt overwhelmed with gratitude for her mother, her father and Duke, because their words and actions all helped her figure it out. It wouldn't kill her to share her body; it would give her more power.

But right now, all she wanted to do was curl up in the curve of Duke's body and sleep for days. She hadn't slept in half a week, but finally, she was safe in this sexy cocoon of silk and strong man, where a deep sleep in his arms would bring the same mind-numbing euphoria as the lovemaking she just shared with him.

He pulled her into the spoon position. Lying on his side, he drew her back to his chest, her ass into the L-shape of his torso and legs, the backs of her thighs on the tops of his. It felt so good, she closed her eyes.

But her lids raised just as quickly as she thought, *He wants me to work for him. If he makes love to me like this all the time, I'd rob a bank if he asked me to.*

Not really, but what did he possibly want her to do that could be so bad? He was breathing softly in her ear, his cheek nestled in her hair on the fluffy pillows.

No, she couldn't sleep now. This sheltered suburban girl had to figure out how to play this game without losing to his slick street smarts, without letting sex influence her common sense or jeopardize her future.

She lay awake for hours, savoring every sensation of his long body behind hers. Her butt on his hard thighs. Her back against his stomach. His broad chest embracing her shoulders, his long arms wrapped around her, his hot breath on her neck. Their ankles twisted together. His scent all over her.

She lay awake for another reason: fear. A little voice inside her was laughing. Alice in Ghettoland just danced past the DO NOT ENTER signs on the door marked HOME. And there was no EXIT sign.

Chapter 33

It was 6:15 p.m. as Knight Johnson rose from the hard brown couch in the rec room. The TV news was blaring, but Knight was too excited to hear it. He had to go call Duke. One step and he felt like he was floating over the beige tile.

I've called Duke every Monday night since I've been in here. But tonight's call is different, more important than ever.

"Yo, Knight," Lonnie shouted. "Eitha tha's yo' baby brotha or yo' papa's rollin' stone jus' turnt up a secret pebble on da news."

Lonnie, sitting on the couch at the edge of a dozen men on couches and chairs, turned his round, acne-scarred face. "Check 'im out." Lonnie pointed at the TV. His legs stretched over the chipped wooden coffee table strewn with sections of today's local newspaper. Knight usually read the paper in the morning, but today his energies had focused on something bigger. And better.

"An' drivin' a Porsche wit' gold rims!" Lonnie shifted, making the front page of the *Detroit News* crinkle under his leg. "I know The Duke ain't that stupid to pose up in the middle o' that mess. The media an' five-oh? He askin'—"

"You right, Lon," Knight said with super-cool nonchalance.

"The Duke ain't about to get sprung up in that chick's media storm. An' you should know better. E'ry dark-skinned bald dude don't all look alike."

"Depend who lookin'," Marvin Dinkins grumbled from the other end of the couch. "Some look-alike the reason I be up in this shit hole. An' don't none o' dese cocksuckas in charge wanna hear 'It wasn't me.'" Marvin pointed a long, black finger and deepened his voice, imitating authorities. "'It was you, nigga. Fi'teen years! No para'e!'"

"Who you tellin'?" Lonnie scolded. "If anybody know dat, it's Knight. That was some 1950s Emmitt Till shit they pulled on ma boy." Lonnie focused back on the TV.

"Dey go that white choc'lit chick who daddy be French kissin' Smith an' Wesson," Marvin said.

Lonnie pointed up to the TV, where the news report showed the young lady walking right past Duke and Beamer in the Porsche. Knight had seen reports about her father's suicide over the past several weeks.

"They talkin' 'bout she look white," Lonnie said.

"Ssshhhheeeee-it. One look at that ass oughtta erase e'ry question mark on that page." Lonnie nodded toward the newspaper, which Knight picked up.

Nearly a whole page of articles and pictures surrounded a bold headline:

CULTURE SHOCK: MILLIONAIRE'S DAUGHTER FALLS FROM WHITE PRIVILEGE TO BLACK POVERTY.

Under that, a smaller headline said:

VICTORIA WINSTON'S BIRACIAL LIFE SHOWS HUGE GAP BETWEEN RACES.

Knight bit down, making his jaw muscles flex. *Why didn't Li'l Tut know better than to sit in the middle of a media beehive? Didn't matter if it was the Thanksgiving Day parade coming through the neighborhood. Duke did not need his face in the newspaper or on TV, even if he was wearing dark sunglasses. He wanted to run Babylon, but didn't have the common sense to stay out of the spotlight?*

He was thinking with the head in his lap.

Was Duke just naively enjoying the spectacle of Victoria being dropped off at Miss Green's house? Was he trying to meet her? Recruit her to work for The Squad? If so, Li'l Tut knew the recruitment of Sluts was always done on the down low, not in front of the media!

The media was making sport out of this poor girl's tragedy. Knight glanced at the newspaper, which even had a satirical sidebar and scoreboard, comparing what her white life was and what her black life would be like now.

The TV newscaster drew Knight's attention to the screen.

"You may recall," said preppy black anchor Orville Smith, "on Sunday, Victoria Winston was taken from this lakefront mansion in an elite, gated community in the suburbs to this decrepit house in one of Detroit's worst neighborhoods. The business-savvy eighteen-year-old, who worked closely with her father, Daniel Winston, says he is wrongly accused of embezzling ten million dollars from his investors."

Knight was mesmerized and impressed by the young lady's incredible poise as her elegant stride took her past a mob of reporters outside her lakeside mansion. She exuded womanly maturity and intelligence, yet the long, black ponytail bouncing just above her Betty Boop butt maintained her girlishness.

As reporters shouted questions about her dead parents, her race, and her life, she stopped and looked straight into the camera. Incredible confidence flashed in her big blue eyes, set in a buttermilk face with very ethnic, come-kiss-me lips whose natural red color had the power to put cosmetics companies out of business.

Knight was awe-struck by how she tilted her chin upward just a little bit. With a voice that was all at once sultry and brilliant, she told reporters, "I refuse to justify or even acknowledge your nonsensical, insulting questions with a response."

That girl has the power. He held the newspaper in front of his khakis. His dick was instantly erect.

One look from me an' she gon' melt into some white chocolate fondue so I can dip my lead pipe in it. Victoria Winston is mine.

That girl was way too much for Li'l Tut to handle. The potency in her eyes—the raw sexuality burning in that voice and that dewy face that had to be virginal—radiated with incredible force from the TV screen. The longer Knight stared, the more bewitching her power became.

I can't breathe. In or out.

It felt like the day, years ago, when he made his first and last mistake relating to Babylon money. Prince slammed him against the exposed brick wall of the penthouse with such force, Knight slumped to the floor, not breathing. He thought he was dead.

Finally, he coughed and never made that, or any other mistake, again.

"Eh, y'all know what happen to a snowflake when it hit black pavement?" Marvin grunted. "Tttttssssssttttt! It melt." He let out a sinister laugh. "She a snowball in hell right now. Ain't got half a muthafuckin' chance."

Marvin cast a cruel smile up at Knight and said, "Yo, G, if I was you, I'd hate any bitch wit' mo' dan two drops o' honkey blood."

"I don't hate white people," Knight answered.

"You should," said Pete Washington, slouching in a chair with his arms crossed.

"Jesus turned the other cheek," Pete said, "an' they beat the shit outta him."

"Condemning a whole race for the act of one gets us nowhere," Knight answered, not so much for hopeless Pete but for the dozens of other men listening. "If a black man hurts a white person, should that victim hate the whole race?"

A chorus erupted. "Hell naw!"

"No, 'cause all black people ain't bad," Lonnie added. "Is jus' some bad seeds sprinkled in the barrel."

"So we shouldn't think this biracial girl is bad until we know more about her," Knight said.

"Y'all be quiet," Lonnie said. "Now she wanted by the FBI!"

"Federal investigators are still searching for Miss Winston," the news anchor said. "They believe she may have crucial information about her father's controversial business practices. But police say Miss Winston has disappeared."

Knight bit down hard, flexing his jaw muscle. Now there was no doubt Li'l Tut was all stirred up in her creamy mix.

Otherwise, Duke would've told Knight all about the media spectacle on Babylon Street. He always told Knight everything that was going on in the hood, whether it was who was having whose baby or how Milan's behavior was composing her own pink slip and eviction notice or who died or whose grandmother died or how the fallen powerline sparked a fire in an alley dumpster last week. Everything.

Except that every media outlet in the city was there to watch a half-white rich girl find her black roots, and Li'l Tut was front and center.

It ain't right. Bringing someone that high profile and notorious inside the doors of Babylon no matter what purpose his horny little brother had in mind. It would only be trouble. Big, big trouble. It would be bad enough when Duke found out Knight was going to seize control of Babylon. When little Victoria took one look at Big Brother and fell madly in love, that would only make things worse for Duke.

She was made for me. That voice inside Knight's head spoke loud and clear. Knight had a gut feeling to follow his intuition. Right now, his intuition was telling him Victoria Winston is the One.

"This just in to the Channel 3 newsroom," Orville Smith said.

"Victoria Winston is now apparently a fugitive of the law. Let's go to reporter Lisa Plateman. She's live on Detroit's east side."

Knight watched intently as live video showed a young black man in a suit on Miss Green's porch, which was surrounded by at least a dozen reporters, TV cameras, and still cameras. He was holding up a purse, a suitcase, and a hand-written note.

"This is a spokesman for the family," the reporter said, sticking a microphone in his face. "Is it true that Victoria Winston ran away?"

The guy held up the note. "Her grandmother found this this morning on her bed. It's written in Victoria's handwriting. It says she's so grief-stricken by the loss of life as she knew it that she's going to a warm, sunny place to escape the media spotlight."

"Can you be more specific?" the reporter asked. "Where is she?"

"Her grandmother says Victoria left with her passport and just enough cash for a one-way ticket to Miami. She kept talking about her friends there, who were gonna loan her keys to a vacation home in the Caribbean."

"Where in the Caribbean?" the reporter asked.

The young spokesman knit his brows.

"Br'a-man need some schoolin'," Marvin said. "Can't lie worth a damn."

"He a'ight," Lonnie said. "Just nervous."

The spokesman stared at the note then looked up. "It doesn't say here, but the family thinks she might be either on the island St. John, St. Barts, or Antigua."

Knight bit down a smile.

Or perhaps Miss Winston had slipped way below the white man's radar, into the secret chambers of Babylon.

Chapter 34

I fucked her to death.
Duke's big hand shaking her arm did nothing to wake her.
"Victoria!" he shouted. "Duchess! Wake up!"
He slapped her cheek.
Nothing.
He put his ear to her mouth. Couldn't feel her breath. He pressed his fingertips to her neck for a pulse. Couldn't find it. Not on her wrist, either.
"Baby girl!" Duke's insides felt like they were turning inside out. Right now, his whole body stung with fear.
Why didn't I listen to whateva the fuck she was sayin' about a sex curse? 'Bout how her daddy fucked her momma to death? I was so busy tryin' ta get my nut, wasn't listenin' wit' my head.
"Baby girl!" he cried, sitting on the edge of the bed, rocking with her hand in his, raising it up to kiss her fingers. The gold blanket was tucked around her neck; her head rested on one of the gold pillows. One shoulder and arm were exposed, the one connected to the hand he was squeezing.
"You gotta wake up. I'ma die if I lose you this fast." Duke hated feeling like somebody else's life had this much power over his. If something really had happened to his Duchess, if she really were dead—
I'm gon' be th'ough.
He squinted in the bright beams of sunshine slicing into the room from the floor-to-ceiling sliding glass doors leading out to the terrace. Even that bright-ass light on her face hadn't awakened her.
Damn, she looked like an angel. Her face was pure. It didn't have one mark or blemish or pimple. But something wasn't the same, like her skin was a little more yellow and

her red, pucker-fish lips looked swollen. Her thick eyelashes still looked like black fringe, and her perfectly arched black eyebrows looked the same, as did all that hair fanned around her head like the prettiest peacock at the zoo.

"Massa Duke," Beamer said, rushing in. "Doc Reynolds here."

Duke barely looked back at the purple glasses on her fine-ass face, with her black hair all swirled up into a French roll. She wore all white, with white Nikes and a leather doctor bag. She pulled out a stethoscope and a little bottle with clear liquid inside.

"How long has she been unconscious?" the doctor asked, pulling back the gold sheer fabric. The bottle was the size of her pinky finger. She set it on her lap.

"More than twenty-four hours." He scooted over so Doc Reynolds could sit on the bed. She leaned down, listening for breath. She took Duchess' pulse at her neck. She used a stethoscope to listen to her heart. She felt her cheeks, her forehead. She pulled back the gold blanket to look at her whole body.

"She dead?" Duke asked, hating the high-pitched panic in his voice. "Tell me she ain't dead."

"She's alive," Doc Reynolds said. "But I need to know if she has any health problems that could cause coma."

"Shit!" The last thing he needed was some EMS ambulance crew coming up in here. It would be all over the news, and the heat would be all over him.

Stop it, ma'fucka. She gon' be fine. Just sleepin', like she need.

"Master Duke. Tell me exactly what happened."

"I went to sleep. Musta been four-fifteen yesterday morning."

"No, before that."

"We kicked it," Duke said. "For a couple hours."

"Was she a virgin?"

"Tight as a vise."

"Did she bleed?"

Duke pointed to the aqua blue towel heaped on the white marble stairs leading up to the bed. "Not a drop. But ain't no question—"

"Does she have health problems? Is she diabetic?"

Duke shrugged. "At dinner, she ate like it was no tomorrow. Salmon, salad, ice cream. Didn't say nothin' 'bout sugar."

"Asthma?"

"She run track."

"That would account for her slow resting heart rate. Runners who are physically fit often have a nearly undetectable pulse."

"She said she hadn't slept in half a week. Some whack shit had happened in her life."

Doc Reynolds nodded. "Victoria Winston. I saw her on the news. Exactly how long has she been sleeping?"

"She was layin' next to me when I went to sleep, but I don't know if she was 'sleep yet. Then when I woke up at ten-fifteen yesterday morning, she was still 'sleep. I kept checkin' on her all day. I did my business by phone, right here, so she was never alone."

"She's the millionaire's daughter," Doc Reynolds said. "I just heard on the news the feds are questioning her grand-mother. They're aggressively searching for this girl, Master Duke."

"I already took care of it." Duke had Henry's nerdy-ass brother, Mike, who worked at a public relations company downtown, send all those reporters an official press release saying Victoria Winston had run away.

Duke had told Mike to hold a press conference yesterday on Miss Green's porch. He told Mike to say that Victoria Winston had left with her passport and just enough cash for a one-way ticket to Miami. That would keep them investigating motherfuckers scrambling for clues at U.S. Customs down in Miami, not on Babylon Street in Motown.

"Obviously you missed the latest report about her leavin' the country," Duke said, casting a Doc Reynolds' intelligent brown eyes. She wore no makeup but she was proof that black don't crack because she was almost forty-five and didn't have near a wrinkle. Even after all those years in the pen for prescription fraud.

"Doc, I didn't bring you up here to play fuckin' Colombo," Duke said. "An' I know you always put Babylon confidentiality first."

"Of course, Master Duke. That goes without saying."

"Within Babylon, too. That mean Milan don't need to know the who, what, when, where, how or why of nothin'. She 'bout to get transferred anyway, an' don't need no info'mation bein' transferred wit' her skinny ass."

"Understood," Doc Reynolds said.

"Now, tell me what Duchess need."

Doc Reynolds's eyes cut to Duchess' pale face like she was trying to figure out that this was Duchess.

"This girl needs rest," Doc Reynolds said. "When she wakes up, make sure she gets plenty to eat and drink. She'll be disoriented and dehydrated, so give her orange juice, bananas, healthy food to get her strength back up."

"Her strength was fine night befo' last," Duke said. And she needed to be strong now. He was going to start Hoodology 101 yesterday, so they were already a day behind now that it was Tuesday.

My birthday party Friday night. We got six days to make or break Babylon Monday morn in wit' them Moreno ma'fuckas. She gotta be on so when Knight come back, he see The Duke be rulin' this shit! By my damn self!

"We gotta wake her up an' get her energy back, pronto," Duke said.

Doc Reynolds shook her head. "Let me take this moment to let you know about Janelle. She's retired. HIV and genital warts. Milan gave her walking papers."

"Dang," Duke said. "Nasty bitch. Put out an alert to the B'Amazons an' Barriors so she can't creep up in here."

Doc Reynolds looked serious when she said, "Of course, sir. And Janelle is aware of the penalty for such an offense."

Beamer came jogging back in with a scary look in his eye.

"Massa D, newsflash."

"I'll newsflash yo' ass if you think it's more important than—"

"It might be." Beamer never looked that alarmed.

Duke stepped down. "What?"

"A Barrior jus' dropped a dime on Knight. He out. Now. Plottin' a take-over."

Duke bit down hard. His voice was cool and calm as he said, "Yo, B, go tell yo' girl Milan to stop startin' bullshit rumors that could get somebody killed."

Beamer's eyes got almost as big as his BMW medallion.

Duke made a shoo motion with his hand, making his diamond ring sparkle. "Go. You on evac. Now."

As Beamer huffed away, Duke spun on a heel and dashed back up the steps to Duchess. He shook her arm. "Wake her up!"

"Sometimes after situations of extreme emotional duress," the doctor said, "coupled with extreme sleep deprivation, the body can shut down into an almost comatose state."

"Aw, hell no!" Duke shot up to his feet, pacing the white marble platform around the bed. "Wake her up!"

Doc Reynolds took that clear vial off her lap. She unscrewed the black cap, held the opening of the bottle under Duchess' pretty little nose. Nothing. Duchess slept just as peacefully as she had before.

"Can't you give her a shot or somethin'?" Duke demanded.

"She doesn't need—" She held the bottle to her nose and cupped her hand around it so Duchess had to breathe in the bottle vapors.

"Ah!" Duchess cried out. She coughed and tried to sit up.

"Baby girl!" he cheered, punching his fist in the air like he was at a Pistons game.

"Where am I?" Her voice was raspy and sexy as hell, but her blue moon eyes were huge, full of panic.

"You wit' me, Sleepin' Beauty," Duke said, leaning down to stroke her hair. He sat next to her. "This Doc Reynolds."

"Good morning, Duchess," the Doc said.

Duchess held the blanket over her chest, looking back and forth at everybody like she didn't know up from down.

"Duchess, baby girl, you been sleepin' for a day an' a half," he said. "Worryin' a ma'fucka half to death."

She focused on Duke. Her eyes were still as intense as blue flame blow torches. Now, his whole body prickled with sweat. And Timbo was on swole!

She froze. The blanket dropped from her chest. Her cinnamon-colored nipples looked so good, they made Cinnabons look like dog biscuits. They were pointing straight out from her round, creamy curves of plump, round titties over her little tapered ribs.

Duke shifted on the bed, letting Timbo roll to a more spacious spot in his jeans.

Her lips curled a little. Something flashed in her eyes as she looked right at him.

"Duke, why the fuck you got all these people in our room?" Her voice sounded deeper. "You said you'd make love to me soon as I woke up." She smirked.

Chapter 35

Milan Henderson threw her cell phone onto the shiny, hardwood floor of the Sex Squad headquarters. It broke into two silver pieces at the base of the reception counter where three Sluts were checking in for their weekly exams.

Milan didn't care that they and the other Sluts and Studs were gawking at her as they sat on the couches, waiting for their exams. They hadn't even turned on the TV. They were too busy watching her flit around, trying not to lose her mind.

I will not become a stark raving lunatic in front of all these people, like they expect me to be. I will not!

It was no secret that something outrageous and scandalous was going on. After all, nobody could miss the two big, barbaric prison wardens who'd been her constant companions since Sunday night, watching her every move, both yesterday and today. Now everybody was looking at her like she stole something. Whispering when she walked past. Laughing when she left the room. The hundreds of people in this building knew that Duke had been locked upstairs with that white bitch he brought here on Sunday. They were actually calling that girl The Duchess.

Two days! Duke had been fucking that bitch for forty-eight hours straight! She couldn't remember the last time she had Duke to herself for two hours. Even when she did, he was constantly answering his phone, making calls, telling her to "hurry up an' cum."

Now he had obviously turned off his phones, because Milan had called dozens of times over the past few days. His voice mail was full. That was why she just pitched the phone.

Not to mention, Beamer hadn't spoken to her since their hotel room tryst. He hadn't returned the phone messages she left, threatening to show Duke the videotape if Beamer didn't call her to talk about their plan. *Was he crazy? Peanut obviously had some other kind of plan of his own, but stupid as he was, it wouldn't get anywhere. But why did Peanut come down here all in a fluster, escorting Dr. Reynolds out when she had important work to do?*

Duke had better not let somebody up in here get a sexually transmitted infection. If word got out that Babylon's Sluts and Studs weren't as squeaky clean as they were reputed to be, it would be the kiss of death for this multimillion-dollar empire.

Milan smiled. What a shame that would be. She could always call Janelle back for a job or two, or send her up to Duke's bedroom so she could lay some HIV and warts on Duke and his new Duchess. See how long they live happily ever after with that shit.

She clapped. Everybody turned, giving her their undivided attention. *There, that was better. The way it should be.*

"Due to some unforeseen circumstances," she announced, looking at all fifteen Sluts and Studs, "your exams for this week are cancelled."

"Naw," a chick on the couch said. "I got some burnin' an' I don't know if it's just bladder irritation or chlamydia or what kinda shit goin' on. I need to see Dr. Reynolds."

"Ain't no way," said the Stud sitting next to her. "All my years o' workin' here, we ain't neva missed a exam. I'd get my dick checked e'ry damn day o' the week, as many pussies as I be drillin' in a day." He shook his cornrowed head. "Half these bitches be beggin' me to hit it raw. An' they tip a couple hun'ed extra if I do! So I say, well, I'ma see Doc Reynolds to make sure I ain't caught nothin'. So—" He crossed his arms, lifted the heels of his cow boy boots slightly, and banged them back on the floor. "I'ma wait 'til the doc come back."

"I'm here," Dr. Reynolds said.

How had Milan not heard or seen the entry door open?

"And when The Duke hears about this," Dr. Reynolds said, "I guarantee he will not be happy, Madame Milan."

Milan snapped, "I thought you had abandoned the premises. I was going to call in another doctor for today or reschedule everyone here."

"Naw, that ain't what she said," the Stud in cowboy boots said. "My cock ain't fallin' prey to her hate. She jus' mad The Duke—"

Dr. Reynolds glared at him. "That's enough, Johnny. You can come with me." She led him into the office. "Milan, you'd be wise to resist the urge to sabotage any computer files or employee records." She shut the door.

Milan's cheeks stung. That bitch would be wise not to answer the phone when the IRS called to inquire about how she earned a high six-figure salary at the storefront clinic—which she owned—for indigent patients in the ghetto. She never went there, just let three employees, who may or may not be doctors, operate it. But even all that Medicaid and Medicare reimbursement couldn't pay for her Benz, her big house in the suburbs, or her timeshare in Barbados.

What was she talking about anyway? Did she just see Duke? Had Duke said something about Milan's status here, or lack thereof? As partner? His children's mother? His top executive?

Milan stomped toward the door.

I am going to see him right now to take care of this! I can not have people inferring that my status is anything but superior around here.

She grabbed the doorknob, but the barbarians wedged in front of the door before she could pull it open. And she screamed.

Chapter 36

Duke's body, glistening in the shower, was so beautiful Duchess couldn't stop staring at him. Everything about him mesmerized her. She watched the way the water streamed over the succulent dark chocolate skin on his bald head, over his ears, those perfectly arched black eyebrows, his thick lashes, down his black Roman warrior nose, his high chiseled cheekbones and wide, clean-shaven jaw, to his thick, smooth neck.

He look fine as hell. An' he mine.

Timbo was poking at her stomach, and Duchess couldn't wait to feel him poke back inside Celeste. How could her pussy feel even more hungry for Duke's delicious dick? How could she feel this wicked craving after hours and hours of fucking this absolute god?

It's called addiction, baby. You was a freak by yo' damn self an' you knew once you let Celeste loose, you'd be a worse sex fiend than yo' freaky-ass parents. Good thing you hooked up wit' a Mandingo stud ma'fucka who can han'le it.

"Oh my God!" Victoria cried out into the hiss of the shower.

It was like Duke was inside her head, talking through her voice.

"Baby girl, you a'ight?"

She took Timbo into her hands, stroking the shaft, loving the satin-over-rock feel of this giant magic wand she would worship until her last breath. Especially when it made Duke look down at her like she was his reason for living. Because that's how she felt.

No, I'm not all right. There's a new voice in my head, making me talk black. Ghetto. Ebonics.

Like all the people I've been around for the past two days.

Her mind was spinning a million miles a minute . . . Thank goodness she didn't have to stay at Gramma Green's house of hell, and that Duke's penthouse was as luxurious as home was. And she finally got some sleep. And she finally got some dick!

Her heart felt like it skipped a beat. With terror.

What now? I did what I said I'd never do. I unleashed the mixed race sex powers. Now I know this is the way to get whatever I want or need in life. But what do I want?

Duke had just told her about the Miami-Caribbean story they'd fed to the media. Victoria Winston didn't exist anymore, unless she wanted to face the feds who would turn around and accuse her of helping Daddy do something wrong. Could she go to the penitentiary for a white collar crime that she unknowingly committed? Would her own father have involved her in something illegal? Or was he truly wrongly accused as he'd claimed?

Right now, after seeing the power of the federal prosecutor who was after Daddy and the power of the press to destroy a man to the point that he took his own life, Victoria had no desire to find out.

I am Duchess, hear me roar!

"Duke," she whispered, wrapping her arms around his firm, tapered waist. She buried her face in that hot, velvety crevice at the center of his chest, where the soft mounds of his pecks came together. "This space was made to cradle my face."

Duke tossed his head back, laughing into the streaming water. "You rhymin' again baby girl? Tol' you I was gonna go raw dog on that ass 'til you couldn't talk!"

"Yeah, lobotomize me, baby," she said.

"Timbo musta banged all the way up in yo' brain to flip the black switch," Duke laughed, "'cause you talk black now. Did you see Doc Reynolds and Beama's eyes pop when you woke up?" Duke was cracking up. "Day-um. That was some hilarious shit right there." He kissed the top of her head, ran his hands down the wet black cape that was her hair, tickling the top of her ass.

"It's like the little voice inside my head," she said, "has been reprogrammed to speak hood."

"Yeah, that's that Mandingo dick," Duke said, "woke the sleepin' black diva within."

Victoria pressed her cheek to his chest as she laughed. His voice vibrated in her ear as he said, "The way you talk, that's still gonna be part of yo' Hoodology 101, to get you ready."

"Ready for what?"

"Yo' work for Babylon. As Duchess. This weekend I'm presentin' you to Babylon at my birthday party. Then we got the meetin' of the millennium comin' up nex' Monday. A week from Friday my brotha Knight comin' home, so we gotta make you into the baddest bitch this side o' the moon."

"Duke," she whispered, real sultry, staring up into his beautiful eyes. "Every other minute that you're not hosting my extreme ghetto makeover"—she reached down to stroke Timbo—"can I be the first contestant on Extreme Pussy Takeover?"

Duke's deep laugher echoed through the shower.

"Yo' sex coma already got us a day behind in yo' trainin'."

"Kiss me."

As the water streamed over their faces, he pressed his satin hot lips to hers.

How could one guy's kiss feel so different than another?

Brian's lips were hard, puckered in a way that felt uninviting, tense. But Duke's lips were relaxed, soft, moving gently, like little nibbles. Her plump lips against his plump lips equalled one sensuous dance of hungry mouths finally tasting the flavor they'd both been craving.

He kissed her forehead then cupped her jaw in his giant hands, tilted her face up so he could focus those beautiful, black kaleidoscopic eyes down at her.

"Duchess, I ain't neva even thought this befo', but when you was 'sleep and I thought you was dead," his voice cracked, "I realized I can't—don't wanna live wit'out you."

"You never have to," she whispered. "In my eyes, you're like this masterpiece of manhood and I was made for you," she whispered. "I could stare at you forever. Kiss you forever. Make love with you forever."

He French kissed her so good, she felt dizzy. Then with his hands on her slippery waist, he turned her around.

"Put your hands on the wall," he said, spreading her fingers against the warm, wet stone. He bent her at the waist, grasping her hips like they were hinges he was adjusting to just the right angle. She looked back. Timbo pointed like Cupid's big black arrow at her milky round ass.

"The prettiest sight on the planet," he groaned as he slid his dick up and down her perfectly round ass. She arched her back aching to feel him inside her. As if he heard her yearning, Duke reached between her legs from the back. He cupped his hand over her pussy so that his fingertips were at the top of the hair and the heel of his hand was at her asshole. He pressed his palm down onto her clit.

"Oh yeah," she moaned. "I need that."

He made his hand move in a way that was covering her entire pussy from front to back, and he was stimulating every square millimeter with his hand. In seconds, Victoria convulsed, legs trembling, nipples squeezing, shivers dancing over her skin, mind flashing blue, green, yellow— Slam!

"Aaaahhh!"

The size and force of Timbo surging up into her pussy was so fucking luscious, Duchess could die right now and be happy.

His fingertips pressed into her hips. He banged ferociously. Did sex feel this good to everyone?

Hell no! That new black voice shouted in Duchess' head.

She closed her eyes, as her brain was a wild whirl of words, thoughts, pictures, with that new narrator trying to add sassy commentary every which way. Duke's dick ramming her with the relentless force she craved made it hard to focus. She didn't want to make thoughts about anything but the pleasure of the moment, but would it crank up the volume even louder on the black voice?

Victoria opened her eyes. She wasn't going to worry about all that for now. She was in the shower with Duke, making love.

She glimpsed his feet;huge, dark, perfect, with long toes and pedicured nails that shined with polish. They raised up and down slightly, splashing the gold stone floor on each side of her much smaller white feet topped with shiny red toenails. She glanced back, her black hair a cape over her back, tumbling to the left side of her waist. On her right hip, his long, elegant fingers contrasted against the soft, creamy curve leading to a long leg.

Ooooh, the most magnificent sight of all was her ass bouncing against his groin. Round, ivory flesh flattening just a little against the hard, ebony plane of muscle, over and over and over.

Wait, Duke's face. That was the most magnificent. She loved how lust was turning his cheeks red, parting his lips. Tenderness and love glowed in his eyes.

Duchess closed hers again. She filed that snapshot away to the most cherished chamber of her heart because this sense of paradise couldn't possibly last in the wicked world.

"If something seems too good to be true," Daddy used to always say, "it probably is."

Chapter 37

It felt like a museum or some wild adventure into Ancient Egypt as Duke stood in front of a floor-to-ceiling King Tut mask;shiny gold-and-black stripes on the headdress, the big eyes with thick black liner, the asp at the forehead. Within the center of the fifteen-foot-wide piece of art: double doors.

"Welcome to Babylon HQ," he said, opening the doors. "I got my vision from Ramses' court on The Ten Commandments."

The floor was shiny white marble, just like in the bedroom.

A huge glass desk dominated the same kind of platform, which was four marble steps up, just like the bed. Two chairs behind the desk, as well as two satin couches against the walls leading to the desk area, were styled like gold thrones with arms that curved into spirals and gold satin seats. Behind the desk, lighted glass shelves stretched between huge, gold-and-black-striped mummy cases.

From a side door, which was open to a vast office space with desks and cubicles, four gorgeous girls came strutting out, all in costume with Cleopatra-style hair and makeup. They wore little white dresses with gold hip belts and gold spike sandals that laced up their bare calves, gold bands holding their hair back, and serpent-style cuffs in the curves between their sculpted biceps and deltoid muscles.

The girls were a gorgeous spectrum, from almond to caramel to milk chocolate to iridescent blue-black. In the adjacent office, all the women who were answering phones, working at desks and typing on computers were dressed that way.

These girls ooze sex. It was in the way they walked, the expressions on their faces and in their eyes. The four of them stood directly in front of her and Duke, holding their hands up as if they were praying.

They said in unison, "Master Duke, Madame Duchess." They bowed.

Duchess' eyes devoured their shapely bodies, how they radiated sensuality, from their red painted lips to their hoisted up breasts to their round butts and long legs. They looked good enough to eat. Where she lived, girls were all super-skinny and horrified by any trace of fat on their bodies. That made Victoria self-conscious about her round butt that was bigger and rounder than anyone else's she knew. Brian's pressure for her to diet and lose weight only made her more self-conscious.

But these girls here had meat on their bones and carried themselves with so much confidence. They looked incredible, solid, not fat at all. Just sensuous and comfortable with themselves. It was another affirmation for Duchess to showcase and celebrate her natural shape.

Her pussy was going wild at the sight of these women.

I wanna eat their pussies. I wanna see them naked, with their juicy thighs spread wide open so I can see if their pussies are as pretty as mine. I wanna see them press their fingertips to their clits then fuck those crazy-sexy studs from in thee gym.

"Master Duke, where you find this sweet sista?" The girl scorched the length of Duchess' body with a fiery stare.

Duchess' lips parted as the girl stepped close. The tops of her glitter-dusted breasts were as mouth watering as golden baked dinner rolls glistening with yellow butter.

Celeste was blowing steam into the crotch of Duchess' jeans. Her panties were soaked. Her mind spun with images of herself, Duke and this beautiful girl having a threesome right here in the office. So many girls at school were into that two guys and one girl, or one guy and two girls.

They all thought I was such a prude 'cause I wouldn't even fuck. If they could see me now!

Her reflection in the mirrored wall on the right made Duchess smile. Duke had stocked his closet with clothes for her, even before he met her. It was the hottest in urban wear, including these Fubu faded denims that hugged her ass like no jeans had ever done before. The pink glitter on the thighs and butt were super sexy, and it matched the snug pink tank top and pink stiletto ankle boots she was wearing with it. Her hair swayed just above what Duke called the "ka-pow!" curve of her ass.

These clothes were fine for now, but Duke said they were going shopping as part of her training to get the wardrobe of her choice. Looking at these girls in the little outfits, they reminded her of the women who worked at Caesar's Palace in Las Vegas.

Victoria had been there several times with Daddy when he had conventions. He'd always take her, Melanie, and Nicholas and let them hang out at the pool or shop in the Foreign Shops.

"Duchess," Duke said. Two syllables from his mouth and she broke out in a sweat all over. He was so damn sexy, and the love in his voice when he said her name emphasized her power.

It reminded her that she was really the one in control here, that she was learning, planning, pretending to let him be in power until she could wield it entirely herself.

"Yeah, baby," she responded, turning to him with perfect posture that showed him that her nipples were hard because she was thinking about him bending her over that desk and fucking her right here in front of these girls.

"This is your personal assistant," Duke said, turning his palm toward the girl with the glitter dusted breasts, the one who was standing just a little closer to Duchess than the other three, who were still lined up facing them.

"I'm Honey," she said, pressing a satin soft hand into Duchess' palm. "Welcome to Babylon. You need anything, I am here to serve."

"The pleasure is mine," Duchess said. "You must be named after your eyes."

Honey lowered her thick black eyelashes. Her full lips, glossed with coral colored lipstick, parted to reveal perfect white squares for teeth. Her cheeks rose like little round apples; her nose was like a mini mushroom. She glanced back up, her honey-brown eyes sparkling, framed by flawless skin as dark as molasses. Her face was round, framed by straight black bangs and hair pulled back in a gold band. Her big, juicy boobs poked toward Duchess.

This is thee sexiest girl I have ever seen. Duchess wanted to open up her mouth and take a bite of Honey.

"Anything you need typed," Duke said, "appointments, travel arrangements, phone calls, Honey can han'le e'rything for you. When you got off-site meetings, shopping, pedicure, anything, Honey can go wit' you."

"I'm looking forward to it," Duchess said.

"The other girls," Duke said, "they're back-up. DaLinda, Rochelle, an' Tamika." Each girl bowed as he said her name.

"How you doin'?" Duchess said, undressing them with her eyes. Whatever work Duke wanted her to do up here, how in the world did he expect her to concentrate with these sex kittens around? Did he think she wouldn't be attracted to girls too?

I didn't think I was attracted to girls until I walked up in this peice! And if there was any question, one look at Honey and it's done. I will eat that pussy. She smiled, thinking of how Duke said, "And so it is written, and so it is done."

Duke watched her closely. He knew. Once he set Celeste free to reign over his dick and Babylon, she'd have to swing both ways to capture the full flavor.

And these four girls definitely represented every flavor.

Duchess knew she wanted to see all of them naked. What did their nipples look like? Their clits? Did Duke fuck them? The way he devoured them with his eyes meant the answer was probably yes. What did that look like? Her insides were electrified with curiosity and a twinge of jealousy that oddly turned her on even more. Did they have orgies right here in his office? If she was responding like this as a girl, she couldn't imagine what a man would be thinking, especially when he was the boss.

Duke clapped. The girls closed their eyes, bowed, then turned and sashayed back into that big office space, where they closed the doors.

Duchess immediately turned to Duke, who was wearing jeans, baby-soft black loafers and a black silk tunic that hugged his muscles and tapered waist. She ran her hands over his black belt and over the log in his pants.

"Celeste needs to talk to Timbo about Honey," Duchess whispered.

Duke kissed her forehead, removing her hands from the bulge of his dick.

"What?" she snapped. Her mind spun. Was he about to say no? Her cheeks burned at the idea of him ever denying her that delicious dick, anytime, anywhere.

"I'll slam you over this desk," Duke said, "and fuck you senseless just like you need, after we talk bidness. Can't think straight after I lay it on yo' fine ass. Can't even wake up for a day or two." He laughed, taking long strides to the throne chairs behind the glass desk.

"Come sit at our desk so I can teach you how to rule."

Chapter 38

Ain't no way she can look at me like that an' I don't fuck her!

Timbo got even bigger and harder as Duke looked down at Duchess' long, elegant giraffe legs straddling the gold arms of this throne. The chair was pushed back from the glass desk so her back didn't hit the edge.

"I loooove this position," she whispered, cupping his face in her hot hands as her big, blue metallic eyes glazed and rolled back a little like she was buzzing off too much Cristal. She was riding him so tough right now, he wouldn't be surprised if she shouted, "Giddyup, mothafucka!"

Her right fingertips rubbed her clit, making her pussy drip hot cream all down Timbo. Good thing Duke had pulled his jeans down to his ankles and pulled his shirt up to his chest.

Duchess' titties, which she pulled out of the scoop-neck of her pink T-shirt, were poking over the edge like torpedoes aiming at Duke's mouth. The cinnamon-colored circles with sweet little points made him suck like tomorrow would never come. He loved how those suckers went in soft and got hard against his tongue.

She loved it, too, because her pussy was starting to squeeze like she was about to cum.

Her eyes were half-closed now as she moaned, "Oh, Duuuuke." In fact, she looked like she was drunk. He was afraid to see how wild Duchess would be if she got some champagne in her. And a blunt? She would tear Timbo up. Break it off.

No, Duchess would stay intoxicant-free for now. This was all the intoxication she needed, right here. Duke slammed his hips up, up, up. Her long, straight black hair bounced all over the glass desktop, her shoulders, arms, and the tops of her milky white thighs.

She was just wild right now because it was new. This was her first dick, and last dick, so she wanted to try it out every way possible. Then her ass would calm down. Otherwise, if they fucked all day, every day, his work would come to a standstill.

They wouldn't get everything ready in two weeks for when Knight was supposed to come home.

Her sex coma had already put them behind schedule a day and a half. All of Monday was wasted. Half of today, Tuesday, was eaten up by having Doc Reynolds come and give her smelling salts or whatever the fuck that was. Now they could have been halfway through the tour if she hadn't muzzled him with that big red clit she shoved in his mouth as he was describing her job duties up in this Egyptian palace.

I wonder how long do it take for Duchess to concentrate after I hit it? If I leave her up here to work, I know she gon' start messin' around wit' Honey. My girl looked at her new executive assistant like she wanna sop her up wit' a biscuit an' slurp her down whole. Lips, titties, ass, legs, from head to toe! If Duchess was this addicted to dick already, how would she act after she got her first taste of pussy?

She gon' lose her ma'fuckin' mind between Honey legs.

She was losing her heart and soul between his. Duchess was going to cum any second now. Duke could tell by the way her pussy was squeezing around Timbo like a hand milking a cow, just like Mama Johnson had showed him as a kid down on her farm in Alabama. If his dick were an udder and Duchess was the hand that was milking it, then she would suck him dry at this rate.

Naw, I gotta make her cum so we can get back to bidness.

Duke grabbed the sides of her hips. He fucked up, up, up, like an upside-down jackhammer on that pussy. He was beating it up, giving it a black eye. Maybe if she were sore, she wouldn't want to fuck for a while. But damn, she didn't even get sore the first time.

"Yeah, Duke. Pound that pussy! Pound it!"

Her titty fell out of his mouth. She kissed him softly. Her lips were so sensuous and hot, he could suck on them all day long.

Neva tasted anything so good. Just like Adam must have said when Eve gave him a bite of that sweet apple. This kiss was sucking the life out of Duke Johnson. He was breathing hard, heart pounding, ass muscles burning, abs aching.

She gon' kill me. Maybe that sex curse she was rambling about, maybe it was true. Maybe it zig-zagged through generations, so like her daddy fucked her momma to death, now when the daughter found a man, she would fuck him to death.

Timbo went soft.

She got still. Her eyes opened real wide. Her pretty black, arched eyebrows drew together. She looked down.

Timbo flopped out with a silvery shine, like a dead fish plopped on a tangle of wet black seaweed. Duke's chest rose and fell as he tried to catch his breath. Beads of sweat on his forehead trickled down, itching all over his face. His shirt was soaked. He didn't sweat this much during their sweet-ass cherry pick-a-thon.

The way she was looking at him felt like her eyes were slicing straight through his heart. Like he failed. Like he tricked her. Like he don't love her.

Hell naw. Timbo surged. His dick rose straight up, like Frankenstein did when the mad scientist flipped the switch and made the lightning bolt jolt life into the creature made of dead body parts.

"Yeah, baby," Duchess purred like a damn cat.

She raised up, speared her pussy down on Timbo, and got that mellow smile back. "Oh, Duke, I love it. Loooooove it."

Duke loved it too.

Even though I'm creatin' a ma'fuckin' monsta.

Chapter 39

Duchess held back a scream every time Duke said "baby mommas" with so much pride in his voice. As if someone who was not even old enough to buy beer should be proud to have five kids by three different girls! But she was laughing too hard right now as five adorable little kids pinned him to the floor here in the playroom. Carpeted with a plush A-B-C pattern of red, yellow and blue, the huge room had murals of jungle scenes, a giant fake tree whose hollow trunk had cushions for reading, and enormous stuffed animals-lions, giraffes, gorillas, flamingos, tigers. They were all arranged amidst a kid-sized Hummer and Barbie Jeep that really drove, and a movie theatre area with mini recliners, a popcorn machine and a state of the art flat screen monitor. This playroom was a stop on her tour of Babylon's fifth floor, where the three "baby mommas" lived in their own apartments.

"Attack!" shouted one little boy who was a fifty-pound clone of Duke, from the bald head to the genie eyes to the tiny silver hoop earrings.

"Daddy down! Daddy down!" shouted another Duke clone, this one about a year younger than the other.

A chubby girl, about the same size as Victoria's two-year-old cousin, giggled as she climbed up Duke's shoulder.

"Help me!" Duke cried playfully, flailing his arms, which two more toddlers—a twin boy and girl—grabbed. "It's attack of the babies!"

A tooth-sucking sound drew Duchess' attention to the three nannies who were sitting on a nearby plush red couch flanked by book cases.

"Is gon' be attack o' some baby mommas when they see a snowstorm done blew up in Babylon," said the one with long, brown braids. All of them wore black jeans, crisp white cotton blouses and white leather loafers. No jewelry. No long fingernails. Just snarls on their faces as Duchess glanced their way. Duchess' cheeks stung, slapped by their negative energy.

"I got a cousin who lighter 'n her," said the small, plain nanny. "We can't hold it against somebody for how God made them look."

"Yes, we can!" The other two high-fived each other. They were whispering so Duke couldn't hear them.

"Renee, you always tryin' ta make nice," the girl with braids said. "Even though you work wit' Queen Evil. Milan already half crazy, but she gon' be triple crazy—"

"Not if she remember what happened to Sunnie," one nanny said. "Kicked out on her ass 'cause she didn't act right. Now little Precious think I'm her momma. But l ain't mad at nobody. I love that baby like she mine."

"Plus you got Sonnie's apartment," Renee said with a big smile. "An' clothes. An' maybe even a taste o' The Duke."

The girl made a zipper motion over her lips, but her laughing eyes flashed a big "Yes!"

"Where white girl stay?" one of them whispered.

"Penthouse," another mumbled.

"I escaped!" Duke shouted. He stood. All the kids screamed with delight. They were latching onto his legs like he was a pole they wanted to climb. "Gimme kisses. I need ten. Zeus, do the math. How many kisses each baby gotta give they daddy?"

"Two!" the boy exclaimed. Duke raised him with one arm like a forklift. The boy kissed Duke's beautiful cheeks. Duke did the same for each smiling child.

"Bye-bye, Daddy!" the apple-cheeked girl giggled, waving as he and Duchess stepped into the hallway and closed the door.

"Take care o' mine," Duke said as she walked ahead of him toward the elevator. The hallway had plush black carpet, exposed brick walls and gold Egyptian-style sconces lighting the way past doors stained a rich shade of red.

Duchess' legs felt like pistons being pumped by red-hot sparks of jealousy.

"You 'take care of mine' what?" Duchess asked. Her insides were vibrating with attitude. *If Duke fucks all these women, then he's gotta fuck me double what he gives them.* Duchess privileges.

"My kids. My baby mommas."

"Why are you so proud that you musta been fifteen when you became a father?" Duchess crossed her arms and stared hard at him as they stood at the sleek stainless steel elevator framed by the same exposed beams and sandblasted brick as she'd seen throughout this former warehouse building.

"I'm proud because I'm doin' right. My kids and they mommas got the best o' e'rything. I take care of my own, right here, where I can make sure they fed and not growin' up around the kinda bullshit I saw." Duke's jaw muscles flexed. "An' all my baby mommas know. Bring anotha nigga up around my kids? That particular female, she out. Evicted. I keep my kids."

"Like Sunnie."

The muscle rippled harder over his jaw. "Sunnie set a good example. Since Knight been in jail, my top boy was Big Moe. But Big Moe an' Sunnie, they storybook romance was turnt into a horror flick. They attraction turned fatal. They liaison turned dangerous."

Duchess wanted to smile at his clever play on movie titles, but the words twisted painfully in her gut, like a sharp gas bubble. Did that mean they were dead?

"Tell me they pulled a Romeo and Juliet and not—"

"Not!"

"Well, who are they, your baby mommas?"

"They gon' hate you," he said. "But long as they get theirs, they straight."

"Their what? Their sex?"

"Money. Apartments. Clothes. Dancin' in videos an' at concerts. Some of 'em doin' a video shoot today, downstairs. An' they practicin' fo' my birthday party. Tha's when I'ma present The Duchess."

"Present?"

"Yeah, once they see you a sista on the inside an' the outside, they gon' respec' you jus' like e'rybody respec' me.

All my females dream o' bein' picked as The Duchess. You so clueless, you ain't even hip to how much pull you got."

"All *my* females?" Duchess busted out laughing, but she got dead-serious just as quickly. "Don't ever lump me into the 'my females' category. Like they're your fleet of sports cars and you just pick which one you want to drive for the moment!"

Duke pulled a phone from his belt. A blue light was flashing on the front until he pushed a silver button on the side then clipped it back to his waist.

All of a sudden, Duchess felt another twinge of jealousy. His phone was constantly ringing. Was it business or booty calls?

How could she ever know? Part of her was submitting to this situation as a business deal so she could learn to be just like The Duke. But her emotions were raw, front and center, too, and they were getting in the way when it came to all these women.

"Yeah, girl!" a female voice echoed in the distance, down the hall. She was one of many in a huge crowd of voices that were getting louder. Duchess kept her glare locked on Duke, who was staring into his phone and pushing the button as if to check who had called.

"An' I was like, 'Fo' real?'" one girl said, shooting words out of her mouth with dizzying speed. Duchess turned slightly. A stream of girls—all as flashy and pretty and sexy as if they'd just stepped out of a music video—poured into the small elevator area. Giggles erupted as they approached.

"Hi, Massa Duke," they said, a chorus of sweet voices.

His eyes glowed the same way Victoria's and her friends' eyes used to glaze over with temptation when they walked into Mrs. Fields cookies.

The girls packed the six-foot-by-six-foot space between Duchess, Duke, and the exposed brick walls. Duke was like a tower of machismo in a swirl of pretty faces, perfect hair, and wild clothes.

The sultan amidst a tiny fraction of his harem. *What if someday I become a sultaness with a harem of equally sexy guys? Then I wouldn't have to worry about whether Duke would give me some dick when I wanted it. Like I did today upstairs. I could have my pick of studs all to myself.*

"Wha'z up?" Duke's deep voice vibrated through the sex cloud that was rising along with the fruity, floral, and spicy scents of the girls' perfumes, lotions, hairspray, and gum.

The sultan was surveying it all, especially all the butts packed in tight jeans. One girl's backside was freakishly large, each cheek literally rolling up-down, up-down like two basketballs in a bag that was bumping against someone's leg as they carried it. She stopped near the elevator.

Her side view reminded Duchess of that horrible day, just a few weeks ago, when Brian shoved pictures of the Hottentot tribe in Africa into Victoria's face. The otherwise thin women had enormous buttocks that protruded at a ninety-degree angle from the smalls of their backs. Some of the women were even captured and put on display in carnival-like, traveling freak shows throughout Europe.

Brian, who was apparently doing a paper on it, shouted, "I saw this in the library today and it reminded me of your ass!" Then he busted out laughing.

"If you think I'm so fat, why are you so proud to be with me?" Victoria had shouted back.

"Because you're brilliant. And beautiful. And I'm just teasin' you, sweetie."

Why was I with that jerk? Because his family was so prestigious? Because Daddy said it was important for my future to stay connected to one of the richest and most powerful families in not just Detroit and Michigan but in the country? "Old money speaks louder and deeper than the whisper of the nouveau riche," Daddy used to say.

"I am fo' real," said the girl who first caught Duchess' attention. She kept talking a mile a minute through lips glossed pink. A fountain of maroon-tinted braids danced over her head as she said, "An' he was like, 'Fo' real, doe!' It all jes' happen' so fas'!"

The girl had giant, hot pink letters splashed all over her impossibly tight jeans and denim jacket, which was open to a pink rhinestone camisole in front that was so tight and skimpy, two brown arcs of nipples dotted its top edge.

"Guuuurrrrllllll," her platinum blonde friend responded. She had false eyelashes and a see-through white mesh tank top with white jeans. Her nipples pointed through the mesh like brown peanut M&M candies. "You ain't gotta take dat shit, fo' the simple fact that—"

Duchess glanced at Duke, whose eyes were devouring every one of these gorgeous girls. His stare was like an open mouth under a delicious piece of pizza when the cheese dripped, steaming hot. He looked like he wanted to slurp down every drop of the sex that was oozing from these girls, even from the one in the yellow rhinestone bustier. She wore auburn-hued side ponytails that swayed as she talked about testifying in court for some complicated legal matter. The flawless skin on her toned shoulders, and the beautiful curves of her waist above her jeans made it impossible to think straight. If Duchess felt this entranced as a girl, then what in the world was Duke thinking?

His dazed and seduced expression left no doubt.

Those jealousy sparks popped through Duchess' whole body and prickled up through her skin. She was mesmerized, though, by all these girls. Who were they? What were they doing here? Did they always dress like that? Duchess couldn't look away from the girl in white leather daisy dukes and a tiny bolero jacket with knee-high boots.

"Then I sent his rims," the girl said. "Twennie-foes like you ain't neva seen. An' I was like, I'ma get wit' him if it kill me!"

"Guuuurrrrllll, you lay some o' yo' sweet shit on dat ma'fucka, he gon' be out cold." She held up her hand like a stop sign. "Guuurrrlll, you know I'd be like, talk to the hand, Negro."

"You know I did! When he pull up, he was like," the girl deepened her voice, "'Dang mami, you thick!' An' I was like, 'Is yo' dick thick?'"

Her friend giggled.

"An' my ass," the girl said, slapping her butt, "Sssssttttt. Hot. Gucci, head to toe. Nails, hair, did like a queen. One look an' he was los'!"

Duchess smiled. These girls had so much personality and excitement.

"Duke, we heard 'bout you finally found you a Duchess," said a girl in jeans with rhinestones down the outer seam. The girl raked her fake-lashed eyes up from Duchess' feet to her eyes. Nutmeg-hued eyes smouldered as she stared at Duchess then Duke. "She look soft. Let us show her some moves."

"She'll see all o' y'all dance at my party," Duke said with too much lust in his eyes.

I bet Duke fucks all of these chicks.

Duchess' cheeks burned as she imagined all of these girls shimmying their asses around Duke as he stood there with his hands crossed like those rappers did in videos. As if he were the king and all the women in the world were simply born to serve him.

"Y'all goin' to rehearsal?"

"Yeah," said another chick who blew him a kiss then glanced at Duchess with hazel eyes a glow with mischief.

Naw, that bitch a ho and she wanna fuck Duke. Period.

Duchess shook her head to stop that black voice in her mind that kept rewording everything she thought. The voice was just echoing the speech cadences she was hearing around her.

"Bang Squad in'a house!" the girls cheered, raising hands over their heads, flashing long acrylic fingernails painted metallic gold. Their voices thundered as they sang, "Babylon rule, wit' Dtown cool, urban jewel, win any duel, jack a fool, sexy seductive, serve an' protect. In Babylon, Duke an' Duchess get respect." An equal number of girls were smiling and scowling at Duchess as they sang. Why hadn't Duke introduced her?

He was nodding to the beat as the elevator doors opened. A dozen girls packed in, but a crowd remained. The girls kept singing, but one girl glared at Duchess and sang, "In Babylon, Duke love constant sex." The girl stuck her tongue out at Duchess in a way that was both snotty and seductive.

"C'mon." Duke pulled Duchess' hand toward a door. "Let's take the stairs up."

In the stairwell, their singing was still loud and their sex energy was just as strong. It made words and jealousy and fear shoot up from Duchess' gut so powerfully, her shoulders twitched as she spoke.

"Duke, we haven't finished talking about our agreement for me to work for you." She was racing up two flights of stairs behind him. Were big Moe and Sunnie dead? And if so, was death the penalty for anyone who crossed Duke? "You need to tell me what exactly you do here besides have sex and get mad when other people do."

"I don't have to tell you shit 'cept what you need to know," Duke said.

Slam! Duke pushed the bar on the stairwell door marked 7. The sound echoed like a sinister exclamation point after his last word.

"Well, don't take it out on me," Duchess snapped, following him into the stairwell. "This place is like all sex, all the time. All those girls! The sex in the gym! How can you blame anybody for wanting to fuck twenty-four/seven under the influence of this place?"

He turned, glaring down. "Bidness always come befo' booty."

"Say business."

"Bizz! Ness!" Duke tossed his head back. Deep laughter echoed up through the stairwell. "No, you the one who 'bout to get schoo'ed on Ebonics. The Duchess gon' speak the queen's English when she negotiate for Babylon, but here at home, you gon' learn to speak fluent homegirl."

Duchess thought about the swarm of girls they just left. She put a hand on her hip, tilted her head forward with a slight neck snap, and said with a slow, controlled and very urban cadence,

"Den you gon' show me all yo' baby mommas." Duke blinked. "Wait, lemme close your eyes an' you can hear it again." She covered his eyes with her hands then repeated it.

"A-plus!" Duke smiled, leading her into the hallway. "But we still gon' have a Ebonics tutorial."

"Answer my question," she said. "Who are all these girls? I mean, do you fuck them? I am not tryin' to catch bumps, blisters, burning or some three-letter death sentence."

The first time they made love, she had insisted on a condom.

The time in the shower and the office, she had not, even though Duke ejaculated on her ass or stomach.

Duchess remembered reading news articles about how Detroit was ranked one of the country's "most infected cities" with gonorrhea, syphyllis, genital warts, chlamydia, herpes, and HIV. And if Timbo took a dive in those infected waters, then I'd have that shit. *Oh my God.*

"Duke, we have to use condoms every time if—"

Duke was walking fast, his jaw muscle flexing.

"Duke, tell me your dick is a hundred percent healthy. All these girls—"

He stopped at an unmarked door, turned. Something wicked glinted in his genie eyes.

"Whatever you're thinking," Duchess said, "that's how the nannies and half those girls looked at me. Like they wanna slap me down a couple shades."

"Ain't nobody gon' touch The Duchess." His words sliced the air like knives.

"Who is Milan?"

"Somebody you ain't neva gon' meet."

Duchess asked more forcefully. "Who is Milan?"

"She my first baby momma. Zeus an' Hercules, the two bigger boys."

"Is she moving? Because I'm not."

Duke pulled her close for a hug. They'd gone upstairs, showered—where they fucked some more—and changed into fresh clothes. She pressed her ear to the center of his chest as he said, "Damn, girl, I love yo' sassy ass. You come up in here two days ago, an' you rulin'!"

"Well, since I'm staying, but I'm never gonna meet Milan, then she must be leaving."

"This a big building."

"I don't like non-answers," she said, pulling back to look straight up into his eyes. "So, Milan may or may not be leaving. Where is she?"

"Workin' here on the seventh floor."

"Is this where you keep baby mommas during the day?"

"There you go," Duke said with an equally sassy tone.

Duchess rolled her eyes, stepping toward the door as she said, "I guess I have to see for myself since you're so stingy with information."

He swatted her butt as they stepped through the door.

"Miss Hot Booty," he groaned, leading her through yet another hallway.

"So, Duke, tell me, if all these employees and 'mommas' are your harem and they give you sex, then do I get to fuck those hot guys in the gym?" She shrugged and spoke in a stern tone. "I mean, I'm hoping that this tour includes an orientation period so you can clue me in on this new game of life. 'Cause so far, I'm playing without a rule book."

"We makin' our own rules, baby girl!" His onyx eyes sparkled down at her, but something else flashed there.

Something that twisted wrong in her gut.

She added, "I take that as a Duchess-makes-her-own-rules kinda response."

"There is no 'I' in 'we,'" Duke said, pinching her nipple through the aqua blue tank top, ruffled around the V-neck with tiny pearl buttons down the front. The quick pain punctuated what he said.

"Then let's agree right now. If you get to have sex with all those women, then I get to pick a dick or two and try that out."

Duke laid his hand over his crotch, making his diamond "D" ring sparkle. "My million-dolla dick don't like it when Miss Celeste make him jealous."

"Well, my clean, healthy pussy doesn't want Timbo spearin' bad meat that makes me sick. Or dead!" She cocked her head to one side. "I can't believe I didn't make you wear a condom every time. My head is so fucked up right now. You've probably screwed hundreds of—" Duke put his hand over her mouth. Her moving lips brushed against his palm. "You got the prettiest pucker-fish lips on the planet, baby girl, but they need to be still right now."

Duchess' eyes got huge. She didn't even try to pry his enormous fingers off.

I'm gonna remember this moment, motherfucker, because I have no idea what you've helped me get myself into. I might have AIDS! I might be pregnant! And I was so caught up in the heat of the moment, I didn't even think about it.

But now because of her hurriness she could end up on the fifth floor in a "baby momma" apartment with a wicked nanny and a job for life on the seventh floor of this mysterious place called Babylon.

Why aren't I scared right now? Because I have no control. None. Whether Duke is telling the truth that I'm about to become the grand dame of this bizarre place, or whether I'm about to become his personal sex slave, I have no idea. But if I make it through this, someday I will have all the power, so now I'm a student at this urban school that's knockin' hard on any sense of security I thought l had in life.

Duke pressed his lips to her forehead. She closed her eyes, loving the warmth and tenderness, and knowing that her emotional state was so out of whack that she was going along with a guy who was literally muzzling her. But it was all an act on her part, getting her toward a mega power play in the grand finale. She still didn't have the details of how that would play out—she had a lot to learn here at Babylon—but someday, she would rule.

Now, she moaned the same way as when they'd made love.

Pressed her hips toward his. Spread her knees, squeezing his thigh between hers. He pulled his hand from her mouth, replacing it with his open lips. The hot wetness was like soothing balm on a cold sting. She ground her pussy into the top of his thigh, craving the mind-numbing slide down his tree trunk into timberland, where Alice could climb, swing, and bounce for as long as she wanted.

He squeezed her ass upward, thrust Timbo once—he was rock-hard even through their clothes, and whispered into her mouth, "Duchess gon' be queen o' the baby mommas."

She froze from head to toe. Disgust zig-zaggged through her, even though she understood that being a Duke baby momma was a prestigious position. Being anybody's baby momma at age eighteen was just wrong. She had to go to college. Start her career. Get married. Then have a baby. The old-fashioned order of things.

She cast a playful stare into his eyes and let laughter explode through her lust trembling lips.

"Why you bust out laughin' when I'm dead serious?" His eyes were laughing with her, but his face was stiff.

"Because I am not having a child until I get my M.R.S. degree. If that happens to be Mrs. Duchess Johnson, cool. But I will not be a teen pregnancy statistic."

"You a trip an' a half," Duke said, shaking his head. "And you a whole bunch o' other statistics, now that you fallen way down below the poverty line."

Duchess tilted her chin up. "But then I became Duchess just as fast." She ran her fingertip over his beautiful lips. "Livin' in the lap of luxury with my Duke. Now, what's behind door number three?"

Duke put his hand on the doorknob.

Duchess smiled. "Let me guess. Is this the baby momma work zone?"

"Ding! Ding! Ding!" Duke imitated a game show host. "The triple bonus prize goes to the lady with the scorching pussy and sassy mouth!"

He opened the door onto a lobby-type area with hardwood floors. To the left, sunshine streamed through windows over a TV and plush orange couches. About a dozen men and women, a few who looked familiar from the sexercise on Sunday evening were lounging on the couches, reading magazines. Everybody sat up straight when they saw Duke. They were downright gawking at Duchess.

They turned to the left. A petite woman in a green silk pantsuit sprang at Duchess like those daredevils at the circus who shot out of cannons.

"White bitch!" the woman screamed. Two giant men, one on each side, grabbed her thin arms. She recoiled.

"Duchess, this Milan," Duke said flatly. He nodded to the big men who were holding the woman. They picked her up and carried her through a door to what looked like an office.

Duke knocked on the door marked EXAM ROOM. That woman with purple glasses who'd given Duchess that disgusting smelling stuff to make her wake up this morning, opened the door.

Duke led Duchess inside.

"Doc Reynolds, Duchess need to hear 'bout the strict health code here at Babylon."

The doctor nodded. "You're looking much better, Madame Duchess. Everyone, including The Duke, gets weekly check-ups, on top of using condoms for any sexual contact. Anyone who becomes infected in the line of duty is either treated or given a reprieve until they're cured, or they're retired and tracked to make sure they don't return."

Duchess' stomach flipped. "What do you mean, 'in the line of duty'?"

The doctor cast a probing look at Duke, who sat on the exam table with Timbo in his hand.

"Doc, I need tests right now. Everything. An' show Duchess my HIV results from last week. Test her too."

The doctor stepped to a computer on the counter. She clicked the keyboard for a few seconds, then a printer hummed as she went at Duke with several giant Q-tips. "Any burning, itching, discharge or odors?"

"I'm as perfect as I've always been," Duke said.

"Good," the doctor said. "How should I explain 'in the line of duty,' Master Duke?" she asked while sticking a swab in his mouth.

He shrugged. "You could say 'While fuckin'. While screwin'. While drillin'. While engaging in sexual relations.'"

"So, sex is their line of duty?" Duchess' brain was spiraling down, down, around a flashing pink neon sign in her imagination that said PROSTITUTION.

Drugs, she would've believed, or illegal gun trafficking, or that bodyguard story. But selling sex? Was that what all those people in the gym were practicing for? And all those men and women in the lobby, were they waiting for their weekly STD check-ups?

The doctor examined Duke's penis. He grimaced as she shoved a Q-tip into the tiny hole at the head.

Duchess asked, "Wait, is the sex for business or pleasure?"

"C'mon, Miss Daisy," Duke said, zipping his jeans. "Don't go clueless on me again. You was really startin' to catch on." He stood up then glanced at the doctor. "Doc Reynolds, you can do the whole deal on her. Blood culture, e'rythang."

"I told you I'm a virgin," Duchess said.

Duke laughed. "Not no more!"

"But I don't need to get tested because—"

"Any type of sexual activity can spread STDs," the doctor said. "Even oral sex."

"Wait," Duchess said. She stepped to Duke, her boobs at the center of his chest. She was taller now in her red sandals. She stared hard into his eyes and accused, "So, you're a pimp? And the work you want me to do for you—"

Duke tossed his head back, his deep laughter ricocheting off the walls of the exam room.

Duchess was not laughing. She was numb. Ice cold. "You came to Gramma Green's house acting like you were rescuing me, just so you could put me on a street corner. As a prostitute! After you took me on a test drive for a Motor City minute!"

This was the curse. It was really happening.

I'll be satisfying Celeste's constant craving for orgasm. I'll be following Celeste's order to share my sex. And somehow, I'll be responding to Mommy's whisper that I'm using that power to get what I want. What that is, I have no idea, but it would prove the curse true, because being a prostitute will definitely kill me.

"It's not funny!" Duchess screamed, pounding Duke's chest.

Stinging tears dripped from her eyes. She sobbed, hitting him. Hating him.

He grabbed her wrists, pulled her trembling hands to his lips, kissing them.

"Sssshhh, baby girl, baby girl. Sssshhh." He drew her into his chest, where his voice vibrated through her. "You got it so wrong, baby girl. Listen up!"

She closed her eyes.

"Excuse me," the doctor said. "I'll come back when it's time for the test." She opened the door and left the exam room.

Why should Duchess believe anything Duke said?

"Does Streetology include acting classes? Because Duke Johnson, you get an Oscar for most convincing role as a lover."

She opened her eyes, glaring at him. "You tricked me in the worst way. And I was so naive!"

"Duchess," he pleaded, gently cupping his hand around the back of her head.

"How stupid was that, believing you really wanted to help me! Your bogus good samaritan act, it was all a trick! The dinner, the ice cream, the sunset kiss, taking me to meet your mother!"

"Baby girl—"

"And making love," she whispered. Her insides felt like they were melting with sadness and disappointment. "I thought that was real."

"It is real." Duke's glassy eyes radiated tenderness. His voice was raspy with a sort of desperate plea that she had not heard from him. "It's all real, baby girl."

That needle in her arm was real, too, when the doctor returned a few minutes later to draw blood for the STD tests. She also did a pelvic exam and took a culture from inside her vagina. All that, the doctor said, would test for stuff like gonorrhea, syphyllis, genital warts, herpes, pelvic inflammatory disease, and chlamydia. Another swab in her mouth tested for HIV.

"As long as you've had no odors, burning when you urinate, itching or discharge," the doctor said, "you're probably fine. You look perfectly healthy."

"Madame Duchess," the doctor said, "you know sexually transmitted infections can cause major damage to your insides but never give you any symptoms. That's why we're vigilant about testing every week."

Victoria studied the woman in purple glasses. Her vibe was totally trustworthy. "Dr. Reynolds, do you think since Duke gets tested so much, it's safe for me not to use condoms with him?"

The doctor nodded. "Duke deals in sex. He is vigilant about health with himself and everybody here. So yes, I think you're safe. However, if you both have other partners, that creates some risk."

Victoria's father always warned, the number one thing people lied about was sex. She could never know if the man she was fucking—even her husband—was being faithful. Her dad said she couldn't be with somebody around the clock, and it only took a few minutes, really, to sneak a screw.

Victoria wrapped her arms around her waist to hug herself, as if that would help her figure this out.

"You look worried," the doctor said. "I think Duke will protect you." She cast a concerned look down at Victoria. "But let me say, Madame Duchess, unless you're planning to get pregnant, I can prescribe birth control pills."

Victoria nodded. "Definitely."

Chapter 40

The fresh scent of hot pussy rising up from Miss Daisy's flowering pussy made Duke smile as he inserted the security key into the golden door lock. It didn't matter whether Duchess was happy, sad or mad, her pussy always reacted before she did. If she got an attitude, like she had now, her pussy would be on swole. When she smiled, her pussy creamed. When she imagined crazy shit about what he was going to do with her here, her pussy shot flames.

She was jealous of all those hotties downstairs, but her pussy was curious as hell about how every one of them got their freak on. Now that she finally got some dick, she was like an undercover investigator trying to expose the who, what, when, where, why, and how of sex.

Right now, she was going to learn the five W's and H of Duke Love, along with her first official Ebonics lesson. They were already way behind schedule, but Duke had to let her know none of what she was saying in the exam room was true. He knew she was clean, but he wanted her to get tested just to show there was an equal partnership. And now he was going to use body language to tell her just how much he loved her.

Timbo 'bout to speak louder, better an' bolder than any words could say. She gon' be a shiverin' lump o' jelly when I lay on this mack daddy powa.

"We gon' talk in here," Duke said as the little green light flashed in the silver box on the gold door. "This the Cleopatra suite."

"I love how the door is just like the Babylon offices upstairs, but this is Cleopatra's mask, right?" she asked, staring up at the enormous gold-and-black mask of the Queen of the Nile. "I've dressed up as Cleopatra every Halloween since third grade when I wrote a paper on her. She was so sexy and confident and powerful."

Duke smiled as he pushed open the door. "Just like you. This where I was gon' have you stay, but now that you made yo'self at home in my penthouse. . . ." He laughed, remembering how she hadn't hesitated saying "our room" this morning. "I'm gon' have Knight stay here when he come."

"No one would believe this is here." Her voice echoed with her footsteps. Her juicy booty bounced as she stepped onto the 3,000 square foot suite. She gawked at the open loft with high, exposed ceilings, brick walls and sunshine shooting down through all the high paned windows. "I love this place."

"All them windows new," Duke said. "Three years ago, jus' before Knight took a fall, we sandblasted all the walls, redid all the plumbing. This building a hun'ed years old."

Shiny hardwood floors stretched to a black marble fireplace framed by a mantle that was a huge version of the Egyptian mask on the door. Plush white couches faced it around a zebra-skin rug.

In the corner was the sleek kitchen with stainless steel appliances, black marble countertops, dark cherry cabinets, and an island with black stools with black-and-gold striped satin cushions. Next to that was a dining table with similar seats and a huge gold bowl overflowing with fresh fruit on the glasstop.

Nearby, a beautiful desk and computer.

"Oh my God," Duchess said, running her fingers over the frosted glass wall leading to the bedroom. "This etching of Cleopatra, her flowing white gown, her elaborate headdress. Oooh, love that!" She pointed to Cleopatra and the two men in Egyptian-style loin cloths and two ladies in waiting. She traced the design to the edge of the glass door, touched the gold hinges, and went inside.

"Duchess." Duke touched the back of her upper arms.

She jumped.

"Ah! I didn't hear you. Don't do your panther walk up behind me!" Her pucker-fish lips pulled back into the prettiest smile. She glanced at the bed and smiled bigger. "So, you brought me in here so you can explain"—her voice got hard and loud—"what the hell you want from me?"

He pressed his fingertip to her pretty lips. "Damn, I wish I had a camera," Duke groaned, running his hand over the tent that Timbo was making of his jeans. He adjusted his gat in his waistband under his black shirt. "The way yo' hair fannin' out all ova them white pillows, an' yo' body all stretched out, you look like the mos' innocent an' sexy playmate ev'a."

"Duke, what do you want from me? Is this like a mini honeymoon where you fuck my brains out then toss me into the masses of girls you keep here?"

Duke pulled his gat from his jeans. Her eyes got as big as her fist. He laid the gun on the nightstand beside a big vase of white flowers.

"I know you ain't that naive, baby girl," he said, pulling another gun from his left black gator cowboy boot, which he set beside the other.

"Tell me your daddy didn't have security." Duke lay beside her, his left elbow on the pillows, his chest pressing into her right shoulder. "I know, as high profile as he was, y'all had at least one gun in that big-ass palace in the middle o' the woods. On yo' own lake!"

"And in his office," Duchess said softly. She closed her eyes. Her lashes were so long, thick and black, they looked like fringe against beige china. "Actually, Daddy loved guns. He had a cabinet full in the house, for hunting, target practice. He even went on a safari in Kenya, after Mommy died." Her voice cracked in a way that stabbed Duke's heart.

He kissed her forehead. "I'm sorry, baby girl. Let's talk about somethin' happy."

She opened her bloodshot eyes, looking at him like he was crazy.

"Duchess, I know this sound whack as hell, since we been knowin' each otha forty-eight hours, but I know you my soul mate." Duke's lips felt hot. His eyes felt extra big, and his heart was banging.

Her eyelashes lowered so her eyes were half-closed, staring down at his mouth. She raised her hand to the back of his neck, pulled him down, and kissed him like he had never been kissed.

Like his mouth was hot loaf of fresh-baked bread, split down the middle and steaming, and her lips were the sweet cream butter, melting right into him, making the perfect flavor so one wouldn't taste right without the other. She tasted it too, because she was kissing him for what felt like forever.

They were naked in a Motor City minute. Duchess stood over him, one foot on each side of his hips, staring down at Timbo like he was the chrome exhaust pipe on a Harley she was about to straddle and ride into the next millennium.

She took a long step toward his head, putting her right foot beside his ear, then she moved her other foot to his other ear Duchess' knees folded down, lightning quick. She squatted so his face was right at her opening. He inhaled the scent of sweet-salty incense.

"Talk to the pussy." Duchess' voice was hard, like every word came out dipped in gold. She said it just like the sistas would hold up their palms and say "talk to the hand."

"Celeste wants to hear it straight from the source," Duchess said, but he couldn't see her face because a big, wet pussy was blocking his view, "what this urban sex lord has to say about The Duke and The Duchess."

Ain't no girl ev'a talked to me like that or taken this bold-as-hell stance over my body.

He couldn't talk right now to save his life. His eyes got big, like hers did in the hall when he put his hand over her mouth.

"I didn't think you'd have anything to say," Duchess said in that same sista-girl-power way. She made her hips circle so the pussy went 'round and 'round in his face. Not touching, just going 'round and 'round like she was going to hypnotize him with it.

And ain't nobody ev'a been hypnotized by somethin' so pretty.

Duke felt like his heart was going to explode. It was pumping so hard and fast with fear, with adrenaline, with excitement, with rage that this lily white girl was mackin' The Duke! *I gotta get up. Get on top. Dominate!*

But that pussy, going in circles in his face . . . the scent . . . the hot dampness like a warm washcloth, the thrill that this was where every motherfucker wished he could stay twenty-four/seven, face to face with a hot, hungry pussy, had him paralyzed

Slam!

A groan like Duke had never heard from his own mouth shot out from between his wet lips because she just slammed down on Timbo like she was a big cube of filet mignon poking herself on a skewer. Ready to sizzle.

The shock of hot, tight pussy that was so wet he just slid in, made his whole body shiver and convulse like he was cumming, and she just got down on it. Her blue blowtorch eyes shot down at him in a way that was hotter than ever. She took a position like she was leaning forward on a motorcycle, so her ass pooted up.

Timbo was deep up in the pussy. Damn, Celeste was sucking him in, squeezing him around, steaming right through this thick dick.

"I'm gonna ride you," Duchess moaned, "'til you beg me to pull over an' let you rest."

She pumped her hips at just the right angle so Timbo slid in and out. Faster, faster, faster. . . . She bounced now. That ass on his thighs, slapping.

"What cha wanna tell me, Duke?" she teased. "Thought you wanted to rap."

She fucked him harder, and he still couldn't talk. Didn't want to talk or think.

Her whole body glistened with sweat now, from her long, pretty neck to her titties pressed between her fingers, her toned stomach, her thighs. Clumps of hair stuck to her shoulders. Some strands fell and caught between her fingers. He couldn't have scripted a more sensuous scene if he were Hugh Hefner.

"Rap," she whispered, keeping a steady beat of her butt pounding his thighs. "I wanna rap as I slap my ass."

He smacked her butt, one hand on each cheek. It was so loud the slaps startled them both. She laughed but didn't stop fucking.

"Yeh, I'm crass. Jus' ask the mask." She nodded at the Egyptian artwork over the bed. "Witness this kiss"—she leaned to suck his mouth—"as I whisper my love like a glove on Timbo. I know he's so fat, so I sat like a cat, with my pussy soft and squooshy . . ."

Her pussy was pulsating like she was about to cum.

"Oooohhhhh, yaaaaay-yaaaaahhhhh."

Celeste squeezed so hard around Timbo, it was like the head was going to pop off. Duchess was cumming so hard, it felt like an earthquake was shaking up inside that temple, threatening to break off this great black obelisk.

"I love this dick," she moaned. She sounded just like Duke would be thinking while he fucked, whether he was with Duchess or any other of the hundreds, if not thousands of pussies he'd had. Some were just OK, but right now Duchess was saying "I love this dick" the same way he would rate some really good pussy, even pussies that he couldn't remember the name or the face they were attached to. Just good-ass pussy.

"I love this dick."

Yeah, girl. Get yo' groove.

"I loooooooove this Duke."

It felt like fire was spreading all over his skin. In a bad way. Like she had just lit a match on The Duke.

I gotta flip her over an' fuck her senseless, squirt so much nut up in that pretty head it drown out any crazy-ass way o' thinkin' like a dude. Hell naw. The Duchess got juice, but it ain't ev'a gon' be equal to The Duke juice. Neva.

He grabbed her thighs. He would just raise her up, now that she was weak from cumming, and tackle.

"Seems like the better angle," she whispered, glancing back at his knees. "Yeah."

Before he could grab her thighs, she spun on his dick like a toy top and faced his feet. It looked like two moons were rising over his stomach.

All I can see is ass. Look almost as good as a face full o' pussy.

Duchess tried a stroke, thrusting her hips forward.

"Oh yeah, tha's it," she moaned, sounding all black now.

She made some round motions, like her hips were going in circles. Her ass was just grinding into him like she would never get tired. Then she moved faster, looking like a rabbit up there. His fingertips danced up her back, tickling her flawless skin. She shivered, moaned. "Ooohhhh, touch me so good."

Duke wanted to ask, "Damn, how can a girl be so erotic she shiver when you just touch her back?" But he still couldn't talk. *I ain't even tryin' to spend a ounce o' energy on anything but gettin' fucked wit'out movin' a single muscle.*

She raised up so her upper body was upright all the way. She moved her feet out at his sides, put her hands on her knees, and raised up in a squat position, just like she had seen the Sluts do in the gym.

Duke smiled. She couldn't wait to try this shit. Without letting Timbo out of the pussy-vise grip, she squatted down, up, down, up.

Dis da bomb! Faster, faster, she was shaking, moaning and crying out like she was cumming, banging down on his dick like she was nailing her soul to his.

"Ah," she sighed like her muscles were sore. She slid down to her knees and bent just a little bit, sucking Timbo up in that creamy pussy tunnel. Her hair was all clumped on her back. Sweat dripped down her ass, onto him, making a pool of hot, salty sweat in his belly button.

Ma'fuck me! Something jolted through him so strong, his head suddenly filled with the image of sticking Timbo in a big electric socket.

I'm gettin' electrocuted up in here. Pussy shock treatments. That gon' fry my brain an' make me dumb as Frankenstein.

He would be a kitten in her lap as she sat at the throne of Babylon with just a shell of The Duke at her side. She could rule and just have him fuck her whenever she wanted.

Slam! She was ruthless, bouncing that booty, taking all of this dick and all of The Duke.

Hell naw!

"Ddddd . . ." Her name came out through his mouth as a grunt. "Ddddduuuuu . . ." What was worse, saying nothing or sounding retarded when he tried to talk?

The scent of their sex made him as mellow as when he breathed in second-hand ganja smoke. Except Timbo was about to blow. Duke's whole body was trembling. Her electric jolts made him convulse, making his dick feel like it was about to shoot with the force of a firehose.

She was cumming again, shaking so hard her shoulders were shimmying, her legs twitching, and her hands were trembling. She was pounding the pussy like there was no tomorrow.

Timbo was taking it, too.

Oh shit, yeeeaaahhhhh. A ma'fuckin' seizure takin' ova The Duke.

"I got this dick!" she moaned. "I got all this dick."

He groaned. Deep. Raw. Like he had never heard himself groan before. Like a bubble was rising up from the deepest part of his core. Like that sound that came out of Prince's mouth as he died. It was a sound he never wanted to hear again, especially from his own mouth. Like a part of him was dying.

Duchess glanced back. Her eyes looked supernatural, all glazed with lust, chunks of hair stuck to her wet cheeks, lips red, open, like a lion that just took the juiciest bite out of the panther it killed.

She was still fucking. Her pussy squeezed as she came. His dick throbbed as he blew his nut, and their sex power juice mixed into some toxic chemical that was going to make both of them crazy.

Duchess banged down more, more, more, until Timbo got tingly like his elbow when he hit the funny bone. He wanted to scream "Stop!" but pussy shock treatments stole his voice. He wanted to grab her, push her off, but his arms felt like lead. He wanted to buck up and toss her off, but the stallion was tame.

So all I can do is lay here like a pussy an' get fucked.

Duchess shot up, letting Timbo slip out and collapse like a dead seal on his groin, which looked like a black sand beach frothing with their salty sex juice.

Duke trembled, every muscle in his body. And he couldn't stop, not even when she stepped off the bed and walked toward the bathroom. Duchess glanced back at him with so much power in her eyes, Duke felt sick. *Look like my body language spoke loud an' clear all right . . . that I'm the punk mafucka who layin' here like some limp-ass jelly. Hell naw!*

Chapter 41

Duke is crazy if he expects me to concentrate on super fly girl clothes, Ebonics, and ghetto psychology while Honey is prancin' around in a tight little white dress.

Duchess strutted across the white marble floor in blood-red patent leather stiletto boots and a sleeveless black cat-suit. She stepped up the stairs to the raised area where Duke was sitting on a gold throne behind the huge, thick glass desk.

"So, you're making me into a thugstress, right?" she said playfully, strutting the way runway models did it on TV reports of fashion shows in New York. "That's a cross between a temptress and a thug, with a sort of Cleopatra feline look."

"You my chameleon who can switch between ghetto fabulous, Wall Street white girl, an' sexy diva," Duke said. "Damn, baby girl, yo' booty be poppin' in nat. Bend over an' shake that ass." His hand was over a huge bulge in his lap.

"Oooohhh, I've never looked so sexy," she said as the designer, Gregor, rolled that giant mirror in front of her. In it, she could also see the rack of equally seductive jeans, dresses, skirts, and jackets she had already tried on.

"Especially with this tan," Duchess said, loving her darker skin thanks to the tanning booth Duke had installed in the penthouse for her. "I feel like one o' those sexy comic book women with superhuman powers. Duke . . ."

He looked pale.

A soft cloud of Honey's perfume—musky with a hint of floral—enchanted Duchess' nose moments before she turned to see the girl's titties come to halt just inches under Duchess' mouth.

I'm gonna drip pussy juice all over these clothes.

Honey's fingertips on Duchess' arms brought to mind that lightning ball at the science center. The girl's touch made purple bolts shoot through Duchess' skin, through her body, lodging in a hot, sizzling glow between her legs.

She attached two gold armbands in the inward curves just above her biceps.

"Just like Cleopatra wore," Honey said with a husky voice that flowed like slow molasses over her lips. Her honey-brown eyes mirrored the lust that was making Duchess feel like she could touch her finger to the bottom of a lightbulb and make it glow.

"I love it," Duchess said, glancing down at the gold cuffs on her arms and Honey's fingers on her skin.

"That cuff is superb," the designer, Gregor, called across the white marble floor here in the Babylon HQ offices. The slender, cocoa-brown guy pushed his silver glasses up into a mop of black ringlet curls. Wearing a blue suede pantsuit, he made "OK" signs with each hand.

"Duchess," he said, turning toward the rack of clothes that Victoria Winston wouldn't have taken a million dollars to wear in public. "The whole Cleopatra look is just spectacular with your long hair. I've got one more thing. Honey, get her some eyeliner."

Duke laughed. "The finishin' touches on the sex monsta we creatin'. You still so horny, you turnin' yo'self on jus' lookin' at yo' own damn thighs in the mirror. You finally free to love how yo' round ass curve up like two big buttered buns, makin' yo' pussy drip."

She threw a satin glove at him. "Stop!"

"Gregor, you see Duchess musta hid yo' iron between her juicy thighs. Honey, don't y'all see steam shootin' outta her pussy? Whoosh! Hot steam burnin' e'rythang in sight. Come burn me, baby!"

Honey giggled as she strutted over to one of the mummy cases flanking the desk. Duke's eyes were on Duchess. She could see him in her peripheral view, while she watched Honey's round, plump ass move under the flowy white chiffon of her little dress. Her thighs caused automatic mouth opening and watering.

When Duchess looked at them, all she could do was imagine her open mouth sucking on that soft, flawless skin.

As the designer jingled something behind Duchess, Honey opened the money case, which contained shelves. She bent over at the waist. The dress rode up, and wet, molasses-brown pussy lips smiled at Duchess. Honey's pussy was fat and bare; shaved hairless, nestling a sweet brownberry treat with a side of fresh cream, displayed right under perfect curves of a plump ass.

Duchess wanted to crawl up behind her and just eat. Her knees weakened; her whole body felt like she just fell into a hot bathtub. Celeste shot hot gusts of steam into the crotch of this sleeveless black bodysuit.

"Here we go," the designer snarled over that jingle sound. "You all can have a little sexcapade on your own time. I have three more clients."

"We'll take e'rything." Duke's voice boomed across the office. He did not stop staring at Duchess as she watched Honey strut back to her. "Leave the rack."

Duke pitched a hand and tossed the money case. Gregor caught it. The suction sound of a tin being opened then closed inspired the designer to whisper, "Every day is Christmas at Babylon. I'm most grateful, Master Duke." There was the sound of the clothes rack wheeling out, doors opening and closing, and Gregor was gone.

"Yeah, all them clothes make me wanna have a sexcapade," Duke said, "wit' my chameleon. Hope you know how lucky you is. My baby mommas would suck dick for days to get all this loot for free."

Honey giggled, sending gusts of hot breath against Duchess' neck. Honey's mouth stayed slightly open as she leaned up with a black cosmetic pencil. Duchess closed her eyes as the soft tip lined her lashes, with one outward stroke at the comers of her eyes.

The heat of Honey's body drew Duchess' nipples to hard points in the black cat-suit. Her chest rose and fell.

"See, yo' body heavin' 'cause that homegirl within tryin' to bust free," Duke said, his hand on his dick. "Now you got a ghetto space ranger to the rescue."

"Here, let me adjust this," Honey whispered, unfastening the halter top at the back of Duchess' neck. It fell open.

Gregor dashed back in, jingling. "Wait, one more"—he stopped in his tracks—"thing." He was holding a gold chain with coins attached.

Duke nodded.

"Here," Gregor said, attaching the belt around Duchess' waist. "Hell, who needs clothes anyway?" Then he dashed out.

"You gotta stay a chameleon," Duke said. "I seen it on my kids' videos, a lizard that change colors to match the background."

"Our colors match nice," Honey whispered, curling her fingertips into the belt, gently scratching Duchess' waist. She stuck out her tongue, and while staring into Duchess' eyes, Honey tickled her tongue across those exposed nipples.

"Mmmmm," Duchess moaned and twisted, making the necklace jingle. "My pussy could boil an egg right now."

"I bet it would come out gold," Honey whispered.

Duke's tone was all lust as he talked. "Wit' Moreno, you gon' be lily white in a pinstripe suit, an' the baddest black bitch crossed wit' yo' daddy business brains on the inside."

Honey's face was like a doll. Her lips were so perfect, Duchess had to taste them.

"You smell like sugar," Duchess whispered.

"My lotion and lip gloss," Honey said. "It's called Brown Sugar. Taste." She leaned close.

Duchess' head spun. She closed her eyes. She had kissed Tiffany so many times, but she'd never been so excited. Oh my God. Honey's lips were soft fire. They parted when they met Duchess' trembling mouth, and Honey just placed them there for a long moment, like she knew this was all new to Victoria, so she was taking it slow.

Deliciously slow. Dizzying. Satin soft, hot, loving she could suck on these lips all day long.

Victoria's pussy convulsed. One touch and she could cum.

Her entire being felt so electric, she felt like she could look up at the sky and make lightning shoot from her eyes. Touch her pussy right now, or let her just see Honey's sweet playmate for Celeste, and thunder would pound the sky.

Honey pulled back just a few inches. She was pouting. Her beautiful eyes glowed with lust, mirroring Victoria's emotions exactly. Her back arched, rising and falling with heavy breathing.

"Right now, we fadin' to black," Duke said. "An' seein' how you can become one wit' female beauty."

Duchess was drunk, as if Honey's lips were a champagne fountain. Honey pulled back then purred, "Aren't we s'posed to be teaching you how to talk like a sista? As your executive assistant, it's my responsibility. So," she whispered, "if you ev'a meet up wit' one o' dem fed pinpricks, what cha gonna say?"

"Ahm gon' say," Duchess jerked her neck a little, tightened her lips, "hell naw, I ain't neva heard o' no white bitch name Victoria Win—what?"

Honey's deep, raspy laughter was infectious. Duchess and Duke cracked up.

"She don't need coachin'," Honey told Duke.

"Yeah, she do," he answered. "Let me sprinkle some wisdom on Miss Daisy. In the hood, rule numba one: Anything you say or do and anything anybody make up about you can and will be used against you, so don't tell nobody nothin'."

Duchess could stare all day at Honey's plump, dark brown breasts. They were all hoisted up in her face, mounds that invited her to rub her face all in the crack, on the soft parts, suck on those nipples forever.

"I always had a 'no information' policy," Duchess said.

"Most things are nobody's business, for sure."

Honey pulled both sides of her dress so that her nipples popped out. With her mouth open, Duchess moaned as she dove toward them.

Oh my God, the sensation of stiff nipple against the soft, wet inside of my mouth . . .

"For sure, Miss Daisy," Duke mocked. "Now say, 'fo' sho'. Where you come from, Miss Daisy say 'fer shewer.' Now The Duchess say 'fo' sho.'"

"Maybe you didn't notice the big, pretty tittie that was in my mouth," Duchess said, playing mad. She pressed her lips together, drew the corners of her mouth back, tilted her head slightly and said, "Quit pissin' me awf, ma'fucka!"

"Day-um," Duke exclaimed with sparkling eyes. "You quick. Com'ere, bof y'all."

As they went up the steps, Duchess watched Honey's ass, her juicy legs and the hump of her plump ass in that little Cleopatra dress. The hot, wet swell between Duchess' legs created torturous friction.

"Duchess," Duke said, patting her throne. "Come sit next to me. Honey, show her what you got."

Duchess sat on Duke's thigh, facing the desk. Honey sat on the desk. She leaned back, stuck her legs in the air, and with a flash of those gold lace-up sandals, she spread her legs.

The round curves of her ass cheeks against the glass desktop formed a sort of platter for Honey's sweet meat. All those shiny folds of pink-brown flesh, it was like those party trays with ham and roast beef sliced so thin it looked like a crumpled piece of satin.

That was what this girl's big, brown clit and shaved pussy lips looked like. All Duchess could do was bend down to indulge in this most feminine delicacy. First, she ran her tongue up one lip, down the other. All the while she was grinding her pussy against Duke's leg.

Honey cupped her big, juicy breasts, sticking her tongue out to lick her own nipples. Duchess wrapped her lips around the plump brownberry, and delicious shivers wracked Duchess' body.

I'm cumming at first bite.

Duke felt it, so he raised her a little, yanked down the bottom half of the cat-suit, and shoved his huge, rock-hard dick inside her. She gasped into Honey's pussy. Then she did the windshield wiper motion. Honey quivered immediately.

"Ooooh, Duchess, you do that good." Honey frantically sucked her own nipples, staring with hungry eyes down at Duchess, who was peering over a bald brown hill, the dress crumpled around her waist and under her boobs. "You eat pussy like a pro."

As Duke thrust up into Celeste, he reached around and stuck his index finger inside Honey's pussy. His knuckles bumped Duchess' wet chin. Duchess pulled back to watch, loving Honey's round, juicy ass pressed down on the glass desk, two circles forming a base for that fat, plump, bald pussy dripping honey as sweet as the name implied.

Duke's fingers pumped in and out of her pussy. His dick slammed up into Duchess' pussy. She shivered faster, more intense. Her nipples were hard as rocks between her fingertips.

She loved the sight of his beautiful brown hand contrasting with Honey's meaty folds.

Honey's pussy was wide open in her mouth; it was a dream.

So was Timbo inside her right now, giving Celeste what she needed.

The fireball between Duchess' legs was about to explode.

Honey was quaking, moaning, shrieking, clawing, pulsating around Duke's finger.

Duchess screamed as orgasm melted her core. But she was terrified, because her veins were pumping red-hot opium. It just melted her mind into a raw, fiendish mass that would make her do anything to get more of the sweet stuff she just sampled with Duke and Honey.

Chapter 42

Duchess was now Alice in Pleasureland, and behind every door lay something even sexier. But these stripper dance lessons were going too far. No way in the world would she ever dance like those girls in videos.

"Madame Duchess," Honey said, guiding her into the gym, "you be doin' these dance moves like a pro. I can tell by the way you flow when you walk."

"I don't know why Duke wants me to—"

Duchess' mouth watered at the sight of dozens of beautiful, bare derrieres lined up at the ballet bar in the mirror and across the red floor mats. Thongs in every color rose up and out of each luscious crack and double bubbles of black velvet, caramel suede, and creamed coffee.

Duchess' breath caught in her throat. At the end of the bar, stretching her thin arms over her head, was Milan.

The main baby momma who got hysterical at the sight of me today.

But those two bodyguards were still with her. Maybe that was why she was making that snarling expression instead of charging at Duchess like she'd done earlier today.

Now I'm definitely not gonnna do this in front of her.

"Welcome, Madame Duchess," said Lee Lee, the tall Asian black woman who was leading Victoria's sexercise session.

"Can I just watch?" Duchess asked.

Something red flashed to her right.

"Put this on," Lee Lee said.

A red thong formed a silky cloud in Victoria's outstretched hands.

"I ain't givin' nasty dance lesson number one with you lookin' like a nun all covered up," Lee Lee said playfully.

"Didn't Duke tell you? When you come to Hood School, we got a certain dress code."

Duchess felt dizzy. The kinds of moves she was learning to make with Duke, and now with Honey, were not something she wanted to do in front of anyone else, especially while she was wearing a thong in a room full of girls.

"An' hurry up," said India, the tall, blue-black girl from the office who handled the fleets. Her stare was seductive as she said, "We all wanna see how much black showed up on that ass. Once you start to bounce it, we'll know."

Laughter echoed through the gym.

"That white girl probably can't dance her way out of a paper bag," Milan snickered. "Probably doesn't have an ounce of rhythm anywhere."

A few girls laughed, including one who looked like Honey with short, straight black hair. She was already doing really sexy exercises, raising her leg all the way up so her foot pointed up beside her face like a ballerina, except she was wearing a thong.

Lee Lee glared at them; they got quiet. If it weren't for that, they'd be cracking up. Duchess wanted to disappear. Why had she felt so comfortable with her newly blossoming sex-until now? Because Milan was here. She was radiating so much hate, Duchess didn't want to be in the same room with her, much less feel sexy or dance or do anything scandalous in front of such a hostile wetness.

I'd feel safer if Duke were here. He said he had to go handle some details about his birthday party coming up in a few days.

India bent to touch her toes. The bulge of baby blue thong stretched over her pussy, making it look like a sling full of plump meat. That little strip of fabric could barely cover the fat lips and big clit within.

Duchess squeezed her pussy lips again, but rather than calm Celeste, they only stimulated a hot, cream-colored throb. A gust of steam heated her jeans.

Why was she suddenly finding women so beautiful? So delicious-looking? Why did she keep staring at and thinking about Honey's boobs, how one look made Duchess want to bury her face in all that soft, round, creamy flesh? Rub her cheeks in it, lick them all around, suck on the pretty tips pointing through that paper-thin black cotton.

Right now, Honey's toned arms looked just as creamy and shapely as they had in her Egyptian maiden mini-dress in the office. Her legs were toned, bare and holding up that super round, firm butt. That sexy bubble looked just as smooth and pretty as Duchess had imagined as she stared at the white chiffon of her dress whooshing back and forth, from the gold belt cinching her waist to the tops of her thighs.

Duchess balled her fists to keep from reaching out and cupping her hands around Honey's ass in front of all these girls, especially Milan, whose stare was so angry she could start a fire with one glance.

Suddenly, Duchess wondered if what she did in Babylon would stay in Babylon. She wasn't going to stay here forever, so what if one day, when she had become a successful business woman, her pussy-slurping activities with Honey came back to haunt her? If former presidents could confess that they had experimented with weed, then certainly she could say she had fully explored her sexuality. But she'd twist it around if she were ever called on it, saying her critics wished they could have watched her, or anything else that went on at Babylon.

Right now she had no choice but to stay in this place of wild, sexy abandon, but when the time was right for her to go back out into the world as Victoria Winston, go to college, start her own business, she would make sure her activities inside this nondescript building in the hood never caught up with her. Duke would teach her how to cover her tracks.

Daddy used to always say, "Never do anything you don't want to see in the newspaper, on TV or over the Internet." She'd have to be extra careful, not let her lust overrule her mind. Who knew? Maybe Milan had a camera phone that could download a picture of Duchess and shoot it all over the world saying, "Here's Victoria Winston! I found her, butt-ass naked, dancin' like a stripper! Eating pussy too!"

But if Duke had so much power and Milan was involved in the mysterious work he did here, she wouldn't want to cross him. Plus, she'd be busting on herself. Still, that didn't mean Duchess wanted to give that hater any ammunition, especially while she wrestled with the meaning of her life over the past forty-eight hours.

Am I in love with Duke? Is it love or lust or both.? How do I feel different? Black, white, both? Am I a dyke? Do other girls feel like this when they look at other females? Touch them? Kiss them?

Dance lessons, she could do without. If Duke thought she was going to shake what her momma gave her like those video chicks, he was the one who was clueless. Why was he so adamant about her getting this tutorial from the B'Amazons?

"Don't just stand there droolin'," Lee Lee snapped. "Let's work."

Victoria clutched the thong and headed into the locker room.

"Where you goin'?" India teased. "We gon' see it all anyway."

A minute later, Victoria's cheeks burned with embarrassment as she watched herself strut across the gym in a red thong. Her super-long legs looked toned and lean, as did her stomach and butt in the mirror. Her nipples were like two copper pennies showing through her tight white jog bra.

"I see why they call it a ponytail," Honey said, running her hands over Duchess' hair. Honey's body heat made Duchess relax, but Milan's angry stare in the mirror made her step out of Honey's reach. If Honey was her assistant and Milan saw their relationship was both business and pleasure, then she could poison that.

"Honey, I really don't feel like dancing."

"Do it for Duke. He'll love it, sweetie."

Lee Lee blasted the music, a hard-driving bass beat with girls singing nasty lyrics.

The rhythm made Duchess want to dance and have fun, but the way Milan's eyes were boring a hole through her backside chilled any notion of enjoyment. If those big men weren't standing on each side of Milan, what would she be doing?

"Line up, hold the bar," Lee Lee commanded. "Madame Duchess, just do what we do."

The girls gripped the bar. With legs straight, they tiptoed a little, bent at the waist, and bounced their butts.

Victoria was frozen, standing up straight.

No way.

Next to her, Honey's butt was going up and down beautifully. When she bent, her butt cheeks parted, revealing the black thong that arched up over her cheeks and around her hips.

"Just try it, sweetie," Honey whispered as she grasped Duchess' waist and bent her over. She put a hand on each hip and lifted them, helping them roll. Like fucking air.

"Puuurrrrrrfect." Honey smiled, resuming her own sensuous movement.

Lee Lee shouted, "Now roll it!"

Honey bent down a little, stuck her butt way out, then rolled it up. Duchess was sure her own wet pussy would soak right through the thong as she watched Honey. Lust was melting her inhibitions, and the movements felt fun and natural.

Forget Milan. I'm gonna dance to my heart's content.

Duchess felt sorry for her. Milan looked so unhappy. Had Duke made her crazy or had she started off that way? Would Duke someday put Duchess down for the next horny new toy and leave her bitter and sad-looking, just like Milan?

I can't worry about all this right now. Because this new freedom and excitement were delicious. People in her town would be appalled to see girls dancing like this, but it felt so good, especially when she suddenly felt hands on her ass. Her eyes bulged. "What—"

"Stick your ass way out," Lee Lee ordered. She was cupping her ass, pulling it up. Her fingertips were dangerously close to Duchess' wet, throbbing pussy. "Rrrrrooolll it, girl. Think of your hips as havin' wheels inside. Smooth, rolling motion."

Duchess did it.

"There you go. Beautiful, girl. Make my cunt drip."

Duchess couldn't wait until this was over so she could go up to the penthouse with Duke and make love again. Just one touch, she was sure she'd be having a damn sexual seizure all over the place. Away from any mean stares or curious eyes.

"You got it, sweetie!" Honey exclaimed, staring back to watch her own cheeks rise and roll. "Work that pretty ass."

A couple more demonstrations and Duchess was actually joining them to do a group dance. They formed a circle facing each other, sticking their butts out, shimmying from shoulders to hips, and swinging their hair. Never had she felt such wild, wonderful abandon. The loud, pulsating music, her body totally exposed in a thong, and the incredible beauty of these women.

"Simulate!" Lee Lee shouted.

"Simulate what?" Duchess asked Honey.

"I wanna show, not tell," Honey whispered. She took Duchess' shoulders, danced with her, pressed her forehead to hers, and then eased her to the floor.

Oh, hell no. This is about to become way too much of a public display of nasty-girl freak show.

Duchess stood up. "I gotta go," she said, glancing toward the door.

I am not having sex with a girl in front of all these people.
Especially that most hostile witness, Milan.

"Relax," Honey said. "I know what you thinkin', but Duke is not about to let that connivin' bitch touch you." Honey ran her hands down her own body. "Plus you know I'll take good care of you."

Duchess' pussy throbbed. The way Honey's crotch was filling out that thong, her nipples were poking through her top, and her lips were all shiny and parted, Duchess couldn't wait to get another taste of her.

Duchess balanced back on her elbows, her palms on the floor beside her body stretched out flat. Honey hovered over her, kneeling with each leg straddling Duchess' hips. Her thong was wet, throbbing with plump female filling that made Celeste drip.

The soft, round flesh of Honey's boobs, with that flawless creamy skin. Her nipples were two hard points just inches from Duchess' face. She was panting, her head spinning at the sensory shock and excitement of this experience. She was even more excited this time.

"Mmmm," she moaned, letting the opium of lust melt away all worry. She felt absolutely euphoric right now. All her fears and anxieties were gone.

Honey bent down, rubbing her nose over Duchess' nipple.

Then she bit it, gently. Duchess tossed back her head, feeling her hair dance over the backs of her hands. Honey licked her neck; rubbed their boobs together. Tingles shot through her.

Then Honey rose up, cupped her boobs, and pulled down the tank top, revealing those succulent brown cones. She stuck out her tongue, raised them up to her mouth, and licked both at once.

"Wanna taste some more?" she whispered.

Duchess nodded seconds before a soft, sweet nipple that smelled like sugar and tasted even more so poked through her lips. She sucked softly.

Honey pulled her nipples out, tracing the outer edge of Victoria's mouth with it. Then Honey rubbed her face in Duchess' chest. She wanted to scream. This was the first woman who had ever touched her nipples. It felt so soft, so beautiful. Her face was all over Duchess' stomach, and, pushing her back, she rubbed her face in her crotch.

Honey's nose rubbed against Duchess' clit.

"Aaahhh," she moaned. "I looooove this."

Honey spread her legs, yanked the thong up so that it went between her butt cheeks and was tight against her swollen pussy.

She thrust it up into Duchess' face several times. The sweet-salty scent made Duchess pant. She wanted to bite at that pussy.

"Wanna see it again?" Honey purred. "I know you like it. You wanna suck on it."

Duchess nodded with eyes at half mast. Honey pulled the thin strip of fabric away from her pussy.

"Yes, just as pretty as before." Honey raised it to Duchess' face then pulled away.

Every cell in her body was on fire. All she wanted to do was put her mouth on that pussy. What did this mean for the mix-race woman power? Did it come out doubly strong when pressed with another woman-power source?

"Kiss my pussy," Honey whispered as she raised it up to her face. Duchess' parted lips pressed into the fat flesh. It tasted sweet, like orange juice. She opened her jaws wide, slurped all over it.

Honey moaned but then pulled away, aiming her swollen clit straight toward Duchess' wet pussy.

Chapter 43

Near the door, about twenty feet from Victoria and Honey, Milan was lying on her back, on a floor mat. She had a mouth full of Lee Lee's pussy meat. The head female B'Amazon soldier was straddling Milan's face, grinding her pussy around her mouth.

"That bitch is getting turned out," Milan said as she drilled her fingers up into Lee Lee's hole and licked at the silver ball piercing her clit. "But now we know she's got a big weakness. She likes Honey."

Lee Lee moaned. "We all love Honey."

"I love money more," Milan said, reaching down to rub her own hungry, aching stuff. Finally, the nausea had subsided, but her horniness had not. "I love Duke, too, and that white bitch is not about to take what's mine. This whole supervision thing is only temporary, until Duke sees the error of his ways and puts me in my proper place."

"Shut up and eat my pussy," Lee Lee ordered.

"You know better 'n anybody," Milan said. "Duke and I have been together since we were in diapers. He and Babylon are mine."

"You a crazy bitch."

"A damn good crazy bitch. And I am going to do whatever I have to do to keep what's already mine and that's Duke and Babylon." Lee Lee pressed her knees into Milan's ears. "I'll squeeze if you don't shut up and lick, bitch."

Milan laughed. Lee Lee loosened her knees.

"That's right. Suck it like that. The secret walls o' my pussy are the only place you need to talk like that. If Duke hears that shit, you're gonna have a boot in that pretty ass o' yours before it lands on the street. Without your kids."

"Beamer and I have a plan, but Duke can't know," Milan said, using her fingers to rub her own clit. "You'll be addressing me as Duchess in a minute."

"Zip it, girl. I do not want to be an accessory to the suicidal shit you rattlin' off into my pussy. Then again, you wouldn't be under supervision if you was actin' right. You already in trouble." Lee Lee muzzled Milan with her pussy by grinding hard. Trembling, the sexercise coach tossed her head back, moaned, and opened her eyes.

"Duke!"

Milan's teeth clamped around Lee Lee's clit. Lee Lee shot up. "Stupid bitch! Don't bite my meat like you a pit bull!"

Milan went numb. She just signed her death warrant in pussy juice. A rigor mortis stiffness froze her every cell.

Duke would understand, pregnancy makes my imagination go wild. He'll remember the crazy stuff I did during my last two pregnancies, and he'll laugh, this off too. Besides, how could he have heard me talking over that loud music?

"Duke, baby," Milan called up, her lips wet with hoochie cream. "Finally we get to talk."

He stared down with a stiff face, the same way he stared down a gangsta or 5-0 or anybody he didn't trust. But now, his eyes were laughing. At her. She could almost hear him thinking, *You stupid-ass skank ho, too ill in the head to keep a scheme quiet.*

"Duke, you caught me under the influence of pussy. You know I lose my mind when I put my face up in it. I'm jus' dreamin'."

Not a flicker of response showed in his eyes. She pressed a hand to her stomach to squeeze down a sudden heave.

No, I will not vomit here at Duke's feet.

"Duke," she said with a nervous laugh. Her voice sounded high-pitched and weak.

He raised his eyes as if she suddenly turned invisible. He stroked his dick through his jeans and looked across the room at Honey and that girl.

Chapter 44

Duke stepped away from Milan then stood over Duchess and her new favorite playmate. Chanel and India were playing Twister right beside them.

He stroked Timbo with lightning speed. His long fingers met the tip of his thumb to form a tube that moved up and down, up and down his legendary dick that he couldn't wait to slide up under the creamy ass of his Duchess. He blew hot air through his almost-smiling lips. *Look at my baby girl! Gettin' to know her inner freak!*

That thong up her crack was spreading each round cheek.

He couldn't wait to take one in each hand and squeeze while he plunged this tree trunk up into that gushing canal. Right now, though, it looked like Honey was getting it in shape and keeping it warm.

Since she loved his dick, she was obviously becoming a fiend for pussy too.

My baby girl will lose her pretty little mind up in that pussy with dick at the same time.

He jacked his dick, watching Honey and Duchess intertwine their pretty legs. Chanel sashayed toward him in a black thong and bare titties. She pressed her back to him, rubbed the tip of his dick against her juicy ass then bent over.

This some o' the sexiest shit I ev'a seen in my life. It was just a preview of a lifetime of new freaky-ass stuff every day. *Duchess gon' be through when she learn all the ways o' this world.*

She would be through in a good way, unlike the bitch across the room, laying there like the corpse that she already was in her heart. Empty. Cold.

Milan was an evil back-stabber. Just like Brutus did Julius Caesar. He could put her out right now. But no, it wasn't like he trusted her before. She was always scheming. Now he just caught her in the act, so he had a plan to make her work even harder for him. She'd be so scared, she'd bend over and eat her own pussy if he told her to.

Right now, her punishment would be the whack thoughts she was having, worried about what Duke was going to do or not do. He could put her out like Sunnie, or keep her here, or transfer her to another place to work. Send her ass off to work for Moreno.

Damn, look how Honey an' Duchess kissin'. Her ponytail was down her back, her legs were spread, and that ass was grinding into the red mat. While that was going on, India and Chanel were grinding against him. They were both bent over in front of him, offering some double Dutch muffs. He shoved Timbo straight into two hot pussies he had been neglecting ever since he first saw Duchess on TV. He blasted two strokes up under India's beautiful blue-black booty then he plowed two strokes up under Chanel's gorgeous honey-colored ass.

"Ohhhhh, shit!" Chanel rolled her booty back, 'round and 'round to the beat of that nasty-ass music.

"Nothin' like Duke dick . . ." India moaned.

Duke put his hands on his hips, like he was bucking on a bull in a rodeo, loving his ride and loving the view of the other one on the floor. Honey was showing his Duchess the many dimensions of life at Babylon.

"Oh, fuck!" Duke groaned. Delicious waves of hot shivers washed through him. He felt like he could fuck all night.

Duchess mine. All this pussy mine. Babylon mine.

He pulled out, spraying his nut like a fountain all over Duchess and Honey, like raindrops on the sexy seeds he was planting to grow the juiciest fruit ever.

Chapter 45

Duchess hardly noticed Duke standing there because her spirit was dancing around the tangle of limbs that was herself and Honey. This was woman-power at its best.

The ultimate power source. If Celeste already had the power, then pressing her into another hot, hungry hooch, especially one as beautiful and clean as Honey's, could only make her stronger. If there were a fountain of youth, this was the fountain of woman-power. Add the extra mix-race potency that her grandmother spoke of, and Duchess would get anything she ever desired.

Right now, cumming with this beautiful nymph was all she wanted. She tilted her head back and cast a mellow smile up at Duke. He probably knew this would happen, and he no doubt would want to watch. It seemed like everything Duke did was strategized then orchestrated exactly to his vision.

"Make our bodies like an X," Honey whispered, weaving one thigh under Duchess' and the other thigh over hers.

If a mouth on her pussy was pleasure paradise, then this was hedonistic heaven. The only thing better was Duke's big, black dick pounding up into her hot, wet pussy. And she would get that as the grand finale.

"How can this be real?" Duchess moaned. "Oooohhhh, Honey, what are you doing to me?"

"Shhh." Honey smiled, grinding so that every circular motion of her hips sent a shiver through Duchess. "It's a secret."

Duchess tossed back her head, looked up at Duke. He smiled back down on her with love and lust. But he was turned slightly, and his whole body was moving, like he was fucking! *He's giving my dick to that girl who looks like Honey. And India. At the same time!*

Duchess couldn't believe her eyes. Duke was fucking two girls right in front of her! Was he serious? Delicious sensations were still radiating between her legs, but her body froze.

"Hey, sweetie," Honey whispered. "It's okay. She's my sister. And India's cool."

Duchess' eyes felt big as baseballs as she stared up at Duke pounding those chicks with great pleasure on his face.

If he's fuckin' two right in front of me, what does he do when I'm not looking?

And Honey thought this was okay since it was a family affair? For a split-second, Duke looked so sexy, she actually felt a burst of pride. It made her pussy even wetter.

That fine-ass man who can fuck two like a pro is all mine, as much as I want, anytime, in our beautiful Egyptian palace bed upstairs.

But the fact that they didn't talk about this first, or any effort she made to talk about sex with other people was dissed with non-answers, made Duchess sting with betrayal. If this is an open relationship, let's make that verbal agreement. Duke disappeared behind her closed eyelids.

"Oh, Honey, you do that so good," Duchess whispered, mimicking Honey's motions to intensify the pleasure.

"X marks the spot," Honey said playfully.

The feeling was unbelievable, like a hot mash of velvet-soft girl stuff. Wet pussy against lips, clit, juice. Steaming. Building the starburst into what would be the most psychedelic, ridiculously intense orgasm.

For now, she would let Duke go on with his wild cowboy on the range self, acting like he could hop on and ride any female in his herd of hotties. He said they were partners, so this cowgirl was definitely going to sample a wide range of black angus of her own, after she savored this sweet, honey-covered appetizer.

Honey's lips were pouting as she stared seductively at Duchess and stuck out her tongue to lick the tips of her beautiful nipples.

Duchess was loving the visual image of that big, juicy pussy that was in her face, now pressing against Celeste, making her feel absolute euphoria.

"Oh, yeaaaahhh," Duchess cried as violent shivers wracked her body. Honey did the same. Together they trembled, moaned, and gasped.

Duchess shivered once again, but this time with fear. Celeste was screaming. She would never be the same. Now she would be cursed to constantly crave dick and pussy. All day, all night. Always.

I'm about to become a sex addict, nymphomaniac. I just bit into the Mrs. Fields brownie on the diet of life. I cannot, and will not, resist.

Chapter 46

Knight had no trouble slipping into Babylon unnoticed, thanks to all the keys he kept stashed at Momma's house, and the secret tunnels and staircases that he and Prince had built into the basement and upper walls of Babylon.

Knight's shoulders brushed the smooth cement walls of the tunnel. Their huge flashlights illuminated Big Moe's pear-shaped nose and small eyes set in a ruddy brown face framed by a black skullcap.

"I'm cool from here," Knight whispered as he unlocked the gate leading up to the building. "I'll be back here to get you at midnight."

"Ya mon," Big Moe said with his gentle Jamaican accent. His enormous hand extended another flashlight. "Take dis in case de udda one go out."

Knight took it. The turning motion in his full stomach made him smile. "I feel it is settin' in. Full stomach, fresh air, and I'm ready for a nap. All I need is some pussy."

Moe flashed bright, white, jagged teeth. "Ya mon, get some pussy an' you'll be out like a light."

Knight turned off his flashlight. The little silver coil inside burned red for a moment then went entirely dark. The light came back on. "Den, you wake stronga dan ev'a!"

"That's how I view my whole time away," Knight said, stepping up into the narrow stone staircase. His flashlight sliced golden beams through the thick blackness. Despite the adrenaline pumping through him, he yawned. All that food at Momma's was hardly making him light on his feet to stealthily navigate the bowels of Babylon.

As he ascended, he burped, loving the sensation of his stomach full of Momma's roast beef, macaroni and cheese, and greens. His mouth still tasted sweet from that big bowl of peach cobbler he had devoured. It was the best food he'd had in two and a half years. And she, fuming over Duke's new half-white, high profile girlfriend, promised to let him surprise Duke in a way that would, as Momma said, "Knock some big brotha sense into that boy's head."

The stairwell went on and on, up and up. Even Duke didn't know about the maze of narrow staircases throughout this massive, ten-story building, or the underground tunnels that connected to a house Knight owned around the block.

He and Prince had built these secret tunnels and stairwells for two reasons: to protect in case of outside turbulence, and to safeguard control of Babylon in case of internal misman-agement and out-of-control power trips, as evidenced, lately, by Li'l Tut.

First, he had evicted Sunnie and Big Moe. Then there was all that drama with Milan and Beamer. Now he was making Babylon sanctuary for a fine-as-she-can-be fugitive from the feds.

Both Prince and Knight knew that one day, if they had to go away for a while, they'd eventually come back and pull in the reins on Li'l Tut's buck wild ruling style. Li'l Tut sure tried to do it right, but his way simply lacked the maturity to run the empire that was the brainchild of his big brothers, and their domain.

And since Prince is only here in spirit, it's on me, Knight. Stepping back into my penthouse in the dark of night. Friday night, just in time to make my appearance at Li'l Tut's birth-day party an' let him start his twenty-first year as assistant to The Knight. I'm not going anyplace other then where I belong, inside what's mine.

Before Knight left the penthouse for jail, Duke had his own suite on the ninth floor, just like Knight did until Prince died.

Finally, Knight reached the waist-high door marked 10. It led into one of the enormous mummy cases flanking the dresser inside the penthouse master suite. Little did Duke know, the cases each had a false back that worked like a trap door. Knight would be able to press a latch and release the panel so he could step right into his bedroom.

But here in the stairwell, he heard voices. Male and female. Arguing. As he calmed his heavy breathing from climbing eleven flights of winding stairs, he listened.

"Oh please, Duke, please," said the female voice that sounded as rich and soft as butter melting in his ears. The sound of her words was so sensuous to Knight's woman starved senses, his pipe turned to lead instantly. His dick hadn't been this hard in years.

Talk to me like that and the world is yours, sweetheart.

Was that the girl from the news? Victoria Winston? Milan tried to talk white but didn't sound that authentic. This girl was the opposite; white trying to sound black, and succeeding.

"I haven't seen you all day, Duke. And it's your birthday!" Fabric rustled. Either somebody was getting undressed or lying across the sheets. "We didn't even make love this morning, you blew outta here so early."

"Baby girl, I'm savin' it for the party." A jostling lock noise preceded a deep hum. It sounded like the lowering of built-in, bulletproof shields that descended over the floor-to-ceiling windows to the terrace.

"Expecting ghetto ninjas to come droppin' in?" the girl asked with an attitudinal tone. "A helicopter drive-by? Duke, who could possibly get up on the tenth floor terrace?"

"A nigga or a bitch on a mission."

"And who might that be?"

"Always got extra security during a party. These niggas get wild an' e'rybody lookin' for a place to get they superfreak on."

Something thudded softly.

"If you need me," Duke said, "or the two Barriors, I got out by the elevator—"

"Duke, baby, I really don't like this Scarface-type atmosphere."

"You'd like the shit better than the morgue. Just push one number. Six."

More rustling fabric. A loud kiss.

"Stop, baby girl. I got serious bidness to han'le. That man eater between yo' pretty thighs can wait a hour or two."

Why did Li'l Tut have to ruin her romantic moment with his thug-talk? Couldn't he see or hear this girl was scared?

She needed some real love. Love and lust. That didn't mean she should have the status Duke thought he was giving her, but why would he bring that beautiful girl here and not take advantage of every moment to make love to her?

"I'm scared," she said." At least hold me for a minute."

The stereo came on playing that damn song that had been all over the radio about Babylon. It was another of Duke's bad decisions, drawing too much attention to what they did. She said louder, "Duke, please just hold me."

"Naw, baby girl." Heavy footsteps echoed. "I got too much shit to han'le befo' I can enjoy my own damn party."

"Duke, I know you're not about to leave me here naked, scared an' creamin' all over my damn thighs!"

"Ain't a safer place in the world than my bed," Duke said, "for all o' dat."

His footsteps echoed across the floor, followed by the sound of a closing door.

Knight eased into the mummy case. He moved the latch so he could step into the front and peer out through tiny holes in the ornate yoke around King Tut. That gave him a perfect view of the sheer gold panels around the bed. They were opened slightly, with a long, light caramel leg hanging to the floor, where a pretty foot with red toenails contrasted with the white marble.

On the bed lay a goddess. She was sitting so that she faced the end of the bed, her left foot curled up under her thigh as she rested back on her hands, staring up at the ceiling. A cascade of straight black hair fell to the golden bedspread, making a wild swirl behind the round curve of her bare ass.

Tears streamed down a face that was too young and innocent to have been talking like she just did. Her straight black bangs and her black eyeliner extended from the corners of her eyes. Gold cuffs hugged her upper arms. A gold belt with coins adorned her waist and soft, creamy belly. She was like a vision of Cleopatra.

Li'l Tut done gone all the way wild!

This was the ghetto version of the witness protection program: Take a rich, suburban, half-white girl who was hiding from the feds and turn her out. She was a woman who always got what she wanted from powerful men, especially when she got that look in her eye, like the one that girl had right now, staring at the flames crackling under the white marble mantle.

Li'l Tut is playin' with fire.

"Motherfucker!" She sobbed with a voice that was sultry but hard. "I hate it when he's stingy!" She snatched up a silver remote and aimed it toward the ceiling. The music cut off.

Silence. Except Knight could hear his own heavy breathing and the blood surging toward the hot pipe between his legs.

Damn, the sound of her voice only made his dick even harder. If there were any justice in two and a half years without any pussy, this would certainly be the reward; jamming this giant cock up between those pretty, creamy thighs, satisfying that girl's ache for love, and his own, all at once.

She belongs to me now, just like this penthouse and all of Babylon.

Knight's pipe was about to blow steam. He knew he was perfectly healthy, thanks to a battery of tests and a full check-up a week ago. Now his dick was hot, healthy, and horny as hell. It hadn't been laid inside a woman or anywhere else for what felt like an eternity, which he would make up for with that Cleopatra goddess right there. She could handle it.

There's a love-starved Cleopatra look-alike on my bed! I know I must've taken a tunnel straight to my Paradise Found. Elysium. Yeah, we need to rename this place The Elysium Suite.

She slid her other foot to the floor and stood, stretching her long, elegant arms over her head. Those copper penny nipples were hard and pointing straight at Knight. Her body was long and curvy, toned in horizontal lines along her abs, a perfect belly button, a little black puff of hair above juicy thighs, not too thick, not too thin.

"I'll show him!" she announced.

In a flash, she grabbed the pole at the end of the bed so that her ass was facing Knight, who was silent and concealed. He was worried that his dick would get so hard it would shoot through his khaki pants and bang on the inner wall of this mummy case.

He struggled to breathe slowly. *I'm gon' pass out.* Every drop of blood in his body was in his dick. Cleopatra's ass was flawless.

She grabbed the pole with both hands then raised her hips up to it.

She started to grind, ass popping in slow, sensuous circles against the bedpost. That gold coin belt around her waist jingled and shone with her perfect movement. Maybe her pussy was touching the post to stimulate her. But from this angle, Knight imagined that pole was his face, smeared and steamed with pussy.

A deep groan escaped his lips.

Cleopatra froze. She turned around with huge blue eyes glowing with fear. "If that motherfucker has someone watching me in here too—" She stomped toward the mummy case, titties bouncing, belt jangling, red lips set to a natural pucker like she was hungry, horny and mad all at once. She grabbed the side of the case. Rattled the latch.

"Doesn't Duke know this creepy shit is for dead people? I'm telling him we need to take the coffins out of the bedroom. Don't care how pretty they are."

She rattled harder, but it wouldn't budge because Knight locked it from the inside. She was close enough to smell. Her natural perfume was lemony-flowery. That made Knight's steampipe vibrate.

Damn, her pussy smelled like fresh picked flowers. Can a nigga cum from jus' smellin' good pussy after this long?

If his appetite for sex was anything like his hunger for food an hour ago at Momma's table, he was going to gorge on pussy until he passed out.

Cleopatra huffed away, her beautiful ass glowing like two full moons in the peachy bedroom light. She strode with that elegant walk into the bathroom. The shower hissed against the stone floor then sounded softer as the hot water streamed against her body.

Knight reached into his pocket for the tiny key that would unlock the mummy case door.

So I can step back into what's mine and take it.

Chapter 47

If this run-away train of thoughts went any faster, it would crash and burn with Duke in the furnace. That was what it felt like right now in HQ, as every motherfucker in the house came at him with a crisis. All while his twenty-first birthday party was rockin' Babylon like never before.

Sitting behind the desk, he wanted to wave a magic wand and make all the problems disappear. Make all these fifteen ma'fuckas in his office walk out, problem stamped SOLVED. Then he'd wave the wand again and make Milan and Knight appear from wherever they were hiding inside this fortress. Were they trying to double team The Duke?

He didn't want to believe that Knight was there with an overthrow scheme. With Beamer acting crazy with Milan, and dudes who was tight under Prince and Knight showing signs of trickery, he didn't trust anybody. Dudes who had more juice under his older brothers probably wanted Knight back in charge so they could rise from the lower spots where Duke had put them.

Now Duke had an APB out amongst his trusted Barriors. Any sign of trouble, the battle would be on. Brother or not, he shouldn't be trying to stage a coup during Duke's birthday party at the Babylon that he ruled.

I ain't got time for all this shit. I gotta go back upstairs an' give my baby girl what she need. Can't stand the look in her eye when I blew outta there.

But he had to take care of everything now, or else there wouldn't be a Babylon for The Duke to have a Duchess in. *I don't need all this shit happenin' right now, 'specially if Knight really out early.*

Duke's heart banged in his chest. His whole body was shaking. It couldn't be a good sign if Knight were free and trying to creep back into Babylon. Ain't no beef or was there? Deep down, Duke already knew what would be going down tonight. His birthday, his party, his girl, his people, and his big brother trying to usurp the power.

Hell naw. I'm runnin' this empire smoov as hell. An' I'll keep running it, starting right now, by replacing all these knucklehead ma'fuckas who let these problems pop in the wrong place at the wrong time.

One of the Hulk-ass bodyguards who was watching Milan said, "It don't make no sense, see what I'm sayin', dat she could jus' be gone. We was like, dang, how she get out?" Scheme shined in this stupid-ass ma'fucka's eyes.

Duke rose from his golden throne. He stepped from behind the big glass desk. His black cowboy boots pounded the white marble as he approached Tweedle Dee and Tweedle Dum.

"I told both you ma'fuckas. Do not let Milan suck yo' dick. Weak-ass punks." He pointed to the door. "Go find her! Inside, outside, just find the bitch an' bring her to me."

"Yes, Massa Duke," they said then ran out.

No way could she hide for long in this high-tech temple and not show up on the security cameras.

Next, a Barrior lieutenant, wearing brown from head to toe, approached. "We checked all the security camera video. Nothing shows that Milan has left the building, but we don't have any video so far of where she is. But we did catch this."

The Barrior held up a wireless video monitor the size of a shoebox. It showed two men, one dark and bald, the other in a black skullcap, holding flashlights.

"It's dark," the Barrior said, "but that looks like Big Moe and Knight down in the tunnels. You recall the hidden security cameras we put in last year. Knight wouldn't know."

"Knight know e'rythang." *And I'm supposed to know more.*

A lot of punks were about to get jacked for letting this happen. Duke's mind ticked down a list of all the locked-up motherfuckers on his payroll who were about to get cut off.

Nobody took his money without providing a service in return. Even if it was about blood. Family blood.

The Barrior said, "You know this main tunnel leads to the garage, and we have video of Knight up to the door. But he vanishes after that. Nothing."

Duke asked, "You seen him anyplace else? The garage, the ninth floor apartments, the penthouse?"

"No, Massa Duke."

"No my ass! E'ry hall, e'ry staircase, e'ry elevator got a camera!" Duke shouted. His enraged voice echoed through the marble-floored office. He felt like steam was shooting from his ears. A high pitched panic was distorting his voice so tough, it sounded like train wheels screeching against a metal track.

"What the fuck?" Duke shouted. "How you gon' miss a six foot ma'fucka wit' a big, black bald head an' shoulders as wide as fuckin' Mr. Universe?"

Everybody in the office froze, turned pale, and made their eyes big.

"Go find Knight Johnson if it kill e'ry one o' y'all ma'fuckas!"

The doors at the front of the office opened. Beamer ran in, all of his redbone braids loose and bouncing over the shoulders of his white Detroit Lions jersey. He pulled up his sagging jeans.

"Massa Duke, two things," he said, out of breath. "First, Barriors got these two black dudes. FBI tryin' to crash yo' party."

"Hell naw."

"They got bogus VIP passes from the band. No warrant, no ID, but they fed, fo' sho'."

Duke's heart pounded so hard, it sounded like flames were hissing inside his ears. "Tell the lawyer to stop havin' his dick sucked up in the VIP suite. Send him down to talk to the young men. Tell 'em we'll prosecute they asses for trespassing if they don't get the fuck up outta my buildin' in a Motor City minute."

Beamer nodded. At least his thinking cap was on snug too.

"What's the second thing?" Duke asked.

"A TV crew," Beamer said. "Downstairs. Talkin' about somebody in the hood said Victoria Winston livin' here. No joke."

"Hell naw. That shit got Milan name all over it." Milan would kill Duchess with her bare hands if she had the chance. *Probably kill me too.* Duke glanced at the phone on his belt that he told Duchess to dial if she needed anything. "Hold up." He dialed. It rang. And rang. And rang. He tried again.

"Hello?" Attitude shot through the phone.

"Baby girl, just checkin' on ya."

"I'm taking a shower."

"Pick up quicker when I call."

"And call you Massa Duke?" The sass in her voice made him almost smile, but he didn't because all these leery-eyed motherfuckers were watching him, waiting for directions to solve their respective bullshit.

"Holla." Duke hung up then turned to Beamer. "Where the media at now?"

"It's a black chick reporter an' a camera dude." Beamer talked fast. "The Barriors caught 'em tryin' to sneak in wit' all the niggas goin' to the party. So now the Channel Six jokers is on the sidewalk out front."

Duke paced the white marble floor. "Where they gon' be videotapin'? All the limos an' cars? They can hear the music. An' they gon' be sniffin' around. Fuck!" *If Knight were in the house and he saw media here, he'd have a fit!*

"Don't no neighbors complain about the traffic an' loud noise, 'cause they know Barriors be patrollin' the streets, the schools, the stores, makin' e'rybody feel safe. So, no matter what else go on, don't nobody snitch on Babylon."

"That's a lie," Duke said. "If you talkin' to Milan, which I know you ain't, tell the bitch that if she called the media on my ass, then she will be dog meat for Pound to come collect for the midnight feedin'."

Beamer's eyes got as big as those chocolate truffles he was always eating.

"But first," Duke said, "call Pound Dog cousin, Mike, the spokesman. Tell him to talk to the media, say Miss Green got a postcard from Victoria in Barbados."

Beamer scrunched his face. "They talkin' about customs ain't got no record of her leavin' Miami."

"Then Mike gon' tell 'em she got a lotta connections wit' folk in Florida who got yachts, wit' lots a places to hide a pretty young girl."

Knight. Milan. The feds. The media.

I am the one under siege ma'fucka. But I'm gon' beat 'em all down. The Duke rule.

Chapter 48

Duchess stared into space as the hot water beat down on her bare back. It was so relaxing after a week of intensive transformation and almost constant sex. She was ready to sleep another two days straight. Her mind, body and spirit were aching with fatigue, but Celeste was roarin' to go.

Am I addicted? It seems the more I get, the more I want. And why is Duke trying to ration his dick? Didn't he know he'd have to finish what he started? I warned him.

His attitude did not make her want to celebrate his birthday party tonight. Was he out getting so much birthday booty and blow jobs from all his females that he didn't have the time or energy for Duchess?

"That is totally unacceptable," she snapped into the steam.

And what about Milan? What in the world did he have to do with her right now?

Duchess turned off the water. She hadn't even washed or shampooed her wet hair. She was too tired.

I'm gonna get in bed, make myself cum, and take a nap until Duke gets back to dress for the party. Their matching black leather jeans and cream tops were all ready. *I have to cum by myself for the first time since Sunday at the restaurant.* "Duke," she said. The sight of him and the surprise of his return made her heart pound with excitement. And it made her pussy hot and wet, instantly. "He is so beautiful," she whispered.

Through the gold sheer around the bed, he reminded her of an enormous Greek god, lying so that the luscious back of his bald head and all the rippling muscles down his back were facing her. The gold blanket was folded under his huge, muscular right arm and hand, which rested on the bulge that was his right leg, bent slightly at the knee on top of his other leg.

Duchess stuck her fingertips between the gold panels. The back of her hand parted the wispy fabric. She put one knee on the bed.

In the dim light, he looked darker. And bigger. He must've had a mega workout down in the gym today. She stared in awe at the little indentions of muscle around his deltoids, his triceps, and biceps and forearms, and those big, beautiful hands. The valley of muscle up his spine was deep and marked by muscle around the vertebrae. His back muscles rose up in graceful curves that made her mouth water. Ripples of strength marked his shoulder blades.

He was nothing short of a masterpiece. His smooth head was so big and round and shiny, flanked by perfect ears; he must've taken his earrings out. And that thick neck, so smooth. *I never noticed that scar before.* She felt a scar toward the back of his neck. As many times as she'd sucked on Duke's neck and touched him there and slept holding onto him from the back, why hadn't she noticed that?

Because I was delirious from dick.

She smiled because she was about to get some more right now. Celeste was screaming for all that Timbo had to offer, and more.

I can climb on, ride to my heart's content then take a nap, and he'll never even know.

Duchess walked quietly to the other side of the bed. She slipped through the gold panels. How could a man be so breathtaking? His face looked like a statue of a black god.

He must have spent time in the sun today, because he looked darker and luscious. Duchess pressed her lips to his forehead, loving the sensation of his smooth, hot skin under the fleshy spread of her lips. He showed no reaction except slow and steady breathing, hard breathing, like he was in a deep sleep.

Slowly, Duchess slid head first under the gold blankets. It was dark, and that intoxicating aroma of man was strong as hell.

She inhaled deeply, holding it in. "Mmmmmm," she moaned.

I need to bottle this stuff so I can smell it all day long. Essence of Duke.

Victoria pressed forward in the darkness with her mouth open until her lips landed at the head of his dick. She kissed it, loving it for the pleasure she knew she was about to take from it. She wrapped her lips around it. He didn't move. She opened wide, sucked the whole thing in until it banged the back of her throat.

He flinched a little, let out a slow groan.

This sensation of a hot marble dicksicle with that delicious aroma made her pussy drip. Her nipples were rock-hard, rubbing against the tops of his legs. *I am so wet right now.* The tops of Duchess' thighs felt steamy and sticky. All she had to do was push his leg with her left hand.

He'd roll onto his back, she could climb on, and in a flash, he rose. He was an enormous shadow of man, quick as lightning, with the grace and stealth of Duke's best panther walk. Giant hands damped her waist. Lifting her up, he rolled onto his back. His arms raised her like they were the front scooping part of a bulldozer, effortlessly, higher and higher.

She gazed down, half-smirkng at the enchanted genie eyes staring back up at her with the hungriest, sexiest, most powerful look she had ever seen in Duke's eyes. Suddenly his eyes radiated a new maturity, a new intelligence.

Maybe he really was working today and accomplished something important.

I shouldn't have been so hard on him.

He was still staring up at her like she was the most precious creature on the planet that he would always love and cherish. He held her up for a long time, as if examining her for the first time.

"Tinkerbell in the hood!" She giggled, shaking her head so that the ends of her hair tickled his right nipple. It pointed up hard at her. She stared into his eyes. Her voice got deep and sultry. "An' I'm gonna sprinkle my pixie dust, my pussy dust, all . . . ova . . . you!"

Like a laser-quick robotic arm on a machine that attached parts, he pulled her forward.

"I'm flying," she cooed.

He held her in that soaring bird position, with her hips an arm's length above his face. Those strong arms yanked her down. She spread her legs, which made a "V" extending out from his head. Her heels landed softly on the fluffy gold pillows.

And he breathed fire air onto her pussy.

"Oooohhh," she moaned.

He inhaled loudly, even louder than she breathed him under the blankets. The tip of his tongue made an "X" across her pussy.

"Yay-yaaaahhh," she moaned as he swirled his tongue around her clit.

"Mine," he groaned in a way that was deep and potent.

The depth of passion and protection in his voice felt so strong and overwhelming, it sparked tears in her eyes. He held her up so that they were face to face, just inches apart. She squeezed the tears to see him more clearly.

Whoosh!

His arms lowered her at turbo-speed.

Duchess screamed. She shivered violently.

I'm cumming at first stroke.

Nipples pinching. Skin quivering. Muscles trembling. And her pussy was one big convulsion. Celeste was pulsating at triple speed, as if her insides were spastic ripples of wet velvet, erotic muscle spasms set off by superhuman sex.

This is the best.

She wanted to scream that she'd bow at his feet forever if he gave her this. What was it? It was not normal. Definitely not just sex. Or making love. This was some abnormal, freaky-ass, supernatural love. Maybe all that Ancient Egyptian stuff they had around here was giving them extra sex powers.

Duchess froze. She opened her eyes without focusing.

This the power. My power. My mix-race woman power.

When blended with true Mandingo warrior sex-power of equal magnitude, it created cataclysmic forces that could move the world.

"With talent comes great responsibility to use it in a way that helps people," Daddy used to say.

"But how?" Victoria used to ask all the time. "What's my talent and what should I do with it?"

"When you find your calling," he said, "you'll just know."

Now, Duchess smiled.

Now I know. I want everybody to let go of their sexual inhibitions and enjoy the most spectacular gift we can share with another person: an orgasm. Yeah, that's my responsibility to help people. And I'm in just the right place to share my passion and my purpose with the world.

Chapter 49

Duchess felt wobbly as she and Duke stepped into the elevator to go down to the party. The music in the garage was so loud, even from here on the tenth floor the relentless bass beat was actually vibrating the elevator. It was making it even harder to walk on legs still tremoring from the meteor that had just shot up into her pussy and sprayed intergalactic stardust so thick she couldn't see straight.

"You obviously don't know your power," she snapped at Duke, whose eyes were as tense as his face. "You should be smilin' not stressin'. It's your birthday."

They were both facing the mirrored wall inside the elevator.

Dressed alike in snug, black leather jeans, black leather boots, and cream tops, Duke towered beside her. His beautiful, dark chocolate face, neck and bald head were clean-shaven and radiant. He had put his little silver hoop earrings back into his ears.

"I gotta look gangsta cool at the party." His tone was flat.

His eyes focused on the piece of lint he was plucking from his chest.

"I loooove the way we look together," Duchess said, extending her left hand to his crotch to squeeze. Her fingers were trembling, just like every other muscle in her body. Even her lips felt like she was shivering in the cold, but her soul was smouldering in heat.

So, why wasn't his? There was no way in hell he could be nonchalant about the cosmic sextravaganza that just exploded in their bed. She pulled her hand from his nonresponsive crotch.

"Duke, why you stressin' on your day? I'm the one who should be scared, the way you were battenin' down the hatches, calling to check on me, putting bodyguards—" She crossed her arms.

Her eyelids felt heavy. She let them fall as a fresh quiver shot through her body. It happened every time she thought of that first dick-stroke. Why was this time different? Did he take some kind of dick-growing endurance drug? He didn't need it.

"Duke, tell me you don't use drugs."

"You the one who look drunk," he shot back, turning to face her. "An' we ain't even at the party yet."

"I'm tipsy on Timbo," she whispered, giggling.

"Baby girl, you trippin'." His jaw muscles flexed as he stared down hard at her. He was looking at an entirely different person than the scared girl he had plucked out of urban hell and delivered into this twenty-four-hour-a-day temptation.

"Duke, you need to chill an' enjoy."

"My gangsta chill for my public, an' the private Romeo chill I show you, they two different looks."

She cut her eyes back at him. "Duke, you got more than a look goin' on. It's a vibe. An' it ain't pretty, baby."

He glanced down at the phones on his belt, flashing red, flashing blue.

And she looked past him at her reflection because that black sounding voice that just came out of her mouth sounded like someone else.

Is this me? Who is me?

Staring at herself, she saw the same eyes she arrived with, but they were now painted with thick black liner like Cleopatra.

She saw the same face, but bronze now, thanks to the tanning booth. Same hair, but with straight bangs on her forehead. Same necklace, but with gold serpent bracelets around the upper arms. Same voice with a new cadence. Same body, same lust, but now addicted to ghetto-licious black dick and pussy. Same mind?

Celeste was laughing, cackling, roaring with laughter. That big black dick got so high up in your brain, it made it as mushy, as wet and as insatiable as your pussy. You just wanna get fucked!

"Hell no!" Duchess said aloud.

Duke, who was on the phone speaking in code as usual, looking wide eyed with stress, made a "ssshhh" gesture with his index fingertip to his sucka lips.

She turned around, pressed her ass into Duke's hard thighs, her back into his chest. Her stiletto-heeled boots stood between his black cowboy boots. She pressed his open palm to the front of her leg. She nuzzled the back of her head into the body-fitting long-sleeved shirt over his chest, inhaled the sexy cloud of his Black Cashmere cologne mixed with her Cashmere Mist perfume.

He raised the bottom of the phone and said, "Yo' I'ma freak comin' out in full effect." His free hand rose up to grip her tits, which were raised in a chiffon camisole with flowy fabric that danced over the top of her pants. Like a reflex, she arched her ass harder into him, loving the hard outline of that big, hot tree trunk in his pants.

"When my tongue hit that pussy, you knew it ain't no turnin' back. That sayin', 'once you go black, you never go back,' got a whole new meanin' fo' yo' sexy ass."

"Yeah," he said into the phone then flipped it down, clipped it back to his belt. "Baby girl, it's gon' be a couple Barriors watchin' you at all times. Can't risk nothin'."

Duchess spun to face him. "What risk? I know you don't let undercover FBI or the media or anybody else into your party!"

"Milan got out." His words hit the air like darts.

"And?"

"We gotta watch yo' back in the crowd. She crazy."

Duchess crossed her arms, tilted her head. "I been meanin' to ask you, Duke, which came first, the chicken or the egg?"

Her Ebonics accent was just right. "I mean, was Milan crazy when you met her, or did you make her crazy?"

Duke smiled. "There you go! Baby girl, sista-certified."

She stuck her head forward slightly. "Answer my question."

"Baby girl, when I introduce you tonight, talk like that. Don't be talkin' like Victoria. You The Duchess now. Say a few words, but you gotta sound cool."

"Look at my forehead." She lifted her bangs. "The word 'clueless' got erased in Streetology 101 class. So—" She tiptoed, wrapped her arms around his neck, kissed his lips soft and slow.

"Happy birthday, baby," she purred. "I'm so glad you came back so I could give you some Celeste-cake."

That kaleidoscope of color and texture in his eyes shifted in a strange way. The rich, dark chocolate hue of his cheeks turned gray.

"That shit was supernatural," Duchess said, smiling as she hugged him and pressed her cheek into his chest. "The best ever. I swear we been fuckin' so much it pumped up your dick muscles. 'Cause Timbo felt like he grew an inch wider and an inch longer. I'm still shakin'."

Chapter 50

Knight fucked my Duchess. He snuck up to the penthouse while I was gone an' he fucked the girl I picked right outta the headlines for myself!

Wait, hold up. That shit can't be true. Ain't no way in hell any nigga, even one as cool as Knight, could pull that off. He couldn't sneak past all the security cameras in the building, including the terrace, the elevator entryway and the bedroom.

But what about that drunk look on Duchess' face when he came back to the penthouse and she was just getting outta the shower? She took two showers, or one long one? It was at least ninety minutes between when he called and when he came back.

And she was walking funny across the room to get her leather pants, like she did after he had banged her booty for an hour straight. When he asked her about it, she just giggled in a way like, you know the answer, silly rabbit!

Duke closed his eyes. He couldn't turn into some Othello motherfucker, overanalyzing every little detail, letting his imagination slip down into a stinking slop jar of suspicion and jealousy. Maybe Duchess was so tired and so overwhelmed by the past week of fucking, eating pussy, seeing Milan, and everything else, she just dreamed that he was fucking her bigger and better than ever. Maybe now she liked fucking so much, she was hallucinating about it. She was the kind of girl who kept liking it more and more. Some girls would fuck once and say, 'Oh, I had enough dick for the week.' But Duchess, it seemed like every bang just cranked her appetite up to a higher notch. And she had a wild way of thinking, so maybe she wanted it so bad tonight, she imagined she got it.

"Baby girl," he whispered, grasping her upper arms and pulling her back so he could look at her face. But MANDINGO DICK AFTERGLOW was stamped all over everywhere. Her cheeks were extra pink, lips were blood-red, ready to smile when nothing was funny. Eyelids were heavy, but her eyeballs were dancing in the wet memory of that dreamy dick-down.

Naw, my girl would know if it wasn't me. Duchess would know if some other dick had been in Celeste, and she wouldn't want it.

Unless she liked it better.

Duke ground his teeth so hard it hurt.

Hell naw. I ain't believin' Knight could be that bad of a ma'fucka. Until I see him, Duchess be innocent until proven guilty.

The elevator doors opened.

"C'mon, baby girl, this party is on!"

She was in freeze-frame, staring out with spooky big eyes that were even bluer in the glow of the neon light tubing around the elevator. Here, there, everywhere, the garage was crammed with dozens of guys and girls fucking, sucking, dancing, bouncing, licking, drinking, and giving off a cloud of vapors of cigarette and marijuana smoke, expensive perfume and cologne, booze and the salty-sweet smell of sex.

Duchess coughed. He wouldn't have heard her if he hadn't been staring right at her, because the Bang Squad was stupid loud down on stage. They were doing their hit, "Dick Chicks." Duke looked down at Duchess as she stepped in front of him to walk on legs that might still be trembling from taking Knight's giant dick. Now she was shaking her whole body with the beat, making her ass say "kapow!" in her tight black leather pants.

Duke's mind flipped to a filmstrip of her riding Knight like she did Duke in the Cleopatra Suite. What if she saw Knight at this party? Could she smell or feel that it was him who gave her that extra big dick upstairs?

Now she probably thought she was a dick chick, specializing in Johnson dicks. She was looking straight ahead at a chick taking three dicks—one in her mouth, one in her ass, and one in her pussy. Two other girls watched the action and stuck out their booties like, "Gimme some too!"

Duchess wasn't wasting any time trying to leave this elevator.

Chapter 51

Yeah, come right at me, bitch.

Milan hid behind Flame's huge body as he fucked some girl on the table. It was so dark over here in the corner of the VIP balcony, none of the Barriors had noticed Milan.

Not one person had recognized her behind these big gold glasses and this wig. She shook her shoulder to free her elbow from a tangle of brown ringlets, which caught on the studded belt securing her green leather Daisy Dukes. The long hair covered her bare titties so Duke and Beamer and anybody else who'd seen the unique slope of her breasts and the points of her nipples couldn't identify her.

She coughed, which wrenched up a heave. The thick fumes of smoke, sex, and booze wrapped around her neck like a deadly python. A coughing fit made her double over, holding one hand to her gagging mouth, the other hand to her nauseated gut.

This air is gonna kill me and the baby.

But losing Duke to some light-skinned bourgeousie bitch that he picked off the six o'clock news would kill her anyway.

He won't even talk to me long enough to find out that I'm pregnant. She smirked. *But I'm a high class dick chick. Always have been. Always will be. I'm the one who deserves to be treated like royalty. I know how to handle it. How to keep it. These people need a leader like me, who ain't scared to let her true bitch reign. They'll see.*

It pissed her off to see Duke walking so tall and proud as the tangle of bodies parted like the fucking Red Sea for him to lead that tacky-ass Cleopatra wannabe up to the silver throne. The throne where Milan Henderson should have been sitting.

Soon as Duke and his cream puff sat back and enjoyed this circus, all those freaks down in the garage would see a surprise trapeze act starring the death defying Duchess with no trapeze.

Chapter 52

Duchess felt like she was stepping into a giant, X-rated rap video called "Urban Babylon." The music was so loud, it vibrated her body. The beat was so hot, she couldn't help but snap her fingers and rock her body to the beat as Duke led her past Barriors three deep on each side of the elevator.

"We stayin' here in VIP," he shouted in her ear as two Barriors guided them through the crowd. "We got the bomb balcony spot."

Familiar faces dotted the mass of bodies: Lee Lee, India, Beamer, and Honey, who blew a kiss. Duchess stopped. "Duke, I'm not ready for an orgy."

His seductive eyes smoldered down at her. He looked like he was about to kiss her. His eyes were lusty, lips parted, head coming down, but his left hand rose up to the top of her camisole.

He yanked it down. Her titties popped out. He sucked both of them, hard, and squeezed her crotch.

Then with a hot, open mouth, he breathed intoxicating fire into her pussy and her soul. His kiss sucked the strength from her knees. She gripped his rock hard arm to keep steady on her spike heels. He pulled back.

She moaned, loving that melting butter sensation from her head to her toes, making her pussy a throbbing, soaked mess.

"Now you ready," he said with bad ass Duke style.

They walked past boobs, butts, big dicks of every size, shape, and shade. He led her to the silver railed edge of the balcony where two silver thrones sat on a raised platform overlooking the party below.

"This the shit!" Duke exclaimed into her ear, the last word rising to a pitch that was a good two octaves higher than his usual deep voice. "An' I'm rulin' all of it! The Duke!"

Why was his whole body trembling behind her? What was he scared of? And why did he sound like he was trying to convince himself that he was in charge?

"Baby girl, let's toast."

He turned back to take gold goblets from trays held by their attendants, two girls and two guys who stood on each side of the thrones. The guys were both in that first sexercise class that drove Duchess to carnal indulgence just five days ago. Now they were wearing gold sandals, wrist cuffs, and short, white loin cloths with gold belts around their six-pack abs. Their thighs bulged under the flowy skirt fabric, which was open about two inches in front, like white curtains around a window display of cocks for sale. They were semi-hard, but both dicks stood at attention as Duchess stared. She squeezed her throbbing pussy that only got hotter and wetter as she checked out the females.

They were styled with Egyptian jewelry. No clothes, just turquoise and gold yokes that came down to their naked nipples. A similar style adorned their waists and hips. They wore about a dozen gold necklaces, connected at the sides of the waist and draped in C-shaped arcs across their abdomens, from their belly buttons down to their bare shaved pussies Peacock feathers sprayed up from the girls' short, straight black hair and bangs. They batted thick, black fake eyelashes and extended gold braceleted arms, offering gold goblets to Duchess and Duke.

"After I present you to the masses," Duke said, handing Duchess a cold goblet, "we gon' sit an' watch niggas an' hoes fuck like it ain't no tomorrow."

Duchess let him clink his goblet to hers as he said, "You always gon' be mine, baby girl." Something hard glinted in his usually tender stare. The possessiveness in his tone, like she was his property, made the cold gush of bubbly taste bitter against her tongue.

She steadied herself by grasping the rail and pressing her right shoulder into his left tricep as they surveyed the orgy below. A wild sexcapade filled every inch of the huge garage, from the stage with the live rap band to a wide-open space for sex-dancing. There were rows of men and women fucking on Hummers and sports cars. Neon blue tube lights across the length of the ceiling cast a smoky blue haze that illuminated bare asses, bouncing boobs and big, hard dicks glistening with cum and saliva on plush couches and satin green pool tables.

Dancing on the bar, strippers popped big, bare butts against silver poles. A guy stood spraying bottle after bottle of champagne, making their nipples, butts and bare skin glisten in the blue light. On stage, members of the superstar rap group Bang Squad, whom Duchess knew from the videos Brian was constantly watching and mimicking, strutted back and forth across the stage. Some of them fucked girls on pink, round beds inside giant acrylic champagne glasses. The lead singer was screwing a girl who was standing and touching her toes. He pulled out, yanked off his condom and squirted cum toward the crowd. It dotted the stage. A girl near the stage had white-looking skin and short, straight black hair, stuck out her tongue as if to catch a white glob with as eager a smile as if it were a snowflake falling from the sky.

That girl made Duchess imagine herself acting like that, losing all decorum, self-respect, dignity, becoming a certified hood ho, fiending for any scrap of sex spewed her way. Disgust cramped her stomach, even though her pussy was gushing. How could it not amidst this flesh-pounding, mind-numbing sexual chaos?

She could not look away from the woman on stage who was facing one of the rappers. It was Honey's sister.

The one Duke was fucking in front of me.

Duchess' pussy was so hot, wet and swollen, she could cum with just a couple of squeezes of her pelvic muscles. She wanted to make love with Duke like they did a little while ago. But not in front of all these people.

"Duke! I wanna leave!" she shouted over the deafening music. "Duke!" He did not look up from an electronic pager. He was frantically pressing buttons. She grabbed his arm.

The music stopped.

Everybody in the garage turned toward them, up here on the balcony, as if she and Duke were the stars of a concert. Except most of them were either naked or had glistening dicks sticking out of peeled back jeans or had big nipples pointing up from open jeans jackets.

Beamer came out of the mass of bodies behind them and handed Duke a cordless microphone. Beamer stood beside Duke.

"Yo, y'all!" Duke shouted into the mic. "Ha y'all doin'?"

Wild screams pierced the air.

"E'rybody know Duke da boss. And when Knight come back, he gon' be right back beside me, buildin' Babylon to conquer the world."

The crowd roared.

"Is gon' be three of us." He raised Duchess's hand. "The Duke foun' his Duchess. Y'all got to bow to her jess like you bow to me."

The hundreds of faces below were solemn and silent, some nodding slightly. A guy shouted, "You need a real sista!"

"She black as you, baby!" Duke bellowed. "The rest o' y'all, just know she ain't white. So zip dat shit now. Duchess a sista jess like y'all."

"Y'all be nice, now!" the lead singer of the band shouted into his microphone on stage. "Don't judge a book by the cover you can't even see through yo' own hate."

Cheers and boos shot up from the crowd.

"So, all y'all plantation mentality ma'fuckas," the singer, Jamal, shouted, "thinkin' about you stuck in the cottonfield of life while that long-hair, light-skin bitch livin' large up in the big house wit' Massa Duke!"

"Yeah!" too many people shouted.

Jamal laughed. "You right! An' ain't shit y'all can do about it 'cept love this sista like she one o' us. 'Cause she is."

The band played a deep chord. Smiles and smirks rose up from the crowd.

"Preach that shit!" Duke shouted. "Yeah!"

Duchess shivered. Had she been taken from a normal day in her past life and transplanted to this spot, she would faint. So would everyone else she knew back then. Even Brian. This would scare the shit out of his punk ass. He thought he was so tough, knowing all the latest rap, blasting it in his Porsche and Land Rover. But his hip-hop clothes and backward baseball caps were fake. He was such a punk deep down that once when a black guy walked up and asked directions to the nearby bookstore, Brian was trembling afterward, saying, "Man, I thought he was gonna whip out a gat and car jack me."

That's how too many girls were still glaring up at Duchess now. Ripping her to shreds with their stares.

Those bitches have so much nerve, cuttin' their eyes at me while they're standin' there naked with nut drippin' down their chins and thighs.

And Duke wanted her to say something? The last time she addressed a crowd, besides all those wicked reporters, was to introduce the debate team at the awards ceremony at the yacht club. But this here wasn't the time for the traditional "Good evening, ladies and gentlemen." Victoria Marie Winston's white girl cadence would spark an uproar of laughter, or worse.

No, this was the official unveiling of The Duchess. Even though half the people down there were staring at her like she was Marie Antoinette and they were the citizens of France who wanted to haul her off to the guillotine out back.

This is where I belong. This is how I can help people. This is the stage to share my purpose and passion that I just discovered in bed with my soul mate.

But how to connect through the hostility?

"Find common ground," Daddy used to always say. "Disarm your enemies by finding common ground. Then, don't just extend the olive branch, hand 'em a fondue fork with the juiciest chocolate-dipped strawberry you can find. You'll have 'em in the palm of your hand forever."

Duke was already on the subject, with his deep voice booming through the huge, silent space. "Think of her as the male version of me," he told the crowd. "Anybody thinkin' about tossin' up some hate gon' face the same brute as if you messed wit' me. Duchess in charge, so e'rybody make her feel welcome at Babylon."

Duke handed her the mic. She wrapped her hot, damp palm around the metal.

Yeah, I have the power. Celeste's mix-race woman power. Black power. Duke power. Love power.

She took a deep breath and looked out at the sea of faces.

"A sista inside," she said, deep and sultry, "who been tryin' to hide . . . won't be denied." She stepped in front of Duke, raised a knee to one side, and ground her hips into the side of his rock-hard thigh. "My sexy ride."

The crowd exploded. Duke's beautiful, white teeth sparkled down at her as brightly as his eyes. She spun back toward the rail. "Look in my eye, a butterfly, broke out a white coccoon, flutter to black so soon . . . singing a new tune." Her tone and cadence were perfect spoken word sista-girl.

"From suburban to urban, virgin to vixen, caucasian to mixin' the black"—she turned so that her side was toward the audience then pressed her titties into Duke's arm—"to the top o' my stack. Step back before I attack"—he strutted in front of him, grinding her ass into the tree trunk in the crotch of his leather jeans—"and jack, your dick."

The guys and girls in the audience shouted, "Yeah!" as they thrust fists up.

"My slick candle wick, you stick in my swirl of melted mix-race girl . . . vanilla-chocolate squaw in us all . . ."

She strutted back and forth along the rail, holding the mic and cutting a flat hand through the air to emphasize her words, just like Jamal did while he rapped. Duke crossed his arms, with a quick point down to Jamal, then nodded to her beat.

"In life's game, we're all the same by any name," she said as a bass beat boomed up from the band. The crowd started dancing, rubbing, and kissing.

Suddenly, with the sexy music and the cool vibe from the crowd and the potency of Duke's eyes and the power of her pussy that was wild and free now, she was having a mind-gasm, loving this! She shivered with the thrill of it as she rapped her rhymes.

"I can't blame those lame ma'fuckas who wanna tame my fame and shame . . . me." She stopped, turned to Duke, let her eyes slowly devour him from his boots to the top of his sexy bald head. "You see," she teased toward the audience, where some guys and girls were back to fucking. She ground her hip into Duke's thigh.

"Do dat!" a guy shouted amongst cheers.

"Sexy and free." She turned her butt to the crowd, smacked the round of her ass and said, "A certified Double D."

The crowd whooped.

"So let me shout, this sista comin' out! Beside your Duke, it's no fluke, up in this juke joint. Make a point to anoint yo'self with Babylon juice. Get wild and loose!"

The sea of people roared. The music got louder. Jamal punctuated her rhymes with a deep "Fuck, yeah!"

"Get hot," she said. "Do not waste a drop of that sweet treat . . . from yo' meat. You gotta beat in this heat 'til yo' feet curl, girl, make yo' mind swirl, 'round the world."

Several girls extended their arms into the air and clapped to Duchess' beat.

"Get yo' sex on, chick. Flex on that dick, yo' slick joy stick."

She pressed her ass back into Timbo, who was pointing straight out of the open zipper of Duke's pants. The black satin flesh against the leather and brass zipper made Duchess' pussy shoot steam. She would be on that in a minute.

"You can lick and do your trick. Get yours, give 'im his and don't miss," she almost whispered, "a single kiss."

She turned around, kissed Duke's sucka lips. The noise of the crowd could blow off the ceiling, screaming, cheering, clapping, and fucking.

Duke took the mic, raised Duchess' fist in the air and shouted, "Duchess, baby! Babylon, rock on!"

The band cranked the bass. Bodies twisted back together.

And something, someone, knocked Duchess to the floor.

Chapter 53

Knight's pipe was steaming again, about to bust after watching Tinkerbell rap the house with her clever spoken word rhymes. It took a minute, but now the masses were screaming for The Duchess like she was the hottest superstar around. And she would be, on many fronts.

My goddess aced both tests, in my bed and in front of Babylon.

Now all Knight had to do was make his chivalrous rescue of the damsel in Duke-stress, and let her sprinkle that pixie dust all over this urban empire and every territory that Knight wanted.

All night, he'd been watching her and Duke from this plush couch near the rail, shielded just enough by a circle of two dozen strong Barriors and B'Amazons. He had a clear view of her ass in those tight leather pants, now and when she rapped. And she took that knock-down by Milan like a champ. She shot back up onto the heels of those sexy-ass boots then body-slammed Milan into submission. The B'Amazons hauled away that poor, emaciated victim of her own manipulative evil and Duke's neglect. All while the Barriors carted Beamer's stupid ass away with her.

If Tinkerbell was scared on the inside, she don't look or act like it. Her soft, innocent appearance, yet sexy, strong behavior were making Knight want her so bad, he could taste her again.

He didn't brush his teeth on purpose so when he talked to Li'l Tut, he'd have Duchess pussy on his lips and on his breath.

Once she goes black as Knight, ain't no way she goin' back. Anywhere. She was physically standing next to Duke right now, but the chemical and spiritual reaction going on inside her was like an internal branding by the fire that started during that intergalactic star show as their bodies and souls united. His sperm was still up there. Now her uterus, her ovaries, her heart, her soul were branded in words of fire spewed by Knight's big, black pipe: PROPERTY OF KNIGHT JOHNSON.

And ain't no doubt my turbo sperm is makin' itself at home; at least for nine months, up inside the luxury accommodations of the most exquisite pussy I'll ever need.

"Let's move," Knight said, his deep, sex-powered voice cutting through the ear, splitting cheers and bass rumble of the band.

Big Moe's hand grasped his arm. "Naw, man, we got this easy. But let him get all the way vulnerable for full effect."

Easy was right. With all of Li'l Tut's mismanagement and failure to take action on plans laid years ago by Prince and Knight, the Barriors and B'Amazons couldn't wait for Knight to come back and make things right.

They operated entirely under Duke's stealth radar, giving Knight detailed reports about Milan—keeping her on the job despite blatant violations of trust. Izz's thievery. Duke's hot head flash and dash all over TV and the newspapers, drawing fed heat and reporters to Babylon. It was all because he brought that media magnet/federal fugitive, despised rich-mix girl up in the heart of the hood.

Knight was sure, when he first heard about it, that she'd have to go out with yesterday's trash along with Milan and Beamer. But Victoria Winston was gone. This chick was someone else entirely. She looked different, sounded different, felt different on the inside. Tonight wasn't just a test, where you drop a substance on chemical-treated paper to see if it sizzles or smokes or turns colors.

"Tonight is her blackness test," Knight said.

Big Moe held up his hand, pressed his fingertips together at the top of his thumb then flicked his hand open like a magician tossing sparkle dust. "Black magic, mon. Ttttsssst! She sizzlin' an' smokin' an' sexin' like dis where she belong."

To have and to hold, from this day forward.

Chapter 54

Beamer shook just as hard as Milan as they knelt on the basement floor. She had already thrown up some green shit on his shirt. She was a mess with that long, curly-haired wig hanging on one side of her head, her real hair sticking out in a rat's nest that was so close it was scratching his cheek. She stared him down with eyes so wild and crazy, she looked like she would snap at him and bite down on the dick that got him into this trouble in the first place.

"I now declare you man and wife," the two-dollar preacher from the corner church said over them with all seriousness in his voice. But who could take him seriously, standing there with no shirt and just black leather chaps that let his still wet dick hang loose at Beamer's eye level?

"Mr. Beamer, you get to kiss the bride now."

I'd rather tell her to kiss my stupid ass.

His childhood dream to kiss Michelle Henderson was now finally coming true in the worst fucking nightmare he could have imagined. Driving his Hummer into that semi-truck the other night would have been a better future than locking down with this bitch and chain.

An' I ain't got no choice.

Duke stood by him with arms crossed over his chest, looking down at him like he wasn't shit.

'Cause I ain't. Finally proved it to myself and e'rybody else by tryin' to cross The Duke.

"Y'all can take 'em to they honeymoon suite now," Duke said, "so I can get back to my birthday party."

The Barrior who grabbed Beamer's handcuffed wrists said to the other, "Bet, dude. Which one gon' kill tha otha one first?"

The other Barrior laughed. "I think they gon' get locked up in that room and make like Romeo and Juliet and end the drama right there with a double suicide."

Beamer already knew the only way outta this was to stop breathing, because no way was Milan going to be in the mood for love when she was growling at Duke like that.

"Yeah, they gon' make war, not love." The Barrior laughed. He turned to Beamer. "Yo, dude, a word of advice on yo' wedding night. I'd keep my dick on lock-down if I was you."

Chapter 55

Duchess sat on her throne, holding Duke's hand as they watched a writhing tangle of male and female strippers perform up close and personal. Beyond the dancers, a wall of Barriors and B'Amazons in head to toe ninja black formed a half-circle around them.

Duchess was still quaking with fear. The sinister, pounding rhythm of the music echoed her racing heart.

"Duke, baby," she shouted so close to his head that her lip brushed his silver hoop earring. "I can't get our freak on when some other crazy bitch might come flyin' outta the crowd at me!"

He shook his head. "You don't ev'a have to worry about Milan again."

"What about someone else?" she shot back. "The way you keep lookin' around, it's like you know some other whack shit is 'bout to break."

"It won't." He turned toward those bodies in black, caramel, and brown. They were making a long sandwich of bodies pressed together, all facing forward so their sides snaked in a slow-sexy groove for Duke and Duchess.

"Duchess," he said with a delicious gust of his Black Cashmere cologne and natural musk. "All these pussies and dicks in here for me an' you. An' you love they stuff just as much I do. They all clean, so do yo' thang."

He nodded at another girl who wore a tiny, light blue crocheted bikini and a silver belly chain that said BABY BLUE.

With the help of a gorgeous brown hunk behind her, she put her foot on the arm of the throne, yanked back her bikini crotch and opened her pussy in Duchess' face. The guy ran his big hand over it as if he were in a jewelry store waving a hand over the pearl counter for customers to pick one.

"Lick that pussy," Duke ordered.

She stared at the Brazilian bikini-waxed flesh. Flawless.

The woman ran a fingertip over her pussy then sucked it loudly. Celeste was twitching, screaming.

Duchess touched the tip of her nose to the clit. Rolled her head so that her nose stimulated the chick just right.

"Damn girl, do dat."

Duchess made a peace sign with her fingers, licked them then ran them down the pussy lips. Suddenly, another stripper was at her feet, another at her waist. They were taking her pants off.

Duchess ran the tip of her tongue from the bottom of the pussy up to the clit. The stripper sucked air and spit through her teeth. "Oooh, shit!"

At the same time, other girls helped Duchess ease out of her pants and thong. Duke, at her side, stroked Timbo.

He stuck his tongue out and they both chewed on Baby Blue's filet mignon. After a while, Duke slurped on Duchess' tongue then sat back to watch.

One stripper raised Duchess' right leg up to the arm of the throne, the opposite side as Baby Blue. On her knees, the stripper dove into Duchess' pussy.

"Oh yaaaay-yaaaaaah," she moaned. The double pleasure was incredible, a mouth on her pussy while she sucked on a clit.

Her head spun. She was fueling her woman-power with double intensity, and Celeste was loving it. From suburban virgin to Detroit dick-lovin' dyke. Just keep it comin'.

Duchess peered over Baby Blue's thigh. Her eyes locked with Duke's. Who knew you could have such intimacy with a group? But the look in Duke's eyes screamed, I am yours. Forever.

This is all for you, baby girl.

Duchess was lapping it up like a kitten. Baby Blue groaned like it was her first time, or her best time. Nina licked Duchess' pussy with perfect precision. She hit that fire spot at the tip of her clit that Duchess could never hit herself. Brian always found it and made her cum quickly. Duke and Honey did too.

Now Nina was there, on it. Damn, her clit felt like the center of the universe as Nina worked her tongue all over it.

From the sound of Baby Blue, Duchess was doing just as well. She imitated the way Duke made that windshield wiper motion, from light to harder pressure, all while finger-fucking her.

Baby Blue's thigh quivered. "Oooohhh shit, girl!" Her nipples stiffened. Her whole body trembled, and her pussy walls pulsated around Duchess' fingers. Another stripper sucked Baby Blue's nipples as she came.

"Damn, girl, I ain't neva cum so fas'." Her leg was still up.

Her pussy was a beautiful swell of soft, glistening folds of brown satin, like a flower.

Duchess' open lips pressed onto that perfect clit.

"Oooohhh!" Baby Blue shivered. "You my new girlfriend."

"Stay right there," Duchess ordered. "While I cum."

Nina was giving her butterfly fingers in her pussy while she made tiny licks, still on the tip of her clit. Every lick rubbed away the pain of Duchess' recent past and the terror of tonight. Now her mind was a mellow flow of lust clogged by a head full of question marks.

If Alice loved Ghettoland, would she ever want to go back to where she came from? Duchess moaned. The inner dialogue from Celeste made the corners of her mouth rise up.

Why'd you make me wait this long to get some tongue? You know you've been wantin' it for so long. Why didn't you and Tiffany experiment? They'd talked about it, but they had both chickened out.

"Puuurrrrfect." Duchess lay back on her throne, staring up into the beautiful pussy spread wide open between Baby Blue's legs. She loved that Duke was watching every second, and that they would finish this interlude off with each other, upstairs, in the privacy of the penthouse.

Seize this power, a soft voice in her head whispered.

It was Celeste, her sex power. Seize this power right now. Store it. Summon it whenever you need it. You will always win. This power right here is magic. It's yours.

The words . . . the pussy in her face . . . Duke's attention . . . and Nina's licking . . . "Oooohhh. Oooohhh." Her pussy exploded into an orgasm seemed to go on forever.

"My turn," a deep voice said. The girls moved.

Duke stepped between her legs, his dick huge and hard, pointing at her. The dark chocolate skin on his stomach was smooth, hairless, and beautiful.

She closed her eyes to focus on a repeat of the supernatural euphoria she experienced a few hours ago, upstairs in their bed. Now Timbo was poised to make her cum again with just one stroke then make love to her again . . . better than ever.

Wham!

Duchess stiffened. Opened her eyes wide.

No, Timbo ain't it. But who the fuck made love to me like that?

Chapter 56

Duke pounded up into that pussy, even though the look in Duchess' eyes right now might as well have been graffiti across her ass saying: I LIKE KNIGHT'S BIG, BLACK DICK BETTER THAN YOURS, YOU PUNK MA'FUCKA.

She don't even know she fucked Knight. She just know somethin' ain't right.

Love still glowed in her blue-flame blow torch eyes that first cast her spell over him. But now, that knowing look was about to kill him.

If Knight bum rush me up in front of all of Babylon and steal the Duchess that I picked! I made! I love! Then my heart gon' stop right here, right now, on my twenty-first birthday.

He made it to old age for the average inner city nigga, but love hurt worse than bullets. That sounded corny as hell, but the fact that he was thinking it and couldn't control it, that showed he was a true punk.

But a pussy-whipped punk by any other name would still curl up and die if his girl left for the bigger, better, badder, blacker warrior.

There was no way she could know who fucked her, but just the fact that she knew somebody did it better than Duke was blowing her mind. As soon as she took a look at Knight, she'd know all too well who tried to impersonate Timbo and gave her the ultimate fuck.

Penis impersonation. That ma'fucka just committed the ultimate felony in my book.

Duke radiated his most mack look down at his Duchess. She was his, and she was innocent. She was the victim here, taken advantage of in her horny state, tricked by a dude in the dark who looked just like her man, even to their own mother in the bright light of day.

I'm gon' fuck her so good right now, my nut gon' brain-wash any idea that it wasn't Timbo who gave her "the best ever."

"I love you," he mouthed down to her. Bang Squad started playing the song he had made for her, "Duchess," slow and sexy.

He lifted her up, making her legs higher around his waist so he could bang his way back up into first place. He stood in front of the thrones, watching the fuck frenzy in the crowd below as he bounced Duchess on Timbo.

Yeah, he was clearing her mind with the brute force she loved right now. Smashing every question mark to bits with this most mack motion. Her hands gripped his shoulders, her eyes stared down with a new message: YOU THE MAN . . . YOU MY MAN . . . MY ONLY MAN.

All those strippers, males and females, now circled around them like flower petals, swaying in a sexy motion with their arms up in the air and their bodies rolling as gracefully as underwater plants on a coral reef.

Duchess leaned close with those pucker fish lips open, ready to kiss. She looked up, over his shoulder. She sucked in air and turned white as a ghost.

'Cause now she sittin' on the wrong dick, lookin' at the bigger, better, blacker one she want.

Chapter 57

I have to see his neck, that scar, then I'll know if he's the supernatural god who made me cum at first stroke. The one who connected with my spirit in a way that's still got me breathless.

The shock of this moment, as Duchess sat speared through the pussy by Duke and speared through the soul by his brother, knocked her brain into an Alice in Double Pleasureland tailspin.

Knight and a whole crew of Barriors and B'Amazons were marching this way. Knight and his boys could pull a Scarface style gun battle right here in the middle of an orgy. He could blast his brother to bits, and all the bullets would have to make Swiss cheese of Duchess' booty, back, and brains first.

Duke could figure out that I fucked his brother, and he'll just shoot me.

Or, if Knight was going to be more chivalrous with his plan of attack, because there was no doubt in his eyes that this was a siege, then he'd use words and wisdom to wield his power over Duke.

And I'll use words to wield my power over both of these sex gods. Then I'll be queen of Babylon. Of course they wouldn't know that. She'd let them think they were both in charge, or keep them in an endless race where they each jockeyed for top position. That would be their distraction while she reigned supreme.

As Knight got closer, Duchess almost smiled as her vision came to mind. Yeah, Cleopatra down, with Duke and Knight at her sides as she walked into the Moreno meeting or the West Coast negotiations, working it just like Duke envisioned.

As the music continued to blast, and as she sat frozen-stiff on Duke's dick, the air was suddenly so thick with hostility and suspicion, she could slice right through it. Knight stood right behind them now. His voice was deep as he said, "Victoria, I need you to excuse yourself so me and Li'l Tut can talk business."

He said "business," not "bidness." And that was the first time anyone had called her Victoria in nearly a week.

She stared wide eyed into his coffee bean brown face, a richer roast than Duke. His eyes were more serious, more mature, and so potent, her vision blurred with the sunburst that flashed when he made her cum at first stroke. Her pussy got hot and wet. It squeezed from the inside out, pushing Duke's limp dick out like a squishy little wet fish.

"Aw, hell naw!" Duke shouted into the still blasting music.

Suddenly Duchess was spinning. Duke was still holding her, but he pivoted so she could look at both beautiful, dangerous men.

"Pick one!" Duke shouted. The veins on the sides of his neck bulged. His eyes were glassy.

She smiled. I know he's not serious, 'cause if he is, he'll kill me before he lets me get wit' Knight.

"Pick which Mandingo stud ma'fucka named Johnson you want for Duchess."

"Oh baby, you're no fun," she said playfully. "What if I want both?"

Duke's voice went down another octave. "Whoever you pick, he get to run Babylon."

"You so silly!" Duchess tightened her legs around his waist.

"Don't just sit on my dick here lookin' dazed!" Duke shouted. Craziness glowed in his eyes. "I said pick one!"

Knight's laughter boomed over the loud bass beat. He put an enormous hand on Duke's bare shoulder.

"Listen up, Li'l Tut. My name is not eenie, meenie, miney or moe. And nobody's gonna catch this nigga by the toe. So, Victoria, if you'll please leave us to talk."

"She about to say somethin'," Duke said. "Now."

"I'll run Babylon myself." Duchess tilted her chin up to hide the earthquake of fear inside her. "You two," she said with a strong, serious voice, "can be my board of directors. We'll actually all make decisions together. But e'rybody know," she said with all the charm, sensuality and power of Cleopatra, "Duchess da boss!"

Chapter 58

Duke felt like a million big, black scarab beetles were eating him alive. He gripped Duchess' thighs hard to keep her juicy booty as a cover over his naked ass.

The look in Knight's eyes said it all. He looked disappointed, excited and too much more for Duke to figure out all at once.

He was just standing there like the new fuckin' sheriff in D-town.

All six-foot-seven inches of his ass looked ready to take back all of Babylon. One look into that bigger, better mirror image of himself set Duke's brain off on a game of emotions; tossing his brother around, shouting "Love" and "Hate" all at the same time.

Right now, the "Hate" was screaming so loud, "Love" had almost left the game.

What if I was wrong about him plunderin' my female treasure? What if Knight just wants to surprise me on my birthday? Don't nobody here know nothin' about Knight plottin' a coup. Is that just my crazy-ass imagination?

Duke wanted to find out right away by going with Knight to a quiet spot to talk. But he couldn't just put down Duchess, who was shaking like she was naked in the snow. He wasn't about to flash the smaller, weaker mirror image of whatever the fuck Knight had between his legs!

The music stopped. The sounds of sex continued; moaning, groaning, nasty talk, skin slapping skin. Then that stopped too.

"Happy birthday, Li'l Tut." Sheriff Knight's voice boomed like a cannonball through Duchess' backside then through Duke's chest. Babylon felt like the dusty street in an Old West movie, where everybody froze in place to watch the showdown.

Two cowboys.

One turf.

A girl in the mix.

Only here, it was the two baddest urban cowboys this side of the Mississippi. And they were blood brothers. The only thing funny about the whole situation was to see Duke standing there butt ass naked while Knight was fully decked out in brown leather outfit. . . Would it be a happy reunion? Would they hug and rule together like they were supposed to? Or did big brotha come back to D-town for a hostile take-over from Li'l Tut?

And how could Duke draw a gun if all he was wearing was a butt-naked Duchess?

"I said happy birthday, Li'l Tut."

"Happy birthday to you!" Jamal shouted up from the stage.

Then the band played the funkiest birthday song ever, and everybody in Babylon screamed along at the tops of their lungs.

Duchess, she stayed curled up around his waist, pressing that hot pussy into his stomach, hiding Timbo with her plump ass.

While the song rocked the house and Knight's deep voice sang along, Duchess pressed her pretty lips to Duke's cheek. "I love you, Duke, baby."

The song ended. Silence.

Jamal's amped voice boomed through the garage. "We all know the birthday boy one o' the baddest cats in town, but now big br'a in'a howooose!"

The bigger, badder, blacker version of himself stared hard into Duke's eyes. They were still at the edge of the balcony, so the masses of people were watching them.

"Welcome to the new Babylon!" Knight's voice blasted through speakers. A cordless mic was clipped to his lapel! No doubt, this siege was orchestrated in advance, in secret-with the band, the Barriors and B'Amazons. Maybe Duchess was even in on the plan of attack. *E'rybody knew but me.*

His brother announced, "The Duke's been han'lin' things, but it's time for The Knight to rule again!"

The crowd exploded. The band played the Babylon theme song. Knight unclipped the mic, handing it to Big Moe. Then the huge brown leather tubes that were Knight's arms came down with long fingers spread on giant hands. He almost looked like a robot the way his arms both moved down at the same angle toward the back of Duchess' waist.

Knight clamped down on her baby-soft flesh like he was about to pull her off and leave Duke standing at his own party with his wet, limp dick in his hand.

Knight pulled, making Duchess' legs unwrap from around Duke's hips. He lifted her up and off, causing a cold wind to hit Duke's dick.

And Knight said, cool as a ma'fuckin' cowboy, "I got Babylon and yo' bitch."

Chapter 59

The Queen shivered with a "powergasm" as she surveyed the hundreds of women and Studs who were fucking and sucking on every plush surface of The Playroom. "Damn, I love my job." The words floated over her hot, parted lips and blended with the blasting sound of her own voice singing nasty lyrics over the funky electric beat of the *Dick Chicks Party Mix,* which she had recorded with the Bang Squad as the signature hip-hop album for all Babylon sex parties from New York to Los Angeles.

"Couldn't be nothin' sexier than this on the whole planet right now." She loved the way the relentless beat synchronized with her excited heartbeat and the rhythm of so much fucking around her. "And all hail The Queen up in this mug."

All around the huge industrial loft of this converted warehouse building overlooking the Detroit River, nude bodies writhed on rows of giant beds. "Yeah, lick those pussies," The Queen said, glancing to her right. In the soft pink haze, a dozen Studs knelt before as many women who were lying spread eagled on the edge of a long, low couch. "Love that shit."

The lyrics, which she had written, were a musical tribute to what she watched and craved.

The Queen moaned, squeezing her pussy muscles to make her clit throb. Damn, the black satin of her thong was marinating in hot cream, but Knight would suck it dry later on. For now, she was loving the way the wet sling of fabric massaged her pussy as she swayed slightly with the beat of the music.

"Love it," she whispered, as female clients and Studs twisted into "fucknastics" on the leopard-print benches and Cleopatra style chaises.

Against the exposed brick walls sat giant framed mirrors, which rested on the floor and angled slightly upward, and reflected a multidimensional freak frenzy. Oversized swings hanging from the exposed beams and pipes of the high ceilings allowed couples to fuck face to face as they swung back and forth.

"Oooh, pound that pussy!" a sista shrieked from just a few feet away. On a huge white mink pillow, the woman convulsed with orgasm as a Stud named Antoine jackhammered her so hard. "Damn," The Queen whispered.

Antoine was gorgeous, but nobody could compare to her beautiful African god named Knight. If she weren't so happy in love, she would definitely get a taste of some of that creamy milk chocolate called Antoine.

He glanced up at her, and the lust in his brown eyes made her shiver. He was a big piece of candy, from those cheeks and lips, down to a perfect dick that didn't quit.

She'd seen his long, fat, big-headed hose in "sexercise" class, but everybody knew Knight would kill a muthafucka who even thought about competing with his lead pipe. The last one who tried, well, nobody even remembered his name, since he had disappeared. Never came out how Knight found out. But Knight knew everything.

Antoine is up to somethin', whispered Celeste. And Celeste was never wrong. *That was just* too *bold the way Antoine looked at you.* The Queen cast a "don't-even-try-it" look down at the Stud and mouthed to him, "Fuck on."

Antoine smiled, flipped his long braids over his shoulder, and banged that booty even harder.

The chrome points of her stiletto heels and her long legs in black leather pants made her feel a mile tall, which intensified her sense of being the baddest bitch in charge of the most erotic enterprise ever heard of in D-town and beyond. And nobody but the right folks would hear about it. Nobody would know who she was, where she came from, or where she was going, even though her sexy rhymes with the Bang Squad were blazin' up the music charts and every hip-hop media outlet wanted to know who The Queen was. But they would never find out who she used to be, who she was now, or how she planned to rule this sexy underworld forever.

Victoria who? Rich prep-school white girl, who? A fugitive wanted by who?

The Queen smiled as she remembered how much life had changed over the past year.

I'm The Queen now. Black, blingin', and bold as hell. Rulin' with my Knight to the infinity. The Queen turned as her assistant, CoCo, approached.

The five foot three inch, cinnamon-hued nymph wore a white leather mini-dress and pointed thigh high boots. That were as sharp as her business minded brain. Her short, curly hair smelled like coconut shampoo.

"Queen," CoCo said close to her boss' ear, "these bitches don't play. They all paid up. Three hundred K, plus the fee." CoCo tapped her pink rhinestone-covered ink pen on the white papers on her clear pink clipboard. A red light flashed at the top of her pink rhinestone-covered cell phone, whose holster hooked to the top of the clipboard. "We got the full half-mil tonight." CoCo's sharp eyes, framed by black awnings of fake lashes, scanned her list of names and payments. Pink circles on her cheeks highlighted her round face not because she wore blush, but because the excitement of her job gave her a natural glow. Chanel set diamonds sparkled in the big gold hoop earrings Jamal had given her.

"Check wit' Mikki at HQ," The Queen ordered. "See if everybody over there paid up."

"It's done." CoCo shot a look at the two B'Amazons and two Barriors at her sides.

The Queen glimpsed all the bodyguards positioned throughout The Playroom, which was the entire top floor of this building known as The Playhouse. Every B'Amazons and Barriors wore a ninja black uniform.

The ones at the door were making sure the line of women still entering each wore a pink wristband and a health card. When scanned through a small black machine, a computer chip inside, confirmed that the client had been checked downstairs at the clinic for pregnancy, major health problems, and all sexually transmitted diseases, including HIV.

They didn't want any pregnant women up here risking their baby's safety with wild sex. Other health problems they needed to avoid included weak hearts and neurological problems. One ground-shaking orgasm, and a bitch could fall out or drop dead. And Babylon didn't need any ambulances pulling up to the pussy party.

Near the entrance, another door led to the locker room. There, Lee Lee Wilson glanced up and winked at The Queen. The chief B'Amazon was gorgeous tonight, with her wild mane of curly black hair that was highlighted with maroon streaks around her dark, slanted eyes, button nose, and full cheeks. Hip and sexy, Lee Lee had a sort of *Bride of Frankenstein* look, but her glamour didn't stop her from being tough as she oversaw the B'Amazons, checking in every woman's purse and giving her a key to a locker for her clothes. The B'Amazons also waved each woman's nude body with a metal detector; no weapons, phones, cameras, recording devices or other electronics were allowed in the party, for privacy and security reasons. If anything went wrong, a deafening alarm would ring. That would put all Barriors and B'Amazons on red alert lockdown until the culprit was caught and dealt with accordingly.

"I just did a security check," CoCo said. "Lee Lee handled one little disturbance with a chick who wanted to bring her cell phone into the party. Turns out it had a built-in camera. She wanted a picture of herself fuckin' Flame 'cause she heard the legend. We took it, an' she changin' right now."

"Keep an eye on her," The Queen said.

"It's done, Queen."

CoCo turned to the four bodyguards with the money. Each held a small gold treasure chest, which they inserted into large Coach leather bags that hung diagonally over their shoulders and chests. All of them rested one hand on the bag, the hand on the opposite side, gripping the black metal shafts of gun power strapped to their solid muscle thighs.

"We on schedule," CoCo said, meaning that the money would be delivered as planned to the vault down on the third floor.

"You always on point, girl." The Queen stroked CoCo's bare shoulder.

Trust was hard to come by in this business, but CoCo and The Queen were tight; they had history.

What a pleasant shock it was for The Queen to see CoCo at Babylon's HQ, about a year ago when Knight took charge, asking if she could work for her. The twenty-six-year-old had said that the feds had questioned her about Dan Winston's work and The Queen's whereabouts. But rather than snitch on the family that had saved her life, CoCo's loyalty had taken her straight to The Queen's side; literally and lustfully.

CoCo's eyes locked to the right. "That Stud wit' an attitude, Flame, he cuttin' a look that ain't right; we betta check that shit."

The Queen loved the way CoCo's maroon-glossed lips looked so soft and sparkly in contrast to the hard tone of the words shooting up out of her mouth. "I'm 'bout to splash Flame's ass with some ice water. Make that muthafucka show some respect."

CoCo burst out laughing.

"What, girl?" The Queen asked playfully.

"If your daddy could see you now. You did a 180 into your dark side, and you all the way there now, like you could do a TV show called *Extreme Black Makeovers*." CoCo laughed.

The Queen did too.

"Sometimes I forget you little Victoria wit' the preppy school uniform and proper English."

"Love it," The Queen said. "Remember all those suited business people in Daddy's office? If I saw 'em now, I could say real prim and proper, 'Hi, I'm The Queen. My product is pussy and dick. My service? All the orgasms you could never even imagine, in a secure, confidential, and medically safe environment."

CoCo laughed as she and the money bags went to make a deposit in the vault on the third floor.

The Queen felt a sly smile raise the corners of her mouth as she scanned the bare asses, the flailing legs, the titties of every size, the spread-open pussies, and the perfectly manicured toes pointing up over the Studs' shoulders. These beautiful body parts belonged to some of the most powerful business women in America.

"Girl," a naked sista shouted into The Queen's ear, "I been dreamin' of this since the day my law degree started turnin' every man I meet into an intimidated, domineering, or social climbing prick. Dicks for hire! Now this is a way for a sophisticated sista to get her freak on, no strings attached."

The woman, whose face was well known as a legal analyst on Global TV News Network, kissed The Queen's cheek. "You need to do this from coast to coast; I'll help spread the word."

The Queen loved the raw, wild pleasure in the eyes of every woman in this room. Including this famous face.

The well known anchor, Trina Michaels, now wore a birthday suit instead of her usual TV business attire, a sheen of sweat highlighting her sleek, toned body. One of her nipples, which pointed out from big, perky boobs like chocolate kisses, brushed The Queen's bare arm.

Damn, Celeste is soakin' wet. Can't wait to slide down on Knight's lead pipe and ride into morning. The Queen wondered how many other women in the room named their pussies and let them come to life to the point that they had conversations with *all* that woman power between their legs. *Probably none.*

"Just don't call me when my network does a story about the latest craze," Trina said. "I can hear it now: 'A new epidemic strikes women across America. A rabid addiction to sex from the hood.'" Trina laughed. "I'm not tryin' to get featured on my own show as the legal chick who broke the law by soliciting for prostitution!"

The Queen smiled. "Here at Babylon, we provide a service that clearly"—she waved her right hand over the crowd—"is making the world a better place by giving pleasure to those who crave it. And this is much safer than picking up a random dude in the bar. Here, you know our Studs are clean, it's supervised; the perfect hook-up."

"Fantastic!" Trina exclaimed. "And as fucked up as our economy is, you're giving our fine brothas from the neighborhood some phenomenal employment opportunities."

The Queen smiled as dozens of naked Studs walked around with platters of martinis, champagne flutes, and raw oysters. Others carried trays offering silver bowls to collect used condoms and neatly rolled, warm, white washcloths to clean up after sex. All in a day's work.

The girls from the hood were cashing in too. Right now, a hundred of Babylon's best sluts were enjoying the same employment boom at Babylon HQ. A major rap group was holding its concert after party in The Garage and on the club balcony. They were "orgifying" the very place where, one year ago tonight, The Queen had connected face to face with her soul mate and said good-bye to the man who'd saved Alice from Ghettoland.

The Queen scanned Trina's beautiful body. "This is my purpose in life, to help you and everybody pursue their pleasure. No shame, no worries, no double standard bullshit. Just wild, free fucking."

Trina ran her fingertips over the chiseled, caramel and charcoal hued chest one of the Stud's. "It ain't free at all." She tugged on the silver hoops in the caramel dude's nipples.

"No, baby, but you get what you pay for," The Queen said, giving a subtle nod to the Studs, who immediately led Trina to a nearby giant bed.

"It's all for you, baby," The Queen whispered as the darker Stud with waist-length braids laid back, his cock pointing up like Cupid's arrow.

Trina stood over him, squatted, and speared herself down on it. His dick disappeared between the two arcs of her pretty little ass.

For a split second, The Queen wondered if the TV star had any clue that her hostess tonight was the fugitive whose face had appeared many times on GNN. Trina had even done an in depth report on the mysterious suicide scandal of Dan Winston and the ensuing federal investigation, and the disappearance of his bi-racial daughter in Detroit's worst ghetto.

I am not that scared, sheltered little girl anymore. I'm a badass bitch who's runnin' things now with the finest man, who loves me more than oxygen. Couldn't be happier. My erotic empire in full effect. Duke created a monster Madame in me, and Knight's giving me free reign. Now I just gotta keep some of these muthafuckas in check 'cause they can't deal with a woman in charge. But it's a new day at Babylon.

So mothafucka's better fall in line, or they'll have to answer to me and Knight in a minute.

The Queen was snapped out of her thinking when her eyes met with CoCo's. She got the nod from CoCo that meant the money was safe and sound.

"Send me Ping and Pong," The Queen said. She nodded at the Barriors and B'Amazons, including Lee Lee, who had transported the cash.

As paranoid as Knight had become lately, because of all this money and fools tryin' to jockey for his power, he still trusted the six people around her right now with their lives and their bank. Their job, after the party, would be to take the money to the main vault at Babylon HQ, where it could be processed into the overseas accounts.

"I'll be in the Champagne Room," The Queen said with her cold business voice. It contrasted with the sexy sultry tone from just minutes ago, as her voice reflected what Knight called the yin and the yang of this erotic enterprise. The ancient Chinese philosophy said that everything had both bad and good, negative and positive, dark and light. And she was about to deal with the ugly side. All the electrifying fucking around her, and the millions she made from it, was the yang, the positive energy, and a direct result of her brilliant business plan to expand Babylon to the untapped women's market.

This 100 women strong national sorority party was a taste of things to come, for sure. Every women's convention coming to Detroit, and the cities where she and Knight were running Babylon, were getting a tour from a visitors and convention bureau of a different sort, offering the kind of extracurricular diversion that was usually reserved for their husbands, boyfriends, fathers, and brothers.

Like Daddy always said, "Get rich in a niche. So now it's the ladies' turn. The Queen scanned the throng of bodies for the organizer, a high-powered CEO from Chicago, who had orchestrated this night. There she was, kneeling on a window ledge, her hands gripping the sheer white drapes like a rope, as a Stud gripped her hips and drilled her so hard, her close cropped head snapped back with every thrust.

"You should win a businesswoman of the year award," a white female voice shouted into her ear. "We finally get to enjoy the oldest profession in the world, and hey, this brings new meaning to the term, 'diversity training.'"

The suntanned woman, with a milky white butt where her bikini bottoms must have been, slinked past, holding hands with a dark chocolate Stud.

"This is for you, Queen," the woman shrieked as the Stud lifted her up and slammed her blond haired pussy down on his huge dick. Her blue eyes closed, her pampered face crinkled in pleasure.

The Queen's pussy pulsated as the Stud's long fingers wrapped around the woman's thighs, and he yanked her up and down, pounding up into a place that was previously uncharted territory for Babylon.

As the couple fucked, The Queen looked past them to the buffet. The serving platters were gorgeous, naked men whose chests, thighs, and open palms served up decadent mounds of grapes, pineapple chunks, shrimp, scallops, and wedges of brie. All around them, naked women perched on the pillows, chatting and nibbling with abandon. A few women dared to eat with their mouths, directly off the Studs!

I am brilliant. These high-powered women have needed some good dick for a long time. Now I'm fulfilling an important role in the world by providing it. And gettin' mine at least twice a day with the sexiest man alive, because I am Queen of the Knight. The Queen focused on the couple fucking before her.

The woman's eyes opened, and she smiled.

Damn, my pussy is hot. But this was business. Pleasure would come later. Because Knight knew his job description as King of Babylon and as The Queen's soul mate meant he had to fuck her good after every event. And he would tonight, later, on the boat.

Now, for the yin—the negative shit that she had to handle within this unique line of work; dealing with difficult workers; like Flame.

No sooner did The Queen turn to glance at him, when he stood up, wiped his mouth with the back of his hand, and made a face like he was disgusted. His client crouched on the couch and sobbed into her hands. Flame was one of Duke's boys. Ever since Knight had come back and taken over, Flame was having a hard time adjusting to the new chain of command. He made it obvious he had a problem with The Queen and he was demanding he get a "no pussy eating" clause in his job description just because he was one of Babylon's first workers.

The Queen nodded to one of the Studs sipping an energy drink beside the giant fireplace. With a subtle point of her index finger, he walked over to the crying chick, pulled her into his arms, and carried her to a plush window seat overlooking the river. He rocked her in his lap then turned her toward him. Her long, brown hair tossed down her back, her tiny ass slid down over his big dick, and he bounced her troubles away.

That's exactly what The Queen was about to do with Flame. "Get the fuck in the Champagne Room wit' me," she said with a hard, grinding tone in his ear.

"Bitch, you crazy."

"Get the fuck in the room unless you'd rather talk to Knight."

Johnny "Flame" Watts flashed his famous, smoky-gray bedroom eyes. His black as licorice linebacker body stiffened. Then he turned and walked butt naked toward a red door to their right. Even though he was pushing forty, his body was perfect. The Queen drew power from the fact that Knight's two most trusted Barriors, Ping and Pong, followed right behind her. In their black ninja uniforms, guns strapped to their bulging thighs, their earpieces assured her that they could be summoned in a split second if she needed their brawn to beat down this unruly Stud named Flame.

Now, as The Queen and Flame went through the red door and closed it, Ping and Pong stayed outside. They'd be on her in a flash, if necessary; plus the closed-circuit TV would allow Paul and Gerard, codirectors of Babylon security, to watch and listen to their every word and movement. The champagne fountain in the middle of the room gurgled as Flame stood near white couches and cube-shaped chairs that glowed pink under red lights.

A flat-screen TV on the wall blasted a bank robbery story on the ten o'clock news. "In other news tonight," the anchor said, "Federal agents are still searching for fugitive Victoria Winston. It's been one year since the eighteen-year-old disappeared after her father's mysterious suicide. New information in the case of embezzlement and money laundering against her father has investigators desperate to find the teen; now it's believed that she helped her father launder money for a powerful crime family—"

The Queen snatched up the remote from the glass coffee table. "Turn that shit off." Her picture, so different from the woman she was now, flashed on the screen. That girl with the innocent smile and the starched white-collared school uniform and pearl earrings was someone else. Victoria Winston had stepped into the hood as a terrified, virginal, white girl, but sex with two Mandingo warrior studs, a crash course in "streetology," and the discovery of her racial roots had transformed her into a sexy, black diva running a multimillion-dollar urban empire with the sexiest man on the planet.

"Stupid bitch!" Flame's deep laughter assaulted her ears as he doubled over with hysterics. "You can run, but you can't hide."

She stepped close to him. "You can talk, but call me a bitch one more time and you won't be able to walk."

"Listen, quit your corny ass rhymin' on me."

His legendary dick was still semi-hard, forming a perfect black arc from a close cropped frame of black hair between the V of his groin muscles and the iron hard bulges of his thighs. His dick reminded her of the triangle shaped head of a python lying still before pouncing on its prey.

"Listen, the only reason you got a record deal was 'cause Knight told the Bang Squad to do it; ain't 'cause you can sing."

"You seem to have forgotten that I'm your boss." The Queen's black leather pants made a crinkling noise as she strode angrily toward him. "This is your job, and it ain't shit for you outside o' Babylon."

Flame smiled at the TV. "One phone call and your wannabe ghetto ass would be on lockdown with Uncle Sam. Think you tough now that you found your black side, but you ain't never been and won't never be nothin' but a prissy, white bitch who got turned out by some 'soul brotha' sex in the hood."

A mirror over the couch behind him, caught The Queen's attention. She glimpsed the expression that she was casting down on him. Her straight, black hair hung down her back and over her forehead in bangs that hit just above her perfectly arched black eyebrows. Big gold hoop earrings tickled her cheeks, which were suntanned deep bronze. Her high, Indian-priestess cheekbones glowed as naturally red as her full, puckering lips.

Damn. I look tough as hell, and so sexy. I'd lick my own pussy if I could reach her . . . because I love my life.

That passion sparkled with power in her silver-blue eyes, which were ringed by thick, black lashes and Cleopatra-style liner extending from the corners. Her little round nose crinkled as Flame's words tried to penetrate her thoughts, but she wasn't hearin' it. Her mouth watered at the sight of her blue and gold striped halter top, which squeezed her creamy titties together. She loved the way her newest tattoo played up the phrase *Cleopatra of the Nile* by announcing, in cobalt blue script-style letters that rolled up and over the hills of her chest, with two words on each breast.

And her low-cut pants offered a succulent slice of smooth stomach and showed off the sparkling diamond in her pierced belly button. Black leather hugged her hips just low enough to flaunt her first tattoo, *QUEEN OF THE KNIGHT,* in Gothic script across her lower back.

Yeah, this was the woman The Queen wanted to become. The woman who wasn't scared anymore. Not scared of the mixed-race sex power that killed her mother, not scared of her black side, not scared of punk-ass thug wannabes like Flame here, trying to flex with his bad-boy talk.

She glared into his eyes. "It's your decision." Her fingertips danced over the choker Knight had given her last night for their first anniversary. The diamonds scratched the back of her index finger as she underlined the thick gold block letters and said, "Read this,QUEEN, whether Duke or Knight is beside me. So you can do your job without the prima donna bitch routine, or leave Babylon."

"I ain't eatin' no more pussy." He plopped down on the couch and crossed his arms. "That bitch out there stank!"

"Babylon allows dental dams if both parties agree—"

"Listen, ain't no bitch gonna pay for me to lick her pussy through some plastic." His gray eyes flashed with rage as he glared up at her.

"You're one of the highest paid Studs at Babylon. You can retire at forty and you'll be well taken care of."

"I came to Babylon when Prince, Duke, and Knight was a team. And when Knight was down for a while, Duke was handlin' it just fine. Even Milan with her twisted ass was takin' care of bidness, but you—"

"I'm in charge, period."

"Wish Duke was back."

"Duke could be dead for all we know, so get back to reality. And get back to work."

Flame shot to his feet. His nose touched The Queen's nose, and his pussy breath steamed her lips. And his eyes burned with hostility as he glared into hers.

"Step the fuck off." The Queen pressed her fingertips into his shoulders.

Flame grabbed her wrists. "I'm gon' step the fuck in." He twisted her around, bent her over, and grabbed her pants just over her ass.

The Queen yanked her wrists, twisting them like Lee Lee had taught her in self-defense classes at the Babylon gym, but his grip was too tight. She stabbed her heels into his bare shins.

"Bitch!" His fingertips scraped the soft skin at the base of her back, stinging her. "I'm gon' cum all over that tattoo. See if you call yourself The Queen after I beat this shit up." He dug under the waistband of her pants.

"Stop!" she screamed. In an instant, she realized just how quickly shit could turn on her. *Did Ping and Pong not hear me outside the door with that music blasting? Damn! I should've had them come inside.* She had all the power, in the business sense of the word, but Flame was still a man with strong muscles and a pleasure stick that he could turn into a weapon against any woman he chose.

Panic jolted The Queen's every cell. *This is some dangerous shit I'm into right now. Flame could rape me, kill me right now.* But she loved it. And Knight would never let anything happen to her. "Let me go, or you'll be swimmin' in the Detroit River," The Queen said with a deep, cool voice.

He laughed. "Who gon' stop me?"

That soft voice inside her head, Celeste, spoke from the core of her woman power, *Knight will stop you, muthafucka. Knight won't let you harm a single hair on The Queen's head.*

And then she heard his beautiful, bad-ass voice inside her head. *I got your back, baby girl. Always.*

The Queen's eyes widened, not from fear, but from complete faith. Knight had always said they were so deeply connected, soul to soul, that one day they'd communicate without talking or even being in the same room. And now it was happening. Her muscles suddenly relaxed. She was safe. She knew intuitively that Knight was on it.

Flame pulled harder on her waistband. It yanked up into her gut, making an animal grunt escape her mouth. He leaned down to her ear and, with his pussy breath, said, "I'll be doin' Duke a favor for you turnin' on him. He saved you, and you fucked him by fuckin' his brother. You slut-ass bitch, you 'bout to get your due."

Chapter 60

In the sleek, silver surveillance room that felt like the cockpit of a space ship, Knight Johnson watched Flame on the closed circuit TV security system. That nigga was about to get zapped for forgetting his place in the new Babylon, for speaking Li'l Tut's name, and for daring to touch The Queen.

Knight had to crack down on all renegade muthafuckas who interfered with the smooth operations of Babylon, both inside and out, coast to coast. *'Cause I'm a visionary with thirty days to Manifest Destiny as the boldest king of the universe, and nobody, nothing will stop me. Not Li'l Tut, not the gold diggin' bitches, not the scheming gangstas, not my health, and not this testosterone crazed fool.*

A cold fist of pressure clenched Knight's chest as he sat still as a statue in his high-backed, black leather chair at the wide silver console.

"You think Knight gon' save yo' mixed-up ass?" Flame growled at The Queen. He bent her over. His huge dick swung up, ready to stab.

"Now!" Knight commanded into the microphone on the console before him. The deep bass of his voice crackled on the line. He imagined his words shooting like lightning into Ping and Pong's earpieces.

In a flash, the two enormous men burst into the Champagne Room. With braids bouncing and huge, ninja black bodies moving as gracefully as quarterbacks, Ping and Pong each hooked a giant hand under Flame's armpits then slammed him up against the wall.

"Yeah, corral that buck wild muthafucka!" Knight said coolly. "Gerard, gimme a close up on The Queen."

Knight kept one eye on Flame and another eye on the monitor zooming in on The Queen. *I gotcha back, baby girl.*

As if she had heard him, she looked into the camera hidden above the mirror, her blue blow-torch eyes burning straight through him with erotic power.

His skin danced with tiny flames of love and lust that threatened to explode the pipe bomb between his legs. Yeah, Shane was about to blow from just looking at her deep-bronze face, the *Cleopatra of the Knight* tattoo curving over her swollen C-cups, and those two juicy bubbles of her ass under that baby-soft black leather.

Knight let one hand fall to the heat blast in his lap. All that was for her, and tonight he'd make it official for life with a diamond engagement ring.

"Don't that crazy *MF* see they guns?" Paul exclaimed as Flame kicked each of the Barriors' chests. "He seen too many Jackie Chan flicks."

"Dang! He strong," Gerard said, "must be on somethin'."

Flame broke free. He screamed, "Bitch!" and charged The Queen.

With a shocked expression, she spun to face him, and the screen went black.

That pressure fist of stress squeezed Knight's chest. "Get her back," he ordered Gerard.

The slim, freckled dude with an auburn "twist" hairstyle, turned knobs and pushed buttons. "Queen on camera three," Gerard squeaked.

She appeared, eyes glowing with terror, chest rising and falling with panicky breaths. Ping and Pong slammed Flame into the wall. He slid down and crumpled to the floor.

Knight spoke into the mic, "Send that muthafucka south of the border," then stood slowly.

He wore black jeans, cowboy boots with silver tips on the pointed toes, a big silver belt buckle that said *KNIGHT,* a brown suede leather jacket with fringe, and a matching cowboy hat. As his six foot, seven inches of brawn rose up, he felt pumped with all the cowboy machismo he'd loved watching on all those western movies he'd studied as a boy. He even stood with his knees slightly bowed and his huge hands at his sides, like he could double-draw and blow away ten outlaws at once.

He took one step toward Gerard. "Why the fuck did that monitor just black out?" Knight's words electrified the cool air.

The men and women in the room froze.

"I-I-I-I'm sorry, B-b-b-boss Knight." Gerard's eyes grew huge. His bushy eyebrows raised up, making stress lines on his forehead. "S-s-s-sos-s-sorry—"

"Sorry don't do CPR if some shit goes down. Sorry don't excuse the fact that you were supposed to test every monitor in Babylon before the parties tonight. Did you?"

Gerard's lips flapped well before any sound came out. "N-n n-na, b-b-boss," Gerard said. "I was so busy riggin' Hummer One wit' the new n-n-navigation system—"

Knight's eyes were as lethal as six shooters. He blasted a disgusted glare at the man who'd helped him secretly slip back into Babylon and take over a year ago. "Now," Knight lowered his voice to reverberate a new work ethic into this muthafucka. "If I find out you were having your sex addicted dick sucked instead of handling our top priority here at Cairo," Knight paused then yelled, "Security!"

Gerard jumped, his lips trembling.

"Then you'll get jacked so bad, even your dick will be in a Mummy wrap. Then you'll be able to concentrate."

Paul, who sat on the other side of Gerard, ran a hand over his thick black beard and exhaled. He turned to Knight. "Boss Knight, man, I can vouch for Gerard." Paul's narrow, dark eyes glowed with concern. "He's been workin' his tail off, getting ready for tonight and The Games."

Knight shot him a hard look. "Nobody works as hard as I do. And if the greatest among us can be a servant to all, then the servants need to strive to be the greatest they can be too." Knight loved the way his words sounded so clear and clean, thanks to his crash course on the King's English while in prison. "That means you, Gerard!"

Gerard shuddered.

Paul shook his head. "All due respect, Boss Knight, but don't nobody else have yo' superhuman powers. The rest of us need sleep. We make mistakes—"

"Don't nobody else? That's a double negative. Say, 'nobody else.'"

Paul stood, making his chair shoot back and bump the console beside a B'Amazon. "I'll be straight wit' you, Boss Knight, no doubt, you're king of Babylon, but a lotta folks feel like you done got too righteous . . . power-trippin'."

Knight respected Paul's courage to speak up. His childhood buddy had always called Knight out on himself.

"My power trippin' has always been a good thing for you."

Paul shook his head. "You goin' overboard, Boss Knight. Folks say you paranoid, moody, unpredictable. That's why we're on red alert half the time. Folks be tryin' to strike back, make it like it was under Duke; relaxed, and without all these new rules."

The tension in the room felt like a vise around Knight's chest. Hearing them speak of Li'l Tut with longing in their voices created a tight sensation in his throat. But he would not allow these inferior-minded followers who lacked his discipline and vision to block his noble mission. So he imagined his eyes were like flame throwers, casting fiery stares down on Paul and Gerard that would singe them into submission.

This situation required Knight's big brother's unwritten rules of domination. The Prince Code said, *Say as few words as possible. Less is more.*

So he said nothing. He just let them know, with his eyes, that their asses were on probation right now. One more wrong move and they would be royally fucked up.

Knight turned his back to them then did a 360 glance around the room to check on every monitor. *Gotta keep an eye on everything my damn self. Can't trust these sneaky muthafuckas who might be scheming with Li'l Tut or Moreno to take what's mine.* The dizzying array of pictures and the enormity of all he had to keep in check made his chest squeeze harder. He struggled to inhale against the pressure. Especially when he looked at the red metal panel that controlled the emergency mechanisms that would turn this ten-story building into a fortress, complete with a flaming moat and rooftop snipers. *We ready to rock.*

Knight coughed. One more month couldn't pass soon enough, so he could Houdini himself and The Queen into a new life. Like magic, they would vanish, and there'd be so much smoke and confusion, nobody would notice until they were already relaxing on a Caribbean island. Had to keep his plan under wraps from The Queen, too, because her nymphomaniac, sweet self was loving every pussy-throbbing second of their orgasmic lifestyle here in Babylon. Knight's dick would stay as hard and heavy as lead. *Shane can lay a lifetime of pipe inside my Queen to make up for any thrills she thinks she's missing away from here.*

Yeah, his top-secret plan, called "Manifest Destiny," gave him one month from right now to bank fifty million. *Five parties a week like this in ten cities across America, then The Games, and the sale of Babylon to Jamal, and it was a done deal—if all this bullshit don't kill me first.*

Knight's heart hammered so hard, he felt his heartbeat to the rhythm of the Bang Squad's funky bass from the party on The Playroom floor above. These physical symptoms made Knight believe that his body was responding to the growing pains that Babylon was experiencing, thanks to the combined brilliance and business savvy of himself and The Queen.

Over the past year, they'd expanded their erotic empire to cities across the country. They were raking in huge bank, controlling thousands of Sluts and Studs. Plus they were collecting even more dough from the personal protection services and security details that the Barriors and B'Amazons were providing for musicians, athletes, and politicians, as well as sporting events, concerts, and rallies.

He scanned the video screens that showed Babylon parties all across the country. They also showed the outside of this building, a ten-story tower of sandblasted brick and tall, multi-paned windows. In front, the building faced a street and many abandoned buildings here in the uninhabited warehouse district. A wooden bridge for cars rose over the ten-foot-wide stream that formed a horseshoe of water around the building's expansive lawn, the circular driveway that was now crammed with limos. The horseshoe-shaped stream created a security moat, because its ends flowed into the river, where boats bobbed in Babylon's private marina.

Still more cameras also provided video for entryways, hallways, and the vault on the third floor. Another bank of monitors provided twenty-four-hour surveillance for the tropical-style swimming pool and jacuzzis, the auditorium, and the game rooms. Some important zones, like the tunnels, were deliberately not wired with cameras. No evidence, no knowledge, no problem.

Other screens showed Babylon's headquarters, about two miles from here. The building was similar, but it stood in the middle of the hood. Next door was the Cape Cod style house, where the Johnson brothers had grown up. The vacant lots, broken glass, and abandoned cars were cleaned up on Babylon Street, where soldiers patrolled the sidewalks to keep children, grandmothers and everybody else safe.

Right now, a VIP rap concert after party was rocking HQ. Cameras showed the apartments, the Penthouse that Knight shared with The Queen, the corporate offices, and the gym. Other video screens showed the entire first floor, called The Garage. The football field sized, three-story room was wall to wall sex. Every dick and pussy in there, represented thousands of dollars. Bank that could only be trusted with Big Moe.

Knight dialed his top lieutenant. "Still rainin' hard?"

Big Moe answered with his soft Jamaican lilt, "Yeah, mon, some shade cleaned out wit' my special sunshine." That meant he'd had some problems but wielded the appropriate influence to check the niggas.

Big Moe's deep laughter made Knight smile. He didn't even need the details. He just knew the problem was fixed. "Twenty-five an' comin'," Big Moe said.

Knight had projected a two hundred thousand dollar profit at that party, so the prosperity gods were smiling down with an extra fifty grand. But the bigger Babylon got, the longer the list of suspects grew.

As he hung up, Knight's chest clenched as his mind ticked down a list of muthafuckas who were scheming to usurp power as boldly as he'd taken this exotic underworld from Li'l Tut a year ago. *I know that was him who called me.* Right now, tiny needles of pain assaulted his heart, as they had since earlier today when that sinister voice had shot through his phone.

Knight inhaled as deeply as when he meditated every morning and night. All that fresh oxygen expanded his muscular belly, filled his lungs, and amped his brain to superhuman intelligence and intuition. This power resulted from all the reading, studying, and meditation he had done in prison to tap into the infinite powers in his mind, body, and spirit. Now he could use those powers to build his Babylonian dynasty with his Queen.

Knight rested a giant hand on his crotch, discreetly massaging Shane as he watched The Queen return to the party. Their combined sex power was another secret to their success in expanding Babylon nationwide. With tantric sex visualizations, they practiced tuning into each other's thoughts, so that they could communicate without words. They also concentrated on mental pictures of their dreams as they reached orgasm. That allowed the most powerful energy in their bodies, to fuel their dreams into reality.

That was all part of a year long training for The Queen to become as big and bad as Knight, even though she didn't always know when he was putting her through a drill. Like tonight, this bullshit with Flame was a test for her, to see how she'd handle it, to test her trust and her toughness.

On the screen, she walked through the party with a new expression. Her eyes were hard; her chest was still rising and falling from her brush with terror.

Good. He'd scared some reality into her for a hot minute. Because even though The Queen had toughened up over the past twelve months, her sheltered upbringing had blessed and cursed her by making her naïve. It was a blessing in that she was oblivious to the real danger of her life here in Babylon; a curse, because it might be too easy for a bitch or a nigga to get over on her. So a few split seconds of the gritty low-down with Flame's animal instincts would get her primed to happily accept Manifest Destiny when the time was right.

She's feelin' it now; she knows this ain't no joke. Knight's insides melted. Heart pounded. If anything ever happened to her, he would have no reason to live. Not for the millions they were making together, not for the fulfillment of providing jobs and security in his neighborhood, and not for the satisfaction of using his money to feed a village of hungry, AIDS and war-orphaned children in Africa.

After tasting the sweetest love with a woman who was truly his other half, the death of her would be the end of him. Anxiety stabbed his heart then radiated throughout his whole chest. The pounding pulse in his ears, and its irregular rhythm, let him know something was very wrong. Those little bouts of something, the tight chest, the dizziness, the pounding heart; it would come and go in terrifying episodes that lasted for thirty seconds or thirty minutes. His doctor said it was anxiety attacks. But there was no way a six foot, seven inch survivor of D-town's meanest streets and now king of Babylon, was having punk ass anxiety attacks.

No, something was wrong. And it had gone wrong in jail, when the doctors had injected him with what they called a flu shot, despite his objections.

A flu shot, my ass. The oppressors poisoned me.

Knight was countering its effects everyday with meditation, exercise, and a healthy diet. But he needed to step up his visualizations of himself in perfect health, and never let The Queen know about this heart crisis that he feared could kill him at any moment. No, he had to cure it before she ever knew. And in the meantime, his every thought focused on protecting his Queen and preparing Babylon for their dramatic exit. *Soon I'll put her through the ultimate test.*

The phone vibrated on his waistband. REBA flashed across the bluescreen.

"I told you not to call me," Knight said, watching The Queen.

"Oh, Daddy, you know you missed this good pussy while you was down."

Reba's high-pitched, little-girl voice always made him think she'd just eaten some cotton candy or put away her Barbie dolls.

"You gotta make up for what you lost. An' I know 'miss white chocolate' ain't gettin' down like you know this ebony sista can."

Knight glanced at three couples fucking on top of a Hummer in The Garage. "Reba, you're the lead dancer at the Bang Squad's after party. Why the hell aren't you working?"

"Came up to my apartment to call you."

"We don't pay you to play on the phone. Get your ass downstairs to work. And one more call like this, we won't need your services any more at Babylon."

"I'm one of y'all's best Sluts," Reba said. "Shoot, I'll go toVegas, make my own fortune, 'steada bein' a trampoline for every rapper that hit D-town."

"Those were Willie Mae's last words," Knight said, "before she ended up working five-dollar johns on Eight Mile. That'll be you, if you keep forgetting where I stand."

"But where The Queen stand?" Reba snapped. "I seen her standin' on top of a fat dick this mornin'. She was doin' sexercise wit' Antoine an' his fine ass. An' I ain't just talkin' about sit-ups."

Knight took a deep breath to flush out the image of his Queen fucking anybody but him. He knew for a fact she hadn't. Because he knew her every move, her every spoken word, and every word spoken to her. He knew with technological sureness that she had never, not once in a year, even talked about flirting or fucking with someone else. But the image of Antoine and Queen tonight at the party, and of her squatting down on that Stud's chocolate dick made Knight's heart pound with pain. Felt like all the little muscle fibers were sharp needles poking into each other.

"My pussy drippin' right now, Knight," Reba whispered. "Just yo' voice make me wanna cum all ova yo' face."

"This is our last conversation," Knight said. His ears tuned out, and he focused his attention on The Queen.

He handed the phone to Gerard and said, "Truce, my brotha, let me share some of the wealth of Babylon." As far as Knight was concerned, Gerard was through, but he'd keep him on board so he could keep tabs on him and put Paul in charge of security.

Gerard said playfully as he took the phone. "Man, I'm married."

"Reba's clean as a whistle," Knight said. "Since her sister died of HIV, she's vigilant about safe sex."

Gerard smiled as he pressed the phone to his ear, his eyes glazing with lust when he was supposed to be watching the monitors.

Yeah, Paul's in charge. Gerard is oblivious to his work when his dick gets hard. Knight watched The Queen, who was having a serious conversation with the woman Flame had dissed. The woman was smiling, thanks to the Stud who picked up the slack and was holding her hand, but was still going off about something.

Gerard groaned, "Yeah, the jacuzzi, when I get off at three tonight. Yeah, baby, I can hook you up at the mall tomorrow. Big Daddy rollin' like that."

Knight thought Gerard was a ridiculous, unprofessional muhafucka. Five minutes ago he was being reprimanded for slacking on the job; now he thought everything was cool since Knight passed some pussy off to him. Just like everybody else, Gerard didn't need to have a clue about what Knight was planning.

Paul was watching the monitors, but his eyes were moving back and forth in a way that showed he was trying to figure out what Knight would say or do next. Scratch that, mutha-fucka, because Knight was master of The Prince Code—be unpredictable.

And Gerard was too dumb to know that, looking all pussy whipped. "Knight, thanks for the pussy man."

"Dig that," Knight said with a cool nod as he took his phone back. "He who giveth, receiveth the kingdom."

"Say it any way you like." Gerard scanned the monitors. "I'll receive a kingdom of pussy all day long. 'Specially from Reba. She act like she in heat twenty-four/seven."

"She's in heat for 'benjamin,' just like all of them are," Knight said as two white women with business-style haircuts sauntered over to the buffet, knelt with their hands behind their backs, and plucked shrimp off the bare body of a Stud. As the women stood, chewed and burst into laughter, the diamond wedding rocks on their left hands sparkled in the pink and purple light. The Queen's necklace glistened too.

"Paul, I'll have her collar tomorrow so you can do a sound check an' upgrade the lo-jack chip," Knight said. Yeah, he trusted his lady. But he needed to keep her on 'round the clock radar for her own protection. If anything ever happened, he'd be able to find her in a heartbeat. And she never needed to know she was being tracked.

"Sure thing, bossman," Paul said.

Gerard punched several green buttons and studied the screens. "All your admirers, they jus' jealous you might kill they ghetto girl dreams an' marry 'miss suburbia' instead; you the most eligible bachelor, so you gotta take the heat."

The heat of the cell phone on Knight's palm made his heartbeat quicken. Heat was a bad word these days.

"Seems like every woman I meet is in heat," Knight said, "degrading themselves as they dig for some gold key to my heart."

"It ain't that deep, brotha," Gerard said. "'Scuse me." He punched a red button then shouted into a microphone. "Where the fuck the Barriors on door two?" He frantically scanned the screens. "Y'all tryin' to let any damn fool walk up in here wit' all these executive pussies gettin' they freak on?"

Three Barriors appeared on camera, in front of door two, a fire exit leading to the patio facing the river and marina.

Intuition spoke, loudly and clearly, in Knight's mind. *They're scheming.* They used to be Li'l Tut's boys and were pissed when Knight took charge.

"We here," one said. "We was just checkin' somethin' out."

"What?" Gerard demanded. "You s'posed to call it in then check it out. In case somethin' go down."

"Wasn't nothin'," the Barrior said.

"They out," Gerard said. "Some heat coulda come creepin' through while they messin' around. Probably suckin' each other's dicks. They out like a mug."

"Not yet," Knight said. "Have them followed 'round the clock. Get me their phone and computer records. Search their apartments. The feds is sniffing hard for The Queen and Babylon in general. And Duke's at large. We need to know what we're dealing with."

"Over and out, boss," Gerard said.

Knight's phone vibrated once more. His chest tightened. He stared at The Queen as if his eyes could protect her from the violent words recorded inside this tiny device that he refastened to the clip on his belt. He had to save her from those vile threats hissed from the mouth of someone who once loved them both.

Manifest Destiny will save us both. We'll steal away to our own secret heaven before anybody tries to send us to hell. That was *all* Knight knew for sure. Didn't know how long he'd live. Or how long his empire could evade the heat's radar. Or how long The Queen could defy the FBI by living the glamorous life at Babylon. Or how long it would take his bad-ass brother, Li'l Tut, to resurface and come back to stake his claim on his Duchess and Babylon.

Despite Knight's careful planning, any of the above factors could topple the kingdom in a heartbeat, literally, if Knight's condition were as serious as he feared.

"Show me the back," Knight said.

Gerard zoomed in on the delivery dock leading down to the marina. Ping and Pong prodded Flame into the back of a white van marked *Feast for Your Eyes,* Babylon's own catering company, which provided food for all its events.

Damn, his phone was blowing up. He glanced down. PRIVATE CALLER flashed on the display. That's what it read when the threat came in. Knight's heart pounded. He had the power. He was unstoppable. But in order to stop this fool, he'd have to wield the ultimate power. And he didn't want to do that to his little brother, no matter what a hot-headed punk Li'l Tut had become.

Knight flipped the phone open. Sirens blared into his ear. Then a male voice quaked, "We gotta talk."

"Who is this?"

"It's the beginnin' of the end, muthafucka."

Knight grabbed his BlackBerry from the console. He texted messaged "YELLOW" to the four Barriors, whose job was to watch The Queen at all times, in The Playroom.

On the monitor, she was holding hands with that TV analyst who looked like she wanted The Queen to lick her pussy right there in the middle of the party. But The Queen never mixed business with pleasure. And she never ate pussy unless Knight could watch, in person, and fuck her while she feasted.

Four stars flashed across Knight's cell screen, one at a time. That meant each Barrior got the message and would respond accordingly. No telling where this joker was calling from.

"You decide," Li'l Tut said. "Give me what's mine, an' e'rybody be cool. Keep fuckin' me an' my Duchess, an' dawn gon' shine on Babylon. Knight gon' be all over an' done wit'."

Knight's heart ached. Seizing control of Babylon was a business decision, so he could take care of Mama and provide jobs for thousands of young black men and women. "Li'l Tut, let's meet."

"Midnight. On the boat."

Knight glanced at his silver Cartier watch which he had bought in New York with The Queen. She wore a matching one, only hers had a pink alligator band and a mother of pearl face surrounded by diamonds. Both had their favorite saying engraved on the back: *LOVE YOU TO THE INFINITY*. A watch, they both agreed, was the intimate symbol of time, of love, of life. Every day, they made sure their watches ticked identically, right down to the second hands.

Now, Knight's watch said 11:45 p.m. He and The Queen had planned to make love tonight on the boat, after the party, which wouldn't end until three. "Check, baby bro'. See you in a quarter."

Knight slipped his phone back onto his belt then turned to Paul. "I'm makin' a run for a hot minute. I put out a yellow. Any trouble, handle it then call me."

Paul nodded. "Over and out, boss Knight."

Knight strode into the back hallway then took the steps, two at a time, up to the next level. In the ammo room, he packed another Glock in his waistband and a fourth one in his boot. That, on top of the one in the holster under his brown leather jacket. His head spun. He got that dizzy feeling again, and his chest felt tight. He leaned over and grasped the edges of a table. *No. I am a warrior. My goddess and I will make our escape and live long and happily. This is just stress, my body is strong.*

Knight stood up straight and took a deep breath. "Mind over matter," he whispered as he hurried down the back staircase to meet Li'l Tut.

Chapter 61

Duke peered from the cabin door of the fifty-foot Sea Ray. He and his two brothers had bought the top-of-the-line boat, which they christened *Babylon Beauty* across the bow, just before Prince died. Right here on deck, they'd spoken their most intense words of bonding, three black powerbrokers, between the black of the sky and the river.

So now, on this warm Indian summer night in September, on that patch of gray-carpeted plexi glass, and on those gray leather bucket seats, was the best place for Duke to let Knight know. *It's my birthday, and I'm 'bout to get back in the captain's chair. I'm a year older, a year wiser, and I'm takin' Babylon back. Got my team ready for a hostile takeover and I'll fight to the death to get my Duchess back too.*

Duke stared up at The Playhouse, the building on the river that he was getting ready to buy when he lost everything. Now Knight had transformed it into "party central." Lights flickered on the third floor. That meant the Barriors and B'Amazons were delivering all that loot to the vault, which would be transported later to HQ on Babylon Street.

Duke smiled. His inside sympathizers had dollar signs in their eyes and loyalty in their hearts, and were ready to help him make the heist of the century. *One month to The Games, an' I'm gon' win the gold.* Then he could have what was up behind those steamy windows of the top floor.

My Duchess was up there in The Playroom. Maybe one of those silhouettes moving in the dim purple and pink light was her.

Timbo throbbed at the thought of diving into that sweet pussy. She was a freak, and Duke needed to tap into her power to take charge.

He stared hard at the top floor, imagining her coming to a window and blowing a kiss down at him. His gaze lowered to the middle windows. "All that money just sittin' there," he groaned.

On the ground floor, the only activity, took place a few minutes ago, when the doors opened, and Ping and Pong took Flame away in that white catering truck.

I'll get back wit' my boy later. I'll need him. But why the catering truck?

That was another of Knight's entrepreneurial endeavors. He wanted to own shit himself, instead of paying other folks, because he always wanted to make all the money himself.

Always so smart, that muthafucka.

The deep rumble of a cigarette boat sliced past on the water, causing a sudden wake that rocked *Babylon Beauty.*

Duke gripped the doorway to steady himself. "Damn, muthafucka!" he shouted. The boat sped away so quickly, it left only the white fishtail pattern in the water. "Slow the fuck down!" Duke grabbed the wide dashboard to steady himself.

Another boat whizzed past, and the force knocked Duke into the captain's chair.

"Can't even stand up right in this mug," he exclaimed.

Suddenly, female laughter from a pleasure boat made him grind his teeth. He could feel his jaw muscle flex hard as he watched three lovey-dovey couples smile and cuddle on a sleek blue cabin cruiser. The soft tinkle of jazz, the champagne glasses in their hands, and the black urban professional look about them set off something inside Duke.

Duke glared at one clean cut guy on the boat, who wore a pink polo shirt, plaid shorts, and gold-rimmed glasses. "Preppy-ass muthafuckas. Act like you ain't neva seen the hood." Duke gripped the steering wheel. Even his fingers were trembling. Just like the rest of his body, from head to toe. All six foot, six inches of his once mighty brawn was shaking in his black Tims, because he was about to do something he'd never done; stand up to his big brother, Knight.

So where the fuck is he? Duke snatched his cell phone from his waistband. His fingers touched the warm metal butt of his gun. He was ready to rumble, if necessary. He held up the phone. The tiny blue display said eleven fifty-eight. "Oh, shit."

Knight stepped out of the doors leading to the back patio, which was softly lit by tropical-style torches. They cast a fiery glow around Knight's six foot, seven inches of power.

That made Duke's leg muscles feel as wobbly as the Ramen noodles that kept him alive for much of the past year, that is, when he ate at all during that 365-day hiatus into hell. At least now, his stomach was full of Mama's best pork chops and potatoes. She promised not to tell anybody, especially Knight, that he was living in the room over her garage.

Suddenly Duke's mind reeled with a wicked flash back to that night a year ago when Knight walked out in the middle of his birthday party and announced he was taking over. *And didn't nobody stop him. Including my punk ass.*

No wonder Knight looked just as ominous and powerful tonight, striding down the dock like a black cowboy, his big silver belt buckle shimmering with diamond block letters which spelled out *KNIGHT* giving just a hint of that "wild west" machismo.

Duke hated the way Knight walked. *Like he own the whole muthafuckin' planet!* Every step of his long legs and boots radiated with cockiness, confidence, and stealth precision, like he never took one stride without analyzing its impact first.

Duke laid his fingers over the metal bulge under his baggy white tee and jeans. *Analyze this, muthafucka.*

Knight's boots thudded on the wooden planks.

Duke's pulse hammered in his ears. He forced himself to focus on the best image of his life him, sitting back in his golden throne ruling the empire with his goddess, Duchess on his lap.

The image faded as Knight came into closer focus.

That muthafucka's face is glowing like the sun! Like he's in love. Like he got the juice and the bank to do any and everything he damn well pleased.

Duke's muscles trembled harder. He bit the inside of his lip to stop the mile long barrage of verbal bullets that were cocked to shoot and kill. He ground his teeth. The words ricocheted back down into his chest, making his heart pound harder.

No doubt Knight had half an army of Barriors lurking in the shadows, plus his own ammo, strapped on every limb.

Duke concentrated on his vision, so the sight of Knight didn't push all his mad buttons, but when Knight stopped on the dock, right at the stern, Duke felt a tornado ripping through his mind. Could hardly think of a sentence to speak. Could hardly see straight.

Because the way Knight stared down at him, the way his bright, black eyes glowed with brotherly love and affection, for a split second but turned instantly to disgust, revealed that Knight knew. His bigger, badder, more brilliant brother knew exactly where little Duke had been and what unspeakable things he'd been doing for the past twelve months.

That stare was so potent, Duke wanted to cower in self disgust like a beat down dog. *I hate what I did!* Duke's throat swelled with tears. He'd rather die before letting them fall. His tongue felt thick and slimy, his eyes burned as he stared at his brother's clean cut face, with its perfectly healthy, dark chocolate complexion and "good-living" fullness to his cheeks. No chance folks would confuse the two of them now. Not the way Duke's skin was looking these days.

He ground his teeth so loudly, he could hear a cracking sound in his ears. Because the mirror image before him was like looking at a reflection of how he used to be. Now he rarely even looked in the mirror. Even though he'd quit that shit and was living clean, his face, eyes, and body hadn't caught up with him yet.

And the disgust in Knight's eyes pulled the trigger on all those wicked words cocked on Duke's tongue. "It's your fault, muthafucka!" Duke shouted. He shot up from the captain's chair. His boots thudded on the floor as boats roared in the background. "You gon' give me back what's mine! I hate your ass, muthafucka! I hate your ass!"

A boat zoomed past, causing a wake. The waves slapped the side of *Babylon Beauty,* causing Duke to wobble.

Knight stood perfectly still, his big hand on his waist, his eyes radiating pity and disgust.

"I want Babylon!" Duke screamed. His lips felt wet; little bits of spit sprayed into the night as he yelled. "I want

Duchess! An' I'm gon' take it!" He knew he was ruining his moment; hysterics would get him nowhere, especially with an always calm, Knight. He was acting like a whacked out crackhead but couldn't stop it. The chemicals, the craziness, that's what was talking.

"You ain't gon' keep me down!" Duke screamed. His head spun so hard, his vision blurred with silvery lights, like just before those horrible migraine headaches came. His tongue felt like it was moving with a mind of its own, and his muscles trembled so hard, it felt like a convulsion would knock him down any second.

Knight just stood there, watching him self destruct.

"You ain't gon' play me like a punk no more!" Duke screamed. His hand slipped into his waistband. He pulled out his gun and aimed it at Knight. His finger spasmed on the hard metal trigger.

Ka-pow! Pow! Pow! The shots echoed off the black eternity of water and sky. Coldness, darkness, numbness.

Chapter 62

Her hot, hungry pussy was poised over Knight's giant dick. This was the moment in life that The Queen loved. This intense anticipation of being just an inch away from fucking scored a close second place to the actual orgasm, and the shit was so good with him, he could make her cum with one stroke.

Right now, in the candlelit master suite of the yacht, she was focused on Knight as she squatted above his massive lead rod, ready to fit herself on it with the perfect grip, then slide down and ride.

She loved to look into his onyx eyes, as her pussy sucked him inside to stroke her soul. She could feel the love and lust burning in her gaze as she stared into his eyes.

But his mind was a million miles away. He was thinking about Babylon, and money and safety and security and other cities and whether Duke was about to sneak into D-town to try and take Babylon back.

I gotta work some magic on my baby; make him forget about everything but us.

All that sexercise she was getting at the Babylon gym had strengthened her quadriceps to the point that she could pump down on him for hours if she wanted to without getting tired or feeling that burn in her muscles that once forced her to stop when she was on top. No, tonight she would do all the work to soothe his mind, body and spirit with supersonic sex and lobotomizing lovemaking.

"Knight, baby," The Queen whispered as she squatted over him, "you stressin'; don't be thinkin' business when you gettin' booty."

Knight laced his fingers with hers. He was lying on the king-sized bed on the white, 500-thread-count Egyptian sheets.

The yacht rocked gently, the silence between R. Kelly's best love songs allowing them to hear the soft slosh of water against the hull. Knight squeezed tight; his fingers were so long they covered the backs of her hands and reached the tops of her wrists. "That was a close call tonight with Flame," Knight said. "Got me thinking about—"

"Oh, man," she groaned. The Queen didn't want to hear anything about thinking. She wanted to hear the sloshy, slurpy sounds of fucking.

She gently sat on his rock-hard stomach, leaning forward and "pooting" her ass back as if she were sitting on his motorcycle, her steamy, wet pussy creaming all over his hot stomach.

"Oooh, baby girl," he said playfully, "you sure know how to change a man's train of thought."

She ground her hips just enough to make her cherry-sized clit slip into his innie belly button. The sensation sent an erotic ripple up through her core that exploded on her skin. Her nipples hardened, lips parted, and her eyes burned down lustfully at him.

Shane's giant head whipped up against the soft curve of her bare ass.

She leaned down to kiss him. ""Mmmm." God couldn't have made a more perfect fit for two pairs of lips.

She loved the way his lips were always so hot and soft, so inviting, so nurturing; even a quick peck promised a lifetime of love.

Right now, though, Knight pulled back. Her lips felt cold and abandoned as his beautiful genie eyes sparkled up at her. Something in them glinted like he'd seen something bad and couldn't shake it from his mind.

"Knight, baby, what's wrong?" She ran her fingertips with a feather soft touch over the sculpted planes of his gorgeous face. "This is our one year anniversary. We should be celebrating."

But Knight's laptop full of work, plus his four guns on the dresser, and the way he kept looking toward the bedroom door here on the yacht, let her know something was wrong.

"Baby, you been so paranoid lately," she said softly. "Like, we were s'posed to take a ride on the Sea Ray tonight; then you all of a sudden switched it to the yacht."

"More luxurious accommodations for my Queen," Knight said, kissing her forehead.

"That sounds real nice, but you ain't bein' straight-up."

"Baby girl," Knight whispered, staring intensely up into her eyes, "you know I love you to infinity."

The Queen's insides melted. His voice was so deep and sexy. "Yeah," she cooed. "Say it again."

"I love you to infinity."

She closed her eyes, letting his deep voice vibrate through her chest, then come to rest in her heart. She inhaled his delicious scent, his Black Cashmere cologne, and the gardenia scented candles glowing around the cabin.

"Baby girl?" His expression was different than any she'd seen on his face.

She drew her eyebrows together and asked, "You didn't meditate today, did you? You got your karma all twisted around. And you look pale."

Knight touched his fingertips to her jaw. He gently pulled her down for another kiss, but she pulled away.

"What's wrong, Knight? You know if something happens to you, I'll just die."

Knight shook his head, but his gaze softened as if he loved hearing this declaration of her love. Then, with a tone half playful, half somber, he asked, "So if I dropped dead right now, what would you do?"

The Queen tapped her fingertip to his nose and said matter-of-factly, "I'd strap myself to your big fine ass, drag us out that door to the water"—she pointed to the French doors leading to the boat's sports deck—"and I'd slide us both into that black infinity forever."

Knight covered her cheeks with feather soft kisses.

His comfort felt so good, it made her lips part. A soft moan escaped up from her soul. Because this tenderness was love. He pressed his hot cheek to hers; she put her hand on the back of his satin smooth head and stroked softly. "Baby girl, I think you played Juliet in the school play one too many times. And this Romeo ain't goin' nowhere. I'm yours for life."

"Life," The Queen whispered. "You *are* my life."

"My Queen." His hot breath tickled her ear. "We have what every other man and woman on the planet dreams about. And I'll fight to the death to make you always feel like my Queen."

She pressed a finger to his full lips. "Ssshhh. Let's celebrate." His face was so beautiful, and the emotion radiating from it was so intense, she felt dizzy. Without him, she had no one. Two dead parents. A brother who had disappeared when they got split up a year ago, and her look alike, older sister, Melanie, who had chosen a convent instead of life in the hood with Gramma Green.

He's trying to tell you something serious, Celeste said, *something that will change your life.*

Her heart pounded with that same panicky feeling when she'd lost all the people who were supposed to love her, in the space of a day. She remembered how she felt when her boyfriend and so called best friend, Tiffany, turned their backs on her and cut her off like she never existed.

If I ever see either of 'em again, I'ma show 'em how I really feel. Hoodstyle.

Suddenly her whole body burned with the anger, betrayal, disappointment, and sadness that she had stuffed down for the past year. Everyone she had known and loved had abandoned her, tossing her out like a pretty doll that had suddenly been ruined by a big, ugly smudge of dirt. Worthless. Disgusting. Black.

Here at Babylon, and in Knight's bed, she had found amazing love that she thought could make up for all the pain she'd endured.

But what if he's about to toss me out too?

The Queen shook her head, to exorcise those emotional demons from her past. Why did she have this sudden terror of rejection? Had he discovered something awful about her, and now it was time to trade her in for a blacker model? He was always talking about The Prince Code, how number one was trust no one. Should she not trust him, and did he not trust her? Was one of those scheming bitches who were always putting their panties in his pocket or blowing up his phone or sticking their titties in his face actually succeeding in stealing her man? Could that be why, despite all his deep declarations of loving her forever, she was getting the same vibe that he was about to cut her off?

Everybody turns on you eventually. Love doesn't last. And it's only a matter of time before you get the boot so they can move on to someone new. But my Knight too?

The Queen had often wondered, if he could come in and do his little brother the way he did, could he be that ruthless to his woman too? And with the long line of pussy constantly trying to hook him, maybe it was time they had a conversation. Perhaps it was time for Alice to pop a little pink pill marked "Reality" to end this Ghettoland fantasy that she was loving so much. But the white Wonderland that she'd wished for a year ago no longer appealed to her. She had faded to black and dropped off the world's radar by slipping into an urban underworld. *And I love it.*

Yet in her mind, she could hear Daddy warning in his deep but gentle voice. "If something seems too good to be true, then you can be sure that it is."

The Queen slid off Knight's stomach, stood beside the bed, and turned on the lamp on the nightstand.

"If you're about to break up with me," The Queen said, glaring down at Knight as he shifted to sit on the edge of the bed, "then I might as well go jump in the Detroit River. My life here with you is everything, Knight Johnson. And—"

"Baby girl!" his voice bellowed like the fog horn on a passing tanker ship. He reached for her hands. "How'd you jump from *A* to cra-*Z*-y with one glance?"

She snatched her hands back and squeezed the tears from her eyes. "Don't call me crazy! If you went through what I—"

Knight shook his head. "Baby girl, stop. You're still hurting; you're afraid to trust even now."

She crossed her arms. Her mind fast forwarded through all her options if she were to leave right now. Her plan to attend the University of Michigan was impossible. One flash of her social security number in their computer system, and the feds would eat her for lunch.

Her lifestyle, her money, it was all through Babylon. Plus, this wasn't the kind of work where you finish your contract and move on to the next company. Who knew what had happened to that ho, Janelle, last year who dared scheme against Duke?

And Milan. Duke made his own baby momma, wicked as she was, marry his back-stabbing boy, Beamer. Then when Duke disappeared and Knight took charge, Knight sent the two of them off to some brothel in Mexico. Duke's children, however, little Zeus and Hercules, plus his three other kids, were on the East Coast at a boarding school that Knight financed, to keep his blood safe while they got educations far away from Duke's drama.

Plus, The Queen realized, she knew way too much. She knew about the money, the Caribbean accounts, the laundering through the catering company and the security business. Her mind was a virtual file cabinet of the men and women who worked as prostitutes and gigolos for Babylon. And worse, she had a mental Rolodex of all the folks who solicited their services, from city officials to business people to celebrities to just plain married muthafuckas tryin' to get some extra booty.

"My queen," Knight whispered, grasping her trembling shoulders, "I see a hurricane tearin' you up inside. C'mon, Tinkerbell, sprinkle some of your magic pixie dust on those worries." He pulled her close.

Oh my God. She nestled into the soft spot at the core of his being, his solar plexus, where the round curves of his pecks came together to form a little indention that was a perfect fit for her hot cheek. But the better place was his neck. *Yeah, his neck is my Nirvana.*

"Are you alive?" she giggled into his neck. "How come I can never feel your pulse in your neck?"

Knight stiffened. "My resting heart rate is slow, almost silent, because I'm so in shape; my heart is conditioned to stay on reserve."

"It scares the hell outta me," The Queen said softly. "My big strong warrior should have a heartbeat that pounds like a Bang Squad song."

Knight let out a low, sexy laugh as he ran his fingertips over her nipples. They immediately stood at attention and sent an electric jolt down to her pussy.

"It will be bangin' in a minute."

The Queen nestled her face deeper into his neck. "Mmmmm . . . this is where I belong. Nowhere else. Ever."

Knight kissed the top of her head. "That's my baby girl. And to prove it," he whispered, his eyes sparkling down on her like black diamonds as he reached behind his back, "I have this for you."

He took her left hand. Whatever he was about to slip on her ring finger, she couldn't see it. He blocked it under his fingertips as it slid on. Then, in one smooth move, he bent down on one knee.

"The Queen. My queen," Knight said with a deep, quaking voice. He pulled back his hand to reveal the ring. "Be my partner in life, here on earth and in eternity, as my wife."

The sound that came up out of The Queen's soul was a blend of a shriek, a cry, a sob, and a purr. He held his open palms under her hand, framing her caramel fingers with his huge, dark hands.

"I feel dizzy," she said, sinking back onto the soft bed, where the silky gold spread caressed her bare ass. She sat upright, facing him. But he was still so tall, just kneeling, that she had to look up into his eyes, their onyx sparkle even more brilliant than the incredible diamond on her finger. She gasped. "Oh my God, Knight, always look at me like that."

He leaned close with parted lips. She leaned forward with an open mouth. And like two, one of a kind puzzle pieces, their lips locked with perfect precision. Intense heat fused them together. And the power of that union sent electric jolts through her every cell that ricocheted back to make pink and purple bolts of lightning behind her closed eyelids.

"Promise you'll always kiss me like this."

"Promise you'll always look at me the way you're looking at me now," Knight said.

"I promise," she purred. "Promise me you'll always see that we can be, you and me, into eternity, for all to see. Never flee, but always be free to be in unity. Fly high with me; cry, sigh, lie with me; die with me as our souls float into infinity."

"Let's go to the studio tomorrow," Knight said. "Have Jamal lay a soft beat with that. So we can play it at the wedding."

The Queen shrieked. "Oooh, the wedding! I love it!" She held up her hand. Her eyes bugged at the breathtaking ring. The center stone was shaped like a heart. This ring was spectacular.

"Knight, it's beautiful," she purred, "I've always wanted a heart-shaped diamond."

Knight smiled. "I know it sounds corny as hell. But when I saw it, I said, 'That's perfect for The Queen of my heart.'"

"You're right," she said, "it is corny as hell, but I love it!" She studied the sparkling stone. It was about three carats secured in platinum prongs on a platinum band, whose sides glistened with tiny baguettes.

"There's more." Knight took her hand and turned it over. In her sweaty palm, he placed a platinum band. "Put this on me," he said softly, "to show the world that I'm yours forever. Read the inside." His stare penetrated her eyes so deeply that it raised the tiny hairs on the back of her neck.

She picked it up. THE QUEEN'S KNIGHT was inscribed inside. She slid it onto his ring finger. "So now are we married?" She stared into his loving eyes.

Knight smiled. His big, white teeth contrasted against his full, dark lips. Now, she stared, trance like, at his mouth.

"We're married as far as I'm concerned," Knight said, "but here's what I propose."

The perfectly curious and attentive expression on The Queen's face gave no hint of the tornado of thoughts ripping through her brain. *Marriage means I'm here to stay. Forever. And I'm only nineteen!*

But did Alice want to stay in Ghettoland, even as The Queen of Hearts, forever? Did she ever want to pop a "back to white" pill and return to her previous life? Was it possible to take the chocolate out of the milk once it had been stirred up, sipped, and savored?

Hell no! The Queen loved every taste, every sip, and every decadent sensation of her life as it was right then. With this gorgeous Mandingo warrior who was pledging the tenderest love forever.

Gone was the naïve, innocent little white girl that arrived at Babylon a year ago. The second she lost her virginity to Duke and got her first real taste of sex, she was turned out, and ready to be the femme fatale she was born to be.

Now, she couldn't imagine life without the mind blowing sex, love, power, and adventure that she enjoyed here every day as The Queen. Hidden far away from the feds who were looking for her after crucifying her daddy. She was now the baddest bitch in Babylon, helping Knight grow it bigger and better every day. Her eyes sparkled at him as he described his plan for their wedding and future.

"First," he said, "we get married on the sexiest day in Babylon. The day of The Games."

"Love it!" The Queen exclaimed. "That's in a month!"

"Four weeks from tonight," Knight said. "First we have a wedding ceremony on the rooftop terrace at The Playhouse. All our guests will be under a white tent overlooking the river, and we'll have a reception on the patio."

The Queen nodded. "Everybody will already be in town for The Games."

"You got it, Tinkerbell. And The Games will actually be our reception, but even more of a celebration because everybody'll be watching the competition. Then we take a boat ride away to paradise and it's all over."

The Queen's face drooped into a sad expression. "Love it," she whispered.

"You don't sound like it," Knight said, tapping a fingertip under her chin to raise her face. "Tinkerbell looks like she lost her pixie dust."

"My parents are dead," she said, her insides aching that they would not see her on the day that she dreamed about as a little girl.

Knight sat on the bed and scooped her onto his lap. Shane pressed against her hip. And the heat of his lap against the bottom of her thighs, along with the firm warmth of his chest against her left arm, inspired her to nestle her cheek into his solar plexus and close her eyes.

"Your parents are watching," Knight said, his deep voice vibrating through her ear down to her soul. "This is all predestined baby girl. Everything that's happened to you was fate's purpose. To bring you to me. And help us do great things together."

She smiled and said in a sultry tone, "To help folks get their freak on."

"To build our empire and secure our future," he said. "I couldn't do it without your brilliant business mind, Miss Female Marketing Genius. Them chicks tonight, boy, they looked like they were in Nirvana and never wanted to leave."

The Queen smiled. "Daddy always said, 'Get rich in a niche. Figure out what nobody's doing, and do it as bold and beautifully as you can.' And nobody was providing dick to the professional ladies."

Knight's deep laughter boomed into her ear. "We'll see if that TV anchor Trina Michaels can keep this little secret to herself after the sexcapade she had the other day." The Queen stiffened. "She made a joke about doing a report about our product. I let her know that shit was not welcome at all."

"Not if she knows what's good for her," Knight said half smiling. As The Queen heard the tone in his voice, and felt a strange surge in her body and something deep down in her gut cramped.

All of a sudden she felt an uncertainty of the unknown. Knight was ruthless. One wrong move on her part and she could find herself in exile from Babylon, just like how it went down with Duke. Till this day she still didn't even know if Duke were still alive. And suddenly, Knight's words echoed back into her thoughts. "You said a boat ride away and it's all over. What do you mean by that?"

"The wedding day," Knight said. "Life as we knew it before marriage is all over. And we start our new life on our honeymoon."

The Queen pulled her cheek away. It felt cold as she turned and stared up into his eyes, probing for more information. Something about the way he'd said "all over" made her gut cramp.

He's hiding something, Celeste said.

The Queen had learned, since Knight was so slick, that questioning him about something was pointless. He was master of the art of deception and evasion. She would have to investigate in more cunning ways. She kissed his cheek. "I want a tropical island honeymoon. So I can lay on the beach with my bare ass pointing up at the sun."

Knight ran a giant hand over her hair, smoothing it down from the crown of her head to her shoulders and back. "I'll find us a remote house on an obscure island. After the wedding, we can sail down Lake Erie to the Erie Canal to the Atlantic and down to the island of your choice."

The Queen caressed the beautiful black skin on his bald head. "Someday I'm gonna climb up into your brilliant mind so I can sit down and look around. I need to see what a bionic brain looks like on the inside."

Suddenly Shane hardened and poked into her hip.

She wrapped her fingers around all that lead pipe, watching her ring glisten brightly against the huge black dick snaking over her thigh. "I'll take a bionic blast from that, too."

"Baby girl, be honest," he whispered. "Do you have any desire, even an ounce, to fuck another man? And do you have any yearning to return to the white world you left behind?"

"Hell no to both."

Knight stared hard into her eyes, as if invisible hooks were shooting into her brain to pry out the truth. "You've made love with two men in your life," he said. "Me for a year, and Duke for five days before that, is that it?"

The Queen stiffened. "Why would I want to sample chicken nuggets when I get to savor the juiciest lobster in the sea all day, every day?"

Knight tossed back his head. Deep laughter echoed off the shimmery turquoise and beige Egyptian design that was hand painted on the leather ceiling. "That, baby girl, is exactly how I feel about you; this man don't ever need any pussy other than the sweet, creamy meat right here." His brows drew together. "I haven't heard you say yes."

The Queen's pussy throbbed. She said with a sassy, sexy tone, "Celeste wants to whisper it to you."

In one graceful movement, Knight grasped The Queen at the sides of her waist, tossed her into the air as he stood up, and caught her by cupping his open palms under her thighs. He pressed his open mouth and extended his tongue, between her legs.

"Whew!" The Queen shrieked playfully.

His tongue fucked her with lightning speed, while his upper lip pressed into her clit with expert precision.

"Oh my God!" The Queen moaned. Her fingertips gripped the back of Knight's smooth, bald head.

He moved his palms to cup right under her butt.

"Yeah, squeeze my ass like that," she said, grinding her hips to intensify the pressure of his lip on her clit. "Can you hear Celeste screaming the answer?"

Knight groaned deeply.

The Queen's whole body trembled as she was about to cum. She tossed back her head, letting her long black hair tickle down her back.

Knight gripped her harder, digging his fingers into the flesh of her ass.

"I'm yours!" The Queen moaned as her heels dug into his back, her fingertips gripped his head, and her pussy pulsated around his tongue.

In a flash, she was falling. Down, down, down. Was he dropping her? Had he been pale earlier because he's sick? Was he fainting and losing his grip? Was her pussy suffocating him? Or sucking the life out of him?

No, God please don't let my mixed-race woman sex powers kill Knight like they killed Mommy.

Her eyes flew open. She stared into Knight's lust widened gaze.

That mischievous smile curling up the corners of his beautiful lips let her know, everything was okay.

The Queen's pussy landed on Knight's huge, hard, dick.

He tossed back his head, busting out a laugh. "I scared you!" he teased.

She wrapped her legs around his waist and gripped his shoulders. She gripped her knees around him and bounced up and down. She was fucking the shit out of that big dick.

"Damn, baby girl," he moaned. "Fuck that shit." He cupped the round curves of her ass, from the sides, and helped her slam that pussy down on it.

Her pussy was extra wet right now. Sex felt so much better when you did it raw. Knight didn't like using condoms and a few months ago, she'd stopped taking the pill, because Knight had said that a love as powerful as theirs, should create new lives to carry on their legacy and their DNA.

Panting, sweating, trembling, screaming, The Queen slipped into an erotic zone.

"Make love to me, Tinkerbell. Make love to me!" Knight's deep voice boomed so loud, the boat rocked.

"Now," The Queen whispered, "cum with me."

She pumped harder. Shivers wracked her every cell.

"This pussy mine for life," Knight panted. "This baby girl mine for life." He stared into her eyes and whispered, "My wife." Their mouths smashed together as Knight squirted up into the core of his Queen, to baptize their union forever.

Chapter 63

Knight had to make his heart stop pounding, and his chest stop squeezing, as he obsessed over that "kill-or-be-killed" moment five hours ago. Even though he'd chosen the first option, the thought of killing his baby brother made his heart ache. Here in bed, he hadn't slept a wink.

Li'l Tut might be dead right now. And I pulled the trigger. Twice. But if he's alive, and he survives that fall into the river, and recuperates, he'll be back with a vengeance.

But if Knight had hesitated, he wouldn't have been laying here watching his Queen sleep more peacefully than an angel. He cherished the sensations of the plush sheets, the warmth of her body, and the gentle rocking of the yacht. It was silent except for the lapping water and his heartbeat.

She could see that I didn't feel well. It scared the shit out of her.

No, his job was to make sure the future Mrs. Johnson never worried another day in life. He didn't have to tell her that after their wedding they'd be leaving Babylon, Detroit, and the United States forever. Stuff was just too crazy around here. For both, it was in their best interests to start a new life together in an exotic place, with a fortune in the bank.

Knight's fingertip traced the dark arc of her eyebrow. Her sun tanned skin was so clear and smooth, as fresh as a baby's. What if he'd planted a seed in her tonight?

Intuition said, *Your child is growing inside her right now. A human being created from the kind of soul-deep love that you never saw between your parents or anybody else.*

Knight's chest ached. If he felt this strongly about protecting his beautiful angel Queen from the evils of the world, how would he feel about his own child? That only emphasized the importance and brilliance of starting over, far away. It wasn't even a choice.

Knight was twenty-five and had no children yet. His mother had been asking him to give her grandkids for years.

And what about Mama? They could take her with them. She couldn't live without any of her baby boys. First, Prince got shot to death. Then Knight went to jail. Then Knight came back, but Li'l Tut disappeared. No more disappearing acts for Mama. After all that struggling by herself to raise her kids in the hood, it was time for her to relax and enjoy life too. Plus, when everything went down, the feds would come to her too. But not if she were playing nanny on a sun splashed island with Knight's first baby.

Knight's chest squeezed. He struggled to suck down air.

All of them had to get away. Too many question marks kept popping up here. The top among them, *Is Li'l Tut alive?*

Knight knew he'd shot Li'l Tut because he saw the red stain on his baby brother's white T-shirt before he fell backward into the Detroit River. The Barriors had searched the marina and surrounding areas of the river but found nothing. But the current could have carried his body down river toward Toledo, or into Lake St. Clair. A freighter or fishing boat could drag him somewhere. Or he could wash up on the island park of Belle Isle, or across the river in Canada.

But what if Li'l Tut were alive? What if he fell into the water with only a graze wound, crawled up on land somewhere nearby, and made his way to someplace where he could recover?

Be for real, intuition said. *You know damn well that boy was as whacked out on crack as he could be.*

The dark circles under his eyes, sunken in cheeks, and dark splotches on his skin said it all. His shirt and pants were hanging off his skinny body like he was a fucking clothes hanger.

Knight massaged his chest over his heart. It had raced uncontrollably while they made love, especially when he tossed her up to eat her pussy. He had only half-planned the drop; he had actually gone weak and lost his grip. Panic shot through him now, as it had then.

What if I fall out and can't protect her? What if I drop dead? Or what if she thinks that crazy curse shit is comin' true and she rations out the pussy to me but gets some dick from another muthafucka?

"Stop!" he said out loud. He tried to remember all the visualization and meditation techniques he learned while he was locked up. "Stop," he whispered. He closed his eyes to visualize himself free of any discomfort. But all he saw was Li'l Tut's drug ravaged face. His heart raced even more intensely.

Perhaps what disturbed Knight most about that, was the eerie resemblance they shared. Seeing his mirror image whacked out on crack made him shudder because that's what he would have become if he had taken that hit some fellas in the neighborhood offered when he caught that rape case. Wrongly accused; yes. Wrongly convicted; yes. But vilified in the media nonetheless.

But Knight was strong. He remembered one of the few words of wisdom their father had offered during his brief appearances during their early childhood, "A man's character is defined by how he handles the bad times."

That muthafucka's character must've been defined as a certified loser, because he disappeared and left Mama to do a man's job. Now Li'l Tut was following in his footsteps. Knight pressed his lips to The Queen's forehead. Never would he hand this goddess back to the young punk who couldn't appreciate her or treat her the way she deserved.

The same went for Babylon. Li'l Tut had been running the family empire into the ground when Knight came back. But ever since Knight had taken over, it had been nothing but prosperity and expansion.

Knight felt a sharp pain and gripped his chest.

He had to check his accounts online, to make sure that everything was in order for Manifest Destiny to happen on schedule. He slowly rose from the bed, trying to breathe away the pain, but every time he inhaled, the chest cramp squeezed more tightly.

Bending over as he walked, he slowly made it across the room to the dresser, turned on the laptop, and brought it back to bed. The clock on the upper right corner of the screen said 4:42 a.m.

His fingers clicked across the silver keyboard as the screen danced with numbers for his various over seas accounts. Accounts that in one month would have a balance of fifty million, which would secure his family's future forever, far away from life in the big city.

He clicked on to the high security Web site for his world class financial institution, which handled accounts for Greek shipping moguls, inner city thugs in hiding, and English royalty alike.

Knight's Manifest Destiny accounts had been opened in the Bahamas under the name of Julius Mark Anthony. With several more secret passwords and a fictitious profile of a California real estate baron, Knight had set up the accounts with the help of a kinky Caucasian couple, Mr. and Mrs. Marx. The West coast couple whom he had met years ago, had helped him expand Babylon to the Pacific and were his mentors.

But their high-profile multimedia company, which made adult films and ran a soft-porn cable TV channel, was currently being investigated for tax evasion. And if the feds actually indicted the Marx's, Knight worried that his accounts would be traced back to them and seized.

A lightning bolt of pain shot through his chest.

Somehow he would have to get these elaborate accounts switched once again to avoid all risks. He had worked so hard, sleeping only a few hours every night for the past year, to build Babylon to what it was now. So it wasn't an option to leave it all behind without taking the financial fruit of his labor with him.

His brain spun over all the scenarios that could break wide open on his wedding night; the feds still searching for Victoria Winston; a raid; Moreno; Li'l Tut plotting a coup with board members and others.

Knight did a mental checklist of his offense and defense. *The moat of fire that would create a wall of flames around The Playhouse while he and The Queen disappeared; rooftop snipers; the tunnel to the river; a motorcycle escape, if necessary, down to yacht #2.*

He remembered a rule from The Prince Code, *Think from the end*. He had to envision every detail of those final minutes then plan accordingly, right now. But time was whizzing at the speed of light.

"Fuck," he whispered. The clock on the upper right hand corner of his laptop screen said 5:55 a.m. He'd already spent more than an hour online and still hadn't figured out a solution for protecting these accounts.

Time is going too fast. The pain radiated from the sharp clutch around his heart, up his neck, down his arm.

He felt like he was on the verge of a panick attack. He set the computer on the blankets, then laid back, holding The Queen's hand. The heat of her fingers comforted him. But when he shifted, the needles pierced his heart.

No, she couldn't wake up to find him dead.

I can control this with my mind. Mind over matter.

Intuition echoed those same words. But the pain intensified.

He took long, deep breaths to calm himself. But his heart was racing. And it hurt. So Knight laid staring wide eyed at the ceiling.

Am I dying?

Chapter 64

The Queen sat behind her glass desk at Babylon HQ, punching numbers into her sleek, silver laptop computer. She had just finished a conference call with L.A., Chicago, New York, and Dallas. Now, finally, it was quiet enough for them to concentrate. Seemed like the phones had been ringing nonstop and employees had been coming in all morning, interrupting their work. She pulled off her gold framed glasses.

"Knight," she said, focusing on him as he hung up the phone. He'd been hammering out the details of the meeting with Moreno tomorrow afternoon and the board meeting after that. Their every move right now was putting Babylon closer to domination over their competitors.

They had so much work to do between now and the wedding, so they could take off and not give Babylon a single worry. But The Queen was worried that all this work was taking a toll on Knight. He hadn't looked right this morning.

Plus they were going to Jamal's studio this afternoon to record their wedding song, which she'd written last night. Seemed like there weren't enough hours in the day. The Queen's muscles tensed. And that triggered her body's automatic urge to relieve stress; have an orgasm.

She glanced at Knight. Maybe she could slide down on it for a minute and let Shane take care of this.

Damn, he looks pale. Somethin' ain't right.

She froze. Were her mixed-race sex powers taking a toll on Knight? Despite Knight reassuring her that he was fine, she didn't think he looked good, so she decided to leave him be. She could take care of it herself. A quick flick of the fingers and boom, she'd cum and be good to go. However, she'd rather enjoy the sensations of somebody wrapping their lips around it and sucking for a while. Then her muscles would loosen up. Where was Honey when she needed her?

The thought of tasting some of Honey's sweetness made The Queen's pussy throb even harder. *Focus!* The Queen studied the green numbers on the computer screen.

"These numbers don't make sense," she said, shifting to make her thong rub against her pussy. "Look at the net and the gross for the past three Bang Squad gigs in The Garage. Somethin's outta whack."

She stood up to let Knight sit down and let his math whiz mind do some calculations. He looked pale, like he had last night.

Maybe he's stressin' about the meetings. But Knight never lets it show. She massaged the back of his shoulders through his crisp white shirt. "Knight, baby, you okay?"

His brows drew together as he focused on the numbers. "Maybe it's time to add more meat and dairy back into your diet," she said. "Maybe all those vegetables just aren't enough for my African god warrior."

Turning toward her, "I get all the meat and cream I need," he smiled and winked.

"But maybe you're anemic, not enough iron," she said, pressing her cheek to his, "Your cheeks feel hot."

"My whole body's been hotter since I first saw you," he said. "I see the problem here. Somebody neglected to add in the tips and fees. That skewed the numbers."

The Queen could almost hear Knight's mind ticking down a list of suspects. Because if they had done this deliberately, they were stealing money from Babylon. And the last person who had done that, had joined Milan and Beamer for a life of sexual servitude down in Mexico.

"CoCo," Knight said without looking up from the screen, "call the accountants to do a computer history on who entered these figures. Not just whose names were on the report, but who logged in and jacked up my dollars."

"Yes, sir," CoCo said, flipping open her phone. She walked through the double doors to the back offices.

The Queen kissed the top of his bald head. "Brilliant man!" She pressed her lips to his ear. "I love you to the infinity."

He turned to kiss her mouth. Anytime their lips touched, it felt like time stopped.

"A month can't come soon enough," The Queen whispered. "I bet all you need is some rest and your beautiful face will start glowin' like rich, dark chocolate again. We'll get that pink blush back on your cheeks, like when we make love."

He grasped her hands then raised her ring to his mouth to kiss it. "Mrs. Johnson, you got a brotha feelin' so unbelievable."

"Believe it. I'm yours for life."

Big Moe walked in through the front office doors. "Must be nice bein' in love, mon," he said, setting an envelope on the desk. "Phone records. I won't interrupt nothin'."

"I appreciate cha, man," Knight said.

As soon as he left, someone else knocked on the side door leading to the secretarial cubicles.

"Damn! All these interruptions," The Queen said.

The door opened. In walked Honey in a short white dress, gold sandals with straps laced up her juicy calves, and gold bands snaking around her upper arms. Her juicy titties bounced under the sheer fabric as she approached the desk. She curtsied Knight, who nodded back without looking away from the computer.

"Queen," Honey said through full, peach-glossed lips, "here's today's mail and that credit card report you asked for."

"Thank you," The Queen said, inhaling Honey's brown sugar, vanilla scent. She was one of the prettiest women The Queen had ever seen. "And there's a woman who wants to see you," Honey said. "She's in the lobby. Says she met you at the sorority party at The Playhouse."

The Queen stiffened. "How'd she find her way over here?"

"Coco invited her."

"That doesn't sound right," The Queen said. "What's her name?"

"Trina Michaels."

Knight glanced up. "Hell no," he bellowed. "Client or not, no journalist is welcome in Babylon HQ. I don't care if she hires every Stud and Slut for a month long party. This building is off limits to outsiders. Bring CoCo's little ass back in here."

"Yes, sir," Honey said.

"Baby girl, turn on the insurance."

The Queen stepped toward the eight foot, black and gold striped mummy cases flanking the glass shelves behind the desk. After opening each one, she pressed a red button and saw a crimson light flash. She did the same with two mummy cases flanking the double doors facing the desk.

CoCo walked in and she spoke before being spoken to. "I made an exception," CoCo said, "because Ms. Michaels wanted to meet the man behind this enterprise."

"We coulda done that over lunch downtown," Knight said, standing. He stepped down from the marble platform that held the desk. Down three steps, and he towered over CoCo. "What up, CoCo?"

She stared up at him with her usual business toughness. "Well, Ms. Michaels wants to hook up a deal for her annual Christmas party in Washington, D.C."

"Coulda done that elsewhere too. Next."

"She kinda got the hots for The Queen." Knight shook his head. "Like I said—"

The Queen stepped between them. "What is the deal, CoCo? Did she lick your pussy so good you agreed to violate Babylon protocol?"

CoCo smiled. "Actually . . ."

The double doors opened and in walked Honey with Trina Michaels. She wore dark jeans, high-heeled sandals and had a pink pedicure that made her toes look like little pieces of candy. Her nipples poked through the thin fabric of her green blouse, and her long brown hair bounced as she strode in.

"Queen," she exclaimed, smiling. Her big brown eyes glowed with lust and excitement as she shook The Queen's hand. "Nice to see you again." The Queen's gut cramped at the idea of this nationally known TV reporter stepping into the nerve center of Babylon.

Knight stepped behind the desk and turned off the computer. "How can we help you, Ms. Michaels?" Knight asked.

Trina looked up at him like she wanted to slurp him down whole, the same way she'd checked out the Studs at the party. But Knight stared down at her like he didn't even notice. "I understand you enjoyed the party," he said with a complete business tone.

"Had the time of my life!" she exclaimed, taking The Queen's hand. "This woman has a magnificent mind!"

Honey and CoCo stared with confused expressions.

"What can we do for you?" Knight asked with a more stern tone. "We don't normally hold meetings here. If you'd like to arrange a party, we can do that in our downtown offices."

"Actually, I have an unusual proposal for you," the TV chick said. "I want to do a special on the sex industry, and I—"

Knight nodded so subtly to The Queen, no one could have noticed.

Honey closed and locked the double doors. And CoCo sat down on one of the black and gold striped satin couches against the side wall.

The Queen raised Trina's hand to her mouth, then trailed the woman's knuckles over her hot, parted lips.

Trina gasped.

At the same time, Honey went to the sound system on the glass shelves behind the desk. One of Bang Squad's sexiest slow songs began to play.

Knight sat in the chair behind the desk.

The Queen stepped closer to Trina. She leaned into her soft brown hair, by her ear, and whispered, "You got the prettiest pussy. Made me think of a pink and brown flower." Trina's eyes widened. Her nipples poked even harder through her shirt as The Queen stepped closer. Her arm brushed against one titty, making the woman close her eyes.

She glanced around nervously. "All these people . . ."

"This is what you wanted, isn't it?" The Queen teased. Then her voice hardened. "This is why you schemed your way up where nobody is allowed to enter. Isn't it, Trina?"

The woman stepped back, her eyes wide with worry.

The Queen felt the rhythm of the sexy music. Her pussy throbbed at the thought of what was about to go down. Fresh meat.

The Queen stepped closer to Trina. Standing nose to nose with her, she pouted her lips and stared seductively into her eyes. "Trina, you ever ate some pussy?"

"No," she whispered, glancing at Knight and CoCo.

Honey sat on one of the marble steps leading up to the desk. She leaned back on the heels of her hands, offering her beautiful titties up into the air, legs wide so that her bare knees offered a delightful view, down to her thighs, where her white dress fluffed in her lap. Honey swayed gently to the music as she held a gold lighter to a long blunt. Squinting, she sucked down the sweet smoke, then offered it to Trina.

The reporter shook her head. "This isn't what—" Then she shrugged and took the blunt. Sucked down some smoke like a pro. She moaned as smoke poured out of her mouth and her whole body visibly relaxed. She gazed longingly at The Queen and said, "I didn't expect to—"

"I know how you feel," The Queen said, her lip slightly brushing Trina's mouth as she spoke. "Wasn't quite what I expected when we saw you either."

Trina kissed her. She pressed those pretty brown lips straight onto The Queen's mouth. Like she'd been hungering for a girl all her life but was too scared to make it happen.

"Yeah," Knight groaned. "CoCo, call Twister."

"Yes, sir."

Before The Queen closed her eyes, to love the sensation of this new, beautiful woman kissing her, she glimpsed in the corner of her eye, Knight's giant hand stroking the crotch of his pants.

My pipe is steamin' now.

The Queen raised Trina's palms up to the V of her blouse. Slid them inside, let Trina feel the hard points of her nipples under her lace bra. "Take your clothes off," The Queen whispered as she led Trina toward the couch.

Both women undressed.

Damn, her pussy looks good.

The Queen straddled one end of the couch. "Come taste," she whispered, sliding down to offer her bare pussy up to this hungry bitch.

Trina straddled the couch, too, facing The Queen. She leaned down, mouth open.

"Oooh, seems like you've done this before," The Queen whispered. "Or does eating pussy just come naturally to you?"

A soft moan was all the response she got.

"Sit up," The Queen said, as she spread Trina's legs.

"Ooh, just look at that pretty sight," The Queen said, loving the image of another juicy pussy about to press into hers. "Knight, baby, you see this?"

Suddenly Trina looked embarrassed. She must have forgotten that Knight was there, and CoCo.

Honey offered Trina another hit on the blunt.

The Queen delighted in watching this prim and proper professional woman suck down smoke and relax.

Yeah, now she's ready to get turned out in a new way.

The Queen closed her eyes, grinding in a slow circle, her whole body trembling with the extreme pleasure of her clit rubbing against another one. Trina moaned as she began grinding and rotating her hips to match The Queen's motions. "Yeah, work that pussy," The Queen whispered, staring into Trina's eyes.

"Good gracious, I had no idea," Trina whispered, "no idea it could be so divine."

The Queen laid back, so that her back arched and her titties poked up. Honey came to the rescue. She knelt at her side, sucking one hard point into her hot mouth.

CoCo did the same with Trina.

In just a few minutes, Trina convulsed all over the place. Her pulsating pussy made The Queen's throb even harder; she shuddered with orgasm.

That's when Knight stepped in.

Trina laid back on the couch, legs spread.

"Oh," The Queen groaned, loving the sight of Trina's pretty pink pussy. The Queen shoved her fingers in it and Trina screamed in ecstasy.

The Queen knelt on the carpet, then lowered her face into the pussy.

Behind her, Knight knelt, too.

Just as The Queen's lips wrapped around Trina's cherry sized clit, Knight's big dick rammed up into The Queen's pussy from the back.

The Queen sucked like her life depended on it. She licked and finger fucked, as she moaned and shivered with the pleasure of Knight's pipe, pounding into her sweet canal.

On the carpet, nearby, Honey spread her sweet stuff for CoCo to lick as CoCo's finger fucked herself from behind, her beautiful dark ass poked up in the air, her titties dancing over the carpet as she sucked.

"I'm 'bout to blow," Knight groaned. He pounded harder and harder.

The Queen licked ferociously.

CoCo and Honey came all over the floor.

"Damn!" Knight exclaimed as he nutted inside The Queen.

Trina panted, then collapsed.

They all laid quiet for a few minutes.

Then, when they were dressed, Trina revisited the TV interview question.

Knight walked to the mummy case. He pulled out a videotape and said, "The answer is no. Hell no. And neva in a million years, unless you'd like to see this on national TV to preview your legal analysis of the day."

Chapter 65

Jamal was diggin' the way CoCo was sucking his dick while he worked the board in his music studio. Life for a twenty-two-year-old brotha from the hood didn't get much better than this fantasy hook up as a hip-hop music mogul. He was sitting in his big chair, getting blown by his lady, and watching Knight and The Queen through the glass in the sound booth, where they were jammin' on their wedding song, and each other.

The world gon' cum jus' by watchin' the sexiest couple groove in my studio. Knight a bad dude, plannin' his disappearing act like this.

The soft light of white candles all around the soundbooth cast the most seductive glow over their nude bodies. They looked like a huge licorice twist around a long caramel sucker, and their love was so hot that they both glistened as if they were melting into one.

As Knight planted his lips on The Queen's shoulder and sucked her skin, making her pretty cinnamon nipples point straight at Jamal, he moaned.

"The world ain't neva seen that kinda love," Jamal whispered. "But I'm 'bout to show 'em." He glanced at the panel of knobs and red lights to his right. Yeah, the cameras were rolling on four angles, including the ceiling, to capture that from every angle. They'd have to edit to make it clean enough for TV, but the Bang Squad knew all kinds of ways to show a lot of bumpin' and grindin' without showing the whole body part.

Jamal swayed his body to the sexy beat he had laid to The Queen's song. It started with The Queen whispering, "Promise you'll always kiss me like this."

The hook jammed on their hit theme song, "Love You to the Infinity," which had been rocking the charts since its debut.

The fact that Knight and The Queen had refused all media interviews from the hottest hip-hop magazines and TV shows out there only made fans want more. All kinds of rumors were burnin' up cell phones, e-mails, and Internet Web sites about the real identities of The Queen and her Knight.

Some said it was Tupac and Aaliyah reincarnated. Or that they had faked their deaths and were recording from some remote hideaway under aliases.

But nobody except folks at Babylon knew the truth. And they also knew that if they snitched that'd be their ass. So the secret was kept. And sales and rumors would shoot through the roof as soon as Manifest Destiny went into effect.

"Millions," Jamal whispered.

Do I really wanna buy Babylon? Yeah, it would be crazy dough. But Bang Squad, Inc. makin' mad money too. Dang, I can't let my boy Knight down. I gave my word.

Just like Knight, Prince, and Duke had given Jamal their word three years ago that they would bankroll his music until he became the next P. Diddy or Jay-Z. And the three brothers had stuck by their word. They'd done everything, from financing his studio time, to sponsoring his national concert tour, to using their underground network and power plays to get him on the hottest radio stations across America.

So by the time Knight had gotten out of lock-up, Jamal and Bang Squad were so rich and famous that their nasty beats were rockin' in cars, flowin' off lips from the cities to the suburbs, and even playing on the soundtrack to a couple in-the-hoodstyle Hollywood movies.

Jamal's dick threatened to turn to mush. Because if he turned on Knight, he'd be through just as quickly.

I'd be a dead, out of bidness muthafucka.

But the idea of taking on an illegitimate business, now that Jamal had huge, legitimate record deals, made something sharp and wicked slice through his gut. Then again, the idea of raking in all those millions that Babylon was making across the country, suddenly made Jamal's dick stand to attention and pledge allegiance to his boy and their deal.

His dick got even harder as The Queen moaned, "Yeah, baby, promise me we can be wild and free and love to the infinity."

And the video of them, right now, making love like a man and a woman was so hot, a magical glow lit up the studio like The Queen really was Tinkerbell sprinkling her pixie dust all over the two of them.

"Millions," Jamal whispered, shifting his hips to shove his dick deeper into CoCo's sexy little mouth.

Yeah, this video would show the hip-hop generation what real love was all about.

"CoCo, you doin' it jus' like Daddy love it," Jamal groaned. His phone vibrated on his hip. DICKMAN flashed on the red screen. Raynard would have to wait.

I'll holla back in a minute.

Right now Jamal only had two things on his mind; music and making love. 'Cause CoCo had a way of letting lots of spit cover her lips and the inside of her mouth while she slurped up and down on Beat.

I love the way CoCo give head.

Unlike some girls who act like a dick's gonna lurch up and bite them, or get stuck in their throat, or make them sweat out their hair, CoCo always got down and dirty, and acted like she loved that shit. A sexy shiver rippled through his six-foot frame as he watched Knight and The Queen through the glass in the sound booth. The Queen's earphones held her hair back over her shoulders as she moaned into the mic that descended from the ceiling. Her hair swayed back and forth, over her bare shoulders as Knight drilled her fine ass from the back. So the sexy sounds everybody would hear at the wedding reception would be real. Because they were really fuckin' in the sound booth.

As CoCo squeezed her slippery lips over his dick, up and down, he shifted his hips in the red suede chair.

Jamal slid up the bass to capture the full range of The Queen's sexual sounds.

Ain't no betta life than this shit. He couldn't even see CoCo under the board. She had a pillow down there in the darkness, to cushion her knees as she sucked his dick. As good as she sucked, he might consider making her his queen when he officially took over Babylon from coast to coast. This king would soon be ruling his kingdom. His Grammy award-winning musical empire was quickly expanding with hit making new artists, a clothing line, a custom Bang Squad SUV, cell phones, male and female fragrances, and even restaurants in New York and L.A.

Adding sex to the enterprise would help him make his billions even faster. And it would be easy to hide under all his legitimate and highly respected business endeavors. He was about to become the most revered and feared gangsta anywhere, ever.

Jamal nodded to the sexy beat that he had laid for their wedding song, "Promise Me." He had promised Knight that their deal would be top secret and not revealed until well after he had disappeared into tropical oblivion.

"Damn, look at that muthafucka," Jamal exclaimed, watching Knight jackhammer The Queen nonstop. Her erotic moans into the mic made Jamal shiver. "Yeah, suck that," he said down to CoCo.

She sucked faster. "Come up here," he said.

She climbed out of the darkness with eager eyes and wet lips. Her black denim mini-dress was already hoisted up over her thighs.

"Come sit on it."

She was so tiny, she could sit back on Beat and not block his view of the sexiest couple he'd ever seen gettin' it on in his studio.

"Oh, fuck," he groaned as her pussy squeezed around Beat.

She ground, round and round, knowing just how to move so that he could still have his hands and forearms on the console.

"Work that shit."

She licked her fingers and pressed them down to her clit. That made her pussy squeeze harder as she rubbed herself.

"Yeah, cum wit' me," Jamal groaned. "Cum wit' me, sweet CoCo."

They faced forward, getting their freak on, watching their best friends do the same, and making beautiful music all at the same time.

Chapter 66

The Queen felt so wild and rebellious as her ass poked out and back toward the traffic. Riding through downtown Detroit on the back of Knight's Suzuki motorcycle, it was as if she were telling the wicked world to kiss her black booty.

The bike lurched forward. The Queen held on tight. And Knight took off, screeching through the intersection as the traffic light glowed green on Jefferson Avenue. The Queen closed her eyes as the power rumbled through her so strongly, rousing shivers.

"Yeah, rev me like that, baby," she purred into the microphone wired inside her black helmet. She needed to write a song called "Lifegasm," about the spasms of love and orgasms she constantly experienced. Knight was driving so fast, the momentum and speed gave her a buzz. Maybe he was zipping through downtown to find a spot where they could park the bike and she could straddle him right there on the seat.

She kept her eyes closed to let that fantasy play out in her mind. The vibrating seat was getting her ready to cum again. Plus, Celeste was still throbbing from the sensuous, candlelit lovemaking and singing in Jamal's studio. It seemed like the more they made love, the more she wanted it.

She gripped the insides of her thighs along the outsides of his legs. They were touching all the way down to her black boots, which were just behind his. All her hair was tucked into her helmet because Knight had said they stood out enough and didn't need any more attention. The last time they had taken the bike out, and she'd let her long black hair fly in the wind behind them, somebody in a van had followed them and asked if he could take their picture for the newspaper.

"Je regrette que je ne parle pas anglais," The Queen had cooed, later laughing that she'd told the photo journalist in French, "I'm sorry, I don't speak English."

Knight didn't laugh though, because he said it could have completely blown their cover.

That's why today, when Knight had at first refused to take the bike out, The Queen had pleaded with him saying the fresh air would make him feel great. And it did, because he'd seemed much more relaxed now.

The Queen opened her eyes. They were speeding west on Jefferson. She smiled behind the tinted glass of her helmet. She began singing their wedding song. "Promise me you'll always—" All of a sudden a deep rumble all around them made her stop.

"Don't turn around," Knight said. "It's a gang."

Beside them, a lime green bike pulled up on their left, along with an orange one. Two black ones stopped to their right.

"Moreno's muthafuckas."

The Queen froze. *I'm pregnant.*

She knew Knight would handle it like a Hollywood stunt man. The light was still red. They were in the middle of five lanes, surrounded by bikes. City Hall was on their right. TV trucks and police cars usually lined the curb, but today there was only a meter maid, a cab, and a bunch of hoodies.

"Hold on, baby girl." Knight proved that his bike really could go from zero to eighty in the blink of an eye. He screeched at the speed of light, making a bold right turn onto Woodward from the middle lane. The revving engine beneath them was all the noise they heard.

The Queen's heart pounded as she gripped Knight with her arms around his waist. *We are safe.* She knew Knight was thinking that he should not have let her talk him into taking the bike to the studio. She could hear him thinking, *The days of reckless abandon for the sake of fun are over. Until we get to paradise forever. And we will.*

But what did "paradise forever" mean? Marriage? Or something else? This telepathic love connection was kind of a bitch. Because she got these hunches that raised questions that maybe she didn't want to know the answers to.

"Biker One to Cairo," Knight said as he sped toward a park at the city's center. Campus Martius outdoor café was bustling with business people and families as Knight sped over the patterned red brick of the circular boulevard.

The deep roar of bikes behind them made her heart hammer.

"Ramses, over," Gerard answered from the security post back at The Playhouse.

"HO delivery. Copak."

The Queen knew that meant "Hummer One pick-up at Comerica Park," the downtown baseball stadium where the Detroit Tigers played.

"Ramses, over."

The Queen also knew that Babylon's security system had a lojack installed in every vehicle, including the catering trucks. So that right now, Paul or Gerard, could be watching exactly where their motorcycle was, along with the fleet of Hummers and cars. That way, he could direct Hummer One to the exact spot where they'd meet.

"Hold on, baby girl." Knight whipped the bike around the circular park. He zipped between a Mercedes and a UPS truck. Then he shot into an alley between two office buildings. He cut a sharp right into another alley, then a left into another.

A few bikes followed; several others rumbled on the streets at the ends of the alleys.

The Queen could hear him thinking, *Here we go. Grip me good.*

His mind was ticking down options at the speed of light as he turned down another alley between tall office buildings. Pedestrians jammed the sidewalk at one end. It was an art fair. Vendor booths and food stations packed the streets. That was virtually a dead end. With brick walls at their sides and bikers behind them, it appeared they were stuck.

Suddenly The Queen realized that her fingers, gripping tightly around Knight's waist, were trembling.

This is some dangerous shit!

For all the exhilarating highs, they were marked by sudden flashes of terror.

Were all the super high moments of exhilaration worth these life threatening lows? Was this the type of lifestyle in which she and Knight wanted to raise a child? But if they were to pick up and leave Babylon, where would they go? What would they do? How could they possibly finance this glamorous life that they loved in a way that was safer, legal, and more low profile?

The questions whizzed through her head as fast as they passed the people, buildings, and vehicles around them. They veered a pasta delivery truck with its back ramp open. A private valet parking lot nestled behind the buildings offered a wide open space.

In one dizzying flash, Knight spun the bike 180 degrees. Two dozen bikers were heading toward them, straight on. He stopped. His black boots touched the brick alley in a way that said, "Bring it on, muthafuckas!"

They zoomed close. And Knight revved the engine. The bike sped straight between the gang.

The Queen imagined she and Knight on the bike were like a bullet shooting past those losers.

She pressed her cheek into Knight's back as he wove between dumpsters, delivery trucks, and people. On the street, he zipped between cars. Not a single biker appeared in the rearview mirrors or at the front or sides.

Knight ripped back up Woodward Avenue. He sped past restaurants, a drug store, chic nightclubs, and lofts. Then he turned right at Grand Circus Park, just south of the fabulous Fox Theatre where Motown greats once played. He whipped toward the giant stone tigers that greeted fans to Comerica Park.

He followed the shiny black stealthiness that was Hummer One, just down the street, as it turned onto a back street for their rendezvous.

Chapter 67

Reba and another Slut, Baby Blue, sashayed amongst the mostly black clientele of Northland Mall.

"Girl, admit it," Baby Blue said as a half dozen teens stopped in their tracks and watched the women switch on high heels, "you a hater."

In a skintight, denim bodysuit, Reba led her best friend into their favorite leather shop that sold the most blingin' styles in D-town. She was treating her girl to an impromptu shopping spree, thanks to the thick stack of Benjamins that Gerard gave up after their sexy splash in the jacuzzi last night.

Reba's whole body felt tingly, because by the end of the day, Baby Blue would be her partner to move up and out of hoin' and into positions of power.

"I don't hate, I plan." Reba stopped at a rack and fingered an orange opalescent leather mini-skirt with cubic zirconia studs. She snatched it and its matching cropped jacket. "I know what I want. I'm gon' get it. An' ain't nobody gon' stop me."

She pointed a long, acrylic nail toward the chick who wore a store name badge but looked as uninterested as a gay dude in Victoria's Secret.

Reba ordered, without making eye contact. "Sweetheart, get me the matching boots in size seven. In orange and black." As her expert shopping vision zoomed in on the sexiest shirts, pants, and dresses, Reba thought about all the steps she'd have to make for her plan to become reality. She was already working every angle.

Reba held up some low cut Baby Phat jeans with a sparkly pattern on the butt. "Ooohh, girl, these would hug your cute little ass just right." She handed them to Baby Blue, who smiled. "And take that bustier top too."

Baby Blue's eyes got big, making her blue contacts look extra bright against the whites of her eyes. Her long, sandy blond weave hung straight over the fronts of her shoulders in two ponytails. Her lips as full and red as Betty Boop's lips on her tight black T-shirt pulled back as she smiled. "Reba, since when does Christmas come in September? You act like you hit the lottery."

"I'm 'bout to," Reba said, tapping the Louis Vuitton bag over her shoulder. She glimpsed her phone in a side pouch; in a minute her partner would be calling to check the progress of her recruitment for Plan B. "Yeah, we can both hit the lottery if you help me."

"How?"

"Aw, shit!" Reba exclaimed, striding quickly on her high heeled sandals to pick up a royal blue crochet dress. "Ain't you got a bikini like this? Girl, wear that under this dress. You'd have niggas lickin' yo' toes."

"I already do." BabyBlue giggled.

"Ain't that the truth," Reba said. "I heard The Queen turnt you out the otha night. Why you didn't tell me? Ain't I still yo' girl?"

Baby Blue turned away like she was looking at the baby T-shirts against the wall. "It ain't somethin' I like to talk about."

"How you gon' go from bein' the freak of the week, puttin' all kin' o' stuff up in yo' pussy while you on stage at The Garage, and now you shy wit' yo' girl?"

Baby Blue's cheeks turned red. She stepped to a nearby table displaying a rainbow of lace thongs. She chose three, each a different shade of blue. "I hit the jackpot. These are my favorite brand. This stretch material don't cut into my crack like the regular ones."

"You ain't hearin' me," Reba said playfully to hide her pissed off feelings inside. Maybe Baby Blue wouldn't be as easy to convince as she thought. "Knight and his snowball got you on some kinda gag order?"

Baby Blue snapped. "Don't ask me what I do wit' them. Just 'cause you saw her eat my pussy last year at Duke's birthday party don't mean somethin's goin' on now."

"Yeeeeaaah . . . right!" Reba flitted toward a fur bikini in the corner. "Girl, the yacht party comin' up. Check this out!"

"I like the blue leather one better," Baby Blue said, picking up a thong bikini with turquoise beads sewn in star patterns over the nipples. "I can wear this in the Sexiest Slut contest during The Games. Girl, if I win all that money, I can seriously think about retiring."

"That's chump change compared to what you can make wit' me," Reba said.

Baby Blue laughed. "I wouldn't call a hundred grand chump change. Plus, last year's winner impressed one of the celebrity judges so much, he married her. Now she lives in some mansion in New Jersey."

Reba fingered the blue leather bikini and said, "Dream on, girlfriend."

"So what else you wanna ask me?"

"Be my partner," Reba said. "I can't tell you the details just yet, but know that you'll get paid when it all go down in a couple weeks."

"Sounds too vague," Baby Blue said. "And if you tryin' to buy me in"—she put the bikini back—"then I can buy my own shit."

"Naw, girl!" Reba grabbed the bikini and put it back in Baby Blue's hands.

I'm gon' make this bitch cooperate wit' my plan one way or the other. She the only one I trust enough to make it *happen now, 'cause Duke only gave me three days to recruit my team.* Smiling, Reba said sweetly, "This just a treat 'cause you my girl. C'mon, let's go try this on."

As Reba marched toward the dressing rooms with an armful of clothes, the Bang Squad's hit song, "Freakalicious," blasted from her phone. "Girl, just a minute. It's Gerard. This pussy gave him a lobotomy last night. Bet he callin' to ask for help rememberin' his own damn name."

Reba held the phone so Baby Blue couldn't see ANTOINE flash on the display. "Hey, big daddy. We shoppin' thanks to you." Reba smiled at Baby Blue, who looked tense. "Yeah, I do. Ain't nothin' like help from a fine-ass man to save the day for D-town's workin' girls."

Baby Blue drew her brows together and mouthed, "Fine?" She rolled her eyes, knowing damn well Gerard was not fine.

"Yeah, big daddy, I'll keep it hot." She hung up.

"Girl, you dangerous," Baby Blue said. "The chief of security ain't a smart choice to be fuckin' around with. He can watch your every move."

"Why you so scared about every damn thing?" Reba snapped as a store worker led them into the dressing room. "An' why you all of a sudden followin' the rules when you shit on Slut Rule number five. Never date your clients."

"I haven't seen Brian in six months," Baby Blue said, staring at the floor. "That crazy white boy loved black booty an' rap music an' dressin' like a thug. But he was racist as hell."

"But he was a Babylon client till you started givin' it away for free."

"He wanted to marry me," Baby Blue said as they stepped into the spacious dressing room with red velvet chairs and mirrored walls, "but his parents said if he married a black chick, he wouldn't get his trust fund money when he turnt twenty-five."

Reba admired herself in the mirror. "Sheee-it. If I was him I'd wait too. Keep the love tip on the down low from my parents 'til I get the money then say, 'Guess who's comin' to dinner?'" Her ponytail bounced as she laughed.

"I don't want no part of that," Baby Blue said. "Besides, I'll do dick for work, but personally, I'd rather get wit' a girl."

Reba rolled her eyes. "You know damn well you'd be all ova some dude who wanted to get married, have babies, and live large in the suburbs."

Baby Blue shook her head. "It's not even like that for me. I like pussy over dick so I ain't tryin'a be wifed up by a man."

"Shit, I am," Reba said. "I'm on a serious man gettin' mission right now. And it will be accomplished."

"Who's the man?" Baby Blue asked, hanging clothes on hooks.

"Knight."

"You dream on, girl! You sound like Milan when she was goin' after Duke. You can only lose; look what happened to that stuck-up snob."

"Got her due for lookin' down her nose at us for so many years," Reba said as she pulled off her jump suit.

"You playin' wit' fire. I don't care how prissy you think Miss White Chocolate be. She don't mess around when it come to her man."

"I ain't scared o' that bitch," Reba said, admiring her big, brown titties in the mirror. "Neither was Janet."

Baby Blue peeled off her T-shirt and low-cut jeans.

"Damn, girl! You ain't got no panties on under them jeans?" Reba exclaimed.

"I like the way my jeans rub up on my clit." Baby Blue tapped her fingertips to the top of her fat pussy.

"Hey now, how I'm gon' resist all that shit in my face?" Reba moaned. She dropped to her knees. "Tell me you ain't givin' me leftovers after snow white took a bite of this juicy apple," Reba said.

"Eat!" Baby Blue ordered, falling back on a chair, spreading her legs.

Kneeling on the zebra striped carpet, Reba rubbed her fingertips on top of that slippery brown berry. "Damn! Yo' pussy wet," Reba said right before she slid her tongue up and down on Baby Blue's pussy lips.

Baby Blue moaned, "Oh, that feels so good!" Reba slid her tongue in and out of Baby Blue's wet opening while she kept rubbing her clit with her fingers.

"Don't stop! I'm wanna cum like that." Baby Blue felt her walls contract as she closed her eyes and enjoyed the sensation.

"I got yo' ass now," she said. "Say you gon' help me."

Suddenly, a knock on the door interrupted their pleasure.

"Ladies, a man is coming here to see you," the store owner said with a heavy accent.

Reba faked a confused expression.

"Can't they wait 'til I get my nut first?" Baby Blue moaned.

"You will." Reba didn't bother to cover up as she opened the door.

Antoine stood there with a big bulge in his jeans. His brown sandals matched the mesh style of his long-sleeved shirt, which showed off his flat stomach and upper body muscles.

Reba said, "You like Superman, you know when it's some bitches in need an' you show up wit' just the right tools."

"At your service," Antoine said, stepping in. The manager rolled his eyes and walked away.

Reba closed the door. "Shoot! As much money as I spend in this joint, he bet' not say nothin'."

Baby Blue sat up, closing her legs. "Is this just a coincidence or a set-up?"

"I was shopping next door and I saw you two fine ladies stoppin' traffic out in the mall," Antoine bullshitted. "I knew you'd get freaky up in here, so I came to offer my services."

"I don't fuck Studs," Baby Blue said.

"A Slut standing on high moral ground," Antoine said. "Betta watch out. A flash-flood can come along, cause a mudslide, and you'll be slippin' into the cesspool with the rest of us unscrupulous muthafuckas."

Baby Blue glared at Reba. "Girl, you know I can't stand his pretty ass. I'm outta here." She stood and reached for her clothes.

"Sit the fuck down," Reba said with a hard tone. "I was tryin' to be nice, but now I see I gotta go ghetto on your seditty ass."

Antoine sat on the arm of the chair beside Baby Blue and cast a fake smile down at her.

"Why you look all jumpy an' nervous?" Reba teased. "I'm 'bout to make you rich."

"I have enough money," Baby Blue said. "My life is just fine the way it is."

"Don't think small," Reba said. "You an' me, as little girls in that rathole apartment our trick-ass mommas shared, they taught us to think small. Like yo' little hook-up at Babylon all you need."

Antoine laughed. "Time to get your juicy slice of Babylon's pie. You'll never have to work again."

"Yeah," Reba said. "Think big."

Baby Blue crossed her arms over her bare titties. Then she crossed her legs. "You both crazy. If you think bum rushin' me with a hot pussy in a dressing room will intimidate me into doing your death wish, forget about it."

Reba snatched her phone out of her purse. "I'll call Knight right now and tell him about you dating a Babylon client for six months, giving away thousands of dollars worth of pussy."

Baby Blue shrugged. "Call him. I'll pay it back. I learned my lesson. And Knight would understand."

"You ain't hearin' me, bitch!" Reba raked her fingernails into the back of Baby Blue's head, grabbed a fistful of hair, and pulled back hard.

Baby Blue's eyes got huge.

"You gon' help us an' you gon' get paid, so listen," Reba said.

Chapter 68

In the small apartment over his mother's garage, Duke searched the doctor's eyes for more answers than the vague words that were coming out of her mouth. He needed to recover from this bullshit ASAP so he could get back to the work of taking what was his.

"It looks nasty as hell," he said, laying on the bed and staring at the shredded skin near his right ribcage. "Tell me it ain't as bad as that shit looks."

Doc Reynolds dabbed a cotton ball with white cream on the wound where Knight's bullet had grazed him. "I'm afraid you need stitches," she said, examining him through her purple framed glasses. "And all that time in the water, you were exposed to bacteria and possibly toxins that are causing a bad infection." She leaned down to his leg. She shook her head. "And this wound; I'm afraid you shouldn't walk on this."

"It's just a cut," Duke said, remembering the ripping sound as he went overboard and the sharp tip of the rope notch sliced open his thigh. "Good thing ain't no sharks in the Detroit River. I woulda been cum like a mug."

Doc Reynolds shook her head. "I'm afraid you need stitches there too."

Duke tried to get up. "I ain't got time to lay up in bed."

Her gentle hand on his chest pushed him back down. "Duke, if you were as healthy as you were a year ago, you'd recover quickly and easily. But the drugs have severely compromised your body's ability to heal. And the blood test, I'm afraid—"

"Quit sayin' you afraid; just tell me, goddammit!" Duke cut her off.

"Sometime over the past year, you contracted HIV," the Doctor said. "Whether it was from unprotected sex or sharing a needle."

"Muthafuck me!" Duke shouted. "How long I got to live?"

"If you get on medication now, it can prolong the onset of AIDS. But those drugs are costly."

Doc Reynolds knew what she was talking about. She was a good doctor. But for whatever reason, Knight had ousted her and replaced her with fancier doctors. Now Duke was recruiting her to work for him again, once he got things back up and running. After he got his body back up and running.

"Give me all the drugs I need," Duke said.

Doc Reynolds shook her head, making her smooth black French roll move from side to side. She crossed her arms over her all-white uniform. "I can start you off with the small supply, maybe a month's worth, that I have at the clinic, but since I left Babylon, I don't have unlimited access to free meds."

Duke ground his teeth. "I'll get the money." And he'd get it from the folks running Babylon in two of America's sexiest cities; Miami and Las Vegas. Shar Miller and Leroy Lewis were sick of Knight's totalitarian regime and all his tight-ass rules. They were ready to bust out on their own, or bolster their bank as part of Duke's new empire, Oz.

And I'm the new muthafuckin' wizard.

Duke had just spoken with Shar and Leroy, who had both promised to put out feelers to recruit more Babylon controlled cities into Oz. Next, Duke was going to talk with sleazy-ass Moreno. Not for the meeting he'd planned a year ago in which Duke would seize all power from their family's empire. This time, Duke would be teaming up with them, to bring down their common enemy: Knight. But first, Duke had to get his body back in top shape to run an empire and win back his Timbo lovin' Duchess.

"Now I'm going to prep you so I can stitch up those wounds," Doc Reynolds said. "I have to go to my car for supplies." As she opened the door, Mama stood there crying. The dinner plate in her hand trembled so badly, the doctor grabbed it.

"Mrs. Johnson, I'm so sorry," Doc Reynolds said, leading her inside.

"Boy, look at the mess you done made!" Mama shrieked. "No wonder Knight took control of e'rythang. You can't no more run a business than stay alive. Now gone and caught the

AIDS?" She grabbed a pillow and whacked him in the head.
"Boy, you nothin' but a dead junkie now. Ain't no point sewin'
you up."

"Mama, admit it. I can't neva be as good as Knight in yo'
eyes. You, him, an' Prince always looked at me as nothin' but
a knuckle-headed punk!"

Duke wanted to stand but his body hurt too much. All the
rage from twenty-two years of feeling lesser than his brothers
in their mother's eyes suddenly surged up and shot out of his
mouth like bullets at the woman who had both birthed him,
and now, killed him inside. "You think I'm such an' ain't shit
muthafucka', Mama. I'll be better off dead anyways. So go on
back to church, tell God thank you for knockin' off your no
good baby boy. You and Knight can live happily ever after."

Duchess' face flashed in his mind.

"You even like his lady now, but you hated her when she
was wit' me!" He snatched the pillow and threw it at his
mother. "Get the fuck out, Mama! You ain't neva gotta look at
this muthafucka again."

Mama burst into tears. "Baby, I'm sorry. I'm just so mad
you don' throwed yo' life away." She spread her arms and
leaned down to hug him. "I'm sorry, baby."

Duke pushed her away. "Doc, take me outta here."

"Baby!" Mama shrieked. "Baby, stay! You need rest! I'll
take care of you."

Duke grimaced and gripped his leg and side as he angled
his body to the edge of the bed. He pressed on the nightstand
and forced himself to stand up, despite the blinding pain.

"Baby, stay!"

"I'm sorry, Mrs. Johnson," the doctor said as she put Duke's
arm over her shoulder and led him toward the door.

Duke turned back, focusing on the floor. "I ain't stayin'
where don't nobody love me. Bye, Mama."

She screamed as he slammed the door.

Chapter 69

The Queen had never met the Moreno Triplets, but she strutted toward them like she owned the whole damn universe. Because after she got through with them, she would. At least the universe of organized sex for sale anywhere near D-town and a dozen big cities across America.

And that little bike chase this afternoon had shifted her all the way into bitch overdrive. If ever she wanted to use her mixed-race sex powers, she was about to whip some *femme fatale* on these muthafuckas.

When I get done, they'll be beggin' for scraps. And I won't even toss 'em a muthafuckin' thing.

Knight's contacts had done extensive research on just what the Morenos controlled and wanted to acquire. They had massage parlors, escort services, and strip clubs. Now they were trying to muscle in on the traditional pussy party circuit. The kind that entertained men. But it turned out, Babylon had them beat in a big way, thanks to The Queen's aggressive thrust into the female market. Only problem was, Moreno wanted what Babylon had. And this was the day to fuck them out of business entirely.

"Now it's time for us to execute Prince's Rule number four. *Crush your enemies entirely,*" Knight had said as they were chauffeured here by Ping and Pong in Hummer One. "But at the same time, they'll never know they're being smashed. The trick is to make them feel like they're being praised as the kings."

The Queen kept that in mind as she led Knight, Ping, and Pong into the private room of a five star restaurant on the seventy-second floor of the Renaissance Center. The all glass walls offered a breathtaking view of downtown Detroit, Windsor, and far beyond.

I love this shit. We're on top of the world. And we're stayin'.

The Queen loved the way her spiky, high gold heels cut into the carpet with every step.

A hostess led them to the sleek meeting room with walls made of beige suede and glass blocks. Inside, at a large, square glass table sat the notorious Moreno Triplets, along with a heavyset, light-skinned guy with thick facial features and a bald head. Beside him, a freakishly skinny blond chick in a tight white pantsuit perched on one of the brown suede chairs. Behind them stood one bodyguard; he was a handsome, African giant wearing a brown suit. A glass wall that shielded them from the sophisticated crowd in the bustling restaurant set a chic backdrop for this gang of six.

Now, The Queen loved how all of their eyes became enchanted and danced all over her as she entered. A rhyme popped into her head; she'd have to write it down later and put it into a song she'd call "A Bad Bitch."

A painfully horny expression radiated from their eyes as they checked her out from head to toe.

They neva seen nothin' like me.

The Queen held back a smile as these new onlookers downright ogled the explosion of titties in the scandalously low-cut lapels that pressed two humps of hot bronze decadence up and into their faces. She had spread some iridescent lotion over her titties to make them shimmer as they bounced with her strut walk. All of them looked at her like she was the lunch that would be served on the table full of cream colored china, silverware, and crystal glasses.

Yet their lust mixed with evil was so strong in the air, she could taste it. In fact, a chill hung inside this small room, even though the rest of the restaurant felt warm and cozy as they'd entered from the elevator. While she had savored the scents of garlic, steak, and seafood cooking as they approached, this room had the choking odor of cigar smoke and too much expensive cologne.

"Queen," the men said in unison, rising to bow slightly. Each wore a white suit, shirt, and silk tie. Their skin was beige, which could have made them Bolivian, Italian, Arabic, Yugoslavian, or even Spanish.

Knight had said they were from a small island in the Mediterranean Sea, but they had lived in Colombia and South Africa before joining an elderly uncle here in Detroit to stake their claim on his underworld empire before he died.

The Queen forced herself not to shiver as she checked out the diabolical vibe in their identical hazel eyes set in fleshy, clean-shaven faces with hook noses and thick black brows that were professionally sculpted. Their lips were unnaturally red, and their skin looked so pampered, it shone as if it were made of wax.

There was something familiar about them. Had she seen them before, or had Duke and Knight mentioned them so many times that she felt she already knew them? Or had she seen their faces and heard their names even before she'd come to Babylon? Had Moreno been among the names on those files that Daddy had asked her to feed into the shredder on that frantic Wednesday night before he blew his brains out?

The Queen's mind spun, but her face was as cool and seductive as a Cleopatra mask. She stared hard into the redhead's eyes as she purred, "You're as gorgeous as legend has it."

He stood and extended his hand. His manicured, polished fingernails shined under the light of the modern chandelier. And his white jacket fell open to reveal a huge bulge in his pants. The white fabric was thin enough to reveal that he wore no boxers or briefs; the rim of the head of his big dick pressed like a face against glass inside the pleated polyester of his pants beside his front zipper.

"*Enchante,*" he said, his eyes blazing with lust. "I meet beautiful women of every race around the world, but you are by far the most exquisite specimen of the black female I have ever had the delight of meeting."

I ain't a muthafuckin' specimen in a science lab, but I'm glad you're taking the bait. The Queen's lips felt hot as she smiled and made her eyes glow with seduction. She did a slow body scan over him, holding her gaze at his bulge, before she looked back into his eyes.

This dude was gorgeous. He reminded her—wait, maybe he *was* the man she had always seen at those super rich, prestigious parties at her ex-boyfriend Brian's mansion and at gatherings hosted by the parents of her ex-best friend, Tiffany. Daddy had even greeted that man, who always had dark, slicked back hair. And she had definitely seen the Asian chick on his arm before. The Queen remembered staring at that woman, wondering what her life was like as the sex kitten arm ornament for a gangster who was hooked into that very legitimate circle of CEOs, lawyers, doctors, and moguls.

Now I'm just like her. Only I got more power. That world, The Queen remembered, would accept a quiet, passive Asian ornament. But they rejected the bone colored China that was actually black on the inside.

Right now, somehow, the Morenos were guilty of racism by association. Looking at them right now, and feeling their very bad vibe, roused up all the horrible feelings that The Queen had kept buried for more than a year.

Suddenly, a red mist of rage in The Queen's mind cast a sinister haze over this creepy cast of characters. All the anger, disappointment, and sadness that she had felt when Brian, and Tiffany and their parents kicked her out of their lives came surging up in a tongue load of cuss words that she now knew how to launch with precision and power.

Naw, hold that. These muthafuckas ain't Brian or Tiffany. They just punks cut from the same sleazy, back stabbin' cloth.

Behind her, Knight must have sensed her angst. Because she heard him speak in her mind, *Keep complete and constant control of your emotions.* "Thank you," The Queen said to the auburn haired Moreno.

"I'm Red," he said, his long, hot fingers still gripping hers. "These are my brothers, Marco and Liam. We've been greatly anticipating this encounter with the singular woman who could meet Knight's superhuman standards of excellence." Red nodded at Knight, who was still behind her. The man gripped The Queen's hand harder and bowed toward her.

The Queen allowed him to continue holding her hand as she stared into his eyes. They were like a marquis flashing DEVIL. The attractive shade of hazel coloring his irises did nothing to hide the violence and betrayal and greed that roiled in his soul. In fact, an aura of malice radiated around the three brothers so intensely. The Queen could almost see pale green vapors rising up around them, like she'd seen in a picture book around an evil dragon that Mommy would read to her as a little girl.

In that story, the beautiful princess always defeated the dragon with her charms, so she could free the handsome prince inside the dragon's scary cave. In the end, the prince and princess tamed the dragon as their pet; he even sang sweet songs instead of breathing fire.

That was their plan with Moreno. But he didn't breathe fire. No, he spoke with an accent that to anybody else, would be a dramatic smoke and mirrors type distraction to trick them into thinking he was an international aristocrat.

It didn't work on The Queen, though. Working with Daddy at his business, she had met authentic rich people and royalty who spoke with beautiful accents from all over the world.

She could see right through this fake, British wannabe. She bit her lip to stop a sudden burst of laughter. In her eyes, despite his expensive suit and impeccable grooming, he was a Eurotrash perpetrator who deserved nothing more than to get double crossed so Babylon could keep all that it had and get whatever else it wanted.

"These are my partners in charge of operations here in southeast Michigan," Moreno said. He nodded toward the heavyset brunette guy and the skinny blond chick. "We met on holiday in Monaco, when they were celebrating their honeymoon at my favorite casino. They both possess brilliant business minds, thanks to their pedigreed family backgrounds."

The Queen froze.

The guy and the chick stared back with equal intrigue. Brian and Tiffany. Those snobby, racist punks were working for a gangster now? Was this man the same dude she'd seen at the fancy parties with her friends from her white life? And was there a connection to Daddy's death?

The Queen's insides reeled with shock. If any of them identified her, they would be able to trump her power play by threatening to tell the feds exactly where she was. Plus that would crush Knight's leverage because they would hold all the juice in the deal.

That would kill us. And Knight has no idea how much more risky this operation just got.

The Queen smiled.

Ain't no way in hell they can recognize me right now. None of 'em.

She looked nothing like she did a year ago. She now sported a deep, honey brown complexion, fifteen extra pounds of thickness and she spoke completely different than how she used to. Now, she was tough, assertive, nasty, and possessed a sexual aura that could dominate anyone; man or woman.

I am someone else. I am The Queen. And I'll crush all their racist asses.

"How y'all doin'?" She nodded toward them. Her former boyfriend and best friend had never seen Victoria in this light before. Even CoCo was unrecognizable from her days working with her Daddy when she went by the name Marlene.

Brian and Tiffany were staring. If they had recognized her, it didn't seem like they were planning on saying anything.

Backstabbing punk-ass muthafackas. They deserve each other.

Knight stepped forward to shake Red's hand. He pulled out a chair for The Queen so that she could sit close to Red.

"We've got a proposal that creates a triple win for all of us," Knight said as he sat beside The Queen. "We keep an open mind and work together. Then the billions are ours for the taking." He looked over at The Queen before continuing, "We propose that immediately following The Games, we create a collaboration."

Red's gaze lowered for a second. He nodded then looked back into her eyes. "Tell me more."

"It's essentially a situation where you keep yours, we keep ours, but together we create something much more powerful."

Brian and Tiffany were staring very hard at The Queen. *They can't possibly know who I am.*

She took a good look at Brian and noticed how terrible he looked. All the weight Tiffany had lost, Brian had found, times ten. It distorted his face, thickening his nose, his lips, and the skin around his blue eyes, which still glinted with the same malice.

"Why should we trust you?" Brian asked, twirling his gold ring imprinted with the Martin's family coat of arms. His voice raked over the scars he had left on her soul.

She imagined herself getting up from the table, walking around the Moreno Triplets, and raising her stiletto heel with the lightning speed and lethal force that Lee Lee had taught her. Her heel would bash straight into his nose and he'd shut the fuck up.

Yeah, I will find the chance to whip some revenge on that muthafucka. And he won't even know what hit him.

"Trust," The Queen said playfully. "What do you feel in your gut right now?"

Brian let out a sexy laugh. "I don't want to get crass while we're doing business. Because what I feel in my gut has nothing to do with trust."

"I believe it does," she says. "You feel sex." The word sex came out of her mouth in such a seductive and powerful way that everyone at the table visibly winced.

"And sex is the name of this game," The Queen said. "Trust *that.*"

Knight watched her speak. His poker face hid his expression from the others, but The Queen saw a sparkle of pride that she was doing her thing. *Teamwork makes the dream work baby.*

As her seductive words hung in the silent, still air, Brian grinned. Tiffany's nipples poked against the chest of her tight suit jacket.

"Trust is not a question," Red said to Brian. "If it were, we would not be sitting here right now. The question is"—he turned to The Queen—"how will this collaboration work?"

"We structure events based on the already established territorial lines," she said. "Anything you host within the city limits, we split fifty-fifty. Anything we host in the suburbs, we split fifty-fifty too." The Queen radiated a smile from her eyes. "And to make it fun, we add a high-stakes gamble to the mix to show our good will."

Liam shifted in his chair, casting a nervous glance at Red, who remained perfectly still.

"I like gambles." Red cast a hungry ogle down on the tops of The Queen's titties. "Tell me more."

The Queen said, "In the past, Babylon has banned Moreno Enterprises from participating in The Games."

Red's lips tightened as he began grabbed his ponytail and began sliding his hand on it. "This year," The Queen said, "to celebrate this historical collaboration, we invite you to participate in The Games. As you know, there's a million dollar prize for each team that can perform in each event with the best style, endurance, and technique."

The triplets grinned all at once.

"We bring our own security," Liam said nervously with that same whack accent. "We don't go into that territory—"

Red cut his hand through the air. "Winner gets the convention circuit, Detroit, New York, Miami, L.A., and Chicago. Male and female."

The Queen cast a charming gaze at him. *Hell naw! That's mine!*

But the Morenos weren't going to win The Games anyway, so it was a moot point to oppose it.

"Bet," Knight said. "Then we make the same toss at next year's Games. Upping the ante will make for more exciting competitions."

"And hotter sex," Marco said, holding a martini glass so that the red liquid swirled over the edge onto his hand. He licked it slowly, staring at The Queen.

"Let's add a little more excitement to the deal," Red said, devouring The Queen with his eyes. "The winner gets an evening alone with this Cleopatra of the Knight." Red raised his eyebrows to underscore this scandalous question as he looked at Knight.

The Queen could feel Knight's rage so strong, she heard his thoughts echo inside her mind.

He's through, Knight was thinking. *This muthafucka betta enjoy his last gulps of oxygen.*

Knight didn't move. His face remained cool and calm. And he let out his most charming laugh, the kind that Daddy would always use when he was annoyed as hell at a client.

"All men should strive for your level of confidence," Knight said with a charming, almost chuckling tone. "However, this territory is not open for negotiation. Right now. I'll have to discuss your proposal with The Queen in private and get back with you on that." Knight glanced at The Queen. "I'm sure you can appreciate that it takes teamwork to make the dream work," he said, turning back to Red. "She may in fact be open to your request."

The Queen let her lips part as she widened her eyes at Red. His waxy beige cheeks grew pink.

"I like your style," The Queen said, smiling at that disrespectful muthafucka.

"Security," Brian said. "We need to work out protection for us as we watch and our teams as they arrive, compete, and leave with several mill."

Red nodded back to the enormous black man behind him. "Nikolai handles that. Our only duty at this time is to agree to this historical collaboration that will fill the coffers of both Babylon and Moreno Enterprises with even more riches. And perhaps bring with it some extraordinary opportunities for pleasure." Red raised a shotglass full of light brown liquid.

"To the deal of the millennium," he said. Without waiting for anyone else to raise a glass, as The Queen and Knight had not even been served, he chugged back the shot. He did not wince before he said with glistening lips, "The truce is a new beginning for all of us, my brother."

"Bet," Knight said.

For the next twenty minutes, they chatted about The Games, the weather, and the upcoming wedding.

"Excuse me," The Queen said. "I'm going to the ladies room."

Tiffany stood. "Me too." She was so skinny that when she turned sideways in that white pantsuit, she almost disappeared against the wall. She had no ass; the dark red pinstripes on her pants made her backside look like a wishbone.

Pong followed as The Queen left the room. She took long strides through the restaurant, loving the way men and women froze to stare at her. She was a diva and radiated sex power that made every person in the room stare at her as she walked.

All hail The Queen. Yeah, her ego was out there. But she was lovin' it.

"I've never met anyone like you," Tiffany said, taking quick, tiny steps to catch up and keep The Queen's pace. "Ever."

Yes, you have. We used to be best friends, bitch.

"What was your name again?" The Queen asked. "Red never mentioned you and your husband's names."

"I'm Birdie; he's B-boy. And we're not really married."

As The Queen pushed open the bathroom door, she saw in her peripheral that Brian was going into the men's bathroom. She didn't have to look to know that Pong would wait outside the women's lounge to listen for any problems and escort her back to Knight.

When she entered, another woman came in from a door at the opposite side of the restaurant.

Be careful, Celeste said. *This bathroom isn't as secure as you thought.* She thought about letting Pong know that, but she had Smith & Wesson strapped to her waist, so she'd be fine. Even with tiny Tiffany in tow.

The Queen dashed into a stall. Lately it seemed she had to pee a lot.

"Does everybody call you The Queen?" Tiffany asked from another stall. "I mean, like what's your real name? I guess something about you seems so familiar."

All the negative emotions that Tiffany's speech cadence was rousing inside The Queen made her pussy ache. She needed sex to pound down these thoughts and feelings. But the girl with whom Victoria Winston had shared so many secrets and pledged to be best friends for life, kept clanging against her senses.

"When my best friend died last year," Tiffany said, "it was so tragic. You remind me of her."

"How'd she die?" The Queen forced the words up and out like sour, slimy chunks of vomit.

"Oh, my gosh! It was so tragic, like," Tiffany continued, "her dad, he died, and she got sent to live in the worst part of Detroit. And she, couldn't handle it. Her dad had been like, really into some shady deals that she helped him hide from the IRS. Red says Dan Winston was really a shady dude who did him wrong."

The Queen wanted to puke. Daddy did business with Moreno? Had that gangster threatened her father when the feds closed in with their audit? Had they threatened to hurt him or his three kids? The Queen choked out the words. She had to relieve these feelings, quickly. "Did him wrong, how?"

Tiffany let out a disgusted sigh. "Oh, I'm not supposed to talk about this, but they're all dead, so it doesn't matter. Red had hired Mr. Winston to handle some of his deals. But the money got mixed up and the IRS clamped down—"

The Queen coughed. Just like other people craved a cigarette when they were stressed, and some folks smoked a joint, while others gambled, The Queen needed to calm herself by cumming. She pressed her middle finger to her clit. Yeah, the ultimate mind mellower. "Mmmmmm," she moaned softly.

"You okay?" Tiffany chirped while hitting the toilet paper dispenser and unrolling it.

"Mmmmm-hhmmmm.""Well," Tiffany said, "it all worked out because I remember my friend said her dad had her shred some papers. The feds never found anything on Moreno, but he was highly pissed."

The Queen's fingers danced over her clit with lightning speed. Her mind swirled with thoughts of Knight's giant dick slamming up into her slippery hole and banging, banging, banging until The Queen couldn't think straight or walk across the room or even say her name. Yeah, right now she needed love to smash away this pain. And shut Tiffany the fuck up.

"So my friend, she was so sweet, but she killed herself. They found the body of a girl who fit her description inside her dad's mansion, like, a few weeks after the funeral."

The Queen gasped. She shoved the fingers on her other hand up into her pussy, fucking herself so that she wouldn't have to let those words register.

They think I killed myself? And they found a body in my childhood home?

This was the first she'd heard of that. A year ago, she had followed news reports about herself and the feds' movement on her case. But after a while, as she immersed deeper into the Babylon world, she stopped paying attention to media lies about Victoria Winston.

Truth was, that girl was in fact, dead. And reincarnated as The Queen. But whose body had they found in the Winston's abandoned mansion? Could it have been her sister Melanie? After all, The Queen had not seen her since the funeral, when Melanie had vowed to enter a convent.

"It was weird," Tiffany said over the rustle of clothes that must have been her pulling her pants up. "They showed the girl's picture on the news and said it was Vikki. But I woulda bet money that it was her sister Melanie, 'cause Vikki had eyes like yours but Melanie had brown eyes, and the girl on the news had brown eyes."

The Queen stabbed her fingers inside the creamy heat between her legs to numb her pain. She wished she had four hands so that she could work her pussy and cover her ears all at once. So she wouldn't have to hear Tiffany's mile-a-minute chatter that was jackin' her cool.

"Plus the news said she hung herself from the banister, but I heard it was blunt force trauma to the head." Tiffany let out a nervous laugh. "I don't know why I'm telling you this. I guess 'cause I don't have anybody else to talk to about it."

Who would kill Melanie to trick the world into thinking Victoria were dead?

Duke. No one else cared.

The Queen let her fingertips circle her clit, 'round and 'round, to still the horrific hurricane in her mind.

But Celeste spoke loud and clear, *Duke had them find a female body in the mansion so they'd stop tracking you. And he must have done it before Knight had rolled back into town.*

The outrage of Duke killing her sister, and anguish of knowing that her sister was dead, made her ache from head to toe.

So The Queen tickled her swollen pussy with expert precision on that fire spot at the tip of her clit. That was the most sensitive place of all. And it protected her from having either, the energy, the ability, or the desire to think about the fact that Duke had committed murder to protect her new position in Babylon.

"I don't know why they keep saying on the news that they're still looking for Victoria when we know she's dead." Tiffany flushed. She unclinked the stall lock. Her heels tapped across the tiles, then the water hissed in the sink.

"What makes it, even more sad, is that Vikki had tricked so many people. We thought she was white, but she was tricking us. She was actually black, and her mom had died in this sex scandal. So me and my family, well it wasn't, like, the black part bothered us. I mean I have a lot of black friends, but the fact that she lied."

A low moan escaped The Queen's trembling lips.

"Victoria pissed us all off by not fessin' up to the fact that she was black," Tiffany said. "I mean, you're beautiful and you're black. But you're not trying to hide it."

The Queen moaned again.

"You okay in there?"

Damn, I wish Knight were in here to slam it real quick.

The Queen raised one foot onto the closed toilet seat so she could open her legs wider. With the thong pulled to one side, and her gun perfectly poised, the waistband of her red leather skirt, she leaned against the stall wall and stuck her left fingers even deeper up her pussy. All the while, her right fingertips danced over Celeste with expert precision and speed.

"Hello?" Tiffany called again.

"I'm fine, sweetheart," she said as the little fireball between her legs radiated up her abdomen, down her trembling legs and arms.

"See ya back there," Tiffany said as she walked out of the bathroom.

The Queen's pussy walls pulsated around her wet fingers. Her clit convulsed under her fingertips. And the starburst exploded. She lay back her head, panted quietly, and let her body's opium mellow her mind. She heard the door close behind Tiffany. The silent stillness of the bathroom was just what she needed before heading back into the bad vibes of those three gangsters.

Damn, I feel better.

All the junk that Tiffany had just spewed had vaporized under the sizzlin' sex power of The Queen's mind and body. So, after wiping the hot cream from between her legs and putting her thong back in place, she stepped out of the stall.

Oh, fuck.

Brian was standing against the shimmery blue wall facing her. "Vee, I thought you were dead," he groaned, rubbing his open palm over the crotch of his pants. "I'm still yours forever. You've never looked better."

The Queen raised her chin and strutted to the sink. "It's The Queen," she said calmly, watching him in the mirror. "And unless you're trying to get kronked beyond recognition, you betta show some respect and get the fuck out."

She could hear Knight reciting one of the rules of The Prince Code, *Kill or be killed.*

Brian stepped close behind her. In the mirror, his eyes glowed with lust from his puffy face. "Congratulations on your music," he said. "Who knew my little lilly white, prep school prude with the coffee-house rhymes would rock her way up the charts with some freakin' black girl beats?"

The recessed lights over the vanity glowed down on his head, casting eerie dark shadows around his eyes while his nose became extra bright.

"You got me sadly and dangerously confused wit' anotha bitch," The Queen said. "So unless you gon' change into a dress up in this *ladies* bathroom, punk, you betta step the fuck on."

He said with a low, sinister tone, "Vee, your acting skills are superb. All that practice in the school plays really paid off. You could win an Oscar for best actress. Let's call your movie, *Ho in the Hood* or *New Black Titty.*" He laughed by himself.

The Queen rolled her eyes.

"Or you could put your Hollywood skills to work for me and Red. Travel the world with us. You saw the way he looked at you. The globe is yours on a silver platter."

The Queen squeezed her still throbbing pussy to calm her emotions. Especially the rage at his bold disrespect of her and Knight. "Sorry," she said, coolly washing her hands and meeting his stare in the mirror. "You're making me an offer I'm afraid I'll have to refuse."

Brian's eyes sparkled. "You can make the world be your playground. Vee, think of it, the whole world at your fingertips with—"

The Queen spun on her sharp heel to stare into his ridiculous eyes. She rapped with a slight neck jerk. "For the last time, you got me confused wit' anotha chick. And I don't be makin' bathroom deals wit' a dude who's wasting my time. Now, please, get your shit out my face." The Queen raised her chin and strutted past him.

His chubby hand gripped her elbow, just below her Cleopatra bracelet on her upper arm.

Oh, no he didn't.

He pulled her close, breathing sour alcohol breath on her. "Vee, you promised we'd be together forever. You're mine. And I know you're givin' it up to that ghetto thug."

She spat in his eye. Saliva dripped down his pudgy cheek. He leaned close to kiss her.

Right now she could scream, and Pong would come in here and squash this punk muthafucka like a bug. She could pull the gun out of her waistband and blow him away, but that would draw too much attention. "You got one last chance to get ya hands the fuck off me," The Queen said coolly. "My dick is so hard," Brian said, yanking out his dark-pink dick. "Sweet little Victoria is such a tough girl."

"Put that shit away. If Knight comes in here, he'll cut it off." Brian laughed with a sinister glow in his eyes. "Oh, I'm real scared of that illiterate gorilla. I bet he shoves his big black cock up the sweet pussy you refused to give me."

The Queen smiled, "And I *loooooove* it." She smirked.

Brian's cheeks turned red as if her words had slapped him. "Think of it, Vee. You and me together again. Promise you'll come back to me. We can travel the world with Moreno till I'm twenty-five. Then I get my trust fund and we can get married. Set for life with millions. You and me, Vee."

The Queen pressed her hands to his shoulders. "You sick. Firs', you don't know who the fuck you fuckin' wit'; secon', you obviously didn't see my fiance; an' third, why the fuck would I want to leave my African god to get wit' yo' fat ass?"

His hand grabbed her left tit. He smashed his slimy mouth into hers.

She pushed his shoulders back.

He fell backward, but lurched back at her.

As she had been trained by Lee Lee and the soldiers, she extended a lightning quick and brutally hard heel of the hand right into his nose. At the same time, her knee slammed his groin.

He doubled over, groaning.

The Queen stepped back. Her whole body tingled with excitement. She felt super human strength as rage, disappointment and sadness pumped through her red hot veins. She blasted her pointed heel into the side of his fleshy gut.

He let out a grotesque groan and stood, glaring at her with glassy eyes. His left hand cupped his nose. Blood dripped down his chin. "Vee, you'll come to your senses," he said with a calm mouth but eyes glowing like a rabid dog.

"So will you," she said, balling her fist and she whacked his left jaw with a punch, followed by an uppercut to his chin and a final punch to the center of his chest with her right hand.

Blood dripped from his vile mouth that had spewed racist insults at her. He slumped on the floor like the pile of trash that he was.

"Stupid racist punk," The Queen whispered. "You just fucked with the wrong nigga bitch. Hope you ain't mixed up no more about who I am. I'm The Queen, bitch. The one and only."

The sweet taste of revenge delighted her mouth as if she'd sucked on a Jolly Rancher. She strutted to the sink, ran cold water over her throbbing knuckles, smoothed down her hair, and strode out of the bathroom humming her song, "A Bad Bitch."

Chapter 70

Later that evening, Knight stood at the head of the sleek black conference table, looking at each of the fifteen board members in the eye.

"I'm always glad to see our top brass gathered in one room," Knight said, looking each one in the eyes.

Tonight I'll bedazzle them with bullshit. The less they know about anything right now, the better.

"On the agenda tonight, we're focusing on The Games and the rapid growth of Babylon over the past year," Knight said.

The Board members knew Babylon was extremely vulnerable to inside and outside forces, because rapid expansion always had the potential to cause serious growing pains. Most of these cats loathed the idea of playing anything but war with Moreno. So the positive outcome of today's meeting was not on the agenda with the board.

And no one, not even The Queen, now seated beside Knight, knew about the mega deal to sell Babylon in one month's time. Nor did anyone even know about their meeting with Moreno today.

Knight wore his best mask of mystery and power while his insides bubbled with love and pride as he gazed at The Queen. Paul had been monitoring every second of her encounter in the bathroom and he had made sure to inform Knght of it. Knight was very happy with how The Queen had handled herself. What he wasn't happy about, was the sleazy shit that punk-ass B-boy tried to pull. Right now, arrangements were being made to secretly alert his parents of their beloved son's underworld lifestyle, so that he could stop counting on his trust fund at age twenty-five. And Brian was also being informed in the most convincing way that any more attempts to contact The Queen or even speak her name to anyone would result in swift and permanent consequences for him.

The theme song for Babylon played on the hidden Bose speakers throughout the conference room. Several people rocked in their seats as they tapped expensive Mont Blanc pens to the agendas and jotted down notes in their mono-grammed leather organizers. Some of these folks knew and loved Jamal; others didn't. With him as the proud new owner of Babylon, they would all be well taken care of, and still earn their fortunes in their respective cities.

But with all those millions on the line, Knight had no time for mutiny in the ranks. So secrecy was the name of his game for the next four weeks. Then he'd do the deals, get married, and disappear before the announcement was made that Babylon was under new management.

Plus, Mama's tearful visit just minutes ago to the Penthouse had him rattled. Li'l Tut was alive, HIV positive crazed, and on the run. Now the Barriors were on a mission to finish what Knight had started on the boat.

Li'l Tut is capable of anything now. He has nothing to live for except a nasty date with death.

The Queen had heard it all as Mama had sobbed into Knight's shoulder. Knight had immediately called Paul to put all of Babylon on Red Alert, the highest security level. It also meant that The Queen would be packing at all times. In fact, after this meeting, Knight would take her to the firing range downstairs, to make sure her shot could blow a muthafucka's block off, if necessary; because if Duke somehow got to her, and took what he wanted, his poisonous dick was as good as a gun to her head.

Gotta take him out. Now! But where the fuck was he?

Suddenly Knight's chest squeezed. He froze. Didn't even want to inhale. Because any movement, he feared, might make those tiny needles stab harder into his heart.

The Queen's eyes locked on him. Her lips were tense and tight; her eyes flashing fear. In his mind, he heard her voice say, *I can feel your pain.*

He could see the worry and concern in her eyes. Knight inhaled deeply. *My body is a precision-tuned, superhuman machine. I am well. It's just stress. It'll all be over in twenty-nine days. I can make it to paradise.*

He inhaled again, very slowly. And the pain dissolved to a dull ache. But this health crisis, he feared, was eroding the cool, calm confidence that was his trademark as the CEO of Babylon.

Now, in the board meeting, he had to walk a tight rope to keep the members happy without revealing the secret deal. Or that Li'l Tut was back with a vengeance, armed and dangerous. Telling that would give the schemers in the room ammunition to make a power play. They also didn't need to know that one of his fed sources had tipped him off to a possible raid during The Games.

Knight had to finesse this meeting so that no wild cards got tossed into the mix.

"Excuse me." Reba came through the door with a silver tray holding glass bottles of water and crystal tumblers. "How's everybody doin'?" She placed a bottle and glass before Knight's seat. She wedged between him and The Queen, brushing her ass against Knight's leg.

He immediately stepped back.

"Hey, boss lady," Reba said, smiling down and sticking her pushed up titties inches from The Queen's face as she served the water. "That pantsuit is sharp."

The Queen cast her eyes up at what she knew was a ho, scheming to steal her man.

Knight focused on his typed agenda.

Reba is through. Can't have her agitating like this.

All eyes in the room were on Reba's highly glossed lips, her titties, and her ass.

"Reba," Knight snapped. "We're about to get started. You can greet everybody at the party down in the garage, after our meeting."

Reba continued serving around the table.

Knight got on with the task of feeling out everybody's state of mind. Some of the members looked calm and collected but others seems anxious and fidgety. Intuition told Knight to be careful with the nervous ones because it could mean they were up to something; or working with Li'l Tut.

As Reba left the room, Knight ignored the tightness in his chest. He had to fake it till he made it.

"I'm grateful that all of you were able to make it today," Knight said, "because our plan for the next month is extremely ambitious. But I believe it's attainable, given the rapid growth of the past year."

He held up the schedule; papers rattled throughout the room as everyone else followed suit. "These are the major deals and events on the horizon," Knight said. "Skip down to the bottom. If you haven't heard, you'll see that The Queen and I are getting married the day after The Games, on October first. The Games will be our bachelor/bachelorette party."

Leroy Lewis' angry tone cut through the chorus of congratulations. "Your planning is fucked-up." His diamond pinkie ring sparkled as he twisted the edge of his pencil-thin mustache. "A huge distraction. Babylon can't afford to derail our focus on the frivolity of a wedding."

Several people let out annoyed groans.

"I agree," Shar Miller said, shaking her spiky black hair. "Makes us vulnerable to outside forces. The feds, the competition, and Moreno's wicked tricks. Too many wild cards out there could deal us a fatal blow. And everybody knows if Duke is still alive, he could come back with a vengeance."

Marcus Reed shot up to his feet and threw his silver pen down on the table. "Why y'all gotta hate on a brotha wit' good news? Damn! Can't stand a hater!" He slapped the back of Leroy's chair. "If you got a legit beef wit' the brotha, speak on it. But if you just gripin' to flex, then shut the fuck up."

Most people around the table applauded.

"What Knight done wit' Babylon over the past year ain't nothin' but a miracle." Marcus strode toward The Queen and stood behind her chair. "An' this young, talented lady done made millions for all o' y'all in the women's market. So e'rybody, let the brilliant brotha speak."

Knight nodded. "I couldn't have said it better myself. That was exquisite, my brotha."

Several people laughed.

But Leroy and Shar were like two smoke stacks. Fuming toxic vapors. Knight didn't even look at them. "Between the wedding and The Games, we have the Moreno meeting tomorrow. And the last yacht party of the season, to recruit clients and associates, will be next week at The Playhouse."

Leroy raised his hand and spoke at the same time, "I heard a rumor around here today that Duke is back. Is that true?"

Knight's chest squeezed. He swallowed a cough. Shooting pains radiated like poison darts from his heart, up his neck, down his arm.

I'm having a heart attack. Can't breathe.

His face remained as stiff as a mask, but he could hear The Queen's panicky thoughts.

I cannot, will not, fall out in this meeting. My power depends on my strength.

Knight took three long strides to the door. He felt like he was holding his breath; just had to swim faster up to the surface, so he could gulp down air. Opened the door. Stepped out. Closed the door. Inhaled.

The pain eased.

The four Barriors and B'Amazons who had been guarding the meeting watched attentively but gave him space.

Then a gush of alarmed voices shot out from the room as the door opened again.

Out came The Queen, eyes wide and rolling with questions. In them, he saw that she felt his pain and fear as intensely as he did. "Knight, baby," she cried, stroking his back as he coughed to hide that he was gasping for breath. She held up her cell phone. "I'm calling an ambu—"

"No, I'm fine. Handle the meeting," he wheezed, holding his chest. "Say I got stomach flu. I'll be upstairs."

A sound he'd never heard shot out from between her lips. It was like a cry of pain, a shriek of horror, but muted so only he could hear it.

It made his heart ache more.

Chapter 71

I'm killin' him with my pussy. The Queen studied her terrified eyes in the mirror. She had locked herself in the huge, marble bathroom of their Penthouse. *We make love so much, it's sucking the life out of him. I have to stay away from him. No more pussy for Knight until he's better.*

She had warned him, but he, like Duke, had laughed when she told them about the killing powers of her pussy. *Poison fruit. Like Eve's poison apple. Taste it in heaven, end up in hell.*

"Baby girl!" He pounded on the locked door. "Let me in."

"Will you go to the doctor?"

"We need to talk."

That meant no, but she had to convince Knight to get medical help. A doctor or specialist could figure out what was going on. Maybe it was something as simple and controllable as asthma. He could just get an inhaler and some breathing treatments, and he'd be fine. Or perhaps he had some type of virus that could be cured with rest. As much as he was working lately, he hardly slept. Maybe he was just fatigued.

The Queen crossed her legs more tightly, as if she had to pee and was holding it in.

My biggest fear is coming true. He's gonna die. And it's partly my fault.

The Queen raked her fingers through her loose hair.

"Baby girl," Knight called through the locked door. "Baby girl, you okay?"

"No, I'm not okay and neither is your ass."

"Come out or I'll come in."

She rolled her eyes. "You can't. It's locked."

He was silent. But in her mind, she could hear him say, *You know a lock never stopped me. I snuck into Babylon, and into my brother's bed, to get to you.*

The Queen shook her head. Why was she hearing his thoughts?

Because the two of you are one, Celeste answered. *It defies logic. It's supernatural.*

A click echoed over the marble bathroom, and the door opened.

Knight walked in.

She didn't bother to ask how he had entered. "It's my curse," she said, facing the mirror, looking into his tired eyes. They were bloodshot and dull, as if dusty rocks had replaced the sparkling gems in his irises. Plum arcs of fatigue framed his lower lashes, and a grayish pallor covered his normally radiant and dark skin.

"Knight, admit it. My curse is suckin' the life outta you."

Wearing a plush white robe with KNIGHT embroidered in gold on the left breast, he stood behind her, resting his chin on the top of her head. His huge, black hands rested on her waist, tickling her bare skin.

She was nude, her long black hair falling over her shoulders and breasts and over Knight's hands. A diamond sparkled in her pierced bellybutton.

"Look in my eyes," he said. Even his delicious sucka lips looked thinner and tense. "What do you see?"

"Sadness, fear. All the things I've never seen there before. All because my pussy power is killing you."

Knight shook his head. "Baby girl, that's ridiculous. How can you think that?"

She cocked her neck. "Because I've been thinking about it ever since I was six years old and I went to my young, healthy mamma's funeral and my cousin said she got fucked to death"

Knight took her hands into his. "Baby girl, there's no medical ailment showing you can die from making love. It creates life, literally and figuratively. It heals. Since I've been with you, I've felt more alive than—"

"Yeah, I could tell how alive it's making you feel when you almost fell out in the meeting tonight," The Queen snapped sarcastically.

"It's just the pressure of everything piling up."

"Right on your chest. You hardly sleep, you're constantly working, you're running yourself ragged, and you won't even go to the doctor."

"I'll go tomorrow."

"You need to go right now." The Queen spun around. His face blurred through her tears. "Knight, if anything happens to you, I'll just die."

"Tinkerbell, watch your words; they have power. Anything you say can and will come true, baby girl, if you put it out there."

"Then read my lips, Knight. If anything ever happens to you, I'll just die. You hear me? I'll scream it while we're making love, to give it that extra power."

Knight scooped her into his arms. "I'm going to make love to you right now to prove that I'm fine. We'll concentrate on the good things we want. Don't speak those words again."

As he walked, she cupped her hands over his jaw and stared into his beautiful eyes. She had to make him well again.

She imagined he were a picture that she could airbrush back to perfection. "Look at my Knight," she whispered. "I gotta get the color back in your cheeks. And erase those dark circles."

"Give me some love therapy."

"No," she said softly. Just the idea of him not feeling his best because of her made her stomach ache. "I don't want to make love until you feel better and look better."

Their sensuous theme song, "Love You to the Infinity," which she'd recorded with the Bang Squad, played softly in the huge bedroom. She led him to their bed and straddled his lap so she could face him.

"I'm gonna heal you of whatever is wrong, but not with sex," The Queen whispered, pressing her lips to each of his cheeks for long moments. Her bare behind rested on his thighs. Her hair was long and loose down her back, tickling the tops of his hands around her waist. "If you hurt," she said, "I hurt. If you cry, I cry. If you die, I die."

He groaned. "Baby girl, don't say that."

"If you die, I die," she said more forcefully. "It's the honest 'Romeo-and-Juliet' truth, so hear it."

"No, no, baby girl."

"Yes, yes, beautiful Knight. You're all I got in this whole world. One million lifetimes of love all rolled into one."

A tear rolled down his cheek.

"I've never seen you cry," she whispered, licking the tear with the tip of her tongue.

"I don't," he said. "But where I come from, you don't see a love this pure and untainted by insecurity and jealousy."

The Queen laughed softly. "I was ready to knock that Reba bitch's block off when she rubbed her fat ass up against you in the meeting."

Knight smiled. "But you didn't 'cause you're secure. You know even the sexiest woman can't steal a man unless he's already put himself at risk for theft."

"My parents had this kind of love. Love so good it kills."

"We'll use our lovemaking power together to make me feel invincible again," Knight said. "And we'll exorcise your mind of that ridiculous curse."

"It's not ridiculous," she snapped. "Kiss me, baby girl."

"Not until you—"

Knight pressed his lips onto hers. His warm lips sent shivers down her spine. The Queen and Knight synchronized their breaths. Both breathed in deeply, slowly, with the same pace and rhythm, then they breathed out just the same, all the while never separating their mouths from each other. They held their hands up, pressing their fingertips and palms together.

She stared into his beautiful black eyes and concentrated on the words *ridiculous curse*. Curse or no curse, they would live and love together or share their final breath.

She closed her eyes. Blue and purple sparks glittered like tiny stars behind the blackness of her closed eyelids. Her mind went numb, and her body tingled; she felt her spirit rise up and dance with Knight's, around their bodies.

Opening her eyes, she gazed lovingly into his eyes. She loved every detail of this man.

I love you to the infinity, The Queen thought.

Knight's eyes sparkled. *I love you to the infinity, baby girl.*

Though their lips were still connected in a kiss, The Queen couldn't stop herself from gasping.

Knight's lips felt like they were twisting into a smile too. He pulled back. "You heard me think," he whispered.

"You heard me first." She giggled.

"We are one mind," he said. "One heart. One soul." Knight smiled at her. The energy between each other right now, she was sure, was so strong, it could melt gold.

Then surely it could heal whatever ailed him.

She kissed him back passionately, feverishly, hoping her heart, lungs, and brain would become his life support until his own body jolted back to normal. They had to. Or she'd die right along with him.

Chapter 72

As he left the dentist's office, all Brian wanted to do was punish the black bitch that his sweet Victoria had become. He ran his tongue over the new caps and veneers to replace the jagged front teeth that had remained after his run in with the so called Queen.

"Kill the bitch!" his favorite gangsta rappers shouted from his stereo as he climbed into his new Range Rover and turned the key in the ignition.

The pounding beat made him clench his fists with the need to blast her back in the mouth, and other places, as she had done to him. She'd become the dirty whore of that inner city kingpin whose cock was probably like a black python, poisoning the pussy that Brian had once wanted so much.

But she never gave it to me. The fat-ass bitch!

And now he didn't even want the tainted shit. He just wanted to destroy it.

All that time, after he'd seen her look alike sister Melanie's picture on TV, he'd thought Victoria was dead.

She tricked me.

His stomach gurgled. He hadn't been eating because his teeth were hurting so bad. And now he hungered for vengeance.

Nobody treated Brian Martin like that. Not only was he working for one of the most powerful men in the world, but his pedigreed, white blood entitled him to respect.

Every inch of him, from his chubby fingers down to his swollen dick, throbbed with rage. It blinded him to the fact that he'd be double crossing his boss, Red Moreno, who wanted her for himself.

Brian flipped open his cell phone, punched in the code that would make his call untraceable, and dialed the FBI. They finally connected him with a dude named Rick Reed.

Brian imitated the way his father spoke when handling the details of multimillion-dollar business deals. He deepened his voice and said, "Good afternoon, Mr. Reed. I'm calling to alert you of the whereabouts of Victoria Winston, who's been wanted for more than a year after—"

"I know who she is." The dude cut him off.

Brian couldn't tell if he were black or white.

"I thought her body was found in her father's house?"

"Mr. Reed, I'm about to make you a hero. Victoria Winston is alive and well. Find her, and you'll solve the murder of Melanie Winston. You'll also crack open an inner city prostitution ring that's bigger and more organized than you'll believe. And I can tell you exactly how and when to do it."

"Let's deal."

Chapter 73

The "gold-digger glint" in Reba's eyes let Duke know she was his for the taking. And she'd do anything to get what she thought he could give her. Even though he was a shot-up, cracked out, HIV infected muthafucka right now, who was letting her foot the bill for this hotel room while he recovered from Knight's gunshots.

She stood over the bed, pulling down the sheets to inspect his wounds.

Duke was laying on his good side, resting his cheek on the pillow. "Reba," he called playfully. He sang, "Suga, suga, how ya get so fine?"

His gaze raked over her skin tight jeans that were so low cut, they revealed the top of that little heart shaped poof of hair over her pussy. Her nipples poked through her orange cropped top that matched her baseball cap. He reached out to touch the orange rhinestone star in her belly button.

"Quit, boy!" she played with her high pitched, little girl voice. "You need to rest. Get yo' strength. So you can be king again."

Duke stared up into the dollar signs flashing in her eyes.

She wanted nothing more than to be at his side as he fought his way back to the top of Babylon. So she could live her ghetto fabulous fantasy as his wife.

She fine, but she ain't Duchess.

And his dream wouldn't be complete without is woman back at this side.

That was the best pussy I eva had in my life.

But for now, Reba would do. She was devious enough to carry out any command he ordered in his war against Knight. And she was mad enough at Knight, for rejecting her, to enjoy his execution.

She's using me, I'm using her; we even. An' we gon' get rich together, or die tryin'.

He watched her ass pop like two round balloons covered in denim. Every step toward the bathroom made one rise up, and then the other go down.

Timbo swelled like a tree trunk thick, hard, and long. But now his dick was a killing machine. Nobody would fuck him if they knew, so he wouldn't tell.

Duke's insides felt like a whirlpool of dirty water spinning down into a drain in the gutter. Because he was filthy. How could he have let himself get this bad?

"Reba," he said playfully. "Reba Sheba be my girl."

Her little girl laughter echoed from the bathroom. "Why you sayin' my name like you wanna fuck?" she cooed over the sound of water wringing out of a washcloth into the sink. She giggled, peering from the doorway. "Boy, you could kill yo'self tryin' to fuck right now. Bleed to death. Pass out from no strength. You betta quit!"

She strutted back toward him with the washcloth and bandages. The warm cotton on his face, and her gentle touch, made him close his eyes and wish he were a little boy getting some "Mama love," but Mama had kicked him out, and this was a ho polishing up her ticket to the jackpot.

"Dang, Duke!" She flitted her long ponytail over her shoulder. A whiff of expensive perfume overwhelmed him. "Every time I look at you, I have to remember. You don't hardly look like—naw, let me stop." She folded her big, juicy lips inward, then nodded. "Knight always says, 'Make it positive.' So, we gon' fix you back up so you even more healthy and fine than you was a year ago."

"You gon' be my nurse?" he asked, rubbing his knuckles against her right nipple. "You gon' help me?"

"Read my lips," she whispered, her face just inches from his. "Reba at your service. Ain't nothin' too much to ask. I'ma do any an' everything to get us where we need to be."

Duke grinned.

"That's my suga pie." She smiled and pressed those juicy lips to his forehead. "We the new Bonnie an' Clyde. Takin' Dtown by storm, baby!"

Duke roared, "Oh, shit!" He grimaced. "I forgot. I can't laugh like that no more. That muthafucka fucked me up!"

Reba shot up, stepping toward the dresser. "Let me get you another pill." She pulled open the drawer where the doctor had stashed all of his medicine. Painkillers, antibiotics, and his HIV cocktail were all in the top drawer under his shirts. "Damn! You got a whole drug store in here."

"No!" Duke shouted. "Don't nobody but the doctor need to give me my drugs. She gon' be here at four."

"That's in three more hours." Reba's tone was sassy. "But you need some now. How we gon' make plans an' you can't barely see straight 'cause it hurt so much?"

Time stood still as she pulled back the sweaters and stared down. If she knew the name of an HIV drug when she saw one, he'd be busted. An' his plan wouldn't work 'cause she be outta there in a hot minute. "Bitch, shut the drawer. Come back ova here."

Reba sucked her teeth and slammed the drawer.

A hard knock on the door made Duke reach under the blankets and grip his gun.

"Who the fuck?" Duke whispered.

Reba had already canceled maid service in this upscale, downtown Detroit hotel. And it wasn't room service because she had already brought in a pizza and salad for lunch.

And Shar, Leroy, and Raynard Ingalls of Chicago all knew better than to show up at his hotel room. Their scheming plans on taking over Babylon was all being handled over the phone for now.

Duke gripped his gun ready to blast off if he had to, even while he was fucked up in his bed. "It's probably Antoine," Reba whispered as she tiptoed to the peephole. "Yup."

"I don't want that muthafucka to see me."

"We can't make a plan without him." Reba unhooked the chain lock and turned the bolt.

Duke had already suffered the shame of his brother, his mother, his doctor, and Reba staring into his face with pity and shock. Now he didn't want one of the finest Studs in Babylon to do the same. "Reba don't open that muthafuckin' door."

She opened it quickly.

Antoine glanced both ways down the hall and slipped in. "Yo," he said with a quick wave, "Duke, good to see you, man."

Duke glared at that caramel-colored pretty boy with a healthy dick. No bullet wounds. No crack-ravaged blood, bones, and body.

A healthy Stud muthafucka like I used to be. The kind a stud that The Duchess couldn't wait to fuck.

Duke closed his eyes to escape this nightmare, but Reba's girlie voice, talking about the time schedule, snagged him back to reality.

Duke stared hard into Antoine's eyes. "How we know you ain't got an allegiance wit' Knight?"

"You don't." Antoine shrugged. "All I got is my word. An' you remember from back in the day, we was tight like that." Antoine stared back hard in a way that said, "Follow me if you need to."

Reba play slapped his hand. "Duke, I ain't gon' bring somebody up in here who ain't on the team. An' you ain't in no position to go out recruitin'. Antoine all right."

"Bet." Duke shot him a hard look. "You play right an' you gon' get ova real good."

"I'm in," Antoine said, pulling up a chair for himself and another for Reba.

"Now, this the way it"—Duke grimaced in pain—"its gon' go down the night o' The Games. An' anybody who stand in my way gon' get steamrolled."

Chapter 74

Knight stood beside The Queen, studying how the clear safety glasses made her eyes look extra big and beautiful. With her hair pulled back in a ponytail, and the orange plugs in her ears, she focused straight ahead, over the tiny view finder above the barrel.

All his chest crushing anxiety about Manifest Destiny had dissolved the moment they had stepped down into this gun range in the basement of Babylon HQ; they had an arsenal that could arm a small country. But right now he had to make sure that The Queen's target practice, twice a month, was preparing her to fight to the death if necessary. Her self-defense classes with Lee Lee were doing the same, as she'd proven with that punk, Brian, after their Moreno meeting.

Knight was making plans to take care of Brian and Moreno, too. They'd be out of the way for Babylon to thrive under Jamal's reign, as Knight and The Queen would flee their urban underworld and live in the sunshine in peace forever.

Just in case all hell broke loose on their wedding night; a power coup, a robbery, a siege, he had to make sure The Queen could handle herself and get out alive.

Knight's thoughts popped as quickly and as intensely as the gunfire of two dozen B'Amazons and Barriors who were doing target practice in adjacent lanes.

"No emotion," Knight said close to her ear. "Kill or be killed."

The Queen's diamond engagement ring glistened as she gripped the pistol with both hands. She aimed at the man-sized target. *Pow!*

The bullet blasted into the red bull's-eye on the man's chest.

The Barriors and B'Amazons around them stopped to admire The Queen's sharp shooter skills.

"You doin' it, baby girl!" Knight exclaimed.

Pow! Another bullet pierced the heart zone on the target. "Baby girl!" Knight said with awe. "You shoot better than some of the B'Amazons."

"'Cause I'm The Queen," she said without taking her eyes off the target or lowering the gun. "I dare a muthafucka." She turned to look into Knight's eyes.

The potency in her stare was so powerful, Knight shivered. It was like looking in the mirror, on his best days, when he felt like the African god that he was, ruling over his kingdom and making his minions quake in their boots with a glance.

The Queen smiled.

She knows what you're thinking, Intuition said. *You're the perfect power couple. Gotta be careful, though.*

There was a glint in The Queen's eyes.

"Your cry for help is *'Isis! Osiris!'* You yell that out if anything happens while you're in The Penthouse, the wedding suite, or anywhere else. Shout it over and over until the Barriors and B'Amazons get there."

The Queen stared back with a suspicious glint.

"We're monitoring every sound and every movement in The Playhouse and HQ. So know that somebody will be there. Until they arrive, though, you can handle it. Stay armed at all times. Does your holster fit okay?"

"It's fine."

"Good. Stay armed at all times, even if you're with security. Even if you think you're in a place that's completely safe."

"Even with you?" she said with a flat tone, staring hard. She put the gun on safety and slipped it into the brown leather holster belt around the waist of her low-cut jeans. "You won't go to the fuckin' doctor, you could fall out any minute. An' I'm just standin' there like a sorry bitch outta muthafuckin' luck."

The anger in her voice made Knight's cheeks burn as if he'd been slapped. He took a deep breath.

"Baby girl—"

"Naw, don't 'baby girl' me right now." She jerked her neck. "I'm a grown-ass woman who's worried about her man who supposed to keep my ass safe, but the way you—"

Knight grasped her arm. Nobody needed to see anything other than complete harmony among them. He pulled her into the small office where men and women had to scan their ID cards to gain entry and check out extra weapons if necessary. Then he guided her with a tight grip on her arm, through a small door to the gun room. Knight closed the door behind them, staring hard at The Queen as she stood framed by a row of rifles. "Never show a public display of anger like that again. This a dangerous time at Babylon. We can trust no one. Because they will divide and conquer if we show even the slightest crack in the veneer."

The Queen rolled her eyes. "You actin' way too paranoid lately. Like you ain't bein' straight wit' me about what's really 'bout to go down when we get married."

Knight took another deep breath to force down any conscious thoughts about his plan.

She had heard something broadcast over their telepathic love connection. And it had tipped her off but she still had no real information.

"I see some scheme, Knight. An' I ain't diggin' it."

Knight squinted slightly as he looked down at her. "Baby girl, you're acting real paranoid right now."

She crossed her arms. "How the fuck else am I supposed to be acting when you walking around looking sick and worried like you expectin' some shit to go down? How the fuck you expect me to be acting right now Knight? You want me to act like an innocent little white girl? Like the way I was a year ago?"

"Baby girl, now you're going a little overboard. I'm just asking you to calm down. I know you worried about me, but you can't let them see you sweat. Hang in there 'til the wedding and then you won't have to put up such a front when we—" Knight stopped himself. He was about to say, "When we disappear," but he stopped himself. Knight cleared his throat. "When we get through Game day," Knight said softly and reassuringly.

"You're right Knight," she said through tight lips. "I guess all this stuff going on lately has me feeling weird." Her eyes became shiny and silvery as they filled with tears. "I love you, Knight. I love the idea of spending the rest of my life here in

Babylon beside you, runnin' things an' raising our family. I
don't want anything to happen to you"—she paused—"or us."

Knight's throat burned. He wanted to pull her into his
arms, cover her with kisses and whisper that he would always
protect her, make her smile, make her cum, and be the perfect
mate. But he was frozen by guilt. It sliced through his gut like
a giant knife.

*I'm deceiving her. She trusts me with her life, and I'm
tricking her. If she fooled me, it would forever destroy my
trust. So how will she forgive me once everything shakes
down and we wake up in another life?*

Something flickered in her eyes. "I got this feeling with
Duke too," she said with a weak tone, as if she were about
to vomit. "You betta tune your thoughts back to a better
frequency where you ain't givin' off that vibe I just felt. I don't
like it. An' I'll slip off your radar before I let you or anybody
else play me. The Queen don't get played."

Knight stepped close to her and rested his hands on her
shoulders. "Everything I do is for us." He lowered an open
palm to the soft, warm swath of belly exposed by her low-cut
jeans. The diamond in her belly button seemed to wink up at
him. "For us and for Baby Prince." Knight kissed her.

Their lips did not move. But the heat and the energy passing between them caused The Queen's tense shoulder to relax
under his hand, and her belly quaked slightly. She gripped the
crotch of his black jeans.

Shane surged to attention.

"Make love to me," she whispered, grabbing the big silver
belt buckle that said KNIGHT. She dropped to her knees,
unfastened his belt, unzipped his pants, and pulled Shane out
in front of her face.

He surged out like a black python.

The Queen had the power and concentration of a snake
charmer in her eyes as she stared at his dick as if it held all the
secrets to the meaning of life and love.

Knight almost smiled. He couldn't think of any situation
in a relationship that didn't get resolved with some good dick
therapy. Because sheer bliss glowed in The Queen's eyes as
she parted her lips and stuck out her tongue to slide it under

the giant black head and lure him into the hot chamber of her mouth.

This is the answer.

Having her mouth on Shane twenty-four/seven was the remedy for his health crisis, because as soon as her steaming hot mouth closed around his cock, it sparked a chemical reaction in his body. The stress and worries that caused tight sensations in his muscles and made his mind reel, suddenly transformed into a warm swirl of liquid opium.

He threw his head back with his eyes closed and enjoyed the sensation of Shane sliding in and out of The Queen's warm, moist mouth.

Evrything's gonna be all right as long as I have my Queen by my side.

Chapter 75

Trina Michaels hurried into her office at the Global News TV Network in Washington, D.C. She was trembling with a nasty mix of emotions, ranging from fear to excitement and anticipation, to disappointment and rage.

I'm never gonna fuck again. Sex never led to anything but trouble.

That was the whole reason she had married her first husband. And her second husband. And that jerk she left at the altar last year, when she realized that sex was her only motive for wanting to tie the knot with him too.

Otherwise, she didn't give half a shit about those cavemen. Cavemen who had gone to the best schools and came from the best, most bourgeoisie families on the East Coast, but cavemen, nonetheless. They all were. Just big apes playing with the bananas between their legs, hoping to hump it into any and every female they encountered while swinging from tree to tree.

"So why does sex make me so stupid too?" she asked aloud as she set down her suitcase and perched on the chair at her desk. "Why do I think that in order to feel clean and respectable, I have to marry the dick of the day?"

And how come, the first time she decides to indulge her curiosity for sex with women, she gets mixed up with some inner city bandits who try to blackmail her by videotaping the female sexcapades? When in her thirty-five years on this planet did Trina Michaels ever have sex that didn't end up a mess?

That abortion just before the senior prom, so she could go to college; Chlamydia after pulling a train at that frat party during her sophomore year at Georgetown University; the rumors and lies that the married anchor spread about her at the first TV station where she worked, in that dusty little hick town in Kentucky; the catfight in the newsroom at her next station, in Atlanta, when she and another female reporter had gone to blows over the hottest guy in TV news at the time.

"Talk about drama," Trina said out loud as she logged on to the blue screen of her computer.

This last situation clearly took the cake over everything else. Even that white network TV headhunter who promised an extra $25,000 in her contract if she fucked him after the interview. When she negotiated it to $35,000, she thought of it as a signing bonus, which helped her get a luxury sports car that projected the appropriately glamorous image for a serious TV reporter in the nation's capitol.

So there was no way that anybody especially that "thug" and "thugette" in Detroit, was going to stop her now. Nope, onward and upward. Alone and without sex.

"Those niggers in Detroit think they got somethin' on me, but I'm gonna do a report that blows them outta the water."

Yes, when The Queen and her caveman, The Knight, first threatened her, Trina felt scared for her safety, her career, and her reputation. But as she fumed on the plane ride back to D.C., she realized, in this day and age of technology and computer manipulation of video, nobody could ever prove that was GNN's Trina Michaels on that nasty tape. Plus, she did so many negative reports about vile people, and the court cases they generated, dozens, if not hundreds, of people in America would've loved nothing better than to destroy her so she could say it was just someone making stuff up to get revenge on her.

I'll say they forged the video using my face from TV and another woman's body. Another woman who was smoking marijuana. Then they'll be busting on their own asses, after my report blasts their little empire to smithereens.

Trina wasn't stupid. She'd grown up with street hoods just like that on the South Side of Chicago, always hustling to make a dollar. No matter what toll it took on someone's body, mind or soul.

A pimp and a ho were a pimp and a ho, no matter how classy, sophisticated, or beautiful their whole spiel appeared to be. They were breaking the law. And they would have to stop. Soon. And she wasn't buying that sob story 'bout growing up in the hood and not having any opportunities. *Stupid idiots.* Her parents were both honest, hard-working people, who taught her the right values. Mother worked downtown as a seamstress at a clothing boutique, and Father had a good job in the U.S. Post Office. Her brother was a lawyer, thanks to Harvard, and her sister was a stay-at-home mom, married to a stockbroker.

Yep, the Michaels family was as American as apple pie. Whereas The Queen and The Knight represented the dark, rotting core that threatened to bring this great country down through moral corruption and blatant disregard for the law.

But not if Trina could stop them first.

"Now, where is that picture?" Trina said out loud as she typed the name Victoria Winston into the GNN video archives.

No, Trina had busted her ass to get where she was. And she wasn't going to allow it to be ruined by that horny mulatto bitch living some ghetto girl dream. Or nightmare, depending on who was talking. And that Knight guy. *Whew! What a piece of work!*

Trina hated the way he just sat there silently like the king, as if everybody should read his thoughts and act accordingly, or else.

Men. The male ego knew no bounds as far as being selfish and self-centered. He should be ashamed of himself, too. Hiding that girl from the authorities.

Trina shivered under her dark brown pantsuit. Her nipples poked through her lace bra and pushed into her white satin blouse.

Babylon, schmabylon. Blackmail or not though, that was undoubtedly the best sex she'd ever had.

Chapter 76

Duke wanted to fuck Reba right away, but she was acting all in a hurry to leave and do a party at The Garage.

"Why you gotta leave?" Duke stroked Timbo. He was nude, sitting up on the bed, his back against the headboard, his legs outstretched, and his dick in his hand.

"Ooooh, you got a pretty dick." Reba stepped closer.

"I need some sexual healing," Duke said. "Doc said it was okay."

"I say it ain't."

"If you gon' marry me," Duke said, "I need a test-drive first. How I know you can't grind down on it like I like?"

"You do know," Reba said, straddling the top of his thighs. Her hot ass in tight jeans against his skin made his dick throb harder. "Or did fuckin' Miss White Chocolate erase all memories of the sistas you used to kick it wit'?"

Duke wrapped his hands around her thighs and stared at her crotch. "Why don't you remind me? Take off yo' top."

Reba pressed her fingertips to her nipples, caressing them through her shirt. They got even harder, poking like juicy grapes through her top. "Why you wanna see my titties?"

Duke stroked his dick. "Its gon' make me heal faster."

She shifted to his kneecap then ground her crotch into him. "Work that shit," he said. "An' suck on Timbo."

Reba leaped off and stood beside the bed. "Duke, you ain't in no condition to mess around. You can't even laugh without pain."

"Get on top," he said, "take a ride. Gimme some sexual healing."

"You been checked?" Reba asked. "Lemme see yo' card, 'cause I'm still workin' for Babylon. But if I catch somethin',

I'm out on my ass. An' this plan ain't gon' work from the outside. So—"

"You think I'm some kinda infected muthafucka?"

"Duke, you know damn well that half the shit out there, ain't got no symptoms. Especially HIV."

"You know how careful I was when we was fuckin' before."

"But when you out on the street, doin' what you was doin' . . . no offense, Duke, but y'all gets sloppy."

"Y'all'? What the fuck you mean?"

"It mean Reba don't fuck no dick that ain't been checked. My pussy clean and I'm keepin' it that way." Reba cupped his face in her hands. "Duke, this can wait. I don't think—"

He grabbed her face and pulled her close. He planted a hot, juicy kiss on her lips.

She resisted, grabbing his wrists to pull away.

He didn't let go; her lips were tense and shut. But he pressed harder. Then he grabbed her ass and pulled her closer so that her crotch nibbed up against Timbo.

She moaned. And her lips relaxed. He slid his tongue into her mouth. She moaned and ground on his dick.

He pulled her ponytail back, yanked her head. Pulled up her shirt, buried his face in those big, delicious titties. Then his fingers pried at the metal button on the waist of her jeans.

She protested. "Duke—"

"I'll wear a condom, then I'll have Doc check me out." Duke wanted the pussy, but he could get by without it.

Truth was, he was sleepy as hell from the painkiller. But he needed to see just how far Reba would go to prove her loyalty to him and his plan. "Baby, I promise I'm clean," he whispered, pulling her close again for a kiss.

Chapter 77

Something in Reba's gut told her don't play with fire, because as bad as Duke looked right now, somethin' wasn't right. Maybe it was just hard life wherever the hell he had been for a year. Maybe it was the drugs. Maybe HIV was the reason he was so skinny and pale, and his skin was all jacked up with blemishes.

Reba didn't want any money so bad she'd risk her life for it. What good would that do? Getting what you want and then dying with it in your hands? And dying from AIDS was no joke. AIDS took its time, like it was a felon of fate inside your body, gloating at the horrible ways that it vandalized your skin, maliciously destroyed your body functions, and attempted to kill many terrifying times before finally committing a homicide. That's what it seemed like when some muthafucka pulled his trigger inside her sister Lucille and shot up her insides with a spray of HIV infected sperm.

Reba had watched her sister waste away into a skeleton with chronic diarrhea and throat infections. Hearing her gasp for her last breaths convinced Reba that HIV was nothing to play with. That's why she loved Babylon. If she was gonna trick, then she had the best case scenario.

That computer card with the chip in her purse, the one that all the Sluts and Studs were required to carry and get updated weekly, was her life insurance. Clients carried the cards too, and had to get checked before every party.

Reba thought of her sister every day, to remind her how precious her health and life were. Yeah, this girl from the hood was doing just fine right now. A nice apartment at Babylon HQ, plenty of money, and tons of men to fuck her, flatter her, and buy her anything she wanted.

I ain't drivin' my yellow Corvette outside an' wearin' designer clothes 'cause I'm strugglin'.

Shit, she was living a better life than she could've ever dreamed of growing up with her mama. When you grow up watching your ho-ass momma do her business in your face, the word *trick* takes on a whole new meaning. Trick or treat wasn't about Halloween. It was about the treats that Momma would buy for Reba and Lucille if she let a trick come while the girls were home.

Momma would give each daughter a dollar from the money that she'd earned for suckin' some crusty negro's dick, then she'd send the girls skipping down to the corner liquor store to buy whatever she and her trick wanted.

Baby Blue's mother, who used to stay in their tiny extra bedroom, while all three girls curled up to sleep together every night on the sofa bed in the living room, did the same thing; treats for their daughters after their tricks left.

Reba's favorite was a long red popsicle, which she would lick and suck the same way she'd seen Momma do all them dudes dicks. Momma took all those muthafuckas into the bedroom, but Reba and Lucille would still watch through the keyhole in the door.

Lucille's treat, though, was barbecue potato chips. She'd eat so many that her lips would burn, crack, and bleed from the salt and spices, because Lucille had the idea that love should hurt. So she followed in Momma's nasty footsteps, as a street ho. She dropped out of school, got hooked on drugs, and worked for a pimp who put blue marks on her black ass.

But Reba wanted to live a nicer life, like the white people she saw on TV. Somewhere out there was a better way. And all the boys and girls on TV who grew up to be somebody had to finish school first. So Reba kept going to middle school and high school.

But when Baby Blue took her to a party at Babylon, and she saw all those rappers and dancers and fine-ass niggas with rolls of dough in their pockets, Reba felt like she'd just stepped into ghetto paradise.

Then Baby Blue, who was already working as a Slut since dropping out of ninth grade, introduced her to Duke. Reba fucked him that night, and it was all over.

She loved his stuff so much she joined the Sex Squad and started working the next day. She even moved into Babylon, sharing an apartment with Baby Blue. It was a nicer place than she'd ever had. Shoot, just the fact that she had heat, hot water, plenty of good food, and no roaches made it an inner city Taj Mahal when compared to the rat hole Momma had kept her and Lucille in.

At Babylon, to keep living this glamorous life, all Reba had to do was do what she already loved to do; fuck, and everything was taken care of. But now, so many years later, she was tired of humpin' for a living. She didn't want to do this hard work for the rest of her life. No, she was looking for early retirement. And Duke, sitting here in a hotel room with bullet wounds, a big dream, and his dick in his hand, was her 401K plan.

"Get some papers or your card from Doc, an' this pussy yours for life," Reba said. "Until then, I can polish yo' knob wit' my hands."

"Naw, baby," Duke said with a deep, almost sinister tone. "If we ain't down all the way like this, it ain't a done deal."

Reba watched his chapped lips as he talked. She remembered how the girls used to say Duke had sucka lips. They were so sexy, that when he talked, all you could think about was wanting to suck on his bottom lip or his top lip or both at once.

But now, the dry skin made little vertical white lines up and down his lips. And while he talked, Reba thought she saw a red sore just inside his mouth. That could be a herpes blister or a syphilis chancre or a burn from a pipe or blunt. And all that made the thought of kissing him about as appetizing as licking a public toilet seat.

"Duke, I got rules for myself. You know how strict it be at Babylon." Reba got a whiff of funk from his underarms. "Don't ask me to toss 'em to the wind jus' so you can blow yo' nut."

"Bye." His word shot through the air like a bullet. "Get yo' ass outta here. Bonnie an' Clyde splittin' up. Clyde gon' get anotha bitch to get paid wit'."

Reba stared into his angry eyes. "You bluffin'."

"Bye."

She stood up, turned her back to him and unzipped her jeans to reveal her bare pussy since she didn't like wearing underwear. She pulled her pants down, and bent over at the waist.

"Now that's what I'm talkin' 'bout. Pussy wet as a mug."

As she faced the floor, she pulled off her shirt, letting her titties dangle. Then, as she stepped out of her jeans and shoes, she pulled a condom from her front right pocket. She ripped it open, then turned around.

"Da-yum!" Duke stroked Timbo.

She stepped onto the bed. With lightning speed, she rolled the condom down on his dick and slid down on it. "You slick," he said, "da's a'ight."

He grimaced in pleasure and pain as he pounded up into the pussy; she slammed down at the same time.

Reba gripped his shoulders. But the sensation of rough scabs on his back made her raise her hands up to the back of his head. Normally shaved bald, it was prickly with a week's worth of hair growth. "Oooh, you know how to fuck," Reba moaned.

"This some good pussy." Duke stared up into her eyes. "Say you love me."

The desperation in his eyes made Reba's gut cramp. "I love you," she said as sensuously as a movie star in a love scene would. "I love you, Duke."

"Say it while I cum," he said, fucking her harder. And harder. And frantically. Breathing hard, like he'd just run down the block.

Damn, he didn't even try to let me cum first. But whatever. The sooner this dangerous shit was over with, the better. She could relax and enjoy it when she knew he was healthy.

But the way he was drilling up, he could split steel with that dick. Plus, she was getting dry because she wasn't that into it. And a dry pussy, hard fucking, and a huge dick created the perfect formula for a broken condom and possible infection with whatever the fuck he might have.

"Duke, wait, let me check the condom," she said. He pulled out. The whole condom still covered every inch of him.

"Okay." She spat into her hand then rubbed the spit all up and down the outside of the condom. Then she slid Timbo back into her pussy.

"Oh, baby, I'm 'bout to cum," he groaned. Sweat beaded on his forehead. He was breathing so hard, he was wheezing. All that smoking.

Reba glanced at the clock on the nightstand. Her heart was pounding, but it was out of fear. The image of her sister Lucille, laying on her deathbed, trembling, sweating, and making unhuman groan noises, flashed through her mind. For a second, Duke's face even transformed into Lucille's, her paper-thin skin stretched so tight over protruding cheekbones, it looked like the bone would slice right through.

"Ah!" Reba cried out. Not in pleasure but in terror. She never took risks like this. Didn't have to, because everything at Babylon was so medically checked and safe. She couldn't wait to get this over with. She'd carefully slide off the condom, go take a long, hot shower, and never put her life on the line again.

"Oh, fuck!" Duke shouted. He threw his head back.

She noticed his teeth were a dull yellow and his breath smelled like medicine. "Say you love me, girl!"

Reba stared at him. Was any money worth this? She did not love this nigga. She loved what this deal represented.

She saw herself in a black Benz convertible, shopping, taking fancy trips, bein' the baddest bitch around, and loaded with cash. "I love you," she whispered, staring into his eyes.

"Yeah, love me!" he shouted. "Fuck!" Finally, he trembled with orgasm. "Damn," Duke smiled, still huffing. "That was the best fuck I eva had. 'Cause we was makin' love, not fuckin'."

Reba couldn't wait to get off this muthafucka. She knew damn well he had said those same words to countless women. Reba pinched the top of the condom around the base of his dick. She started to slide upward.

"Wait," Duke said, pressing down her thighs. "I love you, Reba Sheba." He stared tenderly into her eyes.

For a split second, the idea of a man saying he loved her and looking at her like that, made her want to cry. But she knew this love wasn't real. She knew this was a business exchange where both of them would be getting what they wanted. Right now all she wanted from Duke was, no viruses, no infections, and no bogus-ass words.

"I can't tell you," Duke said, "how good it feel for somebody to give me some love. Not just pussy, but some real love. I ain't felt that since fo'eva."

Reba wanted so desperately to feel that, she kissed his forehead. Because his ass was as pathetic as she was. And they were both perpetrating like they were tough. But at the core they were just two sorry-ass fools trying to play each other to get the prize.

After a long moment of pretending this was her husband who adored her for her, she pinched the base of the condom again. Holding tight to keep it in place and not spill sperm around her pussy, she carefully slid up and off but shredded rubber flopped down the sides of Duke's cum covered dick.

Chapter 78

Knight's deep voice echoed off the damp, black walls of the tunnel as he spoke to Crew Q. He had hand-picked these fifty Barriors and B'Amazons to execute important tasks during the wedding and The Games, or so they thought. Knight knew Li'l Tut, and these muthafuckas were scheming to steal his secret maneuvers and plans, report them back to his brother and his team of bandits, and dare to think they could plunder the riches that Babylon would accumulate the night of The Games.

Knight could hear his older brother, Prince, urging him to follow one of his rules of power, "Crush your enemies." Actually Knight was about to let them crush themselves as they attempted to execute their most misguided, knuckle-headed plan that would backfire in the most tragic of ways as Manifest Destiny triumphed.

"Twenty-one days," Knight said in the dim fluorescent light that flickered from a square panel on the ceiling.

In black scuba suits, Ping and Pong stood at his sides, along with his most trusted B'Amazons, Lee Lee and Dayna. All four of them held rifles. And they needed to know the bogus plan for Crew Q for when they carried out the real deal to whisk the money, Knight, and The Queen far away from Babylon.

"We have zero tolerance for error," Knight said over the sound of dripping water. Though the air was rank with mold and musk, he breathed calmly and deeply.

After years in a prison cell, he felt perfectly at ease in the confines of this hot, humid chamber, its metal walls glistening with greasy grime and patches of green moss. His face and body felt cool, his black ninja suit dry. But sweat glistened on the tense faces and bare, muscular arms of the troops to whom he spoke.

"Hesitation will get you killed." Knight knocked on the wall behind him in the twelve by twelve footwide area "Down here, thirty feet below the water's surface, the Detroit River shows no mercy."

He stared into the serious, yet scared eyes of the soldiers, especially Antoine's look-alike brother, Ben. He, like the others, wore fatigues, black boots, and black tank tops.

"So when this door goes up," Knight said, "it's game time. Anybody who misses their play will get a permanent time out for life." Knight looked over the heads of the men and women, into the thick blackness of a dozen more feet of tunnel behind them.

"Everybody hear me?"

They answered with military punctuality and speed, "Yes, sir!"

Knight took a large canvas backpack from Pong. He pulled open a zippered slot. "Remember, this holds your flotation device. Any heat, your enemies on the water will shoot first, ask questions later, after they snatch the cash." Knight held open the backpack's large inner bag.

"This waterproof pouch will hold the money. Lose it—put on some cement shoes and don't try to float. Your goal is to make it the half mile down the river to the boat with the underwater hatch."

Knight glared into the shifty eyes of that face that looked too much like Antoine to be trusted. "You got that, Ben?"

"Yes, sir!" he boomed back.

"Good." Knight probed his eyes with a hard gaze. The cat's only crime was nature's cruel trick of modeling him after his brother, whose misdirected lust at The Queen was about to get him jacked.

That didn't make him exempt, from Knight questioning his loyalty. Every man and woman down here right now had some mark against them. That mark could have been a rumor that they were Duke sympathizers, or a glance toward Knight that flashed hostility or game. Perhaps they'd shared phone conversations, e-mails or personal contact with Babylon board members who were contemplating a power coup.

So giving directives to Crew Q was the best way to divert all the Barriors and B'Amazons who were vulnerable to conspiring with competitors, especially Duke. Informants had clued Knight in on his baby brother's plan for a heist, followed by the rape and plunder of Babylon's riches. And anybody who helped make it happen would share the wealth, power, and future of Babylon. At least that's what Duke had promised.

Now, the eagerness in several of the soldiers' eyes confirmed Knight's suspicions. They were looking at him but mentally ticking down all the details they would report back to Duke.

"I'm glad I've got your attention," Knight said. "Now, if at any time during that twenty-four-hour period, you get the star signal, you are to report immediately to this tunnel. Not from the outside port, but from the basement inside The Playhouse. Everybody hear me?"

Knight could call this little exercise a test or a diversion or a trick. But he had to do whatever was necessary to make sure Manifest Destiny unfolded with perfect precision.

"One mistake could be your last." Knight's words reverberated through his chest. A dull ache was all that remained there now, thanks to the sexual healing powers that he and The Queen had conjured up while making love every morning and night since the board meeting.

Plus, in his mind, he found strength by envisioning that baby boy growing inside the warm, nurturing flesh of The Queen's womb.

I have the power to heal myself and slip away with my wife and unborn child to a better place.

Knight tapped the metal door wall. "Out in the river," Knight said, "that current is ruthless. There's boat traffic too. But here at the edge, you're safe. Just watch for floating debris; sometimes it's sharp or toxic."

Someone let out an annoyed groan.

"So wear your goggles," Knight said. "And just like we did in the drill over the summer; grab onto the metal handles in the river wall. Hold tight or that current will suck you down to the Rouge Plant and your bones will end up in the metal frame of somebody's new Ford."

One of the B'Amazons at the back of the group sucked her teeth and whispered, "Sheeit, this ain't worth it."

"Officer Sykes, step forward," Knight commanded. He had not seen her face.

Crew Q parted like water in the Red Sea. The woman slunk between them. Her muscular brown shoulders slumped; her close cropped head hung shamefully in front of Knight.

He spoke softly, "Get the fuck out."

The rest of the crew was silent as Lee Lee took her arm.

Pong aimed a small silver remote at the blackness at the rear of the tunnel. Squeaking hinges and the sound of a rising metal gate echoed with spine-chilling screeches.

"Lee Lee, bring me back her discharge papers." Knight stared hard into the eyes of Crew Q.

They stood still and silent as statues. Everybody knew life after Babylon was hell. Even if you left town. It was the ultimate black list.

"Anyone else?" Knight raised his hand toward the blue light dancing on the thick, humid air now that that the back gate had risen. His laughter echoed in a way that made Crew Q look spooked. "After all, we are standing in a tunnel that led to freedom on the Underground Railroad."

Ping nodded and said with a chuckle, "Find freedom or get fucked up, or both."

Knight smiled. "Now's your moment. Whether you're looking for a freedom ride or to smuggle your way out of here, speak now or forever hold"—He tapped the black Glock strapped to his hip—"your piece."

He took the remote from Pong's hand. His finger poised over the red button, he said, "Any defectors are welcome to take the water way out." Knight pointed to the silver square at the metal wall leading to the depths of the Detroit River. He pushed the button. With a deafening squeak, the door began to rise. Water crashed in, flooding the floor.

Several Barriors and B'Amazons jumped to avoid the frothy white water that filled the chamber with a strong fish odor. But Knight remained perfectly still. His waterproof boots rested firmly on the metal floor.

Suddenly his mind was illuminated with a thrilling "Ah-ha moment."

I have no ache in my chest. No sensation in my heart, except for normal, healthy beating. I can do this!

He was in the zone. And for Knight, the zone meant total concentration and focus on a goal. No distractions. No hesitation. No second thoughts.

With this and everything else, he set a goal and accomplished it. And that's what he would do the night of his wedding; accomplish his plans of moving on to a better life with his wife and unborn child. "Ben!" he shouted over the loud splashing sounds. "Ready to swim?"

Ben's huge eyes peered down at the rush of water under the metal door.

"Yyyyyy-eeeehhhh, sssssssiiiirrrr," Ben stammered without stepping forward.

Knight tossed his head back; his laughter echoed off the wet metal walls. The door slammed down. The only sound was the soft fizz of calming waves and bubbles around their feet. And Knight's deep laughter.

"Crew Q," he shouted. "How can I trust you to execute this plan when you're all standing here quaking like a bunch of pussies?"

Ben squared his shoulders. "Master Knight," he said. "What if it's somebody in the basement? Like they followin' us or somethin'?"

"Stop them in their tracks," Knight said. "And follow through." He stared hard into Ben's pretty-boy face, knowing that he would snitch every detail back to his conniving brother. Who would then tell Reba, who would then tell Duke.

Don't they know I'm ten steps ahead of them and everyone else?

There was one glitch though. Knight didn't know where Duke was staying. The Barriors had followed Reba to The Suites downtown hotel, and even identified Duke's room. But when they busted in to take care of him and eliminate this need for plan Q altogether, the Barriors found the room abandoned.

All they found were a used, broken condom on the disheveled bed and some bloody bandages in the bathroom. The Barriors had reported back that fresh funk and sex vapors hung heavily in the warm air, so it was clear that Duke and a now infected female had just fled.

We'll find him.

But plan Q would still be in effect. Just in case the likes of Shar Miller and other conspirators had any ideas about claiming the millions in cash that would be on the premises the night of The Games.

"Now, assuming that you do not get the star signal, and everything is going smoothly," Knight said, "I'm dividing you into driving teams for the drop."

The men and women nodded.

"When Ping and Pong make the drop in Hummer One," Knight said, "we'll have three decoy vehicles. Three other black armored Hummers will take separate routes: one to the vault at HQ; another to a boat down river; and the third to the warehouse."

The warehouse owned by Jamal, who by then, would be the rightful owner of Babylon.

But these turncoat backstabbers didn't need to know that. Nobody did.

Until I'm gone with my Queen and little Prince.

Knight's insides smiled while his face maintained a serious expression. He and The Queen had decided that they would name their son after Knight's older brother. Baby Prince would live a life far away from the violent streets, gunfire, and turf wars that had claimed his uncle. On their island paradise, Prince would study, smile, play, and prepare for a life of greatness. *Our Prince of Peace.*

The night before, Knight and The Queen had thought, then said exactly those words, "Our Prince of Peace" at the same time. Their simultaneous thoughts and spoken words were so sudden and supernatural. Now, suddenly Knight felt warm inside. The Queen was thinking the same thing, feeling the same amazing sensations. This time their soul deep connection had transcended words.

He'd have to be careful, though, so she didn't get any hunches about his real plans for their wedding night and the rest of their lives.

"This information does not leave the confines of these slimy walls," Knight commanded. "Does *everybody* hear me?"

A Barrior named, Deuce, stepped forward with a grim expression. "Master Knight," he said softly, "I can't swim. I need a reassignment up in The Playhouse, or I'll drown in a Motor City minute."

Knight glared at him, not just because the cat just used one of Li'l Tut's favorite references for time.

"All of you took rigorous swimming tests as part of Boot Camp," Knight said with an accusatory tone. He nodded at Pong, who stepped close to the cat. "If you somehow cheated, give me the name of the Sergeant who helped you commit fraud against Babylon."

The Barrior squealed like a girl. "Sir, I ain't tryin' to get nobody in trouble. I take full responsibi—"

Pong whacked him across the mouth.

"Do you realize that your cowardice could have put your fellow Barriors and B'Amazons at risk?" Knight shouted. "Gett 'em outta here!"

Knight's phone vibrated. REBA flashed on the display screen. He pushed the little silver button to put her to voice mail. Didn't that bitch remember he'd told her never to call him again? "Now everybody hit the gym," Knight ordered. "Sixty minutes of cardio kickboxing. Now!"

The phone vibrated again. REBA. He flipped it open. "What?" he snapped.

"I ain't tellin' you nothin' you don't already know when I say Duke tryin' to bring you down," she said with a nasal tone, like she'd been crying. "But that nasty ho playin' wit' people lives."

"Reba," Knight said calmly, "have you talked with him?"

"Yeah, 'bout how he gon' take Babylon back. But he sick. He crazy. He done gone renegade!"

"Where is he?"

"I ain't tellin' you nothin' else wit'out cuttin' a deal. So I can *g-t-f-o* when I need to."

Knight started to propose that she meet him somewhere to talk. But was this a set-up? Was she going to lure him to a remote place so that Duke could pounce on him?

She's for real. His intuition said. *Go.*

But where? He needed someplace where nobody would see them, and if prying eyes did catch a glimpse of their meeting, he'd have a legitimate explanation.

"Reba, meet me by the bar in The Garage. Fifteen minutes."

Chapter 79

As they stepped into the elevator and its doors closed, The Queen, CoCo, and Honey talked about plans for the dickfest that was scheduled for tonight in The Garage. Babylon would be hosting the VIP after-party for some of the country's hottest female rappers, who were giving a sold out concert downtown.

"Make sure the bar is stocked," The Queen said as CoCo used her pink rhinestone pen to check-off tasks on her clipboard. "We need some extra Studs to walk around with bowls of condoms, hot wash cloths, and bags for the wrappers."

As her mind reviewed all the tasks they had to complete that day, The Queen stared at the way Honey's tits curved up and out of the top of her dress.

A hot, swollen sensation delighted her between her legs. But Celeste was feeling something else too. Something about Knight. It was hazy and vague, like he was deliberately blocking their supernatural mind connection right now, which he seemed to be doing a lot lately so she wouldn't know what he was thinking or doing.

The stomach flipping sensations of the descending elevator intensified this out-of-whack vibe that she didn't like. She had to figure out what the hell was causing this, so she could squash that shit. With all the work they had to do, the last thing she needed was this distraction.

But deep down, it wasn't that she thought he was fucking around or anything like that. It was more like he was scheming, or plotting something that would affect her. Like he was making decisions about her life and Babylon without consulting with her first. If they truly were a team, working as partners to make Babylon all that it could be, then she needed to contribute to any and every decision and plan.

"Queen," CoCo said, "come back to Babylon. You lost in outerspace."

The Queen shook her head to focus her thoughts back on that night's party. "The last time Emcee Sexarella and her crew were up in here," she said, "they wore the Studs out. These girls some crazy nymphomaniac bitches. So I want extra Barriors and B'Amazons on hand to keep they shit in check."

CoCo nodded. "I have here that she ordered fifty Sluts as well."

The Queen smiled. "Yeah, the freaky bitch."

As the elevator hummed past the VIP balcony, The Queen noticed how the recessed lighting cast a soft glow around her and her inner circle. "Hey, y'all, look." The Queen smiled and motioned for them to turn and face the mirror next to the row of elevator buttons. "Check us out. Fine, fabulous an' runnin' the shit!"

The Queen loved the sense of camaraderie she felt with CoCo and Honey. Sometimes the three of them would sit in flannel pajamas up in The Penthouse, pop some corn, and watch corny romantic comedies on the huge, flat-screen TV in her and Knight's home theatre. Other times, they'd hit the upscale Somerset Collection to shop, go to the Nordstrom Spa, and have lunch at P.F. Chang's. And they always worked out together in the Babylon gym for sexercise, exotic dance lessons, cardio, and strength training.

"Friends for life," CoCo said, holding both their hands.

The Queen smiled. "Oh, before I forget," The Queen said, "we gotta meet wit' the seamstress after this. Up at The Penthouse."

CoCo nodded. "I told her to bring your veil and our shoes and purses. This is the final fitting before the big day."

Honey's face beamed, "Queen, you inspire me so much. You got the fairytale we all dream about."

The Queen kissed their cheeks. "You're both livin' it too. So let's get this work done so we can play!"

Everything was running smoothly but she just couldn't' shake that strange feeling in her gut about Knight. Was he all right?

Knight, baby, talk to me.

All she heard was the tapping of their heels on the floor as they walked quickly past rows and rows of Navigators, Hummers, and Escalades. On raised platforms, a red H2, a gold Lamborghini, and a baby blue Bentley sparkled like new.

In a matter of hours, every inch of this giant space would be "orgified" with hundreds of girl rappers, their groupies, and as many Studs fucking them up, down, and sideways. Sitting on top of cars, bending over the bar, twisting up on the plush cobalt blue couches situated in cozy seating areas, and on the stage.

"Where the hell are the cages?" The Queen demanded as she pointed to the huge, black stage that was framed by towering speakers. "Emcee Sexarella specifically ordered four cages, two on the stage and two on raised platforms with dancing Studs inside."

CoCo checked her clipboard. "The cages are scheduled for installment within the hour." She pointed to a bed that was the size of a boxing ring, sitting in the center of the stage. "The crew set up the bed first."

"Ok, great. Make sure they stock the bar with all what the girl drinks. Supplies too." The Queen scanned the glass shelves holding hundreds of bottles of booze and glasses. "Emcee Sexarella only drinks shit that's blue, but her crew loves them green apple cosmopolitans."

"Mmmmm," Honey said. "Me too. I personally made sure this morning that we've got extra cases of the mix. And the bartenders know how to mix 'em just right." Her nipples hardened and poked through the front of her dress. "I'll never forget the party she had last year when she had those four Studs fuck her so long, one of them passed out."

CoCo laughed, but The Queen stiffened.

Could Knight be passed out somewhere right now?

A low rumble echoed through The Garage. The sound underscored The Queen's worries. Blinding sunshine poured in as the huge metal door rose.

Knight, baby, how come the telepathic shit don't work when I'm stressin'? Celeste answered, *Relax. He's handling business.*

"Babylon!" The deep chorus of many voices boomed into the huge, hollow space. Their cadence made it sound like a military chant as they exclaimed, "Babylon" with a proud upward swing at the end, like U.S. military leaders bark, "Attention!"

The Queen, CoCo, and Honey turned to watch part of the army file in with a gust of strength and sex power that was so strong, every tiny hair on The Queen's body stood on end.

"Damn, that's sexy as hell," The Queen whispered as CoCo and Honey watched on.

Jogging toward them were four columns of twelve shirtless men in black-white-gray camouflage pants. Their black combat boots hit the floor in unison to create a powerful rhythm.

These were Barriors, whose work originally, was strictly security. But Babylon was growing so fast, she was recruiting many of them to work as Studs as well.

She checked out the sexy contours of the men's broad backs as they marched up the staircase in the far corner, making their way to the gym. That valley of muscle around a man's spine was so damn sexy, she just gawked at the marvels of the male anatomy. But no man was as sexy as Knight.

Thinking of Knight brought that bad feeling in her gut again.

"Babylon!" a female chorus chanted over and over as the B'Amazons now marched into the garage. Also sporting fatigues and boots except they wore tank tops and bras.

"Huuuuuut!" a deep female voice called.

This cornucopia of women was a beautiful sight. They radiated an aura of woman power so strong that The Queen wished she could bottle it and hand it out to every insecure girl on the planet. That was the power of Babylon, which was tattooed on the women's chiseled biceps. They followed the men up the stairs. Not far from them, a circular staircase led up to the VIP balcony.

"Honey," The Queen said, "make sure they got buckets for jimmy wrappers up there. And ashtrays."

She did a 180 to face the row of doors in the wall leading out from the bar. "CoCo, make sure they locked those doors. We don't need nobody fuckin' in the supply rooms and offices—"

An ear-splitting siren blared.

"Oh my God!" The Queen shouted. She cupped her palms over her ears as the noise echoed horribly off the floor and walls of The Garage.

"It's a test of the alarm system," CoCo shouted.

The Queen read her lips because it was impossible to hear her.

"Gotta check it for The Games."

The siren amped up that vibe that something wasn't right with Knight. How long would that noise last? She, CoCo, and Honey stood covering their ears, looking around.

Knight, where are you?

The Queen wanted to phone Paul and tell him, "Yes, the alarm works in The Garage—now turn that shit off!" But he'd never hear her over the phone, so she looked around helplessly. She noticed that one of the office doors was opening.

And out stepped Knight with Reba.

Chapter 80

The crimson velvet couches inside one of D-town's hottest nightclubs set the perfect tone for Duke to hold this first meeting with the leaders of his coup. Up here in the VIP lounge, with its sexy Moroccan decor, Duke took a minute to congratulate himself. Because downstairs in the many private rooms, lounges, and dance bar areas of the club, the first pussy party thrown by Oz was in full effect. And the folks who would rake in all that bank were sitting right here before the young wizard of their new Emerald City.

"How e'rybody feel tonight?" Duke asked, raising his crystal flute as butt-naked waitresses poured Cristal for him and his new crew. Timbo was staying hard at the idea that Duke was in another world, one very different from the crack houses where he'd puffed away his troubles over the last year.

The Duke back to rule like the king that I am.

The light of low hanging, fringed red lamps cast a sexy pink glow over the waitresses' asses and titties as they walked on clear spike heels to pour bubbly for everybody. Shar Miller with her Stud and Baby Blue, Leroy Lewis, Raynard "Dickman" Ingalls, Red, Marco, and Liam Moreno with that big black bodyguard, their white local operations managers, B-Boy and Birdie, the Stud Antoine, and Duke's lady, Reba Sheba.

She'd been one crazy bitch after that condom broke. But a gold-digging ho always got what she deserved. He was using her just like she was using him, and they'd both get their due in the end. Plus, her days were numbered anyway, because she'd get tossed out like yesterday's meat scraps once he got his Duchess back.

But I ain't gonna stop fuckin' in the interim.

Since Doc Reynolds had gotten him all that medication and he'd been eating better, his skin was clearing up and he was putting on a little weight. At twenty-one, Duke was already middle-aged for a brotha from the hood. So if he lived another ten, or twenty, years on the HIV drugs, he'd be doing better than a lot of other muthafuckas he knew.

Plus, whoever he infected, whether Reba or even his Duchess, their status would keep them together in life and in death.

I won't have to worry about her givin' my fortune to some otha nigga after I go, 'cause she'll go wit' me.

Duke suddenly stood taller and felt stronger than he had in a year. Even the constant ache of his healing bullet wounds subsided. He suddenly felt ridiculously powerful and invincible. It was his destiny to rule like a king. And if he had to knock off his brother and steal his lady back to do that, then so be it.

And so it is written, and so it is done.

"Here's a toast to the zillions we gon' make from D-town to 'round the world," Duke said, raising his glass. "Bigger an' better an' bolder than Babylon."

Glasses clinked as everybody toasted each other.

"Now, we gon' talk bidness for a hot minute to make sure we all on point for the night of The Games when the real shit go down. Then we gon' celebrate."

Something in Moreno's eyes still didn't feel right. Yeah, this was honor among thieves. And yeah, Moreno had the overseas contacts and expertise to handle the bank accounts where they'd deposit the millions from The Games. But Duke had to find some leverage to wield over Moreno's sneaky ass.

Let that muthafucka know The Duke don't play.

The funky electric beat from the party downstairs was loud enough in there to get several folks bobbing their heads. And not just in the dancing way.

Three of the waitresses were already on their knees in front of the Moreno triplets. Their pretty asses aimed back at Duke as they sucked dick.

"I said we'd party after we talk bidness," Duke said loudly.

"We heard you," Red said, smiling, and squinting behind the smoke of a Cohiba cigar. "Talk on, my brother. I am very gifted with the ability to multitask."

Duke stared back at him with a look that said, *I don't like that shit one bit.* But that night he'd let it slide.

Moreno kept a hard stare on Duke as the chick's head rose and fell in his lap. His feet were wide apart on the crimson carpet as her suntanned body rested between his legs.

"Now," Duke said. "We gotta handle the logistics of the money drops. Antoine, tell us what you know."

Wearing denim overalls with no shirt, Antoine stood and shared everything that Ben had heard in the tunnel when Knight explained how they'd deliver the loot by boat.

"Who gon' be at the vault wit' you?" Duke asked.

"He ain't tol' us yet," Antoine said, "but Crew Q got a meetin' in a couple days. Then I'll know."

"Cool," Duke said. "Shar, you in charge of—"

She was following Moreno's bad example. Her Stud, who never seemed to wear a shirt, was kneeling on the floor in front of her, eating her pussy. Baby Blue was sitting next to her, licking all over her titties. "Transportation," she said, opening her eyes. "Here's a list of the vehicles and boats, the drivers and their cell phone numbers, their locations and their projected pick-up times."

Baby Blue turned forward without closing her mouth. She bent down and pulled a folder from the black leather briefcase beside the Stud's hip. Then Baby Blue stood. She strutted forward and handed the folder to Duke.

He rested his huge hand on her hip.

"Sorry, Massa Duke," she said, casting a tender gaze down at him. "I don't like dick no more. Yo' girl turnt me out at yo' birthday party. I ain't fucked no dick on my own time since she made me cum like it was a lightnin' storm between my legs."

"Quit clownin'," Duke said. "Girl, you used to beg me for a beat-down wit' Timbo. An' I saw you suckin' Red's dick in the limo."

"That was work, baby; this pleasure." She smiled then pivoted so that her booty was in his face. Smooth patches of skin peeked out from her round, tight ass under the blue, knitted fabric skirt she wore. She walked back to the couch. Real quick, she let the crocheted skirt fall to the floor. She pulled strings at the side of her thong, so it fell too. Her ass bare, she extended one long leg around Shar's head then put both knees over the back of the couch and over Shar's shoulders. And she ground her pussy into Shar's mouth.

"Dam," Duke exclaimed. "She ain't lyin'!" Now Shar was hidden by bodies, except for her lower legs and feet over the Stud's shoulders and her hands cupping the bottom of Baby Blue's juicy ass.

But Timbo didn't respond because Duke had business to take care of. And these nymphomaniac muthafuckas were acting like they had all damn decade to make a plan for the heist.

No surprise that Leroy already had a bitch in his lap too.

"Leroy!" Duke shouted. "I need a report on all the preparations you makin' for backstage during The Games."

Leroy's knees twitched. He opened his eyes and leaned his head forward from the spot where it had been resting on the back of the couch. "We all set to rig the lubricants. They gon' be burnin' like they got army ants up they pussies an' all ova they dicks. Won't be no victories for Babylon."

Duke nodded. "What about the body oils for the Sexiest Slut and Sexiest Stud contests?"

"Same deal, boss. They skin gon' be bubblin' like pork rinds. Nothin' sexy 'bout that shit."

The disgust that Duke felt inside over all these muthafuckas who couldn't hold they nut long enough to have a meeting only intensified when he checked out B-Boy and Birdie on the long, low coffee table. B-Boy's chubby ass looked like Buddha laying on his back with his big, pale belly bulging up from his open dress shirt that hung over the edges of the table. And that white skeleton on top of him with the bones for an ass.

They were on the table at an angle where Duke could see Birdie's back. Her skinny legs were all bone, with loose skin and knobby knees.

Is she sick? Is that the "waif" look that white girls think is fashionable?

She reminded him of his first baby momma, Milan, starving herself from just-thick-enough down to skin and bones, to look like a fashion model.

Duke watched in disgusted fascination as B-Boy's chubby hands gripped her bony hips and raised her up and down. The bitch probably didn't have any strength of her own.

Damn, Duke remembered that day in the Cleopatra Suite when Duchess had climbed on and taken a ride into a place that left him paralyzed and speechless. Her legs had been like pistons, pumping up and down, slamming down on his dick with relentless force, speed, and stamina.

Timbo swelled. He couldn't wait to get Duchess back. His plan was to wait until the night of The Games. That would be the night he would take his brother out and be back on top.

I can't wait. If I take her now, Knight gon' lose his mind. An' it'll be easier to take him out.

Duke stood. He would go outside where it was quiet, get with his contacts inside Babylon, find out where she was, and go take what was his. Tonight.

And so it is *written. And so it is done.*

Chapter 81

The water was pitch black as Knight pretended his body was dead weight, sinking deeper and deeper into the iciness of the Detroit River. His chest felt like it would explode if he didn't suck down a breath of air. But he couldn't go up to the surface. Because he was dead. Or at least pretending to be dead, for the sake of this exercise.

Ping, in a black scuba suit and flippers, wrapped his arms around Knight and dragged him up toward the light shining from the bottom of the cigarette boat. Ping struggled to pull Knight's six foot, seven inches, and 275 pounds of mostly muscle.

Nearby, Pong was having no problem pulling the five foot, eight inch, 125 pound body of The Queen. So he deposited her, then returned to help Ping pull and lift Knight's limp body.

Finally, the brothers had pulled both Knight and The Queen up into the cigarette boat, and they sped away toward the golden lights of the Ambassador Bridge. They'd take the Detroit River to Lake Erie, where they'd transfer into a bigger boat. Then they'd sail through the Erie Canal to the Atlantic Ocean, then down to the Caribbean. Just like they would do on their wedding night, after everything played out the way that Knight had secretly scripted it, starting with the love scene. And he knew from previous conversations that The Queen would play her role perfectly, so that they could enjoy their final act together in paradise.

Everything was in place including the decoy bride and groom who would ride away from The Playhouse in the limo and the second decorated wedding yacht. And nobody had a clue, not even The Queen.

Guilt clenched like an angry fist around his chest.

I'm tricking her, but she'll be glad I did.

Chapter 82

Trina Michaels shivered with a mischievous sense of adventure and revenge and spoke with her long-time FBI source inside her office at GNN in Washington. "Not only can I hand deliver Victoria Winston to you," Trina said, pointing to The Queen's picture on her computer screen, "but I can lead you into the hottest prostitution ring you'll have to see to believe.

"I'm ready to deal." Rick Reed, a Baltimore native and former classmate from Georgetown, ran a hand over his close cropped fade. His gold wedding band shone as he straightened his tortoise shell glasses. In a khaki pantsuit with a white shirt and Burberry plaid tie, he sat with his legs crossed, so that one of his penny loafers almost touched Trina's bare calf. "Sounds like we can both score on this."

"Exactly." Trina scooted her chair closer to his, in front of the TV. "But I need your help."

Rick drew his thick brows together and leaned forward. His glasses magnified his light green eyes that looked bright in contrast to his round, brown face. "I'm all ears."

"Security at Babylon is like Fort Knox," she said. "They've got all these barbarian looking guards who are armed and dangerous. Men *and* women!"

Rick nodded, letting his gaze roll down the front of Trina's navy blue dress. She had deliberately worn this today because it hugged her body just right, and pushed up her titties into two creamy brown mounds in a way that Rick could not overlook. She wore it as insurance, just in case he needed any convincing to help her land *the story* of the century.

"Now," Trina said, grasping his arm, "the only obstacle I have is their super tight security. They don't even allow cell phones into the parties. Everyone has to pass through a metal detector, even if you're naked. Can't even hide a tiny camera in there," she pointed to her crotch, "If you know what I mean."

Rick's serious stare melted into a lusty gaze that focused on her crotch. "So what do you need from me?"

"Well, I want this to be a win-win situation for all of us. You're an ambitious man, with your sights set on advancing to the director's chair at the FBI, right?"

"That's no secret."

"If you ask me, you got robbed last time the chair was open. You deserved it."

"Why, thank you. Tell me more."

"Well," Trina said seductively, "I know you've been looking for a high-profile case to thrust you into the headlines. And that would help you get named and confirmed as leader of this institution."

Rick leaned closer. Nodding, he ran a manicured hand over his close cut beard. "So what do you need from me, Trina?"

"I need Rip Masta Mac."

Rick's eyes became as big as jumbo green olives. Shaking his head, he pulled off his glasses.

"Don't be surprised," Trina said, loving the power of the inside information she had raked up from various confidential sources.

Trina thought about The Queen, and the way her tongue had worked her clit with expert precision. She shifted in the chair, arched her back, and poked out her chest. Trina shivered, and that made her nipples harden under the lace of her Victoria's Secret bra.

Rick's gaze fell to her chest.

"I know all about the plea bargain that you so brilliantly crafted with Rip Masta. If he testifies against Mix Meister in that deadly embezzlement case that killed three innocent white people and a baby, then you'll grant complete immunity to Rip Masta and his boys. You can imagine that type of story will not gain a lot of support for Rick Reed in the hearts and minds of Congress or middle America."

Rick shook his head. His hands gripped the arms of the chair. "How'd you—"

"A great reporter has her sources," Trina said playfully. She traced his knuckles with her fingertip. "So if you want to keep your little deal with Rip Masta a secret, and be the force behind the capture of Victoria Winston and a raid on the wild sex underworld of Babylon then—"

"What do you want?"

"Rip Masta and his crew are friends with Knight and the folks at Babylon," Trina said. "The next big event there is like the sex Olympics. I heard them talking about it when I was in Detroit. It's called The Games."

"Tell me something I don't already know." Rick took her hand and put it on his crotch.

"I've been there," she moaned, rising up to sit on his lap, without taking her grip off his dick. "I've seen it. Felt it. Now I want you to help me get video inside The Games, before you do the raid. But I can't go."

"Why not?"

"They know me and it sort of ended badly," Trina said. "Rip Masta, however, is one guy they'll be glad to see. And he'll want to go visit his homies in the Motor City to take his mind off his legal troubles."

She stroked his dick in case his mind wasn't grasping all her ideas. "All I need you to do is to promise Rip Masta that if he gets us secret video of The Games, then you'll convince the Federal prosecutors to cut him the sweetest deal ever."

Rick's dick went limp for a minute. "I wanted an exclusive on this. I don't know if—"

She slid to her knees, dropped her face in this lap. She sucked that little spongy soft link sausage into her mouth, and slurped on it until it swelled into a fire roasted jumbo bratwurst. It was like a microphone pointing at her mouth as she pulled away to speak. "Wire Rip Masta and his crew with hidden cameras. He and Knight went to school together and they're still friends. So they'll be able to get past the metal detectors. We get video, they come out, and boom! You do your raid and I get my story of the century. Works out for both of us."

Rick's dick swelled bigger and harder.

Trina stood and lifted up her dress, revealing a navy blue lace garter belt that held up her thigh-high stockings and no panties.

Rick's eyes glazed as he stared at her bald pussy, which was just a pull away from his dick.

Trina thought about taking a slide down on it right then. And when he gripped the sides of her hips to pull her closer, she felt dizzy with lust. But no, for once she would have some control when faced with a big, juicy dick.

"This is your reward when we celebrate the fruits of our teamwork. I can write my own ticket as the hottest TV journalist in America, and you'll be director of the FBI. Deal?"

Rick stood, turned her around and bent her over her desk. He quickly rolled on a condom. His dick slammed up into her love starved, power hungry pussy. "Deal," he said with a deep groan. "It's a deal, Miss Michaels."

Chapter 83

The Queen's head throbbed as relentlessly as the driving bass beat blasting through the gym. Here on the second floor of Babylon HQ, just one floor above The Garage, her entire being ached with questions about why the fuck Knight and that Slut had come strutting out of the offices in The Garage in the middle of the day.

Naw, my Knight don't want that ho, does he?

Celeste answered, *Hell no.*

But a hurricane of questions still ripped through her mind as The Queen surveyed the hundreds of beautiful bodies that were fucking in sexercise class on the red floor mats. All around them, even more men and women were pumping, sweating, and cycling on silver and black weight machines and rows of cardio equipment.

"Three minutes!" Noah stood in front of the class with a silver whistle.

The Sluts' pretty, muscular asses slammed down on the dudes' stomachs. Their titties—big, small, firm, floppy, bounced with the force of their thrusting. Tiny beads of sweat rolled between their breasts and down their muscle-toned backs. Some of them glistened with perspiration from head to toe.

The Queen glanced over at Knight as he watched the action. What was he thinking? Did he feel powerful knowing that all this is his? This all-you-can-eat buffet of fresh pussy meat was steaming 'round the clock with any flavor or variety that his appetite craved, so that when he got his fill of her white chocolate, he could spice it up with some peach or licorice or cinnamon.

When did I become so insecure? I want my confidence back! Is this some whack mind trip being fueled and navigated by pregnancy hormones? I need to find an exit. Quick!

But watching all that raw booty in action threatened to bring back the barrage of images of Knight and Reba that had been torturing her mind. And it made that horrible feeling creep into her mind again. *Everybody turns on you eventually.* And on top of that, she was still worried about Knight's health. If something was really wrong with Knight's health, besides the stress that The Queen believed was stealing his color, his breath, his strength, then what if he had decided to get as much pussy as he could before he died?

The dizzying image of Knight walking through this fucking field and plucking out the juiciest bitches to fuck, made The Queen's head hurt even worse.

She hardly heard CoCo, standing beside her, ticking off names and events on her clip board. "Sheila and James won the three top events at The Games last year, but"— tender expression washed over CoCo's face—"Queen, you aw'right? We can take a break if—"

"Let's work." The Queen still wasn't showing any reaction, but she knew Knight was aware that she was all twisted up inside. Because she could hear him telepathically urging her to calm down and believe what he had just explained to her, in the elevator, that what she had just witnessed, was all business, and that Reba was an important link to Li'l Tut's takeover plot.

But Duke had HIV. And if Reba was fuckin' Duke, and screwing Knight, then that three letter death sentence would spray right up into The Queen's heart, soul, and bloodstream too.

And kill our baby.

An overwhelmingly protective urge made her every cell feel like it was exploding with rage. She wanted to march over to Knight right now as he stood beside the superstar Stud named Bam-Bam who was training for The Games. Yeah, The Queen needed to just get it out. She'd scream to that muthafucka that if he wanted her for life, he'd better put on a hazmat suit before he even talked to rank bitches like Reba.

Now Knight stood about twenty feet away, touching that Slut, Pebbles, pretty arching back as she and her husband Bam-Bam did lunges. That bitch fucked other men for a living, so being married didn't make her off limits to Knight either.

Some horrible rage bubbled up so wickedly inside The Queen, it propelled her forward, toward Knight. If he didn't act right, she'd take this rock on her hand, transfer a lot of money out of Babylon accounts and into a private one somewhere far away, and escape the insanity of this morally corrupt world of erotic abandon. She and Knight needed to live, love, and raise their baby far and away, in a safe, normal place.

Suddenly the gym felt as mind blowingly scary. Did she want all that for the little baby growing in her belly? Hell no. But was Knight crazy to think they could be a family in the middle of all this?

I've had enough. Being pregnant and raising a child in a place like this is just too dangerous.

Her feet stomped over the spongy floor. Her mind went *rattat-tat* with the bullet-words that she was about to shoot up at the man she thought was different from all the other lying, cheating muthafuckas of the world. Her chest rose and fell with the kind of overwhelmingly heavy breathing that helped a bitch go off. Her heart pounded.

Daddy's voice boomed through her mind. *"Anger is only one letter away from danger."*

Pick your battles, Celeste warned. *Give Knight the benefit of the doubt 'cause your little arsenal is a BB gun compared to his mighty battalions.*

The Queen turned her back to him and quickly walked toward the locker-rooms, as if she had to pee urgently. She did, actually. Her stomach was still flat, but her bladder was working overtime; this headache was wicked, her titties felt sensitive and sore like just before her period, and her mind, maybe the extra hormones were giving her this paranoid whack attack.

Was this what Knight felt like when he got those panic attacks? Completely out of control of himself? I gotta get a grip.

As she stepped into the locker-room and went to the bathroom, her thoughts reeled at the disastrous outcome she would have created by riddling her beautiful fiance with the vile words and ideas that had poisoned her mind. They had what everybody else in the world wanted. Showing anger toward Knight here in the gym with all these witnesses who could be Duke defectors, would be dangerous. Like Reba conniving to trick Knight into thinking she could play spy, when her real goal was to seduce him and oust The Queen. Or rouse some type of gratitude in Knight that would, in her distorted mindset, make him feel obligated to succumb to her seduction. So if Reba saw or heard about an argument between The Queen and Knight, it could fuel her man stealin' quest.

Plus, The Queen had to keep her cool as a test of wills with Knight. She had seen too many examples of women turning into jealous, suspicious bitches because they claimed to love their man so much. But ultimately their possessiveness had the opposite effect pushing their man away, right into the conniving arms of the bitches who were trying to hook their men.

"Never let anyone see your anger," Daddy would say. "Never let 'em see you sweat or you'll lose."

The Queen took several deep breaths. That fresh oxygen and slow breathing calmed her nerves. Then she walked back out into the gym, where Knight was watching sexercise and talking with Big Moe.

The Queen returned to CoCo, who was checking off names on her clipboard.

"With training like this," CoCo said, "Babylon will win every event in The Games, hands down. Check out Bam-Bam and Pebbles." CoCo nodded toward the muscular couple as they held dumbbells in each hand and did multiple sets of lunges. They both grimaced because that shit hurt when you extended one foot forward then lowered your other knee to the floor over and over.

Bam-Bam cast a loving glance at Pebbles as sweat poured down their temples and their pulses throbbed in their neck veins.

CoCo smiled. "Check out the champs. Pebbles and BamBam are the projected winners of the top three events. Longest

Fuck, Longest Slut on Top, and Longest One-Knee Stud Fuck." Now that The Queen had calmed down, her perception of Pebbles and Bam-Bam was different. They looked like a loving couple who was working hard to master their craft.

Just like me and Knight.

The Queen shivered. "Love that."

"Look like you lovin' that shit or you out," Noah shouted down at one of the women. .

Peaches bit down on her bottom lip in a way that could be construed as an expression of pleasure. And she pumped and pumped some more.

The whistle blew. Noah shouted, "Okay, ladies, on your knees!"

"Gentlemen, three minutes." Noah blew the whistle.

The men lined up in perfect alignment with the women. They thrust forward in unison while the women sucked and slurped in sync. The Queen felt dizzy. Her pussy creamed. And all that lust melted away her headache.

Noah's whistle blew. He shouted, "Switch!"

The women laid down and spread their legs. The men got on their knees and dove face first into steamy, hot pussies. *I need that now.*

The Queen shivered with the need to feel Knight's tongue stroking her insides.

She looked around the room until she spotted him. Knight's back was turned to her as he talked with Noah and surveyed the class. But why were his shoulders moving up and down like that? The Queen hurried over the pathway between the cardio machines and the mats. Knight looked up at her reflection in the mirror as she approached.

No!

He looked gray. He was breathing quickly and holding his chest with one hand.

The curse.

She stepped toward him.

"Excuse me, man," Knight said to Noah, who nodded.

The Queen walked him to the men's locker-room. She pushed through the white door. She guided him to a long bench.

As he held his chest and struggled to breath she sat beside him, stroking his back. "Knight, baby, what is wrong?"

He was looking down. "Knight?"

He turned slightly.

She gasped at the expression in his eyes fear.

Something is wrong with me, Baby girl. What can I do? Love me. Trust me. See me through the wedding and The Games and we'll be all right, baby girl.

"Breathe," she whispered. "All the tests turned out normal at the doctor. It's just panic attacks. So attack it back. Say, 'I am a warrior. I am a warrior. I am a warrior.'"

Knight sat up straight. He inhaled deeply, making his broad shoulders rise and fall.

"There you go," she whispered as he gripped her hands in his trembling fingers. "I am a warrior."

The Queen had researched panic attacks on the internet. Turned out, they could make somebody feel like they were having a heart attack: squeezing chest, struggling to breathe, racing thoughts of doom. Some people fainted. And others rushed to the hospital fearing they were about to have cardiac arrest and drop dead. But it was just a reaction to stress. Or a person allowing stress to take hold of the mind and body.

What The Queen didn't understand was how a person like Knight who meditated and carried himself with cool, calm confidence at all times, and practiced positive affirmations, could allow himself to fall victim to this invisible beast called stress.

"Knight is a warrior," she whispered in a soft lullaby mantra. Her hand stroked gentle circles on his back. "My Knight baby is an African god warrior." Her mind spun in an effort to make sense of this. A panicky feeling burned in her gut, too. Because what if something was seriously wrong with Knight and the doctor's tests just hadn't found it? What if he were to just mysteriously drop dead? What would she do? Where would she go?

Naw, that ain't an option. I gotta heal him.

"Knight, baby?"

"Yeah, baby girl."

"You know that Psalm you love so much? 'Weeping may endure for a night, but joy cometh in the morning'?"

Knight nodded.

"Well, I believe that this, whatever it is, this weeping may endure for my Knight, for a minute, but joy is about to *cumeth* in the morning, in our favorite way." She let out a sexy laugh as she realized her play on words. "But seriously, let's make like the morning is now. The weeping is over. We got each otha, to the infinity. We can't waste another minute feelin' anything less than hype in love and all we got."

Knight's beautiful onyx eyes sparkled back at her. He pulled her into his arms and held her like she was a swaddled infant. With her behind on his lap, he wrapped his arms around her and cupped his giant hands around hers, her cheek resting on his shoulder. "Baby girl," he whispered softly but happily, "thank you."

She smiled slightly, staring up into the black jewels that were his eyes. "For what?"

"For loving me for me. For letting me let my guard down and show that I ain't perfect. For loving me even more when I hurt."

The tenderness in his glassy eyes made The Queen's throat burn. His face blurred as hot tears stung her eyes. All those ridiculous, paranoid thoughts about Reba dissolved under the intense heat of this karmic connection with her soul mate. All that internal drama she'd just experienced about Knight plucking a new Slut from the luscious fields of Babylon, all that dissipated under his loving gaze too.

She squeezed out the tears and stared deep into his eyes. "I love you to the infinity," she whispered, knowing that there would be no life for her without this other half of her soul.

"Love you to the infinity," they said in unison.

Chapter 84

Knight led Jamal into the silent, empty auditorium, which filled the entire first and second floors of The Playhouse. In just a few weeks, it would be packed to capacity for The Games. That was also the time that they would do the multimillion dollar buyout for Jamal to take charge of Babylon, so Knight could flee into the safety and security of a tropical eternity with his Queen and their baby Prince.

Manifest Destiny is so close, I can taste the fresh-cut pineapple that I'm gon' feed into my baby girl's hungry mouth on the beach.

But right now, Knight needed to stop Jamal's second thoughts in their tracks. He also needed to let Jamal know that conspiring with the likes of Raynard "Dickman" Ingalls who was on Li'l Tut's payroll was a good way to follow in the bullet-riddled footsteps of a whole lot of dead musical geniuses.

After he knocked some sense back into Jamal's dreadlocked head, Knight still believed that this trusted friend was the only man who could take over the reins of his urban empire in a way that would continue its goodwill endeavors.

"A thousand seats on this level," Knight said as they walked down the purple carpeted aisle. "Plus, the balconies and the box seats, and we'll have two thousand."

Knight stared hard down into Jamal's eyes. "You hear me, man? Ten grand a seat, times two thousand people. Do the math. And the other folks payin' five K a head to swim, dance, and party in this building during The Games. That's ridiculous bank for one night."

"But I'm gon' take the admissions money," Knight said. "Just this year. Next year it's all yours."

"Dig that," Jamal said. "Yo, dog, if I bail, how come you can't fin' somebody else to buy Babylon? Like Mr. and Mrs. Marx out west, or even Moreno."

Knight stared down at Jamal, who was framed by the ornate gold figures carved into the balconies. "Jamal, it's not about the money; it's about the principle. I need to know that for the next fifty years, at least, proceeds from Babylon will continue to feed and shelter children in the village I've adopted in the Sudan, and fund college scholarships for twelve graduates of Detroit public schools every year."

Jamal shoved his hands in the pockets of his baggy jeans. "This my beef wit' it. All my bidnesses legit, right? I'm wonderin' why I wanna take on somethin' that could bring me down?"

Knight's chest squeezed. His mind lurched forward to the moment of transfer, of money and ownership, just minutes before he and The Queen would execute the exit plan. If Jamal reneged at that moment, or didn't show up, or acted wishy washy, it could jeopardize Knight's entire strategy.

No! I see him the night of The Games, on the yacht, transferring the twenty-five million into my account, as I give him the keys and papers to takeover.

For now, Knight would keep it diplomatic. But if Jamal persisted like this, Knight would have to go ghetto on the young brotha. Yeah, he'd remind that muthafucka where he came from and who *made* his music mogul ass.

"Every detail will be in place for you to take over once I'm gone," Knight said.

"Coo'," Jamal said. "Man, this some hype shit you 'bout to do. Bad as I think I am, I don't know if I could do it. 'Specially if my lady don't have a clue."

Tiny needles of pain shot around Knight's heart. Guilt.

"Yo' dog, you ain't worried yo' lady gon' be so pissed, she gon' kill yo' ass right there on the beach? Like, 'What the fuck you mean, nigga, we ain't goin' back?' Damn, between that an' Duke, no wonder you be lookin' so pale lately."

"No sleep," Knight said coolly. "I been workin' twenty-four/ seven. It's a lot of work planning a Houdini act and running an empire at the same time."

Jamal shook his head. "See, I'm worried that runnin' Babylon will jack my music vibe. I don't know, dog. I'm still havin' second thoughts. Gimme a minute to think. I worked so hard to build up what I got in the music business. I ain't no pimp."

"We don't use that term at Babylon; we're far and above that gritty, degrading image for both black men and women. We don't even say prostitute. We provide a much needed service that creates win-win situations for all parties."

Jamal laughed, making his long dreads shift over his shoulders. "You make it sound so professional."

"It is. The security company is a legitimate front. You know our Barriors and B'Amazons provide protection for your concerts all over the country. Plus sporting events and political gatherings."

Jamal shrugged. "It sound sexy as hell to rule ova Babylon. But music be my numba one—"

"I have directors in place for every city to handle the day to day operations. You, your name, and Bang Squad Incorporated will be well insulated from any risk involved in Babylon's main source of revenue."

Jamal nodded. "Dang, dog! You be spittin' some big words dese days. Yo' Queen daddy blood mus' be rubbin' off some white boy speech lessons."

That "white boy" comment flipped a switch inside Knight's brain from the blue zone labeled DIPLOMATIC into the yellow zone marked PISSED OFF. Knight resented the commonly held belief among too many of his people that speaking correct English meant acting white. He was bilingual, he spoke Ebonics when necessary and proper English when appropriate. That had nothing to do with his racial allegiance. But that was a debate for Jamal on another day.

Knight put his hand on Jamal's shoulder. "The best thing about this deal is that you'll be the figurehead who makes the most money."

"Yo, dog, say it all like that an' I'm all in." Jamal scanned the wide, shiny pine stage. "Where the judges gon' sit?"

Knight extended his arm over the purple velvet seats. He pointed to the empty space between the stage and the arc of bolted-down chairs. "Up there, at a long table, we'll have security stationed across the front of the stage. And under cover every where else."

After a quick tour of the dressing rooms backstage and downstairs, and a glance at where the deejay would spin the tunes for each routine, Knight led Jamal up the stairs to one of the plush box seats overlooking the stage.

"The Queen and I will be here until eleven forty-five," Knight said as they sat on a purple velvet couch in the box closest to the right side of the stage. "You'll be in the next box." Knight pointed to the balcony like seating area to their left. "At eleven forty-seven, you slip back into these curtains with us, and I hand it all over to you."

"Check," Jamal said. Something in his eyes glinted in a way that kept Knight's suspicion running high. As if Jamal were going through the motions of this conversation with no intention of following through.

Did Jamal think that if his punk ass disappeared when the deal was to go down that Knight would carry on and "Houdini" himself and The Queen away regardless?

Jamal's eyes looked a million miles away as he said, "An' you got e'rythang set in case it's mutiny in the ranks?"

Knight stared back hard. "Everything is set."

"Yo, dog, what about Duke? Y'all's search an' destroy mission accomplished yet? I don't want no shit."

"I guarantee," Knight said with a sinister chuckle, "there won't be any."

Jamal stiffened. His eyes grew a little bigger. "Well where that Duke muthafucka at? I want that shit done now. He crazy as hell. I ain't takin' ova, 'less I know e'rythang runnin' smoov."

"We're watching him."

Thanks to Reba, Knight was monitoring Li'l Tut's every move. Knight knew that Moreno, Shar, Raynard, and Leroy were all conspiring with his brother. What he didn't know yet was whether Reba was telling him the truth about what that "motley crew" was actually planning to do. Were they plotting to start their own sex empire? Seize Babylon? Or both?

"What you fin' out?" Jamal asked in a way that pushed Knight's mental mad meter into the red zone marked RENEGADE.

Knight's fist shot out with lightning speed and grabbed the collar of Jamal's white tee, twisted it up against his Adam's apple. Raised that muthafucka an inch or two off the floor and looked down in his eyes with six-gun brutality in his stare. "Jamal, tell me straight-up," Knight groaned through tight lips. "Who'd your punk ass come to when you needed bank to start the Bang Squad?"

Jamal's eyes bugged. "You."

Knight twisted his shirt harder and shook him.

"You an' Prince an' Duke."

"Who gave you the money?"

"You an' Prince. Duke didn't want to—"

"Nice." Knight loosened his grip.

Jamal exhaled with relief.

But just as quickly, Knight snatched him up even higher. The heels of his Air Force One hit the side of a chair. "Who *made* your hip-hoppin' ass?"

"You!" Jamal's voice was high-pitched due to the fact that he was being choked by his shirt. His face bulged and turned red.

"Who has the power to destroy you just as fast?"

"You! You!" His teeth chattered like it was ten degrees below zero outside.

"What you gon' say next time Dickman call?"

"F-f-f-f-f-fuck that muthafucka."

Knight nodded. "And if you talk to him."

"Jamal a dead muthafucka."

Knight threw him down to the aisle.

Jamal thudded on his back. His eyes opened wide, staring up as if he were trying to figure out if he were still alive.

"Jamal," Knight said coolly, "Tell me what you're gonna do at eleven forty-five the night of October first on the other side of those curtains." Knight pointed to the purple velvet drapes framing the stage.

Jamal coughed. He grabbed his throat, massaging the red marks.

"Tell me!" Knight's bellow echoed through the auditorium.

"I'ma sign the papers." Jamal coughed.

"I'ma give you a fat-ass check. An'?"

"I ain't neva gon' tell nobody nothin' about Manifest Destiny."

Knight stared down. "Remember them magic words for the rest of yo' life. They yo' bulletproof vest as far as I'm concerned." The power pumping through Knight's veins made him feel eight feet tall. His chest was clear. His heart was pumping slowly, calmly.

I am king. An African warrior king who will never be defeated.

Chapter 85

In the dark paneled office inside The Penthouse at Babylon HQ, Knight huddled in front of his computer with Larry Marx. The California media mogul and his wife were in town to discuss the final details of Manifest Destiny. Now he and Knight were switching accounts to protect Babylon's assets, just in case the Marxes got indicted.

"Julius Mark Anthony, meet Moses Alexander," Larry said as he typed account numbers in the global banking Web site. "This is switching all your assets into another account that's handled by our company in Sweden. It's untraceable."

Knight patted Larry on the back of his snug fitting brown sweater that matched his brown linen trousers and polished, lace-up brown and white shoes. "I appreciate all the wisdom over the years, man," Knight said, hoping this money maneuver was the remedy for relieving the tightness in his chest. "You helped me work a miracle."

"I'm about to." Larry said, glanced up with a sparkle in his brown eyes. His curly dark hair shook as he laughed. "I cannot wait to see how you pull this off."

Knight's chest squeezed. "I've been working my ass off for years. I need to get away."

"I hear you," Larry said. "Me and Prissy have been so worked up over this indictment, we're thinkin' about doing the same thing. Latest word is, the heat's off. But this is a wakeup call. Can never be too careful."

Knight nodded, watching as Larry worked the keyboard to make page after page pop up with seven-figure bank balances.

"All you have to do after The Games is log on with that same password, *Caesar,* and transfer the money from Jamal's account into this new account, and *voila* lifetime of luxury."

"Thanks for eveything man," Knight said, "you a cool cat."

"Of course Knight," Larry said, looking up from the computer.

"You're the boss," Larry said. "And I'm proud of you, dude."

He's sincere, intuition told Knight.

Still, Knight stared hard into Larry's eyes. "Nothin' like trust. Nothin' like trust."

Larry nodded. "Speaking of trust, this dude, Jamal, you really trust him?"

That band of tension squeezed around Knight's chest. "Jamal knows that any deviation from this plan will earn him a life long visitor's pass to see Prince at Elmwood Cemetery."

"What's the latest on Duke?"

"He's planning an eleventh hour heist, but I'm ten steps ahead of him."

"Stay there." Larry stood. "Mission accomplished. Now let's go see what that pretty little Cleopatra of yours is up to."

Knight's heart pounded as he took long strides to the door. He would be down on his Queen faster than Larry could say, "Swing."

Chapter 86

The Queen moaned as the woman's long fingernails raked through her long, black hair and massaged her scalp over and over.

"Knight told us you were even more beautiful than you were last year." Mrs. Marx stared at The Queen in the mirrored wall of the dining room in The Penthouse at Babylon. "But you are absolutely breathtaking."

The Queen, sitting in her Louis XIV chair at the head of the table, leaned her head back and looked up into the intrigued blue eyes that were on a thin, upside-down face with bright pink lip gloss. "Thank you. I always loved Egyptian stuff and playing dress-up with my mom. So this—"

The Queen's throat burned so much, stealing her words. This was the first older woman she'd encountered in more than a year. Except for Duke's mother, who'd hated her until Knight brought her home, and Mrs. Johnson suddenly loved The Queen. Because, as she learned, their mother praised anything Knight did, while in her eyes, Duke could never be as good as his big brother.

The housekeeper, Nina, pushed through the swinging door to the kitchen and began to clear the table. "Madame Queen," she said with a curtsy that made the tops of her nutmeg-brown breasts jiggle, "I'll serve dessert soon as Master Knight and Mister Marx come back from the office."

"Thank you, Nina," The Queen said, bending her head forward to look into Nina's pretty almond shaped eyes. "You got some French vanilla ice-cream and caramel sauce to go over the pecan pie, right?"

"Yes, ma'am." Nina curtsied again, then piled up dinner plates from the table.

The Queen leaned her head back.

Mrs. Marx, standing behind her chair, cupped a warm hand over The Queen's cheek and stared into her eyes. "You okay, sweetie? You look sad."

As Nina clinked china and silverware, The Queen squeezed hot tears from her eyes, which dripped down onto Mrs. Marx's wrist. She kept her eyes closed, and loved the sensation of Mrs. Marx's hands stroking her face, from each side of her nose, down to her jaw, over and over.

"I think you need to relax," Mrs. Marx said. "Let's go into the living room."

"I'll bring coffee and dessert out there," Nina said.

As they walked toward the plush all-white couches, Mrs. Marx massaged The Queen's shoulders. Perhaps because of the affectionate and grateful way Knight had always spoken of the Marxes, The Queen felt extremely comfortable with this woman. She wanted to tap into her wisdom and learn the ways of a married woman that she'd not been able to learn from her mother.

"Mrs. Marx?"

"Priscilla, please," she said playfully, laying The Queen face down on the couch.

"Priscilla, do you think too much sex can kill a woman or a man?"

"If it can, then Larry and I have nine lives." She laughed, pushing up the Queen's dress to massage her calves. "Or more. Why do you ask?"

"Mmmmm, that feels good," The Queen whispered as the woman kneaded the flesh of her hamstrings.

All through dinner, The Queen had been getting hornier and hornier as she watched Malibu Barbie and her gorgeous husband, eating dinner at the table.

She got the same feeling she'd had when Rip Masta Mac and his harem of hotties had joined them, along with Jamal and CoCo, for dinner last week. They'd barely made it through the lamb chops before Rip Masta put one of his girls in front of him on the table, spread-eagled, and started eating her pussy like it was a pie-eating contest.

That sparked an oral extravaganza around the table, as The Queen had slurped down Knight's dick with wild abandon, and they all ended up on the mattress style chaises on the outdoor terrace, fucking to the funkiest beats of the Bang Squad and Rip Masta, until the sun rose in an explosion over the Detroit River.

Tonight's dinner had been much more reserved, but the twinkle in Mrs. Marx's blue eyes let her know this guest from the West Coast was saving the best for last.

Now The Queen wished Knight would return from whatever serious conversation he was having with Mr. Marx, so they could cap off the evening with dessert. Because Mrs. Marx's hands were massaging her butt cheeks now, and her pussy was as hot and creamy as the steaming coffee that she could smell brewing in the kitchen.

"Your ass is so round."

"Oooh, squeeze my ass," The Queen whispered. "I *loooove* that." She always could cum extra good when Knight took each cheek in one hand, then squeezed and massaged her ass, while he fucked her.

All of a sudden, something hot and wet pressed into The Queen's booty. It was a pussy. Waxed satin-smooth. Creamy, and steaming hot.

Mrs. Marx ground her clit in sultry circles into the round curve of The Queen's juicylicious booty. Meanwhile, her hands massaged The Queen's bareback.

Celeste screamed, loving this new sensation.

Mrs. Marx grinded and rotated until she screamed, shivered, and creamed all over The Queen's ass.

The Queen needed Knight right now. She needed Shane to slam up into her hungry pussy and take care of this ache for love.

She felt Knight's hands on the backs of her knees. He pulled them apart, pooted up her ass with Mrs. Marx still on it, and rammed Shane into the swollen, slippery jellyfish that Celeste had become.

His dick was like an electric eel, slithering up into her and sending jolts through her every cell. Lightning crackled behind her closed eyelids. She spasmed with the shock of his size and speed, and she shuddered, cumming with one magic stroke.

Chapter 87

Duke took one look into Shar Miller's devious eyes and felt pumped with power. And here, inside this white stretch Navigator limousine, Shar looked fine as hell. She sat with Leroy Lewis from Miami, Raynard Ingalls from Chicago, and Red Moreno himself.

"Vegas look good on you, girl," Duke said, glancing over her body. He'd hardly gotten a look at her at the last meeting at the nightclub, when she'd been covered by her Stud and Baby Blue.

Now, Shar wore a skintight black dress that pushed up her big chest and showed off a tattoo that said *SHAR* scrolled across the top of her left tittie. Next to that, her tiny red cell phone poked from between her nutmeg-brown boobs. She had to be damn near forty-five, but her smooth skin proved that black don't crack.

Timbo became as long and hard as a log inside Duke's baggy jeans. "How you gon' look betta wit' age?"

She smiled, glancing at the bare-chested Stud beside her. His brown biceps bulged as she stroked the leg of his jeans. He was holding her steaming coffee cup with one hand and picking a piece of lint off her arm with the other.

"This is my fountain of youth." She glanced at the Stud. "The secret lies in womanly wisdom and a daily regimen of sex. And thank you, Massa Duke. I am so honored to work with you as a partner to put you back in charge of Babylon. We can't let all that business sense you got go to waste."

Duke shrugged, but sat tall. The sound of somebody calling him Massa Duke again made Timbo throb so hard he hurt. "I'm back in full effect."

Moreno flicked his wrist to make his watch fall down from under his crisp white shirt sleeve. How he could even tell time with that blinding sparkle of diamonds was a mystery. And how he could concentrate with Baby Blue sucking his dick was even more baffling.

Duke wanted to see if Moreno's dick looked as waxy as the rest of his skin. That muthafucka looked embalmed; cold, hard, and chemically preserved. Like Prince in his casket. And with that spooky accent, maybe he was some kind of vampire that would live forever until someone drove a stake through his evil heart.

Leroy shifted on the seat. He rested his gold-ringed hand on his crotch and watched Shar in action.

It was hard enough to look at the top of the crack of Baby Blue's fine ass as she knelt in front of Moreno, her jeans holding that bubble-booty of hers just right. The way her head bobbed on his lap and her mouth made little sucking sounds made Timbo stand up like a tree trunk. And the scent of sex filling the limo didn't help much.

Concentrate, muthafucka. Intoxicants, includin' pussy, done already got you in enough trouble. You clean, now.

Moreno's hazel eyes looked as sharp and alert as he rested his waxy-looking right hand on Baby Blue's head and said, "Duke, my brother, Shar, Leroy, and Raynard, pardon my promptness, but the time is short. We can reminisce once the fortunes are in our respective bank accounts."

Shar sipped her coffee, which seemed to deepen her voice and harden it into a razor-sharp tone. "Massa Duke, your brother seems to have forgotten where he came from. Others on the Board are ready to pluck him out, so we'll just be doing them a favor tonight to expedite the process." She raised her long red fingernails to her mouth, parted her red-painted lips, and poked a nail into the gap between her front teeth. She made a sucking sound like she was disgusted. And she moved her hand like she was trying to pull out a piece of sausage that had gotten caught there during breakfast.

She looked elegant and business-like, but the bitch was bad as she needed to be. And the hard glint in her eyes as she spoke of Knight reinforced Duke's belief that Shar wasn't about to play pussyfoot and fuck anything up. She was serious as a heart attack.

"Knight's righteous act," she said, taking the coffee cup from the Stud, "strikes the wrong way, when you remember what a ruthless renegade muthafucka he was before he got locked up." She sat with her ankles together so that the pointed tips of her red patent leather boots looked like they could make a brotha cry—either in lust or in pain. Or both.

Duke had already had her like that. But this was strictly business now.

Now this is the kind o' bitch who can help me make stuff happen, yeah.

She already was. Their phone conversations for the past several months had laid the foundation for the coup of the century.

The muthafuckin' heist of the millennium.

If Knight had strutted in like the new sheriff in town, then Duke was about to swoop down on his ass like a global superpower.

"My operations around the world," Moreno said, "will be greatly enhanced by this partnership. I need it to work out to the finest detail tonight." Moreno's tongue flicked over his blood-colored lips. "Your brother has promised me the ultimate delight when my teams win The Games."

Duke stared into Moreno's sleazy eyes. There could be only one thing that could make Moreno glaze over like that.

Dream on, muthafucka. By the time you think you can get wit' her, The Duchess will be mine again. An' I'll kill yo' ass befo' you lay them embalmed lookin' hands on my goddess.

"It's gon' be wild, fo' sho'," Duke said.

"You'll be glad to know," Shar said with a smooth, deep voice that was nothing like the ghetto-girl twang she'd had while working as a Slut here at Babylon. "That every aspect of Oz is playing out like a well-rehearsed movie; it's almost too perfect." Her dark eyes focused hard on him in a business like way. They looked into his face without a glimmer of disgust or disdain or pity or any of the other fucked up attitudes people had been projecting on him since he came back.

Now, he was a phoenix rising out of the ashes of his own pipe, reinventing himself, bigger and badder than ever.

And Leroy Lewis from Miami was picking up on that. Leroy smiled without showing any reaction to Duke's appearance, and that made Duke feel pumped even bigger and better. "Duke, baby," Leroy said, wringing his gold-ringed hands together, "I been waitin' for this day to come. No disrespec', but I can't stan' that scoundrel who came out yo' momma hoochie befo' yo' sweet ass." Wearing a lemon yellow suit with matching alligator shoes, silk tie, and a feathered hat in the same color, Leroy looked like the pimp he was.

"We gon' make this happen so big an' bad, we gon' make Babylon look like a backalley, boot leg."

Shar rolled her eyes. "Right now we need action, not words. I have to warn you, though"—Shar glanced toward the dark tinted window at the blue Detroit River sparkling in the morning sunshine—"your girl Reba was having serious doubts about this venture. In fact, her absence right now indicates a serious problem. She should be actively participating in every conversation."

Duke ground his teeth. That bitch had better make right and get her act together. He had no place or patience for a snitch or a defector.

Shar added, "I talked some sense back into her, but Duke, you'd be wise to keep an eye on her."

"Already on it," Duke said. "E'rybody in position for tonight? The Barriors and B'Amazons?"

"We've had two drills, both successful," Shar said.

Duke nodded. "And the inside info you got e'rythang pinpointed, how to take down the dudes wit' the bank?"

Shar nodded down to her phone between her titties. "Just had them on my hotline," she said with a deep laugh, "and we're all set."

"What about Gerard and security?"

Leroy's shoulders shook up and down as he laughed. "We sendin' him the kind o' poontang that'll make him think sweet Jesus done turned into a girl an' come to escort him through the pearly gates."

Raynard "Dickman" Ingalls, wearing a green Pelle Pelle leather jacket covered with rhinestones and Benjamins, cracked his knuckles. The twenty-year-old from Chicago was notorious for running a gigolo ring that was thrusting into the upscale market, just as Duchess was doing for Babylon. "I been studyin' the demographic in all the cities we gon' take." He fingered the bill of his baseball hat that matched his jacket. "The Queen ain't got nothin' on what we gon' do." He cracked his knuckles again then flashed a golden grill that had DICKMAN etched in diamonds over his front teeth.

"Coo'," Duke said as he ticked down his mental check-off list for Oz. "What about the Hummers and the drop-off?"

"We've got the schedule and a double backup plan," Shar said. "As soon as The Games officially end at midnight, you and I will meet with Reba and Antoine in the tunnel. Leroy will be in the boat with the crew. We'll target each diver and take their moneybags. Those who may have already reached the boat—"

"We gon' be pirates like a mug," Duke said with an ecstatic tone. But a tremor rippled through his thin body as the image of his bigger, badder, blacker brother, Knight, came to mind. Duke shook his head to banish the thought. He ground his teeth, loving the strong, powerful feeling of his jaw muscles flexing. He couldn't wait to look down on Knight and make him pay for his lifetime of abuse.

Yeah, pretty soon Knight would be Duke's servant. He might even make big bro' sleep on a cot every night so he could watch Duke make love to his Duchess over and over and over again.

I'm The Duke! And I'll be rulin' in a Motor City minute!

He savored the power of his new court here in this limo. "Yo, Dickman, how y'all's crew handlin' the take-down?"

Raynard cracked his knuckles. "Yo, rock dis, I got a exact map showin' the spot where we gon' get his black ass. My crew flawless. Yo' boy, Knight, gon' be right where you want him in about"—Dickman checked out his watch—"twelve hours."

"Coo', coo'." Duke bit down a smile. By daybreak, he would be back in charge of Babylon. His insides tingled. *With Knight out of the way, the Duchess will be mine when all this shakes down tonight.*

Timbo jumped and flipped under his jeans. His dick was like an excited fish that couldn't wait to dive into the deepest, warmest, sweetest waters, and frolic for a lifetime.

Chapter 88

Inside The Playhouse, where one of the private suites was transformed into a bridal boudoir and dressing room, The Queen stepped into the sexiest wedding gown she'd ever seen.

"Damn, I feel turned on just looking at myself in this mug," The Queen said with a seductive tone.

"Put *that* into an etiquette book for brides on their wedding day!" CoCo giggled. Then CoCo said with the kind of prim and proper English that she had used while working for The Queen's father, "Every bride should feel so excited and happy on her wedding day, that her entire genital area should become aroused with a moist, swelling sensation. In addition, her nipples should tingle, and her mouth should pucker slightly, to indicate that she is ready and available to receive her husband's penis on their wedding night so that she can get fucked into a delirious stupor."

"Love it!" The Queen laughed.

CoCo lifted an already-open, dark-green bottle of Cristal from the silver ice bucket on the vanity. She poured a steaming stream into The Queen's crystal flute, then her own.

"Cheers!" CoCo said, as they clinked glasses. "Here's a toast to the sexiest bride marrying the sexiest groom on the sexiest day in Babylon history!"

The Queen raised her crystal champagne flute to her lips and took a long sip. She couldn't wait for the sweet bubbles to dance on her tongue and through her whole body. The cool fluid would relax her tense muscles and erase all thoughts of the high security alert on this stressful-ass day of The Games. "To tell you the truth, girl," The Queen said, "I can't wait to get the fuck outta here and enjoy my honeymoon. I wish they'd just catch Duke and take care of his ass so we can get on with our lives."

"As many Barriors and B'Amazons they got outside this room," CoCo said, "and all the security cameras, you got nothin' to worry about. Knight wouldn't let nothin' happen to you, girl."

The Queen remembered all the terrifying moments over the past month that had made her question whether she wanted to remain in Babylon as a married woman raising a child with Knight. "Sometimes I wonder if I'm in the right place."

"It don't matter where you at." CoCo brushed a loose thread from her pink maid of honor dress. "As long you wit' the man you love. That's how I feel about me an' Jamal. Much as I love Babylon an' his music, I'd drop it all an' live in a barn wit' him if he wanted me to."

The Queen giggled. "Girl, you crazy."

"Money don't buy love or happiness, but love make you happy."

"I'm gonna talk to Knight on our honeymoon about our future," The Queen said. "If I ever surrender my throne, it's yours, CoCo."

CoCo's eyes glowed with appreciation as they filled with tears.

The Queen raised the glass to her lips and took a sip of the sweet, bubbly liquid. A golden spray of champagne shot from between The Queen's lips and into the warm beams of sunshine pouring in from the warehouse windows. "Oh, shit!" She slammed the glass down on the vanity. Her other hand instinctively grasped her stomach.

CoCo's eyes widened with alarm. "What's wrong? Girl, I didn't think you'd get wedding-day jitters."

"Just a cramp."

The Queen wanted to share the good news for weeks, but Knight insisted that she keep the pregnancy a secret until she was actually showing. Plus, the first three months were the most high-risk time for miscarriage anyway.

"We'll wait until it's safe," he'd been saying for the two weeks since her period was late.

The home pregnancy test confirmed what Celeste had already told her, and the doctor down in the clinic had proven it with a blood test.

Her and Knight's baby didn't need to be swimming around in Cristal. "Damn!" The Queen exclaimed. "My mind is so fucked up right now, I can't think straight to save my life."

"Don't say that, girl. You know Knight says our words have power. Every bride is whack on her wedding day; it's normal."

"How many brides you know who got armed guards outside their dressing room door?"

CoCo shrugged. "This life in the big city. But you The Queen of Babylon, so be glad about it. Look at you!"

The Queen checked herself out in the mirror. But she didn't really see herself, except for the brilliant sparkle off her QUEEN choker necklace as the sunshine lit up every diamond. It was so bright, it created silver blurs in her eyes as if someone had just snapped her picture with a flash.

From here on out, she would drink only bottled water, juice, and milk. And most of all, she'd keep her head straight so this wouldn't happen again.

"You and Knight got what everybody else wants but can't even think about having," CoCo said. "It's too rare. So smile. Celebrate, sweetheart!"

The Queen imagined staring into Knight's eyes at the altar. She believed that the only time she could feel more intoxicated and euphoric than that moment was when she was making love with Knight. Otherwise, the thrill of every little girl's dream coming true, in this most sexy, blingin' way, was so over the top, she felt dizzy.

"Knight's gonna love this dress so much." The Queen giggled. "He'll be at the altar like, 'Uh, 'scuse me, y'all, we got some business to handle.'"

CoCo, who was sipping champagne as The Queen talked, pulled the crystal flute away from her highly glossed lips. She laughed. "Then he'll be like, 'Yo, Rev, move out the way an' lemme jus' drill this fine ass on the altar for a hot minute.' "

The Queen bent down slightly as CoCo adjusted the lace straps of her gown over her shoulders.

"It might be white," CoCo said, "but it ain't innocent."

The Queen grinned and shivered as she looked into the giant, three-paneled mirror set against a wall draped in pink tulle, white roses, and green vines. She pivoted on white satin stiletto slippers, loving how the dress hit every curve just right.

"CoCo, look." The Queen stroked the curve of her chest. Her diamond engagement ring sparkled in the sunshine, and her French manicure with clear, opalescent pink polish matched the dress perfectly.

"Girl, you makin' me hot just lookin' at you." CoCo made her shoulders shimmy as if she had caught a chill. Then she stood in the mirror and untied her robe. It fell open. In the bright sunlight, CoCo's pussy glistened like a melting chocolate rose.

"Damn, girl!" The Queen made a sucking sound. "Look like you need a bitch to take care o' that."

"Naw. I'm savin' it for Jamal tonight. He like it when my pussy be marinatin' in hot cream all day, then when we fuck, it's like so boilin' hot, he almost can't stand it."

"Girl, you talk so prim and proper in business, but get you some Cristal and a hot pussy, an' you just as rank as me." The Queen ran her hands down the lace bodice. Embroidered with tiny pink crystals, the body-hugging fabric shimmered as it curved in a perfect hourglass over her breasts, waist, and hips. Right at her thighs, the dress poufed out in an explosion of pale pink tulle, which was also embroidered with tiny white crystals.

"Can you believe I designed this myself?" The Queen said. "It's like a vision just came to me. And the designer was right on point."

Suddenly, The Queen heard Knight speaking in her thoughts, *You were a vision I saw on TV. And the divine plan was right on point. Now you're about to be mine for life. Love you to the infinity, baby girl.*

Celeste answered, *I'm your Queen forever.*

The Queen's nipples hardened, and her pussy swelled with heat and cream. It wasn't so much lust for the sexiest man alive; she was aroused by a sensation of pure joy. After all she'd been through, she was finally being rewarded with the most amazing gift; the love of a lifetime.

The Queen gathered her long black hair up into a twist, which she secured on top of her head with two shimmery white chopsticks. Then she turned around to glimpse the back of the dress, which was mostly bare skin. The lace fastened behind her neck, forming a halter top with two strips that stretched down over her shoulder blades to support the backless dress. Framed by a scalloped lace edge, most of her back was bare, all the way down to the crack of her ass.

"Damn!" CoCo zipped the side of the dress from The Queen's hip bone up to her ribcage. "That designer got it fittin' like second skin. And look," CoCo ran her finger over The Queen's tattoo at the base of her back. "You gon' walk down the aisle and everybody gon' be starin' at your tattoo."

The Queen cast a seductive glance over her shoulder at CoCo. "Love the way you touch me, girl." Then her gaze lowered to the reflection of her tattoo in the mirror. She read the black, Gothic-style letters aloud, "Queen of the Knight. Damn! You won't see this sexy shit in those prissy bridal magazines."

"I bet you'll see a bunch o' hoes copying your style, though. Hey, girl, don't forget about your garter." She pulled it from the vanity, which was covered with makeup that The Queen had just applied. On it also sat a small beaded purse that held The Queen's pearl handheld pistol. "Here, sit down so I can put it on you."

The Queen sat on the white satin stool in front of the vanity. Fabric rustled as she pulled up her dress.

CoCo, who hadn't fastened her robe, knelt before her. Her tight little body, and juicy, cantaloupe titties with nipples made The Queen's mouth water. "Does it go on your left or right leg?" CoCo looked from The Queen's satin shoes up to her face for an answer. Her eyes grew large. "Oooh, girl I never heard of a bride who just said to hell with panties altogether!"

The Queen spread her legs wider and rested her elbows on the vanity behind her. "I get too hot." She cast a seductive stare down at her assistant. She knew CoCo was clean; she'd just been checked the day before, along with Jamal. And The Queen knew for a fact that CoCo wasn't getting with any other girls. "Hot and horny," The Queen said.

In fact, all those pregnancy hormones were keeping her pussy moist at all times, no matter what she was doing. But Knight looked so weak and pale lately, she was afraid to over tax him by demanding dick every hour on the hour.

"Tell me you love to lick my pussy." The Queen moaned in anticipation of CoCo's hot mouth pressing down on all her hot, swollen meat. "Tell me you love it."

CoCo slid her hand between her own legs as she dove forward with an open mouth. She inhaled loudly. "I love to lick this pussy," she whispered, making her hot breath steam onto the top of the bride's clit.

The Queen loved the sensation of CoCo's nipples rubbing against the insides of her thighs.

CoCo stuck out her tongue and licked the tip of The Queen's clit. She loved the sound The Queen made as she moaned.

"Lick that shit like you a little kitten," The Queen whispered. "Suck up all that milk."

CoCo wrapped her lips around her clit.

The Queen buckled. "Damn! You do that good. You still gon' lick me off after I'm married?"

CoCo licked faster.

"Speakin' in tongues," The Queen said with a mellow, intoxicated moan. "Love it."

"Damn, girl, all that champagne made me have to pee." The Queen giggled.

CoCo stood up.

"Go 'head. Turn on some music."

CoCo walked toward the living room area. The sexy beat of *Diamond Hearts* blasted from speakers built into the walls around the suite.

The Queen stood and danced in her gown. She grabbed her veil from the mannequin, put it on, and spun in a big blur of white.

Thud! Pop!

She froze. Her ears strained against the loud music. Those two sounds were unmistakable. And they came from right outside the door, where at least two Barriors were stationed at all times.

Damn, I knew some shit was gonna go down today. The way Knight's been so paranoid. Gotta call him.

She scanned the vanity for her phone. With the push of a button he'd be here. After all, he was dressing on this same floor, in a suite at the opposite end of the long hallways. But where was the phone under all that makeup?

Knight, baby. Trouble.

If ever she needed to use their supernatural vibe to call him, now was the time. She tiptoed to the entrance hall and peeked through the peephole. Nothing. Except an empty hallway with brick walls and wooden doorways lit by cobalt blue sconces.

Where the fuck were the Barriors? I gotta call Knight.

She spun, holding up her gown. She ran toward the bedroom dressing area. The double doors opened. The Queen's heart raced. The metallic taste of fear burned on her tongue.

Because Reba and Antoine were entering the suite, pushing in a huge armoire.

And not a Barrior or B'Amazon was in sight. Except for the tip of a black boot positioned at the bottom of the doorway. The toe pointed to the ceiling, and the heel rested on the blue carpet, as if he was lying on the floor, shot or dead!

"We got your clothes ready for the honeymoon," Reba said, strutting in wearing a pink spandex bodysuit and matching knee-high boots. Antoine wore a black suit.

The Queen glared at them.

Knight, baby. Help!

Chapter 89

Knight perched on the bed, inhaling deeply. But every breath made those needle sensations in his heart pierce harder. And an aching, burning band of pain extended from the right side of his chest, under his arm, and around his back.

"My body is relaxed," he whispered, yanking at the black bow tie that felt like a noose. His watch said five-forty. So did his cell phone, sitting beside him on the bed, which was supposed to alert him of any security breaches.

five forty-one.

He unbuttoned his shirt. With one hand, he massaged his chest.

Nineteen more minutes.

"I am strong," he gasped. "My heart is strong." But his heart was hammering against his ribs. His lungs were squeezing, barely taking in air. And his head was spinning.

I am a black warrior. I am strong.

Little white dots of light danced before his eyes. He tried to focus on himself in the mirror facing the bed. *Knight! Knight, baby, help!*

Knight's heart pounded harder. Sweat prickled under his starched white shirt.

How long had she been calling for help? His panicky state of mind had been blocking his radar.

"Pong!" Knight called weakly.

The Barrior and his twin, Ping, were waiting in the living room. Jamal, his best man, was dressing in another suite. The plan was for him to come here, then they would all go up to the wedding together.

"Pong!" Knight wheezed. He grabbed his phone. If The Queen was in danger, then it meant that all of Babylon was already in the midst of a serious security breakdown. Knight poised his finger over the single button that would spark Ping and Pong into immediate action, and set off an alarm in the security booth for Gerard to take care of whatever was going down.

Those white lights dancing before his eyes became a blinding flash. Static rang in his ears. And everything went black.

Chapter 90

"Muthafuck me!" Gerard shouted. His fingers raced over buttons and knobs on the console in the security room, where six other men and women concentrated on dozens of video monitors covering three walls.

I gotta get a grip on my sex addiction before it gets me killed.

Gerard blocked out the mental pictures of all the pussy he'd been getting, taking, and buying lately. He had to concentrate on the conversation inside The Queen's suite through the sound chip in her necklace. For some reason, the audio monitors that were hooked up to the cameras in that suite had suddenly gone dead. Good thing Knight was so slick he'd had a sound chip installed in The Queen's diamond necklace, so he could keep an ear on his bitch at all times. Gerard had just replaced the chip with an even more powerful one to prepare for today. And The Queen never knew that it was just inside the clasp.

Damn, I can't even concentrate when she talkin'.

If she and CoCo weren't talking so freaky, Gerard would have had an easier time focusing on the screens in front of him. And if they hadn't been flashing each other's pussy at each other as Gerard watched live, thanks to the security camera that showed the bedroom of the bridal suite, then he would have looked away long enough to study the other monitors. Then he wouldn't be in this panic. He'd just now noticed that the monitors for the hidden security cameras outside The Queen's suite room 515, were actually showing room 415.

"Knight gon' kill me." He tried once more to activate the cameras that would, identify the live video as Room 515.

"Whew!" Gerard said, when he read the words on the monitor, Room 515. "She safe." The monitor showed four Barriors standing in the hallway. And the numbers on the door said Room 415. "How the fuck did somebody—"

"That's just a short circuit, man." Paul reached over to adjust the knobs in front of Gerard, "Look."

The image of four Barriors in front of Room 515 appeared on the video.

"Dang, I just saw my life flash before my eyes. Knight woulda killed me his damn self if I'da let somethin' happen to The Queen."

"Everybody too doggone tense around here today," Paul said calmly. "I just saw your girl Reba. She so nervous, you'd think it was her weddin'."

Gerard went numb. He knew she was up to something. Not for taking the money after their little fun in the Jacuzzi. Or the several other times that she'd sucked his dick like "wifey" never had, even when they was young newlyweds and the bitch was still givin' head.

No, something in Reba's eyes had snitched that she wanted something much more valuable than money. And he didn't like the way she kept blowing her nose, mumbling something about having a head cold that lingered for almost two weeks. But he had let her sexiness blind him to overlooking at why she caused that bad feeling in his gut.

Damn, how could I have been so stupid?

It was the hottest pussy he'd ever had. The way she could sit on top of him and grind her ass down on his stomach while she fucked him. Just thinking about that shit made his whole body feel hot. Those magic moves had the power to make a nigga lose his mind.

Gerard stared at the monitor to make sure it still showed Barriors outside Room 515.

In his mind's eye, though, he could see Reba last night, in this security room where Knight prohibited all visitors, whether they were a Slut, a Stud, or a low-ranking Barrior or B'Amazons.

But Gerard and his dumb ass had been thinking with the head between his legs. And he let Reba in. What man wouldn't, when he saw her wearing a miniskirt and tank top. Right here in this chair, she had rubbed his dick between her titties till he called out for his momma. Shit, he'd never blown that much cum at once.

"Hummer One to Cairo," a Barrior said over the two-way radio. "Hummer One to Cairo."

Gerard pushed a red button on the black two-way box on the console. "Ramses. Over."

Static crackled on the line. "Delivery route clear. Over."

"Roger that."

"How it look?" Gerard asked Paul, who was surveying at least a dozen screens that showed about 250 wedding guests at varying stages of arrival. A few still arrived at valet behind the building.

Even though The Playhouse was situated in an old warehouse district, a lot of new construction was going on around it as the city revitalized its waterfront. So Knight had arranged for the guests to arrive in back, pull up near a white tent between the marina and terrace, and walk a red carpet into the building.

"Damn, emcee Sweet got a sexy lady!" Gerard exclaimed as the famous rapper strutted up the red carpet from his white Bentley and into the building.

The woman wore a wispy purple dress with a sequined, lowcut V-neck so low, you could see the tattoo between her bellybutton and her crotch. The sheer fabric clung to the points of her nipples as if they were hooks.

"Tell me that dress ain't glued to her titties!" Gerard said. "Oooh, an' look at them chicks wit' Rip Masta an' his crew. Damn, he got clearance for all that entourage? Got a whole harem wit' his gangsta ass. They sexy as hell."

"Negro, you betta pay attention," Paul said sternly. "Distracting a knucklehead wit' pretty pussy the oldest trick in the book if somebody 'bout to pull a scheme out they stank ass."

Gerard stiffened. The smile curling up his lips flattened, and he focused on three elevators full of guests. When the elevators opened onto the rooftop terrace, Barriors and B'Amazons searched the guests' bags and waved metal detector wands over them.

Guns were checked at a special, high-security room.

"All these folks stayin' for The Games," Paul said, "but in a minute, we gon' get a shit load o' new folks tryin' to get a good seat in the auditorium. An' we'll have to get all the guests from the roof down to The Games. This shit betta go smoov."

Gerard punched some buttons to zoom in on the area where the wedding would be in about fifteen minutes. He realized his fingers were trembling. He was nervous. Because he felt something was wrong.

Naw, it's just the aftershock of that Room 515 scare on the video. Chill out, muthafucka.

But that had never happened before. And as many times as they'd done video system checks to prepare for this day, never once had a short circuit or camera mix-up occurred.

Gerard cast a quick glance at Paul, whose profile was serious and focused on the screens.

Can't trust nobody.

Gerard dialed Knight. But it rang and rang.

Knight always answered the phone on one ring, if that. Sometimes it was like he had ESP and he'd just flip open his phone like he knew Gerard was about to call.

Otherwise, if he were busy, Pong would answer to say Knight was occupied. But now, a recording came on to say, "I'm sorry, the customer you are trying to reach is unavailable. Please . . ."

Gerard punched the END button. "Damn!"

"Now what?" Paul asked impatiently.

"You talk to Knight lately?"

"Naw, but let the man get ready for his weddin'. He 'bout to marry the finest chick in Babylon, so let him be. You know he like to meditate before he do somethin' important anyway."

Chapter 91

Duke's insides felt like fire as he stared down his bride. Her perfect China doll face was much darker now. And her eyes were harder.

Her blow-torch blue eyes burned into him with the kind of power that he used to flex with one glance. A sucking sensation in his chest made him feel like she'd stolen his power, with Knight's help. She was living the glamorous life here at Babylon, eating like a queen, partying like the boss that she was, and fucking her brains out with his big bro'.

And my sorry ass been out on the street. I been punked by my own goddess.

Duke felt frozen in place, even though his insides were melting under her stare. He was paralyzed by the shock of finally seeing her for the first time in a year. He was just a Motor City minute away from usurping the power and the pussy back under his control.

Muthafuck me! She look like she hate me.

"Duchess, I'm back," he said as he climbed out of the armoire. "Your Duke is back. We can finally be together. Knight's gone, so you can marry me today, the way it's s'posed to be." He grinned, remembering way back a year and a month ago, when he had prophesized their wedding day by saying, "And so it is written, and so it is done."

Now, he felt drunk with excitement that his plan was going so smoothly. They had gotten up here undetected. Took out the guards. Antoine was standing with a rifle by the doors, and Reba had gone to make sure CoCo didn't make it out of the bathroom.

Now all he had to do was make Duchess remember that she loved him. In a Motor City minute those big moon beam gray blue eyes would stop flashing with defiance and hatred. They'd soften into that sexy glow that she used to cast on his while they were making love up in their Penthouse.

But right now she looked like a scared cat. Tryin' to look tough and calm, but she couldn't hide the fear in her eyes. Her mind was spinning a scheme to escape, the way she kept glancing back and forth between him and Antoine's gun at the door.

That pretty pushed-up chest was rising and falling fast as she panted for breath. "Isis! Osiris!" she screamed. "Isis! Osiris!" Her ear-splitting cries set off hot sparks that clawed up Duke's skinny spine and gripped his brain.

"Shut the fuck up!" he shouted. For a split second, he realized how insane he must've looked. Even though he'd gained weight and his skin was clearing up, he still wasn't anything like the radiant god he'd been a year ago. And there was no telling what lies Knight had told her to make her hate her first love.

Antoine dashed into the bedroom. "Yo, boss—"

"Get back to the muthafuckin' door," Duke commanded. "I can han'le this bullshit."

"Isis! Osiris!" Duchess screeched even louder. And she dove for a beaded purse on the vanity.

Oh, hell naw.

"I let you live, bitch!" Duke dove toward her as she grabbed the purse. "You woulda been dog meat if I hadn't saved you from ghetto hell. Helped you hide from the feds. Gave you love—"

Her pretty manicured fingers grabbed the purse. The beaded fabric showed the outline of a gun.

Duke's giant fingers pried her hands off of it. He snapped open the purse and pulled out the pearl handheld gun. He waved it close to her face, but she did not flinch. "This the thanks I get?" he said with such a deep voice that his throat hurt. "I give you everything and you think you gon' shoot my ass?"

She inched back toward the triple mirrors.

Now he got a 360-degree view of her fine ass; bareback, ass all round and juicy in sparkly pink fabric. Duke stepped closer. He said in a sweet tone, "You think you gon' shoot The Duke on our weddin' day?"

He wanted to kiss her right now. Them pretty pucker lips were all pouty and red, her cheeks were pink, and her titties looked like they were about to pop out of all that tight, sparkly lace.

"Look at you," he whispered, mesmerized by her beauty. With her hair in chopsticks up on her head, he could see the length of her pretty neck that he used to kiss and suck on.

But that necklace. "Take that shit off yo' neck," he ordered.

The blinding bling of QUEEN made him close his eyes. "That muthafucka got you wearin' a calla like you his dog, bitch. Take the shit off!"

"Isis! Osiris!" she screamed. She bent slightly at the waist as she screamed. And Duke saw in her reflection that something black flashed on her back.

THE QUEEN OF KNIGHT.

"Oh, muthafuckin' hell naw!" He grabbed her bare arm. Yanked her like a rag doll. Turned her around. "Get me a knife!" he shouted. "Get me a muthafuckin' knife! I gotta cut that shit off my baby before we can go up to the roof an' get married today."

The image of his bigger, badder brother fucking The Duchess cast a red hue of rage over everything in Duke's sight. A whistly sound rang in his ears. And his heart pounded like a drum beat that was ticking down one infuriating realization after another.

"We gon' rewind back to when we met an' start ova," Duke groaned close to her pretty face. "You gon' keep doin' jus' what you doin' by runnin' Babylon. Only you gon' report to The Duke. In HQ. And in bed. Startin' now."

Her face snarled up. "You ain't even a shadow of the Duke I used to love. You look like the muthafuckin' night of the living dead."

She glared so hard into his eyes, Duke felt paralyzed.

His eyes burned with tears as he whispered, "Duchess, baby, I'm sorry." He pulled the Glock from the waist of his jeans. He held it to her head, just below the big twist of black hair held in place by those pretty chopsticks. "Say anotha word," he said, "an' Knight can take both our bodies to the cemetery on his wedding day."

With his left hand, Duke yanked her arm; his rough fingernails digging into her baby soft skin. Oooh, skin so soft it didn't feel human. All smooth and creamy, no scars or dark spots like too many chicks had all over their arms, backs, legs, and bellies from hard life in the hood; she was fresh, clean meat.

An' I'm 'bout to get anotha taste.

Timbo was so big and hard, he made a tent in the front of Duke's baggy jeans.

But how I'm gon' fuck her when I got her arm in one hand an' my gat in the otha?

Duke released her arm and shoved her at the same time. She kept her balance, though, on those pretty spike-heeled pumps.

Damn, Timbo was swole like a mug. Gotta get 'im out.

Even though he wore a black leather belt with a BABYLON belt buckle, he easily pulled his pants down with a quick yank by his left hand. Wearin' no drawers in anticipation of this occasion, Timbo swayed free like a sideways telephone pole. Duke stepped back to get a good look at his bride. He thrust his hips forward and whispered, "Baby Girl, come get some Timbo."

The gun in his right hand just didn't feel right.

"Now how I'm gon' make love to my Duchess at gunpoint?" he asked softly, looking into her eyes. "Tell me I can put it down."

She smiled. "Duke, you know I missed you. And you know how things shook down; I didn't have a choice when he took over."

"You didn't have to stay. You coulda found me."

"Nobody knew where you were," she said softly. "All that matters now is that you're back. So, yeah, put the gun down and come get some Duchess."

He looked at the gun in his hand then back at her eyes.

Full o' scheme! Take that pussy now!

Like a football player hunching down for a tackle, he bent at the waist, gun in hand, and grabbed the bottom of her dress. He wrapped an arm around her ankles and pulled forward.

She fell on her ass, and her back hit the floor. So did her head. And her legs spread wide open. That bald, wet pussy smiled back at him. Ooh, it was so pretty.

"I'm back in muthafuckin' heaven where I belong." Timbo was like a giant steel arrow pointing at the best pussy he'd ever had. Duke fell to his knees. He just had to crawl closer so he could slam inside her. He grinned, staring into her eyes as she laid there looking at him, over her chest.

"Put the gun down, Duke, baby," she whispered, "an' I'll give you the wedding day pussy that you been dreamin' about for a year. Duke an' Duchess."

Her lips looked so delicious and the sound of his name floating up off her tongue made him melt inside.

He set down the gun on the carpet.

But a bad-ass bitch look glinted in her eyes.

Whack! Her stiletto heel smashed into his face, piercing a hole in his cheek all the way into his mouth. Hot blood squirted over his tongue and down his throat.

Wham! The other spiked heel slammed into Timbo.

Duke froze. The pain; it was like a red-hot electric knife had just stabbed him in the dick. Couldn't breathe. Couldn't move. Couldn't see nothin', hear nothin'. His head rang like a siren.

"Biiiittttccchhhh," he groaned.

"I'd shut the fuck up if I were you," Duchess said softly. "It's not nice to call names. Especially on my wedding day."

The plan. My people. Who gon' help me now? Antoine. Reba. Where the fuck are they?

All his other folks were under strict orders not to do anything to carry out their plan until they heard from Duke. No word, no action. But how could he lead a coup while laying here with a wounded dick, with the female version of his ruthless-ass brother standing over him?

She was a blur of white, pink, bronze, and black.

Wham! Wham! She kicked the side of his leg.

He let out a high-pitched whimper like the pit bulls used to do if they lost a fight.

"That's for havin' my sister killed."

Duke wanted to say that that bitch Melanie Winston was about to waste away in a convent anyway. He'd done the Duchess' look-alike sister a favor by sparing her a miserable life without dick. Duchess should've been grateful that his trick had duped those FBI muthafuckas for so long.

His lips moved to let some words out, but he coughed on the blood oozing down his throat. He thought he would faint from the pain. But he had to see if she'd kicked a hole in his dick. He had to look down or feel down, but didn't know up from sideways or backward.

Duke did know one thing, however, the cold metal pressing into his sweaty forehead was his own gun, and his Duchess was holding it there.

Chapter 92

The Queen knew Knight or somebody had to bust in here quick. How the fuck could this have happened? Why hadn't the siren blared? All she knew for sure was that she could guarantee that Duke would never hurt her. All she had to do was squeeze down on this metal and put him out of his misery right now.

She remembered Knight citing The Prince Code by saying, "Kill or be killed," in the gun range. Still, faced with the reality of this situation, it seemed a whole lot more complicated.

I definitely don't want to kill my future brother-in-law on my wedding day, but his diseased dick woulda killed me.

The horror of the moment came crashing down on her senses.

Kill or be killed. Fuck! He was about to rape me, infect me, and our baby.

That meant she'd have to kill the muthafucka because Duke would have stolen the only people in her life who mattered; Knight and Baby Prince.

Muthafucka!

Her index finger curved around the hard, cold metal of the trigger. If nobody came, and if CoCo were dead, and Reba and Antoine were about to come in here and kill her too, The Queen would blast away all their evil asses. Then she'd go get married and get the fuck away from this crazy life in Babylon. Assuming no other crazy shit was breaking loose in the rest of the building.

Knight! Where are you? Knight! Answer me!

"C'mon, girl! Run!" CoCo's shout rang from the hallway. In her white robe, splattered with blood, CoCo ran into the bedroom. She snatched her dress off the mannequin and grabbed The Queen's left hand.

"Where's Antoine? And Reba?" The Queen asked, gripping the gun in her right hand.

"Don't worry about them."

The Queen ran, still in her high heels, behind CoCo into the entryway, where on the wall beside the door, a foot wide smear of blood trailed down the white wallpaper. It went behind Antoine's head but started back up at the hole over his ear. He sat upright, eyes wide open.

"What about Reba?" The Queen asked as CoCo as she opened the door.

"She's takin' a long shower," CoCo gasped as they dashed into the hallway. "The stairs!"

They had to run about a dozen feet to reach the stairwell door.

It flew open.

Several Barriors and B'Amazons, rifles in hand, burst into the hallway.

"We escaped our damn selves," CoCo snapped. "Duke's in there bleeding. And we need to get to the wedding."

One of the soldiers gave orders, "Half of you get Duke. The others, escort The Queen and CoCo to the locker room in The Playroom."

Knight, baby, are you okay? Knight, answer me!

The Queen had no phone. It was still back on the vanity in the bridal suite, so she'd been calling for Knight on their special supernatural love hotline. But no answer.

Did Duke kill him first?

And since nobody had responded to her screams, or seen the chaos on the hidden video security system, then any of these allegedly loyal Barriors and B'Amazons could be snitches or Duke sympathizers, who wanted to kill her, CoCo, and Knight, right now.

The Queen squeezed her grip tighter around the handle of Duke's gun. Part of her thought she should feel scared, but it was so surreal, so adrenaline charged, she felt like she was in survival autopilot. And she wasn't going anywhere or doing anything until she saw Knight alive and safe.

Fuck all these people. If security were doing their jobs, then Duke wouldn't have just busted into her room! The Queen sprinted down the hall. Her dress rustled. The chopsticks came loose; she grabbed them with her left hand as her hair tumbled down her shoulders.

"Queen!" CoCo shouted. "Wait for me!"

The thunder of footsteps sounded like the soldiers were following too.

The Queen kept running. Her toes slammed into the sharp points of her life-saving shoes. Finally she came to suite 501. She turned the door knob.

The door opened.

"Knight!" she shrieked, "Knight, baby!"

But every room was empty. The digital clock beside the bed said five-oh-five.

"Let's go!" The Queen grabbed CoCo's hand, and they ran down the hall, Barriors and B'Amazons in tow. Her mind raced as she dashed up three flights of stairs in her heels and wedding dress.

What would Knight do in this situation? If some deadly conspiracy were going on with Duke or someone else, wouldn't they expect her to run straight into Knight's arms?

Trust no one, she heard his voice inside her head. So it didn't matter. If she ran to him and the bad guys at large caught her too, then that was how she wanted to go down; at Knight's side.

Something had to be wrong with Knight right now, or intuition would have responded to her in their telepathic love connection. She yanked open the door marked rooftop. It led to a covered, glass-walled area beside the elevators. This entrance area faced the beautiful arrangement for the wedding.

But the terrace was packed with people. Security, celebrities' assistants, cameramen and video crews, ready to capture every joyous moment.

"Shit!" The Queen exclaimed. "Where is he?"

All around her, "ooohs" and "aaahs" broke out in every direction. Then The Queen remembered she was in her wedding dress, and she was the star of this show. But she wasn't here to meet and greet right now. And all this would be bullshit if she didn't have the man who made her heart beat.

Knight!

A dark pink carpet stretched from beneath her life-saving stilettos over the brick-patterned floor and into the enormous white party tent. Giant white poles, covered with greenery and pink roses, held up the corners and inside lengths of the scalloped tent. Inside, explosions of pink flowers hung from the peaked ceiling. Rows and rows of pink satin-covered chairs held hundreds of beautiful people.

Celebrities. Musicians. Politicians. Pimps. Madames.

But The Queen didn't care about anybody or anything except laying her eyes on her man.

Knight, baby, where are you?

All those people standing in the aisle, she couldn't see the altar, except for the golden backdrop that cast a shimmery sheer over the wide-open view of the blue river and downtown Detroit's skyscrapers.

"Girl, wait," CoCo took her left hand.

The Queen realized she was still holding Duke's gun. She turned toward CoCo, hoisted up her dress, and slipped it into her garter belt.

"Play it cool," CoCo said, pulling her into an elevator.

"I gotta find Knight," The Queen said.

"Everything looks cool and calm up here," CoCo said. "The Barriors are handling the situation downstairs, so don't let anybody see you look flustered."

Trust no one.

The Queen stared hard into CoCo's eyes.

"Girl, don't even think it." CoCo stared back just as hard.

A B'Amazon stepped onto the elevator and nodded at CoCo, who let the bloody robe fall. She slipped into her pink dress and said, "Now zip me, girl. We got a wedding to be in."

As soon as they stepped out, Jamal and the Bang Squad, who were set up near the altar, began to play the wedding march.

CoCo kissed The Queen on her cheek. "You come right after me," CoCo reminded her.

She nodded as CoCo walked in the soft, late afternoon sunshine toward the tent.

Someone brushed The Queen's hair while someone else handed her a giant bouquet of pink roses. Another person guided her to the edge of the tent.

A hip-hop version of "Here Comes the Bride" boomed.

Everybody turned around with more "oohs" and "aaahs."

The Queen stared straight ahead. She looked down the rose petal-strewn aisle, past the satin ribbons draped on the sides of the chairs, past all the famous faces in the crowd. There, under giant bouquets of pink, purple, and white flowers, she should have seen the sexiest man alive.

The reverend was there. So was Jamal. But Knight was nowhere to be seen.

Chapter 93

A bride wasn't supposed to feel this fucked up on her wedding day. She wasn't supposed to fend off an HIV positive rapist or kick him in the face and dick or hold a gun to his head. She wasn't supposed to have soldiers with rifles surrounding the pretty white tent where she would say, "I do." And she definitely wasn't supposed to have a gun strapped inside the lace and satin of her garter belt.

No, Alice was not enjoying Ghettoland one bit. She wished she could pass through a secret portal into a Wonderland where she'd feel safe to live, love, and raise a baby with her man who would magically appear. Now.

As she walked slowly on trembling legs down the pink aisle, she hated that all these people were staring at her when she wanted to burst into tears or cuss somebody out or both. She hadn't even brushed her hair on her wedding day.

Neither had CoCo, but she still looked gorgeous up there, grinning back at The Queen, like there was something in this nightmarish day to smile about.

Knight, baby, where are you?

Suddenly, Knight rose from a chair in the front row, next to his mother, who wore a giant pink hat with netting over her face. Like an ebony tower rising in front of all the guests, Knight turned around. His eyes sparkled at her, his sucka lips curled up into a smile that broke out into a grin.

Thank you, God! My baby is okay!

The Queen wanted to run down the aisle and throw herself into his arms. She had to feel the long, firm length and warmth of his body; then she'd know that he was safe and that his heart was beating just fine. They could get married and live happily ever after.

Yeah, right.

It seemed like forever as The Queen walked toward Knight, fighting the bad vibe in her gut. Still wearing no panties, her pussy was sweaty and swollen. The friction of her walk rubbed Celeste, just right, to take a tiny bit of the edge off this awful state of mind.

I want him inside me, now. I want to make love to the infinity with the only one who matters.

All these fabulous people didn't matter to The Queen. They had on beautiful dresses and suits. Famous musicians, actors, and politicians dotted the crowd. It was as picture-perfect as the celebrity tabloids, daily newspapers, and hip-hop magazines could imagine, yet Knight had issued a ban on all media, for both the wedding and The Games, even though the who's who of the hip-hop world was here to celebrate her big day.

But they don't care about me.

Not Emcee Sexarella in her rhinestone-studded blue leather dress and her entourage of big-haired beauties. Not Rip Masta and his crew of hardcore gangsta rappers. And not all these other people who were officers and associates of Babylon from across the country. They were just here for the hype factor of the hottest wedding in Babylon history and the sexiest entertainment ever, anywhere, for The Games tonight in the auditorium downstairs at The Playhouse.

Oh, baby, you look like hell.

Hot tears blurred the gray pallor on Knight's face. The closer she got, the harder her heart pounded. Whether it was stress or her curse or panic attacks or PTSD or something worse, she was sure that it would kill him if they didn't get out of here.

He held out his arms as she approached.

Her dress fluffed around her feet as she walked, and her palms got sweaty around the satin-ribboned handle of her bouquet.

Finally, she felt beautiful. Not because it was a gorgeous dress whose price tag could finance the purchase of a small house. No, she felt beautiful because her Knight was staring down with so much love in his eyes. She thought she would faint. If she died right now, she would have experienced more love with him in the past year than some women ever got in a lifetime. It was pure.

And we're perfect together.

The Queen hoisted up her dress and ran the last few steps into Knight's arms.

His eyes grew wide as he glimpsed the gun on her thigh. That wasn't part of his security plan for today, but he played it off by embracing her and lifting her up and spinning her around.

They pressed their lips together and kissed long and hard.

The audience exploded with cheers.

The reverend playfully cleared his throat, his microphone attached to the collar of his black robe amplifying the sound. Laughter erupted among the guests.

The Queen never wanted to stop breathing health and life into her man. She pressed her face into his neck, feeling his pulse beat against her eyelids.

Yes, he's alive. Alive and well.

"May we begin?" the reverend asked playfully.

"Yes, sir," Knight answered. "Let's do this!"

As The Queen looked up into Knight's onyx eyes and he stared down into hers, they faced each other and gripped hands. She just wanted to hear the words *husband and wife* so she could stroll off into the sunset with the man of her dreams.

They were close, because the reverend said, "If anyone here has any objection to this union, speak now or forever hold your peace."

A piercing scream made The Queen's gut cramp. All the guests spun around to look.

Blood-covered Reba stumbled onto the pink aisle. "Watch out for Duke!" she screamed.

A shocked gasp rose from the guests. "Watch out for Duke!" Then she collapsed.

In black, white, and gray fatigues, Barriors and B'Amazons descended on her, plucking her off the carpet and carrying her away.

"Continue, please," Knight said.

Minutes later, the reverend said, "I now pronounce you man and wife. You may kiss your bride."

For a moment, their charmed circle of love made everything around them fade to gray. This was their Technicolor dream, live and in color, as they officially became one and three all at once.

But that bliss was shattered when the ear-splitting sirens blared, and B'Amazons and Barriors around the perimeter of the rooftop terrace drew rifles and ushered all the guests to the center of the tent.

Yeah, this was about the most fucked-up wedding day any girl could ever imagine.

But part of The Queen felt like it didn't even matter. Because her beautiful black Knight was pulling her up against his strong body, and she was burying her face in his neck where his pulsing veins confirmed that he was alive. Now they just had to escape this hell.

Chapter 94

Trina Michaels sat in a surveillance van, watching the outrageous display of gaudy ghetto flamboyance through the eight tiny video cameras hidden on Rip Masta and his fellow thugs. "Imagine a shootout at a wedding, and we have the exclusive video!" she exclaimed to her cameraman, who would leave the van and go inside for more video after the feds rushed in. "This story gets better by the second!"

In a matter of hours, after Rip Masta would get great video of the sex Olympics, Trina would get the media coup of the decade. The plan was for Federal officers to storm into Babylon and capture Victoria Winston.

The agents were waiting right now in vans parked throughout this riverfront warehouse district where Trina had gotten fucked so good a month ago inside The Playhouse.

"Bye, bye, Miss Queen!" Trina giggled as she watched the live video showing those soldiers calming the frantic wedding crowd. "If you think your day is bad now, just wait!"

This would serve both her and her pet gorilla right for daring to threaten the great investigative journalist Trina Michaels. They would see who'd come out on top.

Me!

"This whole story epitomizes the fact that an obsession with sex in the black community is its downfall," Trina said. "HIV, pregnancy, prostitution—these are all manifestations of the sex addiction that's gripping our inner cities."

The cameraman, who was adjusting knobs on the wall of sound and editing equipment, crinkled his beige face at her and said, "You're a racist witch. Do you have any idea?"

"As a white male," she snapped, "you have no right to call *me* racist."

"You're a racist, snobby bitch whose sexual frustrations give you a mega superiority attitude," he said. "You wish you were as wild and free as these folks. At least they don't *try* to pretend they're something else. Isn't that what the term 'ghetto fabulous' is all about?"

Rat-tat-tat!

"Gunfire!" Trina shrieked. "Look at 'em scramble. Nice wedding, Miss Queen. You'd do Martha Stewart and Emily Post proud today."

The cameraman put on a headset that blocked his ears; then he turned back to his equipment. "You got serious issues."

Trina gloated at the screen as The Queen huddled under an arch of pink roses with Knight. "No, I got an award-winning, urban docudrama in the palm of my hands!"

Chapter 95

"Babylon, let's fuck!" screamed the thousand-plus people packing The Auditorium for The Games. They were singing along with the Bang Squad's thunderous theme song for this much anticipated annual event.

It was about to get started, and it couldn't get finished soon enough for Knight.

So we can slip away forever.

As he stood backstage, just inside the huge, heavy, purple velvet curtains, his insides trembled and his chest squeezed almost as horribly as those tense moments during the lockdown after the wedding. The alarm had gone off because Paul had spotted Li'l Tut on the security cameras, limping out of suite 515 with Dickman's assistance. Then Paul reported to Knight that Li'l Tut was holding his crotch with one hand and pressing a towel to his bleeding cheek with the other.

Now we gotta finish what The Queen started.

The Queen had jacked him up good, but Li'l Tut was still alive and lurking somewhere in this building. Big Moe and a team of Barriors who were searching every inch had explicit instructions to call Knight to come and finally put that muthafucka out of his misery when they found him.

Lightning bolts of stress pains shot through Knight's chest at the thought of Li'l Tut cornering The Queen in her wedding suite, trying to shoot her up with the deadly weapon that his dick had become.

All while I was blacking out down the hall.

Anger and frustration at himself threatened to suck away Knight's breath.

I am a warrior. Manifest Destiny is mine.

Just a few more hours.

"Babylon, let's fuck!" The audience thundered with the blasting bass beat as Knight and Jamal stepped onto the stage from opposite sides. At the edge of the shiny pine stage floor, giant glass block letters spelling THE GAMES AT BABYLON glowed cobalt blue. Artificial steam from dry ice cast a sexy-smoky mist around them. The smoke glowed blue and purple, creating an outer-space-fantasy feeling as it wafted over the floor of the stage.

The stage dropped about four feet to the floor, where Barriors stood shoulder to shoulder in ninja black, double strapped with rifles. In front of them stretched a long table where six celebrity judges sat with laptop computers that would record and tally their scores for each event.

Beyond the judges stretched a rolling sea of blingin' urban style and vibrant energy. Every purple velvet seat in the place showcased sexy chicks, thugged-out dudes, glitzy celebrities, huge athletes, famous musicians, and Grammy-winning rappers.

Knight savored a sense of pride at the beauty of his people, as purple spotlights flashed from the stage, highlighting the mass of people. A haze of ganja smoke cast a surreal cloud over the people as they smiled, laughed, drank, and put in orders to waitresses, who strutted up and down the aisles in white Babylon dresses and laced-up gold sandals.

Knight wished folks could do without the intoxicants, but this whole show was about to offer up the most enticing intoxicant of all; booty.

As he took all this in, Knight's mind reeled with images of how he hoped that the Barriors had caught Li'l Tut by now, and how in just a few hours, with this crowd whipped into a frenzy of fucking here and up in The Playroom, he and The Queen would be well on their way to paradise.

His chest squeezed under his black silk Armani suit, under which, he hid four guns.

There's no room for error. If some shit goes down, this is our only chance, or we're stuck.

Knight sucked down gulps of air to disarm this barrage of worries. He had to enjoy his last night of this outrageous carnal indulgence that made Babylon what it was. In a few days, he'd be able to redefine carnal indulgence one-on-one, tropical style, with The Queen.

"How e'rybody doin'?" Jamal shouted, launching into his rapper posture, holding the mic and taking long, excited steps from one end of the stage to the other. He stopped in front of three enormous white beds that were draped with mosquito netting suspended by huge, black-and-gold striped masks of Cleopatra and Tutankhamen.

Jamal, wearing baggy blue jeans, black Tims, a white tank top that showcased his caramel-brown muscles, and the heavy gold chain with a Bang Squad medallion, held the mic toward the audience.

"Babylon, let's fuck!" they responded with the music. "Welcome to The *Gaaaaaaa-mes!*" The audience went wild.

Jamal held out a hand toward Knight. "Now some o' y'all was here las' year when the new sheriff blasted back into D-town, guns blazin'!"

The audience roared.

"All y'all know, this the baddest muthafucka eva, rulin' Babylon like a king! Show some love for Knight Johnson!"

Guys in the audience punched their fists in the air and barked. Girls shrieked. Some yanked up their shirts and shook their titties as they cheered.

"Firs', though, y'all congratulate the King o' Babylon for gettin' married today."

"Babylon, let's fuck!" the audience screamed.

Jamal worked his hips in a sexy love-grind, which made the girls shimmy their titties once more. "Yeah, bet they gon' make love tonight," Jamal said playfully. "There go The Queen, who's blazin' that shit up the charts!" He pointed up at The Queen in the closest golden box seat balcony overlooking the stage, where she sat with CoCo and Mr. and Mrs. Marx. Honey would join them after the first competition.

Emcee Sexarella, sitting with her girls in the balcony next to The Queen, stood. Tall, curvy, and wearing a transparent gold bodysuit with sequined stars over her nipples and pussy, she screamed, "All hail The Queen, y'all!" Her round, brown face sparkled with gold eye makeup. And her high black ponytail, which was long, straight, and silky-looking, flipped over her shoulder as she shouted, "Give it up 'cause she got what all y'all want—the sexiest dude in Babylon!"

The audience cheered.

The Queen, wearing a pink lace and sequined bustier and pink leather pants that showcased her diamond-studded belly button and tattoos, stood, turned around, and slapped her ass with her left hand, making her wedding ring sparkle in the hazy purple light.

As the audience roared, Ping and Pong stood in ninja black behind her, scanning every direction.

Knight noticed that Rip Masta was turning his whole body at an unnatural angle to look at The Queen.

Keep an eye on Rip Masta, intuition warned. *Somethin' ain't right with him and his crew.*

The gangsta rappers filled the box next to Sexarella and the one directly across from The Queen. Knight also didn't like that they'd sported saggy jeans with denim jackets and baseball caps to the wedding. They needed to show some respect.

Next to them, all wearing suits, sat Red Moreno and his brothers, plus B-Boy and Birdie in another private balcony box. Nearby, Raynard "Dickman" Ingalls sat with two chicks on his lap beside Shar Miller and Leroy Lewis. Dickman was about to get excused to answer some questions, but that muthafucka didn't know it yet.

Knight smiled up at The Queen, who moved in sultry slow motion as she puckered, and blew him a kiss.

"That's love, y'all," Sexarella shouted, rousing a whole new cheer from the audience, especially the women.

"Wooo-weeeel!" Jamal exclaimed with a deep, sexual tone. "Sorry, y'all, you gon' miss the real Games tonight when he an' his bride make it official."

The men barked in unison.

"Wait up," Jamal said, "do any o' y'all who was at the weddin' know ain't no party 'til some shit go down, right?"

The barking men imitated the siren sound.

Knight kept a poker face as those tiny needles of pain surged once more around his pounding heart.

"We outlaws." Jamal grinned at Knight. "So we gotta set the mood, you know. Show we got some juice if a muthafucka try to show out up in here."

People in the audience screamed.

"Yeeee-ah!" Jamal boomed. "Now, let's get this party started wit' the Prettiest Titties contest."

The audience hooped and hollered as thirty women strutted onto the stage. Standing midway between the blue block letters and the beds, they wore thong bikinis and high-heeled sandals in every color. And each had a small sign on her thigh with a black number and team name. Honey stood with them; she was not a Slut, but as Babylon staff, she had the option of joining the team.

Knight bellowed into the microphone, "Behold the prettiest titties in Babylon from coast to coast!"

Jamal read from a list, announcing the women's names, their home cities, and the enterprises they represented, including teams sponsored by Babylon, Moreno Incorporated, Question Marx Entertainment, Rip Masta, Thuggalicious, Mob Squad Movies, a group of pro-ballers called Slam Dunk, and Emcee Sexarella.

Jamal announced, "Now our distinguished panel of judges will score these titty queens based on size, shape, firmness, nipples, symmetry, and naturalness."

Knight loved looking at this buffet of female fruits. They were all perfect in their own right; something for every man's taste.

Having sampled every variety and flavor in the fresh market of human temptation, Knight now craved only one flavor. And she was sitting safely up in the balcony, laughing with CoCo as they ogled the contestants. Next to them, Mrs. Marx was sitting on Larry's lap, grinding and presumably, fucking already.

In the next balcony, Moreno and company were watching intently, as were Shar Miller and Leroy Lewis. But Dickman was being escorted out by the B'Amazons for an intensive Q&A about Li'l Tut's whereabouts.

Knight caught Rip Masta's sneaky glance. Something was definitely not right with that cat. Knight looked at his watch, to which he had affixed his phone so that he could discreetly check for text messages on stage. The screen showed only the time and the symbols for a charged battery and satellite function. No word yet from Big Moe about Li'l Tut. Knight used his right hand to type a text message into his phone, strapped to his left wrist, to tell Ping to keep an eye on that muthafucka, Rip Masta. Then he looked once more at The Queen.

She pulled her titties out and rubbed seductive circles over her cinnamon-colored nipples. Then she smiled at him playfully and returned her breasts to her bustier.

Shane threatened to raise the front of his pleated pants. He craved the magical moment, in a few hours, when they would make love and consummate this marriage made in the hedonistic Babylon.

As The Queen focused on the contestants, so did Knight.

What was it about a woman's breasts that made a man lose his mind? Knight loved the squishy-soft, yet warm, firm sensation of The Queen's juicy C-cups. He loved to bury his face in that flawless, creamy skin, breathe in her clean, feminine scent, and lock his lips to the gentle curve on the underside of her breasts.

Jamal announced each woman's name, who then stepped forward.

"This here is Zena Drake of Team Thuggalicious."

The audience went crazy.

Knight glanced up at The Queen. A smile raised the corners of his mouth.

Her eyes glowed with lust as she studied the beauties on stage, including her favorite girl, Honey. She and CoCo were whispering, pointing to the contestants, smiling.

Knight's phone vibrated. A text message flashed, Got him. Knight nodded to Jamal then slipped backstage.

This time, the king was going to get his hands dirty, to make sure the job was done right.

Chapter 96

It would be an inevitable and unfortunate chain of events Red Moreno mused as he watched the luscious breasts on stage, when the Johnson brothers would finally meet their fate. Soon they would be resting right alongside their despicable brother, Prince. *Tonight I will wipe them off the screen so that I may single-handedly rule this underworld by adding it to my global empire.*

Babylon was too large and successful for any black man to own. Moreno had simply gone along with that bogus deal led by that misguided, mixed-up Cleopatra wannabe so that he could legitimately get inside the same building with both brothers at once.

Red glanced at his two brothers as Babylon whores performed fellatio on them. Together they were an international phenomenon. He thought of the Johnson brothers starting with Prince, then Knight, then Duke, always a thorn in the side of Moreno Enterprises, when it came to the lucrative market of inner city Detroit.

Finally, Red would savor the delight of wiping the remaining two Johnsons off the map. Now, the true showdown would occur, and neither Duke nor Knight would have a chance.

I'll make off with all the money. And Cleopatra will make me a fortune as the exotic superstar in one of my pleasure penthouses in Beijing.

Her half-black beauty and theatrical style would gather thousands from the businessmen who traveled to the sleek city every day from around the world. Plus Red would get to savor her succulence whenever he wanted.

Now, his body tingled from the head he was getting from a black chick he'd picked up in the lobby. In his mind, though, he was fast-forwarding to the moment when Cleopatra would be sucking his schlong. She'd have nobody to protect her, and her survival would depend on following the orders of her captors. Just like she'd done, according to B-Boy's account of her life over the past year, when Duke kidnapped her into his urban hell. She'd gone from rich and white to black and poor.

Now she'd go from ghetto fabulous to global fast-lane, courtesy of Red Moreno.

B-Boy had told him all about her real background. By getting her out of the country and relieving her of that federal fugitive status, he'd be doing her a favor. And with his connections, getting past authorities and customs and any other government pests would be done faster than anyone could say, "Kidnapping."

In a short while, Moreno's battalion would be moving in on boats, in trucks, and on foot to bring this building called The Playhouse under siege.

The power, the money, and the pussy will all be mine.

Chapter 97

The Queen thought she'd seen it all, but the way those girls were competing in the Craziest Pussy Tricks event was straight-up mind-blowing. Especially that chick on the Mob Squad Movies team, who was chewing gum and blowing big pink bubbles with her pussy!

"How did she do that?" The Queen gasped.

"She a nasty freak!" CoCo exclaimed playfully, mesmerized by the close-up shots of that bubble-blowing bitch on the two giant video screens on the upper left and upper right of the stage. "She got the smokin' chick beat hands down."

So far they'd watched Sexarella's girl smoke a cigarette with her twat. A Slam Dunk chick had shot marbles out of her cunt, which she aimed at a hole in the center of a target and made every shot! And a Moreno contestant had made herself orgasm by rubbing her clit with her fingers before squirting cum twelve feet across the stage!

If this shit weren't so wild and crazy, The Queen would have been out of her mind with worry over where the fuck Knight had disappeared to. She knew he and his boys were searching for Duke, and that security was of utmost concern tonight, especially after that crazy shooting at the wedding after the alarm had gone off.

Plus she got the feeling that a whole lot more than she knew was going down right now, and it was about to break wide open in a few hours. Her telepathic love connection with Knight told her so. Along with the very worrisome vibe that something was still terribly wrong with his health. And the stress of this evening could knock him out cold. Or worse.

"Hey, girl," CoCo said, putting her arm around The Queen, "Knight don't eva lose so take a deep breath an' enjoy this crazy shit." CoCo pointed to the stage, where a bright green snake was slithering out of a girl's pussy and onto the black-skin of her thigh.

I hope you're right CoCo. With all the craziness going on, The Queen just sat there and wondered what in the world would come next.

Chapter 98

Knight drew one of his four guns before easing open the door to the Champagne Room. That's where, according to Big Moe's second text message, they were holding Li'l Tut with Dickman.

Now, in the silent room, Big Moe sat on the end of the white couch, his eyes wide open, staring forward. Facing him in the plush, cube-shaped chairs, sat two Barriors and two others knelt with their faces touching the carpet.

And they were all dead.

Chapter 99

The intense pain of his cheek and his dick riled Duke into a rabid state of mind. He was on a rampage, and he'd kill and destroy anything in his way. Whether that was Knight or Duchess or anybody else.

I'm gonna take the money then storm the stage and reclaim what's mine. And I got some lead for any muthafucka who try to stop me.

Duke charged down the hallway on the third floor. He had to get to the vault before Knight tried any tricks to move the money collected as admissions, bets, and prizes for The Games. Those millions would be a good start.

Later on, Duke would hack into the computer system to access the millions that were his for the taking.

"Man, you shoulda let me stay up there," Duke said as Dickman hurried alongside him. "Coulda knocked off Knight, put that worry outta our minds."

"No time fo' that, dude," Dickman said. "You already done let a bitch take yo' gun an' jack yo' ass today, so I know you ain't right tonight. Let me han'le the security detail."

Duke spun around and knocked Dickman's leather cap off. "Muthafucka, this my world! You call me Massa."

"I'll call you *crazy*, nigga!"

Duke glared back at his boy. The rage pumping through his thin limbs numbed the pain in his cheek and his dick.

Here I go again. A hot-headed muthafucka who can't control himself long enough to claim my fortune.

Duke imagined Knight walking up on them during their temper tantrum in the hallway and popping both their stupid asses. Duke spun on his heel and ran toward the vault with Dickman following.

Duke had already called Shar and Leroy to mobilize their crew to physically get the cash. *Fuck Moreno.* Duke had only gone through the motions of including him to get a feel for what that international gangster wanted.

E'rythang. And he's gettin' nothin'.

Chapter 100

As Knight text messaged Ping and Pong about what was going down, so that they'd body-block The Queen at all times, his mind spun with options. He could sound the alarm and put the whole building on lockdown; he could get The Queen and leave now, then flee to the safety of a new life with the millions they already had in his overseas accounts; or he could hunt down Li'l Tut, take him down his damn self, then execute Manifest Destiny the way he'd planned.

Yeah, that's it.

So what if his chest ached? So what if he was breathing hard? So what if intuition was telling him that he should be worried about much more than Li'l Tut trying to show out tonight? It was time to fight to the death, defy it, and Houdini the hell outta here.

No way in hell was this black warrior going to punk out and run from his own kingdom, until he decided the time was right.

Chapter 101

Baby Blue knew she would be named Sexiest Slut. Didn't matter that she didn't want dick anymore. Didn't matter that she was about to become part of Shar Miller's harem out in Las Vegas. Baby Blue knew she had the stuff to impress these judges right now. Starting with her sexiest walk. She had modeled it after her mother's naturally seductive strut.

Yeah, like this, with my ass pooted out, my toes pointed in, and a slow-motion roll with every step.

The audience exploded.

"Do yo' thang, Double D!" a dude shouted from the front row.

The Queen smiled.

The mesmerizing power of the walk, Baby Blue knew too, was also in the way she worked her face. The way she radiated sex power from her eyes and her glossed, pouty lips. And the way she projected laser beams of attitude that brainwashed and seduced everyone within a mile radius to believe, Baby Blue is the sexiest bitch around.

Didn't even matter that she was wearing that skimpy blue leather bikini that Reba had bought her; Baby Blue could've worked this magic in a gray sweatsuit.

I just got it like that.

As she strutted through the ankle-deep mist on the stage, Baby Blue caught glimpses of her audience that affirmed she would win.

On top of that, all the judges were staring up, wide-eyed, like they wanted to jump the stage, tackle her onto one of those giant beds, and lick her up, down, and sideways.

Most important, Baby Blue was loving herself. She wasn't doing this to impress anybody else; she was doing this to celebrate herself. She was ready to retire from Babylon and she wanted to go out knowing she'd done good for herself.

She'd been saving her money all these years, and winning the half a million dollars would bolster her savings to create a security blanket in case things didn't work out when she lived the glamorous life with Shar Miller in Vegas.

Right now, Baby Blue knew she had all those other gorgeous women beat, "booty down." Because it wasn't about the big hair or the lip gloss or the perfect titties or the pierced bellybuttons.

Sexiness is all about attitude and confidence. An' I got boat loads of both!

Reba once had it too, but all her evil gold-digging finally caught up with her in the worst way, falling out blood-covered and dead at a wedding! Not just any wedding, but the most important wedding Babylon had ever seen.

Reba had been plotting with Duke so he'd marry her, but fate had just fucked her up the ass on this one.

Baby Blue cast a sexy smile at the roaring audience. She pivoted on a sparkly blue stiletto sandal, poked her juicy ass out toward the judges, wound it just enough, then strutted back to her spot with the other contestants, knowing she was the Sexiest Slut in Babylon and beyond.

Chapter 102

CoCo was about to cum on herself.

Because the whole stage was covered with cocks.

She couldn't remember the last time she was this turned on. It was like her pussy was a faucet, soaking her whole crotch in hot water, making a puddle inside the pink leather dress she'd worn to the wedding reception dinner.

"Ladies and gentlemen," Jamal announced, "now it's time for one of the most popular events here at The Games, the Most Perfect Dick contest!"

The audience roared.

CoCo and The Queen pulled out binoculars to check out close-ups of the twenty-five men standing nude on the stage.

"It's time to announce the five finalists that the judges have chosen." Jamal opened an envelope and called out the names and teams that each man represented.

CoCo wished she could lay spread-eagled on that big bed in the middle of the stage and let those five pull a train on her horny ass. It was just a fantasy, because no way was she going to jeopardize her spot as Jamal's lady. Nope, someday soon she would follow in The Queen's sexy footsteps and become a married woman. Maybe CoCo could even take over the daily operations of Babylon when The Queen started having babies.

Damn, Duke almost got me today.

Suddenly the shock of the day came crashing down on CoCo. She had killed two people today in self-defense to save herself and The Queen. How Reba had lived through two bullet wounds long enough to get upstairs to the roof and expire on the wedding aisle was still trippin' her out. And how Duke had snuck into Babylon and bogarted into their suite was even more mind-blowing. It was a good thing CoCo had a gun stashed in the bathrobe pocket, just in case. Why she'd chosen the one with the silencer on it, she didn't know, but if Duke had heard shots when she took out Reba and Antoine, he could've hurt The Queen.

CoCo shook her head to exorcise those haunting, horrible thoughts. She'd been drinking champagne tonight, which had softened her stress. But sex was her ultimate escape, the most intense intoxicant, the most decadent distraction.

Yeah, all those delicious dicks down there proved that the world was one big buffet of male meat of every cut, grade, and quality. CoCo's mouth watered as she examined the final five contestants up on the stage.

CoCo stared with freakish fascination. Like that time when she was a kid and her parents took her to the Guinness Book of World Records museum.

"Girl, I wanna ride all five of them," CoCo whispered to The Queen. "You okay?"

The Queen's eyes shimmered in the dim light as tears threatened to drip.

CoCo put her arm around her.

"I'm scared." The Queen sobbed into CoCo's shoulder. "Knight disappeared backstage an hour ago. He won't answer his phone, and Ping and Pong won't let me go find him."

CoCo's heart ached for her best friend. She gripped The Queen's bare shoulders. "Listen, girl, you know Knight won't let nothin' happen to you. Just trust that it's all gonna work out perfect tonight. Just perfect."

The Queen whispered, "Perfect."

"Now," CoCo said, turning The Queen's shoulders so that she had to look down at the stage, "forget your troubles by lookin' at *that* shit. Girl, my pussy is so wet I could cause a tidal wave if I spread my legs."

"I hope Jamal is thirsty tonight," The Queen said, even though her voice was quivery like she was scared shitless.

CoCo giggled as she focused on contestant number four. Tall and skinny, with copper-brown skin, his uncircumcised dick arched to the left, the foreskin sort of just hanging there.

"Looks like an elephant's trunk," The Queen said, trying to sound playful. "I like number five, personally."

"Oh, yeah! He's definitely your type."

The Queen cocked her neck. "What's my type?"

"Big and black." CoCo giggled. "Like Duke and Knight."

"Damn, he does look like Knight," The Queen exclaimed, "but not as good looking, or as big."

"Ain't many dudes who are six-seven," CoCo said, "but he comes close. An' when he win that money, chicks gon' be all ova tryin' to play that big joystick."

"I think he could be broke as hell an' still get the pussy." CoCo laughed.

The Queen burst into tears. "I will just die if something happens to Knight."

"Hush, girl!" CoCo held her. "Don't let none o' these muthafuckas see you cry."

Chapter 103

The Queen had to get a grip on herself. Her mind was a movie strip of scenes worse than any horror movie. And they were all of Knight laying somewhere in this building, dead at the hands of his brother. The next scene was The Queen finding him, throwing herself on his giant body that was her sanctuary from the wicked world, then figuring out how she could join her soul mate in the blissful infinity of heaven.

It's so fucked up to have this thought pattern. But I can't help it.

The Queen wanted to run and find her Knight.

"Ladies and gentlemen," Jamal announced as Studs pushed ten, thick, futon mattresses onto the stage, "it's time for one of the most popular events of The Games—The Longest Female Fucking on Top."

The crowd exploded as ten nude couples walked hand in hand and stopped in front of the mattresses.

Jamal introduced their names and teams. "And lastly we have the superstar champs from every year I can remember, Pebbles and Bam-Bam!"

The audience roared.

They look so happy. Just like me and Knight.

The Queen shot up to her feet. She didn't care about the games going on. All she cared about was getting to Knight.

"Where you goin'?" CoCo asked with an alarmed expression. She gripped The Queen's wrist and said, "I know you ain't gon' miss the fuck fest that's about to go down."

"I gotta find Knight."

She just had to figure out how to get past the human wall of muscle formed by Ping and Pong, who shook their heads, cast somber glares down at her, and pointed for her to put her ass back in her seat.

Chapter 104

Trina Michaels' pussy was burning with need, and her brain was even more excited. "Can you believe the perversion of this place? The world media is gonna eat this up!"

"You wish that were you up there," her cameraman shot back. "Maybe you wouldn't be such a bitch if you got your pussy pumped on a regular basis."

"That comment constitutes sexual harassment, according to the GNN company handbook. I'm going to report you when we get back to D.C."

The cameraman adjusted dials on the panel of video editing equipment. "Go for it. Because the NAACP, the GNN diversity committee and the black journalists' association are all about to hear about the real Trina Michaels."

She raised her chin, loving the video feeding in live from the eight cameras hidden on Rip Masta and his homies.

The equipment here in the truck was digitally recording the video of the wild sex taking place in this illegal endeavor.

Later, Trina and her cameraman would send the incriminating video by satellite back to the station in Washington.

And I'll become a superstar.

And her jealous cameraman could do nothing to stop her. Trina raised her chin. "As if the NAACP would support this type of animalistic hedonism. Half those jokers are smoking marijuana, and they're all taking part in an illegal sex ring. Civil rights leaders will praise me for putting an enterprise like this out of business."

The cameraman ignored her as he adjusted the sound on camera three.

Trina loved the idea that she'd have video of the event, thanks to Rip Masta, as well as video taken by the Federal agents when they raided the building. And that was supposed to take place within the hour.

Of course Rip Masta had no idea that hundreds of Federal agents were waiting in nearby vans, helicopters, and boats to interrupt his videotaping tasks. No, he was just a pawn in a game too big for his little mind to get burdened with.

Despite her objections, Trina had surrendered to Rick's demand that his agents also get live video from Rip Masta's hidden cameras.

Trina wanted exclusive access to that video so that Rick couldn't backstab her and give her hard earned scoop to another reporter at another network. But Rick refused and left her with no other choice but to go along with his demands.

Her mouth dropped open as she watched a woman fucking on top of the man. The power of her body and the position of female domination made Trina squeeze her thighs over her soaking wet panties. This was messy work, but she loved it.

Yeah, she and Rick would have a good time reviewing this video together. Because it just kept getting hotter and hotter.

"Hey, what are you doing?" Trina exclaimed. "Why are the screens going black?"

Chapter 105

Duke helped Rip Masta pull off the hidden cameras and wires, while Dickman assisted the rest of the crew in doing the same. It just so happened that Rip Masta, invited to the wedding and The Games by Knight, had called Duke earlier that afternoon to find out if his boy was back in action.

Another sign from the Babylon gods that it was time for The Duke to ascend back to the throne; because Duke's offer to make Rip rich in the Babylon underground had sounded much more appealing to his boy than trusting that fed mutha-fucka who had promised immunity in exchange for hidden video of the hottest action around.

"Fuck them liars," Rip said, tossing the lipstick sized camera onto the floor. He stomped on it.

"Work wit' me, man," Duke said. "Disappear off they radar in a Motor City minute."

"Dig that," Rip said, staring at the silver circular handle on the locked vault. "Now, how we gon' get the loot? The Games end in two hours an' they gon' be comin' down here to pay the winners. All cash. Plus I gotta book, 'cause soon as that Rick prick see I directed his home movie to fade to black, he gon' be up in here lookin' fo' me."

Duke playfully raised a fist over Rip's face. "Man, I oughta fuck you up for bringin' heat"

Dickman grabbed Duke's wrist. "Dude, the vault."

Rip nodded to a slim, beige-skinned brotha. "My boy Jimmy, he a locksmith worst nightmare."

Duke led Jimmy to the safe. "Jam on it, my brotha."

Chapter 106

Knight stood in the center of the surveillance room, scanning each monitor for Li'l Tut. Paul and the rest of the security team had just explained how and where they had seen him.

I'ma find him an' kill 'im wit' my own hands.

"Keep zooming in on the crowds," Knight said as B'Amazons studied live feeds from all over the inside and outside of the building. In the auditorium, one camera stayed on The Queen; Knight glanced back at her on that monitor frequently as he scanned the other screens.

"Here go one of the vans," Paul said, zooming an outdoor camera to focus on a black van a block away. He pointed to several other monitors that showed a convoy of vans and a helicopter lurking in the darkness in the warehouse district around The Playhouse. "They got some boats out on the water too."

Icy feelings of worry shot outward along Knight's spine.

They're gonna raid us any minute.

"When they move," Knight said, staring hard into Paul's eyes, "you know it's time for Inferno." Knight had never used the mechanism that would ignite the water in the moat around The Playhouse into a wall office.

Modeled after Medieval defense tactics for castles; it worked by emptying huge vats of flammable chemicals into the water, which would then be set on fire. The moat was far enough away from the building that no one would get hurt, but no one could get past it either.

Meanwhile, anyone inside the building could leave via the underground tunnels that led to various buildings in a one mile radius.

"It's done, Boss Knight," Paul said. "Soon as you give me the sign."

Knight checked out a monitor that showed the rooftop terrace where people lingered at the reception dinner tables. A band played, allowing folks to slow-dance and sip champagne. At the edges of the roof, sniper-trained Barriors and B'Amazons in black perched with rifles, ready to defend this urban fortress.

Knight had assigned only folks who were veterans of the Persian Gulf War and the Iraq War, and even several older brothas who'd served in Vietnam, for that detail. They weren't scared; their minds were right to execute The Prince Code, *Kill or be killed.*

That's how Knight viewed Li'l Tut. No matter what went down tonight, even if Babylon burned to the ground and had to rise like a triumphant phoenix from the ashes, Li'l Tut would not be part of it.

Knight searched monitors that showed the second floor, where hundreds of people splashed and sexed it up in and around the tropical-style swimming pool and hot tubs. Giant closed-circuit TV screens played The Games at each end of the turquoise playpen.

Gerard sat at the edge of the pool, twisted up under three strippers. One of them was in the water, sucking his dick, while the others gyrated around him.

That pathetic muthafucka will get his due.

"Yeah, Boss," Paul said, "Gerard lost his mind. Abandoned his post and joined the party."

Knight visually scoured the heavily guarded marina where yacht number one and two hummed in their slips, while Barriors loaded the cigarette boat and yacht number two with all the cash, except for the prize money and bet money for The Games. Together, that amounted to fifteen million.

Knight had left it, because he was not going to jack up Jamal's reputation by absconding with the cash owed to the contestants and participants. The winning contestants would get paid, as would the folks who'd bet on them.

Nope, Knight had taken only the admissions money, which totaled twenty-five million. And that money, on yacht number two, was pulling out of the marina right now. His laptop, where he and Jamal would make the transfer, was on yacht number one. That was also where The Queen would think it was all over.

It will be, for a minute.

Both yachts were captained by crews from Florida; they had no idea what was about to go down. Knight had paid Larry Marx a ridiculous fee to secure these crews, experienced in the pirate like world of smuggling everything between the United States and South American countries. They had all the appropriate licenses and paperwork on board to bum through any red tape bullshit that the Coast Guard, Detroit Police marine patrols, or anybody else tried to flex.

Knight watched the Barriors work. They too would be lavishly rewarded for transporting it to a private dock owned by Larry Marx's friend down river. There, the cigarette boat would deliver Knight and The Queen, and they would board yacht number two and sail away forever.

Knight's heart pounded as he thought about Jamal. In just a short while, they would do the deal to exchange ownership of Babylon. That additional twenty-five million would make Knight attain his target jackpot of fifty million. And that would set him and The Queen up to live like royalty with Baby Prince for the rest of their lives. *If we make it out of here.*

He coughed as stress suddenly clenched his chest.

On the lobby level, the Knight look-alike Stud who had competed in the Best Dick event stood with a Latina chick with long black hair and a wedding gown. The decoy couple would walk out through the front doors and get into Hummer One, decorated with a Just Married sign. That vehicle would go to the airport as if Knight and The Queen were en route to their honeymoon.

But Knight still had to find Li'l Tut.

Monitors showed the suites on the fifth floor, where all kinds of people were watching The Games on closed circuit TV and holding their own erotic Olympics on beds, chairs, and floors.

Knight looked to the next screens showing the vault. "There he is," Knight said calmly. He tossed back his head and burst out laughing. Because the vault was empty.

The prize and bet money was being protected by a heavily armed battalion of soldiers in a room under the stage dressing rooms. This would be a piece of cake. All Knight had to do was go to the vault room and squash Li'l Tut like a bug.

It ain't gonna be that easy, intuition said.

Chapter 107

Beat was rock-hard inside Jamal's jeans as he watched the Best Dick Suckin' contest on stage. He couldn't wait to get with CoCo, who looked just as horny as he was up there in the balcony with The Queen.

'Cause good as those chicks givin' head, don't nobody do it as good as my girl.

Despite the sexual excitement of this night, Jamal was still scared shitless about doing this deal with Knight.

This was hype and everything, but Jamal just didn't know if he wanted to own it. The more he thought about Dickman's offer to go with him and Duke and let Duke be the boss of this illegitimate empire, the more he liked the idea.

Knight was always talking about The Prince Code, keeping his hands clean.

Yeah, I'm a music mogul wit' legit bidness. I gotta keep my hands clean too.

But the image of Knight glaring down at him in the aisle when he'd expressed doubts flashed in his mind.

Then again, how would Knight even know if Jamal let Duke take over? He'd be all the way on an island somewhere, bangin' with The Queen, not worrying about what's going on back at Babylon. All that righteous talk about feeding the kids in Africa and protecting the hood. Shit! Jamal could make sure that still happened. Duke had a heart too. Plus, by dealing with Duke, Jamal would still be showing loyalty and appreciation to the Johnson family for bank rolling his music business. Even though Duke originally hadn't wanted to spring with the cash to make it happen.

Bygones are bygones. I'll do the deal wit' Knight on the boat. I'll come back an' hand it all back over to Duke. Then I can get the fuck on my merry way wit' my CoCo an' my bangin' music business.

Chapter 108

The Queen had no choice but to stay where she was with CoCo. Ping and Pong made that clear when they blocked her in when she tried to leave to find Knight.

"They won hands down," CoCo said.

"*Dick* down," The Queen decided to just go along with CoCo and act interested because if she didn't she was sure she'd break down crying. *It's gonna be like Armageddon,* Celeste said. *The end of the world as you know* it.

The Queen didn't know what, but something beyond even her wildest imagination, which she thought had been stretched to the limits here in Babylon, was about to happen.

Didn't any of those people down in the audience feel it too? They were feeling something, because the main floor looked like a tangle of bodies, writhing, grinding, bobbing, bouncing, all with their faces toward the blue glow of the stage, so they could watch the spectacle of sex.

And the people in the balconies around her, didn't they feel the sinister vibe in the air that was making the hairs on the back of her neck stand up? It was as strong as an electrical current pulsing through the air.

The Queen definitely took it as a bad omen that Brian was here inside Babylon, sitting so close to her, staring at her with hate in his blue eyes.

He'd smiled a few times at Tiffany, who had waved her bony hand at The Queen.

The Queen smiled, wondering if Tiffany knew that she was the reason that punk-ass Brian, suddenly had new front teeth. She still didn't understand how Brian hooked up with Moreno, whom she now was convinced, was the same man she'd seen at Brian's and Tiffany's parents' parties. And she'd all seen him at Daddy's office a few times. She just wanted to get as far away from his Lucifer-life aura as soon as possible.

Moreno kept staring at her as he put his embalmed-looking hand on the head of the girl who was sucking his dick. As she went up and down, it looked like he was dribbling a basketball. He cast lustful eyes at The Queen, his tongue flickering between his wet lips. When he mouthed, "You're mine," The Queen shivered.

He knew something she didn't know. Only some sinister secret would give him the gall to act so bold on her husband's turf.

Knight, baby, where are you?

The Queen wanted so badly, to get up and run until she found Knight. She would grab his hand and together, they would run.

A giant hand gripped her shoulder, and she froze.

It was Pong's. He and his brother were motioning for her and CoCo to follow them. The expressions on their faces let them know that they weren't escorting the ladies to a champagne toast at the after party.

Chapter 109

Moreno was on the phone with his commander, who gave a move-by-move report.

The battalion was charging the tunnel leading from the Detroit River. These young men and women whom he had recruited from ravaged areas of Ireland, Bosnia, Israel, and every inner city in America were trained and ready to kill. They specialized in storming buildings full of people and getting them all under control in a matter of minutes. So that Moreno could get what he wanted and leave just as quickly.

The thunder of their feet echoed up the metal staircases into the first floor, second floor, and third floor of The Playhouse.

Red had a floor plan of the building thanks to Flame down in Mexico. A comrade had interviewed the exiled Stud, who had been delighted to share confidential information about the secret tunnels.

A bit of C4 explosives on the vault and the millions would be his. Then his troops would head up to wherever Knight was hiding. They'd kill him, take Cleopatra, and get to work.

Merging this urban empire with Moreno Enterprises, would take work. The transition could get rocky, if they encountered any opposition from the staff, but they were used to being ruled with an iron fist. So it would be only a matter of time before they got used to having a white man call the shots.

Red Moreno watched the dick-sucking contest on stage as he calmly gave orders into his cell phone. Some of his troops were about to barge into the vault room while others were seeking out Knight and Cleopatra.

Then Red would have five minutes to extricate the lovely girl from his lap, meet with his commander, and ride away with Cleopatra and twenty-five million dollars.

Chapter 110

"What the fuck!" Paul exclaimed as dozens of white men and women in brown jumpsuits stormed up into The Playhouse from the river tunnel. But they weren't feds. Then who the hell were they?

Paul stood in the center of Cairo, watching the monitors. He felt helpless, like all the wild cards he'd never even thought of were being played at once. How could he trump all that by himself? Because even the top-security Barriors and B'Amazons here in Cairo were staring wide-eyed at the monitors.

I need Knight back up here! He didn't say nothin' about this shit goin' down!

But Knight was heading down to the third floor to pounce on Duke, while Ping and Pong were bringing The Queen and CoCo up here. All the while, the show was still going on in the auditorium, and thousands of people were partying on every floor of the building.

It looked like the fed vans were starting to move in. The video monitors from the outdoor cameras showed the vans steadily creeping up the street, and the cameras on the roof showed two choppers hovering close, while Coast Guard boats were bobbing just beyond the marina.

Babylon 'bout to blow!

Paul punched a single button on his console to reach Knight's cell phone. "Answer!" he exclaimed.

*If Knight walks up on those white soldiers storming down the third floor hallway, toward the vault—*Paul stood in disbelief. The white folks in brown jumpsuits burst into the vault room.

Duke, Dickman, and Rip Masta all drew guns. Bullets blasted and bodies dropped.

Pow!

The floor shook. A gray cloud rolled up toward the monitors.

"Somebody blew something up," Paul exclaimed. And the vault room monitors went black.

"There's Duke!" A Barrior pointed to another screen. "In the hallway."

A B'Amazon said, "Here comes Knight!"

A gray dust cloud rolled into the hallway, where people were running, coughing, and blasting guns at each other.

Paul's brain was a tornado. Should I ignite the moat? Put the rooftop snipers on alert? Sound the alarm? How far had The Queen and CoCo made it? Since the auditorium was on the first and second levels, and the vault was on the third floor, were they caught in that chaos? Had the explosion blown through the floor?

No, the music was still blasting in the auditorium; those sex-crazed folks didn't hear or see a thing. On the monitors, they were transfixed on the Longest Fuck contest on stage, where five couples remained in a frenzied fuck-a-thon.

He almost laughed. If this joint was about to blow up, then those Studs were the luckiest dudes in the building because they'd die fuckin'.

Paul felt dizzy. "What the hell should I do right now?"

Chapter 111

Knight had to find The Queen. They had to get out now. He could do without waiting on Jamal; he could make do with the twenty-five million he already had.

This is a matter of life and death.

Knight coughed on the gray dust in the dimly lit hallway. He stepped over a white man in brown who was groaning on the floor.

Moreno's people. What fuckin' nerve for that muthafucka to think he could storm my turf and steal my loot!

The Queen. Knight's legs pumped with bionic speed. Holding his breath against the dusty smoke, he ran down the hallway to meet Ping and Pong just as they brought his goddess and CoCo up to Cairo on the ninth floor. He charged into the stairwell, taking the black metal steps three at a time. His heart throbbed with pain as he huffed, finally reaching the eighth floor landing.

One more to go.

He'd get The Queen, tell Paul to ignite the moat, and dash to the boat. As he ran up the final flight, he heard voices. Saw several pairs of black Tims, and pink leather stiletto boots. Two pairs.

His heart stopped, or at least it felt that way.

The Queen was standing there, wide-eyed with fear, as Li'l Tut wrapped his arm around her neck and aimed a gun at Knight. "Deja vu, muthafuckaaaaa!" Li'l Tut teased with a crazed look in his eyes. With that raw wound on his cheek, he looked like Freddy Krueger. His voice echoed off the exposed brick of the stairwell. Then he imitated the twang of a cowboy, "Time for a showdown, sheriff."

Dickman and Rip Masta, plus three of their homies, were all pointing guns at Ping, Pong, and CoCo. The thugs let out deep, sinister laughs.

Knight's chest rose and fell as he tried to catch his breath.

He stared his brother in the eye. Then he glanced at The Queen. The terror on her face, and the tremble of her body which in eight months would deliver their baby Prince of peace, riled up something in his soul.

I'll save my family. And today's not my day to die.

Chapter 112

On video monitors, Paul watched the showdown in the stairwell. He mobilized snipers to take out Duke and his crew.

A rifle-carrying battalion of Barriors and B'Amazons was already stomping those crazy folks in brown jumpsuits down in the tunnel. The lower stairwells, and the hallway led to the already empty vault.

"Paul." A Barrier pointed to monitors showing the vans full of federal agents. They were approaching; some of the SWAT looking officers were piling out in front of the building.

"Inferno!" Paul commanded.

Suddenly all the fear and worry and confusion melted. He knew exactly what he had to do.

The Barrior walked to the red panel and flipped the switch. *Whoosh!*

A wall of fire rose up in front of The Playhouse. The SWAT dudes shielded their faces and ran back.

Chapter 113

As Jamal announced the winners of the Longest Fuck contest, the audience screamed, shrieked and even squirted cum up toward the stage. The whole joint was as orgified as any Babylon party was supposed to be.

What the fuck is going on right now?

Jamal wanted to know why the fuck CoCo and The Queen had disappeared during the hottest event of the night. If they were that horny, they coulda done each other right there in the box and let him glance up for a peek. Or they could've waited another twenty or thirty minutes for him and Knight to all get on the boat and get freaky together before the honeymoon lovebirds left to do their own thing.

Fuck! Deep down in his trembling gut, he knew the reason the girls were gone was much more serious than them wanting to get their freak on. *Somethin' ain't right.*

Duke was supposed to page him but hadn't; Knight was supposed to call him but hadn't.

CoCo normally would've text messaged him something nasty to tease him and tell him where she was, and she hadn't. And why the fuck did the floor shake like that? Even with these superhuman fuck machines on the stage, nothing right could rock the house like that.

Plus, why had that spooky lookin' Moreno dude and his crew just up and left in a huff while their team was winning too? It didn't make sense.

Now, Jamal still had to oversee all the winners as they collected their cash prizes from that little, guarded room backstage. The Barriors and B'Amazons were delivering the cash to each of them in Babylon's trademark gold treasure chests, and they were getting high security escorts out of the auditorium.

In another room, all the cats who were high on booze, booty, and blunts were collecting their winnings for the bets they'd placed on each event.

Jamal loved the excitement and the eroticism and the enterprising spirit of the night. Naw, he didn't need Duke to run this shit. It was too much responsibility to share with that hothead. Plus, the millions of dollars in the house right now, made Beat bang for a hot second.

All this will be mine in a minute. As long as Babylon still standin' long enough for me an' Knight to do the damn deal.

Chapter 114

Knight remembered his favorite scenes in all those wild, wild west movies when the cowboy would draw his guns with lightning speed, blast away his enemies, and make off with the girl, the money, or simply his life.

Right now, as he stared at the defiantly crazy look in Li'l Tut's eyes and the horrifically terrified expression on The Queen's face, he was about to reenact one of those scenes.

Ping and Pong were so quick, they could do the same in a split second, to take care of Li'l Tut's punks.

Question was, which gun should he reach for first? The one in the waistband of his pleated black Armani silk pants? The one in the holster under his shoulder? Or the two in his black leather cowboy boots?

With his free hand, Li'l Tut yanked down The Queen's camisole, and her titties popped out.

"Eh, big bro', remember when you took my bitch? She was sittin' naked on my dick at my birthday party, and you just lifted her off like you used to do when we was small, always stealin' my favorite toy for yourself?" Li'l Tut tossed back his head, making his sinister laughter echo up the stairwell.

Knight half-winked at Ping and Pong. It was too subtle for those knuckleheads, Dickman and Rip Masta, to catch. It meant, "Do like I do, when I do it."

The Queen's mind was racing with thoughts as she crossed her arms over her bare breasts. If she still had her gun in her boot, now wouldn't have been the time for her to try to draw it.

Just before Li'l Tut looked back down, Knight cast a look at her saying, "I got ya back, Tinkerbell."

As he held a gun in his left hand, Li'l Tut used his other hand to yank down the zippers on each hip of her pink leather pants. The fabric fell down, exposing her still flat belly, where her and Knight's baby was growing. Li'l Tut's scarred hand pulled down her hands. He squeezed her breasts, pulling them up to cover her *Cleopatra of the Knight* tattoo. He unbuckled his baggy jeans and let them fall to the floor. His dick, big, hard, and bloody from a nasty gash on the shaft, swung out, and hit her leg.

"Yeah, we gon' do a *deja vu* moment all the way, big bro'. We gon'—"

Pow!

Yeah, that's how the sheriff rules in this town. Waistband was the closest thing to a wild, wild west hip-holster.

Perfect aim. Perfect shot. Right in the forehead.

Like the sharpshooter muthafuckas that they were, Ping and Pong, shot down Rip Masta, Dickman, and the two other thugs in a flash.

Then, like a giant robot switched into bionic gear, Knight swooped The Queen up in his arms, while Ping grabbed CoCo.

The men stepped over the mess on the landing. And headed up to Cairo.

Chapter 115

Trina Michaels could not believe that those ghetto pimps were pulling off this pyrotechnic feat. Her whole story was ruined, thanks to a lying thug named Rip Masta, an incompetent FBI joker named Rick Reed, and a Bonnie and Clyde team who had outsmarted everybody.

"Incredible." Her cameraman gasped as he stood beside her, outside the TV truck, shooting video of the twenty-foot-high wall of fire.

Sure, this would make spectacular story in itself, but it was nothing like what she'd envisioned for her exposé on Babylon and the capture of Victoria Winston. Was she even still inside there? How long would this fire burn?

She dialed Rick on his cell phone. "Have you heard from Rip Masta? Or did he just fuck you up the ass?"

Two helicopters hovered nearby, but they couldn't get anywhere near those flames.

Ping! Pow-pow-pow! Pop-pop-pop!

"Gunfire!" Trina screeched.

"Snipers on the roof," the cameraman said, aiming his camera up where the orange glow of the fire illuminated the black tips of guns aiming down at federal agents still standing on the streets around the building.

Trina ran back into the unmarked TV truck.

"Shit!" She had dropped her phone. She'd thought she was so smart, orchestrating this story, using her body to get what she thought would be the scoop of the century. Now, she felt like a stupid, good for nothing, bitch. She was fucked.

Chapter 116

The siren blared as Emcee Sexarella and her crew hurried down the stairwell with mobs of other spectators. An announcement played over and over on the speaker system, "To escape the raid, proceed down the stairs to the underground tunnels. They will take you to a nearby nightclub, a park, and an outdoor concert pavilion. Blend in with the people there for a while. Then discreetly make arrangements to get picked up."

Sexarella's head throbbed. "We all drunk and fucked up, how we gon' do all that?"

"Better 'n gettin' locked up," her Stud said playfully. "Gotta hand it to my man Knight though. He planned it out, an' took care o' his peeps in case of emergency."

"What they got us on?" Sexarella took off her high-heeled boots so she could walk faster down these damn stairs.

A girl laughed. "Prostitution, drugs, gamblin'—"

"Guurrrl, shut the fuck up!" Sexarella said playfully. "Now, where we gon' party at when we get the fuck outta these damn tunnels? Guuurrrlll, I hope it ain't no rats up in here."

Chapter 117

Babylon was burning behind her, or at least so it seemed, with the ring of fire around the building they had just escaped. The rat-tat-tat of guns echoed off the fire-lit sky. The screams of people in the stairwells and that deafening siren still rang in her ears.

The Queen was shell-shocked but not surprised.

Every minute for Alice in her sexy Wonderland had gotten more erotic and enticing from the first jump into what she'd thought was a terrifying black hole a year ago. But suddenly, over the past month, erotic, and enticing, had nose dived into sinister, and scary. So the turn of events today, her wedding day, was just following that trend.

She stared straight ahead at that boat about twenty feet away in the marina behind The Playhouse. That would be her magic carpet ride up and out of this Terrorland.

She gripped Knight's hand harder as they ran across the lawn toward the water. CoCo, Jamal, Ping, and Pong clustered close as they sprinted.

The marina lights were out, but the fire cast a bright orange glow over the boats and the black water.

Her lungs ached as she gasped for breath, and her toes throbbed from running down the stairs in stiletto boots.

But I'm alive. Duke didn't get me. Neither did Brian or Moreno or anybody else. And Knight is alive.

Finally, their feet pounded onto the wooden dock. To her right and to her left, the fire ring burned all the way to the water's edge. Knight had never told her about this medieval looking defense tactic. As long as it was keeping the bad guys out long enough for them to escape, she didn't care. But what about all those police boats, Coast Guard patrols, and who knew what else was lurking out on the river?

Trust me, baby girl.

Yes, she could hear her Knight speaking again on their supernatural love connection.

The crew on the yacht was pulling in the bumpers and the ropes, ready to speed away as soon as they jumped on board. They stepped onto a plexiglass lip at the back, which was strewn with ropes, boogie boards, and scuba gear. It led to two sets of sliding doors.

Knight hurried them through one door, down into the plush living room area, and the boat took off.

"We're safe," Knight said, breathing hard. He looked pale, dark circles ringing his bloodshot eyes.

If anything had happened to him back there, she would've made like Juliet and followed Romeo to heaven. Hopefully they were on their way to doing that right now. On Earth. She needed a long hug and to make love to her husband.

Knight walked to a sleek, wooden desk built into the flat screen TV console. He pulled out his laptop and huddled with Jamal as they typed quickly and spoke softly.

"What the fuck type of business could you possibly be doing right now?" she demanded.

They ignored her.

So The Queen and CoCo sank into the suede couches, closing their eyes, catching their breath. Ping and Pong stood by the door, securing the outside.

A deeply tanned crewman dashed in. "Everybody into the phantom room," he ordered, pushing a silver sconce on the wall that made a doorway appear in the beige suede wall. Inside was a windowless room ringed by low, cushioned benches. "The Coast Guard and FBI are boarding."

Chapter 118

Knight leaned over The Queen, kissing her in bed. The sleek, dimly lit master suite was silent except for the soft hum of the engines beneath them as they sped south down the Detroit River toward a better forever.

"Baby girl," Knight whispered, "I wanted you to wear your wedding gown as I make love to you for the first time as my wife."

Her eyes sparkled and she smiled. She wrapped her legs around the backs of his knees and said, "I'd rather wear my birthday suit."

She giggled as Shane throbbed against her thigh. Then she asked, "How did you shoot Duke like that so his blood didn't splatter on me?"

"Baby girl," Knight said softly, "I want you to push a delete button in your head, starting with anything that happened before this minute. Forget all about today. Everything."

"Then I want you to promise me that you're okay," she said. "You look pale. And something in your eyes doesn't look right."

Knight's heart pounded. The fist of stress was clenching his chest worse than ever. He kept telling himself it would go away as soon as they got to the beach. He just had to stop that ringing sound in his head and that fuzzy feeling in his brain. "Baby girl, you know I've hardly been sleeping, trying to get everything together."

"No, there's more to it that you're not telling me. Are we still in danger? Are the feds still looking for us? I mean, I've never heard so many helicopters in my life." She glanced up at the ceiling. The chop of helicopters sounded close. The silvery circles of their spotlights flashed now and again on the closed curtains. "See? You look just as worried as I feel. You're not telling me something, just like you didn't tell me about all that shit today."

Knight pressed his mouth to her moving lips. They stilled. Because there was much more to come that he wasn't about to tell her.

Somewhere between this bed and those double French doors leading out to the little patio and the water, she'd figure it out and help them reach nirvana. He could call it the final test if he wanted to, but by now he knew that she was committed to him forever, no matter what.

Her lips parted. And her tongue, reaching into his mouth, let him know that she'd much rather make love. She reached down and wrapped her hand around Shane. "This is my lifeline," she moaned, stroking his dick. "I never want to live without you, Knight."

"You won't ever have to, baby girl. Ever." His mouth wrapped around her open lips, their tongues twirling in a way that made him moan.

But the roar of boats beside them and the beating chop of the helicopter above made Knight's heart pound and ache. His lungs squeezed. Head spun. Limbs felt light and tingly.

Her face blurred.

I'm gonna faint.

"Baby girl," he whispered weakly. No, he had to make love to his Queen as this happened. He knew she was ready; she was always wet as an ocean. So, just like the first time, this last time, he would make her cum with one stroke, and it would all be over. For both of them.

With the stealth and aim that made him who he was in business, in life, and now in bed with his wife, he grasped the backs of her knees, and pushed them forward.

"Yeah," she moaned, tickling her fingertips to the sides of his jaw and staring into his eyes.

He thrust Shane into that hot, tight, slippery paradise. Leaned his bare torso over her, and connected his lips to hers.

All in a split second.

Her body went limp and she shivered all at once. A soft little moan surged up from her soul letting him know she was cumming with one stroke.

He pulled his lips back just enough to whisper into her mouth, so that the air in his lungs would mix with hers as they took their dying breath. "We're going to heaven together, baby girl."

"Oh, yeah," she moaned deeply, sucking on his bottom lip. She was panting, and breathing his air deep down.

His heartbeat was so out of whack, it was making static in his ears. Yeah, his dick felt phenomenal inside his Queen, but every stroke was sapping his energy. The roar in his ears grew louder. Or was that a chopper? Was he hallucinating that voice that said, "Come out with your hands up." Knight's heart was exploding with panic and passion all at once.

Gotta make this so good. The perfect ending to the perfect romance.

He thrust harder and she sucked his breath in deeper. Her eyes were closed, and her body was one with his. He was now safe.

Now, I can let go.

He envisioned the tight pink ball of muscle that was his heart. He imagined it never hurting, never making him worry. He imagined it still and peaceful, his spirit floating up with The Queen's soul up to an eternal playground where they could make love for infinity. He closed his eyes and let that fuzzy, roaring sensation. A numb like, tingling sensation took over his mind and body.

And suddenly his heart stopped hurting.

Chapter 119

"Knight!" she screamed. Shane was still inside her, hard as a rock, pulsating like he was cumming. "Knight! Wake up!" She pressed her face into his neck, to feel for his pounding pulse. The hot skin against her face was still.

He's dead. And he knew he was gonna die right now.

"Muthafucka!"

The roar of boats around them, those damn choppers overhead, and the rage and horror in her head fueled her body as she ran out through the double French doors. She did not feel the chill of the September night on her bare skin as she stepped onto the three-foot ledge designed for watersports. It was smooth plexiglass with a lip that went into the water.

Tonight it would serve a more morbid purpose. She kicked open the gate leading to the black water. From the ledge, she grabbed a boogie board and some rope. She threw them into the room. Then she yanked Knight's arm, to pull him off the bed, but his 275 pounds and six foot, seven inches of African god did not budge. So she pulled harder.

The clock on the nightstand said 3:05 a.m. Someone on the crew had to be awake, driving this boat. But why all the frantic footsteps upstairs? Did they hear her scream?

If they come down here to stop me, I'll shoot.

The Queen laid the rope on the floor under the boogie board. She found superhuman strength to pull Knight off the bed, and onto the board. She tied the rope around his chest then dragged him through the doors onto the ledge.

She felt dizzy from all those boats zig-zagging around them, the choppers, the floodlights, and that amplified voice saying, "Come out with your hands up!" She was so glad the crew wasn't coming down here to bother her.

I told Knight I would do this. I told him.

The Queen positioned his legs so they were already in the water. He was facing up on the boogie board, slippery against the plexiglass. Her whole body trembled as she laid on Knight so she was facing down, pressing her pregnant belly into the warmth of his. With trembling hands, she tied the rope around her waist, fastening it on the small of her back.

She hummed their wedding song as she pressed her ear into the silence of his chest, where his heart should have been beating. Riding him like a surfboard, she pushed her palms into the plexiglass and wrapped her arms around his beautiful, dark-chocolate muscles.

And together, as one, they slipped into the icy black infinity.

Epilogue

The fresh-cut pineapple felt sweet and cold on her tongue, but Knight's fingertip was soft and warm as The Queen bit down.

"Gotcha," she giggled as they lay side by side on the plush chaise. The turquoise water stretched to infinity before them as the sun sizzled on their bare backs and asses.

Knight loved how she sucked his finger into her mouth as he flipped her on her back.

"Oooohh, yeah," she moaned, trembling as her pussy pulsated around Shane. "Make me cum with one stroke every time."

"Sssshh, Mommy," he teased, "don't wake baby Prince."

They glanced over at the white bassinet in the shade of a palm tree. His eyes were closed tightly on his plump, beige face; the gentle ocean breeze jiggled his wild shock of black curls. Knight's whole body tingled with pleasure.

This was Manifest Destiny, live and in color.

He tingled even more with the sexual, emotional, and spiritual thrill of it all. He had all the money he needed in the bank, thanks to Jamal's agreement to buy Babylon and keep it going for the right reasons. His body was relaxed; the chest pains had disappeared the moment they had arrived here on this private island a year ago. All thanks to Ping and Pong, who'd executed the underwater rescue a year ago with perfect precision.

They had plucked him and The Queen from the black depths of the Detroit River, put them on the cigarette boat, then whisked them to yacht number two, a short distance down the river. Knight didn't die; he merely passed out with relief that they'd made it out of Babylon alive. And once The

Queen regained consciousness on yacht number two, and he'd explained Manifest Destiny, she'd been thrilled to learn that a glorious, safe new future awaited them.

Now Ping and Pong were here on the island, up at the luxurious house just a short walk up the trail from this beach. Knight's mother was loving her private cottage nearby.

"Make love to me all day," The Queen whispered, "my beautiful African god named Knight."

"Love you to the infinity," he whispered as he thrust gently and stared into her lusty eyes. "Right here in paradise, baby girl."